The Ghost Pirates
and Other
Revenants of
the Sea

The Ghost Pirates and
Other Revenants of the Sea

Being the Third Volume of
the Collected Fiction of William Hope Hodgson

Edited by Jeremy Lassen

Night Shade Books · New York · 2018

Library of Congress Cataloging-in-Publication Data is available on file.

ISBN: 978-1-59780-941-2
Ebook ISBN: 978-1-59780-369-4
Hardcover ISBN: 978-1-89238-941-1

Cover and interior artwork © 2005 by Jason Van Hollander
Interior layout and design by Jeremy Lassen
Introduction © 2005 by Jeremy Lassen
A Note on the Texts © 2005 by Jeremy Lassen

Printed in the United States of America

This series is dedicated to the readers, editors, publishers and scholars who have worked tirelessly since William Hope Hodgson's death to ensure that his work would not be lost or forgotten. Without their efforts, these volumes would not be possible.

In particular, the editor would like to thank S. T. Joshi, Mike Ashley, Jack Adrian and George Locke for their generous support.

Contents

Contents

Extraordinary Conditions

"...the sea is a wide place, and a lonesome place,
and I have seen it, in my time, breed some extraordinary conditions."
— William Hope Hodgson, from "The 'Prentices' Mutiny"

THE THIRD VOLUME OF the complete fiction of William Hope Hodgson collects the remaining sea stories that were not published in Volumes One and Two. It is anchored by Hodgson's most accessible (and some would argue, his most effective) novel, *The Ghost Pirates*. This novel is his shortest and (unlike his longer novels) is not told in an affected or archaic style. The short stories in this volume range from sensationalistic "true exposés" to vignettes of life at sea, to adventure fiction, to the weird sea fiction Hodgson is most remembered for. All of the fiction in this volume features protagonists struggling (both literally and metaphorically) against forces beyond their control...struggling against *extraordinary conditions*. Sometimes these forces are abusive first mates. Other times they are the cold, uncaring power of the sea itself, or the ravages of time. And sometimes they are something altogether *unnatural*.

How the protagonists of Hodgson's fiction confront these *extraordinary conditions* becomes a theme that unites the seemingly disparate stories of this collection (and, it could be argued, encompasses his entire fictional *oeuvre*). It may be a protracted siege that the protagonists are bound to lose, à la *The Ghost Pirates*, or it may be an abusive First Mate that can be overcome with the right combination of wits and strength. But in either case, it is during these confrontations that Hodgson's characters are defined, and are the these characters that define Hodgson's fiction. The lurid title characters of *The Ghost Pirates* are striking, but it is the reader's close identification with the day-to-day, hour-by-hour struggles of the *Mortzestus'* doomed crew that makes it a remarkably effective piece of literature. Hodgson's work may be filled with *otherness* (cosmic or not), but it is the conflict between this otherness and the personable humanity of his protagonists that gives Hodgson's work its power.

The Ghost Pirates was published in 1909 by Stanley Paul & Company. It received very solid reviews upon publication. It is often cited as both Hodgson's most effective work, and one of the best novel-length works of supernatural fiction in the English language. Unfortunately, like his other novels, it did not find commercial success during Hodgson's lifetime.

"The Silent Ship"—the short story that immediately follows *The Ghost Pirates* in this volume—is an alternate and significantly longer ending for *The Ghost Pirates*. Hodgson tried to sell this as a stand-alone story numerous times, under the titles "The Silent Ship," "The Phantom Ship," and "The Third Mates Story." The Manuscript was discovered amongst Hodgson's papers, and eventually saw publication in 1973, as "The Phantom Ship."

The first four stories in this collection were published prior to the publication of *The Ghost Pirates*, and demonstrate a clear progression of Hodgson's skills as a writer. His second story ever published, "A Tropical Horror," was competently written and suitably breathless, but is lacking some of the magic of his later work. Hodgson was clearly beginning to find his unique (pardon the pun) voice, with "The Voice in the Night," which has gone on to be one of his most oft-anthologized stories; and (as of this writing), is the only Hodgson story to have been the basis for a feature-length movie. In "The *Shamraken* Homeward-Bounder," Hodgson delivers a remarkably effective story that combines his uniquely weird, salt-suffused writing style with a melancholic examination of aging and the passage of time. It is a brilliant story, and by many measures, one of Hodgson's greatest works. "Out of the Storm," published several months before *The Ghost Pirates*, can be seen as a thematic, yet oddly disparate, naturalistic twin to his *The Ghost Pirates*: featuring, as it does, a doomed ship unable to survive the forces that threaten it.

The time between the publication of *The Ghost Pirates* and Hodgson's entry into World War I in 1915 was a period of productivity, as writing had become his primary means of earning a living. During this time, he had over fifty original stories published from a wide variety of genres (The Carnaki, Captain Gault, Captain Jat, and D.C.O. Cagunka Stories all appeared during this time). His final novel (*The Night Lands*) and two story collections (*Carnaki The Ghost-Finder* and *Men Of Deep Waters*) also appeared during this time period.

It was almost exactly two years from the publication of *The Ghost Pirates*, to the publication of "the Albatross," which marked a return, of sorts, to the weird sea fiction that had provided him with his initial commercial success. A return "of sorts," because "The Albatross" was already written, sold, and scheduled to be published in the October 1907 issue of *The London Magazine*—until the editor read "The Mystery of the Derelict" (published in July 1907 at a competing magazine), and was put off by the similarities between the stories. Hodgson was forced to provide an alternate story for *The London Magazine*, and "The Albatross" did not see publication for almost four years, in a different magazine altogether.

While the mixing and reusing of scenes and images proved to be relatively disastrous in the above instance, it was a practice most commercial writers of the time engaged in, and Hodgson was no exception. Another example of remixing and reusing prose elements centered around a mutiny on the *Lady Morgan*. In the 1912 February, March and April issues of *The Wide World Magazine*, a three-part account of a mutiny aboard the *Lady Morgan* was published as " 'Prentices' Mutiny." The framing of this piece and promotional copy in the magazine suggested that " 'Prentices' Mutiny" was a true exposé of the abuses that occurred at sea. It was of course, a classic Hodgson tale of the apprentices' revenge against abusive authority. It also featured a protracted siege aboard ship, much like those found in both "The Albatross" and "The Mystery of the Derelict."

Even more striking than the reused siege imagery was the appearance in August of the same year of a different and more humorous account of a mutiny aboard the *Lady Morgan*, published under the title "The Getting Even of Tommy Dodd." The real confusion over this particular story arises from the unfortunate fact that "…Tommy Dodd" was later reprinted under the title "The Apprentices' Mutiny". Further confusing things, the original " 'Prentices' Mutiny" was published in an abridged form (also in 1912) in *"Poems" and "The Dream of X"* under the title "Mutiny." The original "true exposé" from *The Wide World Magazine* has been reprinted in this volume, and the alternate, cross-dressing account of Tommy Dodd's revenge will be presented in the fifth volume of this series.

From this point forward, the retitling upon subsequent publication of Hodgson's sea fiction becomes a major issue of confusion for the Hodgson scholar and bibliographer. Hodgson continued to publish "real-life vignettes" throughout his career, and one such piece appeared in *The Saturday Westminster Gazette* under the title "The Real Thing: On The Bridge" in April 1912. It was later reprinted in his collection *Men of Deep Waters* under the shortened title "On the Bridge," and is presented here as such.

In December, *Red Magazine*, (which had just published "The Getting even of Tommy Dodd" in August) published "The Derelict," which was as much science fiction story as it was horror, and has become one of the most reprinted, archetypal Hodgson "weird sea" stories. "The Island of the Crossbones," an effective adventure/pirate tale was published almost a year later in *Short Stories* magazine.

Six months later, in July 1914, another landmark Hodgson story was published in *Red Magazine*, under the title "The Mystery of the Ship in the Night," though this published version was cut by about two thousand words. Two years later it was republished in his collection *The Luck of the Strong* under the title "The Stone Ship," in an uncut form, which is presented in this volume.

"The Trimming of Captain Dunkan" was first published in *Red Magazine* in August 1914, and rewritten under the title "We Two and Billy Dunkan" for his collection *The Luck of the Strong*. It is this version that is presented herein.

In March 1915, the *Red Magazine* published "The Waterloo of a Hard-Case Skipper." This story was later renamed and published as "The Regeneration of Captain Bully Keller" in *Everybody's Magazine* in July 1918 and is reprinted here under this later title.

Yet another case of a story being published under different names, "The Mystery of Missing Ships," a tale of modern piracy based on reported accounts of piracy of disabled ships by whaling vessels and their crews. This story was published in *All Around Magazine* in December 1915, and was subsequently published posthumously in a slightly different version, under the title "Ships That Go Missing." It is presented here under its original title.

"The Haunted *Pampero*" was one of the few stories that kept its title intact between its British and U.S. publications, and is a return to the supernatural sea fiction. It was originally accepted in November 1915, but didn't see publication until December 1916, when *Premiere Magazine* printed it in December 1916. The story wasn't published in the U.S. until just before Hodgson's death in 1918.

"The Real Thing 'S.O.S' " is another vignette akin to "On The Bridge," and was published in January of 1917 in *Cornhill Magazine*. Another odd pair of stories appeared during this time—"A Fight With a Submarine" and "In The Danger Zone" were published in *Canada in Khaki*, in January and June respectively. This magazine was a Canadian government publication whose goal was to show the Canadian war effort is a positive light. Hodgson's stories, while not his best, do represent a foray into a form of nautical fiction he hadn't previously had a commercial venue for. The publication of these two obviously related stories also bridges the gap between Hodgson's life, and his untimely death.

In 1915, with World War I underway, William Hope Hodgson entered the British service in the Royal Artillery Corps (refusing to have anything to do with the Navy). In 1916 he was severely injured after being thrown from a horse, and discharged from the military. Hodgson worked strenuously to recover. He was re-admitted to the R.A.C. and was deployed to the front in 1917, where his company saw a lot of action. In May of 1918, Hodgson was killed by enemy artillery fire. The enormity of this literary tragedy was mitigated somewhat by the aggressive promotion of Hodgson's work by his widow, Bessie Hodgson, who not only saw to the publication of numerous unpublished manuscripts but also ensured that reprints of his fiction continued to appear in popular magazines on both sides of the Atlantic. "Old Golly" was one of the first stories that Bessie Hodgson sold and was published in 1919, while "The Wild Man of the Sea" was one of the last (published in 1926). "Demons of the Sea" was published in December 1919, and was later reprinted by August Derleth in a significantly different form under the title "The Crew of the Lancing." This alternate version will be presented in volume five of this series.

Another example of a posthumously published story with multiple titles was "The Storm," which was first published by *Short Stories* magazine in 1919. A different version of this story, based on an original manuscript, was published in *Terrors From the Sea* in 1996, under the title "By the Lee." It is this version of the story with this titling that is present herein.

"The Habitants of Middle Islet" was one of the stories sold to August Derleth and published in the 60's. A final generation of posthumously published stories is made up of "The Riven Night," "The Heaving of the Log," "The Sharks of the *St. Elmo*" (AKA "Fifty Dead Chinamen All in a Row"), and " 'Sailormen.' "

From his second story ever published to the ten stories that appeared after his death, this volume represents a very diverse set of stories—real-life vignettes to ghosts and other supernatural occurrences to straight humor, with war and adventure stories thrown in for good measure. Frankly, this volume also represents a very wide range of quality. Some of the stories here are his most well regarded, and some are of historical interest only. But within these pages, a lifetime is represented. The lifetime of a man who struggled against *extraordinary conditions*…. who struggled as a sailor, a writer, a husband, and (like too many literary voices of his generation), a soldier—whose literary output was cut short in the killing fields of World War I. *The Ghost Pirates*, which opens this volume, and "By The Lee," the vignette which closes this volume both feature men who struggle valiantly against forces beyond their control. These two bookends are, to my mind, the perfect metaphor for William Hope Hodgson's life and his work.

Jeremy Lassen
San Francisco

The Ghost Pirates

To Mary Whalley

"Olden Memories that shine against death's Night —
quiet stars of sweet Enchantments, that are seen
In Life's lost distances..."

The World of Dreams

Table of Contents

Author's Preface

THIS BOOK FORMS THE last of three. The first published was "THE BOATS OF THE 'GLEN CARRIG'"; the second "THE HOUSE ON THE BORDERLAND"; this, the third, completes what, perhaps, may be termed a trilogy; for, though very different in scope, each of the three books deals with certain conceptions that have an elemental kinship. With this book, the author believes that he closes the door, so far as he is concerned, on a particular phase of constructive thought.

The Hell O! O! Chaunty

Chaunty Man	Man the capstan, bullies!
Men	Ha!-o-o! Ha!-o-o!
Chaunty Man	Capstan-bars, you tarry souls!
Men	Ha!-o-o! Ha!-o-o!
Chaunty Man	Take a turn!
Men	Ha!-o-o!
Chaunty Man	Stand by to fleet!
Men	Ha!-o-o!
Chaunty Man	Stand by to surge!
Men	Ha!-o-o!
Chaunty Man	Ha!—o-o-o-o!
Men	TRAMP! And away we go!
Chaunty Man	Hark to the tramp of the bearded shellbacks!
Men	Hush! O hear 'em tramp!
Chaunty Man	Tramping, stamping—treading, vamping,
	While the cable comes in ramping.
Men	Hark! O hear 'em stamp!
Chaunty Man	Surge when it rides!
	Surge when it rides!
	Round-o-o-o handsome as it slacks!
Men	Ha!-o-o-o-o! hear 'em ramp!
	Ha!-o-o-o-o! hear 'em stamp!
	Ha!-o-o-o-o-o-o! Ha!-o-o-o-o-o-o!
Chorus	They're shouting now; oh! hear 'em
	A-bellow as they stamp:—
	Ha!-o-o-o! Ha!-o-o-o! Ha!-o-o-o!
	A-shouting as they tramp!
Chaunty Man	O hark to the haunting chorus of the capstan and

7

.... the bars!
.... Chaunty-o-o-o and rattle crash—
.... Bash against the stars!
Men .... Ha-a!-o-o-o! Tramp and go!
.... Ha-a!-o-o-o! Ha-a!-o-o-o!
Chaunty Man .... Hear the pawls a-ranting: with
.... the bearded men a-chaunting;
.... While the brazen dome above 'em
.... Bellows back the 'bars.'
Men .... Hear and hark! O hear 'em!
.... Ha-a!-o-o! Ha-a!-o-o!
Chaunty Man .... Hurling songs towards the heavens—!
Men .... Ha-a!-o-o! Ha-a!-o-o!
Chaunty Man .... Hush! O hear 'em! Hark! O hear 'em!
.... Hurling oaths among their spars!
Men .... Hark! O hear 'em!
.... Hush! O hear 'em!
Chaunty Man .... Tramping round between the bars!

Chorus .... They're shouting now; oh! hear 'em
.... A-bellow as they stamp:—
.... Ha-a !-o-o-o! Ha-a !-o-o-o! Ha-a !-o-o-o!
.... A-shouting as they tramp!

Chaunty Man .... O do you hear the capstan-chaunty!
.... Thunder round the pawls!
Men .... Click a-clack, a-clatter
.... Surge! And scatter bawls!
Chaunty Man .... Click-a-clack, my bonny boys, while it comes
.... in handsome!
Men .... Ha-a!-o-o! Hear 'em clack!
Chaunty Man .... Ha-a!-o-o! Click-a-clack!
Men .... Hush! O hear 'em pant!
.... Hark! O hear 'em rant!
Chaunty Man .... Click, a-clitter, clicker-clack.
Men .... Ha-a!-o-o! Tramp and go!
Chaunty Man .... Surge! And keep away the slack!
Men .... Ha-a!-o-o! Away the slack:
.... Ha-a!-o-o! Click-a-clack
Chaunty Man .... Bustle now each jolly Jack.
.... Surging easy! Surging e-a-s-y!!

Men	Ha-a!-o-o! Surging easy
Chaunty Man	Click-a-clatter — Surge; and steady!
....	Man the stopper there! All ready?
Men	Ha-a!-o-o! Ha-a!-o-o!
Chaunty Man	Click-a-clack, my bouncing boys:
Men	Ha-a!-o-o! Tramp and go!
Chaunty Man	Lift the pawls, and come back easy.
Men	Ha-a!-o-o! Steady-o-o-o-o!
Chaunty Man	Vast the chaunty! Vast the capstan! Drop the pawls!
....	Be-l-a-y!
Chorus	Ha-a!-o-o! Unship the bars!
....	Ha-a!-o-o! Tramp and go!
....	Ha-a!-o-o! Shoulder bars!
....	Ha-a!-o-o! And away we blow!
....	Ha-a!-o-o-o! Ha-a!-o-o-o-o! Ha-a!-o-o-o-o!

I
The Figure Out of the Sea

HE BEGAN WITHOUT ANY circumlocution.

"I joined the *Mortzestus* in 'Frisco. I heard before I signed on, that there were some funny yarns floating round about her; but I was pretty nearly on the beach, and too jolly anxious to get away, to worry about trifles. Besides, by all accounts, she was right enough so far as grub and treatment went. When I asked fellows to give it a name, they generally could not. All they could tell me, was that she was unlucky, and made thundering long passages, and had more than a fair share of dirty weather. Also, that she had twice had the sticks blown out of her, and her cargo shifted. Besides all these, a heap of other things that might happen to any packet, and would not be comfortable to run into. Still, they were the ordinary things, and I was willing enough to risk them, to get home. All the same, if I had been given the chance, I should have shipped in some other vessel as a matter of preference.

"When I took my bag down, I found that they had signed on the rest of the crowd. You see, the 'home lot' cleared out when they got into 'Frisco, that is, all except one young fellow, a cockney, who had stuck by the ship in port. He told me afterwards, when I got to know him, that he intended to draw a payday out of her, whether anyone else did, or not.

"The first night I was in her, I found that it was common talk among the other fellows, that there was something queer about the ship. They spoke of her as if it were an accepted fact that she was haunted; yet they all treated the matter as a joke; all, that is, except the young cockney—Williams—who, instead of laughing at their jests on the subject, seemed to take the whole matter seriously.

"This made me rather curious. I began to wonder whether there was, after all, some truth underlying the vague stories I had heard; and I took the first opportunity to ask him whether he had any reasons for believing that there was anything in the yarns about the ship.

"At first he was inclined to be a bit offish; but, presently, he came round, and told me that he did not know of any particular incident which could be called unusual in the sense in which I meant. Yet that, at the same time, there were lots of little things which, if you put them together, made you think a bit. For instance, she always made such long passages and had so much dirty weather—nothing but that and calms and head winds. Then, other things happened; sails that he knew, himself, had been properly stowed, were always blowing adrift *at night*. And then he said a thing that surprised me.

" 'There's too many bloomin' shadders about this 'ere packet; they gets onter yer nerves like nothin' as ever I seen before in me nat'ral.'

"He blurted it all out in a heap, and I turned round and looked at him.

" 'Too many shadows!' I said. 'What on earth do you mean?' But he refused to explain himself or tell me anything further—just shook his head, stupidly, when I questioned him. He seemed to have taken a sudden, sulky fit.

"I felt certain that he was acting dense, purposely. I believe the truth of the matter is that he was, in a way, ashamed of having let himself go like he had, in speaking out his thoughts about 'shadders.' That type of man may think things at times; but he doesn't often put them into words. Anyhow, I saw it was no use asking any further questions; so I let the matter drop there. Yet, for several days afterwards, I caught myself wondering, at times, what the fellow had meant by 'shadders.'

"We left 'Frisco next day, with a fine, fair wind, that seemed a bit like putting the stopper on the yarns I had heard about the ship's ill luck. And yet—"

"He hesitated a moment, and then went on again.

"For the first couple of weeks out, nothing unusual happened, and the wind still held fair. I began to feel that I had been rather lucky, after all, in the packet into which I had been shunted. Most of the other fellows gave her a good name, and there was a pretty general opinion growing among the crowd, that it was all a silly yarn about her being haunted. And then, just when I was settling down to things, something happened that opened my eyes no end.

"It was in the eight to twelve watch, and I was sitting on the steps, on the starboard side, leading up to the fo'cas'le head. The night was fine and there was a splendid moon. Away aft, I heard the timekeeper strike four bells, and the lookout, an old fellow named Jaskett, answered him. As he let go the bell lanyard, he caught sight of me, where I sat quietly, smoking. He leant over the rail, and looked down at me.

" 'That you, Jessop?' he asked.

" 'I believe it is,' I replied.

" 'We'd 'ave our grandmothers an' all the rest of our petticoated relash'ns comin' to sea, if 'twere always like this,' he remarked, reflectively—indicating, with a sweep of his pipe and hand, the calmness of the sea and sky.

"I saw no reason for denying that, and he continued:—

" 'If this ole packet is 'aunted, as some on 'em seems to think, well all as I can say is, let me 'ave the luck to tumble across another of the same sort. Good grub, an' duff fer Sundays, an' a decent crowd of 'em aft, an' everythin' comfertable like, so as yer can feel yer knows where yer are. As fer 'er bein' 'aunted, that's all 'ellish nonsense. I've comed 'cross lots of 'em before as was said to be 'aunted, an' so some on 'em was; but 'twasn't with ghostesses. One packet I was in, they was that bad yer couldn't sleep a wink in yer watch below, until yer'd 'ad every stitch out yer bunk an' 'ad a reg'lar 'unt. Sometimes—' At that moment, the relief, one of the ordinary seamen, went up the other ladder on to the fo'cas'le head, and the old chap turned to ask him 'Why the 'ell' he'd not relieved him a bit smarter. The ordinary made some reply; but what it was, I did not catch; for, abruptly, away aft, my rather sleepy gaze had lighted on something altogether extraordinary and outrageous. It was nothing less than the form of a man stepping inboard over the starboard rail, a little abaft the main rigging. I stood up, and caught at the handrail, and stared.

"Behind me, someone spoke. It was the lookout, who had come down off the fo'cas'le head, on his way aft to report the name of his relief to the Second Mate.

" 'What is it, mate?' he asked, curiously, seeing my intent attitude.

"The thing, whatever it was, had disappeared into the shadows on the lee side of the deck.

" 'Nothing!' I replied, shortly; for I was too bewildered then, at what my eyes had just shown me, to say any more. I wanted to think.

"The old shellback glanced at me; but only muttered something, and went on his way aft.

"For a minute, perhaps, I stood there, watching; but could see nothing. Then I walked slowly aft, as far as the after end of the deck house. From there, I could see most of the main-deck; but nothing showed, except, of course, the moving shadows of the ropes and spars and sails, as they swung to and fro in the moonlight.

"The old chap who had just come off the lookout, had returned forrard again, and I was alone on that part of the deck. And then, all at once, as I stood peering into the shadows to leeward, I remembered what Williams had said about there being too many 'shadders.' I had been puzzled to understand his real meaning, then. I had no difficulty *now*. There *were* too many shadows. Yet, shadows or no shadows, I realised that for my own peace of mind, I must settle, once and for all, whether the thing I had seemed to see stepping aboard out of the ocean had been a reality, or simply a phantom, as you might say, of my imagination. My reason said it was nothing more than imagination, a rapid dream—I must have dozed; but something deeper than reason told me that this was not so. I put it to the test, and went straight in amongst the shadows— There was nothing.

"I grew bolder. My common sense told me I must have fancied it all. I walked over to the main-mast, and looked behind the pin-rail that partly surrounded it, and down into the shadow of the pumps; but here again was nothing. Then I went in under the break of the poop. It was darker under there than out on deck. I looked up both sides of the deck, and saw that they were bare of anything such as I looked for. The assurance was comforting. I glanced at the poop ladders, and remembered that nothing could have gone up there, without the Second Mate or the Timekeeper seeing it. Then I leant my back up against the bulkshead, and thought the whole matter over, rapidly, sucking at my pipe, and keeping my glance about the deck. I concluded my think, and said 'No!' out loud.

"Then something occurred to me, and I said 'Unless—' and went over to the starboard bulwarks, and looked over and down into the sea; but there was nothing but sea; and so I turned and made my way forrard. My common sense had triumphed, and I was convinced that my imagination had been playing tricks with me.

"I reached the door on the port side, leading into the fo'cas'le, and was about to enter, when something made me look behind. As I did so, I had a shaker. Away aft, a dim, shadowy form stood in the wake of a swaying belt of moonlight, that swept the deck a bit abaft the main-mast.

"It was the same figure that I had just been attributing to my fancy. I will admit that I felt more than startled; I was quite a bit frightened. I was convinced now that it was no mere imaginary thing. It was a human figure. And yet, with the flicker of the moonlight and the shadows chasing over it, I was unable to say more than that. Then, as I stood there, irresolute and funky, I got the thought that someone was acting the goat; though for what reason or purpose, I never stopped to consider.

I was glad of any suggestion that my common sense assured me was not impossible; and, for the moment, I felt quite relieved. That side to the question had not presented itself to me before. I began to pluck up courage. I accused myself of getting fanciful; otherwise I should have tumbled to it earlier. And then, funnily enough, in spite of all my reasoning, I was still afraid of going aft to discover who that was, standing on the leeside of the main-deck. Yet I felt that if I shirked it, I was only fit to be dumped overboard; and so I went, though not with any great speed, as you can imagine.

"I had gone half the distance, and still the figure remained there, motionless and silent—the moonlight and the shadows playing over it with each roll of the ship. I think I tried to be surprised. If it were one of the fellows playing the fool, he must have heard me coming, and why didn't he scoot while he had the chance? And where could he have hidden himself, before? All these things, I asked myself, in a rush, with a queer mixture of doubt and belief; and, you know, in the meantime, I was drawing nearer. I had passed the house, and was not twelve paces distant; when, abruptly, the silent figure made three quick strides to the port rail, and *climbed over it into the sea.*

"I rushed to the side, and stared over; but nothing met my gaze, except the shadow of the ship, sweeping over the moonlit sea.

"How long I stared down blankly into the water, it would be impossible to say; certainly for a good minute. I felt blank—just horribly blank. It was such a beastly confirmation of the *unnaturalness* of the thing I had concluded to be only a sort of brain fancy. I seemed, for that little time, deprived, you know, of the power of coherent thought. I suppose I was dazed—mentally stunned, in a way.

"As I have said, a minute or so must have gone, while I had been staring into the dark of the water under the ship's side. Then, I came suddenly to my ordinary self. The Second Mate was singing out:— 'Lee fore brace.'

"I went to the braces, like a chap in a dream.

II
What Tammy the 'Prentice Saw

"THE NEXT MORNING, IN my watch below, I had a look at the places where that strange thing had come aboard, and left the ship; but I found nothing unusual, and no clue to help me to understand the mystery of the strange man.

"For several days after that, all went quietly; though I prowled about the decks at night, trying to discover anything fresh that might tend to throw some light on to the matter. I was careful to say nothing to any one about the thing I had seen. In any case, I felt sure I should only have been laughed at.

"Several nights passed away in this manner, and I was no nearer to an understanding of the affair. And then, in the middle watch, something happened.

"It was my wheel. Tammy, one of the first voyage 'prentices, was keeping time—walking up and down the leeside of the poop. The Second Mate was forrard, leaning over the break of the poop, smoking. The weather still continued fine, and the moon, though declining, was sufficiently powerful to make every detail about the poop, stand out distinctly. Three bells had gone, and I'll admit I was feeling sleepy. Indeed, I believe I must have dozed, for the old packet steered very easily, and there was precious little to do, beyond giving her an odd spoke now and again. And then, all at once, it seemed to me that I heard some one calling my name, softly. I could not be certain; and first I glanced forrard to where the Second stood, smoking, and from him, I looked into the binnacle. The ship's head was right on her course, and I felt easier. Then, suddenly, I heard it again. There was no doubt about it this time, and I glanced to leeward. There I saw Tammy reaching over the steering gear, his hand out, in the act of trying to touch my arm. I was about to ask him what the devil he wanted, when he held up his finger for silence, and pointed forrard along the lee side of the Poop. In the dim light, his

15

face showed palely, and he seemed much agitated. For a few seconds, I stared in the direction he indicated, but could see nothing.

" 'What is it?' I asked in an undertone, after a couple of moments' further ineffectual peering. 'I can't see anything.'

" 'H'sh!' he muttered, hoarsely, without looking in my direction. Then, all at once, with a quick little gasp, he sprang across the wheel-box, and stood beside me, trembling. His gaze appeared to follow the movements of something I could not see.

"I must say that I was startled. His movement had shown such terror; and the way he stared to leeward made me think he saw some-thing uncanny.

" 'What the deuce is up with you?' I asked, sharply. And then I remembered the Second Mate. I glanced forrard to where he lounged. His back was still towards us, and he had not seen Tammy. Then I turned to the boy.

" 'For goodness sake, get to looard before the Second sees you!' I said. 'If you want to say anything, say it across the wheelbox. You've been dreaming.'

"Even as I spoke, the little beggar caught at my sleeve with one hand; and, pointing across to the logreel with the other, screamed:— 'He's coming! He's coming—' At this instant, the Second Mate came running aft, singing out to know what was the matter. Then, suddenly, crouching under the rail near the logreel, I saw something that looked like a man; but so hazy and unreal, that I could scarcely say I saw any-thing. Yet, like a flash, my thoughts ripped back to the silent figure I had seen in the flicker of the moonlight, a week earlier.

"The Second Mate reached me, and I pointed, dumbly; and yet, as I did so, it was with the knowledge that *he* would not be able to see what I saw. (Queer, wasn't it?) And then, almost in a breath, I lost sight of the thing, and became aware that Tammy was hugging my knees.

"The Second continued to stare at the logreel for a brief instant; then he turned to me, with a sneer.

" 'Been asleep, the pair of you, I suppose!' Then, without waiting for my denial, he told Tammy, to get to hell out of it and stop his noise, or he'd boot him off the poop.

"After that, he walked forrard to the break of the poop, and lit his pipe, again—walking forrard and aft every few minutes, and eyeing me, at times, I thought, with a strange, half-doubtful, half-puzzled look.

"Later, as soon as I was relieved, I hurried down to the 'prentice's berth. I was anxious to speak to Tammy. There were a dozen ques-tions that worried me, and I was in doubt what I ought to do. I found him crouched on a sea-chest, his knees up to his chin, and his gaze fixed on the doorway, with a frightened stare. I put my head into the berth, and he gave a gasp; then he saw who it was, and his face relaxed something of its strained expression.

"He said: 'Come in,' in a low voice, which he tried to steady; and I stepped over the washboard, and sat down on a chest, facing him.

" 'What was *it*?' he asked; putting his feet down on to the deck, and leaning forward. 'For God's sake, tell me what it was!'

"His voice had risen, and I put up my hand to warn him.

" 'H'sh!' I said. 'You'll wake the other fellows.'

"He repeated his question, but in a lower tone. I hesitated, before answering him. I felt, all at once, that it might be better to deny all knowledge—to say I hadn't seen anything unusual. I thought quickly, and made answer on the turn of the moment.

" 'What was *what*?' I said. 'That's just the thing I've come to ask you. A pretty pair of fools you made of the two of us up on the poop just now, with your hysterical tomfoolery.'

"I concluded my remark in a tone of anger.

" 'I didn't!' he answered, in a passionate whisper. 'You know I didn't. You know *you* saw it yourself. You pointed it out to the Second Mate. I saw you.'

"The little beggar was nearly crying between fear, and vexation at my assumed unbelief.

" 'Rot!' I replied. 'You know jolly well you were sleeping in your timekeeping. You dreamed something and woke up suddenly. You were off your chump.'

"I was determined to reassure him, if possible; though, goodness! I wanted assurance myself. If he had known of that other thing, I had seen down on the main-deck, what then!

" 'I wasn't asleep, any more than you were,' he said, bitterly. 'And you know it. You're just fooling me. The ship's haunted.'

" 'What!' I said, sharply.

" 'She's haunted,' he said, again. 'She's haunted.'

" 'Who says so?' I inquired, in a tone of unbelief.

" 'I do ! And you *know* it. Everybody knows it; but they don't more than half believe it… I didn't, until tonight.'

" 'Damned rot!' I answered. 'That's all a blooming old shellback's yarn. She's no more haunted than I am.'

" 'It's not damned rot,' he replied, totally unconvinced. 'And it's not an old shellback's yarn…. Why won't you say you saw it?' he cried, growing almost tearfully excited, and raising his voice again.

"I warned him not to wake the sleepers.

" 'Why won't you say you saw it?' he repeated.

"I got up from the chest, and went towards the door.

" 'You're a young idiot!' I said. 'And I should advise you not to go gassing about like this, round the decks. Take my tip, and turn-in and get a sleep. You're talking dotty. Tomorrow you'll perhaps feel what an unholy ass you've made of yourself.'

"I stepped over the washboard, and left him. I believe he followed me to the door to say something further; but I was halfway forrard by then.

"For the next couple of days, I avoided him as much as possible, taking care never to let him catch me alone. I was determined, if possible, to convince him that he had been mistaken in supposing that he had seen anything that night. Yet, after all, it was little enough use, as you will soon see. For, on the night of the second day, there was a further extraordinary development, that made denial on my part useless.

III

The Man Up the Main

"IT OCCURRED IN THE first watch, just after six bells. I was forrard, sitting on the forehatch. No one was about the main-deck. The night was exceedingly fine; and the wind had dropped away almost to nothing, so that the ship was very quiet.

"Suddenly, I heard the Second Mate's voice—

" 'In the main-rigging, there! Who's that going aloft?'

"I sat up on the hatch, and listened. There succeeded an intense silence. Then the Second's voice came again. He was evidently getting wild.

" 'Do you damn well hear me? What the hell are you doing up there? Come down.'

"I rose to my feet, and walked up to wind'ard. From there, I could see the break of the poop. The Second Mate was standing by the starboard ladder. He appeared to be looking up at something that was hidden from me by the top-sails. As I stared, he broke out again:—

" 'Hell and damnation, you blasted sojer, come down when I tell you!'

"He stamped on the poop, and repeated his order, savagely. But there was no answer. I started to walk aft. What had happened? Who had gone aloft? Who would be fool enough to go, without being told? And then, all at once, a thought came to me. The figure, Tammy and I had seen. Had the Second Mate seen something—someone? I hurried on, and then stopped, suddenly. In the same moment there came the shrill blast of the Second's whistle; he was whistling for the watch, and I turned and ran to the fo'cas'le to rouse them out. Another minute, and I was hurrying aft with them to see what was wanted.

"His voice met us halfway:—

" 'Up the main some of you, smartly now, and find out who that damned fool is up there. See what mischief he's up to.'

" 'i, i, Sir,' several of the men sung out, and a couple jumped into the weather rigging. I joined them, and the rest were proceeding to follow; but the Second shouted for some to go up to leeward—case the fellow tried to get down that side.

"As I followed the other two aloft, I heard the Second Mate tell Tammy, whose time-keeping it was, to get down on to the main-deck with the other 'prentice, and keep an eye on the fore and aft stays.

" 'He may try down one of them if he's cornered,' I heard him explain. 'If you see anything, just sing out for me, right away.'

"Tammy hesitated.

" 'Well?' said the Second Mate, sharply.

" 'Nothing, Sir,' said Tammy, and went down onto the main-deck.

"The first man to wind'ard had reached the futtock shrouds; his head was above the top, and he was taking a preliminary look, before venturing higher.

" 'See anythin', Jock?' asked Plummer, the man next above me.

" 'Na'!' said Jock, tersely, and climbed over the top, and so disappeared from my sight.

"The fellow ahead of me, followed. He reached the futtock rigging, and stopped to expectorate. I was close at his heels, and he looked down to me.

" 'What's up, anyway?' he said. 'What's 'e seen? 'oo're we chasin' after?'

"I said I didn't know, and he swung up into the top-mast rigging. I followed on. The chaps on the leeside were about level with us. Under the foot of the top-sail, I could see Tammy and the other 'prentice down on the main-deck, looking upwards.

"The fellows were a bit excited in a sort of subdued way; though I am inclined to think there was far more curiosity and, perhaps, a certain consciousness of the strangeness of it all. I know that, looking to leeward, there was a tendency to keep well together, in which I sympathised.

" 'Must be a bloomin' stowaway,' one of the men suggested.

"I grabbed at the idea, instantly. Perhaps— And then, in a moment, I dismissed it. I remembered how that first thing had stepped over the rail *into the sea. That* matter could not be explained in such a manner. With regard to this, I was curious and anxious. *I* had seen nothing this time. What could the Second Mate have seen? I wondered. Were we chasing fancies, or was there really someone—something real, among the shadows above us? My thoughts returned to that thing, Tammy and I had seen near the log-reel. I remembered how incapable the

Second Mate had been of seeing anything then. I remembered how natural it had seemed that he should not be able to see. I caught the word 'stowaway' again. After all, that might explain away *this* affair. It would—

"My train of thought was broken suddenly. One of the men was shouting and gesticulating.

" 'I sees 'im! I sees 'im!' He was pointing upwards over our heads.

" 'Where?' said the man above me. 'Where?'

"I was looking up, for all that I was worth. I was conscious of a certain sense of relief. 'It is *real*, then,' I said to myself. I screwed my head round, and looked along the yards above us. Yet, still I could see nothing; nothing except shadows and patches of light.

"Down on deck, I caught the Second Mate's voice.

" 'Have you got him?' he was shouting.

" 'Not yet, Zur,' sung out the lowest man on the leeside.

" 'We sees 'im, Sir,' added Quoin.

" 'I don't!' I said.

" 'There 'e is agen,' he said.

"We had reached the t'gallant rigging, and he was pointing up to the royal yard.

" 'Ye're a fule, Quoin. That's what ye are.'

"The voice came from above. It was Jock's, and there was a burst of laughter at Quoin's expense.

"I could see Jock now. He was standing in the rigging, just below the yard. He had gone straight away up, while the rest of us were mooning over the top.

" 'Ye're a fule, Quoin,' he said, again. 'And I'm thinking the Second's juist as saft.'

"He began to descend.

" 'Then there's no one?' I asked.

" 'Na',' he said, briefly.

"As we reached the deck, the Second Mate ran down off the poop. He came towards us, with an expectant air.

" 'You've got him?' he asked, confidently.

" 'There wasn't anyone,' I said.

" 'What!' he nearly shouted. 'You're hiding something!' he continued, angrily, and glancing from one to another. 'Out with it. Who was it?'

" 'We're hiding nothing,' I replied, speaking for the lot. 'There's no one up there.'

"The Second looked round upon us.

" 'Am I a fool?' he asked, contemptuously.

"There was an assenting silence.

" 'I saw him myself,' he continued. 'Tammy, here, saw him. He wasn't over the top when I first spotted him. There's no mistake about it. It's all damned rot saying he's not there.'

" 'Well, he's not, Sir,' I answered. 'Jock went right up to the royal yard.'

"The Second Mate said nothing, in immediate reply; but went aft a few steps and looked up the main. Then he turned to the two 'prentices.

" 'Sure you two boys didn't see any one coming down from the main?' he inquired, suspiciously.

" 'Yes, Sir,' they answered together.

" 'Anyway,' I heard him mutter to himself, 'I'd have spotted him myself, if he had.

" 'Have you any idea, Sir, who it was you saw?' I asked, at this juncture.

"He looked at me, keenly.

" 'No!' he said.

"He thought for a few moments, while we all about in silence, waiting for him to let us go.

" 'By the holy poker!' he exclaimed, suddenly. 'But I ought to have thought of that before.'

"He turned, and eyed us individually.

" 'You're all here?' he asked.

" 'Yes, Sir,' we said in a chorus. I could see that he was counting us. Then he spoke again.

" 'All of you men stay here where you are. Tammy, you go into *your* place and see if the other fellows are in their bunks. Then come and tell me. Smartly now!'

"The boy went, and he turned to the other 'prentice.

" 'You get along forrard to the fo'cas'le,' he said. 'Count the other watch; then come aft and report to me.'

"As the youngster disappeared along the deck to the fo'cas'le, Tammy returned from his visit to the Glory Hole, to tell the Second Mate that the other two 'prentices were sound asleep in their bunks. Whereupon, the Second bundled him off to the Carpenter's and Sailmaker's berth, to see whether they were turned-in.

"While he was gone, the other boy came aft, and reported that all the men were in their bunks, and asleep.

" 'Sure?' the Second asked him.

" 'Quite, Sir,' he answered.

"The Second Mate made a quick gesture.

" 'Go and see if the Steward is in his berth,' he said, abruptly. It was plain to me that he was tremendously puzzled.

" 'You've something to learn yet, Mr. Second Mate,' I thought to myself. Then I fell to wondering to what conclusions he would come.

"A few seconds later, Tammy returned to say that the Carpenter, Sailmaker and 'Doctor' were all turned-in.

"The Second Mate muttered something, and told him to go down into the saloon to see whether the First and Third Mates, by any chance, were not in their berths.

"Tammy started off; then halted.

" 'Shall I have a look into the Old Man's place, Sir, while I'm down there?' he inquired.

" 'No!' said the Second Mate. 'Do what I told you, and then come and tell me. If any one's to go into the Captain's cabin, it's got to be me.'

"Tammy said 'i, i, Sir,' and skipped away, up on to the poop.

"While he was gone, the other 'prentice came up to say that the Steward was in his berth, and that he wanted to know what the hell he was fooling round his part of the ship for.

"The Second Mate said nothing, for nearly a minute. Then he turned to us, and told us we might go forrard.

"As we moved off in a body, and talking in undertones, Tammy came down from the poop, and went up to the Second Mate. I heard him say that the two Mates were in their berths, asleep. Then he added, as if it were an afterthought—

" 'So's the Old Man.'

" 'I thought I told you—' the Second Mate began.

" 'I didn't, Sir,' Tammy said. 'His cabin door was open.'

"The Second Mate started to go aft. I caught a fragment of a remark he was making to Tammy.

" '—accounted for the whole crew. I'm—'

"He went up on to the poop. I did not catch the rest.

"I had loitered a moment; now, however, I hurried after the others. As we neared fo'cas'le, one bell went, and we roused out the other watch, and told them what jinks we had been up to.

" 'I rec'on 'e must be rocky,' one of the men remarked.

" 'Not 'im,' said another. ' 'e's bin 'avin' forty winks on the break, an' dreemed 'is mother-en-lore 'ad come on 'er visit, friendly like.'

"There was some laughter at this suggestion, and I caught myself smiling along with the rest; though I had no reason for sharing their belief, that there was nothing in it all.

" 'Might 'ave been a stowaway, yer know,' I heard Quoin, the one who had suggested it before, remark to one of the A.B.'s, named Stubbins— A short, rather surly-looking chap.

" 'Might have been hell!" returned Stubbins. 'Stowaways hain't such fools as all that.'

" 'I dunno,' said the first. 'I wish I 'ad arsked the Second what 'e thought about it.'

" 'I don't think it was a stowaway, somehow, I said, chipping in. 'What would a stowaway want aloft? I guess he'd be trying more for the Steward's pantry.

" 'You bet he would, hevry time,' said Stubbins. He lit his pipe, and sucked at it, slowly.

" 'I don't hunderstand it, all ther same,' he remarked, after a moment's silence.

" 'Neither do I,' I said. And after that I was quiet for a while, listening to the run of conversation on the subject.

"Presently, my glance fell upon Williams, the man who had spoken to me about 'shadders.' He was sitting in his bunk, smoking, and making no effort to join in the talk.

"I went across to him.

" 'What do you think of it, Williams?' I asked. 'Do *you* think the Second Mate really saw anything?'

"He looked at me, with a sort of gloomy suspicion; but said nothing.

"I felt a trifle annoyed by his silence; but took care not to show it. After a few moments, I went on.

" 'Do you know, Williams, I'm beginning to understand what you meant that night, when you said there were too many shadows.'

" 'Wot yer mean?' he said, pulling his pipe from out of his mouth, and fairly surprised into answering.

" 'What I say, of course,' I said. 'There *are* too many shadows.'

"He sat up, and leant forward out from his bunk, extending his hand and pipe. His eyes plainly showed his excitement.

" ' 'ave yer seen—' he hesitated, and looked at me, struggling inwardly to express himself.

" 'Well?' I prompted.

"For perhaps a minute he tried to say something. Then his expression altered suddenly from doubt, and something else more indefinite, to a pretty grim look of determination.

"He spoke.

" 'I'm blimed,' he said, 'ef I don't tike er piy-diy out of 'er, shadders er no shadders.'

"I looked at him, with astonishment.

" 'What's it got to do with your getting a payday out of her?' I asked.

"He nodded his head, with a sort of stolid resolution.

" 'Look 'ere,' he said.

"I waited.

" 'Ther crowd cleared'; he indicated with his hand and pipe towards the stern.

" 'You mean in 'Frisco?' I said.

" 'Yus,' he replied; ' 'an withart er cent of ther piy I styled.'

"I comprehended him suddenly.

" 'You think they saw,' I hesitated; then I said 'shadows?'

"He nodded; but said nothing.

" 'And so they all bunked?'

"He nodded again, and began tapping out his pipe on the edge of his bunkboard.

" 'And the officers and the Skipper?' I asked.

" 'Fresh uns,' he said, and got out of his bunk; for eight bells was striking.

IV
The Fooling with the Sail

"IT WAS ON THE Friday night, that the Second Mate had the watch aloft looking for the man up the main; and for the next five days little else was talked about; though, with the exception of Williams, Tammy and myself, no one seemed to think of treating the matter seriously. Perhaps I should not exclude Quoin, who still persisted, on every occasion, that there was a stowaway aboard. As for the Second Mate, I have very little doubt *now*, but that he was beginning to realise there was something deeper and less understandable than he had at first dreamed of. Yet, all the same, I know he had to keep his guesses and half-formed opinions pretty well to himself; for the Old Man and the First Mate chaffed him unmercifully about his 'bogy.' This, I got from Tammy, who had heard them both ragging him during the second dog-watch the following day. There was another thing Tammy told me, that bowed how the Second Mate bothered about his inability to understand the mysterious appearance and disappearance of the man he had seen go aloft. He had made Tammy give him every detail he could remember about the figure we had seen by the log-reel. What is more, the Second had not even affected to treat the matter lightly, nor as a thing to be sneered at; but had listened seriously, and asked a great many questions. It is very evident to me that he was reaching out towards the only possible conclusion. Though, goodness knows, it was one that was impossible and improbable enough.

"It was on the Wednesday night, after the five days of talk I have mentioned, that there came, to me and to those who *knew*, another element of fear. And yet, I can quite understand that, at *that* time, those who had seen nothing, would find little to be afraid of, in all that I am going to tell you. Still, even they were much puzzled and astonished, and perhaps, after all, a little awed. There was so much in the affair that was inexplicable, and yet again such a lot that was natural and

26

commonplace. For, when all is said and done, it was nothing more than the blowing adrift of one of the sails; yet accompanied by what were really significant details—significant, that is, in the light of that which Tammy and I and the Second Mate knew.

"Seven bells, and then one, had gone in the first watch, and our side was being roused out to relieve the Mate's. Most of the men were already out of their bunks, and sitting about on their sea-chests, getting into their togs.

"Suddenly, one of the 'prentices in the other watch, put his head in through the doorway on the port side.

" 'The Mate wants to know,' he said, 'which of you chaps made fast the fore royal, last watch.'

" 'Wot's 'e want to know that for?' inquired one of the men.

" 'The leeside's blowing adrift,' said the 'prentice. 'And he says that the chap who made it fast is to go up and see to it as soon as the watch is relieved.'

" 'Oh! does 'e ? Well 'twasn't me, any'ow,' replied the man. 'You'd better arsk sum of t'others.'

" 'Ask what?' inquired Plummer, getting out of his bunk, sleepily.

"The 'prentice repeated his message.

"The man yawned and stretched himself.

" 'Let me see,' he muttered, and scratched his head with one hand, while he fumbled for his trousers with the other. ' 'oo made ther fore r'yal fast?' He got into his trousers, and stood up. 'Why, ther Or'nary, er course; 'oo else do yer suppose?'

" 'That's all I wanted to know!' said the 'prentice, and went away.

" 'Hi! Tom!' Stubbins sung out to the Ordinary. 'Wake up,' you lazy young devil. Ther Mate's just sent to hinquire who it was made the fore royal fast. It's all blowin' adrift, and he says you're to get along up as soon as eight bells goes, and make it fast again.'

"Tom jumped out of his bunk, and began to dress, quickly.

" 'Blowin' adrift!' he said. 'There ain't all that much wind; and I tucked the ends of the gaskets well in under the other turns.'

" 'P'raps one of ther gaskets is rotten, and given way,' suggested Stubbins. 'Anyway, you'd better hurry up, it's just on eight bells.'

"A minute later, eight bells went, and we trooped away aft for roll-call. As soon as the names were called over, I saw the Mate lean towards the Second and say something. Then the Second Mate sung out:—

" 'Tom!'

" 'Sir!' answered Tom.

" 'Was it you made fast that fore royal, last watch?'

" 'Yes, Sir.'

" 'How's that it's broken adrift?'

" 'Carn't say, Sir.'

" 'Well, it has, and you'd better jump aloft and shove the gasket round it again. And mind you make a better job of it this time.'

" 'i, i, Sir,' said Tom, and followed the rest of us forrard. Reaching the fore rigging, he climbed into it, and began to make his way leisurely aloft. I could see him with a fair amount of distinctness, as the moon was very clear and bright, though getting old.

"I went over to the weather pin-rail, and leaned up against it, watching him, while I filled my pipe. The other men, both the watch on deck and the watch below, had gone into the fo'cas'le, so that I imagined I was the only one about the main-deck. Yet, a minute later, I discovered that I was mistaken; for, as I proceeded to light up, I saw Williams, the young cockney, come out from under the lee of the house, and turn and look up at the Ordinary as he went steadily upwards. I was a little surprised, as I knew he and three of the others had a 'poker fight' on, and he'd won over sixty pounds of tobacco. I believe I opened my mouth to sing out to him to know why he wasn't playing; and then, all at once, there came into my mind the memory of my first conversation with him. I remembered that he had said sails were always blowing adrift *at night*. I remembered the, then, unaccountable emphasis he had laid on those two words; and remembering that, I felt suddenly afraid. For, all at once, the absurdity had struck me of a sail—even a badly stowed one—blowing adrift in such fine and calm weather as we were then having. I won-dered I had not seen before that there was something queer and unlikely about the affair. Sails don't blow adrift in fine weather, with the sea calm and the ship as steady as a rock. I moved away from the rail and went towards Williams. He knew something, or, at least, he guessed at something that was very much a blankness to me at that time. Up above, the boy was climbing up, to what? That was the thing that made me feel so frightened. Ought I to tell all I knew and guessed? And then, who should I tell? I should only be laughed at—I—

"Williams turned towards me, and spoke.

" 'Gawd!' he said, 'it's started agen!'

" 'What?' I said. Though I knew what he meant.

" 'Them syles,' he answered, and made a gesture towards the fore royal.

"I glanced up, briefly. All the leeside of the sail was adrift, from the bunt gasket outwards. Lower, I saw Tom; he was just hoisting himself into the t'gallant rigging.

"Williams spoke again.

" 'We lost two on 'em just sime way, comin' art.'

" 'Two of the men!' I exclaimed.

" 'Yus!' he said tersely.

" 'I can't understand,' I went on. 'I never heard anything about it.'

" 'Who'd yer got ter tell yer abart it?' he asked.

"I made no reply to his question; indeed, I had scarcely comprehended it, for the problem of what I ought to do in the matter had risen again in my mind.

" 'I've a good mind to go aft and tell the Second Mate all I know,' I said. 'He's seen something himself that he can't explain away, and—anyway I can't stand this state of things. If the Second Mate knew all—'

" 'Garn!' he cut in, interrupting me. 'An' be told yer're a blastid hidiot. Not yer. Yer sty were yer are.'

"I stood irresolute. What he had said, was perfectly correct, and I was positively stumped what to do for the best. That there was danger aloft, I was convinced; though if I had been asked my reasons for supposing this, they would have been hard to find. Yet of its existence, I was as certain as though my eyes already saw it. I wondered whether, being so ignorant of the form it would assume, I could stop it by joining Tom on the yard? This thought came as I stared up at the royal. Tom had reached the sail, and was standing on the foot-rope, close in to the bunt. He was bending over the yard, and reaching down for the slack of the sail. And then, as I looked, I saw the belly of the royal tossed up and down abruptly, as though a sudden heavy gust of wind had caught it.

" 'I'm blimed—!' Williams began, with a sort of excited expectation. And then he stopped as abruptly as he had begun. For, in a moment the sail had thrashed right over the after side of the yard, apparently knocking Tom clean from off the foot-rope.

" 'My God!' I shouted out loud. 'He's gone!'

"For an instant there was a blur over my eyes, and Williams was singing out something that I could not catch. Then, just as quickly, it went, and I could see again, clearly.

"Williams was pointing, and I saw something black, swinging below the yard. Williams called out something fresh, and made a run for the fore rigging. I caught the last part—

" ' —ther garskit.'

"Straightway, I knew that Tom had managed to grab the gasket as he fell, and I bolted after Williams to give him a hand in getting the youngster into safety.

"Down on deck, I caught the sound of running feet, and then the Second Mate's voice. He was asking what the devil was up; but I did not able to answer him then. I wanted all my breath to help me aloft. I knew very well that some of the gaskets were little better than old shakins; and, unless Tom got hold of something on the t'gallant yard below him, he might come down with a run any moment. I reached the top, and lifted myself over it in quick time. Williams was some distance above me. In less than half a minute, I reached the t'gallant yard. Williams had gone up on to the royal. I slid out on to the t'gallant foot-rope until I was just below Tom; then I sung out to him to let himself down to me, and I would catch him. He made no answer, and I saw that he was hanging in a curiously limp fashion, and by one hand.

"Williams's voice came down to me from the royal yard. He was singing out to me to go up and give him a hand to pull Tom up on to the yard. When I reached him, he told me that the gasket had hitched itself round the lad's wrist. I bent beside the yard, and peered down. It was as Williams had said, and I realised how near a thing it had been. Strangely enough, even at that moment, the thought came to me how little wind there was. I remembered the wild way in which the sail had lashed at the boy.

"All this time, I was busily working, unreeving the port buntline. I took the end, made a running bowline with it round the gasket, and let the loop slide down over the boy's head and shoulders. Then I took a strain on it and tightened it under his arms. A minute later we had him safely on the yard between us. In the uncertain moonlight, I could just make out the mark of a great lump on his forehead, where the foot of the sail must have caught him when it knocked him over.

"As we stood there a moment, taking our breath, I caught the sound of the Second Mate's voice close beneath us. Williams glanced down; then he looked up at me and gave a short, grunting laugh.

" 'Crikey!' he said.

" 'What's up?' I asked, quickly.

"He jerked his head backwards and downwards. I screwed round a bit, holding the jackstay with one hand, and steadying the insensible Ordinary with the other. In this way I could look below. At first, I could see nothing. Then the Second Mate's voice came up to me again.

" 'Who the hell are you? What are you doing?

"I saw him now. He was standing at the foot of the weather t'gallant rigging, his face was turned upwards, peering round the after side of the mast. It showed to me only as a blurred, pale-coloured oval in the moonlight.

"He repeated his question.

" 'It's Williams and I, Sir,' I said. 'Tom, here, has had an accident.'

"I stopped. He began to come up higher towards us. From the rigging to leeward there came suddenly a buzz of men talking.

"The Second Mate reached us.

" 'Well, what's up, anyway?' he inquired, suspiciously. 'What's happened?'

"He had bent forward, and was peering at Tom. I started to explain; but he cut me short with:—

" 'Is he dead?'

" 'No, Sir,' I said. 'I don't think so; but the poor beggar's had a bad fall. He was hanging by the gasket when we got to him. The sail knocked him off the yard.'

" 'What?' he said, sharply.

" 'The wind caught the sail, and it lashed back over the yard—'

" 'What wind?' he interrupted. 'There's no wind, scarcely.' He shifted his weight on to the other foot. 'What do you mean?'

" 'I mean what I say, Sir. The wind brought the foot of the sail over the top of the yard and knocked Tom clean off the foot-rope. Williams and I both saw it happen.'

" 'But there's no wind to do such a thing; you're talking nonsense!'

"It seemed to me that there was as much of bewilderment as anything else in his voice; yet I could tell that he was suspicious—though, of what, I doubted whether he himself could have told.

"He glanced at Williams, and seemed about to say something. Then, seeming to change his mind, he turned, and sung out to one of the men who had followed him aloft, to go down and pass out a coil of new, three-inch manila, and a tail-block.

" 'Smartly now!' he concluded.

" ''i, i, Sir,' said the man, and went down swiftly.

"The Second Mate turned to me.

" 'When you've got Tom below, I shall want a better explanation of all this, than the one you've given me. It won't wash.'

" 'Very well, Sir,' I answered. 'But you won't get any other.'

" 'What do you mean?' he shouted at me. 'I'll let you know I'll have no impertinence from you or anyone else.'

" 'I don't mean any impertinence, Sir—I mean that it's the only explanation there is to give.'

" 'I tell you it won't wash!' he repeated. 'There's something too damned funny about it all. I shall have to report the matter to the Captain. I can't tell him that yarn—' He broke off abruptly.

" 'It's not the only damned funny thing that's happened aboard this old hooker,' I answered. '*You* ought to know that, Sir.'

" 'What do you mean?' he asked, quickly.

" 'Well, Sir,' I said, 'to be straight, what about that chap you sent us hunting after up the main the other night? That was a funny enough affair, wasn't it? This one isn't half so funny.'

" 'That will do, Jessop!' he said, angrily.

" 'I won't have any back talk.'

"Yet there was something about his tone that told me I had got one in on my own. He seemed all at once less able to appear confident that I was telling him a fairy tale.

"After that, for perhaps half a minute, he said nothing. I guessed he was doing some hard thinking. When he spoke again it was on the matter of getting the Ordinary down on deck.

" 'One of you'll have to go down the leeside and steady him down,' he concluded.

"He turned and looked downwards.

" 'Are you bringing that gantline?' he sung out.

" 'Yes, Sir,' I heard one of the men answer.

"A moment later, I saw the man's head appear over the top. He had the tail-block slung round his neck, and the end of the ganth'ne over his shoulder.

"Very soon we had the ganth'ne rigged, and Tom down on deck. Then we took him into the fo'cas'le and put him in his bunk. The Second Mate had sent for some brandy, and now he started to dose him well with it. At the same time a couple of the men chafed his hands and feet. In a little, he began to show signs of coming round. Presently, after a sudden fit of coughing, he opened his eyes, with a surprised, bewildered stare. Then he caught at the edge of his bunk-board, and sat up, giddily. One of the men steadied him, while the Second Mate stood back, and eyed him, critically. The boy rocked as he sat, and put up his hand to his head.

" 'Here,' said the Second Mate, 'take another drink.'

"Tom caught his breath and choked a little; then he spoke.

" 'By gum!' he said, 'my head does ache.'

"He put up his hand, again, and felt at the lump on his forehead. Then he bent forward and stared round at the men grouped about his bunk.

" 'What's up?' he inquired, in a confused sort of way, and seeming as if he could not see us clearly.

" 'What's up?' he asked again.

" 'That's just what I want to know!' said the Second Mate, speaking for the first time with some sternness.

'I ain't been snoozin' while there's been a job on?' Tom inquired, anxiously.

"He looked round at the men appealingly.

" 'It's knocked 'im dotty, strikes me,' said one of the men, audibly.

" 'No,' I said, answering Tom's question 'You've had—'

" 'Shut that, Jessop!' said the Second Mate quickly, interrupting me, 'I want to hear what the boy's got to say for himself.'

"He turned again to Tom.

" 'You were up at the fore royal,' he prompted.

" 'I carn't say I was, Sir,' said Tom, doubtfully. I could see that he had not gripped the Second Mate's meaning.

" 'But you were!' said the Second, with some impatience. 'It was blowing adrift, and I sent you up to shove a gasket round it.'

" 'Blowin' adrift, Sir?' said Tom, dully.

" 'Yes! blowing adrift. Don't I speak plainly?'

"The dullness went from Tom's face, suddenly.

" 'So it was, Sir!' he said, his memory returning. 'The bloomin' sail got chock full of wind. It caught me bang in the face.'

"He paused a moment.

" 'I believe—' he began, and then stopped once more.

" 'Go on!' said the Second Mate. 'Spit it out!'

" 'I don't know, Sir,' Tom said. 'I don't understand—'

"He hesitated again.

" 'That's all I can remember,' he muttered, and put his hand up to the bruise on his forehead, as though trying to remember something.

"In the momentary silence that succeeded, I caught the voice of Stubbins.

" 'There hain't hardly no wind,' he was saying, in a puzzled tone.

"There was a low murmur of assent from the surrounding men.

"The Second Mate said nothing, and I glanced at him, curiously. Was he beginning to see, I wondered, how useless it was to try to find any sensible explanation of the affair? Had he begun at last to couple it with that peculiar business of the man up the main? I am inclined *now* to think that this was so; for, after staring a few moments at Tom, in a doubtful sort of way, he went out of the fo'cas'le, saying that he would inquire further into the matter in the morning. Yet, when the morning came, he did no such thing. As for his reporting the affair to the Skipper, I much doubt it. Even did he, it must have been in a very casual way; for we heard nothing more about it; though, of course we talked it over pretty thoroughly among our-selves.

"With regard to the Second Mate, even now I am rather puzzled by his attitude to us aloft. Sometimes I have thought that he must have suspected us of trying to play off some trick on him—perhaps, at the time, he still half suspected one of us of being in some way connected with the other business. Or, again, he may have been trying to fight against the conviction that was being forced upon him, that there was really something impossible and beastly about the old packet. Of course, these are only suppositions.

"And then, close upon this, there were further developments.

V
The End Of Williams

"AS I HAVE SAID, there was a lot of talk, among the crowd of us forrard, about Tom's strange accident. None of the men knew that Williams and I had seen it *happen*. Stubbins gave it as his opinion that Tom had been sleepy, and missed the foot-rope. Tom, of course, would not have this by any means. Yet, he had no one to appeal to; for, at that time, he was just as ignorant as the rest, that we had seen the sail flap up over the yard.

"Stubbins insisted that it stood to reason it couldn't be the wind. There wasn't any, he said; and the rest of the men agreed with him.

" 'Well,' I said, 'I don't know about all that. I'm a bit inclined to think Tom's yarn is the truth.'

" 'How do you make that hout?' Stubbins asked, unbelievingly. 'There haint nothin' like enough wind.'

" 'What about the place on his forehead?' I inquired, in turn. 'How are you going to explain that?'

" 'I 'spect he knocked himself there when he slipped,' he answered.

" 'Likely 'nuff,' agreed old Jaskett, who was sitting smoking on a chest near by.

" 'Well, you're both a damn long way out of it!' Tom chipped in, pretty warm. 'I wasn't asleep; an' the sail did bloomin' well hit me.'

" 'Don't you be imperent, young feller,' said Jaskett.

"I joined in again.

" 'There's another thing, Stubbins,' I said. 'The gasket Tom was hanging by, was on the after side of the yard. That looks as if the sail might have flapped it over? If there were wind enough to do the one, it seems to me that it might have done the other.'

" 'Do you mean that it was hinder ther yard, or hover ther top?' he asked.

" 'Over the top, of course. What's more, the foot of the sail was

35

hanging over the after part of the yard, in a bight.'

"Stubbins was plainly surprised at that, and before he was ready with his next objection, Plummer spoke.

" " 'oo saw it?' he asked.

" 'I saw it!' I said, a bit sharply. 'So did Williams; so—for that matter—did the Second Mate.'

"Plummer relapsed into silence, and smoked; and Stubbins broke out afresh.

" 'I reckon Tom must have had a hold of the foot and the gasket, and pulled 'em hover the yard when he tumbled.'

" 'No!' interrupted Tom. 'The gasket was under the sail. I couldn't even see it. An' I hadn't time to get hold of the foot of the sail, before it up and caught me smack in the face.'

" " 'ow did yer get 'old er ther gasket, when yer fell, then?' asked Plummer.

" 'He didn't get hold of it,' I answered for Tom. 'It had taken a turn round his wrist, and that's how we found him hanging.'

" 'Do yer mean to say as 'e 'adn't got 'old of ther garsket?' Quoin inquired, pausing in the lighting of his pipe.

" 'Of course, I do,' I said. 'A chap doesn't go hanging onto a rope when he's jolly well been knocked senseless.'

" 'Ye're richt,' assented Jock, richt there, Jessop.'

"Quoin concluded the lighting of his pipe.

" 'I dunno,' he said.

"I went on, without noticing him.

" 'Anyway, when Williams and I found him, he was hanging by the gasket, and it had a couple of turns round his wrist. And besides that, as I said before, the foot of the sail was hanging over the after side of the yard, and Tom's weight on the gasket was holding it there.'

" 'It's damned queer,' said Stubbins, in a puzzled voice. 'There don't seem to be no way of gettin' a proper hexplanation to it.'

"I glanced at Williams, to suggest that I should tell all that we had seen; but he shook his head, and, after a moment's thought, it seemed to me that there was nothing to be gained by so doing. We had no very clear idea of the thing that had happened, and our half facts and guesses would only have tended to make the matter appear more grotesque and unlikely. The only thing to be done was to wait and watch. If we could only get hold of something tangible, then we might hope to tell all that we knew, without being made into laughingstocks.

"I came out from my think, abruptly.

"Stubbins was speaking again. He was arguing the matter with one of the other men.

" 'You see, with there bein' no wind, scarcely, ther thing's himpossible, an' yet—'

"The other man interrupted with some remark I did not catch.

" 'No,' I heard Stubbins say. 'I'm hout of my reckonin'. I don't savvy it one bit. It's too much like a damned fairy tale.'

" 'Look at his wrist!' I said.

"Tom held out his right hand and arm for inspection. It was considerably swollen where the rope had been round it.

" 'Yes,' admitted Stubbins. 'That's right enough; but it don't tell you nothin'.'

"I made no reply. As Stubbins said, it told you 'nothin'.' And there I let it drop. Yet, I have told you this, as showing how the matter was regarded in the fo'cas'le. Still, it did not occupy our minds very long; for, as I have said, there were further developments.

"The three following nights passed quietly; and then, on the fourth, all those curious signs and hints culminated suddenly in something extraordinarily grim. Yet, everything had been so subtle and intangible, and, indeed, so was the affair itself, that only those who had actually come in touch with the invading fear, seemed really capable of comprehending the terror of the thing. The men, for the most part, began to say the ship was unlucky, and, of course, as usual! there was some talk of there being a Jonah in the ship. Still, I cannot say that none of the men realised there was anything horrible and frightening in it all; for I am sure that some did, a little; and I think Stubbins was certainly one of them; though I feel certain that he did not, at that time, you know, grasp a quarter of the real significance that underlay the several queer matters that had disturbed our nights. He seemed to fail, somehow, to grasp the element of personal danger that, to me, was already plain. He lacked sufficient imagination, I suppose, to piece the things together—to trace the natural sequence of the events, and their development. Yet I must not forget, of course, that he had no knowledge of those two first incidents. If he had, perhaps he might have stood where I did. As it was, he had not seemed to reach out at all, you know, not even in the matter of Tom and the fore royal. Now, however, after the thing I am about to tell you, he seemed to see a little way into the darkness, and realise possibilities.

"I remember the fourth night, well. It was a clear, starlit, moonless sort of night: at least, I think there was no moon; or, at any rate, the moon could have been little more than a thin crescent, for it was near the dark time.

"The wind had breezed up a bit; but still remained steady. We were slipping along at about six or seven knots an hour. It was our middle watch on deck, and the ship was full of the blow and hum of the wind aloft. Williams and I were the only ones about the main-deck. He was leaning over the weather pin-rail, smoking; while I was pacing up and down, between him and the fore hatch. Stubbins was on the lookout.

"Two bells had gone some minutes, and I was wishing to goodness that it was eight, and time to turn-in. Suddenly, overhead, there sounded a sharp crack, like the report of a rifle shot. It was followed instantly by the rattle and crash of sailcloth thrashing in the wind.

"Williams jumped away from the rail, and ran aft a few steps. I followed him, and, together, we stared upwards to see what had gone. Indistinctly, I made out that the weather sheet of the fore t'gallant had carried away, and the clew of the sail was whirling and banging about in the air, and, every few moments, hitting the steel yard a blow, like the thump of a great sledge hammer.

" 'It's the shackle, or one of the links that's gone, I think,' I shouted to Williams, above the noise of the sail. 'That's the spectacle that's hitting the yard.'

" 'Yus!' he shouted back, and went to get hold of the clewline. I ran to give him a hand. At the same moment, I caught the Second Mate's voice away aft, shouting. Then came the noise of running feet, and the rest of the watch, and the Second Mate, were with us almost at the same moment. In a few minutes we had the yard lowered and the sail clewed up. Then Williams and I went aloft to see where the sheet had gone. It was much as I had supposed; the spectacle was all right, but the pin had gone out of the shackle, and the shackle itself was jammed into the sheavehole in the yard arm.

"Williams sent me down for another pin, while he unbent the clewline, and overhauled it down to the sheet. When I returned with the fresh pin, I screwed it into the shackle, clipped on the clewline, and sung out to the men to take a pull on the rope. This they did, and at the second heave the shackle came away. When it was high enough, I went up on to the t'gallant yard, and held the chain, while Williams shackled it into the spectacle. Then he bent on the clew-line afresh, and sung out to the Second Mate that we were ready to hoist away.

" 'Yer'd better go down an' give 'em a 'aul,' he said. 'I'll sty an' light up ther syle.'

" 'Right ho, Williams,' I said, getting into the rigging. 'Don't let the ship's bogy run away with you.'

"This remark I made in a moment of lightheartedness, such as will come to any one aloft, at times. I was exhilarated for the time being, and quite free from the sense of fear that had been with me so much of late. I suppose this was due to the freshness of the wind.

" 'There's more'n one!' he said, in that curiously short way of his.

" 'What?' I asked.

"He repeated his remark. I was suddenly serious. The *reality* of all the impossible details of the past weeks came back to me, vivid, and beastly.

" 'What do you mean, Williams?' I asked him.

"But he had shut up, and would say nothing.

" 'What do you know—how much do you know?' I went on, quickly. 'Why did you never tell me that you—'

"The Second Mate's voice interrupted me, abruptly:—

" 'Now then, up there! Are you going to keep us waiting all night? One of you come down and give us a pull with the ha'lyards. The other stay up and light up the gear.'

" 'i, i, Sir,' I shouted back.

"Then I turned to Williams, hurriedly.

" 'Look here, Williams,' I said. 'If you think there is *really* a danger in your being alone up here—' I hesitated for words to express what I meant. Then I went on. 'Well, I'll jolly well stay up with you.'

"The Second Mate's voice came again.

" 'Come on now, one of you! Make a move! What the hell are you doing?'

" 'Coming, Sir!' I sung out.

" 'Shall I stay?' I asked definitely.

" 'Garn!' he said. 'Don't yer fret yerself. I'll tike er bloomin' piy-diy out of 'er. Blarst 'em. I ain't funky of 'em.'

"I went. That was the last word Williams spoke to anyone living.

"I reached the decks, and tailed on to the haulyards.

"We had nearly mast-headed the yard, and the Second Mate was looking up at the dark outline of the sail, ready to sing out 'Belay'; when, all at once, there came a queer sort of muffled shout from Williams.

" 'Vast hauling, you men,' shouted the Second Mate.

"We stood silent, and listened.

" 'What's that, Williams?' he sung out. 'Are you all clear?'

"For nearly half a minute we stood, listening; but there came no reply. Some of the men said afterwards that they noticed a curious rattling and vibrating noise aloft, that sounded faintly above the hum and swirl of the wind. Like the sound of loose ropes being shaken and slatted together, you know. Whether this noise was really heard, or whether it was something that no existence outside of their imaginations, I cannot say. I heard nothing of it; but then I was at the tail end of the rope, and furthest from the fore rigging; while those who heard it were on the fore part of the haulyards, and close up to the shrouds.

"The Second Mate put his hands to his mouth.

" 'Are you all clear there?' he shouted again.

"The answer came, unintelligible and unexpected. It ran like this:—

" 'Blarst yer... I've styed.... Did yer think... drive... bl—dy piydiy.' And then there was a sudden silence.

"I stared up at the dim sail, astonished.

" 'He's dotty!' said Stubbins, who had been told to come off the lookout and give us a pull.

" ' 'e's as mad as a bloomin' 'atter,' said Quoin, who was standing foreside of me. ' 'e's been queer all along.'

" 'Silence there!' shouted the Second Mate. Then:—

" 'Williams!'

"No answer.

" 'Williams!' more loudly.

"Still no answer.

"Then:—

" 'Damn you, you jumped-up cockney crocodile! Can't you hear? Are you blooming-well deaf?'

"There was no answer, and the Second Mate turned to me.

" 'Jump aloft, smartly now, Jessop, and see what's wrong!'

" 'i, i, Sir,' I said, and made a run for the rigging. I felt a bit queer. Had Williams gone mad? He certainly always had been a bit funny. Or—and the thought came with a jump—had he seen— I did not finish. Suddenly, up aloft, there sounded a frightful scream. I stopped, with my hand on the sheer-pole. The next instant, something fell out of the darkness—a heavy body, that struck the deck near the waiting men, with a tremendous crash and a loud, ringing, wheezy sound that sickened me. Several of the men shouted out loud in their fright, and let go of the haulyards; but luckily the stopper held it, and the yard did not come down. Then, for the space of several seconds, there was a dead silence among the crowd; and it seemed to me that the wind had in it a strange moaning note.

"The Second Mate was the first to speak. His voice came so abruptly that it startled me.

" 'Get a light, one of you, quick now!'

"There was a moment's hesitation.

THE GHOST PIRATES   41

" 'Fetch one of the binnacle lamps, Tammy.'

" 'i, i, Sir,' the youngster said, in a quavering voice, and ran aft.

"In less than a minute, I saw the light coming towards us along the deck. The boy was running. He reached us, and handed the lamp to the Second Mate, who took it and went towards the dark, huddled heap on the deck. He held the light out before him, and peered at the thing.

" 'My God!' he said. 'It's Williams!'

"He stooped lower with the light, and I saw details. It was Williams right enough. The Second Mate told a couple of the men to lift him and straighten him out on the hatch. Then he went aft to call the Skipper. He returned in a couple of minutes with an old Ensign which he spread over the poor beggar. Almost directly, the Captain came hurrying forrard along the decks. He pulled back one end of the Ensign, and looked; then he put it back quietly, and the Second Mate explained all that we knew, in a few words.

" 'Would you leave him where he is, Sir?' he asked, after he had told everything.

" 'The night's fine,' said the Captain. 'You may as well leave the poor devil there.'

"He turned, and went aft, slowly. The man who was holding the light, swept it round so that it showed the place where Williams had struck the deck.

"The Second Mate spoke abruptly.

" 'Get a broom and a couple of buckets, some of you.'

"He turned sharply, and ordered Tammy onto the poop.

"As soon as he had seen the yard mast-headed, and the ropes cleared up, he followed Tammy. He knew well enough that it would not do for the youngster to let his mind dwell too much on the poor chap on the hatch, and I found out, a little later, that he gave the boy something to occupy his thoughts.

"After they had gone aft, we went into the fo'cas'le. Everyone was moody and frightened. For a little while, we sat about in our bunks and the chests, and no one said a word. The below were all asleep, and not one of them what had happened.

"All at once, Plummer, whose wheel it was stepped over the starboard washboard, into the fo'cas'le.

" 'What's up, anyway?' he asked. 'Is Williams much 'urt?'

" ' 'Sh!' I said. 'You'll wake the others. Who's taken your wheel?'

" 'Tammy—ther Second sent 'im. 'e said I could go forrard an' 'ave er smoke, 'e said Williams 'ad 'ad er fall.'

"He broke off, and looked across the fo'cas'le.

" 'Where is 'e?' he inquired, in a puzzled voice.

"I glanced at the others; but no one seemed inclined to start yarning about it.

" 'He fell from the t'gallant rigging!' I said.

" 'Where is 'e?' he repeated.

" 'Smashed up,' I said. 'He's lying on the hatch.'

" 'Dead?' he asked.

"I nodded.

" 'I guessed 'twere some thin' pretty bad, when I saw the Old Man come forrard. 'ow did it 'appen?'

"He looked round at the lot of us sitting there silent and smoking.

" 'No one knows,' I said, and glanced at Stubbins. I caught him eyeing me, doubtfully.

"After a moment's silence, Plummer spoke again.

" 'I 'eard 'im screech, when I was at ther wheel, 'e must 'ave got 'urt up aloft.'

"Stubbins struck a match and proceeded to relight his pipe.

" 'How d'yer mean?' he asked, speaking for the first time.

" ' 'ow do I mean? Well, I can't say. Maybe 'e jammed 'is fingers between ther parrel an' ther mast.'

" 'What about 'is swearin' at ther Second Mate? Was that 'cause 'e'd jammed 'is fingers?' put in Quoin.

" 'I never 'eard about that,' said Plummer. ' 'oo 'eard 'im?'

" 'I should think heverybody in ther bloomin' ship heard him,' Stubbins answered. 'All ther same, I hain't sure he *was* swearin' at ther Second Mate. I thought at first he'd gone dotty an' was cussin' him; but somehow it don't seem likely, now I come to think. It don't stand to reason he should go to cuss ther man. There was nothin' to go cussin' about. What's more, he didn't seem ter be talkin' down to us on deck——what I could make hout. 'sides, what would he want ter go talkin' to ther Second about his pay-day?'

"He looked across to where I was sitting. Jock, who was smoking, quietly, on the chest next to me, took his pipe slowly out from between his teeth.

" 'Ye're no far oot, Stubbins, I'm thinkin'. Ye're no far oot,' he said, nodding his head.

"Stubbins still continued to gaze at me.

" 'What's your idee?' he said, abruptly.

"It may have been my fancy; but it seemed to me that there was something deeper than the mere sense the question conveyed.

"I glanced at him. I couldn't have said, myself, just what my idea was.

" 'I don't know!' I answered, a little adrift. 'He didn't strike me as cursing at the Second Mate. That is, I should say, after the first minute.'

" 'Just what I say,' he replied. 'Another thing—don't it strike you as bein' bloomin queer about Tom nearly comin' down by ther run, an' then *this*?'

"I nodded.

" 'It would have been all hup with Tom, if it hadn't been for ther gasket.'

"He paused. After a moment, he went on again.

"'That was honly three or four nights ago!'

" 'Well,' said Plummer. 'What are yer drivin' at?'

" 'Nothin', answered Stubbins. 'Honly it's damned queer. Looks as though ther ship might be unlucky, after all.'

" 'Well,' agreed Plummer. 'Things 'as been a bit funny lately; and then there's what's 'appened ternight. I shall 'ang on pretty tight ther next time I go aloft.'

"Old Jaskett took his pipe from his mouth, and sighed.

" 'Things is going wrong 'most every night,' he said, almost pathetically. 'It's as diff'rent as chalk 'n' cheese ter what it were w'en we started this 'ere trip. I thought it were all 'ellish rot about 'er bein' 'aunted; but it's not, seem'ly.'

"He stopped and expectorated.

" 'She hain't haunted,' said Stubbins. 'Leastways, not like you mean—'

"He paused, as though trying to grasp some elusive thought.

" 'Eh?' said Jaskett, in the interval.

"Stubbins continued, without noticing the query. He appeared to be answering some half-formed thought in his own brain, rather than Jaskett:—

" 'Things is queer—an' it's been a bad job tonight. I don't savvy one bit what Williams was sayin' of hup aloft. I've thought sometimes he'd somethin' on 'is mind—'

"Then, after a pause of about half a minute, he said this:—

" '*Who* was he sayin' that to?'

" 'Eh?' said Jaskett, again, with a puzzled expression.

" 'I was thinkin',' said Stubbins, knocking out his pipe on the edge of the chest. 'P'raps you're right, hafter all.'

VI

Another Man to the Wheel

"THE CONVERSATION HAD SLACKED off. We were all moody and shaken, and I know I, for one, was thinking some rather troublesome thoughts.

"Suddenly, I heard the sound of the Second's whistle. Then his voice came along the deck:—

" 'Another man to the wheel!' 'e's singin' out for someone to go aft an' relieve ther wheel,' said Quoin, who had gone to the door to listen. 'Yer'd better 'urry up, Plummer.'

" 'What's ther time?' asked Plummer, standing up and knocking out his pipe. 'Must be close on ter four bells, 'oo's next wheel is it?'

" 'It's all right, Plummer,' I said, getting up from the chest on which I had been sitting. 'I'll go along. It's my wheel, and it only wants a couple of minutes to four bells.

"Plummer sat down again, and I went out of the fo'cas'le. Reaching the poop, I met Tammy on the lee side, pacing up and down.

" 'Who's at the wheel?' I asked him, in astonishment.

" 'The Second Mate,' he said, in a shaky sort of voice. 'He's waiting to be relieved. I'll tell you all about it as soon as I get a chance.'

"I went on aft to the wheel.

" 'Who's that?' the Second inquired.

" 'It's Jessop, Sir,' I answered.

"He gave me the course, and then, without another word, went forrard along the poop. On the break, I heard him call Tammy's name, and then for some minutes he was talking to him; though what he was saying, I could not possibly hear. For my part, I was tremendously curious to know why the Second Mate had taken the wheel. I knew that if it were just a matter of bad steering on Tammy's part, he would not have dreamt of doing such a thing. There had been something queer happening, about which I had yet to learn; of this, I felt sure.

"Presently, the Second Mate left Tammy, and commenced to walk the weather side of the deck. Once he came right aft, and, stooping, peered under the wheel-box; but never addressed a word to me. Sometime later, he went down the weather ladder on to the main-deck. Directly afterwards, Tammy came running up to the lee side of the wheel-box.

" 'I've seen it again!' he said, gasping with sheer nervousness.

" 'What?' I said.

" 'That *thing*,' he answered. Then he leant across the wheel-box, and lowered his voice.

" 'It came over the lee rail—*up out of the sea*,' he added, with an air of telling something unbelievable.

"I turned more towards him; but it was too dark to see his face with any distinctness. I felt suddenly husky. 'My God!' I thought. And then I made a silly effort to protest; but he cut me short with a certain impatient hopelessness.

" 'For God's sake, Jessop,' he said, 'do stow all that! It's no good. I must have someone to talk to, or I shall go dotty.'

"I saw how useless it was to pretend any sort of ignorance. Indeed, really, I had known it all along, and avoided the youngster on that very account, as you know.

" 'Go on,' I said. 'I'll listen; but you'd better keep an eye for the Second Mate may pop up any minute.'

"For a moment, he said nothing, and I him peering stealthily about the poop.

" 'Go on,' I said. 'You'd better make haste, or he'll be up before you're halfway through. What was he doing at the wheel when I came up to relieve it? Why did he send you away from it?'

" 'He didn't,' Tammy replied, turning his face towards me. 'I bunked away from it.'

" 'What for?' I asked.

" 'Wait a minute,' he answered, 'and I'll tell you the whole business. You know the Second Mate sent me to the wheel, after *that*—' He nodded his head forrard.

" 'Yes,' I said.

" 'Well, I'd been here about ten minutes, or a quarter of an hour, and I was feeling rotten about Williams, and trying to forget it all and keep the ship on her course, and all that; when, all at once, I happened to glance to loo'ard, and there I saw it climbing over the rail. My God! I didn't know what to do. The Second Mate was standing forrard on the break of the poop, and I was here all by myself. I felt as if I were frozen stiff. When it came towards me, I let go of the wheel, and yelled and bunked forrard to the Second Mate. He caught hold of me and shook me; but I was so jolly frightened, I couldn't say a word. I could only keep on pointing. The Second kept asking me 'Where?' And then, all at once, I found I couldn't see the thing. I don't know whether he saw it. I'm not at all certain he did. He just told me to damn well get back to the wheel and stop making a damned fool of myself. I said out straight I wouldn't go. So he blew his whistle, and sung out for someone to come aft and take it. Then he ran and got hold of the wheel himself. You know the rest.'

" 'You're quite sure it wasn't thinking about Williams made you imagine you saw something?' I said, more to gain a moment to think, than because I believed that it was the case.

" 'I thought you were going to listen to me, seriously!' he said, bitterly. 'If you won't believe me; what about the chap the Second Mate saw? What about Tom? What about Williams? For goodness sake! don't try to put me off like you did last time. I nearly went cracked with wanting to tell someone who would listen to me, and wouldn't laugh. I could stand anything, but this being alone. There's a good chap, don't pretend you don't understand. Tell me what it all means. What is this horrible man that I've twice seen? You know you know something, and I believe you're afraid to tell anyone, for fear of being laughed at. Why don't you tell me? You needn't be afraid of my laughing.'

"He stopped, suddenly. For the moment, I said nothing in reply.

" 'Don't treat me like a kid, Jessop!' he exclaimed, quite passionately.

" 'I won't,' I said, with a sudden resolve to tell him everything. 'I need someone to talk to, just as badly as you do.'

" 'What does it all mean, then?' he burst out. 'Are they real? I always used to think it was all a yarn about such things.'

" 'I'm sure I don't know what it all means, Tammy,' I answered. 'I'm just as much in the dark, there, as you are. And I don't know whether they're real—that is, not as we consider things real. You don't know that I saw a queer figure down on the main-deck, several nights before you saw that thing up here.'

" 'Didn't you see this one?' he cut in, quickly.

" 'Yes,' I answered.

" 'Then, why did you pretend not to have?' he said, in a reproachful voice. 'You don't know what a state you put me into, what with my being certain that I had seen it, and then you being so jolly positive that there had been nothing. At one time I thought I was going clean off my dot—until the Second Mate saw that man go up the main. Then, I knew that there must be something in the thing I was certain I'd seen.'

" 'I thought, perhaps, that if I told you I hadn't seen it, you would think you'd been mistaken,' I said. 'I wanted you to think it was imagination, or a dream, or something of that sort.'

" 'And all the time, you knew about that other thing you'd seen?' he asked.

" 'Yes,' I replied.

" 'It was thundering decent of you,' he said. 'But it wasn't any good.'

"He paused a moment. Then he went on:—

" 'It's terrible about Williams. Do you think he saw something, up aloft?'

" 'I don't know, Tammy,' I said. 'It's impossible to say. It *may* have been only an accident.' I hesitated to tell him what I really thought.

" 'What was he saying about his pay-day? Who was he saying it to?'

" 'I don't know,' I said, again. 'He was always cracked about taking a pay-day out of her. You know, he stayed in her, on purpose, when all the others left. He told me that he wasn't going to be done out of it, for any one.'

" 'What did the other lot leave for?' he asked. Then, as the idea seemed to strike him— 'Jove! do you think they saw something, and got scared? It's quite possible. You know, we only joined her in 'Frisco. She had no 'prentices on the passage out. Our ship was sold; so they sent us aboard Here to come home.'

" 'They may have,' I said. 'Indeed, from things I've heard Williams say, I'm pretty certain, he for one, guessed or knew a jolly sight more than we've any idea of.'

" 'And now he's dead!' said Tammy, solemnly. 'We'll never be able to find out from him now.'

"For a few moments, he was silent. Then he went off on another track.

" 'Doesn't anything ever happen in the Mate's watch?'

" 'Yes,' I answered. 'There's several things happened lately, that seem pretty queer. Some of his side have been talking about them. But he's too jolly pig-headed to see anything. He just curses his chaps, and puts it all down to them.'

" 'Still,' he persisted; 'things seem to happen more in our watch than in his—I mean, bigger things. Look at tonight.'

" 'We've no proof, you know,' I said.

"He shook his head, doubtfully.

" 'I shall always funk going aloft, now.'

" 'Nonsense!' I told him. 'It may only have been an accident.'

" 'Don't!' he said. 'You know you don't think so, really.'

"I answered nothing, just then; for I knew very well that he was right. We were silent for a couple of moments.

"Then he spoke again:—

" 'Is the ship haunted?'

"For an instant I hesitated.

" 'No,' I said, at length. 'I don't think she is. I mean, not in that way.'

" 'What way, then?'

" 'Well, I've formed a bit of a theory, that seems wise one minute, and cracked the next. Of course, it's as likely to be all wrong; but it's the only thing that seems to me to fit in with all the beastly things we've had lately.'

" 'Go on!' he said, with an impatient, nervous movement.

" 'Well, I've an idea that it's nothing *in* the ship that's likely to hurt us. I scarcely know how to put it; but, if I'm right in what I think, it's the ship herself that's the cause of everything.'

" 'What do you mean?' he asked, in a puzzled voice. 'Do you mean that the ship *is* haunted, after all?'

" 'No,' I answered. 'I've just told you I didn't. Wait until I've finished what I was going to say.'

" 'All right!' he said.

" 'About that thing you saw tonight,' I went on. 'You say it came over the lee rail, up on to the poop?'

" 'Yes,' he answered.

" 'Well the thing I saw, *came up out of the sea, and went back into the sea.*'

" 'Jove!' he said; and then:— 'Yes, go on.'

" 'My idea is, that this ship is open to be boarded by those things,' I explained. 'What they are, of course I don't know. They look like men—in lots of ways. But—well, the Lord knows what's in the sea. Though we don't want to go imagining silly things, of course. And then, again, you know, it seems fat-headed, calling anything silly. That's how I keep going, in a sort of blessed circle. I don't know a bit whether they're flesh and blood, or whether they're what we should call ghosts or spirits—'

" 'They can't be flesh and blood,' Tammy interrupted. 'Where would they live? Besides, that first one I saw, I thought I could see through it. And this last one—the Second Mate would have seen it. And they would drown—'

" 'Not necessarily,' I said.

" 'Oh, but I'm sure they're not,' he insisted. 'It's impossible—'

" 'So are ghosts—when you're feeling sensible,' I answered. 'But

I'm not saying they *are* flesh and blood; though, at the same time, I'm not going to say straight out they're ghosts—not yet, at any rate.'

" 'Where do they come from?' he asked, stupidly enough.

" 'Out of the sea,' I told him. 'You saw for yourself!'

" 'Then why don't other vessels have them coming aboard?' he said. 'How do you account for that?'

" 'In a way—though sometimes it seems cracky—I think I can, according to my idea,' I answered.

" 'How?' he inquired, again.

" 'Why, I believe that this ship is open, as I've told you—exposed, unprotected, or whatever you like to call it. I should say it's reasonable to think that all the things of the material world are barred, as it were, from the immaterial; but that in some cases the barrier may be broken down. That's what may have happened to this ship. And if it has, she may be naked to the attacks of beings belonging to some other state of existence.'

" 'What's made her like that?' he asked, in a really awed sort of tone.

" 'The Lord knows!' I answered. 'Perhaps something to do with magnetic stresses; but you'd not understand, and I don't, really. And, I suppose, inside of me, I don't believe it's anything of the kind, for a minute. I'm not built that way. And yet I don't know! Perhaps, there may have been some rotten thing done aboard of her. Or, again, it's a heap more likely to be something quite outside of anything I know.'

" 'If they're immaterial then, they're spirits?' he questioned.

" 'I don't know,' I said. 'It's so hard to say what I really think, you know. I've got a queer idea, that my head-piece likes to think good; but I don't believe my tummy believes it.'

" 'Go on!' he said.

" 'Well,' I said. 'Suppose the earth were inhabited by two kinds of life. We're one, and *they're* the other.'

" 'Go on!' he said.

" 'Well,' I said. 'Don't you see, in a normal state we may not be capable of appreciating the *realness* of the other? But they may be just as *real* and material to *them*, as *we* are to *us*. Do you see?'

" 'Yes,' he said. 'Go on!'

" 'Well,' I said. 'The earth may be just as *real* to them, as to us. I mean that it may have qualities as material to them, as it has to us; but neither of us could appreciate the other's realness, or the quality of realness in the earth, which was real to the other. It's so difficult to explain. Don't you understand?'

" 'Yes,' he said. 'Go on!'

" 'Well, if we were in what I might call a healthy atmosphere, they would be quite beyond our power to see or feel, or anything. And the same with them; but the more we're like *this*, the more *real* and actual they could grow *to us*. See? That is, the more we should be-come able to appreciate their form of materialness. That's all. I can't make it any clearer.'

" 'Then, after all, you *really* think they're ghosts, or something of that sort?' Tammy said.

" 'I suppose it does come to that,' I answered. 'I mean that, anyway, I don't think they're our ideas of flesh and blood. But, of course, it's silly to say much; and, after all, you must remember that I may be all wrong.'

" 'I think you ought to tell the Second Mate all this,' he said. 'If it's really as you say, the ship ought to be put into the nearest port, and jolly well burnt.'

" 'The Second Mate couldn't do anything,' I replied. 'Even if he believed it all; which, we're not certain he would.'

" 'Perhaps not,' Tammy answered. 'But if you could get him to believe it, he might explain the whole business to the Skipper, and then something might be done. It's not safe as it is.'

" 'He'd only get jeered at again,' I said, rather hopelessly.

" 'No,' said Tammy. 'Not after what's happened tonight.'

" 'Perhaps not,' I replied, doubtfully. And just then the Second Mate came back on to the poop, and Tammy cleared away from the wheel-box, leaving me with a worrying feeling that I ought to do something.

VII

The Coming of the Mist,
and That Which It Ushered

"WE BURIED WILLIAMS AT midday. Poor beggar! It had been so sudden. All day the men were awed and gloomy, and there was a lot of talk about there being a Jonah aboard. If they'd only known what Tammy and I, and perhaps the Second Mate, knew!

"And then the next thing came—the mist. I cannot remember now, whether it was on the day we buried Williams that we first saw it, or the day after.

"When first I noticed it, like everybody else aboard, I took it to be some form of haze, due to the heat of the sun; for it was broad daylight when the thing came.

"The wind had died away to a light breeze, and I was working at the main rigging, along with Plummer, putting on seizings.

" 'Looks as if 'twere middlin' 'ot,' he remarked.

" 'Yes,' I said; and, for the time, took no further notice.

"Presently he spoke again:—

" 'It's gettin' quite 'azy!' and his tone showed he was surprised.

" I glanced up, quickly. At first, I could see nothing. Then, I saw what he meant. The air had a wavy, strange, unnatural appearance; something like the heated air over the top of an engine's funnel, that you can often see when no smoke is coming out.

" 'Must be the heat,' I said. 'Though I don't remember ever seeing anything just like it before.'

" 'Nor me,' Plummer agreed.

"It could not have been a minute later when I looked up again, and was astonished to find that the whole ship was surrounded by a thinnish haze that quite hid the horizon.

" 'By Jove! Plummer,' I said. 'How queer!'

" 'Yes,' he said, looking round. 'I never seen anythin' like it before—not in these parts.'

51

" 'Heat wouldn't do that!' I said.

" 'N—no,' he said, doubtfully.

"We went on with our work again—occasionally exchanging an odd word or two. Presently, after a little time of silence, I bent forward and asked him to pass me up the spike. He stooped and picked it up from the deck, where it had tumbled. As he held it out to me, I saw the stolid expression on his face, change suddenly to a look of complete surprise. He opened his mouth.

" 'By Gum!' he said. 'It's gone.'

"I turned quickly, and looked. And so it had—the whole sea showing clear and bright, right away to the horizon.

"I stared at Plummer, and he stared at me.

" 'Well, I'm blowed!' he exclaimed.

"I do not think I made any reply; for I had a sudden, queer feeling that the thing was not right. And then, in a minute, I called myself an ass; but I could not really shake off the feeling. I had another good look at the sea. I had a vague idea that something was different. The sea looked brighter, somehow, and the air clearer, I thought, and I missed something; but not much, you know. And it was not until a couple of days later, that I knew that it was several vessels on the horizon, which had been quite in sight before the mist, and now were gone.

"During the rest of the watch, and indeed all day, there was no further sign of anything unusual. Only, when the evening came (in the second dog-watch it was) I saw the mist rise faintly—the setting sun shining through it, dim and unreal.

"I knew then, as a certainty, that it was not caused by heat.

"And that was the beginning of it.

"The next day, I kept a pretty close watch, during all my time on deck; but the atmosphere remained clear. Yet, I heard from one of the chaps in the Mate's watch, that it had been hazy during part of the time he was at the wheel.

" 'Comin' an' goin', like,' he described it to me, when I questioned him about it. He thought it might be heat.

"But though I knew otherwise, I did not contradict him. At that time, no one, not even Plummer, seemed to think very much of the matter. And when I mentioned it to Tammy, and asked him whether he'd noticed it, he only remarked that it must have been heat, or else the sun drawing up water. I let it stay at that; for there was nothing to be gained by suggesting that the thing had more to it.

"Then, on the following day, something happened that set me wondering more than ever, and showed me how right I had been in feeling the mist to be something unnatural. It was in this way.

"Five bells, in the eight to twelve morning watch, had gone. I was at the wheel. The sky was perfectly clear—not a cloud to be seen, even on the horizon. It was hot, standing at the wheel; for there was scarcely any wind, and I was feeling drowsy. The Second Mate was down on the main-deck with the men, seeing about some job he wanted done; so that I was on the poop alone.

"Presently, with the heat, and the sun beating right down on to me, I grew thirsty; and, for want of something better, I pulled out a bit of plug I had on me, and bit off a chew; though, as a rule, it is not a habit of mine. After a little, naturally enough, I glanced round for the spit-toon; but discovered that it was not there. Probably it had been taken forrard when the decks were washed, to give it a scrub. So, as there was no one on the poop, I left the wheel, and stepped aft to the taffrail. It was thus that I came to see something altogether unthought of—a full-rigged ship, close-hauled on the port tack, a few hundred yards on our starboard quarter. Her sails were scarcely filled by the light breeze, and flapped as she lifted to the swell of the sea. She appeared to have very little way through the water, certainly not more than a knot an hour. Away aft, hanging from the gaff-end, was a string of flags. Evidently, she was signalling to us. All this, I saw in a flash, and I just stood and stared, astonished. I was astonished because I had not seen her earlier. In that light breeze, I knew that she must have been in sight for at least a couple of hours. Yet I could think of nothing rational to satisfy my wonder. There she was—of that much, I was certain. And yet, how had she come there without my seeing her, before?

"All at once, as I stood, staring, I heard the wheel behind me, spin rapidly. Instinctively, I jumped to get hold of the spokes; for I did not want the steering gear jammed. Then I turned again to have another look at the other ship; but, to my utter bewilderment, *there was no sign of her*—nothing but the calm ocean, spreading away to the distant horizon. I blinked my eyelids a bit, and pushed the hair off my forehead. Then, I stared again; but there was no vestige of her—nothing, you know; and absolutely nothing unusual, except a faint, tremulous quiver in the air. And the blank surface of the sea, reaching everywhere to the empty horizon.

"Had she foundered I asked myself, naturally enough; and, for the moment, I really wondered. I searched round the sea for wreckage; but there was nothing, not even an odd hencoop, or a piece of deck furniture; and so I threw away that idea, as impossible.

"Then, as I stood, I got another thought, or, perhaps, an intuition, and I asked myself, seriously, whether this disappearing ship might not be in some way connected with the other queer things. It occurred to me then, that the vessel I had seen was nothing real, and, perhaps, did not exist outside of my own brain. I considered the idea, gravely. It helped to explain the thing, and I could think of nothing else that would. Had she been real, I felt sure that others aboard us would have been bound to have seen her long before I had—I got a bit muddled there, with trying to think it out; and then, abruptly, the reality of the other ship, came back to me—every rope and sail and spar, you know. And I remembered how she had lifted to the heave of the sea, and how the sails had flapped in the light breeze. And the string of flags! She had been signalling. At that last, I found it just as impossible to believe that she had not been real.

"I had reached to this point of irresolution, and was standing with my back, partly turned to the wheel. I was holding it steady with my left hand, while I looked over the sea, to try to find something to help me to understand.

"All at once, as I stared, I seemed to see the ship again. She was more on the beam now, than on the quarter; but I thought little of that, in the astonishment of seeing her once more. It was only a glimpse I caught of her—dim and wavering, as though I looked at her through the convolutions of heated air. Then she grew indistinct, and vanished again; but I was convinced now that she was real, and had been in sight all the time, if I could have seen her. That curious, dim, wavering appearance had suggested something to me. I remembered the strange, wavy look of the air, a few days pre-viously, just before the mist had surrounded the ship. And in my mind, I connected the two. It was nothing about the other packet that was strange. The strangeness was with us. It was something that was about (or invested) our ship that prevented me—or indeed, any one else aboard—from seeing that other. It was evident that she had been able to see us, as was proved by her signalling. In an irrelevant sort of way, I wondered what the people aboard of her thought of our apparently intentional disregard of their signals.

"After that, I thought of the strangeness of it all. Even at that minute, they could see us, plainly; and yet, so far as we were concerned, the whole ocean seemed empty. It appeared to me, at that time, to be the weirdest thing that could happen to us.

"And then a fresh thought came to me. How long had we been like that? I puzzled for a few moments. It was now that I recollected that we had sighted several vessels on the morning of the day when the mist appeared; and since then, we had seen nothing. This, to say the least, should have struck me as queer; for some of the other packets were homeward bound along with us, and steering the same course. Consequently, with the weather being fine, and the wind next to nothing, they should have been in sight all the time. This reasoning seemed to me to show, unmistakably, some connection between the coming of the mist, and our inability to *see*. So that it is possible we had been in that extraordinary state of blindness for nearly three days.

"In my mind, the last glimpse of that ship on the quarter, came back to me. And, I remember, a curious thought got me, that I had looked at her from out of some other dimension. For a while, you know, I really believe the mystery of the idea, and that it might be the actual truth, took me; instead of my realising just all that it might mean. It seemed so exactly to express all the half-defined thoughts that had come, since seeing that other packet on the quarter.

"Suddenly, behind me, there came a rustle and rattle of the sails; and, in the same instant, I heard the Skipper saying:—

" 'Where the devil have you got her to, Jessop?'

"I whirled round to the wheel.

" 'I don't know—Sir,' I faltered.

"I had forgotten even that I was at the wheel.

" 'Don't know!' he shouted. 'I should damned well think you don't. Starboard your helm, you fool. You'll have us all aback!'

" 'i, i, Sir,' I answered, and hove the wheel over. I did it almost mechanically; for I was still dazed, and had not yet had time to collect my senses.

"During the following half-minute, I was only conscious, in a confused sort of way, that the Old Man was rating at me. This feeling of bewilderment passed off, and I found that I was peering blankly into the binnacle, at the compass-card; yet, until then, entirely without being aware of the fact. Now, however, I saw that the ship was coming back on to her course. Goodness knows how much she had been off!

"With the realisation that I had let the ship get almost aback, there came a sudden memory of the alteration in the position of the other vessel. She had appeared last on the beam, instead of on the quarter. Now, however, as my brain began to work, I saw the cause of this apparent and, until then, inexplicable change. It was due, of course, to our having come up, until we had brought the other packet on to the beam.

"It is curious how all this flashed through my mind, and held my attention—although only momentarily—in the face of the Skipper's storming. I think I had hardly realised he was still singing out at me. Anyhow, the next thing I remember, he was shaking my arm.

" 'What's the matter with you, man?' he was shouting. And I just stared into his face, like an ass, without saying a word. I seemed still incapable, you know, of actual, reasoning speech.

" 'Are you damned well off your head?' he went on shouting. 'Are you a lunatic? Have you had sunstroke? Speak, you gaping idiot!'

"I tried to say something; but the words would not come clearly.

" 'I—I—I—' I said, and stopped, stupidly. I was all right, really; but I was so bewildered with the thing I had found out; and, in a way, I seemed almost to have come back out of a distance, you know.

" 'You're a lunatic!' he said, again. He repeated the statement several times, as if it were the only thing that sufficiently expressed his opinion of me. Then he let go of my arm, and stepped back a couple of paces.

" 'I'm not a lunatic!' I said, with a sudden gasp. 'I'm not a lunatic, Sir, any more than you are.'

" 'Why the devil don't you answer my questions then?' he shouted, angrily. 'What's the matter with you? What have you been doing with the ship? Answer me now!'

" 'I was looking at that ship away on the starboard quarter, Sir,' I blurted out. 'She's been signalling—'

" 'What!' he cut me short with. 'What ship?'

"He turned, quickly, and looked over the quarter. Then he wheeled round to me again.

" 'There's no ship! What do you mean by trying to spin up a cuffer like that?'

" 'There is, Sir,' I answered. 'It's out there—' I pointed.

" 'Hold your tongue!' he said. 'Don't talk rubbish to me. Do you think I'm blind?'

" 'I saw it, Sir,' I persisted.

" 'Don't you talk back to me!' he snapped, with a quick burst of temper. 'I won't have it.

"Then, just as suddenly, he was silent. He came a step towards me, and stared into my face. I believe the old ass thought I was a bit mad; anyway, without another word, he went to the break of the poop.

" 'Mr. Tulipson,' he sung out.

" 'Yes, Sir,' I heard the Second Mate reply.

" 'Send another man to the wheel.'

" 'Very good, Sir,' the Second answered.

"A couple of minutes later, old Jaskett came up to relieve me. I gave him the course, and he repeated it.

" 'What's up, mate?' he asked me, as I stepped off the grating.

" 'Nothing much,' I said, and went forrard to where the Skipper was standing on the break of the poop. I gave him the course; but the crabby old devil took no notice of me, whatever. When I got down on to the main-deck, I went up to the Second, and gave it to him. He answered me civilly enough, and then asked me what I had been doing to put the Old Man's back up.

" 'I told him there's a ship on the starboard quarter, signalling us,' I said.

" 'There's no ship out there, Jessop,' the Second Mate replied, looking at me with a queer, inscrutable expression.

" 'There is, Sir,' I began. 'I—'

" 'That will do, Jessop!' he said. 'Go forrard and have a smoke. I shall want you then to give a hand with these foot-ropes. You'd better bring a serving-mallet aft with you, when you come.'

"I hesitated a moment, partly in anger; but more, I think, in doubt.

" 'i, i, Sir,' I muttered, at length, and went forrard.

VIII
After the Coming of the Mist

"AFTER THE COMING OF the mist, things seemed to develop pretty quickly. In the following two or three days a good deal happened.

"On the night of the day on which the Skipper had sent me away from the wheel, it was our watch on deck from eight o'clock to twelve, and my lookout from ten to twelve.

"As I paced slowly to and fro across the fo'cas'le head, I was thinking about the affair of the morning. At first, my thoughts were about the Old Man. I cursed him thoroughly to myself, for being a pig-headed old fool, until it occurred to me that if I had been in his place, and come on deck to find the ship almost aback, and the fellow at the wheel staring out across the sea, instead of attending to his business, I should most certainly have kicked up a thundering row. then, I had been an ass to tell him about the ship. I should never have done such a thing if I had not been a bit adrift. Most likely the old chap thought I was cracked.

"I ceased to bother my head about him, and fell to wondering why the Second Mate had looked at me so queerly in the morning. Did he guess more of the truth than I supposed? And if that were the case, why had he refused to listen to me?

"After that, I went to puzzling about the mist. I had thought a great deal about it, during the day. One idea appealed to me, very strongly. It was that the actual, visible mist was a materialised expression of an extraordinarily subtle atmosphere, in which we were moving.

"Abruptly, as I walked backwards and forwards, taking occasional glances over the sea (which was almost calm), my eye caught the glow of a light out in the darkness. I stood still, and stared. I wondered whether it was the light of a vessel. In that case we were no longer enveloped in that extraordinary atmosphere. I bent forward, and gave the thing my more immediate attention. I saw then that it was undoubtedly the green light of a vessel on our port bow. It was plain that she was bent on crossing bows. What was more, she was dangerously near—the size and brightness of her light showed that. She would be close-hauled, while we were going free, so that, of course, it was our place to get out of her way. Instantly, I turned and, putting my hands up to my mouth, hailed the Second Mate:—

" 'Light on the port bow, Sir.'

"The next moment his hail came back:—

" 'Whereabouts?'

" 'He must be blind,' I said to myself.

" 'About two points on the bow, Sir,' I sung out.

"Then I turned to see whether she had shifted her position at all. Yet, when I came to look, there was no light visible. I ran forrard to the bows, and leant over the rail, and stared; but there was nothing—absolutely nothing except the darkness all about us. For perhaps a few seconds I stood thus, and a suspicion swept across me, that the whole business was practically a repetition of the affair of the morning. Evidently, the impalpable something that invested the ship, had thinned for an instant, thus allowing me to see the light ahead. Now, it had closed again. Yet, whether I could see, or not, I did not doubt the fact that there was a vessel ahead, and very close ahead, too. We might run on top of her any minute. My only hope was that, seeing we were not getting out of her way, she had put her helm up, so as to let us pass, with the intention of then crossing under our stern. I waited, pretty anxiously, watching and listening. Then, all at once, I heard steps coming along the deck, forrard, and the 'prentice, whose timekeeping it was, came up on to the fo'cas'le head.

" 'The Second Mate says he can't see any light, Jessop,' he said, coming over to where I stood. 'Whereabouts is it?'

" 'I don't know,' I answered. 'I've lost sight of it myself. It was a green light, about a couple of points on the port bow. It seemed fairly close.'

" 'Perhaps their lamp's gone out,' he suggested, after peering out pretty hard into the night for a minute or so.

" 'Perhaps,' I said.

"I did not tell him that the light had been so close that, even in the darkness, we should *now* have been able to see the ship herself.

" 'You're quite sure it was a light, and not a star?' he asked, doubtfully, after another long stare.

" 'Oh! no,' I said. 'It may have been the moon, now I come to think about it.'

" 'Don't rot,' he replied. 'It's easy enough to make a mistake. What shall I say to the Second Mate?'

" 'Tell him it's disappeared, of course!'

" 'Where to?' he asked.

" 'How the devil should I know?' I told him. 'Don't ask silly questions!'

" 'All right, keep your rag in,' he said, and went aft to report to the Second Mate.

"Five minutes later, it might have been, I saw the light again. It was broad on the bow, and told me plainly enough that she had up with her helm to escape being run down. I did not wait a moment; but sung out to the Second Mate that there was a green light about four points on the port bow. By Jove! it must have been a close shave. The light did not *seem* to be more than about a hundred yards away. It was fortunate that we had not much way through the water.

" 'Now,' I thought to myself, 'the Second will see the thing. And perhaps Mr. Blooming 'prentice will be able to give the star its proper name.'

"Even as the thought came into my head, the light faded and vanished; and I caught the Second Mate's voice.

" 'Whereaway?' he was singing out.

" 'It's gone again, Sir,' I answered.

"A minute later, I heard him coming along the deck.

"He reached the foot of the starboard ladder.

" 'Where are you, Jessop?' he inquired.

" 'Here, Sir,' I said, and went to the top of the weather ladder.

"He came up slowly on to the fo'cas'le head.

" 'What's this you've been singing out about a light?' he asked. 'Just point out exactly where it was you last saw it.'

"This, I did, and he went over to the port rail, and stared away into the night; but without seeing anything.

" 'It's gone, Sir,' I ventured to remind him. 'Though I've seen it twice now—once, about a couple of points on the bow, and this last time, broad away on the bow; but it disappeared both times, almost at once.'

" 'I don't understand it at all, Jessop,' he said, in a puzzled voice. 'Are you sure it was a ship's light?'

" 'Yes Sir. A green light. It was quite close.

" 'I don't understand,' he said, again. 'Run aft and ask the 'prentice to pass you down my night glasses. Be as smart as you can.'

" 'i, i, Sir,' I replied, and ran aft.

"In less than a minute, I was back with his binoculars; and, with them, he stared for some time at the sea to leeward.

"All at once, he dropped them to his side, and faced round on me with a sudden question:—

" 'Where's she gone to? If she's shifted her bearing as quickly as all that, she must be precious close. We should be able to see her spars and sails, or her cabin lights, or her binnacle light, or something!'

" 'It's queer, Sir,' I assented.

" 'Damned queer,' he said. 'So damned queer that I'm inclined to think you've made a mistake.'

" 'No, Sir. I'm certain it was a light.'

" 'Where's the ship, then?' he asked.

" 'I can't say, Sir. That's just what's been puzzling me.'

"The Second said nothing in reply; but took a couple of quick turns across the fo'cas'le head—stopping at the port rail, and taking another look to leeward through his night glasses. Perhaps a minute he stood there. Then, without a word, he went down the lee ladder, and away aft along the main-deck to the poop.

" 'He's jolly well puzzled,' I thought to myself. 'Or else he thinks I've been imagining things.' Either way, I guessed he'd think that.

"In a little, I began to wonder whether, after all, he had any idea of what might be the truth. One minute, I would feel certain he had; and the next, I was just as sure that he guessed nothing. I got one of my fits of asking myself whether it would not have been better to have told him everything. It seemed to me that he must have seen sufficient to make him inclined to listen to me. And yet, I could not by any means be certain. I might only have been making an ass of myself, in his eyes. Or set him thinking I was dotty.

"I was walking about the fo'cas'le head, feeling like this, when I saw the light for the third time. It was very bright and big, and I could see it move, as I watched. This again showed me that it must be very close.

" 'Surely,' I thought, 'the Second Mate must see it now, for himself.'

"I did not sing out this time, right away. I thought I would let the Second see for himself that I had not been mistaken. Besides, I was not going to risk its vanishing again, the instant I had spoken. For quite half a minute, I watched it, and there was no sign of its disappearing. Every moment, I expected to hear the Second Mate's hail, showing that he had spotted it at last; but none came.

"I could stand it no longer, and I ran to the rail, on the after part of the fo'cas'le head.

" 'Green light a little abaft the beam, Sir!' I sung out, at the top of my voice.

"But I had waited too long. Even as I shouted, the light blurred and vanished.

"I stamped my foot and swore. The thing was making a fool of me. Yet, I had a faint hope that those aft had seen it just before it disappeared; but this I knew was vain, directly I beard the Second's voice.

" 'Light be damned!' he shouted.

"Then he blew his whistle, and one of the men ran aft, out of the fo'cas'le, to see what it was he wanted.

" 'Whose next lookout is it?' I heard him ask.

" 'Jaskett's, Sir.'

" 'Then tell Jaskett to relieve Jessop at once. Do you hear?'

" 'Yes, Sir,' said the man, and came forrard.

"In a minute, Jaskett stumbled up on to the fo'cas'le head.

" 'What's up, mate?' he asked, sleepily.

" 'It's that fool of a Second Mate!' I said, savagely. 'I've reported a light to him three times, and, because the blind fool can't see it, he's sent you up to relieve me!'

" 'Where is it, mate?' he inquired.

"He looked round at the dark sea.

" 'I don't see no light,' he remarked, after a few moments.

" 'No,' I said. 'It's gone.'

" 'Eh?' he inquired.

" 'It's gone!' I repeated, irritably.

"He turned and regarded me silently, through the dark.

" ' 'I'd go an' 'ave a sleep, mate,' he said, at length. 'I've been that way meself. Ther's nothin' like a snooze w'en yer gets like that.'

" 'What!' I said. 'Like what?'

" 'It's all right, mate. Yer'll be all right in ther mornin'. Don't yer worry 'bout me.' His tone was sympathetic.

" 'Hell!' was all I said, and walked down off the fo'cas'le head. I wondered whether the old fellow thought I was going silly.

" 'Have a sleep, by Jove!' I muttered to myself. 'I wonder who'd feel like having a sleep after what I've seen and stood today!'

"I felt rotten, with no one understanding what was really the matter. I seemed to be all alone, through the things I had learnt. Then the thought came to me to go aft and talk the matter over with Tammy. I knew he would be able to understand, of course; and it would be such a relief.

"On the impulse, I turned and went aft, along the deck to the 'prentices' berth. As I neared the break of the poop, I looked up and saw the dark shape of the Second Mate, leaning over the rail above me.

" 'Who's that?' he asked.

" 'It's Jessop, Sir,' I said.

" 'What do you want in this part of the ship?' he inquired.

" 'I'd come aft to speak to Tammy, Sir,' I replied.

" 'You go along forrard and turn-in,' he said, not altogether un-kindly. 'A sleep will do you more good than yarning, about. You know, you're getting to fancy things too much!'

" 'I'm sure I'm not, Sir! I'm perfectly well. I—'

" 'That will do!' he interrupted, sharply. 'You go and have a sleep.'

"I gave a short curse, under my breath, and went slowly forrard. I was getting maddened with being treated as if I were not quite sane.

" 'By God!' I said to myself. 'Wait till the fools know what I know—Just wait!'

"I entered the fo'cas'le, through the port doorway, and went across to my chest, and sat down. I felt angry and tired, and miserable.

"Quoin and Plummer were sitting close by, playing cards, and smoking. Stubbins lay in his bunk, watching them, and also smoking. As I sat down, he put his head forward over the bunk-board, and regarded me in a curious, meditative way.

" 'What's hup with ther Second hofficer?' he asked, after a short stare.

"I looked at him, and the other two men looked up at me. I felt I should go off with a bang, if I did not say something, and I let out pretty stiffly, telling them the whole business. Yet, I had seen enough to know that it was no good trying to explain things; so I just told them the plain, bald facts, and left explanations as much alone as possible.

" 'Three times, you say?' said Stubbins when I had finished.

" 'Yes,' I assented.

" 'An' ther Old Man sent yer from ther wheel this mornin', 'cause yer 'appened ter see a ship 'e couldn't,' Plummer added in a reflective tone.

" 'Yes,' I said, again.

"I thought I saw him look at Quoin, significantly; but Stubbins, I noticed, looked only at me.

" 'I reckon ther Second thinks you're a bit hoff colour,' he re-marked, after a short pause.

" 'The Second Mate's a fool!' I said, with some bitterness. 'A confounded fool!'

" 'I hain't so sure about that,' he replied. 'It's bound ter seem queer ter him. I don't hunderstand it myself—'

"He lapsed into silence, and smoked.

" 'I carn't understand 'ow it is ther Second Mate didn't 'appen to spot it,' Quoin said, in a puzzled voice.

"It seemed to me that Plummer nudged him to be quiet. It looked as if Plummer shared the Second Mate's opinion, and the idea made me savage. But Stubbins's next remark drew my attention.

" 'I don't hunderstand it,' he said, again; speaking with deliberation. 'All ther same, ther Second should have savvied enough not to have slung you hoff ther lookhout.'

"He nodded his head, slowly, keeping his gaze fixed on my face.

" 'How do you mean?' I asked, puzzled; yet with a vague sense that the man understood more, perhaps, than I had hitherto thought.

" 'I mean what's ther Second so blessed cocksure about?' he said.

"He took a draw at his pipe, removed it, and leant forward somewhat, over his bunk-board.

" 'Didn't he say nothin' ter you, after you came hoff ther lookhout?' he asked.

" 'Yes,' I replied; 'he spotted me going aft. He told me I was getting to imagining things too much. He said I'd better come forrard and get a sleep.'

" 'An' what did you say?'

" 'Nothing. I came forrard.'

" 'Why didn't you bloomin' well harsk him if he wern't doin' ther imaginin' trick when he sent us chasin' hup ther main, hafter that bogy-man of his ?'

" 'I never thought of it,' I told him.

" 'Well, yer ought ter have.'

"He paused, and sat up in his bunk, and asked for a match.

"As I passed him my box, Quoin looked up from his game.

" 'It might 'ave been a stowaway, yer know. Yer carn't say as it's ever been proved as it wasn't.'

"Stubbins passed the box back to me, and went on without noticing Quoin's remark:—

" 'Told you to go an' have a snooze, did he? I don't hunderstand what he's bluffin' at.'

" 'How do you mean, bluffing?' I asked.

"He nodded his head, sagely.

" 'It's my hidea he knows you saw that light, just as bloomin' well as I do.'

"Plummer looked up from his game, at this speech; but said nothing.

" 'Then *you* don't doubt that I really saw it?' I asked, with a certain surprise.

" 'Not me,' he remarked, with assurance. 'You hain't likely ter make that kind of mistake three times runnin'.'

" 'No,' I said. 'I *know* I saw the light, right enough; but'—I hesitated a moment—'it's blessed queer.'

" 'It *is* blessed queer!' he agreed. 'It's damned queer! An' there's a lot of other dam queer things happenin' aboard this packet lately.'

"He was silent for a few seconds. Then he spoke suddenly:—

" 'It's not nat'ral, I'm damned sure of that much.'

"He took a couple of draws at his pipe, and in the momentary silence, I caught Jaskett's voice, above us. He was hailing the poop.

" 'Red light on the starboard quarter, Sir,' I heard him sing out.

" 'There you are,' I said, with a jerk of my head. 'That's about where that packet I spotted, ought to be by now. She couldn't cross our bows, so she up helm, and let us pass, and now she's hauled up again and gone under our stern.'

"I got up from the chest, and went to the door, the other three following. As we stepped out on deck, I heard the Second Mate shouting out, away aft, to know the whereabouts of the light.

" 'By Jove! Stubbins,' I said. 'I believe the blessed thing's gone again.'

"We ran to the starboard side, in a body, and looked over; but there was no sign of a light in the darkness astern.

" 'I carn't say as *I* see any light,' said Quoin.

"Plummer said nothing.

"I looked up at the fo'cas'le head. There, I could faintly distinguish the outlines of Jaskett. He was standing by the starboard rail, with his hands up, shading his eyes, evidently staring towards the place where he had last seen the light.

" 'Where's she got to, Jaskett?' I called out.

" 'I can't say, mate,' he answered. 'It's the most 'ellishly funny thing ever I've comed across. She were there as plain as me 'att one minnit, an' ther next she were gone—clean gone.'

"I turned to Plummer.

" 'What do you think about it, *now*?' I asked him.

" 'Well,' he said. 'I'll admit I thought at first 'twere somethin' an' nothin'. I thought yer was mistaken; but it seems yer did see somethin'.'

"Away aft, we heard the sound of steps, along the deck.

" 'Ther Second's comin' forrard for a hexplanation, Jaskett,' Stubbins sung out. 'You'd better go down an' change yer breeks.'

"The Second Mate passed us, and went up the starboard ladder.

" 'What's up now, Jaskett?' he said, quickly. 'Where is this light? Neither the 'prentice nor I can see it!'

" 'Ther dam thing's clean gone, Sir,' Jaskett replied.

" 'Gone!' the Second Mate said. 'Gone! What do you mean?'

" 'She were there one minnit, Sir, as plain as me 'att, an' ther next, she'd gone.'

" 'That's a dam silly yarn to tell me!' the Second replied. 'You don't expect me to believe it, do you?'

" 'It's Gospel trewth any'ow, Sir,' Jaskett answered. 'An' Jessop seen it just ther same.'

"He seemed to have added that last part as an afterthought. Evidently, the old beggar had changed his opinion as to my need for sleep.

" 'You're an old fool, Jaskett,' the Second said, sharply. 'And that idiot Jessop has been putting things into your silly old head.'

" 'He paused, an instant. Then he continued:—

" 'What the devil's the matter with you all, that you've taken to this sort of game? You know very well that you saw no light! I sent Jessop off the lookout, and then you must go and start the same game.'

" 'We 'aven't—' Jaskett started to say; but the Second silenced him.

" 'Stow it!' he said, and turned and went down the ladder, passing us quickly, without a word.

" 'Doesn't look to *me*, Stubbins,' I said, 'as though the Second did believe we've seen the light.'

" 'I hain't so sure,' he answered. 'He's a puzzler.'

"The rest of the watch passed away quietly; and at eight bells I made haste to turn-in, for I was tremendously tired.

"When we were called again for the four to eight watch on deck, I learnt that one of the men in the Mate's watch had seen a light, soon after we had gone below, and had reported it, only for it to disappear immediately. This, I found, had happened twice, and the Mate had got so wild (being under the impression that the man was playing the fool) that he had nearly come to blows with him—finally ordering him off the lookout, and sending another man up in his place. If this last man saw the light, he took good care not to let the Mate know; so that the matter had ended there.

"And then, on the following night, before we had ceased to talk about the matter of the vanishing lights, something else occurred that temporarily drove from my mind all memory of the mist, and the extraordinary, blind atmosphere it had seemed to usher.

IX
The Man Who Cried for Help

"IT WAS, AS I have said, on the following night that something further happened. And it brought home pretty vividly to me, if not to any of the others, the sense of a personal danger aboard.

"We had gone below for the eight to twelve watch, and my last impression of the weather at eight o'clock, was that the wind was freshening. There had been a great bank of cloud rising astern, which had looked as if it were going to breeze up still more.

"At a quarter to twelve, when we were called for our twelve to four watch on deck, I could tell at once, by the sound, that there was a fresh breeze blowing; at the same time, I heard the voices of the men in the other watch, singing out as they hauled on the ropes. I caught the rattle of canvas in the wind, and guessed that they were taking the royals off her. I looked at my watch, which I always kept hanging in my bunk. It showed the time to be just after the quarter; so that, with luck, we should escape having to go up to the sails.

"I dressed quickly, and then went to the door to look at the weather. I found that the wind had shifted from the starboard quarter, to right aft; and, by the look of the sky, there seemed to be a promise of more, before long.

"Up aloft, I could make out faintly the fore and mizzen royals, flapping in the wind. The main had been left for a while longer. In the fore rigging, Jacobs, the Ordinary Seaman in the Mate's watch, was following another of the men aloft to the sail. The Mate's two 'prentices were already up at the mizzen. Down on deck, the rest of the men were busy clearing up the ropes.

"I went back to my bunk, and looked at my watch—the time was only a few minutes off eight bells; so I got my oilskins ready, for it looked like rain, outside. As I was doing this, Jock went to the door for a look.

" 'What's it doin', Jock?' Tom asked, getting out of his bunk, hurriedly.

" 'I'm thinkin' maybe it's goin' to blow a wee, and ye'll be needin' ye'r oilskins,' Jock answered.

"When eight bells went, and we mustered aft for roll-call, there was a considerable delay, owing to the Mate refusing to call the roll until Tom (who, as usual, had only turned out of his bunk at the last minute) came aft to answer his name. When, at last, he did come, the Second and the Mate joined in giving him a good dressing down for a lazy sojer; so that several minutes passed before we were on our way forrard again. This was a small enough matter in itself, and yet really terrible in its consequence to one of our number; for, just as we reached the fore rigging, there was a shout aloft, loud above the noise of the wind, and the next moment, something crashed down into our midst, with a great, slogging thud—something bulky and weighty, that struck full upon Jock, so that he went down with a loud, horrible, ringing 'ugg,' and never said a word. From the whole crowd of us there went up a yell of fear, and then, with one accord, there was a run for the lighted fo'cas'le. I am not ashamed to say that I ran with the rest. A blind, unreasoning fright had seized me, and I did not stop to think.

"Once in the fo'cas'le and the light, there was a reaction. We all stood and looked blankly at one another for a few moments. Then some one asked a question, and there was a general murmur of denial. We all felt ashamed, and someone reached up, and unhooked the lantern on the port side. I did the same with the starboard one; and there was a quick movement towards the doors. As we streamed out on deck, I caught the sound of the Mates' voices. They had evidently come down from off the poop to find out what had happened; but it was too dark to see their whereabouts.

" 'Where the hell have you all got to?' I heard the Mate shout.

"The next instant, they must have seen the light from our lanterns; for I heard their footsteps, coming along the deck, at a run. They came the starboard side, and just abaft the fore rigging, one of them stumbled and fell over something. It was the First Mate who had tripped. I knew this by the cursing that came directly afterwards. He picked himself up, and, apparently without stopping to see what manner of thing it was that he had fallen over, made a rush to the pin-rail. The Second Mate ran into the circle of light thrown by our lanterns, and stopped, dead—eyeing us doubtfully. I am not surprised at this, *now*, nor at the behaviour of the Mate, the following instant; but at that time, I must say I could not conceive what had come to them, particularly the First Mate. He came out at us from the darkness with a rush and a roar like a bull, and brandishing a belaying-pin. I had failed to take into account the scene which his eyes must have shown him:— The whole crowd of men in the fo'cas'le—both watches—pouring out on to the deck in utter confusion, and greatly excited, with a couple of fellows at their head, carrying lanterns. And before this, there had been the cry aloft and the crash down on deck, followed by the shouts of the frightened crew, and the sounds of many feet running. He may well have taken the cry for a signal, and our actions for something not far short of mutiny. Indeed, his words told us that this was his very thought.

" 'I'll knock the face off the first man that comes a step further aft!' he shouted, shaking the pin in my face. 'I'll show yer who's master here! What the hell do yer mean by this? Get forrard into yer kennel!'

"There was a low growl from the men at that last remark, and the old bully stepped back a couple of paces.

" 'Hold on, you fellows!' I sung out. 'Shut up a minute!'

" 'Mr. Tulipson!' I called out to the Second, who had not been able to get a word in edgeways, 'I don't know what the devil's the matter with the First Mate; but he'll not find it pay to talk to a crowd like ours, in that sort of fashion, or there'll be ructions aboard.'

" 'Come! come! Jessop! This won't do! I can't have you talking like that about the Mate!' he said, sharply. 'Let me know what's to-do, and then go forrard again, the lot of you.'

" 'We'd have told you at first, Sir,' I said, 'only the Mate wouldn't give any of us a chance to speak. There's been an awful accident, Sir. Something's fallen from aloft, right onto Jock—'

"I stopped suddenly; for there was a loud crying aloft.

" 'Help! help! help!' some one was shouting, and then it rose from a shout into a scream.

" 'My God! Sir,' I shouted. 'That's one of the men up at the fore royal!'

" 'Listen!' ordered the Second Mate. 'Listen!'

"Even as he spoke, it came again—broken and, as it were, in gasps.

"'Help! ...Oh! .... God! ...Oh! ...Help! H—e—l—p!'

"Abruptly, Stubbins's voice struck in.

" 'Hup with us, lads! By God! hup with us!' and he made a spring into the fore rigging. I shoved the handle of the lantern between my teeth, and followed. Plummer was coming; but the Second Mate pulled him back.

" 'That's sufficient,' he said. 'I'm going,' and he came up after me.

"We went over the foretop, racing like fiends. The light from the lantern prevented me from seeing to any distance in the darkness; but, at the cross-trees, Stubbins, who was some ratlines ahead, shouted out all at once, and in gasps:—

" 'They're fightin' …like …hell!'

" 'What?' called the Second Mate, breathlessly.

"Apparently, Stubbins did not hear him; for he made no reply. We cleared the cross-trees, and climbed into the t'gallant rigging. The wind was fairly fresh up there, and overhead, there sounded the flap, flap of sailcloth flying in the wind; but since we had left the deck, there had been no other sound from above.

"Now, abruptly, there came again a wild crying from the darkness over us. A strange, wild medley it was of screams for help, mixed up with violent, breathless curses.

"Beneath the royal yard, Stubbins halted, and looked down to me.

" 'Hurry hup… with ther… lantern… Jessop!' he shouted, catching his breath between the words. 'There'll be… murder done… hin a minute!'

"I reached him, and held the light up for him to catch. He stooped, and took it from me. Then, holding it above his head, he went a few ratlines higher. In this manner, he reached to a level with the royal yard. From my position, a little below him, the lantern seemed but to throw a few straggling, flickering rays along the spar; yet they showed me something. My first glance had been to wind'ard, and I had seen at once, that there was nothing on the weather yard arm. From there my gaze went to leeward. Indistinctly, I saw something upon the yard, that clung, struggling. Stubbins bent towards it with the light; thus I saw it more clearly. It was Jacobs, the Ordinary Seaman. He had his right arm tightly round the yard; with the other, he appeared to be fending himself from something on the other side of him, and further out upon the yard. At times, moans and gasps came from him, and sometimes curses. Once, as he appeared to be dragged partly from his hold, he screamed like a woman. His whole attitude suggested stubborn despair. I can scarcely tell you how this extraordinary sight affected me. I seemed to stare at it without realising that the affair was a real happening.

"During the few seconds which I had spent staring, and breathless, Stubbins had climbed round the after side of the mast, and now I began again to follow him.

"From his position below me, the Second had not been able to see the thing that was occurring on the yard, and he sung out to me to know what was happening.

" 'It's Jacobs, Sir,' I called back. 'He seems to be fighting with some one to looard of him. I can't see very plainly yet.

"Stubbins had got round onto the lee foot-rope, and now he held the lantern up, peering, and I made my way quickly alongside of him. The Second Mate followed; but instead of getting down onto the foot-rope, he got on the yard, and stood there holding on to the tie. He sung out for one of us to pass him up the lantern, which I did, Stubbins handing it to me. The Second held it out at arm's length, so that it lit up the lee part of the yard. The light showed through the darkness, as far as to where Jacobs struggled so weirdly. Beyond him, nothing was distinct.

"There had been a moment's delay while we were passing the lantern up to the Second Mate. Now, however, Stubbins and I moved out slowly along the foot-rope. We went slowly; but we did well to go at all, with any show of boldness; for the whole business was so abominably uncanny. It seems impossible to convey truly to you, the strange scene on the royal yard. You may be able to picture it to yourselves. The Second Mate standing upon the spar, holding the lantern; his body swaying with each roll of the ship, and his head craned forward as he peered along the yard. On our left, Jacobs, mad, fighting, cursing, praying, gasping; and outside of him, shadows and the night.

"The Second Mate spoke, abruptly.

" 'Hold on a moment!' he said. Then:—

" 'Jacobs!' he shouted. 'Jacobs, do you hear me?'

"There was no reply, only the continual gasping and cursing.

" 'Go on,' the Second Mate said to us. 'But be careful. Keep a tight hold!'

"He held the lantern higher, and we went out cautiously.

"Stubbins reached the Ordinary, and put his hand on his shoulder, with a soothing gesture.

" 'Steady hon now, Jacobs,' he said. 'Steady hon.'

"At his touch, as though by magic, the young fellow calmed down, and Stubbins—reaching round him—grasped the jackstay on the other side.

" 'Get a hold of him your side, Jessop,' he sung out. 'I'll get this side.'

"This, I did, and Stubbins climbed round him.

" 'There hain't no one here,' Stubbins called to me; but his voice expressed no surprise.

" 'What!' sung out the Second Mate. 'No one ther! Where's

Svensen, then?'

"I did not catch Stubbins's reply; for suddenly, it seemed to me that I saw something shadowy at the extreme end of the yard, out by the lift. I stared. It rose up, upon the yard, and I saw that it was the figure of a man. It grasped at the lift, and commenced to swarm up, quickly. It passed diagonally above Stubbins's head, and reached down a vague hand and arm.

" 'Look out! Stubbins!' I shouted. 'Look out!'

" 'What's hup now?' he called, in a startled voice. At the same instant, his cap went whirling away to leeward.

" 'Damn ther wind!' he burst out.

"Then, all at once, Jacobs, who had only been giving an occasional moan, commenced to shriek and struggle.

" 'Hold fast hon ter him!' Stubbins yelled. 'He'll be throwin' hisself hoff ther yard.'

"I put my left arm round the Ordinary's body—getting hold of the jackstay on the other side. Then I looked up. Above us, I seemed to see something dark and indistinct, that moved rapidly up the lift.

" 'Keep tight hold of him, while I get a gasket,' I heard the Second Mate sing out.

"A moment later there was a crash, and the light disappeared.

" 'Damn and set fire to the sail!' shouted the Second Mate.

"I twisted round, somewhat, and looked in his direction. I could dimly make him out on the yard. He had evidently been in the act of getting down on to the foot-rope, when the lantern was smashed. From him, my gaze jumped to the lee rigging. It seemed that I made out some shadowy thing stealing down through the darkness; but I could not be sure; and then, in a breath, it had gone.

" 'Anything wrong, Sir?' I called out.

" 'Yes,' he answered. 'I've dropped the lantern. The blessed sail knocked it out of my hand!'

" 'We'll be all right, Sir,' I replied. 'I think we can manage without it. Jacobs seems to be quieter now.'

" 'Well, be careful as you come in,' he warned us.

" 'Come on, Jacobs,' I said. 'Come on; we'll go down on deck.'

" 'Go along, young feller,' Stubbins put in. 'You're right now. We'll take care of you.' And we started to guide him along the yard.

"He went willingly enough; though without saying a word. He seemed like a child. Once or twice he shivered; but said nothing.

"We got him in to the lee rigging. Then, one going beside him, and the other keeping below, we made our way slowly down on deck.

We went very slowly—so slowly, in fact, that the Second Mate—who had stayed a minute to shove the gasket round the lee side of the sail—was almost as soon down.

" 'Take Jacobs forrard to his bunk,' he said, and went away aft to where a crowd of the men, one with a lantern, stood round the door of an empty berth under the break of the poop on the starboard side.

"We hurried forrard to the fo'cas'le. There we found all in darkness.

" 'They're haft with Jock, and Svensen.' Stubbins had hesitated an instant before saying the name.

" 'Yes,' I replied. 'That's what it must have been, right enough.'

" 'I kind of knew it all ther time,' he said.

"I stepped in through the doorway, and struck a match. Stubbins followed, guiding Jacobs before him, and, together, we got him into his bunk. We covered him up with his blankets, for he was pretty shivery. Then we came out. During the whole time, he had not spoken a word.

"As we went aft, Stubbins remarked that he thought the business must have made him a bit dotty.

" 'It's driven him clean barmy,' he went on. 'He don't hunderstand a word that's said ter him.'

" 'He may be different in the morning,' I answered.

"As we neared the poop, and the crowd of waiting men, he spoke again:—

" 'They've put 'em hinter ther Second's hempty berth.'

" 'Yes,' I said. 'Poor beggars.'

"We reached the other men, and they opened out, and allowed us to get near the door. Several of them asked in low tones, whether Jacobs was all right, and I told them, Yes; not saying anything then about his condition.

"I got close up to the doorway, and looked into the berth. The lamp was lit, and I could see, plainly. There were two bunks in the place, and a man had been laid in each. The Skipper was there, leaning up against a bulkshead. He looked worried; but was silent—seeming to be mooding in his own thoughts. The Second Mate was busy with a couple of flags, which he was spreading over the bodies. The First Mate was talking, evidently telling him something; but his tone was so low that I caught his words, only with difficulty. It struck me that he seemed pretty subdued. I got parts of his sentences in patches, as it were.

" '…broken,' I heard him say. 'And the Dutchman….'

" 'I've seen him,' the Second Mate said, shortly.

" 'Two, straight off the reel,' said the Mate. '…three in….'

"The Second made no reply.

" 'Of course, yer know...... accident.' The First Mate went on.

" 'Is it!' the Second said, in a queer voice.

"I saw the Mate glance at him, in a doubtful sort of way; but the Second was covering poor old Jock's dead face, and did not appear to notice his look.

" 'It—it—' the Mate said, and stopped.

"After a moment's hesitation, he said something further, that I could not catch; but there seemed a lot of funk in his voice.

"The Second Mate appeared not to have heard him; at any rate, he made no reply; but bent, and straightened out a corner of the flag over the rigid figure in the lower bunk. There was a certain niceness in his action which made me warm towards him.

" 'He's white!' I thought to myself.

"Out loud, I said:—

" 'We've put Jacobs into his bunk, Sir.'

"The Mate jumped; then whizzed round, and stared at me as though I had been a ghost. The Second Mate turned also; but before he could speak, the Skipper took a step towards me.

" 'Is he all right?' he asked.

" 'Well, Sir,' I said. 'He's a bit queer; but I think it's possible he may be better, after a sleep.'

" 'I hope so, too,' he replied, and stepped out on deck. He went towards the starboard poop ladder, walking slowly. The Second went and stood by the lamp, and the Mate, after a quick glance at him, came out and followed the Skipper up on to the poop. It occurred to me then, like a flash, that the man had stumbled upon a portion of the *truth*. This accident coming so soon after that other! It was evident that, in his mind, he had connected them. I recollected the fragments of his remarks to the Second Mate. Then, those many minor happenings that had cropped up at different times, and at which he had sneered. I wondered whether he would begin to comprehend their significance—their beastly, sinister significance.

" 'Ah! Mr. Bully-Mate,' I thought to myself. 'You're in for a bad time if you've begun to understand.'

"Abruptly, my thoughts jumped to the vague future before us.

" 'God help us!' I muttered.

"The Second Mate, after a look round, turned down the wick of the lamp, and came out, closing the door after him.

" 'Now, you men,' he said to the Mate's watch, 'get forrard; we can't do anything more. You'd better go and get some sleep.'

" 'i, i, Sir,' they said, in a chorus.

"Then, as we all turned to go forrard, he asked if any one had relieved the lookout.

" 'No, Sir,' answered Quoin.

" 'Is it yours?' the Second asked.

" 'Yes, Sir,' he replied.

" 'Hurry up and relieve him then,' the Second said.

" 'i, i, Sir,' the man answered, and went forrard with the rest of us.

"As we went, I asked Plummer who was at the wheel.

" 'Tom,' he said.

"As he spoke, several spots of rain fell, and I glanced up at the sky. It had become thickly clouded.

" 'Looks as if it were going to breeze up,' said.

" 'Yes,' he replied. 'We'll be shortenin' 'er down 'fore long.'

" 'May be an all-hands job,' I remarked.

" 'Yes,' he answered again. ' 'Twon't be no use their turnin'-in, if it is.'

"The man who was carrying the lantern, went into the fo'cas'le, and we followed.

" 'Where's ther one, belongin' to our side?' Plummer asked.

" 'Got smashed hupstairs,' answered Stubbing.

" ' 'ow were that?' Plummer inquired.

"Stubbins hesitated.

" 'The Second Mate dropped it,' I replied. 'The sail hit it, or something.'

"The men in the other watch seemed to have no immediate intention of turning-in; but sat in their bunks, and around on the chests. There was a general lighting of pipes, in the midst of which there came a sudden moan from one of the bunks in the forepart of the fo'cas'le—a part that was always a bit gloomy, and was more so now, on account of our having only one lamp.

" 'Wot's that?' asked one of the men belonging to the other side.

" 'S—sh !' said Stubbins. 'It's him.'

" ' 'oo?' inquired Plummer. 'Jacobs?'

" 'Yes,' I replied. 'Poor devil!'

" 'Wot were 'appenin' when yer got hup *ther*?' asked the man on the other side, indicating with a jerk of his head, the fore royal.

"Before I could reply, Stubbins jumped up from his sea-chest.

" 'Ther Second Mate's whistlin'!' he said. 'Come hon,' and he ran out on deck.

"Plummer, Jaskett and I followed quickly.

"Outside, it had started to rain pretty heavily. As we went, the Second Mate's voice came to us through the darkness.

" 'Stand by the main royal clewlines and buntlines,' I heard him shout, and the next instant came the hollow thutter of the sail as he started to lower away.

"In a few minutes we had it hauled up.

" 'Up and furl it, a couple of you,' he sung out.

"I went towards the starboard rigging; then I hesitated. No one else had moved.

"The Second Mate came among us.

" 'Come on now, lads,' he said. 'Make a move. It's got to be done.'

"Still, no one stirred, and no one answered.

" 'I'll go,' I said, 'If someone else will come.'

"Tammy came across to me.

" 'I'll come,' he volunteered, in a nervous voice.

" 'No, by God, no!' said the Second Mate, abruptly. He jumped into the main rigging himself. 'Come along, Jessop!' he shouted.

"I followed him; but I was astonished. I had fully expected him to get on to the other fellows' tracks like a ton of bricks. It had not occurred to me that he was making allowances. I was simply puzzled then; but afterwards it dawned upon me.

"No sooner had I followed the Second Mate, than, straightway, Stubbins, Plummer, and Jaskett came up after us at a run.

"About halfway to the maintop, the Second Mate stopped, and looked down.

" 'Who's that coming up below you, Jessop?' he asked.

"Before I could speak, Stubbins answered:—

" 'It's me, Sir, an' Plummer an' Jaskett.'

" 'Who the devil told you to come *now*? Go straight down, the lot of you!'

" 'We're comin' hup ter keep you company, Sir,' was his reply.

"At that, I was confident of a burst of temper from the Second; and yet, for the second time within a couple of minutes I was wrong. Instead of cursing Stubbins, he, after a moment's pause, went on up the rigging, without another word, and the rest of us followed. We reached the royal, and made short work of it; indeed, there were sufficient of us to have eaten it. When we had finished, I noticed that the Second Mate remained on the yard until we were all in the rigging. Evidently, he had determined to take a full share of any risk there might be; but I took care to keep pretty close to him; so as to be on hand if anything happened; yet we reached the deck again, without anything having occurred. I have said, without anything having occurred; but I am not really correct in this; for, as the Second Mate came down over the cross-trees, he gave a short, abrupt cry.

" 'Anything wrong, Sir?' I asked.

" 'No—o !' he said. 'Nothing! I banged my knee.'

"And yet *now*, I believe he was lying. For, that same watch, I was to hear men giving just such cries; but, God knows, they had reason enough.

X
Hands That Plucked

"**D**IRECTLY WE REACHED THE deck, the Second Mate gave the order:—

" 'Mizzen t'gallant clewlines and buntlines,' and led the way up onto the poop. He went and stood by the haulyards, ready to lower away. As I walked across to the starboard clewline, I saw that the Old Man was on deck, and as I took hold of the rope, I heard him sing out to the Second Mate.

" 'Call all hands to shorten sail, Mr. Tulipson.'

" 'Very good, Sir,' the Second Mate replied. Then he raised his voice:—

" 'Go forrard, you, Jessop, and call all hands to shorten sail. You'd better give them a call in the Bosun's place, as you go.'

" 'i, i, Sir,' I sung out, and hurried off.

"As I went, I heard him tell Tammy to go down and call the Mate.

"Reaching the fo'cas'le, I put my head in through the starboard doorway, and found some of the men beginning to turn-in.

" 'It's all hands on deck, shorten sail,' I sung out.

"I stepped inside.

" 'Just wot I said,' grumbled one of the men.

" 'They don't dam well think we're goin' aloft tonight, after what's happened?' asked another.

" 'We've been up to the main royal,' I answered. 'The Second Mate went with us.'

" 'Wot?' said the first man. 'Ther Second Mate hisself?'

" 'Yes,' I replied. 'The whole blooming watch went up.'

" 'An' wot 'appened?' he asked.

" 'Nothing,' I said. 'Nothing at all. We just made a mouthful apiece of it, and came down again.'

" 'All the same,' remarked the second man, 'I don't fancy goin' upstairs, after what's happened.'

" 'Well,' I replied. 'It's not a matter of fancy. We've got to get the sail off her, or there'll be a mess. One of the 'prentices told me the glass is falling.'

" 'Come erlong, boys. We've got ter du it,' said one of the older men, rising from a chest, at this point. 'What's it duin' outside, mate?'

" 'Raining,' I said. 'You'll want your oil-skins.'

"I hesitated a moment before going on deck again. From the bunk forrard among the shadows, I had seemed to hear a faint moan.

" 'Poor beggar!' I thought to myself.

"Then the old chap who had last spoken, broke in upon my attention.

" 'It's awl right, mate!' he said, rather testily. 'Yer needn't wait. We'll be out in er minit.'

" 'That's all right. I wasn't thinking about you lot,' I replied, and walked forrard to Jacobs' bunk. Some time before, he had rigged up a pair of curtains, cut out of an old sack, to keep off the draught. These, some one had drawn, so that I had to pull them aside to see him. He was lying on his back, breathing in a queer, jerky fashion. I could not see his face, plainly; but it seemed rather pale, in the half-light.

" 'Jacobs,' I said. 'Jacobs, how do you feel now?' but he made no sign to show that he had heard me. And so, after a few moments, I drew the curtains to again, and left him.

" 'What like does 'e seem?' asked one of the fellows, as I went towards the door.

" 'Bad,' I said. 'Dam bad! I think the Steward ought to be told to come and have a look at him. I'll mention it to the Second when I get a chance.'

"I stepped out on deck, and ran aft again to give them a hand with the sail. We got it hauled up, and then went forrard to the fore t'gallant. And, a minute later, the other watch were out, and, with the Mate, were busy at the main.

"By the time the main was ready for making fast, we had the fore hauled up, so that now all three t'gallants were in the ropes, and ready for stowing. Then came the order:—

" 'Up aloft and furl!'

" 'Up with you, lads,' the Second Mate said. 'Don't let's have any hanging back this time.'

"Away aft by the main, the men in the Mate's watch seemed to be standing in a clump by the mast; but it was too dark to see clearly. I heard the Mate start to curse; then there came a growl, and he shut up.

" 'Be handy, men! be handy!' the Second Mate sung out.

"At that, Stubbins jumped into the rigging.

" 'Come hon!' he shouted. 'We'll have ther bloomin' sail fast, an' down hon deck again before they're started.'

"Plummer followed; then Jaskett, I, and Quoin who had been called down off the lookout to give a hand.

" 'That's the style, lads!' the Second sung out, encouragingly. Then he ran aft to the Mate's crowd. I heard him and the Mate talking to the men, and presently, when we were going over the foretop, I made out that they were beginning to get into the rigging.

"I found out, afterwards, that as soon as the Second Mate had seen them off the deck, he went up to the mizzen t'gallant, along with the four 'prentices.

"On our part, we made our way slowly aloft, keeping one hand for ourselves and the other for the ship, as you can fancy. In this manner we had gone as far as the cross-trees, at least, Stubbins, who was first, had; when, all at once, he gave out just another such cry as had the Second Mate a little earlier, only that in his case he followed it by turning round and blasting Plummer.

" 'You might have blarsted well sent me flyin' down hon deck,' he shouted. 'If you bl—dy well think it's a joke, try it hon some one else—'

" 'It wasn't me!' interrupted Plummer. 'I 'aven't touched yer. 'oo the 'ell are yer swearin' at?'

" 'At you—!' I heard him reply; but what more he may have said, was lost in a loud shout from Plummer.

" 'What's up, Plummer?' I sung out. 'For God's sake, you two, don't get fighting, up aloft!'

"But a loud, frightened curse was all the answer he gave. Then straightway, he began to shout at the top of his voice, and in the lulls of his noise, I caught the voice of Stubbins, cursing savagely.

" 'They'll come down with a run!' I shouted, helplessly. 'They'll come down as sure as nuts.'

"I caught Jaskett by the boot.

" 'What are they doing? What are they doing?' I sung out. 'Can't you see?' I shook his leg as I spoke. But at my touch, the old idiot—as I thought him at the moment—began to shout in a frightened voice:—

"Oh! oh! help! hel—!'

" 'Shut up!' I bellowed. 'Shut up, you old fool! If you won't do anything, let me get past you!"

"Yet he only cried out the more. And then, abruptly, I caught the sound of a frightened clamour of men's voices, away down somewhere about the maintop—curses, cries of fear, even shrieks, and above it all, someone shouting to go down on deck:—

" 'Get down! get down! down! down! Blarst—' The rest was drowned in a fresh outburst of hoarse crying in the night.

"I tried to get past old Jaskett; but he was clinging to the rigging, sprawled onto it, is the best way to describe his attitude, so much of it as I could see in the darkness. Up above him, Stubbins and Plummer still shouted and cursed, and the shrouds quivered and shook, as though the two were fighting desperately.

"Stubbins seemed to be shouting something definite; but whatever it was, I could not catch.

"At my helplessness, I grew angry, and shook and prodded Jaskett, to make him move.

" 'Damn you, Jaskett!' I roared. 'Damn you for a funky old fool! Let me get past! Let me get past, will you!'

"But, instead of letting me pass, I found that he was beginning to make his way down. At that, I caught him by the slack of his trousers, near the stern, with my right hand, and with the other, I got hold of the after shroud somewhere above his left hip; by these means, I fairly hoisted myself up onto the old fellow's back. Then, with my right, I could reach to the forrard shroud, over his right shoulder, and having got a grip, I shifted my left to a level with it; at the same moment, I was able to get my foot on to the splice of a ratline and so give myself a further lift. Then I paused an instant, and glanced up.

" 'Stubbins! Stubbins!' I shouted. 'Plummer! Plummer!'

"And even as I called, Plummer's foot—reaching down through the gloom—alighted full on my upturned face. I let go from the rigging with my right hand, and struck furiously at his leg, cursing him for his clumsiness. He lifted his foot, and in the same instant a sentence from Stubbins floated down to me, with a strange distinctness:—

" *'For God's sake tell 'em ter get down hon deck!'* he was shouting.

"Even as the words came to me, something in the darkness gripped my waist. I made a desperate clutch at the rigging with my disengaged right hand, and it was well for me that I secured the hold so quickly; for the same instant, I was wrenched at with a brutal ferocity that appalled me. I said nothing, but lashed out into the night with my left foot. It is queer, but I cannot say with certainty that I struck anything; I was too downright desperate with funk, to be sure; and yet it seemed to me that my foot encountered something soft, that gave under the blow. It may have been nothing more than an imagined sensation; yet I am inclined to think otherwise; for, instantly, the hold about my waist was released; and I commenced to scramble down, clutching the shrouds pretty desperately.

"I have only a very uncertain remembrance of that which followed. Whether I slid over Jaskett, or whether he gave way to me, I cannot tell. I know only that I reached the deck, a blind whirl of fear and excitement, and the next thing I remember, I was among a crowd of shouting, half-mad sailor-men.

XI
The Search for Stubbins

"IN A CONFUSED WAY, I was conscious that the Skipper and the Mates were down among us, trying to get us into some state of calmness. Eventually they succeeded, and we were told to go aft to the Saloon door, which we did in a body. Here, the Skipper himself served out a large tot of rum to each of us. Then, at his orders, the Second Mate called the roll.

"He called over the Mate's watch first, and everyone answered. Then he came to ours, and he must have been much agitated; for the first name he sung out was Jock's.

"Among us there came a moment of dead silence, and I noticed the wail and moan of the wind aloft, and the flap, flap of the three unfurled t'gallan's'ls.

"The Second Mate called the next name, hurriedly:—

" 'Jaskett,' he sung out.

" 'Sir,' Jaskett answered.

" 'Quoin.'

" 'Yes, Sir.'

" 'Jessop.'

" 'Sir,' I replied.

" 'Stubbins.'

"There was no answer.

" 'Stubbins,' again called the Second Mate.

"Again there was no reply.

" 'Is Stubbins here?—anyone!' The Second's voice sounded sharp and anxious.

"There was a moment's pause. Then one of the men spoke:—

" 'He's not here, Sir.'

" 'Who saw him last?' the Second asked.

"Plummer stepped forward into the light that streamed through the saloon doorway. He had on neither coat nor cap, and his shirt seemed to be hanging about him in tatters.

" 'It were me, Sir,' he said.

"The Old Man, who was standing next to the Second Mate, took a pace towards him, and stopped and stared; but it was the Second who spoke.

" 'Where?' he asked.

" ' 'e were just above me, in ther cross-trees, when, when—' the man broke off short.

" 'Yes! yes!' the Second Mate replied. Then he turned to the Skipper.

" 'Someone will have to go up, Sir, and see—' He hesitated.

" 'But—' said the Old Man, and stopped.

"The Second Mate cut in.

" 'I shall go up, for one, Sir,' he said, quietly.

"Then he turned back to the crowd of us.

" 'Tammy,' he sung out. 'Get a couple of lamps out of the lamp-locker.'

" 'i, i, Sir,' Tammy replied, and ran off.

" 'Now,' said the Second Mate, addressing us. 'I want a couple of men to jump aloft along with me, and take a look for Stubbins.'

"Not a man replied. I would have liked to step out and offer; but the memory of that horrible clutch was with me, and for the life of me, I could not summon up the courage.

" 'Come! come, men!' he said. 'We can't leave him up there. We shall take lanterns. Who'll come now?'

"I walked out to the front. I was in a horrible funk; but, for very shame, I could not stand back any longer.

" 'I'll come with you, Sir,' I said, not very loud, and feeling fairly twisted up with nervousness.

" 'That's more the tune, Jessop !' he replied, in a tone that made me glad I had stood out.

"At this point, Tammy came up, with the lights. He brought them to the Second, who took one, and told him to give the other to me. The Second Mate held his light above his head, and looked round at the hesitating men.

" 'Now, men!' he sung out. 'You're not going to let Jessop and me go up alone. Come along, another one or two of you! Don't act like a damned lot of cowards!'

"Quoin stood out, and spoke for the crowd.

" 'I dunno as we're actin' like cowyards, Sir; but just look at '*im*,' and he pointed at Plummer, who still stood full in the light from the Saloon, doorway.

" 'What sort of a Thing is it as 'as done that, Sir?' he went on. 'An' then yer arsks us ter go up agen! It aren't likely as we're in a 'urry.'

"The Second Mate looked at Plummer, and surely, as I have before mentioned, the poor beggar was in a state; his ripped-up shirt was fairly flapping in the breeze that came through the doorway.

"The Second looked; yet he said nothing. It was as though the realisation of Plummer's condition had left him without a word more to say. It was Plummer himself who finally broke the silence.

" 'I'll come with yer, Sir,' he said. 'Only yer ought ter 'ave more light than them two lanterns. 'Twon't be no use, unless we 'as plenty er light.'

"The man had grit; and I was astonished at his offering to go, after what he must have gone through. Yet, I was to have even a greater astonishment; for, abruptly, the Skipper—who all this time had scarcely spoken—stepped forward a pace, and put his hand on the Second Mate's shoulder.

" 'I'll come with you, Mr. Tulipson,' he said.

"The Second Mate twisted his head round, and stared at him a moment, in astonishment. Then he opened his mouth.

" 'No, Sir; I don't think—' he began.

" 'That's sufficient, Mr. Tulipson,' the Old Man interrupted. 'I've made up my mind.'

"He turned to the First Mate, who had stood by without a word.

" 'Mr. Grainge,' he said. 'Take a couple of the 'prentices down with you, and pass out a box of blue-lights and some flare-ups.'

"The Mate answered something, and hurried away into the Saloon, with the two 'prentices in his watch. Then the Old Man spoke to the men.

" 'Now, men!' he began. 'This is no time for dilly-dallying. The Second Mate and I will go aloft, and I want about half a dozen of you to come along with us, and carry lights. Plummer and Jessop here, have volunteered. I want four or five more of you. Step out now, some of you!'

"There was no hesitation whatever, now; and the first man to come forward was Quoin. After him followed three of the Mate's crowd, and then old Jaskett.

" 'That will do; that will do,' said the Old Man.

"He turned to the Second Mate.

" 'Has Mr. Grainge come with those lights yet?' he asked, with a certain irritability.

" 'Here, Sir,' said the First Mate's voice, behind him in the Saloon doorway. He had the box of blue-lights in his hands, and behind him came the two boys carrying the flares.

"The Skipper took the box from him, with a quick gesture, and opened it.

" 'Now, one of you men, come here,' he ordered.

"One of the men in the Mate's watch, ran to him.

"He took several of the lights from the box, and handed them to the man.

" 'See here,' he said. 'When we go aloft, you get into the foretop, and keep one of these going all the time, do you hear?'

" 'Yes, Sir,' replied the man.

" 'You know how to strike them?' the Skipper asked, abruptly.

" 'Yes, Sir,' he answered.

"The Skipper sung out to the Second Mate:—

" 'Where's that boy of yours—Tammy, Mr. Tulipson?'

" 'Here, Sir,' said Tammy, answering for himself.

"The Old Man took another light from the box.

" 'Listen to me, boy!' he said. 'Take this, and standby on the forrard deck house. When we go aloft, you must give us a light until the man gets his going in the top. You understand?'

" 'Yes, Sir,' answered Tammy, and took the light.

" 'One minute!' said the Old Man, and stooped and took a second light from the box. 'Your first light may go out before we're ready. You'd better have another, in case it does.'

"Tammy took the second light, and moved away.

" 'Those flares all ready for lighting there, Mr. Grainge?' the Captain asked.

" 'All ready, Sir,' replied the Mate.

"The Old Man pushed one of the blue-lights into his coat pocket, and stood upright.

" 'Very well,' he said. 'Give each of the men one apiece. And just see that they all have matches.'

"He spoke to the men particularly:—

" 'As soon as we are ready, the other two men in the Mate's watch will get up into the cranelines, and keep their flares going there. Take your paraffin tins with you. When we reach the upper top-sail, Quoin and Jaskett will get out on to the yard-arms, and show their flares there. Be careful to keep your lights away from the sails. Plummer and Jessop will come up with the Second Mate and myself. Does every man clearly understand?'

" 'Yes, Sir,' said the men in a chorus.

"A sudden idea seemed to occur to the Skipper, and he turned, and went through the doorway into the saloon. In about a minute, he came back, and handed something to the Second Mate, that shone in the light from the lanterns. I saw that it was a revolver, and he held another in his other hand, and this I saw him put into his side pocket.

"The Second Mate held the pistol a moment, looking a bit doubtful.

" 'I don't think, Sir—' he began. But the Skipper cut him short.

" 'You don't know!' he said. 'Put it in your pocket.'

"Then he turned to the First Mate.

" 'You will take charge of the deck, Mr. Grainge, while we're aloft,' he said.

" i, i, Sir,' the Mate answered, and sung out to one of his 'prentices to take the blue-light box back into the cabin.

"The Old Man turned, and led the way forrard. As we went, the light from the two lanterns shone upon the decks, showing the litter of the t'gallant gear. The ropes were foul of one another in a regular 'bunch o' buffers.' This had been caused, I suppose, by the crowd trampling over them in their excitement, when they reached the deck. And then, suddenly, as though the sight had waked me up to a more vivid comprehension, you know, it came to me new and fresh, how damned strange was the whole business. I got a little touch of despair, and asked myself what was going to be the end of all these beastly happenings. You can understand?

"Abruptly, I heard the Skipper shouting, away forrard. He was singing out to Tammy to get up on to the house with his blue-light. We reached the fore rigging, and, the same instant, the strange, ghastly flare of Tammy's blue-light burst out into the night, causing every rope, sail, and spar to jump out weirdly.

"I saw now that the Second Mate was already in the starboard rigging, with his lantern. He was shouting to Tammy to keep the drip from his light, clear of the staysail, which was stowed upon the house. Then, from somewhere on the port side, I heard the Skipper shout to us to hurry.

" 'Smartly now, you men,' he was saying. 'Smartly now.'

"The man who had been told to take up a station in the foretop, was just behind the Second Mate. Plummer was a couple of ratlines lower.

"I caught the Old Man's voice again.

" 'Where's Jessop with that other lantern?' I heard him shout.

" 'Here, Sir,' I sung out.

" 'Bring it over this side,' he ordered. 'You don't want the two lanterns on one side.'

"I ran round the fore side of the house. Then I saw him. He was in the rigging, and making his way smartly aloft. One of the Mate's watch and Quoin were with him. This, I saw as I came round the house. Then I made a jump, gripped the sherpole, and swung myself up onto the rail. And then, all at once, Tammy's blue-light went out, and there came, what seemed by contrast, pitchy darkness. I stood where I was—one foot on the rail, and my knee upon the sherpole. The light from my lantern seemed no more than a sickly yellow glow against the gloom, and higher, some forty or fifty feet, and a few ratlines below the futtock rigging on the starboard side, there was another glow of yellowness in the night. Apart from these, all was blackness. And then from above—high above, there wailed down through the darkness a weird, sobbing cry. What it was, I do not know; but it sounded horrible.

"The Skipper's voice came down, jerkily.

" 'Smartly with that light, boy!' he shouted. And the blue glare blazed out again, almost before he had finished speaking.

"I stared up at the Skipper. He was standing where I had seen him before the light went out, and so were the two men. As I looked, he commenced to climb again. I glanced across to starboard. Jaskett, and the other man in the Mate's watch, were about midway between the deck of the house and the foretop. Their faces showed extraordinarily pale in the dead glare of the blue-light. Higher, I saw the Second Mate in the futtock rigging, holding his light up over the edge of the top. Then he went further, and disappeared. The man with the blue-lights followed, and also vanished from view. On the port side, and more directly above me, the Skipper's feet were just stepping out of the futtock shrouds. At that, I made haste to follow.

"Then, suddenly, when I was close under the top, there came from above me the sharp flare of a blue-light, and almost in the same instant, Tammy's went out.

"I glanced down at the decks. They were filled with flickering, grotesque shadows cast by the dripping light above. A group of the men stood by the port galley door—their faces upturned and pale and unreal under the gleam of the light. Then I was in the futtock rigging, and a moment afterwards, standing in the top, beside the Old Man. He was shouting to the men who had gone out on the cranelines. It seemed that the man on the port side was bungling; but at last—nearly a minute after the other man had lit his flare—he got his going. In that time, the man in the top had lit his second blue-light, and we were ready to get into the top-mast rigging. First, however, the Skipper leant over the after side of the top, and sung out to the First Mate to send a man up on to the fo'cas'le head with a flare. The Mate replied, and then we started again the Old Man leading.

"Fortunately, the rain had ceased, and there seemed to be no increase in the wind; indeed, if anything, there appeared to be rather less; yet what there was drove the flames of the flare-ups out into occasional, twisting serpents of fire at least a yard long.

"About halfway up the top-mast rigging, the Second Mate sung out to the Skipper, to know whether Plummer should light his flare; but the Old Man said he had better wait until we reached the cross-trees, as then he could get out away from the gear to where there would be less danger of setting fire to anything.

" We neared the cross-trees, and the Old Man stooped and sung out to me to pass him the lantern by Quoin. A few ratlines more, and both he and the Second Mate stopped almost simultaneously, holding their lanterns as high as possible, and peered up into the darkness.

" 'See any signs of him, Mr. Tulipson?' the Old Man asked.

" 'No, Sir,' replied the Second. 'Not a sign.'

"He raised his voice.

" 'Stubbins,' he sung out. 'Stubbins, are you there?'

"We listened; but nothing came to us beyond the blowing moan of the wind, and the flap, flap of the bellying t'gallant above.

"The Second Mate climbed over the cross-trees, and Plummer followed. The man got out by the royal backstay, and lit his flare. By its light we could see, plainly; but there was no vestige of Stubbins, so far as the light went.

" 'Get out onto the yard-arms with those flares, you two men,' shouted the Skipper. 'Be smart now! Keep them away from the sail!'

"The men got on to the foot-ropes—Quoin on the port, and Jaskett on the starboard, side. By the light from Plummer's flare, I could see them clearly, as they lay out upon the yard. It occurred to me that they went gingerly—which is no surprising thing. And then, as they drew near to the yard-arms, they passed beyond the brilliance of the light; so that I could not see them clearly. A few seconds passed, and then the light from Quoin's flare streamed out upon the wind; yet nearly a minute went by, and there was no sign of Jaskett's.

"Then out from the semi-darkness at the starboard yard-arm, there came a curse from Jaskett, followed almost immediately by a noise of something vibrating.

" 'What's up?' shouted the Second Mate. 'What's up, Jaskett?'

" 'It's ther foot-rope, Sir—r—r!' he drew out the last word into a sort of gasp.

"The Second Mate bent quickly, with the lantern. I craned round the after side of the top-mast, and looked.

" 'What is the matter, Mr. Tulipson?' I heard the Old Man singing out.

"Out on the yard arm, Jaskett began to shout for help, and then, all at once, in the light from the Second Mate's lantern, I saw that the star-board foot-rope on the upper top-sail yard was being violently shaken—savagely shaken, is perhaps a better word. And then, almost in the same instant, the Second Mate shifted the lantern from his right to his left hand. He put the right into his pocket and brought out his gun with a jerk. He extended his hand and arm, as though pointing at something a little below the yard. Then a quick flash spat out across the shadows, followed immediately by a sharp, ringing crack. In the same moment, I saw that the footrope ceased to shake.

" 'Light your flare! Light your flare, Jaskett!' the Second shouted. 'Be smart now!'

"Out at the yardarm there came the splutter of a match, and then, straightway, a great spurt of fire as the flare took light.

" 'That's better, Jaskett. You're all right now!' the Second Mate called out to him.

" 'What was it, Mr. Tulipson?' I heard the Skipper ask.

"I looked up, and saw that he had sprung across to where the Second Mate was standing. The Second Mate explained to him; but he did not speak loud enough for me to catch what he said.

"I had been struck by Jaskett's attitude, when the light of his flare had first revealed him. He had been crouched with his right knee cocked over the yard, and his left leg down between it and the foot-rope, while his elbows had been crooked over the yard for support as he was lighting the flare. Now, however, he had slid both feet back on to the foot-rope, and was lying on his belly, over the yard, with the flare held a little below the head of the sail. It was thus, with the light being on the fore side of the sail, that I saw a small hole a little below the foot-rope, through which a ray of the light shone. It was undoubtedly the hole which the bullet from the Second Mate's revolver had made in the sail.

"Then I heard the Old Man shouting to Jaskett.

" 'Be careful with that flare there!' he sung out. 'You'll be having that sail scorched!'

"He left the Second Mate, and came back on to the port side of the mast.

"To my right, Plummer's flare seemed to be dwindling. I glanced up at his face through the smoke. He was paying no attention to it; instead, he was staring up above his head.

" 'Shove some paraffin on to it, Plummer,' I called to him. 'It'll be out in a minute.'

"He looked down quickly to the light, and did as I suggested. Then he held it out at arm's length, and peered up again into the darkness.

" 'See anything?' asked the Old Man, suddenly observing his attitude.

"Plummer glanced at him, with a start.

" 'It's ther r'yal, Sir,' he explained. 'It's all adrift.'

" 'What!' said the Old Man.

"He was standing a few ratlines up the t'gallant rigging, and he bent his body outwards to get a better look.

" 'Mr. Tulipson!' he shouted. 'Do you know that the royal's all adrift?'

" 'No, Sir,' answered the Second Mate. 'If it is, it's more of this devilish work!'"

" 'It's adrift right enough,' said the Skipper, and he and the Second went a few ratlines higher, keeping level with one another.

"I had now got above the cross-trees, and was just at the Old Man's heels.

"Suddenly, he shouted out:—

" 'There he is! —Stubbins! Stubbins!'

" 'Where, Sir?' asked the Second, eagerly. 'I can't see him!'

" 'There! there!' replied the Skipper, pointing.

"I leant out from the rigging, and looked up along his back, in the direction his finger indicated. At first, I could see nothing; then, slowly, you know, there grew upon my sight a dim figure crouching upon the bunt of the royal, and partly hidden by the mast. I stared, and gradually it came to me that there was a couple of them, and further out upon the yard, a hump that might have been anything, and was only visible indistinctly amid the flutter of the canvas.

" 'Stubbins!' the Skipper sung out. 'Stubbins, come down out of that! Do you hear me?'

"But no one came, and there was no answer.

" 'There's two—' I began; but he was shouting again:—

" 'Come down out of that! Do you damned well hear me?'

"Still there was no reply.

" 'I'm hanged if I can see him at all, Sir!' the Second Mate called out from his side of the mast.

" 'Can't see him!' said the Old Man, now thoroughly angry. 'I'll soon let you see him!'

"He bent down to me with the lantern. Catch hold, Jessop,' he said, which I did.

"Then he pulled the blue-light from his pocket, and as he was doing so, I saw the Second peek round the back side of the mast at him. Evidently, in the uncertain light, he must have mistaken the Skipper's action; for, all at once, he shouted out in a frightened voice:—

" 'Don't shoot, Sir! For God's sake, don't shoot!'

" 'Shoot be damned!' exclaimed the Old Man. 'Watch!'

"He pulled off the cap of the light.

" 'There's two of them, Sir,' I called again to him.

" 'What!' he said in a loud voice, and at the same instant he rubbed the end of the light across the gap, and it burst into fire.

"He held it up so that it lit the royal yard like day, and straightway, a couple of shapes dropped silently from the royal on to the t'gallant yard. At the same moment, the humped something, midway out upon the yard, rose up. It ran in to the mast, and I lost sight of it.

" '—God!' I heard the Skipper gasp, and he fumbled in his side pocket.

"I saw the two figures which had dropped on to the t'gallant, run swiftly along the yard—one to the starboard and the other to the port yard-arms.

"On the other side of the mast, the Second Mate's pistol cracked out twice, sharply. Then, from over my head the Skipper fired twice, and then again; but with what effect, I could not tell. Abruptly, as he fired his last shot, I was aware of an indistinct Something, gliding down the starboard royal backstay. It was descending full upon Plummer, who, all unconscious of the thing, was staring towards the t'gallant yard.

" 'Look out above you, Plummer!' I almost shrieked.

" 'What? where?' he called, and grabbed at the stay, and waved his flare, excitedly.

"Down on the upper top-sail yard, Quoin's and Jaskett's voices rose simultaneously, and in the identical instant, their flares went out. Then Plummer shouted, and his light went utterly out. There were left only the two lanterns, and the blue-light held by the Skipper, and that, a few seconds afterwards, finished and died out.

"The Skipper and the Second Mate were shouting to the men upon the yard, and I heard them answer, in shaky voices. Out on the cross-trees, I could see, by the light from my lantern, that Plummer was holding in a dazed fashion to the backstay.

" 'Are you all right, Plummer?' I called.

" 'Yes,' he said, after a little pause; and then he swore.

" 'Come in off that yard, you men!' the Skipper was singing out. 'Come in! come in!'

"Down on deck, I heard some one calling; but could not distinguish the words. Above me, pistol in hand, the Skipper was glancing about, uneasily.

" 'Hold up that light, Jessop,' he said. 'I can't see!'

"Below us, the men got off the yard, into the rigging.

" 'Down on deck with you!' ordered the Old Man. 'As smartly as you can!'

" 'Come in off there, Plummer!' sung out the Second Mate. 'Get down with the others!'

" 'Down with you, Jessop!' said the Skipper, speaking rapidly. 'Down with you!'

"I got over the cross-trees, and he followed. On the other side, the Second Mate was level with us. He had passed his lantern to Plummer, and I caught the glint of his revolver in his right hand. In this fashion, we reached the top. The man who had been stationed there with the blue-lights, had gone. Afterwards, I found that he went down on deck as soon as they were finished. There was no sign of the man with the flare on the starboard craneline. He also, I learnt later, had slid down one of the backstays on to the deck, only a very short while before we reached the top. He swore that a great black shadow of a man had come suddenly upon him from aloft. When I heard that, I remembered the thing I had seen descending upon Plummer. Yet the man who had gone out upon the port craneline—the one who had bungled with the lighting of his flare—was still where we had left him; though his light was burning now but dimly.

" 'Come in out of that, *you*!' the Old Man sung out. 'Smartly now, and get down on deck!'

" 'i, i, Sir,' the man replied, and started to make his way in.

"The Skipper waited until he had got into the main rigging, and then he told me to get down out of the top. He was in the act of following, when, all at once, there rose a loud outcry on deck, and then came the sound of a man screaming.

" 'Get out of my way, Jessop!' the Skipper roared, and swung himself down alongside of me.

"I heard the Second Mate shout something from the starboard rigging. Then we were all racing down as hard as we could go. I had caught a momentary glimpse of a man running from the doorway on the port side of the fo'cas'le. In less than half a minute we were upon the deck, and among a crowd of the men who were grouped round something. Yet, strangely enough, they were not looking at the thing among them; but away aft at something in the darkness.

" 'It's on the rail!' cried several voices.

" 'Overboard!' called somebody, in an excited voice. 'It's jumped over the side!'

" 'Ther' wer'n't nothin'!' said a man in the crowd.

" 'Silence!' shouted the Old Man. 'Where's the Mate? What's happened?'

" 'Here, Sir,' called the First Mate, shakily, from near the centre of the group. 'It's Jacobs, Sir. He—he—'

" 'What!' said the Skipper. 'What!'

" 'He—he's—he's dead—I think!' said the First Mate, in jerks.

" 'Let me see,' said the Old Man, in a quieter tone.

"The men had stood to one side to give him room, and he knelt beside the man upon the deck.

" 'Pass the lantern here, Jessop,' he said.

"I stood by him, and held the light. The man was lying face downwards on the deck. Under the light from the lantern, the Skipper turned him over and looked at him.

" 'Yes,' he said, after a short examination. 'He's dead.'

"He stood up and regarded the body a moment, in silence. Then he turned to the Second Mate, who had been standing by, during the last couple of minutes.

" 'Three!' he said, in a grim undertone.

"The Second Mate nodded, and cleared his voice.

"He seemed on the point of saying something; then he turned and looked at Jacobs, and said nothing.

" 'Three,' repeated the Old Man. 'Since eight bells!'

"He stooped and looked again at Jacobs. Poor devil! poor devil!' he muttered.

"The Second Mate grunted some of the huskiness out of his throat, and spoke.

" 'Where must we take him?' he asked, quietly. 'The two bunks are full.'

" 'You'll have to put him down on the deck by the lower bunk,' replied the Skipper.

"As they carried him away, I heard the Old Man make a sound that was almost a groan. The rest of the men had gone forrard, and I do not think he realised that I was standing by him.

" 'My God! O, my God!' he muttered, and began to walk slowly aft.

"He had cause enough for groaning. There were three dead, and Stubbins had gone utterly and completely. We never saw him again.

XII

The Council

"A FEW MINUTES LATER, the Second Mate came forrard again.
I was still standing near the rigging, holding the lantern, in an
aimless sort of way.

" 'That you, Plummer?' he asked.

" 'No, Sir,' I said. 'It's Jessop.'

" 'Where's Plummer, then?' he inquired.

" 'I don't know, Sir,' I answered. 'I expect he's gone forrard. Shall
I go and tell him you want him?'

" 'No, there's no need,' he said. 'Tie your lamp up in the rigging—
on the sherpole there. Then go and get his, and shove it up on the
starboard side. After that you'd better go aft and give the two 'prentices
a hand in the lamp locker.'

" 'i, i, Sir,' I replied, and proceeded to do as he directed. After I
had got the light from Plummer, and lashed it up to the starboard
sherpole, I hurried aft. I found Tammy and the other 'prentice in our
watch, busy in the locker, lighting lamps.

" 'What are we doing?' I asked.

" 'The Old Man's given orders to lash all the spare lamps we can
find, in the rigging, so as to have the decks light,' said Tammy. 'And a
damned good job too!'

"He handed me a couple of the lamps, and took two himself.

" 'Come on,' he said, and stepped out on deck. 'We'll fix these in
the main rigging, and then I want to talk to you.'

" 'What about the mizzen?' I inquired.

" 'Oh,' he replied. 'He' (meaning the other 'prentice) 'will see to
that. Anyway, it'll be daylight directly.'

"We shoved the lamps up on the sherpoles—two on each side.
Then he came across to me.

" 'Look here, Jessop!' he said, without any hesitation. 'You'll have

96

to jolly well tell the Skipper and the Second Mate all you know about all this.'

" 'How do you mean?' I asked.

" 'Why, that it's something about the ship herself that's the cause of what's happened,' he replied. 'If you'd only explained to the Second Mate when I told you to, this might never have been!'

" 'But I don't *know*,' I said. 'I may be all wrong. It's only an idea of mine. I've no proofs—'

" 'Proofs!' he cut in with. 'Proofs! what about tonight? We've had all the proofs ever I want!'

"I hesitated before answering him.

" 'So have I, for that matter,' I said, at length. 'What I mean is, I've nothing that the Skipper and the Second Mate would consider as proofs. They'd never listen seriously to me.'

" 'They'd listen fast enough,' he replied. 'After what's happened this watch, they'd listen to anything. Anyway, it's jolly well your duty to tell them!'

" 'What could they do, anyway?' I said, despondently. 'As things are going, we'll all be dead before another week is over, at this rate.'

" 'You tell them,' he answered. 'That's what you've got to do. If you can only get them to realise that you're right, they'll be glad to put into the nearest port, and send us all ashore.'

"I shook my head.

" 'Well, anyway, they'll have to do something,' he replied, in answer to my gesture. 'We can't go round the Horn, with the number of men we've lost. We haven't enough to handle her, if it comes on to blow.'

" 'You've forgotten, Tammy,' I said. 'Even if I could get the Old Man to believe I'd got at the truth of the matter, he couldn't do anything. Don't you see, if I'm right, we couldn't even see the land, if we made it. We're like blind men....'

" 'What on earth do you mean?' he interrupted. 'How do you make out we're like blind men? Of course we could see the land—'

" 'Wait a minute! wait a minute!' I said. 'You don't understand. Didn't I tell you?'

" 'Tell what?' he asked.

" 'About the ship I spotted,' I said. 'I thought you knew!'

" 'No,' he said. 'When?'

" 'Why,' I replied. 'You know when the Old Man sent me away from the wheel?'

" 'Yes,' he answered. 'You mean in the morning watch, day before yesterday?'

" 'Yes,' I said. 'Well, don't you know what was the matter?'

" 'No,' he replied. 'That is, I heard you were snoozing at the wheel, and the Old Man came up and caught you.'

" 'That's all a damned silly yarn!' I said. And then I told him the whole truth of the affair. After I had done that, I explained my idea about it, to him.

" 'Now you see what I mean?' I asked.

" 'You mean that this strange atmosphere—or whatever it is—we're in, would not allow us to see another ship?' he asked, a bit awestruck.

"Yes,' I said. 'But the point I wanted you to see, is that if we can't see another vessel, even when she's quite close, then, in the same way, we shouldn't be able to see land. To all intents and purposes we're blind. Just you think of it! We're out in the middle of the briny, doing a sort of eternal blind man's hop. The Old Man couldn't put into port, even if he wanted to. He'd run us bang on shore, without our ever seeing it.'

" 'What are we going to do, then?' he asked, in a despairing sort of way. 'Do you mean to say we can't do anything? Surely something can be done! It's terrible!'

"For perhaps a minute, we walked up and down, in the light from the different lanterns. Then he spoke again.

" 'We might be run down, then,' he said, 'and never even see the other vessel?'

" 'It's possible,' I replied. 'Though, from what I saw, it's evident that *we're* quite visible; so that it would be easy for them to see us, and steer clear of us, even though we couldn't see them.'

" 'And we might run into something, and never see it?' he asked me, following up the train of thought.

" 'Yes,' I said. 'Only there's nothing to stop the other ship from getting out of our way.'

" 'But if it wasn't a vessel?' he persisted. 'It might be an iceberg, or a rock, or even a derelict.'

" 'In that case,' I said, putting it a bit flippantly, naturally, 'we'd probably damage it.'

"He made no answer to this, and for a few moments, we were quiet.

"Then he spoke abruptly, as though the idea had come suddenly to him.

" 'Those lights the other night!' he said. 'Were they a ship's lights?'

"Yes,' I replied. 'Why?'

" 'Why,' he answered. 'Don't you see, if they were really lights, we *could* see them?'

" 'Well, I should think I ought to know that,' I replied. 'You seem to forget that the Second Mate slung me off the lookout for daring to do that very thing.'

" 'I don't mean that,' he said. 'Don't you see that if we could see them at all, it showed that the atmosphere-thing wasn't round us then?'

" 'Not necessarily,' I answered. 'It may have been nothing more than a rift in it; though, of course, I may be all wrong. But, anyway, the fact that the lights disappeared almost as soon as they were seen, shows that it was very much round the ship.'

"That made him feel a bit the way I did, and when next he spoke, his tone had lost its hopefulness.

" 'Then you think it'll be no use telling the Second Mate and the Skipper anything?' he asked.

" 'I don't know,' I replied. 'I've been thinking about it, and it can't do any harm. I've a very good mind to.'

" 'I should,' he said. 'You needn't be afraid of anybody laughing at you, now. It might do some good. You've seen more than anyone else.'

"He stopped in his walk, and looked round.

"Wait a minute,' he said, and ran aft a few steps. I saw him look up at the break of the poop; then he came back.

" 'Come along now,' he said. 'The Old Man's up on the poop, talking to the Second Mate. You'll never get a better chance.'

"Still I hesitated; but he caught me by the sleeve, and almost dragged me to the lee ladder.

" 'All right,' I said, when I got there. 'All right, I'll come. Only I'm hanged if I know what to say when I get there.'

" 'Just tell them you want to speak to them,' he said. 'They'll ask what you want, and then you spit out all you know. They'll find it in-teresting enough.'

" 'You'd better come too,' I suggested. 'You'll be able to back me up in lots of things,'

" 'I'll come, fast enough,' he replied. 'You go up.'

"I went up the ladder, and walked across to where the Skipper and the Second Mate stood talking earnestly, by the rail. Tammy kept behind. As I came near to them, I caught two or three words; though I attached no meaning then to them. They were: '...send for him.' Then the two of them turned and looked at me, and the Second Mate asked what I wanted.

" 'I want to speak to you and the Old M—Captain, Sir,' I answered.

" 'What is it, Jessop?' the Skipper inquired.

" 'I scarcely know how to put it, Sir,' I said. 'It's—it's about these—these things.'

" 'What things? Speak out, man,' he said.

" 'Well, Sir,' I blurted out. 'There's some dreadful thing or things come aboard this ship, since we left port.'

"I saw him give one quick glance at the Second Mate, and the Second looked back.

"Then the Skipper replied.

" 'How do you mean, come aboard?' he asked.

" 'Out of the sea, Sir,' I said. 'I've seen them. So's Tammy, here.'

" 'Ah!' he exclaimed, and it seemed to me, from his face, that he was understanding something better. 'Out of the sea!'

"Again he looked at the Second Mate; but the Second was staring at me.

" 'Yes, Sir,' I said. 'It's the *ship*. She's not safe! I've watched. I think I understand a bit; but there's a lot I don't.'

"I stopped. The Skipper had turned to the Second Mate. The Second nodded, gravely. Then I heard him mutter, in a low voice, and the Old Man replied; after which he turned to me again.

" 'Look here, Jessop,' he said. 'I'm going to talk straight to you. You strike me as being a cut above the ordinary shellback, and I think you've sense enough to hold your tongue.'

" 'I've got my mate's ticket, Sir,' I said, simply.

"Behind me, I heard Tammy give a little start. He had not known about it until then.

"The Skipper nodded.

" 'So much the better,' he answered. 'I may have to speak to you about that, later on.'

"He paused, and the Second Mate said something to him, in an undertone.

" 'Yes,' he said, as though in reply to what the Second had been saying. Then he spoke to me again.

" 'You've seen things come out of the sea, you say?' he questioned. 'Now just tell me all you can remember, from the very beginning.'

"I set to, and told him everything in detail, commencing with the strange figure that had stepped aboard out of the sea, and continuing my yarn, up to the things that had happened in that very watch.

"I stuck well to solid facts; and now and then he and the Second Mate would look at one another, and nod. At the end, he turned to me with an abrupt gesture.

" 'You still hold, then, that you saw a ship the other morning, when I sent you from the wheel?' he asked.

" 'Yes, Sir,' I said. 'I most certainly do.'

" 'But you know there wasn't any!' he said.

" 'Yes, Sir,' I replied, in an apologetic tone. 'There was; and, if you will let me, I believe that I can explain it a bit.'

" 'Well,' he said. 'Go on.'

"Now that I knew he was willing to listen to me in a serious manner, all my funk of telling him had gone, and I went ahead and told him my ideas about the mist, and the thing it seemed to have ushered, you know. I finished up, by telling him how Tammy had worried me to come and tell what I knew.

" 'He thought then, Sir,' I went on, 'that you might wish to put into the nearest port; but I told him that I didn't think you could, even if you wanted to.'

" 'How's that?' he asked, profoundly interested.

" 'Well, Sir,' I replied. 'If we're unable to see other vessels, we shouldn't be able to see the land. You'd be piling the ship up, without ever seeing where you were putting her.'

"This view of the matter, affected the Old Man in an extraordinary manner; as it did, I believe, the Second Mate. And neither spoke for a moment. Then the Skipper burst out.

" 'By Gad! Jessop,' he said. 'If you're right, the Lord have mercy on us.'

"He thought for a couple of seconds. Then he spoke again, and I could see that he was pretty well twisted up:—

" 'My God ! ...if you're right!'

"The Second Mate spoke.

" 'The men mustn't know, Sir,' he warned him. 'It'd be a mess if they did!'

" 'Yes,' said the Old Man.

"He spoke to me.

" 'Remember that, Jessop,' he said. 'Whatever you do, don't go yarning about this, forrard.'

" 'No, Sir,' I replied.

" 'And you too, boy,' said the Skipper. 'Keep your tongue between your teeth. We're in a bad enough mess, without your making it worse. Do you hear?'

" 'Yes, Sir,' answered Tammy.

"The Old Man turned to me again.

" 'These things, or creatures that you say come out of the sea,' he said. 'You've never seen them, except after nightfall?' he asked.

" 'No, Sir,' I replied. 'Never.'

"He turned to the Second Mate.

" 'So far as I can make out, Mr. Tulipson,' he remarked, 'the danger seems to be only at night.'

" 'It's always been at night, Sir,' the Second answered.

"The Old Man nodded.

" 'Have you anything to propose, Mr. Tulipson?' he asked.

" 'Well, Sir,' replied the Second Mate. 'I think you ought to have her snugged down every night, before dark!'

"He spoke with considerable emphasis. Then he glanced aloft, and jerked his head in the direction of the unfurled t'gallants.

" 'It's a damned good thing, Sir,' he said, 'that it didn't come on to blow any harder.'

"The Old Man nodded again.

" 'Yes,' he remarked. 'We shall have to do it; but God knows when we'll get home!'

" 'Better late than not at all,' I heard the Second mutter, under his breath.

"Out loud, he said:—

" 'And the lights, Sir?'

" 'Yes,' said the Old Man. 'I will have lamps in the rigging every night, after dark.'

" 'Very good, Sir,' assented the Second. Then he turned to us.

" 'It's getting daylight, Jessop,' he remarked, with a glance at the sky. 'You'd better take Tammy with you, and shove those lamps back again into the locker.'

" 'i, i, Sir,' I said, and went down off the poop with Tammy.

XIII
The Shadow in the Sea

"WHEN EIGHT BELLS WENT, at four o'clock, and the other watch came on deck to relieve us, it had been broad daylight for some time. Before we went below, the Second Mate had the three t'gallants set; and now that it was light, we were pretty curious to have a look aloft, especially up the fore; and Tom, who had been up to overhaul the gear, was questioned a lot, when he came down, as to whether there were any signs of anything queer up there. But he told us there was nothing unusual to be seen.

"At eight o'clock, when we came on deck for the eight to twelve watch, I saw the Sailmaker coming forrard along the deck, from the Second Mate's old berth. He had his rule in his hand, and I knew he had been measuring the poor beggars in there, for their burial outfit. From breakfast time until near noon, he worked, shaping out three canvas wrappers from some old sailcloth. Then, with the aid of the Second Mate and one of the hands, he brought out the three dead chaps on to the after hatch, and there sewed them up, with a few lumps of holy stone at their feet. He was just finishing, when eight bells went, and I heard the Old Man tell the Second Mate to call all hands aft for the burial. This was done, and one of the gangways unshipped.

"We had no decent grating big enough, so they had to get off one of the hatches, and use it instead. The wind had died away during the morning, and the sea was almost a calm——the ship lifting ever so slightly to an occasional glassy heave. The only sounds that struck on the ear were the soft, slow rustle and occasional shiver of the sails, and the continuous and monotonous creak, creak of the spars and gear at the gentle movements of the vessel. And it was in this solemn half-quietness that the Skipper read the burial service.

"They had put the Dutchman first upon the hatch (I could tell him by his stumpiness), and when at last the Old Man gave the signal, the

103

Second Mate tilted his end, and he slid off, and down into the dark.

" 'Poor old Dutchie,' I heard one of the men say, and I fancy we all felt a bit like that.

"Then they lifted Jacobs onto the hatch, and when he had gone, Jock. When Jock was lifted, a sort of sudden shiver ran through the crowd. He had been a favourite in a quiet way, and I know I felt, all at once, just a bit queer. I was standing by the rail, upon the after bollard, and Tammy was next to me; while Plummer stood a little behind. As the Second Mate tilted the hatch for the last time, a little, hoarse chorus broke from the men:—

" 'S'long, Jock! So long, Jock!'

"And then, at the sudden plunge, they rushed to the side to see the last of him as he went downwards. Even the Second Mate was not able to resist this universal feeling, and he, too, peered over. From where I had been standing, I had been able to see the body take the water, and now, for a brief couple of seconds, I saw the white of the canvas, blurred by the blue of the water, dwindle and dwindle in the extreme depth. Abruptly, as I stared, it disappeared—too abruptly, it seemed to me.

" 'Gone!' I heard several voices say, and then our watch began to go slowly forrard, while one or two of the other, started to replace the hatch.

"Tammy pointed, and nudged me.

" 'See, Jessop,' he said. 'What is it?'

" 'What?' I asked.

" 'That queer shadow,' he replied. 'Look!'

"And then I saw what he meant. It was something big and shadowy, that appeared to be growing clearer. It occupied the exact place—so it seemed to me—in which Jock had disappeared.

" 'Look at it!' said Tammy, again. 'It's getting bigger!'

"He was pretty excited, and so was I.

"I was peering down. The thing seemed to be rising out of the depths. It was taking shape. As I realised what the shape was, a queer, cold funk took me.

" 'See,' said Tammy. 'It's just like the shadow of a ship!'

"And it was. The shadow of a ship rising out of the unexplored immensity beneath our keel. Plummer, who had not yet gone forrard, caught Tammy's last remark, and glanced over.

What's 'e mean?' he asked.

" 'That!' replied Tammy, and pointed.

"I jabbed my elbow into his ribs; but it was too late. Plummer had seen. Curiously enough, though, he seemed to think nothing of it.

" 'That ain't no thin', 'cept ther shadder er ther ship,' he said.

"Tammy, after my hint, let it go at that. But when Plummer had gone forrard with the others, I told him not to go telling everything round the decks, like that.

" 'We've got to be thundering careful!' I remarked. 'You know what the Old Man said, last watch!'

" 'Yes,' said Tammy. 'I wasn't thinking; I'll be careful next time.'

"A little way from me, the Second Mate was still staring down into the water. I turned, and spoke to him.

" 'What do you make it out to be, Sir?' I asked.

" 'God knows!' he said, with a quick glance round to see whether any of the men were about.

"He got down from the rail, and turned to go up onto the poop. At the top of the ladder, he leant over the break.

" 'You may as well ship that gangway, you two,' he told us. 'And mind, Jessop, keep your mouth shut about this.'

" 'i, i, Sir,' I answered.

" 'And you too, youngster!' he added, and went aft along the poop.

"Tammy and I were busy with the gangway, when the Second came back. He had brought the Skipper.

" 'Eight under the gangway, Sir,' I heard the Second say, and he pointed down into the water.

"For a little while, the Old Man stared. Then I heard him speak.

" 'I don't see anything,' he said.

"At that, the Second Mate bent more forward and peered down. So did I; but the thing, whatever it was, had gone completely.

" 'It's gone, Sir,' said the Second. 'It was there right enough when I came for you.'

"About a minute later, having finished shipping the gangway, I was going forrard, when the Second's voice called me back.

" 'Tell the Captain what it was you saw just now,' he said, in a low voice.

" 'I can't say exactly, Sir,' I replied. 'But it seemed to me like the shadow of a ship, rising up through the water.'

" 'There, Sir,' remarked the Second Mate to the Old Man. 'Just what I told you.'

"The Skipper stared at me.

" 'You're quite sure?' he asked.

" 'Yes, Sir,' I answered. 'Tammy saw it, too.'

"I waited a minute. Then they turned to go aft. The Second was saying something.

" 'Can I go, Sir?' I asked.

" 'Yes, that will do, Jessop,' he said, over his shoulder. But the Old Man came back to the break, and spoke to me.

" 'Remember, not a word of this forrard!' he said.

" 'No, Sir,' I replied, and he went back to the Second Mate; while I walked forrard to the fo'cas'le to get something to eat.

" 'Your whack's in the kid, Jessop,' said Tom, as I stepped in over the washboard. 'An' I got your limejuice in my pannakin.'

" 'Thanks,' I said, and sat down.

"As I stowed away my grub, I took no notice of the chatter of the others. I was too stuffed with my own thoughts. That shadow of a vessel rising, you know, out of the profound deeps, had impressed me tremendously. It had not been imagination. Three of us had seen it—really four; for Plummer distinctly saw it; though he failed to recognise it as anything extraordinary.

"As you can understand, I thought a lot about this shadow of a vessel. But, I am sure, for a time, my ideas must just have gone in an everlasting, blind circle. And then I got another thought; for I got thinking of the figures I had seen aloft in the early morning; and I began to imagine fresh things. You see, that first thing that had come up over the side, had come *out of the sea*. And it had gone back. And now there was this shadow vessel-thing—ghost-ship I called it. It was a damned good name, too. And the dark, noiseless men..... I thought a lot on these lines. Unconsciously, I put a question to myself, aloud:—

" 'Were they the crew?'

" 'Eh?' said Jaskett, who was on the next chest.

"I took hold of myself, as it were, and glanced at him, in an apparently careless manner.

" 'Did I speak?' I asked.

" 'Yes, mate,' he replied, eyeing me, curiously. 'Yer said sumthin' about a crew.'

" 'I must have been dreaming,' I said; and rose up to put away my plate.

XIV
The Ghost Ships

"AT FOUR O'CLOCK, WHEN again we went on deck, the Second Mate told me to go on with a paunch mat I was making; while Tammy, he sent to get out his sinnet. I had the mat slung on the fore side of the main-mast, between it and the after end of the house; and, in a few minutes, Tammy brought his sinnet and yarns to the mast, and made fast to one of the pins.

" 'What do you think it was, Jessop?' he asked, abruptly, after a short silence.

"I looked at him.

" 'What do you think?' I replied.

" I don't know what to think,' he said. 'But I've a feeling that it's something to do with all the rest,' and he indicated aloft, with his head.

" 'I've been thinking, too,' I remarked.

" 'That it is?' he inquired.

" 'Yes,' I answered, and told him how the idea had come to me at my dinner, that the strange men-shadows which came aboard, might come from that indistinct vessel we had seen down in the sea.

" 'Good Lord!' he exclaimed, as he got my meaning.

"And then for a little, he stood and thought.

" 'That's where they live, you mean?' he said, at last, and paused again.

" 'Well,' I replied. 'It can't be the sort of existence *we* should call life.'

"He nodded, doubtfully.

" 'No,' he said, and was silent again.

"Presently, he put out an idea that had come to him.

" 'You *think*, then, that that—vessel has been with us for some time, if we'd only known?' he asked.

" 'All along,' I replied. 'I mean ever since these things started.'

" 'Supposing there are others,' he said, suddenly.

"I looked at him.

" 'If there are,' I said. 'You can pray to God that they won't stumble across us. It strikes me that whether they're ghosts, or not ghosts, they're blood-gutted pirates.'

" 'It seems horrible,' he said, solemnly, 'to be talking seriously like this, about—you know, about such things.'

" 'I've tried to stop thinking that way,' I told him. 'I've felt I should go cracked, if I didn't. There's damned queer things happen at sea, I know; but this isn't one of them.'

" 'It seems so strange and unreal, one moment, doesn't it?' he said. 'And the next, you *know* it's really true, and you can't under-stand why you didn't always know. And yet they'd never believe, if you told them ashore about it.'

" 'They'd believe, if they'd been in this packet in the middle watch this morning,' I said.

" 'Besides,' I went on. 'They don't, understand. We didn't.... I shall always feel different now, when I read that some packet hasn't been heard of.'

"Tammy stared at me.

" 'I've heard some of the old shellbacks talking about things,' he said. 'But I never took them really seriously.

" 'Well,' I said. 'I guess we'll have to take this seriously. I wish to God we were home!'

" 'My God! so do I,' he said.

"For a good while after that, we both worked on in silence; but, presently, he went off on another tack.

" 'Do you think we'll really shorten her down every night before it gets dark?' he asked.

" 'Certainly,' I replied. 'They'll never get the men to go aloft at night, after what's happened.'

" 'But, but—supposing they *ordered* us aloft—' he began.

" 'Would you go?' I interrupted.

" 'No!' he said, emphatically. 'I'd jolly well be put in irons first!'

" 'That settles it, then,' I replied. 'You wouldn't go, nor would any one else.'

"At this moment the Second Mate came along.

" 'Shove that mat and that sinnet away, you two,' he said. 'Then get your brooms and clear up.'

" 'i, i, Sir,' we said, and he went on forrard.

" 'Jump on the house, Tammy,' I said. 'And let go the other end of this rope, will you?'

" 'Right,' he said, and did as I had asked him. When he came back, I got him to give me a hand to roll up the mat, which was a very large one.

" 'I'll finish stopping it,' I said. 'You go and put your sinnet away.'

" 'Wait a minute,' he replied, and gathered up a double handful of shakins from the deck, under where I had been working. Then he ran to the side.

" 'Here!' I said. 'Don't go dumping those. They'll only float, and the Second Mate or the Skipper will be sure to spot them.'

" 'Come here, Jessop!' he interrupted, in a low voice, and taking no notice of what I had been saying.

"I got up off the hatch, where I was kneeling. He was staring over the side.

" 'What's up?' I asked.

" 'For God's sake, hurry!' he said, and I ran, and jumped onto the spar, alongside of him.

" 'Look!' he said, and pointed with a handful of shakins, right down, directly beneath us.

"Some of the shakins dropped from his hand, and blurred the water, momentarily, so that I could not see. Then, as the ripples cleared away, I saw what he meant.

" 'Two of them!' he said, in a voice that was scarcely above a whisper. 'And there's another out there,' and he pointed again with the handful of shakins.

" 'There's another a little further aft,' I muttered.

" 'Where?—where?' he asked.

" 'There,' I said, and pointed.

" 'That's four,' he whispered. 'Four of them!'

"I said nothing; but continued to stare. They appeared to me to be a great way down in the sea, and quite motionless. Yet, though their outlines were somewhat blurred and indistinct, there was no mistaking that they were very like exact, though shadowy, representations of vessels. For some minutes we watched them, without speaking. At last Tammy spoke.

" 'They're real, right enough,' he said, in a low voice.

" 'I don't know,' I answered.

" 'I mean we weren't mistaken this morning,' he said.

" 'No,' I replied. 'I never thought we were.'

"Away forrard, I heard the Second Mate, returning aft. He came nearer, and saw us.

" 'What's up now, you two?' he called, sharply. 'This isn't clearing up!'

"I put out my hand to warn him not to shout, and draw the attention of the rest of the men.

"He took several steps towards me.

" 'What is it? what is it?' he said, with a certain irritability; but in a lower voice.

" 'You'd better take a look over the side, Sir,' I replied.

"My tone must have given him an inkling that we had discovered something fresh; for, at my words, he made one spring, and stood on the spar, alongside of me.

" 'Look, Sir,' said Tammy. 'There's four of them.'

" The Second Mate glanced down, saw something, and bent sharply forward.

" 'My God!' I heard him mutter, under his breath.

"After that, for some half-minute, he stared, without a word.

" 'There are two more out there, Sir,' I told him, and indicated the place with my finger.

"It was a little time before he managed to locate these, and when he did, he gave them only a short glance. Then he got down off the spar, and spoke to us.

" 'Come down off there,' he said, quickly. 'Get your brooms and clear up. Don't say a word!— It may be nothing.'

"He appeared to add that last bit, as an afterthought, and we both knew it meant nothing. Then he turned and went swiftly aft.

" 'I expect he's gone to tell the Old Man,' Tammy remarked, as we went forrard, carrying the mat and his sinnet.

" 'H'm,' I said, scarcely noticing what he was saying; for I was full of the thought of those four shadowy craft, waiting quietly down there.

"We got our brooms, and went aft. On the way, the Second Mate and the Skipper passed us. They went forrard to by the fore brace, and got upon the spar. I saw the Second point up at the brace, and he appeared to be saying something about the gear. I guessed that this was done purposely, to act as a blind, should any of the other men be looking. Then the Old Man glanced down over the side, in a casual sort of manner; so did the Second Mate. A minute or two later, they came aft, and went back, up on to the poop. I caught a glimpse of the Skipper's face as he passed me, on his return. He struck me as looking worried—bewildered, perhaps, would be a better word.

"Both Tammy and I were tremendously keen to have another look; but when at last we got a chance, the sky reflected so much on the water, we could see nothing below.

"We had just finished sweeping up when four bells went, and we cleared below for tea. Some of the men got chatting while they were grubbing.

" 'I 'ave 'eard,' remarked Quoin, 'as we're goin' ter shorten 'er down afore dark.'

" 'Eh?' said old Jaskett, over his pannakin of tea.

"Quoin repeated his remark.

" ' 'oo says so?' inquired Plummer.

" 'I 'eard it from ther Doc,' answered Quoin. ' 'e got it from ther Stooard.

" ' 'ow would 'ee know?' asked Plummet.

" 'I dunno,' said Quoin. 'I 'spect 'e's 'eard 'em talkin' 'bout it arft.'

"Plummer turned to me.

" ' 'ave you 'eard anythin', Jessop?' he inquired.

" 'What, about shortening down?' I replied.

" 'Yes,' he said. 'Weren't ther Old Man talkin' ter yer, up on ther poop this mornin'?'

" 'Yes,' I answered. 'He said something to the Second Mate about shortening down; but it wasn't to me.'

" 'Ther y'are!' said Quoin. ' 'aven't I just said so?'

"At that instant, one of the chaps in the other watch, poked his head in through the starboard doorway.

" 'All hands shorten sail!' he sung out; at the same moment the Mate's whistle came sharp along the decks.

"Plummer stood up, and reached for his cap. 'Well,' he said. 'It's evydent they ain't goin' ter lose no more of us!'

"Then we went out on deck.

"It was a dead calm; but all the same, we furled the three royals, and then the three t'gallants. After that, we hauled up the main and foresail, and stowed them. The crossjack, of course, had been furled some time, with the wind being plumb aft.

"It was while we were up at the foresail, that the sun went over the edge of the horizon. We had finished stowing the sail, out upon the yard, and I was waiting for the others to clear in, and let me get off the foot-rope. Thus it happened that having nothing to do for nearly a minute, I stood watching the sun set, and so saw something that otherwise I should, most probably, have missed. The sun had dipped nearly halfway below the horizon, and was showing like a great, red dome of dull fire. Abruptly, far away on the starboard bow, a faint mist drove up out of the sea. It spread across the face of the sun, so that its light shone now as though it came through a dim haze of smoke. Quickly, this mist or haze grew thicker; but, at the same time, separating and taking strange shapes, so that the red of the sun struck through ruddily between them. Then, as I watched, the weird mistiness collected and shaped and rose into three towers. These became more definite, and there was something elongated beneath them. The shaping and forming continued, and almost suddenly I saw that the thing had taken on the shape of a great ship. Directly afterwards, I saw that it was moving. It had been broadside on to the sun. Now it was swinging. The bows came round with a stately movement, until the three masts bore in a line. It was heading directly towards us. It grew larger; but yet less distinct. Astern of it, I saw now that the sun had sunk to a mere line of light. Then, in the gathering dusk it seemed to me that the ship was sinking back into the ocean. The sun went beneath the sea, and the thing I had seen, became merged, as it were, into the monotonous greyness of the coming night.

"A voice came to me from the rigging. It was the Second Mate's. He had been up to give us a hand.

" 'Now then, Jessop,' he was saying. 'Come along! come along!'

"I turned quickly, and realised that the fellows were nearly all off the yard.

" 'i, i, Sir,' I muttered, and slid in along the foot-rope, and went down on deck. I felt fresh dazed and frightened.

"A little later, eight bells went, and, after roll-call, I cleared up, on to the poop, to relieve the wheel. For a while as I stood at the wheel, my mind seemed blank, and incapable of receiving impressions. This sensation went, after a time, and I realised that there was a great stillness over the sea. There was absolutely no wind, and even the everlasting creak, creak of the gear seemed to ease off at times.

"At the wheel there was nothing whatever to do. I might just as well have been forrard, smoking in the fo'cas'le. Down on the main-deck, I could see the loom of the lanterns that had been lashed up to the sherpoles in the fore and main rigging. Yet they showed less than they might, owing to the fact that they had been shaded on their after sides, so as not to blind the officer of the watch more than need be.

"The night had come down strangely dark, and yet of the dark and the stillness and the lanterns, I was only conscious in occasional flashes of comprehension. For, now that my mind was working, I was thinking chiefly of that queer, vast phantom of mist, I had seen rise from the sea, and take shape.

"I kept staring into the night, towards the West, and then all round me; for, naturally, the memory predominated that she had been coming towards us, when the darkness came, and it was a pretty disquieting sort of thing to think about. I had such a horrible feeling that something beastly was going to happen any minute.

"Yet, two bells came and went, and still all was quiet—strangely quiet, it seemed to me. And, of course, besides the queer, misty vessel I had seen in the West, I was all the time remembering the four shadowy craft lying down in the sea, under our port side. Every time I remembered them, I felt thankful for the lanterns round the main-deck, and I wondered why none had been put in the mizzen rigging. I wished to goodness that they had, and made up my mind I would speak to the Second Mate about it, next time he came aft. At the time, he was leaning over the rail across the break of the poop. He was not smoking, as I could tell; for had he been, I should have seen the glow of his pipe, now and then. It was plain to me that he was uneasy. Three times already he had been down on to the main-deck, prowling about. I guessed that he had been to look down into the sea, for any signs of those four grim craft. I wondered whether they would be visible at night.

"Suddenly, the Timekeeper struck three bells, and the deeper notes of the bell forrard, answered them. I gave a start. It seemed to me that they had been struck close to my elbow. There was something unaccountably strange in the air that night. Then, even as the Second Mate answered the lookout's 'All's well,' there came the sharp whir and rattle of running gear, on the port side of the main-mast. Simultaneously, there was the shrieking of a parrel, up the main; and I knew that some one, or something, had let go the main-top-sail haulyards. From aloft there came the sound of something parting; then the crash of the yard as it ceased falling.

"The Second Mate shouted out something unintelligible, and jumped for the ladder. From the main-deck there came the sound of running feet, and the voices of the watch, shouting. Then I caught the Skipper's voice; he must have run out on deck, through the Saloon doorway.

" 'Get some more lamps! Get some more lamps!' he was singing out. Then he swore.

"He sung out something further. I caught the last two words.

" '...carried away,' they sounded like.

" 'No, Sir,' shouted the Second Mate. 'I don't think so.'

"A minute of some confusion followed; and then came the click of pawls. I could tell that they had taken the haulyards to the after capstan. Odd words floated up to me.

" '...all this water?' I heard in the Old Man's voice. He appeared to be asking a question.

" 'Can't say, Sir,' came the Second Mate's.

"There was a period of time, filled only by the clicking of the pawls and the sounds of the creaking parrel and the running gear. Then the Second Mate's voice came again.

" 'Seems all right, Sir,' I heard him say.

"I never heard the Old Man's reply; for in the same moment, there came to me a chill of cold breath at my back. I turned sharply, and saw something peering over the taffrail. It had eyes that reflected the binnacle light, weirdly, with a frightful, tigerish gleam; but beyond that, I could see nothing with any distinctness. For the moment, I just stared. I seemed frozen. It was so close. Then movement came to me, and I jumped to the binnacle and snatched out the lamp. I twitched round, and shone the light towards it. The thing, whatever it was, had come more forward over the rail; but now, before the light, it recoiled with a queer, horrible litheness. It slid back, and down, and so out of sight. I have only a confused notion of a wet, glistening something, and two vile eyes. Then I was running, crazy, towards the break of the poop. I sprang down the ladder, and missed my footing, and landed on my stern, at the bottom. In my left hand I held the still burning binnacle lamp. The men were putting away the capstan-bars; but at my abrupt appearance, and the yell I gave out at falling, one or two of them fairly ran backwards a short distance, in sheer funk, before they realised what it was.

"From somewhere further forrard, the Old Man and the Second Mate came running aft.

" 'What the devil's up now?' sung out the Second, stopping and bending to stare at me. 'What's to do, that you're away from the wheel?'

"I stood up and tried to answer him; but I was so shaken that I could only stammer.

" 'I—I—there—there—' I stuttered.

" 'Damnation!' shouted the Second Mate, angrily. 'Get back to the wheel!'

"I hesitated, and tried to explain.

" 'Do you damned well hear me?' he sung out.

" 'Yes, Sir; but—' I began.

" 'Get up on to the poop, Jessop!' he said.

"I went. I meant to explain, when he came up. At the top of the ladder, I stopped. I was not going back alone to that wheel. Down below, I heard the Old Man speaking.

" 'What on earth is it now, Mr. Tulipson?' he was saying.

"The Second Mate made no immediate reply; but turned to the men, who were evidently crowding near.

" 'That will do, men!' he said, somewhat sharply.

"I heard the watch start to go forrard. There came a mutter of talk from them. Then the Second Mate answered the Old Man. He could not have known that I was near enough to overhear him.

" 'It's Jessop, Sir. He must have seen something; but we mustn't frighten the crowd more than need be.'

" 'No,' said the Skipper's voice.

"They turned and came up the ladder, and I ran back a few steps, as far as the skylight. I heard the Old Man speak as they came up.

" 'How is it there are no lamps, Mr. Tulipson?' he said, in a surprised tone.

" 'I thought there would be no need up here, Sir,' the Second Mate replied. Then he added something about saving oil.

" 'Better have them, I think,' I heard the Skipper say.

" 'Very good, Sir,' answered the Second, and sung out to the Timekeeper to bring up a couple of lamps.

"Then the two of them walked aft, to where I stood by the skylight.

" 'What are you doing, away from the wheel?' asked the Old Man, in a stern voice.

"I had collected my wits somewhat by now.

" 'I won't go, Sir, till there's a light,' I said.

"The Skipper stamped his foot, angrily; but the Second Mate stepped forward.

" 'Come! Come, Jessop!' he exclaimed. 'This won't do, you know! You'd better get back to the wheel without further bother.'

" 'Wait a minute,' said the Skipper, at this juncture. 'What objection have you to going back to the wheel?' he asked.

" 'I saw something,' I said. 'It was climbing over the taffrail, Sir—'

" 'Ah!' he said, interrupting me with a quick gesture. Then, abruptly: 'Sit down! sit down; you're all in a shake, man.'

"I flopped down on to the skylight seat. I was, as he had said, all in a shake, and the binnacle lamp was wobbling in my hand, so that the light from it went dancing here and there across the deck.

" 'Now,' he went on. 'Just tell us what you saw.'

"I told them, at length, and while I was doing so, the Timekeeper brought up the lights and lashed one up on the sheerpole in each rigging.

" 'Shove one under the spanker boom,' the Old Man sung out, as the boy finished lashing up the other two. 'Be smart now.'

" 'i, i, Sir,' said the 'prentice, and hurried off. Now then,' remarked the Skipper, when this had been done. 'You needn't be afraid to go back to the wheel. There's a light over the stern, and the Second Mate or myself will be up here all the time.'

"I stood up.

" 'Thank you, Sir,' I said, and went aft. I replaced my lamp in the binnacle, and took hold of the wheel; yet, time and again, I glanced behind, and I was very thankful when, a few minutes later, four bells went, and I was relieved.

"Though the rest of the chaps were forrard in the fo'cas'le, I did not go there. I shirked being questioned about my sudden appearance at the foot of the poop ladder; and so I lit my pipe and wandered about the main-deck. I did not feel particularly nervous, as there were now two lanterns in each rigging, and a couple standing upon each of the spare top-masts under the bulwarks.

"Yet, a little after five bells, it seemed to me that I saw a shadowy face peer over the rail, a little abaft the fore lanyards. I snatched up one of the lanterns from off the spar, and flashed the light towards it, whereupon there was nothing. Only, on my mind, more than my sight, I fancy, a queer knowledge remained of wet, peery eyes. Afterwards, when I thought about them, I felt extra beastly. I knew then how brutal they had been.... Inscrutable, you know. Once more in that same watch I had a somewhat similar experience, only in this instance it had vanished even before I had time to reach a light. And then came eight bells, and our watch below.

XV
The Great Ghost Ship

"WHEN WE WERE CALLED again, at a quarter to four, the man who roused us out, had some queer information.

" 'Toppin's gone—clean vanished!' he told us, as we began to turn out. 'I never was in such a damned, hair-raisin' hooker as this here. It ain't safe to go about the bloomin' decks,'

" ' 'oo's gone?' asked Plummer, sitting up suddenly and throwing his legs over his bunk-board.

" 'Toppin, one of the 'prentices,' replied the man. 'We've been huntin' all over the bloomin' show. We're still at it— But they'll never find him,' he ended, with a sort of gloomy assurance.

" 'Oh, I dunno,' said Quoin. 'P'raps 'e's snoozin' somewheres 'bout.'

" 'Not him,' replied the man. 'I tell you we've turned everythin' upside down. He's not aboard the bloomin' ship.'

" 'Where was he when they last saw him?' I asked. 'Someone must know something, you know!'

" 'Keepin' time up on the poop,' he replied. 'The Old Man's nearly shook the life out of the Mate and the chap at the wheel. And they say they don't know nothin'.'

" 'How do you mean?' I inquired. 'How do you mean, nothing?'

" 'Well,' he answered. 'The youngster was there one minute, and then the next thing they knew, he'd gone. They've both sworn black an' blue that there wasn't a whisper. He's just disappeared off of the face of the bloomin' earth.'

"I got down onto my chest, and reached for my boots.

"Before I could speak again, the man was saying something fresh.

" 'See here, mates,' he went on. 'If things is goin' on like this, I'd like to know where you an' me'll be befor' long!'

" 'We'll be in 'ell,' said Plummer.

" 'I dunno as I like to think 'bout it,' said Quoin.

117

" 'We'll have to think about it!' replied the man. 'We've got to think a bloomin' lot about it. I've talked to our side, an' they're game.'

" 'Game for what?' I asked.

" 'To go an' talk straight to the bloomin' Capting,' he said, wagging his finger at me. 'It's make tracks for the nearest bloomin' port, an' don't you make no bloomin' mistake.'

"I opened my mouth to tell him that the probability was we should not be able to make it, even if he could get the Old Man to see the matter from his point of view. Then I remembered that the chap had no idea of the things I had seen, and *thought out*; so, instead, I said:—

" 'Supposing he won't?'

" 'Then we'll have to bloomin' well make him,' he replied.

" 'And when you got there,' I said. 'What then? You'd be jolly well locked up for mutiny.'

" 'I'd sooner be locked up,' he said. 'It don't kill you!'

"There was a murmur of agreement from the others, and then a moment of silence, in which, I know, the men were thinking.

"Jaskett's voice broke into it.

" 'I never thought at first as she was 'aunted—' he commenced; but Plummer cut in across his speech.

" 'We mustn't 'urt any one, yer know,' he said. 'That'd mean 'angin', an' they ain't been er bad crowd.'

" 'No,' assented every one, including the chap who had come to call us.

" 'All the same,' he added. 'It's got to be up helium, an' shove her into the nearest bloomin' port.'

" 'Yes,' said every one, and then eight bells went, and we cleared out on deck.

"Presently, after roll-call—in which there had come a queer, awkward little pause at Toppin's name—Tammy came over to me. The rest of the men had gone forrard, and I guessed they were talking over mad plans for forcing the Skipper's hand, and making him put into port—poor beggars!

"I was leaning over the port rail, by the fore brace-block, staring down into the sea, when Tammy came to me. For perhaps a minute he said nothing. When at last he spoke, it was to say that the shadow vessels had not been there since daylight.

" 'What?' I said, in some surprise. 'How do you know?'

" 'I woke up when they were searching for Toppin,' he replied. 'I've not been asleep since. I came here, right away.' He began to say something further; but stopped short.

" 'Yes,' I said encouragingly.

" 'I didn't know—' he began, and broke off. He caught my arm. 'Oh, Jessop!' he exclaimed. 'What's going to be the end of it all? Surely something can be done?'

"I said nothing. I had a desperate feeling that there was very little we could do to help ourselves.

" 'Can't we do something?' he asked, and shook my arm. 'Anything's better than *this*! We're being *murdered*!'

"Still, I said nothing; but stared moodily down into the water. I could plan nothing; though I would get mad, feverish fits of thinking.

"He was almost crying.

" 'Do you hear?' he said.

" 'Yes, Tammy,' I replied. 'But I don't know! I *don't* know!'

" 'You don't know!' he exclaimed. 'You don't know! Do you mean we're just to give in, and be murdered, one after another?'

" 'We've done all we can,' I replied. 'I don't know what else we can do, unless we go below and lock ourselves in, every night.'

" 'That would be better than this,' he said. 'There'll be no one to go below, or anything else, soon!'

" 'But what if it came on to blow?' I asked. 'We'd be having the sticks blown out of her.'

" 'What if it came on to blow *now*?' he returned. 'No one would go aloft, if it were dark, you said, yourself! Besides, we could shorten her *right* down, first. I tell you, in a few days there won't be a chap alive aboard this packet, unless they jolly well do something!'

" 'Don't shout,' I warned him, 'You'll have the Old Man hearing you.' But the young beggar was wound up, and would take no notice.

" 'I will shout,' he replied. 'I want the Old Man to hear. I've a good mind to go up and tell him.'

"He started on a fresh tack.

" 'Why don't the men do something?' he began. 'They ought to damn well make the Old Man put us into port! They ought—'

" 'For goodness' sake, shut up, you little fool!' I said. 'What's the good of talking a lot of damned rot like that? You'll be getting yourself into trouble.'

" 'I don't care,' he replied. 'I'm not going to be murdered!'

" 'Look here,' I said. 'I told you before, that we shouldn't be able to see the land, even if we made it.'

" 'You've no proof,' he answered. 'It's only your idea.'

" 'Well,' I replied. 'Proof, or no proof, the Skipper would only pile her up, if he tried to make the land, with things as they are now.'

" 'Let him pile her up,' he answered. 'Let him jolly well pile her up! That would be better than staying out here to be pulled over-board, or chucked down from aloft!'

" 'Look here, Tammy—' I began; but just then the Second Mate sung out for him, and he had to go. When he came back, I had started to walk to and from, across the fore side of the main-mast. He joined me, and after a minute, he started his wild talk again.

" 'Look here, Tammy,' I said, once more.

'It's no use your talking like you've been doing. Things are as they are, and it's no one's fault, and nobody can help it. If you want to talk sensibly, I'll listen; if not, then go and gas to some one else.'

"With that, I returned to the port side, and got upon the spar, again, intending to sit on the pin-rail, and have a bit of a talk with him. Before sitting down, I glanced over, into the sea. The action had been almost mechanical; yet, after a few instants, I was in a state of the most intense excitement, and without withdrawing my gaze, I reached out and caught Tammy's arm, to attract his attention.

" 'My God!' I muttered. 'Look!'

" 'What is it?' he asked, and bent over the rail, beside me. And this is what we saw:— A little distance below the surface there lay a pale-coloured, slightly domed disk. It seemed only a few feet down. Below it, we saw quite clearly, after a few moments' staring, the shadow of a royal-yard, and, deeper, the gear and standing-rigging of a great mast. Far down among the shadows, I thought, presently, that I could make out the immense, indefinite stretch of vast decks.

" 'My God!' whispered Tammy, and shut up. But presently, he gave out a short exclamation, as though an idea had come to him; and got down off the spar, and ran forrard on to the fo'cas'le head. He came running back, after a short look into the sea, to tell me that there was the truck of another great mast coming up there, a bit off the bow, to within a few feet of the surface of the sea.

"In the meantime, you know, I had been staring like mad down through the water at the huge, shadowy mast just below me. I had traced out bit by bit, until now, I could clearly see the jackstay, running along the top of the royal mast; and, you know, the royal itself was *set*.

"But, you know, what was getting at me more than anything, was a feeling that there was movement down in the water there, among the rigging. I *thought* I could actually see, at times, things moving and glinting faintly and rapidly to and fro in the gear. And once, I was practically certain that something was on the royal-yard, moving in to the mast; as though, you know, it might have come up the leech of the sail. And this way, I got a beastly feeling that there were things swarming down there.

"Unconsciously, I must have leant further and further out over the side, staring; and suddenly—good Lord! how I yelled—I over-balanced. I made a sweeping grab, and caught the fore brace, and with that, I was back in a moment upon the spar. In the same second, almost, it seemed to me that the surface of the water above the submerged truck was broken, and I am sure *now*, I saw something a moment in the air against the ship's side—a sort of shadow in the air; though I did not realise it at the time. Anyway, the next instant, Tammy gave out an awful scream, and was head downwards over the rail, in a second. I had an idea *then* that he was jumping overboard. I collared him by the waist of his britchers, and one knee, and then I had him down on the deck, and sat plump on him; for he was struggling and shouting all the time, and I was so breath-less and shaken and gone to mush, I could not have trusted my hands to hold him. You see, I never thought *then* it was anything but some influence at work on him; and that he was trying to get loose to go over the side. But I know *now* that I saw the shadow-man that had him. Only, at the time, I was so mixed up, and with the one idea in my head, I was not really able to notice anything, properly. But, afterwards, I comprehended a bit (you can understand, can't you?) what I had seen at the time without taking in.

"And even now looking back, I know that the shadow was only like a faint-seen greyness in the daylight, against the whiteness of the decks, clinging against Tammy.

"And there was I, all breathless and sweating, and quivery with my own tumble, sitting on the little screeching beggar, and he fighting like a mad thing; so that I thought I should never hold him.

"And then I heard the Second Mate shouting, and there came running feet along the deck. Then many hands were pulling and hauling, to get me off him.

" 'Bl—dy cowyard!' sung out some one.

" 'Hold him! Hold him!' I shouted. 'He'll be overboard!'

"At that, they seemed to understand that I was not ill-treating the youngster; for they stopped manhandling me, and allowed me to rise; while two of them took hold of Tammy, and kept him safe.

" 'What's the matter with him?' the Second Mate was singing out. 'What's happened?'

" 'He's gone off his head, I think,' I said.

" 'What?' asked the Second Mate. But before I could answer him, Tammy ceased suddenly to struggle, and flopped down upon the deck.

" ' 'e's fainted,' said Plummer, with some sympathy. He looked at me, with a puzzled, suspicious air. 'What's 'appened? What's 'e been doin'?'

" 'Take him aft into the berth!' ordered the Second Mate, a bit abruptly. It struck me that he wished to prevent questions. He must have tumbled to the fact that we had seen something, about which it would be better not to tell the crowd.

"Plummer stooped to lift the boy.

" 'No,' said the Second Mate. 'Not you, Plummer. Jessop, you take him.' He turned to the rest of the men. 'That will do,' he told them, and they went forrard, muttering a little.

"I lifted the boy, and carried him aft.

" 'No need to take him into the berth,' said the Second Mate. 'Put him down on the after hatch. I've sent the other lad for some brandy.'

"When the brandy came, we dosed Tammy and soon brought him round. He sat up, with a somewhat dazed air. Otherwise, he seemed quiet and sane enough.

" 'What's up?' he asked. He caught sight of the Second Mate. 'Have I been ill, Sir?' he exclaimed.

" 'You're right enough now, youngster,' said the Second Mate. 'You've been a bit off. You'd better go and lie down for a bit.'

" 'I'm all right now, Sir,' replied Tammy. 'I don't think—'

" 'You do as you're told!' interrupted the Second. 'Don't always have to be told twice! If I want you, I'll send for you.'

"Tammy stood up, and made his way, in rather an unsteady fashion, into the berth. I fancy he was glad enough to lie down.

" 'Now then, Jessop,' exclaimed the Second Mate, turning to me. 'What's been the cause of all this? Out with it now, smart!'

"I commenced to tell him; but, almost directly, he put up his hand.

" 'Hold on a minute,' he said. 'There's the breeze!'

"He jumped up the port ladder, and sung out to the chap at the wheel. Then down again.

" 'Starboard fore brace,' he sung out. He turned to me. 'You'll have to finish telling me afterwards,' he said.

" 'i, i, Sir,' I replied, and went to join the other chaps at the braces.

"As soon as we were braced sharp up on the port tack, he sent some of the watch up to loose the sails. Then he sung out for me.

" 'Go on with your yarn now, Jessop,' he said.

"I told him about the great shadow vessel, and I said something about Tammy—I mean about my not being sure *now* whether he *had* tried to jump overboard. Because, you see, I began to realise that I had

seen the shadow; and I remembered the stirring of the water above
the submerged truck. But the Second did not wait, of course, for any
theories; but was away, like a shot, to see for himself. He ran to the side,
and looked down. I followed, and stood beside him; yet, now that the
surface of the water was blurred by the wind, we could see nothing.

" 'It's no good,' he remarked, after a minute. 'You'd better get away
from the rail before any of the others see you. Just be taking those
halyards aft to the capstan.'

"From then, until eight bells, we were hard at work getting the sail
upon her, and when at last eight bells went, I made haste to swallow
my breakfast, and get a sleep.

"At midday, when we went on deck for the afternoon watch, I
ran to the side; but there was no sign of the great shadow ship. All
that watch, the Second Mate kept me working at my paunch mat,
and Tammy he put on to his sinnet, telling me to keep an eye on the
young-ster. But the boy was right enough; as I scarcely doubted now,
you know; though a—most unusual thing—he hardly opened his lips
the whole afternoon. Then at four o'clock, we went below for tea.

"At four bells, when we came on deck again, I found that the light
breeze, which had kept us going during the day, had dropped, and we
were only just moving. The sun was low down, and the sky clear. Once
or twice, as I glanced across to the horizon, it seemed to me that I
caught again that odd quiver in the air that had preceded the coming
of the mist; and, indeed, on two separate occasions, I saw a thin wisp
of haze drive up, apparently out of the sea. This was at some little
distance on our port beam; otherwise, all was quiet and peaceful; and
though I stared into the water, I could make out no vestige of that
great shadow ship, down in the sea.

"It was some little time after six bells, that the order came for all
hands to shorten sail for the night. We took in the royals and t'gallants,
and then the three courses. It was shortly after this, that a rumour
went round the ship that there was to be no lookout that night after
eight o'clock. This naturally created a good deal of talk among the
men; especially as the yarn went, that the fo'cas'le doors were to be
shut and fastened as soon as it was dark, and that no one was to be
allowed on deck.

" ' 'oo's goin' ter take ther wheels?' I heard Plummer ask.

" 'I s'pose they'll 'ave us take 'em as usual,' replied one of the
men. 'One of ther officers is bound ter be on ther poop; so we'll 'ave
company.'

"Apart from these remarks, there was a general opinion that—if

it were true—it was a sensible act on the part of the Skipper. As one
of the men said:—

" 'It ain't likely as there'll be any of us missin' in ther mornin', if
we stays in our bunks all ther blessed night.'

"And soon after this, eight bells went.

XVI
The Ghost Pirates

"AT THE MOMENT WHEN eight bells actually went, I was in the fo'cas'le, talking to four of the other watch. Suddenly, away aft, I heard shouting, and then on the deck overhead, came the loud thudding of some one pomping with a capstan-bar. Straightway, I turned and made a run for the port doorway, along with the four other men. We rushed out through the doorway on to the deck. It was getting dusk; but that did not hide from me a terrible and extraordinary sight. All along the port rail there was a queer, undulating greyness, that moved downwards inboard, and spread over the decks. As I looked, I found that I saw more clearly, in a most extraordinary way. And, suddenly, all the moving greyness resolved into hundreds of strange men. In the half-light, they looked unreal and impossible, as though there had come upon us the inhabitants of some fantastic dream-world. My God! I thought I was mad. They swarmed in upon us in a great wave of murderous, living shadows. From some of the men who must have been going aft for roll-call, there rose into the evening air a loud, awful shouting.

" 'Aloft!' yelled someone; but, as I looked aloft, I saw that the horrible things were swarm-ing there in scores and scores.

" 'Jesus Christ——!' shrieked a man's voice, cut short, and my glance dropped from aloft, to find two of the men who had come out from the fo'cas'le with me, rolling upon the deck. They were two indistinguishable masses that writhed here and there across the planks. The brutes fairly covered them. From them, came muffled little shrieks and gasps; and there I stood, and with me were the other two men. A man darted past us into the fo'cas'le, with two grey men on his back, and I heard them kill him. The two men by me, ran suddenly across the fore hatch, and up the starboard ladder on to the fo'cas'le head. Yet, almost in the same instant, I saw several of the grey men disappear up the other ladder. From the fo'cas'le head above, I heard the two men commence to shout, and this died away into a loud scuffling. At that, I turned to see whether I could get away. I stared round, hopelessly; and then with two jumps, I was on the pigsty, and from there upon the top of the deckhouse. I threw myself flat, and waited, breathlessly.

"All at once, it seemed to me that it was darker than it had been the previous moment, and I raised my head, very cautiously. I saw that the ship was enveloped in great billows of mist, and then, not six feet from me, I made out some one lying, face downwards. It was Tammy. I felt safer now that we were hidden by the mist, and I crawled to him. He gave a quick gasp of terror when I touched him; but when he saw who it was, he started to sob like a little kid.

" 'Hush!' I said. 'For God's sake be quiet!' But I need not have troubled; for the shrieks of the men being killed, down on the decks all around us, drowned every other sound.

"I knelt up, and glanced round and then aloft. Overhead, I could make out dimly the spars and sails, and now as I looked, I saw that the t'gallants and royals had been unloosed and were hanging in the buntlines. Almost in the same moment, the terrible crying of the poor beggars about the decks, ceased; and there succeeded an awful silence, in which I could distinctly hear Tammy sobbing. I reached out, and shook him.

" 'Be quiet! Be quiet!' I whispered, intensely. 'THEY'LL hear us!'

"At my touch and whisper, he struggled to become silent; and then, overhead, I saw the six yards being swiftly mastheaded. Scarcely were the sails set, when I heard the swish and flick of gaskets being cast adrift on the lower yards, and realised that ghostly things were at work there.

"For a minute or so there was silence, and I made my way cautiously to the after end of the house, and peered over. Yet, because of the mist, I could see nothing. Then, abruptly, from behind me, came a single wail of sudden pain and terror from Tammy. It ended instantly in a sort of choke. I stood up in the mist and ran back to where I had left the kid; but he had gone. I stood dazed. I felt like shrieking out loud. Above me, I heard the flaps of the courses being tumbled off the yards. Down upon the decks, there were the noises of a multitude working in a weird, inhuman silence. Then came the squeal and rattle of blocks and braces aloft. They were squaring the yards.

"I remained standing. I watched the yards squared, and then I saw the sails fill suddenly. An instant later, the deck of the house upon which I stood, became canted forrard. The slope increased, so that I

could scarcely stand, and I grabbed at one of the wire-winches. I wondered, in a stunned sort of way, what was happening. Almost directly
afterwards, from the deck on the port side of the house, there came
a sudden, loud, human scream; and immediately, from different parts
of the decks there rose, afresh, some most horrible shouts of agony
from odd men. This grew into an intense screaming that shook my
heart up; and there came again a noise of desperate, brief fighting.
Then a breath of cold wind seemed to play in the mist, and I could see
down the slope of the deck. I looked below me, towards the bows. The
jibboom was plunged right into the water, and, as I stared, the bows
disappeared into the sea. The deck of the house became a wall to me,
and I was swinging from the winch, which was now above my head.
I watched the ocean lip over the edge of the fo'cas'le head, and rush
down on to the main-deck, roaring into the empty fo'cas'le. And still
all around me came the crying of the lost sailormen. I heard something
strike the corner of the house above me, with a dull thud, and then
I saw Plummer plunge down into the flood beneath. I remembered
that he had been at the wheel. The next instant, the water had leapt
to my feet; there came a drear chorus of bubbling screams, a roar of
waters, and I was going swiftly down into the darkness. I let go of
the winch, and struck out madly, trying to hold my breath. There was
a loud singing in my ears. It grew louder. I opened my mouth. I felt I
was dying. And then, thank God! I was at the surface, breathing. For
the moment, I was blinded with the water, and my agony of breathlessness. Then, growing easier, I brushed the water from my eyes, and
so, not three hundred yards away, I made out a large ship, floating
almost motionless. At first, I could scarcely believe I saw aright. Then,
as I realised that indeed there was yet a chance of living, I started to
swim towards you.

"You know the rest—"

*   *   *   *

"And you think—?" said the Captain, interrogatively, and stopped
short.

"No," replied Jessop. "I don't think, I *know*. None of us *think*. It's
a gospel fact. People *talk* about queer things happening at sea; but
this isn't one of them. This is one of the *real* things. You've all seen
queer things; perhaps more than I have. It depends. But they don't
go down in the log. These kinds of things never do. This one won't;
at least, not as it's really happened."

He nodded his head, slowly, and went on, addressing the Captain more particularly.

"I'll bet," he said, deliberately, "that you'll enter it in the log-book, something like this:— 'May 18th. Lat.—S. Long.—W. 2 p.m. Light winds from the South and East. Sighted a full-rigged ship on the starboard bow. Overhauled her in the first dog-watch. Signalled her; but received no response. During the second dog-watch she steadily refused to communicate. About eight bells, it was observed that she seemed to be settling by the head, and a minute later she foundered suddenly, bows foremost, with all her crew. Put out a boat and picked up one of the men, an A.B. by the name of Jessop. He was quite unable to give any explanation of the catastrophe.

"And you two," he made a gesture at the First and Second Mates, "will probably sign your names to it, and so will I, and perhaps one of your A.B.'s. Then when we get home they'll print a report of it in the newspapers, and people will talk about unseaworthy ships. Maybe some of the experts will talk rot about rivets and defective plates and so forth."

He laughed, cynically. Then he went on.

"And, you know, when you come to think of it, there's no one except our own selves will ever know how it happened—really. The shellbacks don't count. They're only 'beastly, drunken brutes of *common sailors*'—Poor devils! No one would think of taking anything they said, as anything more than a damned cuffer. Besides, the beggars only tell these things when they're half boozed. They wouldn't then (for fear of being laughed at), only they're not responsible—"

He broke off, and looked round at us. The Skipper and the two Mates nodded their heads, in silent assent.

Appendix
The Silent Ship

I'M THE THIRD MATE of the *Sangier*, the vessel that picked up Jessop, you know; and he's asked us to write a short note of what we saw from our side, and sign it. The Old Man's set me on to the job, as he says I can put it better than he can.

Well, it was in the first dog-watch that we came up with her, the *Mortzestus* I mean; but it was in the second dog-watch that it happened. The Mate and I were on the poop watching her. You see, we'd signalled her, and she'd not taken any notice, and that seemed queer, as we couldn't have been more than three or four hundred yards off her port beam, and it was a fine evening; so that we could almost have had a tea-fight, if they'd seemed a pleasant crowd. As it was, we called them a set of sulky swine, and left it at that, though we still kept our hoist up. All the same, you know, we watched her a lot; and I remember, even then I thought it queer how quiet she was. We couldn't hear even her bell go, and I spoke to the Mate about it, and he said he'd been noticing the same thing.

Then, about six bells, they shortened her right down to top-sails; and I can tell you that made us stare more than ever, as any one can imagine. And I remember we noticed then, especially, that we couldn't hear a single sound from her, even when the haulyards were let go; and, you know, without the glass, I saw their Old Man singing out something; but we didn't get a sound of it, and we *should* have been able to hear every word.

Then, just after eight bells, the thing Jessop's told us about, happened. Both the Mate and the Old Man said they could see men going up her side, a bit indistinct, you know, because it was getting dusk; but the Second Mate and I half thought we did, and half thought we didn't; but there was something queer; we all knew that; and it looked like a sort of movey mist along her side. I know I felt pretty funny;

but it wasn't the sort of thing, of course, to be too sure and serious about until you *were* sure.

After the Mate and the Captain had said they saw the men boarding her, we began to hear sounds from her; very queer at first, and rather like a phonograph makes when it's getting up speed. Then the sounds came properly from her, and we heard them shouting and yelling; and, you know, I don't know even now just what I really thought. I was all so queer and mixed.

The next thing I remember, there was a thick mist round the ship; and then all the noise was shut off, as if it were all the other side of a door. But we could still see her masts and spars and sails above the misty stuff; and both the Captain and the Mate said they could see men aloft; and I thought I could; but the Second Mate wasn't sure. All the same, though, the sails were all loosed in about a minute, it seemed, and the yards mastheaded. We couldn't see the courses above the mist; but Jessop says they were loosed too, and sheeted home, along with the upper sails. Then we saw the yards squared, and I saw the sails fill bang up with; and yet, you know, ours were slatting.

The next thing was the one that hit me more than anything. Her masts took a cant forrard, and then I saw her stern come up out of the mist that was round her. Then all in an instant, we could hear sounds from the vessel again. And I tell you, the men didn't seem to be shouting, but screaming. Her stern went higher. It was most extraordinary to look at; and then she went plunk down, head foremost, right bang into the mist-stuff.

It's all right what Jessop says, and when we saw him swimming (I was the one who spotted him) we got out a boat quicker than a wind-jammer ever got out a boat before, I should think.

The Captain and the Mate and the Second and I are all going to sign this.

(Signed)   WILLIAM NAWSTON, *Master.*
J. E. G. ADAMS, *First Mate.*
ED. BROWN, *Second Mate.*
JACK T. EVAN, *Third Mate.*

The Silent Ship

Alternate Ending to *The Ghost Pirates*— Published in 1973 as "The Phantom Ship"

IT WAS IN THE second dog-watch. We were in the Southern Pacific, just within the tropics. Away on our starboard beam, distant some three or four hundred yards, a large ship was sliding slowly along in the same direction as ourselves. We had come up with her during the previous watch; but, the wind failing, our speed had dropped, and we were doing no more than keeping abreast of her.

The mate and I were watching her curiously; for, to all our signals, she had paid not the slightest heed. Not even a face had peered over her rail in our direction; though (save once or twice, when a curious thin haze had seemed to float up from the sea between the two ships) we were plainly able to see the officer of the watch pacing the poop, and the men lounging about her decks. Stranger than this was our inability to catch any sound from her—not even an occasional order, nor the stroke of the bells.

"Sulky beasts!" said the Mate expressively. "A lot of blasted uncivil Dutchmen!"

He stood for a couple of minutes and eyed them in silence. He was very much annoyed at their persistent disregard of our signals; yet I think that, like myself, he was even more curious to know the reason of it: and his very bafflement on this point only served to increase his irritability.

He turned to me.

"Pass out that trumpet, Mr. Jepworth," he added. "We'll see if they've the manners to notice that."

Going to the companion-way, I unslung the speaking trumpet out of its becketts and brought it to him.

Taking it quickly, he raised it to his lips, and sent a loud "Ship ahoy!" across the water to the stranger. He waited a few moments; but no sign could I see to show that he had been heard.

131

"Blast them!" I heard him mutter. Then he lifted the trumpet again. This time he hailed the other craft by name, it being plainly visible on the bow— "*Mortzestus* ahoy!"

Again he waited. Still there was no sign to show that they had either seen or heard us.

The Mate lifted the trumpet and shook it towards the strange vessel.

"The devil fly away with you!" he shouted. He turned to me.

"Here, take this back again, Mr. Jepworth," he growled. "If ever I came across a lot of petticoated skunks, it's them. Making a fool of a man like that!"

From all of which it will be conceived that we had become vastly interested in the strange ship.

For the space of perhaps another hour, we continued to view her at intervals through our glasses; but failed to discover that they had become even aware of our presence.

Then, as we watched her, there appeared suddenly a great show of activity aboard of her. The three royals were lowered almost simultaneously, and in a minute the t'gallens'ls followed them. Then we saw the men jump into the rigging and aloft to furl.

The Mate spoke.

"I'm damned if they're not going to shorten her down. What the devil's the matter with them—"

He stopped short as though a sudden idea had come to him.

"Run below," he said, without removing his scrutiny from the other packet, "and take a look at the glass."

Without wasting time, I hurried below, returning in a minute to tell him that the glass was perfectly steady.

He made no reply to my information, but continued to stare across the water at the stranger.

Abruptly, he spoke.

"Look here, Mr. Jepworth, I'm just beggared, that's what I am. I can't make head nor tail of it. I've never seen the likes of it all the time I've been fishing."

"Looks to me as though their skipper was a bit of an old woman," I remarked. "Perhaps—"

The Mate interrupted me.

"Lord!" he said impiously. "And now they're taking the courses off her. Their Old Man *must* be a fool."

He had spoken rather loudly, and in the momentary silence that followed his words, I was startled to hear a voice at my elbow say—

"Whose Old Man is a fool?"

It was our Old Man who had come on deck unobserved.

Without waiting for a reply to his query, he inquired if the other packet had deigned to notice our signals yet.

"No, Sir," the Mate made answer. "We might be a lump of dirt floating about, for all the notice they've taken of us."

"They've shortened her down to top-sails, Sir," I said to the Captain, and I proffered him my glasses.

"H'm!" he said with a note of surprise in his voice. He took a long look. Presently he lowered the glasses.

"Can't understand it at all," I heard him mutter. Then he asked me to pass out the telescope.

With this, he studied the stranger awhile. Yet there was nothing to be seen that would explain the mystery.

"Most extraordinary!" he exclaimed. Then he pushed the telescope in among the ropes on the pin-rail, and took a few turns up and down the poop.

The Mate and I continued to scrutinise the stranger; but all to no purpose. Outwardly, at least, she was an ordinary full-rigged ship; and save for her inexplicable silence and the furling of the sails, there was nothing to distinguish her from any chance windjammer one might happen to fall across in the usual course of a long sea trip.

I have said that there was nothing unusual about her appearance; yet I think that, even thus early, we had begun to realize dimly that some intangible mystery hung about her.

The Captain ceased to pace up and down and stood by the Mate, staring curiously across at the silent ship on our starboard beam.

"The glass is as steady as a rock," he remarked presently.

"Yes," the Mate assented. "I sent Mr. Jepworth to give a look as soon as I saw they were going to shorten down."

"I can't understand it!" the Captain remarked again, with a sort of puzzled irritability. "The weather's just grand."

The Mate made no immediate reply; but pulled a plug of ship's tobacco out from his hip pocket, and took a bite. He replaced it, expectorated, and then expressed his opinion that they were all a lot of blasted Dutch swine.

The Captain resumed his walk, while I continued to scan the other vessel.

A little later one of the 'prentices went aft and struck eight bells. A few seconds later the Second Mate came up onto the poop to relieve the Mate.

"Have you got the lady to speak yet?" he inquired, referring to the unsociable craft away on our beam.

The Mate almost snorted. Yet I did not hear his reply; for, at that moment, unbelievable as it seems, I saw Things coming out of the water alongside the silent ship. Things like men, they were, only you could see the ship's side through them, and they had a strange, misty, unreal look. I thought I must be going dotty for the moment, until I glanced round and saw the Mate staring over my shoulder, his face thrust forward and his eyes fixed in their intensity. Then I looked again and they were climbing up the other hooker's side—thousands of them. We were so close, I could see the officer of the watch lighting his pipe. He stood leaning up against the port rail, facing to starboard.

Then I saw the chap at the wheel wave his arms, and the officer moved quickly towards him. The helmsman pointed, and the officer turned about and looked. In the dusk, and at that distance, I could not distinguish his features; but I knew by his attitude that he had seen. For one short instant he stood motionless; then he made a run for the break of the poop, gesticulating. He appeared to be shouting. I saw the lookout seize a capstan-bar and pound on the fo'cas'le head. Several men ran out from the port doorway. And then, all at once, sounds came to us from the hitherto silent ship. At first, muffled, as though from miles away. Quickly they grew plainer. And so, in a minute, as though an invisible barrier had been torn down, we heard a multitudinous shouting of frightened men. It rolled over the sea to us like the voice of Fear clamouring.

Behind me, I heard the Mate mutter huskily; but I took no notice. I had a sense of the unreality of things.

A minute passed—it seemed an age. And then, as I stared, bewildered, a thick haze grew up out of the sea and closed about the hull of the strange ship; yet we could still see her spars. Out from the mist there still drove that Babel of hoarse cries and shouting.

Almost unconsciously, my glance roved among the spars and rigging that rose straight up into the sky out from that weird clot of mist on the sea. Suddenly my wandering gaze was arrested. Through the calm evening air, I saw a movement among the stowed sails-gaskets were being cast adrift, and, against the darkening skies, I seemed to make out dim unreal shapes working fiendishly.

With a low rustle first, and then a sudden flap, the bellies of the three t'gallan's'ls fell out of the bunt gaskets and hung. Almost immediately the three royals followed. All this time the confused noises had continued. Now, however, there was a sudden lull of silence; and then, simultaneously, the six yards began to rise amid a perfect quietness save for the chafing of the ropes in the blocks and the occasional squeal of a parrel against a mast.

On our part, we made no sound, said nothing. There was nothing to be said. I, for one, was temporarily speechless. The sails continued to rise with the steady, rythmic, pull-and-heave movement peculiar to sailormen. A minute went swiftly, and another. Then the leeches of the sails tautened and the hauling ceased. The sails were set.

Still from that uncanny craft there came no sound of human voice. The mist of which I have made mention continued to cling about the hull, a little hill of cloud, hiding it completely and a portion of the lower masts, though the lower yards with the courses made fast upon them were plainly visible.

And now I became aware that there were ghostly forms at work upon the gaskets of the three courses. The sails rustled upon the yards. Scarcely a minute, it seemed, and the mainsail slid off the yard and fell in loose festoons; followed almost immediately by the fore and crossjack. From somewhere out of the mist there came a single strangulated cry. It ceased instantly, yet it seemed to me as though the sea echoed it remotely.

For the first time, I turned and looked at the Old Man who was standing a little to my left. His face wore an almost expressionless look. His eyes were fixed with a queer stony stare upon that mist-enshrouded mystery. It was only a momentary glance I gave, and then I looked back quickly.

From that other ship there had come a sudden squeal and rattle of swinging yards and running gear, and I saw that the yards were being squared in swiftly. Very quickly this was accomplished, though what slight airs there were came from the southwest, and we were braced sharp up on the port tack to make the most of them. By rights this move on the part of the other packet should have placed her all aback and given her sternway. Yet, as I looked with incredulous eyes, the sails filled abruptly—bellying out as though before a strong breeze, and I saw something lift itself up out from the mist at the after end of the ship. It rose higher, and grew plain. I saw it then distinctly; it was the white-painted "half-round" of the stern. In the same moment, the masts inclined forward at a distinct angle, that increased. The top of the chart-house came into view.

Then, deep and horrible, as though lost souls cried out from Hell, there came a hoarse, prolonged cry of human agony. I started, and the Second Mate swore suddenly and stopped halfway. In some curious manner, I was astonished as well as terrified and bewildered. I do not think, somehow, I had expected to hear a human voice come out from that mist again.

The stern rose higher out from the mistiness, and, for a single instant, I saw the rudder move blackly against the evening sky. The wheel spun sharply, and a small black figure plunged away from it helplessly, down into the mist and noise.

The sea gave a sobbing gurgle, and there came a horrible, bubbling note into the human outcry. The foremast disappeared into the sea, and the main sank down into the mist. On the aftermast, the sails slatted a moment, then filled; and so, under all sail, the stranger drove down into the darkness. A gust of crying swept up to us for one dreadful instant, and then only the boil of the sea as it closed in over all.

Like one in a trance, I stared. In an uncomprehending way, I heard voices down on the main-deck, and an echo of mixed prayer and blasphemy filled the air.

Out on the sea, the mistiness still hung about the spot where the strange ship had vanished. Gradually, however, it thinned away and disclosed various articles of ship's furniture circling in the eddy of the dying whirlpool. Even as I watched, odd fragments of wreckage rushed up out from the ocean with a plop, plopping noise.

My mind was in a whirl. Abruptly, the Mate's voice rasped across my bewilderment roughly, and I found myself listening. The noise from the main-deck had dropped to a steady hum of talk and argument—subdued.

He was pointing excitedly somewhat to the southward of the floating wreckage. I only caught the latter part of his sentence.

"—over there!"

Mechanically, almost, my eyes followed the direction indicated by his finger. For a moment they refused to focus anything distinctly. Then suddenly there jumped into the circled blur of my vision a little spot of black that bobbed upon the water and grew plain—it was the head of a man, swimming desperately in our direction.

At the sight, the horror of the last few minutes fell from me, and, thinking only of rescue, I ran towards the starboard lifeboat, whipping out my knife as I ran.

Over my shoulder came the bellow of the Skipper's voice— "Clear away the starboard lifeboat; jump along some of you!"

Even before the running men had reached the boat, I had ripped the cover off, and was busy heaving out the miscellaneous lumber that is so often stowed away into the boats of a windjammer. Feverishly,

I worked, with half a dozen men assisting vigourously, and soon we had the boat clear and the running gear ready for lowering away. Then we swung her out, and I climbed into her without waiting for orders. Four of the men followed me, while a couple of the others stood by to lower away.

A moment later we were pulling away rapidly towards the solitary swimmer. Reaching him, we hauled him into the boat, and only just in time, for he was palpably done up. We sat him on a thwart, and one of the men supported him. He was gasping heavily and gurgling as he breathed. Atfer a minute, he rejected a large quantity of sea water.

He spoke for the first time.

"My God!" he gasped. "Oh, my God!" And that was all that he seemed able to say.

Meanwhile, I had told the others to give way again, and was steering the boat towards the wreckage. As we neared it, the rescued man struggled suddenly to his feet, and stood swaying and clutching at the man who was supporting him; while his eyes swept wildly over the ocean. His gaze rested on the patch of floating hencoops, spars, and other lumber. He bent forward somewhat and peered at it, as though trying in vain to comprehend what it meant. A vacant expression crept over his features, and he slid down onto the thwart limply, muttering to himself.

As soon as I had satisfied myself that there was nothing living among the mass of floating stuff, I put the boat's head round, and made for the ship with all speed. I was anxious to have the poor fellow attended to as soon as possible.

Directly we got him aboard, he was turned over to the Steward, who made him up a bed in one of the bunks in a spare cabin opening off the saloon.

The rest, I give as the Steward gave it me:—

"It was like this, Sir. I stripped him an' got him inter the blankets which the doctor had made warm at the galley fire. The poor beggar was all of a shake at first, an' I tried to get some whisky into him; but he couldn't do it nohow. His teeth seemed locked, and so I just gave up, an' let him bide. In a little, the shakes went off him, an' he was quiet enough. All the same, seein' him that bad, I thought as I'd sit up with him for the night. There was no knowin' but that he'd be wantin' somethin' later on.

"Well, all through the first watch he lay there, not sayin' nothin', nor stirrin'; but just moanin' quiet-like to hisself. An', think I, he'll go off inter a sleep in a bit; so I just sat there without movin'. Then, all

on a sudden, about three bells in the middle watch, he started shiverin'
and shakin' again. So I shoved some more blankets onter im, an' then
I had another try to get some whisky between his teeth; but 'twas no
use; an' then, all at once, he went limp, an' his mouth come open with
a little flop.

"I ran for the Capting then; but the poor devil was dead befor'
we got back."

We buried him in the morning, sewing him up in some old canvas
with a few lumps of coal at his feet.

To this day I ponder over the thing I saw; and wonder, vainly, what
he might have told us to help solve the mystery of that silent ship in
the heart of the vast Pacific.

Stories of the Sea

A Tropical Horror

WE ARE A HUNDRED and thirty days out from Melbourne, and for three weeks we have lain in this sweltering calm.

It is midnight, and our watch on deck until four a.m. I go out and sit on the hatch. A minute later, Joky, our youngest 'prentice, joins me for a chatter. Many are the hours we have sat thus and talked in the night watches; though, to be sure, it is Joky who does the talking. I am content to smoke and listen, giving an occasional grunt at seasons to show that I am attentive.

Joky has been silent for some time, his head bent in meditation. Suddenly he looks up, evidently with the intention of making some remark. As he does so, I see his face stiffen with a nameless horror. He crouches back, his eyes staring past me at some unseen fear. Then his mouth opens. He gives forth a strangulated cry and topples backward off the hatch, striking his head against the deck. Fearing I know not what, I turn to look.

Great Heavens! Rising above the bulwarks, seen plainly in the bright moonlight, is a vast slobbering mouth a fathom across. From the huge dripping lips hang great tentacles. As I look the Thing comes further over the rail. It is rising, rising, higher and higher. There are no eyes visible; only that fearful slobbering mouth set on the tremendous trunk-like neck; which, even as I watch, is curling inboard with the stealthy celerity of an enormous eel. Over it comes in vast heaving folds. Will it never end? The ship gives a slow, sullen roll to starboard as she feels the weight. Then the tail, a broad, flat-shaped mass, slips over the teak rail and falls with a loud slump on to the deck.

For a few seconds the hideous creature lies heaped in writhing, slimy coils. Then, with quick, darting movements, the monstrous head travels along the deck. Close by the main-mast stand the harness casks, and alongside of these a freshly opened cask of salt beef with the top loosely replaced. The smell of the meat seems to attract the monster, and I can hear it sniffing with a vast indrawing breath. Then those lips open, displaying four huge fangs; there is a quick forward motion of the head, a sudden crashing, crunching sound, and beef and barrel have disappeared. The noise brings one of the ordinary seamen out of the fo'cas'le. Coming into the night, he can see nothing for a moment. Then, as he gets further aft, he *sees*, and with horrified cries rushes forward. Too late! From the mouth of the Thing there flashes forth a long, broad blade of glistening white, set with fierce teeth. I avert my eyes, but cannot shut out the sickening "Glut! Glut!" that follows.

The man on the look-out, attracted by the disturbance, has witnessed the tragedy, and flies for refuge into the fo'cas'le, flinging to the heavy iron door after him.

The carpenter and sailmaker come running out from the half-deck in their drawers. Seeing the awful Thing, they rush aft to the cabin with shouts of fear. The Second Mate, after one glance over the break of the poop, runs down the companion-way with the Helmsman after him. I can hear them barring the scuttle, and abruptly I realise that I am on the main-deck alone.

So far I have forgotten my own danger. The past few minutes seem like a portion of an awful dream. Now, however, I comprehend my position and, shaking off the horror that has held me, turn to seek safety. As I do so my eyes fall upon Joky, lying huddled and senseless with fright where he has fallen. I cannot leave him there. Close by stands the empty half-deck—a little steel-built house with iron doors. The lee one is hooked open. Once inside I am safe.

Up to the present the Thing has seemed to be unconscious of my presence. Now, however, the huge barrel-like head sways in my direction; then comes a muffled bellow, and the great tongue flickers in and out as the brute turns and swirls aft to meet me. I know there is not a moment to lose, and, picking up the helpless lad, I make a run for the open door. It is only distant a few yards, but that awful shape is coming down the deck to me in great wreathing coils. I reach the house and tumble in with my burden; then out on deck again to unhook and close the door. Even as I do so something white curls round the end of the house. With a bound I am inside and the door is shut and bolted. Through the thick glass of the ports I see the Thing sweep round the house, in vain search for me.

Joky has not moved yet; so, kneeling down, I loosen his shirt collar and sprinkle some water from the breaker over his face. While I am doing this I hear Morgan shout something; then comes a great shriek of terror, and again that sickening "Glut! Glut!" Joky stirs uneasily, rubs his eyes, and sits up suddenly.

"Was that Morgan shouting—?" He breaks off with a cry. "Where are we? I have had such awful dreams!"

At this instant there is a sound of running footsteps on the deck and I hear Morgan's voice at the door.

"Tom, open—!"

He stops abruptly and gives an awful cry of despair. Then I hear him rush forward. Through the porthole, I see him spring into the fore rigging and scramble madly aloft. Something steals up after him. It shows white in the moonlight. It wraps itself around his right ankle. Morgan stops dead, plucks out his sheath-knife, and hacks fiercely at the fiendish thing. It lets go, and in a second he is over the top and running for dear life up the t'gallant rigging.

A time of quietness follows, and presently I see that the day is breaking. Not a sound can be heard save the heavy gasping breathing of the Thing. As the sun rises higher the creature stretches itself out along the deck and seems to enjoy the warmth. Still no sound, either from the men forward or the officers aft. I can only suppose that they are afraid of attracting its attention. Yet, a little later, I hear the report of a pistol away aft, and looking out I see the serpent raise its huge head as though listening. As it does so I get a good view of the fore part, and in the daylight see what the night has hidden.

There, right about the mouth, is a pair of little pig-eyes, that seem to twinkle with a diabolical intelligence. It is swaying its head slowly from side to side; then, without warning, it turns quickly and looks right in through the port. I dodge out of sight; but not soon enough. It has seen me, and brings its great mouth up against the glass.

I hold my breath. My God! If it breaks the glass! I cower, horrified. From the direction of the port there comes a loud, harsh, scraping sound. I shiver. Then I remember that there are little iron doors to shut over the ports in bad weather. Without a moment's waste of time I rise to my feet and slam to the door over the port. Then I go round to the others and do the same. We are now in darkness, and I tell Joky in a whisper to light the lamp, which, after some fumbling, he does.

About an hour before midnight I fall asleep. I am awakened suddenly some hours later by a scream of agony and the rattle of a water-dipper. There is a slight scuffling sound; then that soul-revolting "Glut! Glut!"

I guess what has happened. One of the men forrad has slipped out of the fo'cas'le to try and get a little water. Evidently he has trusted to the darkness to hide his movements. Poor beggar! He has paid for his attempt with his life!

After this I cannot sleep, though the rest of the night passes quietly enough. Towards morning I doze a bit, but wake every few minutes with a start. Joky is sleeping peacefully; indeed, he seems worn out with the terrible strain of the past twenty-four hours. About eight a.m. I call him, and we make a light breakfast off the dry ship's biscuit and water. Of the latter happily we have a good supply. Joky seems more himself, and starts to talk a little—possibly somewhat louder than is safe; for, as he chatters on, wondering how it will end, there comes a tremendous blow against the side of the house, making it ring again. After this Joky is very silent. As we sit there I cannot but wonder what all the rest are doing, and how the poor beggars forrad are faring, cooped up without water, as the tragedy of the night has proved.

Towards noon, I hear a loud bang, followed by a terrific bellowing. Then comes a great smashing of woodwork, and the cries of men in pain. Vainly I ask myself what has happened. I begin to reason. By the sound of the report it was evidently something much heavier than a rifle or pistol, and judging from the mad roaring of the Thing, the shot must have done some execution. On thinking it over further, I become convinced that, by some means, those aft have got hold of the small signal cannon we carry, and though I know that some have been hurt, perhaps killed, yet a feeling of exultation seizes me as I listen to the roars of the Thing, and realise that it is badly wounded, perhaps mortally. After a while, however, the bellowing dies away, and only an occasional roar, denoting more of anger than aught else, is heard.

Presently I become aware, by the ship's canting over to starboard, that the creature has gone over to that side, and a great hope springs up within me that possibly it has had enough of us and is going over the rail into the sea. For a time all is silent and my hope grows stronger. I lean across and nudge Joky, who is sleeping with his head on the table. He starts up sharply with a loud cry.

"Hush!" I whisper hoarsely. "I'm not certain, but I do believe it's gone."

Joky's face brightens wonderfully, and he questions me eagerly. We wait another hour or so, with hope ever rising. Our confidence is returning fast. Not a sound can we hear, not even the breathing of the Beast. I get out some biscuits, and Joky, after rummaging in the locker, produces a small piece of pork and a bottle of ship's vinegar. We fall to with a relish. After our long abstinence from food the meal acts on us like wine, and what must Joky do but insist on opening the door, to make sure the Thing has gone. This I will not allow, telling him that at least it will be safer to open the iron port-covers first and have a look out. Joky argues, but I am immovable. He becomes excited. I believe the youngster is light-headed. Then, as I turn to unscrew one of the after-covers, Joky makes a dash at the door. Before he can undo the bolts I have him, and after a short struggle lead him back to the table. Even as I endeavour to quieten him there comes at the starboard door—the door that Joky has tried to open—a sharp, loud sniff, sniff, followed immediately by a thunderous grunting howl and a foul stench of putrid breath sweeps in under the door. A great trembling takes me, and were it not for the Carpenter's tool-chest I should fall. Joky turns very white and is violently sick, after which he is seized by a hopeless fit of sobbing.

Hour after hour passes, and, weary to death, I lie down on the chest upon which I have been sitting, and try to rest.

It must be about half-past two in the morning, after a somewhat longer doze, that I am suddenly awakened by a most tremendous uproar away forrad—men's voices shrieking, cursing, praying; but in spite of the terror expressed, so weak and feeble; while in the midst, and at times broken off short with that hellishly suggestive "Glut! Glut!" is the unearthly bellowing of the Thing. Fear incarnate seizes me, and I can only fall on my knees and pray. Too well I know what is happening.

Joky has slept through it all, and I am thankful.

Presently, under the door there steals a narrow ribbon of light, and I know that the day has broken on the second morning of our imprisonment. I let Joky sleep on. I will let him have peace while he may. Time passes, but I take little notice. The Thing is quiet, probably sleeping. About midday I eat a little biscuit and drink some of the water. Joky still sleeps. It is best so.

A sound breaks the stillness. The ship gives a slight heave, and I know that once more the Thing is awake. Round the deck it moves, causing the ship to roll perceptibly. Once it goes forrad—I fancy to again explore the fo'cas'le. Evidently it finds nothing, for it returns almost immediately. It pauses a moment at the house, then goes on further aft. Up aloft, somewhere in the fore-rigging, there rings out a peal of wild laughter, though sounding very faint and far away. The Horror stops suddenly. I listen intently, but hear nothing save a sharp creaking beyond the after end of the house, as though a strain had come upon the rigging.

A minute later I hear a cry aloft, followed almost instantly by a loud crash on deck that seems to shake the ship. I wait in anxious fear. What is happening? The minutes pass slowly. Then comes another frightened shout. It ceases suddenly. The suspense has become terrible, and I am no longer able to bear it. Very cautiously I open one of the after port-covers, and peep out to see a fearful sight. There, with its tail upon the deck and its vast body curled round the main-mast, is the monster, its head above the top-sail yard, and its great claw-armed tentacle waving in the air. It is the first proper sight that I have had of the Thing. Good Heavens! It must weigh a hundred tons! Knowing that I shall have time, I open the port itself, then crane my head out and look up. There on the extreme end of the lower top-sail yard I see one of the able seamen. Even down here I note the staring horror of his face. At this moment he sees me and gives a weak, hoarse cry for help. I can do nothing for him. As I look the great tongue shoots out and licks him off the yard, much as might a dog a fly off the window-pane.

Higher still, but happily out of reach, are two more of the men. As far as I can judge they are lashed to the mast above the royal yard. The Thing attempts to reach them, but after a futile effort it ceases, and starts to slide down, coil on coil, to the deck. While doing this I notice a great gaping wound on its body some twenty feet above the tail.

I drop my gaze from aloft and look aft. The cabin door is torn from its hinges, and the bulkhead—which, unlike the half-deck, is of teak wood—is partly broken down. With a shudder I realise the cause of those cries after the cannon-shot. Turning I screw my head round and try to see the foremast, but cannot. The sun, I notice, is low, and the night is near. Then I draw in my head and fasten up both port and cover.

How will it end? Oh! how will it end?

After a while Joky wakes up. He is very restless, yet though he has eaten nothing during the day I cannot get him to touch anything.

Night draws on. We are too weary—too dispirited to talk. I lie down, but not to sleep…. Time passes.

A ventilator rattles violently somewhere on the main-deck, and there sounds constantly that slurring, gritty noise. Later I hear a cat's agonised howl, and then again all is quiet. Some time after comes a great splash alongside. Then, for some hours all is silent as the grave. Occasionally I sit up on the chest and listen, yet never a whisper of noise comes to me. There is an absolute silence, even the monotonous creak of the gear has died away entirely, and at last a real hope is springing up within me. That splash, this silence—surely I am justified in hoping. I do not wake Joky this time. I will prove first for myself that all is safe. Still I wait. I will run no unnecessary risks. After a time I creep to the after-port and will listen; but there is no sound. I put up my hand and feel at the screw, then again I hesitate, yet not for long. Noiselessly I begin to unscrew the fastening of the heavy shield. It swings loose on its hinge, and I pull it back and peer out. My heart is beating madly. Everything seems strangely dark outside. Perhaps the moon has gone behind a cloud. Suddenly a beam of moonlight enters through the port, and goes as quickly. I stare out. Something moves. Again the light streams in, and now I seem to be looking into a great cavern, at the bottom of which quivers and curls something palely white.

My heart seems to stand still! It is the Horror! I start back and seize the iron port-flap to slam it to. As I do so, something strikes the glass like a steam ram, shatters it to atoms, and flicks past me into the berth. I scream and spring away. The port is quite filled with it. The lamp shows it dimly. It is curling and twisting here and there. It is as thick as a tree, and covered with a smooth slimy skin. At the end is a great claw, like a lobster's, only a thousand times larger. I cower down into the farthest corner.... It has broken the tool-chest to pieces with one click of those frightful mandibles. Joky has crawled under a bunk. The Thing sweeps round in my direction. I feel a drop of sweat trickle slowly down my face—it tastes salty. Nearer comes that awful death.... Crash! I roll over backwards. It has crushed the water breaker against which I leant, and I am rolling in the water across the floor. The claw drives up, then down, with a quick uncertain movement, striking the deck a dull, heavy blow, a foot from my head. Joky gives a little gasp of horror. Slowly the Thing rises and starts feeling its way round the berth. It plunges into a bunk and pulls out a bolster, nips it in half and drops it, then moves on. It is feeling along the deck. As it does so it comes across a half of the bolster. It seems to toy with it, then picks it up and takes it out through the port....

A wave of putrid air fills the berth. There is a grating sound, and something enters the port again—something white and tapering and set with teeth. Hither and thither it curls, rasping over the bunks, ceiling, and deck, with a noise like that of a great saw at work. Twice it flickers above my head, and I close my eyes. Then off it goes again. It sounds now on the opposite side of the berth and nearer to Joky. Suddenly the harsh, raspy noise becomes muffled, as though the teeth were passing across some soft substance. Joky gives a horrid little scream, that breaks off into a bubbling, whistling sound. I open my eyes. The tip of the vast tongue is curled tightly round something that drips, then is quickly withdrawn, allowing the moonbeams to steal again into the berth. I rise to my feet. Looking round, I note in a mechanical sort of way the wrecked state of the berth—the shattered chests, dismantled bunks, and something else—

"Joky!" I cry, and tingle all over.

There is that awful Thing again at the port. I glance round for a weapon. I will revenge Joky. Ah! there, right under the lamp, where the wreck of the Carpenter's chest strews the floor, lies a small hatchet. I spring forward and seize it. It is small, but so keen—so keen! I feel its razor edge lovingly. Then I am back at the port. I stand to one side and raise my weapon. The great tongue is feeling its way to those fearsome remains. It reaches them. As it does so, with a scream of "Joky! Joky!" I strike savagely again and again and again, gasping as I strike; once more, and the monstrous mass falls to the deck, writhing like a hideous eel. A vast, warm flood rushes in through the porthole. There is a sound of breaking steel and an enormous bellowing. A singing comes in my ears and grows louder—louder. Then the berth grows indistinct and suddenly dark.

EXTRACT FROM THE LOG OF THE STEAMSHIP *HISPANIOLA*.

June 24. —Lat. —N. Long. —W. 11 a.m. —Sighted four-masted barque about four points on the port bow, flying signal of distress. Ran down to her and sent a boat aboard. She proved to be the *Glen Doon*, homeward bound from Melbourne to London. Found things in a terrible state. Decks covered with blood and slime. Steel deck-house stove in. Broke open door, and discovered youth of about nineteen in last stage of inanition, also part remains of boy about fourteen years of age. There was a great quantity of blood in the place, and a huge curled-up mass of whitish flesh, weighing about half a ton, one end of which appeared to have been hacked through with a sharp instrument. Found forecastle door open and hanging from one hinge. Doorway bulged, as though something had been forced through. Went inside. Terrible state of affairs, blood everywhere, broken chests, smashed bunks, but no men nor remains. Went aft again and found youth showing signs of recovery. When he came round, gave the name of Thompson. Said they had been attacked by a huge serpent—thought it must have been sea-serpent. He was too weak to say much, but told us there were some men up the main-mast. Sent a hand aloft, who reported them lashed to the royal mast, and quite dead. Went aft to the cabin. Here we found the bulkhead smashed to pieces, and the cabin-door lying on the deck near the after-hatch. Found body of Captain down lazarette, but no officers. Noticed amongst the wreckage part of the carriage of a small cannon. Came aboard again.

Have sent the Second Mate with six men to work her into port. Thompson is with us. He has written out his version of the affair. We certainly consider that the state of the ship, as we found her, bears out in every respect his story. (Signed)

William Norton (Master).
Tom Briggs (1st Mate).

The Voice in the Night

IT WAS A DARK, starless night. We were becalmed in the Northern Pacific. Our exact position I do not know; for the sun had been hidden during the course of a weary, breathless week, by a thin haze which had seemed to float above us, about the height of our mastheads, at whiles descending and shrouding the surrounding sea.

With there being no wind, we had steadied the tiller, and I was the only man on deck. The crew, consisting of two men and a boy, were sleeping forrard in their den; while Will—my friend, and the master of our little craft—was aft in his bunk on the port side of the little cabin.

Suddenly, from out of the surrounding darkness, there came a hail:—

"Schooner, ahoy!"

The cry was so unexpected that I gave no immediate answer, because of my surprise.

It came again—a voice curiously throaty and inhuman, calling from somewhere upon the dark sea away on our port broadside:—

"Schooner, ahoy!"

"Hullo!" I sung out, having gathered my wits somewhat. "What are you? What do you want?"

"You need not be afraid," answered the queer voice, having probably noticed some trace of confusion in my tone. "I am only an old—man."

The pause sounded oddly; but it was only afterwards that it came back to me with any significance.

"Why don't you come alongside, then?" I queried somewhat snappishly; for I liked not his hinting at my having been a trifle shaken.

"I—I—can't. It wouldn't be safe. I—" The voice broke off, and there was silence.

"What do you mean?" I asked, growing more and more astonished.

150

"Why not safe? Where are you?"

I listened for a moment; but there came no answer. And then, a sudden indefinite suspicion, of I knew not what, coming to me, I stepped swiftly to the binnacle, and took out the lighted lamp. At the same time, I knocked on the deck with my heel to waken Will. Then I was back at the side, throwing the yellow funnel of light out into the silent immensity beyond our rail. As I did so, I heard a slight, muffled cry, and then the sound of a splash, as though someone had dipped oars abruptly. Yet I cannot say that I saw anything with certainty; save, it seemed to me, that with the first flash of the light, there had been something upon the waters, where now there was nothing.

"Hullo, there!" I called. "What foolery is this!"

But there came only the indistinct sounds of a boat being pulled away into the night.

Then I heard Will's voice, from the direction of the after scuttle:—

"What's up, George?"

"Come here, Will!" I said.

"What is it?" he asked, coming across the deck.

I told him the queer thing which had happened. He put several questions; then, after a moment's silence, he raised his hands to his lips, and hailed: "Boat, ahoy!"

From a long distance away, there came back to us a faint reply, and my companion repeated his call. Presently, after a short period of silence, there grew on our hearing the muffled sound of oars; at which Will hailed again.

This time there was a reply:—

"Put away the light."

"I'm damned if I will," I muttered; but Will told me to do as the voice bade, and I shoved it down under the bulwarks.

"Come nearer," he said, and the oar-strokes continued. Then, when apparently some half-dozen fathoms distant, they again ceased.

"Come alongside," exclaimed Will. "There's nothing to be frightened of aboard here!"

"Promise that you will not show the light?"

"What's to do with you," I burst out, "that you're so infernally afraid of the light?"

"Because—" began the voice, and stopped short.

"Because what?" I asked, quickly.

Will put his hand on my shoulder.

"Shut up a minute, old man," he said, in a low voice. "Let me tackle him."

He leant more over the rail.

"See here, Mister," he said, "this is a pretty queer business, you coming upon us like this, right out in the middle of the blessed Pacific. How are we to know what sort of a hanky-panky trick you're up to? You say there's only one of you. How are we to know, unless we get a squint at you—eh? What's your objection to the light, anyway?"

As he finished, I heard the noise of the oars again, and then the voice came; but now from a greater distance, and sounding extremely hopeless and pathetic.

" I am sorry—sorry! I would not have troubled you, only I am hungry, and—so is she."

The voice died away, and the sound of the oars, dipping irregularly, was borne to us.

"Stop!" sung out Will. "I don't want to drive you away. Come back! We'll keep the light hidden, if you don't like it."

He turned to me:—

"It's a damned queer rig, this; but I think there's nothing to be afraid of?"

There was a question in his tone, and I replied.

"No, I think the poor devil's been wrecked around here, and gone crazy."

The sound of the oars drew nearer.

"Shove that lamp back in the binnacle," said Will; then he leaned over the rail, and listened. I replaced the lamp, and came back to his side. The dipping of the oars ceased some dozen yards distant.

"Won't you come alongside now?" asked Will in an even voice. "I have had the lamp put back in the binnacle."

"I—I cannot," replied the voice. "I dare not come nearer. I dare not even pay you for the—the provisions."

"That's all right," said Will, and hesitated. "You're welcome to as much grub as you can take—" Again he hesitated.

"You are very good," exclaimed the voice. "May God, Who understands everything, reward you—" It broke off huskily.

"The—the lady?" said Will, abruptly. "Is she—"

"I have left her behind upon the island," came the voice.

"What island?" I cut in.

"I know not its name," returned the voice. "I would to God—!" it began, and checked itself as suddenly.

"Could we not send a boat for her?" asked Will at this point.

"No!" said the voice, with extraordinary emphasis. "My God! No!" There was a moment's pause; then it added, in a tone which seemed a merited reproach:—

"It was because of our want I ventured— Because her agony tortured me."

"I am a forgetful brute," exclaimed Will. "Just wait a minute, whoever you are, and I will bring you up something at once."

In a couple of minutes he was back again, and his arms were full of various edibles. He paused at the rail.

"Can't you come alongside for them?" he asked.

"No—I *dare not*," replied the voice, and it seemed to me that in its tones I detected a note of stifled craving—as though the owner hushed a mortal desire. It came to me then in a flash, that the poor old creature out there in the darkness, was *suffering* for actual need of that which Will held in his arms; and yet, because of some unintelligible dread, refraining from dashing to the side of our little schooner, and receiving it. And with the lightning-like conviction, there came the knowledge that the Invisible was not mad; but sanely facing some intolerable horror.

"Damn it, Will!" I said, full of many feelings, over which predominated a vast sympathy. "Get a box. We must float off the stuff to him in it."

This we did—propelling it away from the vessel, out into the darkness, by means of a boathook.

In a minute, a slight cry from the Invisible came to us, and we knew that he had secured the box.

A little later, he called out a farewell to us, and so heartful a blessing, that I am sure we were the better for it. Then, without more ado, we heard the ply of oars across the darkness.

"Pretty soon off," remarked Will, with perhaps just a little sense of injury.

"Wait," I replied. "I think somehow he'll come back. He must have been badly needing that food."

"And the lady," said Will. For a moment he was silent; then he continued:—

"It's the queerest thing ever I've tumbled across, since I've been fishing."

"Yes," I said, and fell to pondering.

And so the time slipped away—an hour, another, and still Will stayed with me; for the queer adventure had knocked all desire for sleep out of him.

The third hour was three parts through, when we heard again the sound of oars across the silent ocean.

"Listen!" said Will, a low note of excitement in his voice.

"He's coming, just as I thought," I muttered.

The dipping of the oars grew nearer, and I noted that the strokes were firmer and longer. The food had been needed.

They came to a stop a little distance off the broadside, and the queer voice came again to us through the darkness:—

"Schooner, ahoy!"

"That you?" asked Will.

"Yes," replied the voice. "I left you suddenly; but—but there was great need."

"The lady?" questioned Will.

"The—lady is grateful now on earth. She will be more grateful soon in—in heaven."

Will began to make some reply, in a puzzled voice; but became confused, and broke off short. I said nothing. I was wondering at the curious pauses, and, apart from my wonder, I was full of a great sympathy.

The voice continued:—

"We—she and I, have talked, as we shared the result of God's tenderness and yours—"

Will interposed; but without coherence.

"I beg of you not to—to belittle your deed of Christian charity this night," said the voice. "Be sure that it has not escaped His notice."

It stopped, and there was a full minute's silence. Then it came again:—

"We have spoken together upon that which—which has befallen us. We had thought to go out, without telling any, of the terror which has come into our—lives. She is with me in believing that tonight's happenings are under a special ruling, and that it is God's wish that we should tell to you all that we have suffered since—since—"

"Yes?" said Will, softly.

"Since the sinking of the *Albatross*."

"Ah!" I exclaimed, involuntarily. "She left Newcastle for 'Frisco some six months ago, and hasn't been heard of since."

"Yes," answered the voice. "But some few degrees to the North of the line she was caught in a terrible storm, and dismasted. When the day came, it was found that she was leaking badly, and, presently, it falling to a calm, the sailors took to the boats, leaving—leaving a young lady—my fiancée—and myself upon the wreck.

"We were below, gathering together a few of our belongings, when they left. They were entirely callous, through fear, and when we came up upon the decks, we saw them only as small shapes afar off upon the horizon. Yet we did not despair, but set to work and constructed a small raft. Upon this we put such few matters as it would hold, including a quantity of water and some ship's biscuit. Then, the vessel being very deep in the water, we got ourselves onto the raft, and pushed off.

"It was later, when I observed that we seemed to be in the way of some tide or current, which bore us from the ship at an angle; so that in the course of three hours, by my watch, her hull became invisible to our sight, her broken masts remaining in view for a somewhat longer period. Then, towards evening, it grew misty, and so through the night. The next day we were still encompassed by the mist, the weather remaining quiet.

"For four days, we drifted through this strange haze, until, on the evening of the fourth day, there grew upon our ears the murmur of breakers at a distance. Gradually it became plainer, and, somewhat after midnight, it appeared to sound upon either hand at no very great space. The raft was raised upon a swell several times, and then we were in smooth water, and the noise of the breakers was behind.

"When the morning came, we found that we were in a sort of great lagoon; but of this we noticed little at the time; for close before us, through the enshrouding mist, loomed the hull of a large sailing-vessel. With one accord, we fell upon our knees and thanked God; for we thought that here was an end to our perils. We had much to learn.

"The raft drew near to the ship, and we shouted on them, to take us aboard; but none answered. Presently, the raft touched against the side of the vessel, and, seeing a rope hanging downwards, I seized it and began to climb. Yet I had much ado to make my way up, because of a kind of grey, lichenous fungus, which had seized upon the rope, and which blotched the side of the ship, lividly.

"I reached the rail, and clambered over it, onto the deck. Here, I saw that the decks were covered, in great patches, with the grey masses, some of them rising into nodules several feet in height; but at the time, I thought less of this matter than of the possibility of there being people aboard the ship. I shouted; but none answered. Then I went to the door below the poop-deck. I opened it, and peered in. There was a great smell of staleness, so that I knew in a moment that nothing living was within, and with the knowledge, I shut the door quickly; for I felt suddenly lonely.

"I went back to the side, where I had scrambled up. My—my sweetheart was still sitting quietly upon the raft. Seeing me look down, she called up to know whether there were any aboard of the ship. I replied that the vessel had the appearance of having been long deserted; but that if she would wait a little, I would see whether there was anything in the shape of a ladder, by which she could ascend to the deck. Then we would make a search through the vessel together. A little later, on, the opposite side of the decks, I found a rope side-ladder. This I carried across, and a minute afterwards, she was beside me.

"Together, we explored the cabins and apartments in the after-part of the ship; but nowhere was there any sign of life. Here and there, within the cabins themselves, we came across odd patches of that queer fungus; but this, as my sweetheart said, could be cleansed away.

"In the end, having assured ourselves that the after portion of the vessel was empty, we picked our ways to the bows, between the ugly grey nodules of that strange growth; and here we made a further search, which told us that there was indeed none aboard but ourselves.

"This being now beyond any doubt, we returned to the stern of the ship, and proceeded to make ourselves as comfortable as possible. Together, we cleared out and cleaned two of the cabins; and, after that, I made examination whether there was anything eatable in the ship. This I soon found was so, and thanked God in my heart for His goodness. In addition to this, I discovered the whereabouts of the freshwater pump, and having fixed it, I found the water drinkable, though somewhat unpleasant to the taste.

"For several days, we stayed aboard the ship, without attempting to get to the shore. We were busily engaged in making the place habitable. Yet even thus early, we became aware that our lot was even less to be desired than might have been imagined; for though, as a first step, we scraped away the odd patches of growth that studded the floors and walls of the cabins and saloon, yet they returned almost to their original size within the space of twenty-four hours, which not only discouraged us, but gave us a feeling of vague unease.

"Still, we would not admit ourselves beaten, so set to work afresh, and not only scraped away the fungus, but soaked the places where it had been, with carbolic, a can-full of which I had found in the pantry. Yet, by the end of the week, the growth had returned in full strength, and, in addition, it had spread to other places, as though our touching it had allowed germs from it to travel elsewhere.

"On the seventh morning, my sweetheart woke to find a small patch of it growing on her pillow, close to her face. At that, she came to me, so soon as she could get her garments upon her. I was in the galley at the time, lighting the fire for breakfast.

" 'Come here, John,' she said, and led me aft. When I saw the thing upon her pillow, I shuddered, and then and there we agreed to go right out of the ship, and see whether we could not fare to make ourselves more comfortable ashore.

"Hurriedly, we gathered together our few belongings, and even among these, I found that the fungus had been at work; for one of her shawls had a little lump of it growing near one edge. I threw the whole thing over the side, without saying anything to her.

"The raft was still alongside; but it was too clumsy to guide, and I lowered down a small boat that hung across the stern, and in this we made our way to the shore. Yet, as we drew near to it, I became gradually aware that here the vile fungus, which had driven us from the ship, was growing riot. In places it rose into horrible, fantastic mounds, which seemed almost to quiver, as with a quiet life, when the wind blew across them. Here and there, it took on the forms of vast fingers, and in others it just spread out flat and smooth and treacherous. Odd places, it appeared as grotesque stunted trees, seeming extraordinarily kinked and gnarled— The whole quaking vilely at times.

"At first, it seemed to us that there was no single portion of the surrounding shore which was not hidden beneath the masses of the hideous lichen; yet, in this, I found we were mistaken; for somewhat later, coasting along the shore at a little distance, we descried a smooth white patch of what appeared to be fine sand, and there we landed. It was not sand. What it was, I do not know. All that I have observed, is that upon it, the fungus will not grow; while everywhere else, save where the sand-like earth wanders oddly, path-wise, amid the grey desolation of the lichen, there is nothing but that loathsome greyness.

"It is difficult to make you understand how cheered we were to find one place that was absolutely free from the growth, and here we deposited our belongings. Then we went back to the ship for such things as it seemed to us we should need. Among other matters, I managed to bring ashore with me one of the ship's sails, with which I constructed two small tents, which, though exceedingly rough-shaped, served the purposes for which they were intended. In these, we lived and stored our various necessities, and thus for a matter of some four weeks, all went smoothly and without particular unhappiness. Indeed, I may say with much of happiness—for—for we were together.

"It was on the thumb of her right hand, that the growth first showed. It was only a small circular spot, much like a little grey mole. My God! how the fear leapt to my heart when she showed me the place. We cleansed it, between us, washing it with carbolic and water. In the morning of the following day, she showed her hand to me again.

The grey warty thing had returned. For a little while, we looked at one another in silence. Then, still wordless, we started again to remove it. In the midst of the operation, she spoke suddenly.

"'What's that on the side of your face, Dear!' Her voice was sharp with anxiety. I put my hand up to feel.

"'There! Under the hair by your ear. —A little to the front a bit." My finger rested upon the place, and then I knew.

"'Let us get your thumb done first,' I said. And she submitted, only because she was afraid to touch me until it was cleansed. I finished washing and disinfecting her thumb, and then she turned to my face. After it was finished, we sat together and talked awhile of many things; for there had come into our lives sudden, very terrible thoughts. We were, all at once, afraid of something worse than death.   W e spoke of loading the boat with provisions and water, and making our way out on to the sea; yet we were helpless, for many causes, and—and the growth had attacked us already. We decided to stay. God would do with us what was His will. We would wait.

"A month, two months, three months passed, and the places grew somewhat, and there had come others. Yet we fought so strenuously with the fear, that its headway was but slow, comparatively speaking.

"Occasionally, we ventured off to the ship for such stores as we needed. There, we found that the fungus grew persistently. One of the nodules on the main-deck became soon as high as my head.

"We had now given up all thought or hope of leaving the island. We had realised that it would be unallowable to go among healthy humans, with the thing from which we were suffering.

"With this determination and knowledge in our minds, we knew that we should have to husband our food and water; for we did not know, at that time, but that we should possibly live for many years.

"This reminds me that I have told you that I am an old man. Judged by years this is not so. But—but—"

He broke off; then continued somewhat abruptly:—

"As I was saying, we knew that we should have to use care in the matter of food. But we had no idea then how little food there was left, of which to take care. It was a week later, that I made the discovery that all the other bread tanks—which I had supposed full—were empty, and that (beyond odd tins of vegetables and meat, and some other matters) we had nothing on which to depend, but the bread in the tank which I had already opened.

"After learning this, I bestirred myself to do what I could, and set to work at fishing in the lagoon; but with no success. At this, I was somewhat inclined to feel desperate, until the thought came to me to try outside the lagoon, in the open sea.

"Here, at times, I caught odd fish; but, so infrequently, that they proved of but little help in keeping us from the hunger which threatened. It seemed to me that our deaths were likely to come by hunger, and not by the growth of the thing which had seized upon our bodies.

"We were in this state of mind when the fourth month wore out. Then I made a very horrible discovery. One morning, a little before midday, I came off from the ship, with a portion of the biscuits which were left. In the mouth of her tent, I saw my sweetheart sitting, eating something.

" 'What is it, my Dear?' I called out as I leapt ashore. Yet, on hearing my voice, she seemed confused, and, turning, slyly threw something towards the edge of the little clearing. It fell short, and, a vague suspicion having arisen within me, I walked across and picked it up. It was a piece of the grey fungus.

"As I went to her, with it in my hand, she turned deadly pale; then a rose red.

"I felt strangely dazed and frightened.

" 'My Dear! My Dear!' I said, and could say no more. Yet, at my words, she broke down and cried bitterly. Gradually, as she calmed, I got from her the news that she had tried it the preceding day, and—and liked it. I got her to promise on her knees not to touch it again, however great our hunger. After she had promised, she told me that the desire for it had come suddenly, and that, until the moment of desire, she had experienced nothing towards it, but the most extreme repulsion.

"Later in the day, feeling strangely restless, and much shaken with the thing which I had discovered, I made my way along one of the twisted paths—formed by the white, sand-like substance—which led among the fungoid growth. I had, once before, ventured along there; but not to any great distance. This time, being involved in perplexing thought, I went much further than hitherto.

"Suddenly, I was called to myself, by a queer hoarse sound on my left. Turning quickly, I saw that there was movement among an extraordinarily shaped mass of fungus, close to my elbow. It was swaying uneasily, as though it possessed life of its own. Abruptly, as I stared, the thought came to me that the thing had a grotesque resemblance to the figure of a distorted human creature. Even as the fancy flashed into my brain, there was a slight, sickening noise of tearing, and I saw that one of the branch-like arms was detaching itself from the surrounding grey masses, and coming towards me. The head of the thing—a shapeless grey ball, inclined in my direction. I stood stupidly, and the vile arm brushed across my face. I gave out a frightened cry, and ran back a few paces. There was a sweetish taste upon my lips, where the thing had touched me. I licked them, and was immediately filled with an inhuman desire. I turned and seized a mass of the fungus. Then more, and—more. I was insatiable. In the midst of devouring, the remembrance of the morning's discovery swept into my mazed brain. It was sent by God. I dashed the fragment I held, to the ground. Then, utterly wretched and feeling a dreadful guiltiness, I made my way back to the little encampment.

"I think she knew, by some marvellous intuition which love must have given, so soon as she set eyes on me. Her quiet sympathy made it easier for me, and I told her of my sudden weakness; yet omitted to mention the extraordinary thing which had gone before. I desired to spare her all unnecessary terror.

"But, for myself, I had added an intolerable knowledge, to breed an incessant terror in my brain; for I doubted not but that I had seen the end of one of those men who had come to the island in the ship in the lagoon; and in that monstrous ending, I had seen our own.

"Thereafter, we kept from the abominable food, though the desire for it had entered into our blood. Yet, our drear punishment was upon us; for, day by day, with monstrous rapidity, the fungoid growth took hold of our poor bodies. Nothing we could do would check it materially, and so—and so—we who had been human, became—Well, it matters less each day. Only—only we had been man and maid!

"And day by day, the fight is more dreadful, to withstand the hunger-lust for the terrible lichen.

"A week ago we ate the last of the biscuit, and since that time I have caught three fish. I was out here fishing tonight, when your schooner drifted upon me out of the mist. I hailed you. You know the rest, and may God, out of His great heart, bless you for your goodness to a—a couple of poor outcast souls."

There was the dip of an oar—another. Then the voice came again, and for the last time, sounding through the slight surrounding mist, ghostly and mournful.

"God bless you! Good-bye!"

"Good-bye," we shouted together, hoarsely, our hearts full of many emotions.

I glanced about me. I became aware that the dawn was upon us.

The sun flung a stray beam across the hidden sea; pierced the mist dully, and lit up the receding boat with a gloomy fire. Indistinctly, I saw something nodding between the oars. I thought of a sponge—a great, grey nodding sponge— The oars continued to ply. They were grey—as was the boat—and my eyes searched a moment vainly for the conjunction of hand and oar. My gaze flashed back to the—head. It nodded forward as the oars went backward for the stroke. Then the oars were dipped, the boat shot out of the patch of light, and the—the Thing went nodding into the mist.

The *Shamraken*
Homeward-Bounder

I

THE OLD *SHAMRAKEN*, SAILING-SHIP, had been many days upon the waters. She was old—older than her masters, and that was saying a great deal. She seemed in no hurry, as she lifted her bulging, old, wooden sides through the seas. What need for hurry! She would arrive sometime, in some fashion, as had been her habit heretofore.

Two matters were especially noticeable among her crew—who were also her masters—; the first the agedness of each and everyone; the second the *family* sense which appeared to bind them, so that the ship seemed manned by a crew, all of whom were related one to the other; yet it was not so.

A strange company were they, each man bearded, aged and grizzled; yet there was nothing of the inhumanity of old age about them, save it might be in their freedom from grumbling, and the calm content which comes only to those in whom the more violent passions have died.

Had anything to be done, there was nothing of the growling, inseparable from the average run of sailor men. They went aloft to the "job" —whatever it might be—with the wise submission which is brought only by age and experience. Their work was gone through with a certain slow pertinacity—a sort of tired steadfastness, born of the knowledge that such work *had* to be done. Moreover, their hands possessed the ripe skill which comes only from exceeding practice, and which went far to make amends for the feebleness of age. Above all, their movements, slow as they might be, were remorseless in their lack of faltering. They had so often performed the same kind of work, that they had arrived, by the selection of utility, at the shortest and most simple methods of doing it.

They had, as I have said, been many days upon the water, though I am not sure that any man in her knew to a nicety the number of

162

those days. Though Skipper Abe Tombes—addressed usually as Skipper Abe—may have had some notion; for he might be seen at times gravely adjusting a prodigious quadrant, which suggests that he kept some sort of record of time and place.

Of the crew of the *Shamraken,* some half dozen were seated, working placidly at such matters of seamanship as were necessary. Besides these, there were others about the decks. A couple who paced the lee side of the main-deck, smoking, and exchanging an occasional word. One who sat by the side of a worker, and made odd remarks between draws at his pipe. Another, out upon the jibboom, who fished, with a line, hook and white rag, for bonito.

This last was Nuzzie, the ship's boy. He was grey-bearded, and his years numbered five and fifty. A boy of fifteen he had been, when he joined the *Shamraken,* and "boy" he was still, though forty years had passed into eternity, since the day of his "signing on"; for the men of the *Shamraken* lived in the past, and thought of him only as the "boy" of that past.

It was Nuzzie's watch below—his time for sleeping. This might have been said also of the other three men who talked and smoked; but for themselves they had scarce a thought of sleep. Healthy age sleeps little, and they were in health, though so ancient.

Presently, one of those who walked the lee side of the main-deck, chancing to cast a glance forrard, observed Nuzzie still to be out upon the jibboom, *jerking* his line so as to delude some foolish bonito into the belief that the white rag was a flying-fish. The smoker nudged his companion. "Time thet b'y 'ad 'is sleep."

"I, I, mate," returned the other, withdrawing his pipe, and giving a steadfast look at the figure seated out upon the jibboom.

For the half of a minute they stood there, very effigies of Age's implacable determination to rule rash Youth. Their pipes were held in their hands, and the smoke rose up in little eddies from the smouldering contents of the bowls.

"Thar's no tamin' of thet b'y!" said the first man, looking very stern and determined. Then he remembered his pipe, and took a draw.

"B'ys is tur'ble queer critters," remarked the second man, and remembered his pipe in turn.

"Fishin' w'en 'e orter be sleepin'," snorted the first man.

"B'ys needs a tur'ble lot er sleep," said the second man. "I 'member w'en I wor a b'y. I reckon it's ther growin'."

And all the time poor Nuzzie fished on.

"Guess I'll jest step up an' tell 'im ter come in outer thet," exclaimed the first man, and commenced to walk towards the steps leading up on to the fo'cas'le head.

"B'y!" he shouted, as soon as his head was above the level of the fo'cas'le deck. "B'y!"

Nuzzie looked round, at the second call. "Eh?" he sung out.

"Yew come in outer thet," shouted the older man, in the somewhat shrill tone which age had brought to his voice. "Reckon we'll be 'avin' yer sleepin' at ther wheel ter night."

"i," joined in the second man, who had followed his companion up onto the fo'cas'le head. "Come in, b'y, an' get ter yer bunk."

"Right," called Nuzzie, and commenced to coil up his line. It was evident that he had no thought of disobeying. He came in off the spar, and went past them without a word, on the way to turn in. They, on their part, went down slowly off the fo'cas'le head, and resumed their walk fore and aft along the lee side of the main-deck.

II

"I reckon, Zeph," said the man who sat upon the hatch and smoked, "I reckon as Skipper Abe's 'bout right. We've made a trifle o' dollars outer the ole 'ooker, an' we don't get no younger."

"Ay, thet's so, right 'nuff," returned the man who sat beside him, working at the stropping of a block.

"An' it's 'bout time's we got inter the use o' bein' ashore," went on the first man, who was named Job. Zeph gripped the block between his knees, and fumbled in his hip pocket for a plug. He bit off a chew and replaced the plug.

"Seems cur'ous this is ther last trip, w'en yer comes ter think uv it," he remarked, chewing steadily, his chin resting on his hand.

Job took two or three deep draws at his pipe before he spoke.

"Reckon it had ter come sumtime," he said, at length. "I've a purty leetle place in me mind w'er' I'm goin' ter tie up. 'Ave yer thought erbout it, Zeph?"

The man who held the block between his knees, shook his head, and stared away moodily over the sea.

"Dunno, Job, as I know what I'll do w'en they old 'ooker's sold," he muttered. "Sence M'ria went. I don't seem nohow ter care 'bout bein' 'shore."

"I never 'ad no wife," said Job, pressing down the burning tobacco in the bowl of his pipe. "I reckon seafarin' men don't ought ter have no truck with wives."

"Thet's right 'nuff, Job, fer yew. Each man ter 'is taste. I wer' tur'ble fond uv M'ria—" he broke off short, and continued to stare out over the sea.

"I've allus thought I'd like ter settle down on er farm o' me own. I guess the dollars I've arned 'll do the trick," said Job.

Zeph made no reply, and, for a time, they sat there, neither speaking.

Presently, from the door of the fo'cas'le, on the starboard side, two figures emerged. They were also of the "watch below." If anything, they seemed older than the rest of those about the decks; their beards, white, save for the stain of tobacco juice, came nearly to their waists. For the rest, they had been big vigourous men; but were now sorely bent by the burden of their years. They came aft, walking slowly. As they came opposite to the main hatch, Job looked up and spoke:

"Say, Nehemiah, thar's Zeph here's been thinkin' 'bout M'ria, an' I ain't bin able ter peek 'im up nohow."

The smaller of the two newcomers shook his head slowly.

"We hev oor trubbles," he said. "We hev oor, trubbles. I hed mine w'en I lost my datter's gell. I wor powerful took wi' thet gell, she wor that winsome; but it wor like ter be—it wor like ter be, an' Zeph's hed his trubble sence then."

"M'ria wer a good wife ter me, she wer'," said Zeph, speaking slowly. "An' now th' old 'ooker's goin', I'm feared as I'll find it mighty lonesome ashore yon," and he waved his hand, as though suggesting vaguely that the shore lay anywhere beyond the starboard rail.

"Ay," remarked the second of the newcomers. "It's er weary thing to me as th' old packet's goin'. Six and sixty year hev I sailed in her. Six and sixty year!" He nodded his head, mournfully, and struck a match with shaky hands.

"It's like ter be," said the smaller man. "It's like ter be."

And, with that, he and his companion moved over to the spar that lay along under the starboard bulwarks, and there seated themselves, to smoke and meditate.

III

Skipper Abe, and Josh Matthews, the First Mate, were standing together beside the rail which ran across the break of the poop. Like the rest of the men of the *Shamraken,* their age had come upon them, and the frost of eternity had touched their beards and hair.

Skipper Abe was speaking:—

"It's harder 'n I'd thought," he said, and looked away from the Mate, staring hard along the worn, white-scoured decks.

"Dunno w'at I'll du, Abe, w'en she's gone," returned the old Mate. "She's been a 'ome fer us these sixty years an' more." He knocked out the old tobacco from his pipe, as he spoke, and began to cut a bowl-full of fresh.

"It's them durned freights!" exclaimed the Skipper. "We're jest losin' dollars every trip. It's them steam packets as hes knocked us out."

He sighed wearily, and bit tenderly at his plug.

"She's been a mighty comfortable ship," muttered Josh, in soliloquy. "An' sence thet b'y o' mine went, I sumhow thinks less o' goin' ashore 'n I used ter. I ain't no folk left on all thar 'arth."

He came to an end, and began with his old trembling fingers to fill his pipe.

Skipper Abe said nothing. He appeared to be occupied with his own thoughts. He was leaning over the rail across the break of the poop, and chewing steadily. Presently, he straightened himself up and walked over to leeward. He expectorated, after which he stood there for a few moments, taking a short look round—the result of half a century of habit. Abruptly, he sung out to the Mate....

"W'at dyer make outer it?" he queried, after they had stood awhile, peering.

"Dunno, Abe, less'n it's some sort o' mist, riz up by ther 'eat."

Skipper Abe shook his head; but having nothing better to suggest, held his peace for awhile.

Presently, Josh spoke again:—

"Mighty cur'us, Abe. These are strange parts."

Skipper Abe nodded his assent, and continued to stare at that which had come into sight upon the lee bow. To them, as they looked, it seemed that a vast wall of rose-coloured mist was rising towards the zenith. It showed nearly ahead, and at first had seemed no more than a bright cloud upon the horizon; but already had reached a great way into the air, and the upper edge had taken on wondrous flame-tints.

"It's powerful nice-lookin'," said Josh. "I've allus 'eard as things was diff'rent out 'n these parts."

Presently, as the *Shamraken* drew near to the mist, it appeared to those aboard that it filled all the sky ahead of them, being spread out now far on either bow. And so in a while they entered into it, and, at once, the aspect of all things was changed.... The mist, in great rosy wreaths, floated all about them, seeming to soften and beautify every rope and spar, so that the old ship had become, as it were a fairy craft in an unknown world.

"Never seen nothin' like it, Abe—nothin'!" said Josh. "Ey! but it's fine! It's fine! Like 's of we'd run inter ther sunset."

"I'm mazed, just mazed!" exclaimed Skipper Abe, "but I'm 'gree'ble as it's purty, mighty purty."

For a further while, the two old fellows stood without speech, just gazing and gazing. With their entering into the mist, they had come into a greater quietness than had been theirs out upon the open sea. It was as though the mist muffled and toned down the creak, creak, of the spars and gear; and the big, foamless seas that rolled past them, seemed to have lost something of their harsh whispering roar of greeting.

"Sort o' unarthly, Abe," said Josh, later, and speaking but little above a whisper. "Like as of yew was in church."

"Ay," replied Skipper Abe. "It don't seem nat'rel."

"Shouldn't think as 'eaven was all thet diff'rent," whispered Josh. And Skipper Abe said nothing in contradiction.

IV

Sometime later, the wind began to fail, and it was decided that, when eight-bells was struck, all hands should set the main t'gallant. Presently, Nuzzie having been called (for he was the only one aboard who had turned in) eight bells went, and all hands put aside their pipes, and prepared to tail onto the ha'lyards; yet no one of them made to go up to loose the sail. That was the b'y's job, and Nuzzie was a little late in coming out on deck. When, in a minute, he appeared, Skipper Abe spoke sternly to him.

"Up now, b'y, an' loose thet sail. D'y think to let er grown man dew suchlike work! Shame on yew!"

And Nuzzie, the grey-bearded "b'y" of five and fifty years, went aloft humbly, as he was bidden. Five minutes later, he sung out that all was ready for hoisting, and the string of ancient Ones took a strain on the ha'lyards. Then Nehemiah, being the chaunty man, struck up in his shrill quaver:—

"Thar wor an ole farmer in Yorkshire did dwell."

And the shrill piping of the ancient throats took up the refrain:—

"Wi' me ay, ay, blow thar lan' down."

Nehemiah caught up the story:—

" 'e 'ad 'n ole wife, 'n 'e wished 'er in 'ell."

"Give us some time ter blow thar lan' down," came the quavering chorus of old voices.

"O, thar divvel come to 'im one day at thar plough," continued old Nehemiah; and the crowd of ancients followed up with the refrain:—

"Wi' me ay, ay, blow thar lan' down."

"I've comed fer th' ole woman, I mun 'ave 'er now," sang Nehemiah. And again the refrain:— "Give us some time ter blow thar lan' down," shrilled out.

And so on to the last couple of stanzas. And all about them, as they chaunteyed, was that extraordinary, rose-tinted mist; which, above, blent into a marvellous radiance of flame-colour, as though, just a little higher than their mastheads, the sky was one red ocean of silent fire.

"Thar wor three leetle divvels chained up ter thar wall," sang Nehemiah, shrilly.

"Wi' me ay, ay, blow thar lan' down," came the piping chorus.

"She tuk off 'er clog, 'n she walloped 'em all," chaunted old Nehemiah, and again followed the wheezy, age-old refrain.

"These three leetle divvels fer marcy did bawl," quavered Nehemiah, cocking one eye upward to see whether the yard was nearly mast-headed.

"Wi' me ay, ay, blow thar lan' down," came the chorus.

"Chuck out this ole hag, or she'll mur—"

"Belay," sung out Josh, cutting across the old sea song, with the sharp command. The chaunty had ceased with the first note of the Mate's voice, and, a couple of minutes later, the ropes were coiled up, and the old fellows back to their occupations.

It is true that eight bells had gone, and that the watch was supposed to be changed; and changed it was, so far as the wheel and look-out were concerned; but otherwise little enough difference did it make to those sleep-proof ancients. The only change visible in the men about the deck, was that those who had previously only smoked, now smoked and worked; while those who had hitherto worked and smoked, now only smoked. Thus matters went on in all amity; while the old *Shamraken* passed onward like a rose-tinted shadow through the shining mist, and only the great, silent, lazy seas that came at her, out from the enshrouding redness, seemed aware that she was anything more than the shadow she appeared.

Presently, Zeph sung out to Nuzzie to get their tea from the galley, and so, in a little, the watch below were making their evening meal. They ate it as they sat upon the hatch or spar, as the chance might be; and, as they ate, they talked with their mates, of the watch on deck, upon the matter of the shining mist into which they had plunged. It was obvious, from their talk, that the extraordinary phenomenon had impressed them vastly, and all the superstition in them seemed to have been waked to fuller life. Zeph, indeed, made no bones of declaring his belief that they were nigh to something more than earthly. He said that he had a feeling that "M'ria" was somewhere near to him.

"Meanin' ter say as we've come purty near ter 'eaven?" said Nehemiah, who was busy thrumming a paunch mat, for chafing gear.

"Dunno," replied Zeph; "but"—making a gesture towards the hidden sky—"yew'll 'low as it's mighty wonnerful, 'n I guess of 'tis 'eaven, thar's some uv us as is growin' powerful wearied uv 'arth. I guess I'm feelin' peeky fer a sight uv M'ria."

Nehemiah nodded his head slowly, and the nod seemed to run round the group of white-haired ancients.

"Reckon my datter's gell 'll be thar," he said, after a space of pondering. "Be s'prisin' ef she 'n M'ria 'd made et up ter know one anuther."

"M'ria wer' great on makin' friends," remarked Zeph, meditatively, "an' gells wus awful friendly wi' 'er. Seemed as she hed er power thet way."

"I never 'ad no wife," said Job, at this point, somewhat irrelevantly. It was a fact of which he was proud, and he made a frequent boast of it.

"Thet's naught ter cocker thysel on, lad," exclaimed one of the white-beards, who, until this time, had been silent. "Thou'lt find less folk in heaven t' greet thee."

"Thet's trewth, sure 'nuff, Jock," assented Nehemiah, and fixed a stern look on Job; whereat Job retired into silence.

Presently, at three bells, Josh came along and told them to put away their work for the day.

V

The second dog-watch came, and Nehemiah and the rest of his side, made their tea out upon the main hatch, along with their mates. When this was finished, as though by common agreement, they went every one and sat themselves upon the pin-rail running along under the t'gallant bulwarks; there, with their elbows upon the rail, they faced outward to gaze their full at the mystery of colour which had wrapped them about. From time to time, a pipe would be removed, and some slowly evolved thought given an utterance.

Eight bells came and went; but, save for the changing of the wheel and lookout, none moved from his place.

Nine o'clock, and the night came down upon the sea; but to those within the mist, the only result was a deepening of the rose colour into an intense red, which seemed to shine with a light of its own creating. Above them, the unseen sky seemed to be one vast blaze of silent, blood-tinted flame.

"Piller uv cloud by day, 'n er piller uv fire by night," muttered Zeph to Nehemiah, who crouched near.

"I reckon 's them's Bible words," said Nehemiah.

"Dunno," replied Zeph; "but them's thar very words as I heerd passon Myles a sayin' w'en thar timber wor afire down our way. 'Twer' mostly smoke 'n daylight; but et tarned ter 'n etarnal fire w'en thar night comed."

At four bells, the wheel and lookout were relieved, and a little later, Josh and Skipper Abe carne down on to the main-deck.

"Tur'ble queer," said Skipper Abe, with an affectation of indifference.

"Aye, 'tes, sure," said Nehemiah.

And after that, the two old men sat among the others; and watched.

At five bells, half-past ten, there was a murmur from those who sat nearest to the bows, and a cry from the man on the lookout. At that, the attention of all was turned to a point nearly right ahead. At this particular spot, the mist seemed to be glowing with a curious, unearthly red brilliance; and, a minute later, there burst upon their vision a vast arch, formed of blazing red clouds.

At the sight, each and every one cried out their amazement, and immediately began to run towards the fo'cas'le head. Here they congregated in a clump, the Skipper and the Mate among them. The arch appeared now to extend its arc far beyond either bow, so that the ship was heading to beyond right beneath it.

"'Tis 'eaven fer sure," murmured Josh to himself; but Zeph heard him.

"Reckon 's them's ther Gates uv Glory thet M'ria wus allus talkin' 'bout," he replied.

"Guess I'll see thet b'y er mine in er little," muttered Josh, and he craned forward, his eyes very bright and eager.

All about the ship was a great quietness. The wind was no more now than a light steady breath upon the port quarter; but from right ahead, as though issuing from the mouth of the radiant arch, the long-backed, foamless seas rolled up, black and oily.

Suddenly, amid the silence, there came a low musical note, rising and falling like the moan of a distant aeolian harp. The sound appeared to come from the direction of the arch, and the surrounding mist seemed to catch it up and send it sobbing and sobbing in low echoes away into the redness far beyond sight.

"They'm singin'," cried Zeph "M'ria wer' allus tur'ble fond uv singin'. Hark ter—"

" 'Sh!" interrupted Josh. "Thet's my b'y!" His shrill old voice had risen almost to a scream.

"It's wunnerful—wunnerful; just mazin'!" exclaimed Skipper Abe.

Zeph had gone a little forrard of the crowd. He was shading his eyes with his hands, and staring intently, his expression denoting the most intense excitement.

"B'lieve I see 'er. B'lieve I see 'er," he was muttering to himself, over and over again.

Behind him, two of the old men were steadying Nehemiah, who felt, as he put it, "a bit mazy at thar thought o' seein' thet gell."

Away aft, Nuzzie, the "b'y," was at the wheel. He had heard the moaning; but, being no more than a boy, it must be supposed that he knew nothing of the *nearness* of the next world, which was so evident to the men, his masters.

A matter of some minutes passed, and Job, who had in mind that farm upon which he had set his heart, ventured to suggest that heaven was less near than his mates supposed; but no one seemed to hear him, and he subsided into silence.

It was the better part of an hour later, and near to midnight, when a murmur among the watchers announced that a fresh matter had come to sight. They were yet a great way off from the arch; but still the thing showed clearly—a prodigious umbel, of a deep, burning red; but the crest of it was black, save for the very apex which shone with an angry red glitter.

"Thar Throne uv God!" cried out Zeph, in a loud voice, and went down upon his knees. The rest of the old men followed his example, and even old Nehemiah made a great effort to get to that position.

"Simly we'm a'most 'n 'eaven," he muttered huskily.

Skipper Abe got to his feet, with an abrupt movement. He had never heard of that extraordinary electrical phenomenon, seen once perhaps in a hundred years—the "Fiery Tempest" which precedes certain great Cyclonic Storms; but his experienced eye had suddenly discovered that the red-shining umbel was truly a low, whirling wa-ter-hill reflecting the red light. He had no theoretical knowledge to tell him that the thing was produced by an enormous air-vortice; but he had often seen a water-spout form. Yet, he was still undecided. It was all so beyond him; though, certainly, that monstrous gyrating hill of water, sending out a reflected glitter of burning red, appealed to him as having no place in his ideas of Heaven. And then, even as he hesitated, came the first, wild-beast bellow of the coming Cyclone. As the sound smote upon their ears, the old men looked at one another with bewildered, frightened eyes.

"Reck'n thet's God speakin'," whispered Zeph, "Guess we're on'y rnis'rable sinners."

The next instant, the breath of the Cyclone was in their throats, and the *Shamraken,* homeward-bounder, passed in through the everlasting portals.

Out of the Storm

"HUSH!" SAID MY FRIEND the scientist, as I walked into his laboratory. I had opened my lips to speak; but stood silent for a few minutes at his request.

He was sitting at his instrument, and the thing was tapping out a message in a curiously irregular fashion—stopping a few seconds, then going on at a furious pace.

It was during a somewhat longer than usual pause that, growing slightly impatient, I ventured to address him.

"Anything important?" I asked.

"For God's sake, shut up!" he answered back in a high, strained voice.

I stared. I am used to pretty abrupt treatment from him at times when he is much engrossed in some particular experiment; but this was going a little too far, and I said so.

He was writing, and, for reply, he pushed several loosely written sheets over to me with the one curt word, "Read!"

With a sense half of anger, half of curiosity, I picked up the first and glanced at it. After a few lines, I was gripped and held securely by a morbid interest. I was reading a message from one in the last extremity. I will give it word for word:—

"John, we are sinking! I wonder if you really understand what I feel at the present time—you sitting comfortably in your laboratory, I out here upon the waters, already one among the dead. Yes, we are doomed. There is no such thing as help in our case. We are sinking—steadily, remorselessly. God! I must keep up and be a man! I need not tell you that I am in the operator's room. All the rest are on deck—or dead in the hungry thing which is smashing the ship to pieces.

"I do not know where we are, and there is no one of whom I can ask. The last of the officers was drowned nearly an hour ago, and the

173

vessel is now little more than a sort of breakwater for the giant seas.

"Once, about half an hour ago, I went out onto the deck. My God! the sight was terrible. It is a little after midday; but the sky is the colour of mud—do you understand?—grey mud! Down from it there hang vast lappets of clouds. Not such clouds as I have ever before seen; but monstrous, mildewed-looking hulls. They show solid, save where the frightful wind tears their lower edges into great feelers that swirl savagely above us, like the tentacles of some enormous Horror.

"Such a sight is difficult to describe to the living; though the Dead of the Sea know of it without words of mine. It is such a sight that none is allowed to see and live. It is a picture for the doomed and the dead; one of the sea's hell-orgies—one of the *Thing's* monstrous gloatings over the living—say the alive-in-death, those upon the brink. I have no right to tell of it to you; to speak of it to one of the living is to initiate innocence into one of the infernal mysteries—to talk of foul things to a child. Yet I care not! I will expose, in all its hideous nakedness, the death-side of the sea. The undoomed living shall know some of the things that death has hitherto so well guarded. Death knows not of this little instrument beneath my hands that connects me still with the quick, else would he haste to quiet me.

"Hark you, John! I have learnt undreamt of things in this little time of waiting. I know now why we are afraid of the dark. I had never imagined such secrets of the sea and the grave (which are one and the same).

"Listen! Ah, but I was forgetting you cannot hear! I can! The Sea is—Hush! the Sea is laughing, as though Hell cackled from the mouth of an ass. It is jeering. I can hear its voice echo like Satanic thunder amid the mud overhead—It is calling to me! call—I must go—The sea calls!

"Oh! God, art Thou indeed God? Canst Thou sit above and watch calmly that which I have just seen? Nay! Thou art no God! Thou art weak and puny beside this foul *Thing* which Thou didst create in Thy lusty youth. *It* is *now* God—and I am one of its children.

"Are you there, John? Why don't you answer! Listen! I ignore God; for there is a stronger than He. My God is here, beside me, around me, and will be soon above me. You know what that means. It is merciless. *The sea is now all the God there is!* That is one of the things I have learnt.

"Listen! *it*, is laughing again. God is *it*, not He.

"It called, and I went out onto the decks. All was terrible. *It* is in the waist—everywhere. *It* has swamped the ship. Only the forecastle, bridge and poop stick up out from the bestial, reeking *Thing,* like three islands in the midst of shrieking foam. At times gigantic billows assail the ship from both sides. They form momentary arches above the vessel—arches of dull, curved water half a hundred feet towards the hideous sky. Then they descend—roaring. Think of it! You cannot.

"There is an infection of sin in the air: it is the exhalations from the *Thing.* Those left upon the drenched islets of shattered wood and iron are doing the most horrible things. The *Thing* is teaching them. Later, I felt the vile informing of its breath; but I have fled back here—to pray for death.

"On the forecastle, I saw a mother and her little son clinging to an iron rail. A great billow heaved up above them—descended in a falling mountain of brine. It passed, and they were still there. The *Thing* was only toying with them; yet, all the same, it had torn the hands of the child from the rail, and the child was clinging frantically to its Mother's arm. I saw another vast hill hurl up to port and hover above them. Then the Mother stooped and bit like a foul beast at the hands of her wee son. She was afraid that his little additional weight would be more than she could hold. I heard his scream even where I stood—it drove to me upon that wild laughter. It told me again that God is not He, but *It.* Then the hill thundered down upon those two. It seemed to me that the *Thing* gave a bellow as it leapt. It roared about them churning and growling; then surged away, and there was only one—the Mother. There appeared to me to be blood as well as water upon her face, especially about her mouth; but the distance was too great, and I cannot be sure. I looked away. Close to me, I saw something further—a beautiful young girl (her soul hideous with the breath of the *Thing*) struggling with her sweetheart for the shelter of the chart-house side. He threw her off; but she came back at him. I saw her hand come from her head, where still clung the wreckage of some form of headgear. She struck at him. He shouted and fell away to leeward, and she—smiled, showing her teeth. So much for that. I turned elsewhere.

"Out upon the *Thing,* I saw gleams, horrid and suggestive, below the crests of the waves. I have never seen them until this time. I saw a rough sailorman washed away from the vessel. One of the huge breakers snapped at him! —Those things were teeth. It has teeth. I heard them clash. I heard his yell. It was no more than a mosquito's shrilling amid all that laughter; but it was very terrible. There is worse than death.

"The ship is lurching very queerly with a sort of sickening heave—

"I fancy I have been asleep. No—I remember now. I hit my head when she rolled so strangely. My leg is doubled under me. I think it is broken; but it does not matter—

"I have been praying. I—I—What was it? I feel calmer, more resigned, now. I think I have been mad. What was it that I was saying? I cannot remember. It was something about—about—God. I—I believe I blasphemed. May He forgive me! Thou knowest, God, that I was not in my right mind. Thou knowest that I am very weak. Be with me in the coming time! I have sinned; but Thou art all merciful.

"Are you there, John? It is very near the end now. I had so much to say; but it all slips from me. What was it that I said? I take it all back. I was mad, and—and God knows. He is merciful, and I have very little pain now. I feel a bit drowsy.

"I wonder whether you are there, John. Perhaps, after all, no one has heard the things I have said. It is better so. The Living are not meant—and yet, I do not know. If you are there, John, you will—you will tell *her* how it was; but not—not—Hark! there was such a thunder of water overhead just then. I fancy two vast seas have met in mid-air across the top of the bridge and burst all over the vessel. It must be soon now—and there was such a number of things I had to say! I can hear voices in the wind. They are singing. It is like an enormous dirge—

"I think I have been dozing again. I pray God humbly that it be soon! You will not—not tell *her* anything about, about what I may have said, will you, John? I mean those things which I ought not to have said. What was it I did say? My head is growing strangely confused. I wonder whether you really do hear me. I may be talking only to that vast roar outside. Still, it is some comfort to go on, and I will not believe that you do not hear all I say. Hark again! A mountain of brine must have swept clean over the vessel. She has gone right over on to her side.... She is back again. It will be very soon now—

"Are you there, John? Are you there? It is coming! The Sea has come for me! It is rushing down through the companion-way! It—it is like a vast jet! My God! I am dr-own-ing! I—am—dr—"

The Albatross

I

"CONFOUND THAT BRUTE!" I shouted in sheer desperation. Then I sang out to the 'prentice who was keeping "time" on the lee side of the poop, to bring me a piece of spun-yarn and a marlinspike.

I was First Mate of the *Skylark*, full-rigged ship, and we were off the Horn on a cold, absolutely windless night. It was the twelve to four watch in the early morning, and four bells (two o'clock) had just gone.

All the watch there had been an enormous albatross flying round and round the vessel; sometimes he would actually fly across the decks, which is a thing I have never known to happen before.

When the boy brought the marlinspike and the yarn, I bent on about two fathoms of the latter, so that I had a sort of handy little harpoon. Then I slipped quickly up the mizzen rigging and out onto the cross jack yard, where I waited with the spike ready in one hand and the end of the line held fast in the other.

Presently, away forward in the still night, I heard the dismal *squark* of the great bird, and immediately a spate of blasphemy from the man on the lookout, who was evidently getting as much bothered as I by the actions of the creature.

Not a sound then for maybe ten minutes; and then suddenly I saw something float between me and the dim skyline and come inboard. I lost it for a moment; but immediately there came the loud, dismal *squark* out of the night to my left, and directly afterward I saw vaguely that something was passing under the yard. I raised the marlinspike and drove down at the thing with all my strength, letting the line fly out to its full length. There was a rustle of feathers and a tugging on the line, and the bird *squarked* twice. Then a jerk and the snap of something breaking, and the great albatross was gone free.

I hauled in on the spun-yarn until I had the marlinspike again in my hand; as I passed it between my fingers I felt that there was some-

177

thing caught round the butt, something that felt like a piece of rag.
I loosed it from the spike. Then I went down again onto the poop,
and at once to the light of the main binnacle, to see what it was that
had got caught round the marlinspike. I could not see the thing very
plainly at first, and I took the lamp out of the holder, so as to have a
better light. I found then that it was a strip of red silk, such as might
be torn from a girl's blouse. At one end was a piece of broken tape.
For some minutes I examined the thing very carefully. It was in this
way that I found presently a single long hair, tangled in the knot of the
tape. I picked it loose, gently, and looked at it; then I coiled it round
and round my forefinger. It was a girl's hair, brown, with a glint of
gold in it! What did it mean? We were off Cape Horn—one of the
grim, lonely places of the ocean!

After a while I replaced the lamp in the binnacle and resumed
my ordinary tramp of the weather-side of the poop. All the while I
was turning this matter over in my brain, and presently I went back
again to the light, so that I might have another look at the piece of
silk. I saw then that it could not have been very long since it had been
torn; for it was very little frayed at the tear and had no appearance of
having been weatherworn for more than a few days. Also, the material
was new and seemed to be of very fine quality. I grew more puzzled.

Of course it was possible that there was another sailing-ship within
a hundred miles of us; it was also possible that such a vessel had a girl
aboard, perhaps the Captain's daughter; it was also possible that they
had caught this particular albatross on a line and tied the silk to it and
let it go again. But it was also exceedingly improbable. For sailors will
always keep an albatross for the sake of the wing-bones, which make
pipe-stems, and the webs, which make purses, and the breast, which
makes a gorgeous fire-screen; while others prize the great bill and the
beautiful wing-tips.

Moreover, even if the bird had been loosed, why had some one
torn up a new silk garment, when a piece of old bunting would have
done just as well? You can see how my thoughts were trending. That
piece of silk and that long pretty hair coming to me suddenly out of
the night in that lonely and desolate sea had stirred me with vague
wonderings. Yet I never put my wonderments actually into words, but
went back to my constant pacing fore and aft. And so, presently, the
Second Mate came up at eight bells to relieve me.

The next day, through all the eight-to-twelve forenoon watch, I
kept a pretty keen lookout for albatross, but the whole sea was lonely,
and though there was such an absolute calm, there was not even a

Mother Carey's chicken in sight—only everywhere, so far as the sight might reach, an everlasting grey desolation of water.

The afternoon watch I went below for a sleep. Then, in the first dog-watch, a little before three bells, I saw a great albatross swing and glide against the grey of the sky, about a mile astern. I reached for my glasses and had a good look. I saw the bird plainly, a huge, bony-shouldered albatross, with a queer bulge below the breast. As I stared at him, I grew suddenly excited, for I saw that the bulge was really a packet of some kind tied onto the creature, and there was something fluttering from it.

In the second dog-watch, I asked two of my 'prentices to come down with me into the sail-locker and help me root out an old seine-net that we carried for occasional sport. I told them I was going to have a try for the big albatross that night, if he started flying across the decks again, and they were nearly as keen as I, though I had asked them to do this sail-tossing in their watch below.

When my watch came, from eight until midnight, I did nothing until the "Old Man" had turned in for the night; then I had my boys rig lines for the big net from the main and the mizzen masts, so that we could hoist it up at any moment and let it hang like a curtain between the masts.

The night was very quiet and dark, and though it was difficult to see anything, it would have been easy to hear the bird at a great distance. Yet for over an hour after this there was no sign of anything, and I began to think that we were not to have a visit. However, just after four bells had gone (ten o'clock) there came from far away over the sea the strange lonely *squark, squark* of an albatross, and a few minutes later I had a vague glimpse of him flying silently round and round the ship, in the way common enough with his kind. Presently he gave out a loud *squark* and turned inboard to fly over the poop. The next instant there was a loud *squarking* up in the night, and a constant beating of heavy wings. I shouted to the boys at the lines to lower away, and a moment later I was shining the binnacle light on a fluster of beating wings and tangled net.

I sang out to the nearest 'prentice to hold the lamp while I disentangled the albatross and found out what the package was that was made fast to him. The parcel was done up in layer after layer of oilskin, and from the outside there was another such streamer of red silk as the one that had caught on my spike the night before. Then I had come to the last of the wrappings of oilskin and there were a couple of pages torn from a log-book and folded very tight and compact. I opened them, and found that they were covered with hasty feminine handwriting. And this is what I read:

This is written aboard the *Unicorn,* derelict, on the twenty-first day of March, 1904. She was run down by an unknown steamer ten days ago. I am here alone, living in the chart-house. I have food and water sufficient to last me for about a week longer, if I am very careful. The vessel seems to be floating with her decks just a little above the water, and every time the sea is a bit rough it just pours aboard of her.

I am sending this message tied round the neck of an albatross. The captain shot it the day before we were run down, and hurt the poor creature's wing. I told him he was an inhuman brute. I am sorry now, for he, along with every other soul, is dead, drowned. He was a brave man. The men crowded into the boats, and he stood with his revolver and tried to stop them, saying that no one should leave the ship before I was safe. He shot two of them, but the others threw him into the sea. They were mad. They took the boats and went away; and my maid went with them. But it was terribly rough, and I saw them sink just a little way from the ship.

I have been alone ever since, except for the albatross. I have nursed it, and now it seems as if it should be able to fly. I pray God that this message be found before it is too late! If any find it, come and save a girl from an awful and lonely death. The position of the ship is written down in the logbook here in the chart-house, so I will give it; then you will know where to search for me. It is Latitude 62° 7' S. and Longitude 67° 10' W.

I have sent other messages corked up in bottles; but this is the one in which I have all my hope. I shall tie a piece of something red to it, so that any one seeing my albatross will know it is carrying something and try to catch it. Come, come, come, as quickly as ever you can!

There are enormous numbers of rats about. I suppose the water has driven them up out of the holds and places; but they make me afraid to sleep. Remember, the food I have won't last more than a week, and I am here all alone. But I will be brave. Only don't give up searching for me. The wind has been blowing from the north ever since the night

when the boats sank. It is quite calm now. Perhaps these
things will help you to know where to look for me, as I can
see that the wind must make the ship drift. Don't give me
up! Remember I'm waiting, waiting, and trying to be brave.
      Mary Doriswold.

You can imagine how I felt, when I had finished reading this paper.
Our position that day was 58° S. and 67° 30' W.; so that we were at
least two hundred and fifty miles to the north of the place where the
derelict had been eighteen days earlier; for it was now the twenty-ninth
day of March. And there, somewhere away to the southward of us, a
girl was dying of hunger and lonesomeness! And there was absolutely
no sign of wind.

After a little while I told the boys to clear away the net and take the
albatross down on to the main-deck and tie it to one of the ring-bolts.
Then I took a turn or two up and down the poop, and finally decided
to go down and call the "Old Man" and set the matter before him.

When he had heard what I had to tell, he slipped into his clothes
and came out into the saloon, where he read the letter twice, very
carefully. Then he had a look at the barometer, and afterward came
up with me onto the poop and had a look at the weather; but there
were certainly no immediate signs of wind.

Through all the rest of the watch he walked up and down with
me, discussing the thing, and went several times to the binnacle to
make fresh examinations of the letter. Once I suggested the possibility
of manning one of the life-boats and trying down to the southward,
letting the ship follow on so soon as the wind came. But, of course,
he would not listen to this, and very rightly, too. For not only would it
have been to risk the lives of all who went in the boat, but to risk the
vessel also, because we should have had to leave her undermanned.
And so the only thing we could do was to pray for wind.

Down on the main-deck I could hear presently the murmur of
voices, and I knew that the men had got the news and were talking it
over; but that was all that we could do.

At midnight, when the Second Mate came up to relieve me, he
had already learned the story from the 'prentice who called him, and
when finally I went below, he and the Skipper were still discussing it.

At four o'clock, when I was waked, my first inquiry was about the
wind; but there was not a sign, and when I got on the poop I could
see that the weather still had the same dead, settled look.

All that day we kept waiting for the wind that never came; and at last a deputation of the men came aft to ask to be allowed to volunteer to man one of the life-boats and make a search party. But the Master sent them forward again, quietly enough, and even took the trouble to point out the hopelessness of such an attempt, as well as the tremendous risk. For if the derelict were still above water, she might have drifted sufficiently far to be still lost after weeks of searching in the great unknown seas to the southward.

All that day the wind never came, and all that day there was nothing else talked about aboard except the chances of saving the girl. And when at last night came I do not believe half the watch below turned in, but paced the decks, whistling for wind and watching the weather.

The morning came, and still the calm; and at last I asked the Captain whether he would give me permission to take the little gig, which was a light and handy boat, and make the trial alone. I said that if I failed, and the boat was lost, her value would be amply covered by the wages due to me. But the "Old Man" simply refused to listen to the idea, and told me, kindly enough, that it was madness.

I saw that it was no use arguing with him, for he was perfectly right in what he said; but at the same time I was determined to try, if the wind did not come by the evening. For I could not get the thought of that lonely unknown girl out of my mind, and I kept remembering what she had said about the rats.

II

That night, when the Captain had gone below, I had a talk with the Steward, and afterward I gave orders to get the little gig quietly into the water. I provisioned her thoroughly and added a bottle of brandy and a bottle of rum. The Second Mate fitted her with a boat's compass and binnacle from one of the life-boats, and also attended to the filling of the water-breakers, and saw that all the gear was in place. Then I added my oilskins, some rugs and canvas, and my sextant and chronometer and charts, and so forth. At the last I remembered my shotgun, and ran down for this and plenty of cartridges; for there was no saying how useful it might be.

I shook hands with the Second Mate, when I returned, and went down into the boat.

"We'll be after you as soon as the wind comes," he said quietly. "Good luck!"

I nodded, and afterward mentioned one or two details of ship's work which would need attention. Then I pulled in the painter and pushed off. As I cleared the side of the vessel, there came a hushed cheering, and hoarse whispers of, "Good luck, Sir! Good luck, Sir!"

The lamp in the little binnacle was lit, and I turned the hood round, so that I could watch the compass as I pulled. Then I settled down to my work at the oars, and presently the vessel had faded away from me into the night, though for a long while there would come over the sea to me the odd rustle and flap of a sail, as the ship lifted to the occasional glassy swell. But afterward I rowed on through an everlasting silence toward the south.

Twice in the night I ceased work, and ate and drank; then onward again, keeping to an easy, regular pull that I knew I could keep up hour after hour.

In the morning I had a good look round, but the *Skylark* was lost below the horizon astern, and the whole world seemed empty. It was a most extraordinary and depressing sensation. I had an early breakfast, and rowed on. Later, I got my longitude; at midday I took my altitude and found that I had done nearly fifty miles to the south.

All that day I pulled steadily, stopping only to eat and drink at regular intervals. That night I slept for six hours, from twelve until six, and when I waked there was still the everlasting calm.

Four more days and nights I went onward in this fashion. All the fourth day I pulled steadily, stopping every half-hour to take a look round; but there was always and only the grey emptiness of the sea. All that night I drifted; for I had passed over, and was now to the southward of the position of the derelict given by the girl, and I dared not row in the darkness, for fear of passing the wreck.

Part of the night I used in making calculations, and afterward had a good long sleep. I was wakened in the dawn by the lapping of water against the boat, and found that a light breeze had sprung up from the west. This cheered me immensely for I knew that now the *Skylark* would be able to follow, provided that the wind was not merely a local breeze. And, in any case, there was no longer need to use the oars, for I had a mast and sail in the boat.

I stepped the mast and hoisted the lug-sail; then I shipped the rudder and sat down to rest and steer. And it is impossible to express my gratitude; for my hands were raw with broken blisters, and I ached in all my body with the constant and weary labor at the oars.

All that day I ran to the southward, keeping a lookout; but never a sign was there of anything, so that an utter dismay began to come down on me. Yet I did not give up hoping. That night I made fresh calculations, with the result that next morning, as soon as I had hoisted the sail (for I had let the boat drift during the darkness), I altered my course a few degrees to the eastward. At noon I found that I was a hundred and twenty-seven miles to the south and forty-six miles to the east of the last known position of the *Unicorn*. If I sighted nothing by evening, I would make a long tack next day to the north, a few miles eastward of my downward run.

I ran on until the dusk came; and then, after a final long look round, I dropped my sail for the night and set the boat to ride by the painter to a couple of oars, as I had done on the previous nights of drifting.

I felt desperately disheartened, and began to realise more thoroughly my own position, over four hundred miles from the *Skylark* and in a latitude of hopeless and weary storms and utterly unfrequented by ships. Yet I fought this down and finally settled myself to sleep, well wrapped up in my rugs, for it was bitterly cold, though so fine.

It was some time after midnight that something waked me, and I sat up in the darkness and looked about and listened. I could not imagine what had roused me, but I felt that I had heard something, though there was no sound in all the night, except the low blowing of the wind and the rippling of the water against the boat.

And then, suddenly, as I sat there harking, there came over the sea from the southward the desolate mournful blowing of a foghorn. I stood up abruptly and threw all my rugs from me into the bottom of the boat.

I ran down in the direction of the foghorn, and in ten minutes or so I saw against the sky the spars of a big four-masted vessel. I dropped the sail and shipped the oars. As I pulled toward her, the sound of the horn broke out into the night in a dull roar, coming from the after-part of the vessel. I backed the boat aft, noticing as I did so that the vessel stood no more than three or four feet above the level of the sea.

Then, as I came opposite to the place where the horn seemed to be, I saw dimly that the deck rose here, and that I was come opposite to the poop. I rested on my oars. "Miss Doriswold!" I shouted. "Miss Doriswold!"

The fog-horn gave a short, impotent blare, and immediately a girl's voice called:

"Who is that? Who is that?" in a queer, frightened, breathless way.

"It's all right!" I shouted back. "We got your message! I'm the Mate of the *Skylark*, the ship that got the message. I'm coming aboard."

The answer astonished me.

"Don't come onto the ship!" the voice called back to me, shrill and anxious. "Keep the boat away! Keep the boat away! There are thousands of rats—"

It broke off abruptly, and there was the sound of a pistol shot up in the darkness. At that, I had the painter fast in a moment and, catching up my gun, vaulted aboard. In an instant the girl's voice came again: "I'm all right. Don't come aboard, whatever you do! It's the rats! Wait for the daylight!"

Even before she spoke, I was aware of a sound along the poop like the harsh noise of several saws at work. I walked aft a few steps, groping, and knew suddenly that there was a faint, curious smell everywhere about me in the night. I paused and stared through the darkness.

"Where are you?" I shouted, and then I saw the black bulk of the chart-house vaguely through the darkness. I went forward a pace, and stumbled clumsily over a deck ring-bolt. "Where are you?" I shouted again. "I've come aboard."

"Go back! Go back! Go back!" called the girl's voice shrilly, with a note of utter fear and horror in it. "Get into the boat, *quick!* I'll explain. Go back! Go back!"

III

There came to me in the same moment a strange sense of restlessness all about the decks, and then, suddenly, all the air seemed to be full of an odd whining noise, that rose into a horrible shrill, twittering keening of sound. I heard a massed sound, as of thousands of small scuttering bodies coming toward me at a run through the darkness. The voice of the girl came in the same instant, crying out something in a frightened voice. But I never heard what she said, for something plucked my trousers, and immediately hundreds of creatures sprang upon me and swarmed over me, biting and tearing. My gun was utterly useless, and in an instant I knew that if I would save my life I must go overboard. I made a mad, staggering run to the side of the derelict, the rats flocking about me. With my free hand I was tearing their great bodies from me and keeping them from my face. The hideous little brutes were so thick upon me that I was loaded with them. I reached the rail and got over somehow, and fell souse down into the icy cold water.

I stayed under water deliberately, as long as I could; and the rats left me and went to the surface to breathe. I swam hard until my head felt as if it would burst; then I came up, and found that I was clear of the rats. I discovered that I still had my gun in my left hand, and I was careful not to lose it. I swam forward until I was opposite the boat. I heard the girl's voice calling something to me, but the water in my ears prevented me from hearing what it was.

"Are you safe? Are you safe? Where are you?" the girl was calling.

"I'm all right, thanks!" I shouted back. "I'm in the boat. I'll wait till daylight, if you're sure you are safe."

She assured me that she was all right, now that I had come, and could easily hold out until the morning. In the meanwhile I had stripped off my wet things and got into the spares I had brought with me and for which I was very thankful now, as you can imagine. All the time, as I changed, the girl and I kept up a conversation. I asked her about food; she told me she had eaten nothing for three days and nights but had still some water, and I was not to try to reach her until daylight came to show me the position of everything.

This, however, would not satisfy me, and as I completed my dressing a sudden thought came to me. I struck a match and lit the binnacle-lamp and also the boat's lantern, which was in the midship locker. Then I hooked the ring of the lantern over the spike of the boat-hook and reached the lantern up on to the poop of the derelict, where I set it on the deck. I could see the chart-house plainly now, and a pale but very beautiful face was looking at me through the glass of one of the ports. It was Miss Doriswold, and I waved to her with the boat-hook. She opened the port about an inch and called out to know what I was going to do. I told her she would see very quickly. Then I stuck the boat-hook into the handle of the binnacle-lamp and ran to the other end of the boat, where I was able to set it inboard on the poop-deck, some way farther aft than the boat-lamp.

I got the bottom boards of the boat now and set them across from gunnel to gunnel of the boat, and then, taking my gun and a pocket full of cartridges, I stood on this temporary erection and looked aboard.

I saw a most extraordinary sight, and really a very horrible one; for in the light of the lamps the *decks were literally black and moving with rats,* and the shining of their eyes in the lights made a constant, myriad twinkling from a thousand places at once, as the rats shifted this way and that. All about the base of the house there seemed to be rats, and I could see dimly that they had been at the woodwork of the house, but as there was a steel combing in at the back of the teak, very few had been able to get in, and then only by the door, as I learned afterward.

I glanced at the port, but Miss Doriswold was not there, and as I looked there came the flare of a match and immediately the sharp report of a pistol shot. In a minute she returned to the port and cast out a big rat, which was instantly set upon by hundreds of others in a great black scramble. Then I raised my gun so that it was just a little above the level of the poop-deck and fired both barrels into that struggling crowd of little monsters. Several rolled over and died, and over a dozen ran about wounded and squealing, but in a moment both the wounded and the dead were covered with the living rats and literally torn to pieces.

I reloaded quickly and began now to fire shot after shot among the hideous little brutes, and with every thud of the gun they lay dying and dead over the deck, and every time the living rats would leap onto the dead and wounded and destroy them, devouring them practically alive.

In ten minutes I had killed hundreds, and within the next half hour I must have destroyed a thousand, to make a rough guess. The gun was almost red-hot in my hands. The dead began now to lie about the decks; for most of the rats were destroyed and the living rats had begun to run into hiding. I waved to Miss Doriswold, and we began to talk, while the gun was cooling.

She told me she had been fighting the brutes off for the last four days, but that she had burned all her candles and had been forced to stay in the dark, only striking a match now and again (of which she had several boxes left) when the sounds at the door told her that a rat had nearly gnawed his way through. Then she would fire the Captain's revolver at the brute, block the hole up with coal, and sit quiet in the dark, waiting for the next. Sometimes the rats got through in other places, above the steel combing. In this way she had been badly bitten several times, but had always managed to kill the rats and block the holes.

Presently, when the gun was cool again, I began to shoot systematically at every rat in sight, so that soon I had killed and driven the little monsters clear off the visible parts of the poop-deck. I jumped aboard then, and walked round the house, with the boat-lantern and my gun. In this way I surprised and shot a score of rats that were hiding in the shadows, and after that there was not a rat to be seen anywhere.

"They're gone!" I shouted to Miss Doriswold, and in the same moment I heard her unlocking the chart-house door, and she came out onto the deck. She looked dreadfully haggard and seemed a little uncertain on her feet, but even thus I could see how pretty she was.

"Oh!" she said, and staggered and gripped the corner of the chart-house. She tried to say something further, but I thought she was going to fall and caught her arm to lead her back into the house.

"No!" she whispered breathlessly. "Not in there!" And I helped her to the seat on the side of the skylight. Then I ran to the boat for brandy, water and food, and presently I saw the life begin to come back into her. She told me later that she had not slept for four nights. And once she tried to thank me, but she was dumb that way—only her eyes said all the rest.

Afterward, I got her to the boat, and when I had seen her safe and comfortable, I left her there and walked the poop of the derelict until daylight. And she, now that she felt safe, slept through the whole night and far into the daylight.

When she waked I helped her aboard again and she insisted on preparing our breakfast. There was a fireplace in the chart-house, and coal, and I broke up the front of one of the hen-coops for kindling-wood. Soon we were drinking hot coffee and eating sea-biscuit and tinned meat. Then we went out on deck to walk up and down and talk. In this way she learned my side of the story, and questioned me closely on every point.

"Oh," she said at last, holding out both hands to me, "may God bless you!" I took her hands and looked at her with the strangest mixture of awkwardness and happiness. Then she slipped her hands from me and we went again to our constant pacing. Presently I had to send her to rest, though she would not at first, because she felt too happy to sit still; but afterward she was glad to be quiet.

Through four days and nights we waited for the *Skylark*. The days we had entirely together; the nights she slept in the chart-house, and I in the little alley-way, with just a few feet below me the roll and gurgle of the water going through the waterlogged cabins of the half-sunk vessel. Odd whiles I would rise and see that the lamp was burning brightly in the rigging, so that the *Skylark* would not pass us in the darkness.

On the morning of the fourth day, after we had made our breakfast happily together, we went out for our usual walk of the poop. The wind still continued light, but there were heavy clouds to the northward, which made me very anxious. Then, suddenly, Miss Doriswold cried out that she saw the ship, and in the same moment I saw her, too. We turned and looked at each other. Yet it was not all happiness that was in us. There was a half-questioning in the girl's eyes, and abruptly I held out my arms!

Two hours later we were safely aboard the *Skylark,* under only the main lower top-sail, and the wind coming down out of the north like thunder while to leeward the lonesome derelict was lost in huge clouds of spray.

The 'Prentices' Mutiny

I

IN GIVING THE FOLLOWING account of an actual and distinctly unusual happening, I have discovered, somewhat to my disgust, how awkward crude facts are to recount with plausibility. In fiction one realizses that mere statements are not sufficient; the invented fact must always have a road of plausible lies to aid its journey into the reader's belief. Here, dealing with the bald, naked truth, I am permitted to make no preparatory road of plausible inventions. I am allowed only to present to you the things that actually happened—in short, the truth.

I have also endeavoured to present, along with the narrative of what occurred, a slight though constant picture of the emotions and feelings of the actors in the scenes I have set out.

Finally, I wish the reader to understand definitely that, for the sake of many who are yet living, in different parts of this little world of ours, the names of the personalities mentioned herein have been altered, and certain other precautions taken to safeguard them from any results which might follow upon the publication of this severely unvarnished account of their several actions in the affair of this quite unique mutiny.

The following is, as far as possible, an exact account of the mutiny of the eight 'prentices of the full-rigged ship *Lady Morgan*—a thoroughly serious affair that occurred on the voyage home round Cape Horn.

On the voyage out from England the *Lady Morgan* carried only two apprentices, youngsters of fifteen and sixteen, who endured a very great deal of rough treatment, notably at the hands of William Beeston, the Master; Jan Henricksen, the Second Mate; and Carl Schieffs, the Bo'sun. The indignities and sufferings that these two boys endured go to prove that the harsh treatment of young lads at sea is not so much a matter of the past as one could wish.

The Mate, Robert Jenkins, though stern and brusque, treated the two youths with ordinary fairness, and as a result they had very warm feelings for him. His attitude to them was no better and no worse than that of most officers in well-disciplined vessels; but, standing alone for fairness, amid so much petty and brutal treatment, his conduct appears more humane, by the mere force of the contrast, than was probably the case.

The boys' names were Harold Jones and Mercer Kinniks, and among some of their punishments and inflictions I may mention the following: Having to pace the lee side of the poop with a heavy cap-stan-bar in each hand during the whole of their night watch; having to stay on deck during the afternoon watch below, though the men were allowed to go below as usual; having to go aloft at night and sit on the main-royal yard-arm for the whole four hours of the watch; being constantly kept on deck at nights, when it was properly their watch below; being both kicked and rope-ended on a number of occasions; and having many times a bucket of sea-water hove over them, fully dressed as they were, so that often they had no dry clothes to wear.

This kind of thing was common all the way out to 'Frisco, where, as good fortune would have it, Captain Beeston was cabled to by his company to take aboard six apprentices from another of their vessels. This ship had just been sold to a Dutch timber-carrying firm, and the 'prentices out of her were transferred to the *Lady Morgan* so that they might work their passage home in her in the ordinary way.

Now the six new lads were all of them, excepting the youngest, second and third voyagers—powerful, hefty youths, determined not to knuckle down to the kind of treatment which Jones and Kinniks told them they had received.

It may be that, being indignant at what they heard from the two other 'prentices, and anxious to show that they would not be "hazed" likewise, they really displayed what may have appeared to the officers an attitude of almost wanton insubordination, and so actually invited the rough handling they were determined to resist.

That they endured a harder time than ever they had expected is undoubtedly true; for both the Master and the Second Mate were big men, and could use their hands more than a bit, as the saying goes. So that on those occasions when some one of the new 'prentices made an attempt to stand up for himself the results were neither pleasant to the youth nor to those who had to look on.

In justice to the First Mate, it must be stated that this kind of thing occurred, in the natural course of the ship's routine, largely in his watch below, during the Second's charge of the deck; so that he saw only a part of the rough usage the lads endured. Moreover, when the Master ill-treated the 'prentices during the First Mate's watch on deck the Mate's unspoken disapproval produced a certain amount of restraint on his actions, with the result that he seldom saw the brutal extremes to which things were being carried; for the Bo'sun (an animal of a man) soon discovered that the First Mate had no especial taste for "hazing," and therefore took care to satisfy his appetite for brutality chiefly in the Second Mate's watch.

The name of the senior apprentice was Wyckliffe, but he was always called Jumbo in the berth, on account of his size, and because of his big, slow, good-humoured way of going about things. He was really an exceptionally powerful young man of nineteen, and had so far escaped any personal experience of rough usage, as had also Bullard, the next oldest lad—a strong and well-made youth.

These two, after a consultation, called a meeting of all the 'prentices in the "Glory Hole" ('prentices' berth) one second dog-watch, and told them that they had decided to stand by the next lad who was badly treated, and that they had all better swear to stand by each other every time anyone was knocked about. Jumbo made it plain that he was not proposing they should stand out at any minor act of bullying, such as docking them of their watch below, but only in actual cases of any of them being hit or kicked—a thing that was now becoming of daily occurrence.

As a result of this decision and compact, there was in the morning watch of the very next day a tremendous fight up on the poop between the Captain, Second Mate, and Bo'sun on the one side and seven of the 'prentices on the other.

It happened through the Second Mate catching hold of young Kinniks by the ear and repeatedly kicking him, with his heavy sea boot, from one end of the poop to the other. Kinniks remembered the compact and shouted for help. Instantly, almost, two of the 'prentices in his watch came flying up on to the poop, having first shouted a warning of what was going onto the four of the watch below, who were just about to turn in. These also followed, just as they were, in their pyjamas, the sleepy Jumbo being the first of the lot. Before the Second Mate well knew what had occurred, Kinniks was pulled from him, and he had to face young Jumbo instead.

"We protest, Sir," he said, "against this kind of treatment, which is both illegal and brutal."

The Second Mate almost gasped; then, without a word, he hit the apprentice with all his might, breaking his front teeth and sending him stunned to the deck. He next turned on the others, cursing, shouting meanwhile for the Master, Beeston, and Schieffs, the Bo'sun. The lads all fought doggedly, and Henricksen would have been badly mauled had not Captain Beeston and the Bo'sun come quickly to his aid. The Bo'sun was serving some foot-ropes at the time, and he came running up onto the poop, carrying his heavy teak serving mallet. With this he nearly killed two of the younger boys, named respectively Darkins and Peters, and within a minute the whole seven of the boys were either knocked senseless or being unmercifully kicked by the three men into abject submission.

I had better state here that the opinions of the men (*i.e.*, the A.B.'s for'ard in the fo'c'sle) upon the treatment accorded the 'prentices was divided, some holding that it did boys good to be "handled" a bit, others that it was a shame and ought to be stopped; others, again, thought that the 'prentices were "uppish," and got no more than they deserved.

This, I think, gives very fairly the attitudes of the men, and the reason why there was no attempt to interfere between the after-guard and the lads.

Meanwhile, up on the poop Captain Beeston was shouting to the Steward to bring up the irons. When these were brought, Jumbo, Bullard, and Connaught, the three biggest 'prentices, were trussed up, after which the Second Mate and the Bo'sun carried them down into the pantry and fairly tumbled them into the lazarette. In this way the three most formidable lads were disposed of. Of the others, the two who had been hit by the Bo'sun's serving mallet were put into their bunks to recover, whilst Kinniks and Jones, the two young *Lady Morgan* apprentices, were sent aloft to grease down.

I have said that the three most formidable 'prentices were down in the lazarette securely in irons; but in this I am hardly correct, for the most formidable lad of the lot, as events proved, was at that moment down in the fore-peak (away up in the bows of the ship) routing out paint-drums, and sublimely unconscious of what had just happened to his berth-mates. When he came on deck, however, he was speedily learned.

"Your mates 'ave bin gettin what-for, my son!" one of the men informed him, grinning.

"Yes," said another; "and from what I saw I shouldn't be surprised to hear that them two young'uns won't get better. There'll be the deuce

to pay then, an' serve them three big brutes right. It'll mean hangin';
that's what it'll mean!"

Larry Edwards (generally called "Tommy Dodd") waited for
nothing more, but raced aft, where he found things quite as bad as
the men had pictured to him. Darkins and Peters still lay senseless in
their bunks, breathing with queer little gasps. He ran in through the
saloon doorway, under the break of the poop, for the Steward, and
found him in his pantry.

"Steward," he said, "have you been to Darkins and Peters? Those
brutes have laid them out while I was down the fore-peak, and they
look awful bad."

"Hush!" whispered the Steward, holding up his hand. "The Old
Man's sittin' in the saloon, an' I darsent come yet. I was goin' to have
a look at 'em just now, but he saw me, an' told me to let 'em lie, or
he'd put me the same way. He's just rampin', the drunken old brute.
But I'll come the minute he goes into his cabin to lie down."

"Steward," said Tommy, very earnestly, "Darkins and Peters are
going to die, I believe, unless something's done. You've got to come,
or there'll be a murder trial when we get home, and you'll show up
pretty bad."

This frightened the Steward, and, after much hesitation, he slipped
out of his pantry, along the alley-way, out through the doorway under
the poop, and there waited until he heard the Second Mate's footsteps
going aft in his continual pacing of the poop overhead; then he literally darted for'ard, round the mizzen hatch, and into the small steel
after-deckhouse, where the 'prentices lived.

"Shut the door," he whispered to Edwards, "or they'll see us."
When this was done he drew aside the curtains of the boys' bunks
and looked at the damaged youngsters.

"My word! My word!" he said, drawing in his breath. "They'll
die, sure enough. I can't do nothin' for 'em. It's the Bo'sun did this. I
wouldn't be him for the Mint!"

All the time that he talked he was examining first one boy's head
and then the other.

"They've sure had a terrible bashing," he muttered. "I'll watch
my chance and bring some stuff along to bath 'em, an bind 'em up.
If I'm caught, sonny, I shall be massacred." Yet he managed it, and
finally tried to force a little brandy down the boys' throats; but the
stuff dribbled helplessly away out of the corners of their mouths, and
brought a bubbling sound into their breathing that frightened the old
Steward so that he stopped, declaring that he had done all he could,

and dared try no experiments.

"Just leave 'em be is all we can do now," he said. "If they dies, they dies—an' blow me if it won't serve the Bo'sun right!" With that brief sentiment he left them, after having given Larry a brief outline of how the trouble had originated.

It was Edwards's and Kinniks's watch on deck that night. Darkins and Peters still lay unconscious in their bunks, breathing in the same strange, unnatural fashion that Larry had noticed when he first saw them after the fight. Harold Jones, whose watch below it was, sat wearily on a chest, not even trying to undress and turn in. From time to time he whispered to "Tommy Dodd," who had crept quietly into the berth to see how the two in the bunks were getting on.

For a little while they sat and talked, until suddenly the for'ard door of the house was opened a little and Kinniks pushed his head cautiously into the berth. He was the Timekeeper for the first two hours of that watch, and had just stolen down off the poop for a moment.

" 'S—sh!" he whispered, with a gesture of nervous excitement. "They're going to have old Jumbo and Bullard and Connaught up out of the lazarette at seven bells. And they're goin' to tie them up by their thumbs in the mizzen rigging, before the First Mate is called, and hammer them till they're sick. I heard the Old Man and the Second talking about it on the weather side of the chart-house."

It was then, and at that exact moment, that young Larry Edwards had his inspiration of the plan (the first part of which he actually carried out almost unaided) by which he managed literally to show Captain Beeston that he had met his Waterloo.

He took command from that moment; told Kinniks to get back onto the poop at once, and not to worry whatever he might see. "You'll have to keep my time as well as yours," he told him; and therewith hurried him off. Then he turned to the still-dressed Harold Jones. "Don't ask questions," he said; "but go and get the fresh-water pump shipped, as quiet as you can. If you make a sound they'll hear you, and you'll just get murdered."

As soon as Jones had gone on this errand Edwards turned the lamp a little lower and went out through the for'ard steel door of the little house. He returned in a couple of minutes with one of the boat's empty water-breakers, which he proceeded to wash out. By the time that he had done Jones came in quickly to say that the pump was shipped.

"Right!" said the younger boy. "Now fill this breaker and the berth water-barrel as quick as ever you can; but go slow with the pump, or they'll hear you."

He next went aft himself, as quietly as a shadow, and stole the keys of the lamp-room out of the Second Mate's room. With these he unlocked paint-locker and oil-room, away for'ard, and stepped inside, but, as fate would have it, did not snick it properly. As it fell out, whilst he was routing round in the dark for what he wanted, the Bo'sun happened to walk for'ard on that side of the main-deck, and the door, swinging open with the roll of the ship, caught him a blow on the elbow that set him dancing.

"Curse the door!" he said, and slammed it savagely, without ever thinking to look inside. I suppose he imagined merely that the Second Mate had forgotten to lock it that evening. A minute or so later it was opened ever so cautiously and Larry's head came out to take a survey. Finally the whole of that astute youth emerged, and lifted out onto the deck a five-gallon drum of paraffin. He locked the door, and then swiftly and with infinite care carried his spoils aft to the 'prentices' berth.

He did not bother to return the keys; but, having seen that Harold Jones was managing all right with the water, slipped out of the berth again and away in through the saloon doorway. Here, after listening awhile, he made his way aft to the Steward's room and listened to his snoring; then to the room of Mr. Jenkins, the First Mate, and made sure that he was asleep. Finally, after standing a moment at the foot of the companion-way, listening, he did the thing he was planning—walked right into the privacy of the Captain's own cabin, opened his desk, and took out the keys of the irons. There was a revolver there, which he grabbed up, but failed, in his hurry, to find the cartridges—perhaps a providential failure. There were two Winchester rifles locked in a rack, and these he quickly put out of action by bashing the hammers, which he did with two sharp steady blows from one of the emergency axes, which lay in their rack below the rifles.

The blows had not made much sound, but he was acutely anxious to make sure no one had heard, and so ran again, first to the Mate's door, and then to the Steward's; but both appeared to be sleeping quietly, whilst overheard, to wind'ard, he could hear the steady pacing of the Master and the Second Mate; and so he knew that, for the present at any rate, he was safe.

And now came the most desperate part of his scheme. He ran lightly (he was barefooted, remember) again to the foot of the companion way, listened a moment, and then stole into the pantry. Here he lifted the hatch that led down into the lazarette and felt for the ladder with his feet; then down he went, lowering the hatch cautiously back into place over his head. He felt his way down the ladder, reached the deck of the lazarette, and whispered: "Jumbo! Jumbo!"

"Halloa! Who's there?" said Bullard's voice.

" 'S—sh!" whispered Edwards. "It's me—Larry. I've got the keys. We'll beat them yet!"

He struck a light, and a murmur of muttered exclamations of excitement came from out of the darkness. He walked over towards the sounds, striking another match, and so found his three fellow-'prentices, all ironed brutally. Their hands were handcuffed and their feet lashed together; then they had been doubled forward until their elbows were below their knees, and broomsticks had been thrust in over the elbows and under the knees and lashed securely, thus forcing them to remain always in that one constrained position.

"Larry, you're a little brick!" said Jumbo, and Bullard added another word of praise; Connaught, the third one in irons, said nothing. He just lay silent, partly on his side, where he had fallen. He had been so roughly used that all the spirit seemed to have been knocked out of him.

Edwards drew his sheath-knife and, by the light of several matches, managed to cut Jumbo's lashings; he was then able to get at the irons to unlock them. Whilst he worked he told them that Kinniks had overheard that they were going to be brought on deck at seven bells (near midnight—eleven-thirty, to be exact) and tied by their thumbs in the mizzen rigging and thrashed.

"I'll do murder first," said Jumbo, quietly. Then he caught young Larry in the dark and hugged him savagely. "I'll never forget, kid, while I live. Come on with the others."

Between them they cut out the other two, and in less than another couple of minutes had their irons off. They shook Connaught and rubbed his hands and knees and elbows until he began to take some notice of them; then they went for the ladder. Edwards felt his way up first, lifted the hatch ever so slightly, and peeped out. He lifted it higher and listened; there was not a sound, save the creak of the woodwork and the steady footsteps of the Captain and Second Mate overheard on the deck.

"Come on," he whispered, and lifted the hatch fully. Jumbo came first; then Connaught, helped and urged by Bullard from below. Jumbo stooped, caught him under the arms, and hove him up bodily. Bullard followed, and Edwards lowered the hatch noiselessly into place. They next went quietly out of the pantry into the alley-way, the two bigger lads supporting Connaught. Tommy ran on noiselessly ahead, coming back to report that all was clear. They came out under the break of the poop, waited until the sound of the Captain's and Second Mate's footsteps had gone aft along the poop-deck; then they made a run, half-carrying Connaught, and so got into the berth through the after door.

They shut the door and bolted it. The for'ard one was open, and Kinniks was just entering with the last bucketful of water for the breaker.

"Good for you, Larry!" said Jumbo. "You seem to have enough for a siege."

"Yes," said Larry; "I've brought in five gallons of lamp-oil, too, for our stove and the berth lamp. Unship the fresh-water pump, Kinniks, and bring it into the berth; that'll give them beans. We'll bolt the door after you; scratch three times when you're back again."

Kinniks went out into the darkness and Edwards bolted the door. Then he rummaged in his chest and produced two of his pillowcases.

"I'm going down into the lazarette for some tins of corned beef and some ship's bread," he announced. "Then we'll have to get some lime-juice, and we'll want some sugar. We've got to have enough grub to enable us to hang on in here until the Old Man makes terms and agrees to treat us with ordinary decency, and not like a lot of dogs."

"You're not going alone, my son," said Jumbo, quietly. "I'm coming; so's Bullard. You've done your share tonight. You stay here and open for us."

But this Larry refused flatly to do, and finally, when Kinniks had returned with the pump, the three of them, each with a couple of pillow-cases, stole out of the berth. They waited until the Captain and the Mate had turned to go aft in their constant pacing, then bolted in under the break of the poop and ran silently down the alley-way to the pantry. Here Tommy listened, first at the Steward's door and afterwards at the Mate's, and, finding them fast asleep, signed to the others to open the hatch.

Tommy went last, and lowered the hatch silently into place above his head; then groped down the ladder after the two big lads.

"We'll have to be quick," he whispered, as Jumbo struck a match. "It's twenty past eleven; they'll be down here in ten minutes—perhaps before."

They rummaged round with all speed, striking matches constantly, and it was a mercy that they did not set the ship on fire. At the end of three or four minutes Jumbo had secured six full-sized tins of corned beef and a pillowslip full of hard biscuit. He took off his knife-belt and strapped the tins together, and so was ready. Meanwhile, Tommy had filled one of his slips with ship's biscuit and the other with sugar, a tin of Kiel salt butter, and several handfuls of loose tea, scooped up bodily out of an opened tea-chest. Bullard had filled his slips with biscuit and an assortment consisting of a tin of molasses, a bottle of lime-juice, and a second tin of salt butter.

With this bulky collection they fumbled their way up the ladder and pushed up the hatch a little way to listen. Tommy was first; and as he paused there at the top of the ladder, clear and sharp up in the night came seven bells.

"Goodness!" whispered Tommy, heaving up the hatch. "The bell's gone. We must just scoot. My gracious, they're coming!"

As he said the last word Bullard and Jumbo stood beside him, and he lowered the trap into place swiftly but silently. Then all three of them ran quietly, barefooted as they were, up the alley-way, just as they heard the Captain's foot on the bottom step of the companion-way. Another fraction of a second and they would have been caught. They heard the Master call up to the Second Mate to send aft a couple of the hands, and to call the Bo'sun and tell him to bring aft a couple fathoms of ratlin-line—a thinnish tarred rope, from a third to half an inch in circumference.

The three lads vanished out on deck and reached the berth, where they scratched on the door for Kinniks to open to them.

"That was for you!" whispered Edwards, as they entered. "Those brutes would have just cut you to pieces with that ratlin-line!"

"Stop," said Tommy, as Bullard made to bolt the door again. "There's Jones going for'ard for the Bo'sun. We must get him in! I've a notion," he added, quaintly, "that Mr. Bo'sun won't be needed after all."

He put his head out of the doorway.

"Jones!" he called quietly. "Jones!" But Harold Jones needed no calling for he was already at the door, trembling with excitement.

"Larry," he said, "those brutes are going to do it *now*, they've sent me for the Bo'sun, and he's to bring some ratlin-line. They're—"

"Come inside," interrupted Edwards, catching him by the shoulder. "They're just going to do nothing at all. Come in!" And he hauled him in over the wash-board and bolted the door.

"My goodness!" cried Jones, in astonishment. "Jumbo! and Bullard! Where's Connaught? How did you manage? What are you going to do? Good Lord! Don't you know they're going to lash you up in the rigging and baste you?"

"*Were* going to, you mean," replied Jumbo, calmly, yet with a curious grim gritting of his teeth together. "Connaught's in his bunk. Larry got us out. I guess there'll be murder done before they touch us now." He went to his bunk and, lifting the coil mattress, brought out a Winchester saloon rifle. "On my honour," he said, in a tense voice, "I'll pot the Skipper if he tries to touch me—or that brute of a Second Mate or the Bo'sun either!"

"I've something, too," said Tommy, and threw down the Captain's revolver on the berth table. "Only I couldn' t find the cartridges. But I've got a good old muzzle-loader in my chest, and heaps of powder and shot."

He proceeded to rummage for the weapon and its adjunct of death and destruction. He produced the weapon and exhibited it with pride—a big, old-fashioned flint-lock pistol, such as might well have been carried in Dick Turpin's holster. "I got it in that gun-shop on the right-hand side of Market Street," he explained. "They wanted a dollar for it, but I only had seventy-five cents, so they let it go for that, and seemed to think it a good joke. The boss of the shop made me a present of the shot and the powder, and said he'd come and read the burial service any time for nothing."

Tommy grinned cheerfully and began to load the ponderous weapon, "I'd like to—"

But he never finished his remark, for away aft there suddenly arose a loud shouting. "They've discovered we're missing!" said Bullard, going to first one door and then the other to examine the bolts. "Hark to the Old Man! He's hammering the Steward!"

"Iron covers over the ports—smart, you chaps!" cried Larry, quickly, at this moment, leaving his pistol and springing to the nearest. "There's the Second Mate! Screw 'em up hard!"

As each lad jumped to do this job there came a loud shout outside the after door, and immediately it was shaken and kicked. Then came a roar from the Second Mate.

"Open at once, you young devils," he shouted, "or it'll be all the worse for you!"

II

As the Second Mate shouted, Jumbo held up his finger for absolute silence, and the officer bawled the order again, with foul language, and punctuated by heavy kicks. Abruptly he was silent, listening, as they supposed; for directly afterwards he shouted: "I hear you in there, you—! Just wait five minutes, and we'll murder you!" Then, to some man near him, "Bring the Blacksmith's sled out of the Bo'sun's locker. We'll soon have 'em out, Sir." Evidently he was now speaking to Captain Beeston. "I'll make 'em wish they'd never been born!" In a lower tone he added: "I'm blowed, Sir, if I can understand how they got loose out of the lazarette!"

"Stand clear, Sir," was his next remark, after a few seconds' quietness. Then came a tremendous blow upon the steel door, making the whole of the interior of the little steel-house ring like a monstrous drum. But, though the furious officer struck blow after blow, until he was exhausted, he produced no effect upon the strong steel door beyond slightly denting it.

He stopped and hove the hammer onto the deck, swearing breathlessly. Immediately afterwards he gave an order to some of the men: "Bring the hose aft—smartly, now! Shove it on the nearest nozzle, and two of you man the pump."

"What's he going to do now?" whispered Edwards, staring round and round the berth.

He could not conceive just what was going to be done; how the attack was to be made. Jumbo and Bullard tiptoed silently to the after door and listened. Kinniks and Harold Jones stared at each other, with a queer mixture of terror and nervous excitement. The silence was unbearable.

Suddenly Larry felt something touch his head; he jumped back and stared up. Something was coming down the little ventilator in the decked roof—the brass-coupled end of the hose was being pushed down it into the berth.

"Look!" called Edwards, breathlessly. As he spoke the pump on the fo'cas'le head was manned and a great jet of water came pulsing down into the place.

"Great Scot!" cried Jumbo; "they mean to flood the place!" And he whipped out his sheath-knife, with some vague intention of cutting the hose, which, of course, would have done no good at all.

"No!" shouted Tommy; "twist it up, put a turn in it; that'll stop the water." Which it did at once, the canvas pipe swelling up, above the twist, to bursting point, with the strain of the checked water in it, for the pump-men were working furiously. "Now pull for all you're worth," said Larry; and they tailed onto the hanging length of twisted canvas and pulled.

Abruptly something gave, and they went down in a muddle on the deck of the berth, whilst a confused shouting and cursing sounded out on deck. "Pull! Oh, pull!" shouted Jumbo, getting to his feet with a jump. The hose came in hand over hand, as the sailormen say, and in a few moments the end came switching down on them, slatting water in all directions.

"It's bust clean away from the lashing on the other coupling," said Jumbo, picking up the final part and examining it. "We've done 'em proper; we've got the whole lot. Good boy, Larry! There's no spare hose; the other's rotten; an' Sails will take a week to make another."

Outside on deck there was loud, angry talking between the Second Mate and Captain Beeston. "I'll match them! I'll match them!" the 'prentices could hear the Second Mate saying, time after time, in an excited, furious voice. They heard him go aft into the saloon at a run, and then the sounds of his footsteps returning. He ran to the little house, and they heard him spring up the small steel ladder, and so to the decked roof. Then his voice sounded at the ventilator:—

"Open the doors at once, you young—, or I'll shoot you down for mutiny on the high seas!"

"Don't talk rot," replied Jumbo, staring quietly at the ventilator, but reaching out his right hand until he held his rifle; for there was no saying what the man would do. "Will you promise to stop treating us all like a lot of dogs? That's the first thing to settle."

"Open that door!" was all the Second Mate's reply. "We're going to take the flesh off your backs and see if that won't learn you. Open that—"

"Oh," said Jumbo, angrily, "go to the deuce!"

There was a burst of nervous laughter from the other lads, and this seemed to set the Second Mate off like a light to powder. He literally *screamed* something, and his great hand and arm came down the ventilator. "Flash-bang! flash-bang! flash-bang!" He was shooting madly and indiscriminately among the lads! Three shots he fired. There was a fourth; but it was from Jumbo's saloon rifle. The Second Mate dropped his revolver and ripped his hand out of the ventilator, screaming and cursing as only a man shot in the hand can.

"Anyone hurt?" shouted Jumbo, through the smoke that filled the place. There was a general instinctive feeling-over, to make sure, whilst overhead the Second Mate's feet beat a mad tattoo of pain upon the decked roof of the house; and from the main-deck there was loud shouting in the Skipper's voice, and, finally, the First Mate singing out something.

"Turn up the lamp more," said Larry. "No one's hurt, thank goodness! That's what I call a rank attempt to murder, if you like. We ought to block up the ventilator right away."

This was done, by screwing one of the bottom boards out of a bunk over the opening. Whilst they were doing this they could hear a loud and excited talk under the break of the poop, and presently the First Mate's voice: "No, Sir," he was saying; "you can do what you like in your own ship, of course; but I'll have nothing to do with any of it. You mark my words, Sir, an' you, too, Mister, you'll have sad cause to rue, if you don't ease up on them boys. You'll have a police-court case, an' there's going to be some hanging done, if you don't drop it. There, I've had my say. Please yourselves; but I'm out of it."

"Good old Mate!" said Larry, enthusiastically. "I'll bet we find him useful. We may be able to slip out for things at night in his watch. I'll bet he'll take good care never to see us."

At this moment there came the Captain's voice:—

"Take your watch, Mr. Henricksen, and rig a gantling. Take the old mizzen-royal yard; sling it by the parral, and bash the door in. Use it as a battering-ram. The for'ard door'll be best. I'll teach the young beggars!" and he swore horribly.

"Well," said Jumbo, "we've got to stop that. They'll just murder some of us if they get in now. Get that big pistol of yours finished loading up, Tommy. Don't use those bb's; fill her with some of that broken-up rock-salt instead, and mind you don't shoot at their faces, or you'll blind them for life. Aim at their legs. They'll be close enough, goodness knows.

"Now," he continued, standing up and looking rather pale but very determined, "out with the lamp. You take the other port; I'll take the one in the starboard end of the house. Don't you shoot unless there's a rush that I can't stop. And, for Heavens sake, aim low. You'll be glad afterwards. It makes a horrible mess, that saltpetre." (I had better explain here that the rock-salt had come out of a beef-barrel which the Steward had been emptying.)

The lamp was turned out, and then, very silently, the two of them unscrewed the iron covers of the two forward ports and peered out. They saw that the gantline was already rigged and the men were bending it on round the yard, near the parral. This was done, and the Second Mate gave orders to hoist away until the yard was about half a fathom off the deck and about level with the middle of the berth door.

"Make fast, there!" he shouted. "Come here, all of you, and get hold; on both sides, lads—on both sides. Steady her!"

It was at this moment that Jumbo unscrewed the glass port light itself and put his head out.

"Mr. Henricksen," he said, speaking as calmly as he could, "you've got to stop that, or we shall shoot."

The Second Mate stopped swiftly, caught up an iron-bound snatch-block with his uninjured left hand, and hove it at Jumbo's unprotected head. It would have killed the lad, probably, had it struck; but he drew back in time, and the great heavy block crashed against the brass circle about the port-hole and fell with a thud to the deck.

"Back with it, lads!" shouted the Second Mate. "In with the door!" He caught the far end of the big spar, so as to steer it, for it swayed clumsily with the rolling of the vessel.

"I give you one more warning," shouted Jumbo, from within the house.

"All together, lads! All together!" roared Henricksen, steadying the yard with his left hand. "Now!"

At the same instant Jumbo levelled his rifle and fired. The Second Mate gave a shout, loosed the end of the yard, and caught at his left thigh.

"Now, then, you chaps," cried Jumbo, to the hesitating men; "you clear off and be sensible. We don't want to hurt you; but there's going to be sudden death aboard here if we ain't left alone and treated proper."

Still they hesitated, seeming half-minded to obey the Second Mate's groaning orders: "In with the door!"

"Now, Larry!" said Jumbo, quickly drawing back into the dark half-deck, "shove out your pistol. If they don't move, let 'em have it in the legs, and Heaven help them!"

Edwards pushed his great pistol out through the other port. "Now," he said, "run!" And as one man they loosed the hanging spar and ran, leaving it there to bash and clatter and sway about. Behind them Larry's great weapon roared; for he had fired over their heads to hasten them. In ten seconds not a man was visible, even the groaning and cursing officer having thought it advisable to remove himself to a safer place.

"That's done it!" said Edwards. "Let's screw everything up tight again. They'll not touch us again tonight. Have you seen poor old Darkins and Peters?" He drew back their bunk-curtains, and the five boys stood round solemnly in a semicircle, staring rather helplessly.

"How queer Peters is breathing!" said Jumbo. "Where's he hurt? Who bandaged their heads up?"

"The Steward," said Tommy. "The Old Man wouldn't let him come, but I got him to sneak in and fix them up. Look at the colour of Darkin's face! There's going to be an awful row about all this when we get home. Anyway, I'm glad we didn't start the shooting first."

"Jove!" said Jumbo, "I wish it was all over!" He was old enough to realise the hopeless, dreadful piteousness of it all, and to see something of the awful complications that might lie ahead.

They drew back the curtains of Connaught's bunk and had a look at him, but found him still in a kind of heavy, dull sleep, or stupor.

They drew the curtains again before the three unconscious lads, held a council, and finally decided to turn in.

Edwards proved to be right in supposing that no further attempt would be made on them that night. They were left absolutely unmolested for three days—the work of the ship going on about the closed steel-house as though it held nothing more unusual or tragic than its accustomed set of light-hearted, healthy careless crowd of 'prentices, instead of two lads near death, and a third who was still in a kind of heavy stupor, and all of the others under threat of most brutal reprisal, once they should open the doors of the little house.

Within the berth the lads cleaned up, cooked, ate, and tried crudely and ineffectually to feed their unconscious mates with soup of a kind of mawkish beef-tea which they made on their little oil-stove with water and corned beef. Fortunately they did no harm with these well-meant efforts; and presently they desisted for fear that they should.

At times during those three days they would catch snatches of the talk that went on between the men—talk that came plain to them as odd men happened to pass near the house. In this way they gathered bits of news, there behind their steel barrier. They learned that the Second Mate was very bad in his bunk; that one of the men had actually received a portion of the charge from Edwards's pistol in the back of his neck, and was feeling very sore about it, in more ways than one. Also, the lads learned that they were considered by some of the men to be "plucky young devils," and by others as needing something to "break 'em in"; these latter having evidently, from their remarks, a strong relish in the picture of all the 'prentices being tied up in the rigging and the Bo'sun "easing 'em of their bucko with a fathom of ratlin-line."

In the second dog-watch of the third day, when it was growing dusk, a little before eight bells, the 'prentices had a pleasant little "heartener," for they heard one of the men speaking to them cautiously through the keyhole of the for'ard door. "Good on you, mates!" he said. "Stick to it! There's a lot of us is bettin' you'll win yet. Curse 'em! I says." Which, though no more than an expression of sympathy from a half-developed mentality, was yet a cheering thing to the imprisoned five, upon whom the anxiety and confinement of their position were beginning to tell, as they sat there in the lamplight, playing cards most of the day, and talking in whispers; for they had always the feeling that some spy of the "afterguard" might be near one of the doors listening.

Then, on the night of that same third day, about three bells in the middle watch (half-past one in the morning), something happened. Larry Edwards woke with a sudden feeling that something was wrong. He sat up very quietly in his bunk and looked, first at one closed door and then the other. Both were safely shut. He let his glance wander all round the berth and saw nothing unusual. Keeping absolutely still, he listened intently. As he did so he became aware of a faint, curious sound that he could not locate. It began, continued a little, paused, and then began again—a faint grinding sound, slow and stealthy.

The slight, curious noise, distinct above the faint natural creakings of the bunks and fittings, as the vessel rolled, troubled Larry more than anything that had happened yet. He knew in his heart that the enemy were attacking their security in some way; but he could not imagine how or where. Again and again he let his gaze go slowly round the berth.

Suddenly he looked upwards, and saw something that made him tingle with excitement and apprehension. The end of a big auger was coming slowly through the decked-roof of the berth!

He sat up silently, and let his feet down over the edge of the bunk; then took a closer look. The auger was slowly withdrawn, and Tommy Dodd saw that it left an inch hole that was one of about a score of others, all bored to follow round what would make (when completed) a circle some eighteen inches in diameter.

The lad saw the plan in a moment. When the person on the roof of the house had completed his series of holes, all that would be necessary to finish his work would be a little quiet manipulation of a narrow-bladed saw; then, hey! a blow or two with the Carpenter's heavy maul, and a circle of the roof-planks would be driven clean in, to be followed instantly by Captain Beeston, Schieffs, the Bo'sun, and some of the more brutal of the men, who would thus be upon them before they had fully comprehended the meaning of the noise that had wakened them. A good plan it was, too, and one that would certainly have left them at the mercy of the brutes in authority, but for young Edwards's providential awakening.

As he slid cautiously from his bunk to the chest that lay beneath him he heard the slow grinding of the tool commence again, very gently, and knew that the man above them was continuing his work, all unconscious that he had waked anyone.

Larry reached behind him under his pillow, and brought out his big old flint-lock; then he stepped from his chest to the next, and stooped down to wake big Jumbo, who preferred, for some incomprehensible reason, to sleep in a bottom bunk (hence the reason that Larry, a young 'prentice, was allowed to have a top bunk—a luxury above the heads of first-voyagers, in every sense of the word). He shook the senior 'prentice gently, and the young man heaved himself up instantly, muttering: "What's up? What's up?"

"Hush!" whispered Larry. "They're boring through the roof. Look!"

He pointed, and even as Jumbo looked, with anxious, startled eyes, he saw the end of the auger come through, whilst a few tiny chips and shavings came fluttering down to the deck of the house.

"My goodness!" growled the big lad; and was out of his bunk in a moment, rifle in hand and ready to fire. When, however, he saw that there would have to be bored at least another twenty holes before any immediate danger need be apprehended, he eased the tenseness of his attitude and beckoned Tommy close to him.

"Plenty of time, Larry" he said. "It's lucky you woke up, though, or they'd have been through on us, and I believe that would mean right-down murder, in the spirit they'll be in now."

"Yes," agreed young Larry Edwards. "I've got a notion, too— pepper! Put pepper in my pistol, instead of bb's. Fire it up one of the holes. That'll give 'em snuff!"

Jumbo laughed silently, and held out his hand for the big weapon. Then, with a strand of steel hawser wire, he raked out the paper wad that Tommy had pushed down the barrel to hold in the shot. Next he poured out the shot—a big handful. "My word, Larry!" he said, "you meant to make sure of hitting something!" Afterwards he drew the second wad of paper, that held the powder down, and so was able to empty away about three-quarters of the explosive.

"The pepper-tin!" Jumbo whispered, and found Larry ready with it at his elbow. "Thanks!" he said, and poured a couple of ounces of the stuff down upon the powder, having first rewadded it very loosely.

"Now," he whispered, "I guess we'll just shift whoever's on the roof, my son."

He stepped forward under the holes and listened to the noise of the auger, trying to decide the position of the man who was boring. At that instant, however, the auger ceased to work, and in the succeeding silence he caught Larry's voice, whispering urgently:—

"Quick, Jumbo! Fire! They've spotted you! Get from under the holes! Get from under the holes!"

But the warning came too late, for at the same moment there

came a spurt of fire down through the last hole bored, and something seemed to scald Jumbo's left shoulder horribly, while the bang of the revolver sounded tremendous. Jumbo raised the big pistol, but there came two more shots from above and he was wounded again, one bullet ripping along the whole length of his right arm and the other taking the skin and flesh off his middle knuckle.

"Come back!" shouted Larry, and caught him by his wounded arm and dragged him out of range. "Jumbo," he continued, "are you hurt much? Tell me quick!" For big Jumbo looked ghastly, and the blood was running down both sleeves, whilst the big pistol lay unfired upon the deck of the berth.

"Hey! hey! hey!" they heard the wounded Second Mate laughing, brutally, through the auger-holes. "We're going to shoot you down like rats! Go ahead with the auger, Chips. You needn't bother to be quiet now. The Bo'sun and I will keep them away."

"My gracious!" said Bullard, who, with Kinniks and Jones, had jumped out of his bunk when the Second Mate fired. "What has he done to you, Jumbo? What has he done? Get him on a chest, Larry!" He took the big 'prentice in his arms and steadied him to the chest, for the young man had grown utterly sick and dizzy.

"Oh, you brute!" he shouted, fiercely, up to the Second Mate. "You vile brute! You've killed Jumbo!"

The only reply was a blind succession of shots into the berth, which hit no one, as no one was in view of the auger holes. The result, however, on Bullard was to make him stoop swiftly for the big horse-pistol upon the floor. Then, in a kind of mad rage, he made one spring right under the holes and thrusting the muzzle of the big weapon up against one of them, he fired. It was all done in an instant of time, with the quickness of a wild cat leaping. From the top of the house there came a terrible scream in the Second Mate's voice: "I'm blinded! I'm blinded! Oh, good heavens, I'm blinded!"

They heard nothing further for a number of seconds; for every one of the lads was taken with tremendous paroxysms of sneezing, owing to an enormous quantity of pepper being in the air of the berth; for some had spurted out at the sides, at the juncture of the hole and muzzle.

Abruptly, as the effect of the pepper was easing from them, there came a gigantic sneeze from behind the curtains of Connaught's bunk, and the next instant his curtains were violently switched aside and he sat up—waked out of his long lethargy, sneezing and sane.

Above them, on the roof of the little house, they caught the moaning of the Second Mate, intermingled with violent sneezings from the Bo'sun and Chips.

"What's happened?" asked Connaught, utterly bewildered, and staring at the group of lads about the bleeding Jumbo. "What's happened?" he asked again, and went off once more into a burst of sneezes. But none of the lads had any time to reply to him, for they were all busy with the senior, Larry and Bullard cutting off his coat, and Kinniks and Harold Jones getting water in the berth basin and tearing up shore-going handkerchiefs for bandages.

Presently they had him bound up as well as they could, and so lifted him into his bunk. Above them they heard the staggering, limping steps of the Second Mate and his constant groaning, as the Bo'sun and Chips helped him across the roof-deck of the house and down the little steel ladder to the main-deck. They heard him go staggering aft.

"Now!" said Larry. And they took the teak washboard and, having bored holes in it with a brace and bit which Bullard had in his chest, they screwed it up over the auger-holes and so felt safe once more.

They got Connaught something to eat and drink, for he was ravenous, and explained things to him as well as they could. Afterwards they settled down round the table to talk, anxiously and nervously; for the realisation of serious injuries received and given was weighing upon them, with a dread of consequences. From time to time one or other would tiptoe quietly to Jumbo's bunk, to see how he felt. Fortunately, his wounds were not in any way vitally serious. They were, literally, furrows, or gouges. Yet poor old Jumbo lost a tremendous lot of blood, and was some time before he felt quite his old self again.

It was arranged now, between Bullard, Tommy Dodd, Connaught, Harold Jones, and Mercer Kinniks, that there should be a regular watch kept every night in future, so as to preclude any further chance of a successful surprise. And so, having performed their nightly task of dumping anything not required in the berth through one of the ports out on to the main-deck, they had a final look at their three invalids, and so turned in, all except the watchman.

At times, as can be imagined, the berth got fearfully oppressive and stuffy, with doors, ports, and ventilator all closed; so that, some times at night, having turned out the lamp, the lad who was acting as watchman would open one or two of the ports very cautiously and give the berth a blow through.

It was on the following night when Bullard, the watchman at the time, was doing this very same thing, that he discovered there was some new plan "in the wind" for breaking into the berth. For, instead of the quietness of the decks at night, with the wind steady and only the silence apparent, he heard, away for'ard, a constant subdued bustle and the murmur of voices speaking in low tones.

He listened a long while, trying also to stare through the gloom; and eventually heard the Bo'sun speaking, evidently busy with some of the watch. A little later he heard and saw Captain Beeston go for'ard, tiptoeing past the house, and later on there came a loud crash and a hoarse shout of pain in the fore-part of the ship, as if something very heavy had fallen on to the deck and hurt one of the men. That this was to some extent a correct surmise, Bullard discovered soon; for one of the men came limping aft, supported by two others, and moaning and groaning with every step.

Bullard began to think it time to call the other 'prentices, which he did, and after telling all that he had seen, the lads were stationed at various ports to keep watch about the decks and report anything unusual that they might see, without a moment's loss of time; for it was impossible to say what form this new attack might take, or from what quarter it might come, or when.

It must have been just after four bells (ten o'clock) when Bullard first discovered that something was afoot; and the five boys stood watching and listening at their ports until seven bells had struck before anything definite was reported. Then it was young Larry Edwards who gave the word, in an excited whisper.

"Look!" he said. "On the port side! Don't you see? They've got bare feet; they're sneaking aft! They're dragging something. Listen!"

There was an absolute silence in the berth whilst the lads listened with all their might. Then they heard what young Larry meant—a dull, vague, heavy rumbling sound that came and went intermittently.

"My goodness!" said Bullard. "What is it?"

No one answered. The three other lads had left their stations, and were crowded now round the two for'ard ports, where Bullard and Tommy Dodd were watching. Very slowly the black, indistinct huddle of figures on the port side of the deck came nearer; and all the time the strange, heavy sound grew more ominous.

"What is it? What is it?" Bullard asked again, in complete and frightened bewilderment. "What can it be?"

"Gracious!" said Larry Edwards, suddenly, and burst away from his port, through the 'prentices at his back, and darted to his bunk. He was back in a moment with a pair of good night-glasses, which he possessed.

"What a fool I was! What a fool I was!" he kept muttering, as he adjusted them hastily.

He put them to his eyes and stared along the port side of the main-deck.

"Great Scot!" he cried. "It's the cannon! They're bringing the signal-gun aft! They're going to blow the door in! The brutes mean to kill us! They're mad! They're absolutely *mad*!"

III

A short but awful silence fell upon the lads on hearing the news concerning the cannon; then Larry's voice broke in again:—

"They're sluing it 'round, muzzle this way." He tailed off into silence, staring. The others could make out no more than a vague muddle of moving shadows for'ard, under the lee of the fore deck-house.

"Jumbo's rifle!" said Bullard, suddenly, and ran from his port into the darkness of the berth, groping where the weapon lay in beckets along the inside of Jumbo's bunk.

Jumbo, who was in a sort of feverish sleep, groaned uneasily and gave a little cry of pain; for Bullard must have touched one of his wounds as he leant into the bunk. Then Bullard had the rifle, and was dodging round the table, back to his port, cocking the weapon as he went.

He reached the port just as a general burst of frightened exclamations came from the others. A little flame had spurted out suddenly in the darkness on the port side of the deck.

"Stop that!" shouted Larry, shrilly, out of his port; for the light was that of a match in the Bo'sun's hand, and was being extended to the primed touch-hole of the cannon. "Stop!" he shouted again, and in the same second there came the crack of the rook-rifle; for Bullard had aimed at the light, heedless as to whether his shot brought actual death to any among the attacking crowd or not. He realised that the war between them and orthodox authority had reached such a pitch of bitterness that the Captain and the Second Mate had really lost their heads for the time being, and would literally stick at nothing to have them at their mercy. As for the Bo'sun, the man was a brute, and capable of anything, so long as he was countenanced in his actions by those in charge.

The crack of the light rifle was followed by a queer, half-gasping cry; and the light went out on the instant.

"We'll shoot again if you try to fire that gun!" Larry shouted, shrilly, out of his port. For'ard, to leeward of the other house, there was a curious, disagreeable gasping, and a quick sound of thudding on the deck, that came plainly to them in the succeeding moments of utter silence that followed the shot.

Bullard whitened suddenly in the darkness as he realised what the sound meant; one of the men was lying on the deck, probably kicking the life out there in the darkness by the side of the fore-house. Beyond the broken gasps and the queer drumming there was, as I have said, no sound from the group of men, away in the darkness at the back of the cannon.

Then, abruptly, there came Captain Beeston's voice, mad with half-drunken rage: "Blow the young fiends to blazes!"

There was the flash of another match in the darkness, followed by the sudden scampering for'ard of bare feet, as if some of the watch were running, in fear of another shot. Then, in the berth, the sharp click of the lock of the rifle and a frightened curse from Bullard. "It's empty! It's empty!" he cried, apprehension in his voice.

In the same instant Kinniks fumbled the big, old fashioned horse-pistol into Larry's hand. Larry saw the flame of the match being shielded down to the dark, low bulk on the deck that he knew to be the cannon. He thrust the heavy weapon at arm's length through the open port and pulled the trigger. There was a burst of fire and a huge report, followed almost in the same moment of time by a great flash for'ard and a bang that seemed to shake the ship. With the report something roared over their heads with a vast whooping noise, and there was a crash far away aft and a hoarse screaming.

"They've hit the man at the wheel!" shouted Kinniks, in a voice shrill with excitement and fright. "They've hit the man at the wheel!"

For'ard, there was a riot of shouts of pain, curses, and the noise of a man actually crying, "O-hoo! O-hoo! O-hoo!" and sobbing hoarsely, in a horrible fashion. In addition there was a constant noise of footsteps, as if somebody were running 'round and 'round in a circle.

"Good heavens!" said Bullard, in the utter silence of the dark berth. "We've fixed them!" He broke off in a dumb blank.

"They asked for it! They asked for it! We had to do it to save ourselves!" Larry managed to get out. "Serve them right!" he added in a strange voice, trying to get his courage and nerves under control again. And therewith he broke down hopelessly into a dry sobbing; and curiously enough it was the somewhat nervous Kinniks who attempted to console him, and ease him of his sudden burden of dread responsibility, by preaching vehement justification aloud into the darkness of the berth.

"Shut up, all of you," said Bullard, a little later. "It's done now, and we had to do it. They're mad, and we're being forced to do horrible things to save ourselves. And, anyway, if anyone's killed I've done it with Jumbo's rifle. Those bb's that Larry fired wouldn't be so likely to kill. But they won't try anything more tonight. They've all gone for'ard into the fo'c'sle."

They spent a time further, listening at the ports; but hearing nothing more, beyond the hum of voices coming vaguely aft from within the fo'c'sle, they shut and fastened both the ports and the iron doors that covered them. Then they lit the lamp, sat 'round the table, and talked. After a while, Harold Jones lit the little Rippingille and made some tea; and so, with tea and talk, they managed to get themselves back again into a more normal state.

Later—a long time after midnight—someone struck eight bells, and then corrected it by striking four. It was two o'clock in the morning. At times the whispering lads heard odd footsteps pass the little house very quietly. And once towards the four in the morning, they heard Mr. Jenkins, the First Mate, arguing something in a loud, angry voice. They caught his final words: "I shall have nothing to do with it, Mister. This is going to be a jailing job. I'd have you to mind that I've stood out of it all along!"

This seemed to be followed by sounds as of a scuffle or fight; but, though Bullard opened the after port-cover to have a look, he could see no one at all on the fore part of the poop, which was all that the angle of sight allowed them to see, on account of the port being so much lower than the poop.

As he stood staring he saw the Captain's face come into sight as he came for'ard along the poop-deck. The man saw him in the same moment, and shouted out an obscene oath as to what he meant to do. Then, before Bullard could get away from the port, Captain Beeston had whipped a revolver from his coat-pocket and fired at him. The bullet struck the side of the house, making it ring; and Bullard dodged quickly. In the same instant the drink-unbalanced Master fired again, and hit the glass of the port at the edge, making a perfectly clean hole through it. The bullet passed right under the lad's chin (at least, so they judged afterwards) and struck the other side of the berth, where it flattened in among some rivets in the steel side.

Bullard dropped completely out of sight, and reached up a hand to the iron cover, which he slammed and proceeded hastily to screw up.

"You're not hurt!" whispered Tommy, anxiously. "The old man must be mad drunk. You're sure you're not hurt?"

"No," said Bullard, and finished screwing up the metal cover; yet, when he turned away and came towards the lamp, all the lads exclaimed, for blood was running down his face. An examination showed that the whole of his left cheek, from the corner of his mouth to the temple, was raw with the finely pulverized glass which had been driven in a shower over him by the entrance of the bullet. The wound was not in any way deep or apparently dangerous; but it took an extraordinarily long time to heal; and it was a mercy that his left eye was untouched.

All the early part of that day the lads sat about in the berth, listless and upset, and taking very little notice of the sounds that went on around them about the decks. At four bells, however, they heard a rustle at the for'ard door of the berth, and a piece of old cardboard was pushed in, between the edge of the door and the side of the house. On picking it up, they found a roughly-pencilled message, which—although, of course, I cannot pretend to give it exactly—ran like this: "Look out the old devils goin' to blow the door in they bust the wheel last night and carried away 3 of Jock's fingers here's luck us for'ard ain't havin' no more."

This does not, as I have said, pretend to be an exact duplicate of the extraordinary note; but as far as my memory goes, it gives the true sense and spirit of it, and something of its legal sublimity of punctuation.

As may be thought, the lads in the berth were tremendously excited, and grew sullenly fierce, as they realised how indifferent and callous the Master had grown as to the risk to their lives and limbs, in his attempts to force the berth.

The rifle was reloaded from a box of .22's, which Jumbo had in his chest, and Larry's monstrosity of a pistol was heavily charged with powder and several brass rollers out of patent sheave-blocks; for he had fired away his supply of bb's. Then the port-covers were cautiously opened a little, here and there, from time to time around the house, and a constant watch kept about the decks. Yet never a sign could the lads see of anything unusual on hand. One thing only at last struck Edwards as being curious: there was not a man in sight anywhere about the main-decks.

The thing for which they were watching so blindly came, as might be thought, all unexpected. Larry had just opened the iron cover of the starboard for'ard port, and peeped out along the decks, when he started back, crying: "Great Scot! Look out!" He slammed the cover fiercely and screwed it home with might and main, shouting, "They've lowered a shell thing from aloft. It's burning just outside the door! The—" There came a tremendous stunning thud of sound and force, just without, and a blinding reek of smoke poured into the berth through the interstices about the for'ard door. Many of the lads shouted aloud with fright and shock, and there was a stampede to the after end of the little house, where they clustered for a few moments, waiting, unreasoning.

Eventually Bullard walked for'ard to the other door, and Larry came out from the bunk into which he had jumped. The others followed, and they examined the fore part of the house, to see what damage had been done. They found that the explosion had applied its force most curiously. What I might call the coaming or bottom of the house had been cracked clean through, from the port bottom corner of the door right down to the deck, while the bottom section of the iron or steel had been bowed in several inches, as if it had been hit by a gigantic hammer. Beyond these two evidences there was nothing more to show for the explosion—that is, from the inside of the house; though afterwards the boys learned that quite considerable damage had been done out on deck, one of the skid-supports having been blown away, and the bows of the starboard lifeboat lifted bodily out of the chocks, ripping through two of the lower planks. In addition, one of the iron water-doors in the bulwarks had been punched right out into the sea, leaving a very ugly gap in the bulwarks. Two of the sheep in the sheep-pen, foreside of the house, had been killed, and the pen itself wrecked badly; whilst, most serious of all, a portion of the main-deck in from of the door had been severely crushed and shaken.

It was as the lads all stood about the inside of the door, staring in a dumb, frightened sort of way, and feeling that things had indeed got far beyond anything they had ever intended or dreamed of, that Bullard took sudden action. He stepped to the door and tried to wrench back the lower bolt, which held the lower half of the door shut (the door was in two pieces, divided across halfway up, like most galley doors). However, the explosion had so bent the lower half of the door that he could not move the jammed bolt. He then pulled back the upper bolt, and swung the upper half of the door boldly open. He leant well out over the bent half-door and stared up aloft. The next instant he drew back and made one jump to the table, where Jumbo's saloon rifle lay ready loaded. He caught up the rifle, sprang back to the door, and leant himself out backwards over the edge, aiming upwards with the rifle. In the berth all the lads stood silent, nervous and excited; they could not see what Bullard was aiming at. They saw his finger crook suddenly upon the trigger, and the little rifle cracked sharply. On the instant there was a loud scream of pain aloft, and the rope with which the amateur powder-bomb had been lowered before the door shook violently.

"Got him!" said Bullard, coming forward again into the berth, very white and grim-looking. "If the Skipper's going to murder us all in here, we've got to save ourselves."

He would say nothing more; and immediately closed the door and sat down and was silent for some hours in a tense, moody way on his sea-chest; but all the 'prentices knew that he had shot Captain Beeston aloft. Once, as voices were heard near the main-mast, Bullard picked up the rifle and walked across to the door again; but Edwards ran before him.

"Don't; oh, don't Bullard! It'll do no good; and oh, we're in such a mess! Don't unless they attack us again. Don't, Bullard, don't!"

Bullard looked at the young apprentice for a little, in a strange way, then turned abruptly and laid the rifle on the table; and so went back again to his tense moodiness on his sea-chest.

From time to time the other lads attended to various matters about the berth. Kinniks, who was acting as cook for the day, made a sort of cracker-hash of biscuits and corned beef—the biscuits pounded fine in a canvas bag. But no one seemed to want any. Edwards and Connaught spent part of their time attending on Jumbo, who was muttering feverishly; and two or three times during the day they had a look at Darkins and Peters. To their utter delight—and, indeed, it quite heartened all of them in the berth, except Bullard—Peters was found towards evening, lying quietly with his eyes open, but most extraordinarily weak; so that they fed him with a thick soup which they made with water and boiled corned beef. Yet he never said a word to them; but merely took a few spoonfuls of the soup, and went gently off into a natural-seeming sleep. Darkins, however, seemed to the lads to be no better; but, again, he certainly seemed no worse; so that, as I have said, an atmosphere of comparative brightness seemed to steal into the berth for a time. It did not last, however, for they felt utterly lost and frightened as to what the outcome of their defiance was going to be.

It was as if everything was to culminate on that one day; for, suddenly, just after eight bells (midday), though no bell had been struck, there came a knock on the after door of the berth and the First Mate's voice speaking.

"For goodness' sakes, lads, come out of it!" he said; and they all (except Bullard and the three in the bunks) crowded excitedly aft to speak to the Mate.

"Is it all right, Sir?" asked Edwards, speaking for the others. "Will the Captain promise to treat us properly, sir? We're not coming out to be half killed. I don't mean to be cheeky to you, Mr. Jenkins, but I think the Old Man and the Second Mate have gone mad. They wouldn't mind if they killed us—"

"That'll do, Edwards!" said Mr. Jenkins. "I can promise you that you will none of you come to any harm." He paused a moment, then continued: "Captain Beeston is in his bunk with a bullet in his shoulder."

"Will he live, Sir?" almost shouted Bullard's voice at this instant. "Will he live, Sir?"

"Yes," replied the Mate. "Unless," he added, grimly, "he drinks himself to death. Come out now. I can't stop arguing with you. For Heaven's sake come out of it; and be smart. I'm sick to death of this awful business!"

"The Second Mate, Sir?" asked Connaught, with a kind of stolid fierceness in his voice; for he was in the Second Mate's watch.

"The Second Mate's in his berth, stone blind, and it's odds he'll never take another watch!" rapped out the First Mate, tersely.

"The Bo'sun, Sir?" said Bullard, in a new voice.

"I tell you," said the Mate, almost angrily, "that you will none of you come to harm. You keep clear of the Bo'sun, and he'll keep clear of you, or I'll have him into irons in two shakes. Anyway, he's laid up at present. Come out of that, and don't keep me here talking. Do you hear me, Bullard? Open the door at once."

"Yes, Sir," said Bullard, instantly, and opened the door forthwith. And thus it was, and exactly in this fashion, that authority once more resumed her interrupted sway aboard the *Lady Morgan*.

"How are those two that were hurt?" the Mate said, and stepped into the berth. "Anyone else hurt?"

They told him as he drew back the bunk curtains. He looked at the lads, one after another, and proceeded to issue orders:—

"Get those other ports uncovered and opened. Open that for'ard door. Whoever's turn it is, get a bucket and broom and clean the place out. Kinniks, go aft to the Steward and tell him I want him here at once. Move now, or I shall be losing my ticket over this job, along with those two fools aft there!" This latter was gritted out in an undertone; but the lads heard, and comprehended how the situation might appear to the "Afterguard" in their sane moments. Also that the First Mate, whom they all liked, might suffer seriously in the general clearing up that lay ahead of them all, both the 'prentices and the officers.

Now, it was out of these conditions—plus the Second Mate's blindness and damages, and the Master's still more fortunate wound (for, as it chanced, Bullard had shot better than he knew when he fired aloft in such blind anger at Captain Beeston)—that an amicable settlement eventually came about. The Master, who had been drinking heavily all the voyage, was thoroughly frightened by his bullet-wound, which certainly proved more serious than the Mate had anticipated, possibly on account of his drunken habits. As a result, he grew presently to a frame of mind—aided thereto by an enforced and strict sobriety due to the Mate's dumping all the liquor aboard—quiet way out of the dreadful muddle which had arisen. The 'prentices, on their part, were equally eager to have the matter hushed up, for they could not conceive how they might fare if ever the business entered a criminal court. The Second Mate simply did not count, in the circumstances; and as for the men, none of them had been seriously damaged, except Jock, whose fingers had been crushed by the cannon-shot, which had been a piece of timber rounded by the carpenter to fit the signal-gun. Jock received a handsome present of tobacco; and as his fingers eventually regained something of their previous shape and usage, he ceased—sailor-like, I suppose—to think overmuch about the matter.

Jan Henricksen, the half-Dutch Second Mate, recovered the sight of his right eye, and was thereafter a very much quieter man, and well pleased, after a certain talk with Captain Beeston and the Mate, to go delicately, like Agag. I suppose, until he dies, a limp of a very pronounced type will remain a much untreasured possession. I have little pity for him; he was an unmitigated bully.

It was Carl Schieffs, the Bo'sun, who came worst off in the whole transaction. Bullard's shot cut away his right middle finger and nicked the bone of his shin on the inside of the right leg, for he was in a stooping position when the 'prentice fired. The man was undoubtedly in agony for a little while; it was his feet they had heard drumming on the deck. Then, when Captain Beeston fired the cannon, part of the breech blew clean away in tiny fragments, cutting the Bo'sun frightfully about the face and neck, as he lay there on the deck just behind it. Extraordinarily enough, neither the bursting of the breech of the signal gun nor the handful of bb's from Tommy's pistol touched Captain Beeston, though three of the crew received trifling flesh wounds from the small shot.

Jumbo, under proper treatment, was about in ten or twelve days, and Peters considerably before this time. Darkins, however, was several weeks before he became anything like himself; and it is possible that his share of the business was the worst. I say possible because I cannot pretend to prove a connection between the blow he had from the Bo'sun and the fact that within a week of reaching home the lad fell from aloft and smashed up on the skids. I have often wondered whether he turned giddy and thus met his death as an indirect result of the blow.

The Bo'sun recovered; and I heard some time later that he was killed in one of those cellars which formed underground Chinatown in San Francisco. I am not surprised.

It may interest readers who like the last ounce of detail, in an account of facts, to learn that the securing of the fresh water pump in the 'prentices berth caused no inconvenience, as the ship proved to possess a spare one.

And now, I think, I have told you everything; certainly everything vital. I cannot help something of a smile, as I think of people I have met who will tell you that nothing ever happens at sea nowadays. Possibly this is true concerning the "tame-cat" life of the liners, which is the only sea-life that most of them have any acquaintance with; but the sea is a wide place, and a lonesome place, and I have seen it, in my time, breed some extraordinary conditions.

On the Bridge

(The 8-to-12 watch, and ice was in sight at nightfall)

IN MEMORY OF
APRIL 14, 1912
LAT. 41 deg. 16 min. N.
LONG. 50 deg. 14 min. W.

TWO-BELLS HAS JUST GONE. It is nine o'clock. You walk to wind'ard and sniff anxiously. Yes, there it is, unmistakably, the never-to-be-forgotten smell of ice… a smell as indescribable as it is unmistakable.

You stare, fiercely anxious (almost incredibly anxious), to wind'ard, and sniff again and again. And you never cease to peer, until the very eyeballs ache, and you curse almost insanely because some door has been opened and lets out a shaft of futile and dangerous light across the gloom, through which the great ship is striding across the miles.

For the least show of light about the deck, "blinds" the officer of the watch temporarily, and makes the darkness of the night a double curtain of gloom, threatening hatefully. You curse, and 'phone angrily for a Steward to go along and have the door shut or the window covered, as the case may be; then once again to the dreadful strain of watching.

Just try to take it all in. You are, perhaps, only a young man of twenty-six or twenty-eight, and you are in sole charge of that great bulk of life and wealth, thundering on across the miles. One hour of your watch has gone, and there are three to come, and already you are feeling the strain. And reason enough, too; for though the bridge-telegraph pointer stands at HALF-SPEED, you know perfectly well that the engine-room has its private orders, and speed is not cut down at all.

And all around, to wind'ard and to loo'ard, you can see the gloom pierced dimly in this place and that, everlastingly, by the bursts of phosphorescence from breaking sea-crests. Thousands and tens of thousands of times you see this… ahead, and upon either beam. And you sniff, and try to distinguish between the coldness of the half-gale and the peculiar and what I might term the "personal," brutal, ugly Chill-of-Death that comes stealing down to you through the night, as

219

you pass some ice-hill in the darkness.

And then, those countless bursts of dull phosphorescence, that break out eternally from the chaos of the unseen waters about you, become suddenly things of threatening, that frighten you; for any one of them may mean broken water about the unseen shore of some hidden island of ice in the night... some half-submerged, inert Insensate Monster-of-Ice, lurking under the wash of the seas, trying to steal unperceived athwart your hawse.

You raise your hand instinctively in the darkness, and the cry "HARD A STARBOARD!" literally trembles on your lips; and then you are saved from making an over-anxious spectacle of yourself; for you see now that the particular burst of phosphorescence that had seemed so pregnant of ICE, is nothing more than any one of the ten thousand other bursts of sea-light, that come and go among the great moundings of the sea-foam in the surrounding night.

And yet there is that infernal ice-smell again, and the chill that I have called the Chill-of-Death, is stealing in again upon you from some unknown quarter of the night. You send word forrard to the lookouts, and to the man in the "nest," and redouble your own care of the thousand humans who sleep so trustfully in their bunks beneath your feet... trusting you—a young man—with their lives... with everything. They, and the great ship that strides so splendid and blind through the Night and the Dangers of the Night, are all, as it were, in the hollow of your hand... a moment of inattention, and a thousand deaths upon the head of your father's son! Do you wonder that you watch, with your very heart seeming dry with anxiety, on such a night as this!

Four bells! Five bells! Six bells! And now there is only an hour to go; yet, already, you have nearly given the signal three times to the Quartermaster to "port" or "starboard," as the case may be; but each time the conjured terror of the night, the dree, suggestive foam-lights, the infernal ice-smell, and the Chill-of-Death have proved to be no true Prophets of Disaster in your track.

Seven bells! My God! Even as the sweet silver sounds wander fore and aft into the night, and are engulfed by the gale, you see something close upon the starboard bow... A boil of phosphorescent lights, over some low-lying sea-buried thing in the darkness. Your night-glasses are glaring at it; and then, even before the various lookouts can make their reports, you KNOW. "My God!" you spirit is crying inside of you. "My God!" But your human voice is roaring words that hold life and death for a thousand sleeping souls:—"HARD A STARBOARD!

HARD A STARBOARD!" The man in the Wheel-house leaps at your cry… at the fierce intensity of it; and then, with a momentary loss of nerve, *whirls the wheel the wrong way*. You make one jump, and are into the Wheel-house. The glass is tinkling all about you, and you do not know in that instant that you are carrying the frame of the shattered Wheel-house door upon your shoulders. Your fist takes the frightened helmsman under the jaw, and your free hand grips the spokes, and dashes the wheel round toward you, the engine roaring, away in its appointed place. Your junior has already flown to his post at the telegraph, and the engine-room is answering the order you have flung at him as you leapt for the Wheel-house. But YOU… why, you are staring, half-mad, through the night, watching the monster bows swing to port, against the mighty background of the night.… The seconds are the beats of eternity, in that brief, tremendous time.… And then, aloud to the wind and the night, you mutter, "Thank God!" For she has swung clear. And below you the thousand sleepers sleep on.

A fresh Quartermaster has "come aft" (to use the old term) to relieve the other, and you stagger out of the Wheel-house, becoming conscious of the inconvenience of the broken woodwork around you. Someone, several people, are assisting you to divest yourself of the framework of the door; and your junior has a queer little air of respect for you, that, somehow, the darkness is not capable of hiding.

You go back to your post then; but perhaps you feel a little sick, despite a certain happy elation that stimulates you.

Eight bells! And your brother officer comes to relieve you. The usual formula is gone through, and you go down the bridge steps, to the thousand sleeping ones.

Next day a thousand passengers play their games and read their books and talk their talks and make their usual sweepstakes, and never even notice that one of the officers is a little weary-looking.

The carpenter has replaced the door; and a certain Quartermaster will stand no more at this wheel. For the rest, all goes on as usual, and no one ever knows.… I mean no one outside of official circles, unless an odd rumour leaks out through the Stewards.

And a certain man has no deaths to the name of his father's son.

And the thousand never know. Think of it, you people who go down to the sea in floating palaces of steel and electric light. And let your benedictions fall silently upon the quiet, grave, neatly uniformed man in blue upon the bridge. You have trusted him unthinkingly with your lives; and not once in ten thousand times has he failed you. Do you understand better now?

The Derelict

"IT'S THE *MATERIAL*," SAID the old ship's doctor… "The *Material*, plus the Conditions; and, maybe," he added slowly, "a third factor—yes, a third factor; but there, there…." He broke off his half-meditative sentence, and began to charge his pipe.

"Go on, Doctor," we said, encouragingly, and with more than a little expectancy. We were in the smoke-room of the *Sand-a-lea*, running across the North Atlantic, and the Doctor was a character. He concluded the charging of his pipe, and lit it; then settled himself, and began to express himself more fully:—

"*Material*," he said, with conviction, "is inevitably the medium of expression of the Life-Force—the fulcrum, as it were; lacking which, it is unable to exert itself, or, indeed, to express itself in any form or fashion that would be intelligible or evident to us.

"So potent is the share of the *Material* in the production of that thing which we name Life, and so eager the Life-Force to express itself, that I am convinced it would, if given the right Conditions, make itself manifest even through so hopeless-seeming a medium as a simple block of sawn wood; for I tell you, gentlemen, the Life-Force is both as fiercely urgent and as indiscriminate as Fire—the Destructor; yet which some are now growing to consider the very essence of Life rampant…. There is a quaint seeming paradox there," he concluded, nodding his old grey head.

"Yes, Doctor," I said. "In brief, your argument is that Life is a thing, state, fact, or element, call-it-what-you-like, which requires the *Material* through which to manifest itself, and that given the *Material*, plus the Conditions, the result is Life. In other words, that Life is an evolved product, manifested through Matter and bred of Conditions—Eh?"

"As we understand the word," said the old Doctor. "Though, mind you, there *may* be a third factor. But, in my heart, I believe that

222

it is a matter of chemistry; Conditions and a suitable medium; but given the Conditions, the Brute is so almighty that it will seize upon anything through which to manifest itself. It is a Force generated by Conditions; but nevertheless this does not bring us one iota nearer to its *explanation*, any more than to the explanation of Electricity or Fire. They are, all three, of the Outer Forces—Monsters of the Void. Nothing we can do will *create* any one of them; our power is merely to be able, by providing the Conditions, to make each one of them manifest to our physical senses. Am I clear?"

"Yes, Doctor, in a way you are," I said. "But I don't agree with you; though I think I understand you. Electricity and Fire are both what I might call natural things; but Life is an abstract something—a kind of all-permeating Wakefulness. Oh, I can't explain it; who could! But it's spiritual; not just a thing bred out of a Condition, like Fire, as you say, or Electricity. It's a horrible thought of yours. Life's a kind of spiritual mystery...."

"Easy, my boy!" said the old Doctor, laughing gently to himself; "or else I may be asking you to demonstrate the spiritual mystery of life of the limpet, or the crab, shall we say."

He grinned at me, with ineffable perverseness. "Anyway," he continued, " as I suppose you've all guessed, I've a yarn to tell you in support of my impression that Life is no more a mystery or a miracle than Fire or Electricity. But, please to remember, gentlemen, that because we've succeeded in naming and making good use of these two Forces, they're just as much mysteries, fundamentally, as ever. And, anyway, the thing I'm going to tell you, won't explain the mystery of Life; but only give you one of my pegs on which I hang my feeling that Life is, as I have said, a Force made manifest through Conditions (that is to say, natural Chemistry); and that it can take for its purpose and Need, the most incredible and unlikely Matter; for without Matter, it cannot come into existence—it cannot become manifest...."

"I don't agree with you, Doctor," I interrupted. "Your theory would destroy all belief in life after death. It would...."

"Hush, sonny," said the old man, with a quiet little smile of comprehension. "Hark to what I've to say first; and, anyway, what objection have you to material life, after death; and if you object to a material framework, I would still have you remember that I am speaking of Life, as we understand the word in this our life. Now do be a quiet lad, or I'll never be done:—

"It was when I was a young man, and that is a good many years ago, gentlemen. I had passed my examinations; but was so run down with overwork, that it was decided that I had better take a trip to sea. I was by no means well off, and very glad, in the end, to secure a nominal post as Doctor in a sailing passenger-clipper, running out to China.

"The name of the ship was the *Bheotpte,* and soon after I had got all my gear aboard, she cast off, and we dropped down the Thames, and next day were well away out in the Channel.

"The Captain's name was Gannington, a very decent man; though quite illiterate. The First Mate, Mr. Berlies, was a quiet, sternish, reserved man, very well-read. The Second Mate, Mr. Selvern, was, perhaps, by birth and upbringing, the most socially cultured of the three; but he lacked the stamina and indomitable pluck of the two others. He was more of a sensitive; and emotionally and even mentally, the most alert man of the three.

"On our way out, we called at Madagascar, where we landed some of our passengers; then we ran Eastward, meaning to call at North West Cape; but about a hundred degrees East, we encountered, very dreadful weather, which carried away all our sails, and sprung the jibboom and fore t'gallant mast.

"The storm carried us Northward for several hundred miles, and when it dropped us finally, we found ourselves in a very bad state. The ship had been strained, and had taken some three feet of water through her seams; the main top-mast had been sprung, in addition to the jibboom and fore t'gallant mast; two of our boats had gone, as also one of the pigsties (with three fine pigs), this latter having been washed overboard but some half hour before the wind began to ease, which it did quickly; though a very ugly sea ran for some hours after.

"The wind left us just before dark, and when morning came, it brought splendid weather; a calm, mildly undulating sea, and a brilliant sun, with no wind. It showed us also that we were not alone; for about two miles away to the Westward, was another vessel, which Mr. Selvern, the Second Mate, pointed out to me.

" 'That's a pretty rum-looking packet, Doctor,' he said, and handed me his glass. I looked through it, at the other vessel, and saw what he meant; at least, I thought I did.

" 'Yes, Mr. Selvern,' I said, 'she's got a pretty old-fashioned look about her.'

"He laughed at me, in his pleasant way.

" 'It's easy to see you're not a sailor, Doctor,' he remarked. 'There's a dozen rum things about her. She's a derelict, and has been floating round, by the look of her, for many a score of years. Look at the shape of her counter, and the bows and cutwater. She's as old as the hills, as you might say, and ought to have gone down to Davy Jones a long time ago. Look at the growths on her, and the thickness of her standing rigging; that's all salt encrustations, I fancy, if you notice the white colour. She's been a small barque; but don't you see she's not a yard left aloft. They've all dropped out of the slings; everything rotted away; wonder the standing rigging hasn't gone too. I wish the Old Man would let us take the boat, and have a look at her; she'd be well worth it.'

"There seemed little chance, however, of this; for all hands were turned-to and kept hard at it all day long, repairing the damage to the masts and gear, and this took a long while, as you may think. Part of the time, I gave a hand, heaving on one of the deck-capstans; for the exercise was good for my liver. Old Captain Gannington approved, and I persuaded him to come along and try some of the same medicine, which he did; and we grew very chummy over the job.

"We got talking about the derelict, and he remarked how lucky we were not to have run full tilt onto her, in the darkness; for she lay right away to leeward of us, according to the way that we had been drifting in the storm. He also was of the opinion that she had a strange look about her, and that she was pretty old; but on this latter point, he plainly had far less knowledge than the Second Mate; for he was, as I have said, an illiterate man, and knew nothing of sea-craft, beyond what experience had taught him. He lacked the book-knowledge which the Second Mate had, of vessels previous to his day, which it appeared the derelict was.

" 'She's an old 'un, Doctor,' was the extent of his observations in this direction.

"Yet, when I mentioned to him that it would be interesting to go aboard, and give her a bit of an overhaul, he nodded his head, as if the idea had been already in his mind, and accorded with his own inclinations.

" 'When the work's over, Doctor,' he said. 'Can't spare the men now, ye know. Got to get all shipshape an' ready as smart as we can. But we'll take my gig, an' go off in the Second Dog Watch. The glass is steady, an' it'll be a bit of gam for us.'

"That evening, after tea, the Captain gave orders to clear the gig and get her overboard. The Second Mate was to come with us, and the Skipper gave him word to see that two or three lamps were put into the boat, as it would soon fall dark. A little later, we were pulling across the calmness of the sea, with a crew of six at the oars, and making very good speed of it.

"Now, gentlemen, I have detailed to you with great exactness, all the facts, both big and little, so that you can follow step by step each incident in this extraordinary affair; and I want you now to pay the closest attention.

"I was sitting in the stern-sheets, with the Second Mate, and the Captain, who was steering; and as we drew nearer and nearer to the stranger, I studied her with an ever growing attention, as, indeed, did Captain Gannington and the Second Mate. She was, as you know, to the Westward of us, and the sunset was making a great flame of red light to the back of her, so that she showed a little blurred and indistinct, by reason of the halation of the light, which almost defeated the eye in any attempt to see her rotting spars and standing-rigging, submerged as they were in the fiery glory of the sunset.

"It was because of this effect of the sunset, that we had come quite close, comparatively, to the derelict, before we saw that she was all surrounded by a sort of curious scum, the colour of which was difficult to decide upon, by reason of the red light that was in the atmosphere; but which afterwards we discovered to be brown. This scum spread all about the old vessel for many hundreds of yards, in a huge, irregular patch, a great stretch of which reached out to the Eastward, upon our starboard side, some score, or so, fathoms away.

" 'Queer stuff,' said Captain Gannington, leaning to the side, and looking over. 'Something in the cargo as 'as gone rotten an' worked out through 'er seams.'

" 'Look at her bows and stern,' said the Second Mate; 'just look at the growth on her.'

"There were, as he said, great clumpings of strange-looking sea-fungi under the bows and the short counter astern. From the stump of her jibboom and her cutwater, great beards of rime and marine-growths hung downward into the scum that held her in. Her blank starboard side was presented to us, all a dead, dirtyish white, streaked and mottled vaguely with dull masses of heavier colour.

" 'There's a steam or haze rising off her,' said the Second Mate, speaking again; 'you can see it against the light. It keeps coming and going. Look!'

"I saw then what he meant—a faint haze or steam, either suspended above the old vessel, or rising from her; and Captain Gannington saw it also.

" 'Spontaneous combustion!' he exclaimed. 'We'll 'ave to watch wen we lift the 'atches; 'nless it's some poor devil that's got aboard of 'er; but that ain't likely.'

"We were now within a couple of hundred yards of the old derelict, and had entered into the brown scum. As it poured off the lifted oars, I heard one of the men mutter to himself:— 'dam treacle!' and, indeed, it was something like it. As the boat continued to forge nearer and nearer to the old ship, the scum grew thicker and thicker; so that, at last, it perceptibly slowed us.

" 'Give way, lads! Put some beef to it!' sung out Captain Gannington; and thereafter there was no sound, except the panting of the men, and the faint, reiterated suck, suck, of the sullen brown scum upon the oars, as the boat was forced ahead. As we went, I was conscious of a peculiar smell in the evening air; and whilst I had no doubt that the puddling of the scum, by the oars, made it rise, I felt that in some way, it was vaguely familiar; yet I could give it no name.

"We were now very close to the old vessel, and presently she was high above us, against the dying light. The Captain called out then to:— 'in with the bow oars, and stand-by with the boat-hook,' which was done.

" 'Aboard there! Ahoy! Aboard there! Ahoy!' shouted Captain Gannington; but there came no answer, only the flat sound of his voice going lost into the open sea, each time he sung out.

" 'Ahoy! Aboard there! Ahoy!' he shouted, time after time; but there was only the weary silence of the old hulk that answered us; and, somehow as he shouted, the while that I stared up half expectantly at her, a queer little sense of oppression, that amounted almost to nervousness, came upon me. It passed; but I remember how I was suddenly aware that it was growing dark. Darkness comes fairly rapidly in the tropics; though not so quickly as many fiction-writers seem to think; but it was not that the coming dusk had perceptibly deepened in that brief time, of only a few moments, but rather that my nerves had made me suddenly a little hyper-sensitive. I mention my state particularly; for I am not a nervy man, normally; and my abrupt touch of nerves is significant, in the light of what happened.

" 'There's no one aboard there!' said Captain Gannington. 'Give way, men!' For the boat's crew had instinctively rested on their oars, as the Captain hailed the old craft. The man gave way again; and then the Second Mate called out excitedly:— 'Why, look there, there's our pigsty! See, it's got *Bheotpte* painted on the end. It's drifted down here, and the scum's caught it. What a blessed wonder!'

"It was, as he had said, our pigsty that had been washed overboard in the storm; and most extraordinary to come across it there.

" 'We'll tow it off with us, when we go,' remarked the Captain, and shouted to the crew to get-down to their oars; for they were hardly moving the boat, because the scum was so thick, close in around the old ship, that it literally clogged the boat from going ahead. I remember that it struck me, in a half-conscious sort of way, as curious that the pigsty; containing our three dead pigs, had managed to drift in so far, unaided, whilst we could scarcely manage to force the boat in, now that we had come right into the scum. But the thought passed from my mind; for so many things happened within the next few minutes.

"The men managed to bring the boat in alongside, within a couple of feet of the derelict, and the man with the boat-hook, hooked on.

" ' 'Ave ye got 'old there, forrard?' asked Captain Gannington.

" 'Yessir!' said the bow-man; and as he spoke, there came a queer noise of tearing.

" 'What's that?' asked the Captain.

" 'It's tore, Sir. Tore clean away!' said the man; and his tone showed that he had received something of a shock.

" 'Get ahold again then!' said Captain Gannington, irritably. 'You don't s'pose this packet was built yesterday! Shove the hook into the main chains.' The man did so, gingerly, as you might say; for it seemed to me, in the growing dusk, that he put no strain onto the hook; though, of course, there was no need; you see, the boat could not go very far, of herself, in the stuff in which she was embedded. I remember thinking this, also, as I looked up at the bulging side of the old vessel. Then I heard Captain Gannington's voice:

" 'Lord! but she's old! An' what a colour, Doctor! She don't half want paint, do she!... Now then, somebody, one of them oars.'

"An oar was passed to him, and he leant it up against the ancient, bulging side; then he paused, and called to the Second Mate to light a couple of the lamps, and stand-by to pass them up; for darkness had settled down now upon the sea.

"The Second Mate lit two of the lamps, and told one of the men to light a third, and keep it handy in the boat; then he stepped across, with a lamp in each hand, to where Captain Gannington stood by the oar against the side of the ship.

" 'Now, my lad,' said the Captain, to the Mate who had pulled stroke, 'up with you, an we'll pass ye up the lamps.'

"The man jumped to obey; caught the oar, and put his weight upon it, and as he did so, something seemed to give a little.

" 'Look!' cried out the Second Mate, and pointed, lamp in hand.... 'It's sunk in!'

"This was true. The oar had made quite an indentation into the bulging, somewhat slimy side of the old vessel.

" 'Mould, I reckon,' said Captain Gannington, bending towards the derelict, to look. Then, to the man:—

" 'Up you go, my lad, and be smart…. Don't stand there within'!'

"At that, the man, who had paused a moment as he felt the oar give beneath his weight, began to shin up, and in a few seconds he was aboard, and leant out over the rail for the lamps. These were passed up to him, and the Captain called to him to steady the oar. Then Captain Gannington went, calling to me to follow, and after me the Second Mate.

"As the Captain put his face over the rail, he gave a cry of astonishment:

" 'Mould, by gum! Mould… Tons of it. Good Lord!'

"As I heard him shout that, I scrambled the more eagerly after him, and in a moment or two, I was able to see what he meant—Everywhere that the light from the two lamps struck, there was nothing but smooth great masses and surfaces of a dirty-white mould.

"I climbed over the rail, with the Second Mate close behind, and stood upon the mould-covered decks. There might have been no planking beneath the mould, for all that our feet could feel. It gave under our tread, with a spongy, puddingy feel. It covered the deck-furniture of the old ship, so that the shape of each article and fitment was often no more than suggested through it.

"Captain Gannington snatched a lamp from the man, and the Second Mate reached for the other. They held the lamps high, and we all stared. It was most extraordinary, and, somehow, most abominable. I can think of no other word, gentlemen, that so much describes the predominant feeling that affected me at the moment.

" 'Good Lord!' said Captain Gannington, several times. 'Good Lord!' But neither the Second Mate nor the man said anything, and for my part I just stared, and at the same time began to smell a little at the air; for there was again a vague odour of something half familiar, that somehow brought to me a sense of half-known fright.

"I turned this way and that, staring, as I have said. Here and there, the mould was so heavy as to entirely disguise what lay beneath; converting the deck-fittings into indistinguishable mounds of mould, all dirty-white, and blotched and veined with irregular, dull purplish markings.

"There was a strange thing about the mould, which Captain Gannington drew attention to—it was that our feet did not crush into it and break the surface, as might have been expected; but merely indented it.

" 'Never seen nothin' like it before!... Never!' said the Captain, after having stooped with his lamp to examine the mould under our feet. He stamped with his heel, and the stuff gave out a dull, puddingy sound. He stooped again, with a quick movement, and stared, holding the lamp close to the deck. 'Blest, if it ain't a reg'lar skin to it!' he said.

"The Second Mate and the man and I all stooped, and looked at it. The Second Mate progged it with his forefinger, and I remember I rapped it several times with my knuckles, listening to the dead sound it gave out, and noticing the close, firm texture of the mould.

" 'Dough!' said the Second Mate. 'It's just like blessed dough!... Pouf!' He stood up with a quick movement. 'I could fancy it stinks a bit,' he said.

"As he said this, I knew suddenly what the familiar thing was, in the vague odour that hung about us—It was that the smell had something animal-like in it; something of the same smell, only *heavier*, that you will smell in any place that is infested with mice. I began to look about with a sudden very real uneasiness.... There might be vast numbers of hungry rats aboard.... They might prove exceedingly dangerous, if in a starving condition; yet, as you will understand, somehow I hesitated to put forward my idea as a reason for caution; it was too fanciful.

"Captain Gannington had begun to go aft, along the mould-covered main-deck, with the Second Mate; each of them holding his lamp high up, so as to cast a good light about the vessel. I turned quickly and followed them, the man with me keeping close to my heels, and plainly uneasy. As we went, I became aware that there was a feeling of moisture in the air, and I remembered the slight mist, or smoke, above the hulk, which had made Captain Gannington suggest spontaneous combustion, in explanation.

"And always, as we went, there was that vague, animal smell; and, suddenly, I found myself wishing we were well away from the old vessel.

"Abruptly, after a few paces, the Captain stopped and pointed at a row of mould-hidden shapes on either side of the main-deck.... 'Guns,' he said. 'Been a privateer in the old days, I guess; maybe worse! We'll 'ave a look below, Doctor; there may be something worth touchin'. She's older than I thought. Mr. Selvern thinks she's about three hundred year old; but I scarce think it.'

"We continued our way aft, and I remember that I found myself walking as lightly and gingerly as possible; as if I were subconsciously afraid of treading through the rotten, mould-hid decks. I think the others had a touch of the same feeling, from the way that they walked.

Occasionally, the soft mould would grip our heels, releasing them with a little, sullen suck.

"The Captain forged somewhat ahead of the Second Mate; and I know that the suggestion he had made himself, that perhaps there might be something below, worth the carrying away, had stimulated his imagination. The Second Mate was, however, beginning to feel somewhat the same way that I did; at least, I have that impression. I think, if it had not been for what I might truly describe as Captain Gannington's sturdy courage, we should all of us have just gone back over the side very soon; for there was most certainly an unwholesome feeling abroad, that made one feel queerly lacking in pluck; and you will soon perceive that this feeling was justified.

"Just as the Captain reached the few, mould-covered steps, leading up on to the short half-poop, I was suddenly aware that the feeling of moisture in the air had grown very much more definite. It was perceptible now, intermittently, as a sort of thin, moist, fog-like vapour, that came and went oddly, and seemed to make the decks a little indistinct to the view, this time and that. Once, an odd puff of it beat up suddenly from somewhere, and caught me in the face, carrying a queer, sickly, heavy odour with it, that somehow frightened me strangely, with a suggestion of a waiting and half-comprehended danger.

"We had followed Captain Gannington up the three, mould-covered steps, and now went slowly aft along the raised after-deck.

"By the mizzen-mast, Captain Gannington paused, and held his lantern near to it….

" 'My word, Mister,' he said to the Second Mate, 'it's fair thickened up with the mould; why, I'll g'antee it's close on four foot thick.' He shone the light down to where it met the deck. 'Good Lord!' he said, 'look at the sea-lice on it!' I stepped up; and it was as he had said; the sea-lice were thick upon it, some of them huge; not less than the size of large beetles, and all a clear, colourless shade, like water, except where there were little spots of grey in them, evidently their internal organisms.

" 'I've never seen the like of them, 'cept on a live cod!' said Captain Gannington, in an extremely puzzled voice. 'My word! but they're whoppers!' Then he passed on; but a few paces farther aft, he stopped again, and held his lamp near to the mould-hidden deck.

" 'Lord bless me, Doctor!' he called out, in a low voice, 'did ye ever see the like of that? Why, it's a foot long, if it's a hinch!'

"I stooped over his shoulder, and saw what he meant; it was a clear, colourless creature, about a foot long, and about eight inches high, with a curved back that was extraordinarily narrow. As we stared, all in a group, it gave a queer little flick, and was gone.

" 'Jumped!' said the Captain. 'Well, if that ain't a giant of all the sea-lice that ever I've seen! I guess it's jumped twenty-foot clear.' He straightened his back, and scratched his head a moment, swinging the lantern this way and that with the other hand, and staring about us. 'Wot are *they* doin' aboard 'ere!' he said. 'You'll see 'em (little things) on fat cod, an' such-like…. I'm blowed, Doctor, if I understand.'

"He held his lamp towards a big mound of the mould, that occupied part of the after portion of the low poop-deck, a little foreside of where there came a two-foot high 'break' to a kind of second and loftier poop, that ran away aft to the taffrail. The mound was pretty big, several feet across, and more than a yard high. Captain Gannington walked up to it:—

" 'I reck'n this 's the scuttle,' he remarked, and gave it a heavy kick. The only result was a deep indentation into the huge, whitish hump of mould, as if he had driven his foot into a mass of some doughy substance. Yet; I am not altogether correct in saying that this was the only result; for a certain other thing happened— From a place made by the Captain's foot, there came a little gush of a purplish fluid, accompanied by a peculiar smell, that was, and was not, half-familiar. Some of the mould-like substance had stuck to the toe of the Captain's boot, and from this, likewise, there issued a sweat, as it were, of the same colour.

" 'Well!' said Captain Gannington, in surprise; and drew back his foot to make another kick at the hump of mould; but he paused, at an exclamation from the Second Mate:—

" 'Don't, Sir!' said the Second Mate.

"I glanced at him, and the light from Captain Gannington's lamp showed me that his face had a bewildered, half-frightened look, as if he were suddenly and unexpectedly half-afraid of something, and as if his tongue had given away his sudden fright, without any intention on his part to speak.

"The Captain also turned and stared at him:—

" 'Why, Mister?' he asked, in a somewhat puzzled voice, through which there sounded just the vaguest hint of annoyance. 'We've got to shift this muck, if we're to get below.'

"I looked at the Second Mate, and it seemed to me that, curiously enough, he was listening less to the Captain, than to some other sound.

"Suddenly, he said in a queer voice:— 'Listen, everybody!'

"Yet, we heard nothing, beyond the faint murmur of the men talking together in the boat alongside.

" 'I don't hear nothin',' said Captain Gannington, after a short pause. 'Do you, Doctor?'

" 'No,' I said.

" 'Wot was it you thought you heard?' asked the Captain, turning again to the Second Mate. But the Second Mate shook his head, in a curious, almost irritable way; as if the Captain's question interrupted his listening. Captain Gannington stared a moment at him; then held his lantern up, and glanced about him, almost uneasily. I know I felt a queer sense of strain. But the light showed nothing, beyond the greyish dirty-white of the mould in all directions.

" 'Mister Selvern,' said the Captain at last, looking at him, 'don't get fancying things. Get hold of your bloomin' self. Ye know ye heard nothin'?'

" 'I'm quite sure I heard something, Sir!' said the Second Mate. 'I seemed to hear—' He broke off sharply, and appeared to listen, with an almost painful intensity.

" 'What did it sound like?' I asked.

" 'It's all right, Doctor,' said Captain Gannington, laughing gently. 'Ye can give him a tonic when we get back. I'm goin' to shift this stuff.'

"He drew back, and kicked for the second time at the ugly mass, which he took to hide the companion-way. The result of his kick was startling; for the whole thing wobbled sloppily, like a mound of unhealthy-looking jelly.

"He drew his foot out of it, quickly, and took a step backward, staring, and holding his lamp towards it:

" 'By gum!' he said; and it was plain that he was genuinely startled, 'the blessed thing's gone soft!'

"The man had run back several steps from the suddenly flaccid mound, and looked horribly frightened. Though, of what, I am sure he had not the least idea. The Second Mate stood where he was, and stared. For my part, I know I had a most hideous uneasiness upon me. The Captain continued to hold his light towards the wobbling mound, and stare:

" 'It's gone squashy all through!' he said. 'There's no scuttle there. There's no bally woodwork inside that lot! Phoo! what a rum smell!'

"He walked round to the after-side of the strange mound, to see whether there might be some signs of an opening into the hull at the back of the great heap of mould-stuff. And then:—

" 'LISTEN!' said the Second Mate, again, in the strangest sort of voice.

"Captain Gannington straightened himself upright, and there

succeeded a pause of the most intense quietness, in which there was not even the hum of talk from the men alongside in the boat. We all heard it—a kind of dull, soft Thud! Thud! Thud! Thud! somewhere in the hull under us; yet so vague that I might have been half doubtful I heard it, only that the others did so, too.

"Captain Gannington turned suddenly to where the man stood:

" 'Tell them—' he began. But the fellow cried out something, and pointed. There had come a strange intensity into his somewhat unemotional face; so that the Captain's glance followed his action instantly. I stared, also, as you may think. It was the great mound, at which the man was pointing. I saw what he meant.

"From the two gapes made in the mould-like stuff by Captain Gannington's boot, the purple fluid was jetting out in a queerly regular fashion, almost as if it were being forced out by a pump. My word! but I stared! And even as I stared, a larger jet squirted out, and splashed as far as the man, spattering his boots and trouser-legs.

"The fellow had been pretty nervous before, in a stolid, ignorant sort of way; and his funk had been growing steadily; but, at this, he simply let out a yell, and turned about to run. He paused an instant, as if a sudden fear of the darkness that held the decks, between him and the boat, had taken him. He snatched at the Second Mate's lantern; tore it out of his hand, and plunged heavily away over the vile stretch of mould.

"Mr. Selvern, the Second Mate, said not a word; he was just standing, staring at the strange-smelling twin streams of dull purple, that were jetting out from the wobbling mound. Captain Gannington, however, roared an order to the man to come back; but the man plunged on and on across the mould, his feet seeming to be clogged by the stuff, as if it had grown suddenly soft. He zigzagged, as he ran, the lantern swaying in wild circles, as he wrenched his feet free, with a constant plop, plop; and I could hear his frightened gasps, even from where I stood.

" 'Come back with that lamp!' roared the Captain again; but still the man took no notice, and Captain Gannington was silent an instant, his lips working in a queer, inarticulate fashion; as if he were stunned momentarily by the very violence of his anger at the man's insubordination. And in the silence, I heard the sounds again:— Thud Thud! Thud! Thud! Quite distinctly now, beating, it seemed suddenly to me, right down under my feet, but deep.

"I stared down at the mould on which I was standing, with a quick, disgusting sense of the terrible all about me; then I looked at the Captain, and tried to say something, without appearing frightened. I saw that he had turned again to the mound, and all the anger had gone out of his face. He had his lamp out towards the mound, and was listening. There was a further moment of absolute silence; at least, I know that I was not conscious of any sound at all, in all the world, except that extraordinary Thud! Thud! Thud! Thud! down somewhere in the huge bulk under us.

"The Captain shifted his feet, with a sudden, nervous movement; and as he lifted them, the mould went plop! plop! He looked quickly at me, trying to smile, as if he were not thinking anything very much about it:— 'What do you make of it, Doctor?' he said.

" 'I think—' I began. But the Second Mate interrupted with a single word; his voice pitched a little high, in a tone that made us both stare instantly at him:—

" 'Look!' he said, and pointed at the mound. The thing was all of a slow quiver. A strange ripple ran outward from it, along the deck, like you will see a ripple run inshore out of a calm sea. It reached a mound a little fore-side of us, which I had supposed to be the cabin-skylight; and in a moment, the second mound sank nearly level with the surrounding decks, quivering floppily in a most extraordinary fashion. A sudden, quick tremor took the mould, right under the Second Mate, and he gave out a hoarse little cry, and held his arms out on each side of him, to keep his balance. The tremor in the mould, spread, and Captain Gannington swayed, and spread his feet, with a sudden curse of fright. The Second Mate jumped across to him, and caught him by the wrist:—

" 'The boat, Sir!' he said, saying the very thing that I had lacked the pluck to say. 'For God's sake—'

"But he never finished; for a tremendous, hoarse scream cut off his words. They hove themselves round, and looked. I could see without turning. The man who had run from us, was standing in the waist of the ship, about a fathom from the starboard bulwarks. He was swaying from side to side, and screaming in a dreadful fashion. He appeared to be trying to lift his feet, and the light from his swaying lantern showed an almost incredible sight. All about him, the mould was in active movement. His feet had sunk out of sight. The stuff appeared to be *lapping* at his legs; and abruptly his bare flesh showed. The hideous stuff had rent his trouser-legs away, as if they were paper. He gave out a simply sickening scream, and, with a vast effort, wrenched one leg free. It was partly destroyed. The next instant he pitched face downward, and the stuff heaped itself upon him, as if it were actually alive, with a dreadful savage life. It was simply infernal. The man had gone from sight. Where he had fallen was now a writhing, elongated mound, in constant and horrible increase, as the mould appeared to move towards it in strange ripples from all sides.

"Captain Gannington and the Second Mate were stone silent, in amazed and incredulous horror; but I had begun to reach towards a grotesque and terrific conclusion, both helped and hindered by my professional training.

"From the men in the boat alongside, there was a loud shouting, and I saw two of their faces appear suddenly above the rail. They showed clearly, a moment, in the light from the lamp which the man had snatched from Mr. Selvern; for, strangely enough, this lamp was standing upright and unharmed on the deck, a little way fore-side of that dreadful, elongated, growing mound, that still swayed and writhed with an incredible horror. The lamp rose and fell on the passing ripples of the mould, just—for all the world—as you will see a boat rise and fall on little swells. It is of some interest to me now, psychologically, to remember how that rising and falling lantern brought home to me, more than anything, the incomprehensible, dreadful strangeness of it all.

"The men's faces disappeared, with sudden yells, as if they had slipped, or been suddenly hurt; and there was a fresh uproar of shouting from the boat. The men were calling to us to come away; to come away. In the same instant, I felt my left boot drawn suddenly and forcibly downward, with a a horrible, painful gripe. I wrenched it free, with a yell of angry fear. Forrard of us, I saw that the vile surface was all a-move; and abruptly I found myself shouting in a queer frightened voice:

" 'The boat, Captain! The boat, Captain!'

"Captain Gannington stared round at me, over his right shoulder, in a peculiar, dull way, that told me he was utterly dazed with bewilderment and the incomprehensibleness of it all. I took a quick, clogged, nervous step towards him, and gripped his arm and shook it fiercely.

" 'The boat!' I shouted at him. 'The boat! For God's sake, tell the men to bring the boat aft!'

"Then the mould must have drawn his feet down; for, abruptly, he bellowed fiercely with terror, his momentary apathy giving place to furious energy. His thick-set, vastly muscular body doubled and writhed with his enormous effort, and he struck out madly, dropping the lantern. He tore his feet free, something ripping as he did so. The reality and necessity of the situation had come upon him, brutishly real, and he was roaring to the men in the boat:

" 'Bring the boat aft! Bring 'er aft! Bring 'er aft!'

"The Second Mate and I were shouting the same thing, madly.

" 'For God's sake be smart, lads!' roared the Captain, and stooped quickly for his lamp, which still burned. His feet were gripped again, and he hove them out, blaspheming breathlessly, and leaping a yard high with his effort. Then he made a run for the side, wrenching his feet free at each step. In the same instant, the Second Mate cried out something, and grabbed at the Captain:

" 'It's got hold of my feet! It's got hold of my feet!' he screamed. His feet had disappeared up to his boot-tops; and Captain Gannington caught him round the waist with his powerful left arm, gave a mighty heave, and the next instant had him free; but both his boot-soles had almost gone.

For my part, I jumped madly from foot to foot, to avoid the plucking of the mould; and suddenly I made a run for the ship's side. But before I could get there, a queer gape came in the mould, between us and the side, at least a couple of feet wide; and how deep I don't know. It closed up in an instant; and all the mould, where the gape had been, went into a sort of flurry of horrible ripplings, so that I ran back from it; for I did not dare to put my foot upon it. Then the Captain was shouting to me.

" 'Aft, Doctor! Aft, Doctor! This way, Doctor! Run!' I saw then that he had passed me, and was up on the after, raised portion of the poop. He had the Second Mate thrown like a sack, all loose and quiet, over his left shoulder; for Mr. Selvern had fainted, and his long legs flogged, limp and helpless, against the Captain's massive knees as the Captain ran. I saw, with a queer, unconscious noting of minor details, how the torn soles of the Second Mate's boots flapped and jigged, as the Captain staggered aft.

" 'Boat ahoy! Boat ahoy! Boat ahoy!' shouted the Captain; and then I was beside him, shouting also. The men were answering with loud yells of encouragement, and it was plain they were working desperately to force the boat aft, through the thick scum about the ship.

"We reached the ancient, mould-hid taffrail, and slewed about, breathlessly, in the half-darkness, to see what was happening. Captain Gannington had left his lantern by the big mound, when he picked up the Second Mate; and as we stood, gasping, we discovered suddenly that all the mould between us and the light was full of movement. Yet, the part on which we stood, for about six or eight feet forrard of us, was still firm.

"Every couple of seconds, we shouted to the men to hasten, and they kept on calling to us that they would be with us in an instant. And all the time, we watched the deck of that dreadful hulk, feeling, for my part, literally sick with mad suspense, and ready to jump overboard into that filthy scum all about us.

"Down somewhere in the huge bulk of the ship, there was all the time that extraordinary, dull, ponderous Thud! Thud! Thud! Thud! growing ever louder. I seemed to feel the whole hull of the derelict beginning to quiver and thrill with each dull beat. And to me, with the grotesque and monstrous suspicion of what made that noise, it was, at once, the most dreadful and incredible sound I have ever heard.

"As we waited desperately for the boat, I scanned incessantly so much of the grey-white bulk as the lamp showed. The whole of the decks seemed to be in strange movement. Forrard of the lamp, I could see, indistinctly, the moundings of the mould swaying and nodding hideously, beyond the circle of the brightest rays. Nearer, and full in the glow of the lamp, the mound which should have indicated the skylight, was swelling steadily. There were ugly, purple veinings on it, and as it swelled, it seemed to me that the veinings and mottlings on it, were becoming plainer—rising, as though embossed upon it, like you will see the veins stand out on the body of a powerful, full-blooded horse. It was most extraordinary. The mound that we had supposed to cover the companion-way, had sunk flat with the surrounding mould, and I could not see that it jetted out any more of the purplish fluid.

"A quaking movement of the mould began, away forrard of the lamp, and came flurrying away aft towards us; and at the sight of that, I climbed up on to the spongy-feeling taffrail, and yelled afresh for the boat. The men answered with a shout, which told me they were nearer; but the beastly scum was so thick that it was evidently a fight to move the boat at all. Beside me, Captain Gannington was shaking the Second Mate furiously, and the man stirred and began to moan. The Captain shook him again.

" 'Wake up! Wake up, Mister!' he shouted.

"The Second Mate staggered out of the Captain's arms, and collapsed suddenly, shrieking:—— 'My feet! Oh, God! My feet!' The Captain and I lugged him up off the mould, and got him into a sitting position upon the taffrail, where he kept up a continual moaning.

" 'Hold 'im, Doctor,' said the Captain, and whilst I did so, he ran forrard a few yards, and peered down over the starboard quarter rail. 'For God's sake, be smart, lads! Be smart! Be smart!' he shouted down to the men; and they answered him, breathless, from close at hand;

yet still too far away for the boat to be any use to us on the instant.

"I was holding the moaning, half-unconscious officer, and staring forrard along the poop-decks. The flurrying of the mould was coming aft, slowly and noiselessly. And then, suddenly, I saw something closer:

" 'Look out, Captain!' I shouted; and even as I shouted, the mould near to him gave a sudden peculiar slobber. I had seen a ripple stealing towards him through the horrible stuff. He gave an enormous, clumsy leap, and landed near to us on the sound part of the mould; but the movement followed him. He turned and faced it, swearing fiercely. All about his feet there came abruptly little gapings, which made horrid sucking noises.

" 'Come *back*, Captain!' I yelled. 'Come back, *quick!*'

"As I shouted, a ripple came at his feet—lipping at them; and he stamped insanely at it, and leaped back, his boot torn half off his foot. He swore madly with pain and anger, and jumped swiftly for the taffrail.

" 'Come on, Doctor! Over we go!' he called. Then he remembered the filthy scum, and hesitated; roaring out desperately to the men to hurry. I stared down, also.

" 'The Second Mate?' I said.

" 'I'll take charge, Doctor,' said Captain Gannington, and caught hold of Mr. Selvern. As he spoke, I thought I saw something beneath us, outlined against the scum. I leaned out over the stern, and peered. There was something under the port quarter.

" 'There's something down there, Captain!' I called, and pointed in the darkness.

"He stooped far over, and stared.

" 'A boat, by Gum! A BOAT!' he yelled, and began to wriggle swiftly along the taffrail, dragging the Second Mate after him. I followed.

" 'A boat it is, sure!' he exclaimed, a few moments later; and, picking up the Second Mate clear, of the rail, he hove him down into the boat, where he fell with a crash into the bottom.

" 'Over ye go, Doctor!' he yelled at me, and pulled me bodily off the rail, and dropped me after the officer. As he did so, I felt the whole of the, ancient, spongy rail give a peculiar, sickening quiver, and begin to wobble. I fell onto the Second Mate, and the Captain came after, almost in the same instant; but fortunately, he landed clear of us, onto the fore thwart, which broke under his weight, with a loud crack and splintering of wood.

" 'Thank God!' I heard him mutter. 'Thank God!… I guess that was a mighty near thing to goin' to hell.'

"He struck a match, just as I got to my feet, and between us we got the Second Mate straightened out on one of the after thwarts. We shouted to the men in the boat, telling them where we were, and saw the light of their lantern shining round the starboard counter of the derelict. They called back to us, to tell us they were doing their best; and then, whilst we waited, Captain Gannington struck another match, and began to overhaul the boat we had dropped into. She was a modern, two-bowed boat, and on the stern, there was painted 'CY-CLONE Glasgow.' She was in pretty fair condition, and had evidently drifted into the scum and been held by it.

"Captain Gannington struck several matches, and went forrard towards the derelict. Suddenly he called to me, and I jumped over the thwarts to him.

" 'Look, Doctor,' he said; and I saw what he meant—a mass of bones, up in the bows of the boat. I stooped over them, and looked. There were the bones of at least three people, all mixed together, in an extraordinary fashion, and quite clean and dry. I had a sudden thought concerning the bones; but I said nothing; for my thought was vague, in some ways, and concerned the grotesque and incredible suggestion that had come to me, as to the cause of that ponderous, dull Thud! Thud! Thud! Thud! that beat on so infernally within the hull, and was plain to hear even now that we had got off the vessel herself. And all the while, you know, I had a sick, horrible, mental-picture of that frightful wriggling mound aboard the hulk.

"As Captain Gannington struck a final match, I saw something that sickened me, and the Captain saw it in the same instant. The match went out, and he fumbled clumsily for another, and struck it. We saw the thing again. We had not been mistaken... A great lip of grey-white was protruding in over the edge of the boat—a great lappet of the mould was coming stealthily towards us; a live mass of *the very hull itself.* And suddenly Captain Gannington yelled out, in so many words, the grotesque and incredible thing I was thinking:—

" 'She's ALIVE!'

"I never heard such a sound of *comprehension* and terror in a man's voice. The very horrified assurance of it, made actual to me the thing that, before, had only lurked in my subconscious mind. I knew he was right; I knew that the explanation my reason and my training, both repelled and reached towards, was the true one.... I wonder whether anyone can possibly understand our feelings in that moment.... The unmitigable horror of it, and the *incredibleness.*

"As the light of the match burned up fully, I saw that the mass of living matter, coming towards us, was streaked and veined with purple, the veins standing out, enormously distended. The whole thing quivered continuously to each ponderous Thud! Thud! Thud! Thud! of that gargantuan organ that pulsed within the huge grey-white bulk. The flame of the match reached the Captain's fingers, and there came to me a little sickly whiff of burned flesh; but he seemed unconscious of any pain. Then the flame went out, in a brief sizzle; yet at the last moment, I had seen an extraordinary raw look, become visible upon the end of that monstrous, protruding lappet. It had become dewed with a hideous, purplish sweat. And with the darkness, there came a sudden charnel-like stench.

I heard the match-box split in Captain Gannington's hands, as he wrenched it open. Then he swore, in a queer frightened voice; for he had come to the end of his matches. He turned clumsily in the darkness, and tumbled over the nearest thwart, in his eagerness to get to the stern of the boat; and I after him; for we knew that thing was coming towards us through the darkness; reaching over that piteous mingled heap of human bones, all jumbled together in the bows. We shouted madly to the men, and for answer saw the bows of the boat emerge dimly into view, round the starboard counter of the derelict.

" 'Thank God!' I gasped out; but Captain Gannington yelled to them to show a light. Yet this they could not do; for the lamp had just been stepped on, in their desperate efforts to force the boat round to us.

" 'Quick! Quick!' I shouted.

" 'For God's sake be smart, men!' roared the Captain; and both of us faced the darkness under the port counter, out of which we knew (but could not see) the thing was coming towards us.

" 'An oar! Smart now; pass me an oar!' shouted the Captain; and reached out his hands through the gloom towards the oncoming boat. I saw a figure stand up in the bows, and hold something out to us, across the intervening yards of scum. Captain Gannington swept his hands through the darkness, and encountered it.

" 'I've got it. Let go there!' he said, in a quick, tense voice.

In the same instant, the boat we were in, was pressed over suddenly to starboard by some tremendous weight. Then I heard the Captain shout:— 'Duck y'r head, Doctor;' and directly afterwards he swung the heavy, fourteen-foot ash oar round his head, and struck into the darkness. There came a sudden squelch, and he struck again, with a savage grunt of fierce energy. At the second blow, the boat righted, with a slow movement, and directly afterwards the other boat bumped gently into ours.

"Captain Gannington dropped the oar, and springing across to the Second Mate, hove him up off the thwart, and pitched him with knee and arms clear in over the bows among the men; then he shouted to me to follow, which I did, and he came after me, bringing the oar with him. We carried the Second Mate aft, and the Captain shouted to the men to back the boat a little; then they got her bows clear of the boat we had just left, and so headed out through the scum for the open sea.

" 'Where's Tom 'Arrison?' gasped one of the men, in the midst of his exertions. He happened to be Tom Harrison's particular chum; and Captain Gannington answered him, briefly enough:—

" 'Dead! Pull! Don't talk!'

"Now, difficult as it had been to force the boat through the scum to our rescue, the difficulty to get clear seemed tenfold. After some five minutes pulling, the boat seemed hardly to have moved a fathom, if so much; and a quite dreadful fear took me afresh; which one of the panting men put suddenly into words:—

" 'It's got us!' he gasped out; 'same as poor Tom!' It was the man who had inquired where Harrison was.

" 'Shut y'r mouth an' pull!' roared the Captain. And so another few minutes passed. Abruptly, it seemed to me that the dull, ponderous Thud! Thud! Thud! Thud! came more plainly through the dark, and I stared intently over the stern. I sickened a little; for I could almost swear that the dark mass of the monster was actually *nearer*... that it was coming nearer to us through the darkness. Captain Gannington must have had the same thought; for after a brief look into the darkness, he made one jump to the stroke-oar, and began to double-bank it.

" 'Get forrid under the thwarts, Doctor!' he said to me, rather breathlessly. 'Get in the bows, an' see if you cant free the stuff a bit round the bows.'

"I did as he told me, and a minute later I was in the bows of the boat, puddling the scum from side to side with the boat-hook, and trying to break up the viscid, clinging muck. A heavy, almost animal-like odour rose off it, and all the air seemed full of the deadening smell. I shall never find words to tell anyone the whole horror of it all—the threat that seemed to hang in the very air around us; and, but a little astern, that incredible thing, coming, as I firmly believe, nearer, and the scum holding us like half-melted glue.

"The minutes passed in a deadly, eternal fashion, and I kept staring back astern into the darkness; but never ceasing to puddle that filthy scum, striking at it and switching it from side to side, until I sweated.

"Abruptly, Captain Gannington sang out:—

" 'We're gaining, lads. Pull!' And I felt the boat forge ahead perceptibly, as they gave way, with renewed hope and energy. There was soon no doubt of it; for presently that hideous Thud! Thud! Thud! Thud! had grown quite dim and vague somewhere astern, and I could no longer see the derelict; for the night had come down tremendously dark, and all the sky was thick overset with heavy clouds. As we drew nearer and nearer to the edge of the scum, the boat moved more and more freely, until suddenly we emerged with a clean, sweet, fresh sound, into the open sea.

" 'Thank God!' I said aloud, and drew in the boat-hook, and made my way aft again to where Captain Gannington now sat once more at the tiller. I saw him looking anxiously up at the sky, and across to where the lights of our vessel burned, and again he would seem to listen intently; so that I found myself listening also.

" 'What's that, Captain?' I said sharply; for it seemed to me that I heard a sound far astern, something between a queer whine and a low whistling. 'What's that?'

" 'It's wind, Doctor,' he said, in a low voice. 'I wish to God we were aboard.'

"Then, to the men:— 'Pull! Put y'r backs into it, or ye'll never put y'r teeth through good bread again!'

"The men obeyed nobly, and we reached the vessel safely, and had the boat safely stowed, before the storm came, which it did in a furious white smother out of the West. I could see it for some minutes beforehand, tearing the sea, in the gloom, into a wall of phosphorescent foam; and as it came nearer, that peculiar whining, piping sound, grew louder and louder, until it was like a vast steam whistle, rushing towards us across the sea.

"And when it did come, we got it very heavy indeed; so that the morning showed us nothing but a welter of white seas; and that grim derelict was many a score of miles away in the smother, lost as utterly as our hearts could wish to lose her.

"When I came to examine the Second Mate's feet, I found them in a very extraordinary condition. The soles of them had the appearance of having been partly digested. I know of no other word that so exactly describes their condition; and the agony the man suffered, must have been dreadful.

"Now," concluded the Doctor, "that is what I call a case in point. If we could know exactly what that old vessel had originally been loaded with, and the juxtaposition of the various articles of her cargo, plus the heat and time she had endured, plus one or two other only guessable quantities, we should have solved the chemistry of the Life-Force, gentlemen. Not necessarily the *origin*, mind you; but, at least, we should have taken a big step on the way. I've often regretted that gale, you know—in a way, that is, in a way! It was a most amazing discovery; but, at the time, I had nothing but thankfulness to be rid of it.... A most amazing chance. I often think of the way the monster woke out of its torpor.... And that scum.... The dead pigs caught in it.... I fancy that was, a grim kind of a net, gentlemen... It caught many things.... It...."

The old Doctor sighed and nodded.

"If I could have had her bill of lading," he said, his eyes full of regret. "If— It might have told me something to help. But, anyway.... He began to fill his pipe again.... "I suppose," he ended, looking round at us gravely, "I s'pose we humans are an ungrateful lot of beggars, at the best!... But... but what a chance! What a chance—eh?"

The Island of the Crossbones

I

"BETWEEN THE HORN AND the Cape," said Captain Gaskelt solemnly, "there's an island as you and me'd give our toes to find, Mister. Did you ever hear tell of Crossbone Island?"

Maulk, the Mate of the little wooden brig, said nothing but his eyes had a queer look in them, and the Skipper continued:

"Well, there's no sayin'," he said. "You'll find a man here an' a man there as 'as heard of it; but you'll find a hundred as 'll think you're lyin' if you was to say you'd set eyes on it. An' that's what I done, Mister; just once in all the years I been fishin'. When I was a bit of a lad in the old Marty, one of them old brigantines, away back.... Lord! how one does get old! I seen it once in the middle of a three weeks' snow-storm, and the Master himself had no more notion of where we was than—than, well, than I had. We was fifty days out from Melbourne. Lord! it wasn't like you'd see it today! An' I saw the great peak of the island in a mighty sort of rift through the snow flurry; and there was the great crossbones, cut in the side of the mountain; and then the snow closed in round again, and it was gone.

"I'd heard them talk about there bein' supposed to be this here island somewhere to the south'ard an' I sings out that I'd seen it; and they near clouted my head off. I might as well have talked of ghosts! I'd a lot to learn then about sailormen! I found they never took it as real, you see, Mister, but only as a sort of yarn of a spook island; an' when I got yellin' as I'd seen it, they near came to think of me as the Jonah as was gettin' the ship all her dirty weather. Lord! There's some damn ignorant fools as goes to sea! But I seen it, Mister; mind you that. I seen it with my two eyes, as plain as I see you this minute. An' I've told the yarn up and down, through forty-five years of sea-faring; but I've never had a man believe me, not right down in his heart; only mouth-belief, 'cause he thought maybe I was good for a drink, or maybe as I should turn nasty if I heard what he really thought. An' all these years, Mister, I've never met a man as 'as seen it. But I seen it, Mister. Don't you make no bloomin' error!"

Old Captain Gaskelt terminated a speech that was becoming almost vehement, and viewed the Mate with an aggressive eye, his big, hairy fist instinctively clenched.

But the broad, black-browed, white-haired, grey-bearded Maulk said not a word in reply; only he looked steadily from under his half-closed lids at the Skipper, his eyes shining with an extraordinary gleam in them. It was almost as if some long-forgotten memory had stirred behind them, and waked to life a desire in the back of his grimly silent brain.

"I seen it!" repeated the Captain once more. But the big Mate appeared not even to be listening to him. He was not looking at the Skipper now, but away over the vast grey sea to wind'ard, where nothing showed to the horizon except the lonesome wheel of a ponderous circling albatross. As he looked, that waking gleam of memory still showed in his eyes, and presently he turned abruptly from his place beside the Captain, and walked forward to the break of the poop, evidently in a black study. Yet to old Captain Gaskelt there was nothing peculiar in this; he was already getting used to the morose, unsociable ways of his new Mate. All he would have said, had he been asked, would have been: "The Mate! No, Mister, he don't talk much, but he's a good sailorman." And as the Old Man was both owner and Master of the little wooden brig, *Lady Alice,* in which they were sailing, there was nothing more to be said, if he were satisfied.

II

Dan'l Templet, who acted as Bo'sun of the *Lady Alice,* was waked about five bells in the middle watch a few nights later, by the shaking of a heavy hand, and Maulk's gruff voice.

"Get out, Dan'l!" he was saying. "You'll have to stan' the rest of the Old Man's watch; he's gone a-missing."

It was quite true. Dan'l Templet rolled himself in an upright position in his bunk, and questioned, rubbing the sleep out of his eyes. Maulk explained, with customary moroseness of voice, that he had come on deck a little after four bells, as he couldn't sleep, and found no one on the half-poop except the man who had just relieved the wheel. He asked the man at the wheel where the Captain was, for the Old Man always took his own watch faithfully.

The man explained that he had only just relieved the wheel; and

Maulk had come forward then to question the one who had been relieved. But the relieved man had nothing to tell. He hadn't seen the Skipper since before three bells, when he was standing smoking to wind'ard, near the break of the half-poop. The man had walked round the poop and the main-deck, looking for him, to give him the course, but when he could not find him anywhere had simply ceased to bother and gone forward for his smoke-on.

This appeared to be all there was to it. Maulk had since searched the brig pretty thoroughly, but had soon made quite sure that the Skipper was not aboard; and he had then called the Bo'sun to take his watch, while he went below to try and get some sleep, which he did with the inevitable callousness that seemed his nature, for the boy who called him at four a.m. found him hard and fast in slumber.

Now the men, several of whom had sailed years with old Captain Gaskelt, were enormously puzzled at the Skipper's disappearance. They spoke to Dan'l when he came forward that morning at four o'clock; for he was always one of the "crowd" though he kept a slight aloofness, to help him maintain his position of half authority among them.

"What would the Old Man want to go and dump himself for?" they asked. They summed up all their doubts, and, maybe, indefinable fears in one blunt question; which, of course, had to remain unanswered.

Three nights later an extraordinary thing happened. One of the men who was having a quiet smoke out on the lee side of the dark main-deck suddenly shouted out in a tone of horror, and immediately began to scream something. His voice ceased abruptly, just as the watch dropped their cards round the fo'cas'le table, and came running out on deck. They shouted to the man by name, but there was no answer, and then someone thought to bring out the slush lamp.

As they carried the lamp down to leeward, they heard the Bo'sun singing out away on the poop; and then he came running forward, calling to know what was happening. They began to search the main-deck, and while they were doing this, and calling the man's name, they wakened Maulk, who came up on to the poop, growling angrily and sleepily to know what they were about. Yet among them all, though they searched fore and aft, they found not a sign of any living thing along the decks. The man had vanished as completely as had old Captain Gaskelt, three nights before.

There were a number of circumstances which made the thing more extraordinary. The night was very calm, and the sea as smooth as an enormous pond, with only a long, almost invisible heave, moving periodically under the glass-like surface. Thus the idea of the man's having fallen overboard was incredible, as will be plain in a few words. He had not even been smoking near the rail, as was shown by the position of his pipe, which they found on the deck, near to the caboose, where he must have dropped it when he gave out that shout of horror. There was nothing to make him fall overboard; and if he had, the splash would have been easily heard in the stillness of the quiet night; also, he would have shouted afresh when he came to the surface. And, moreover, he would have been seen, for though the moon was hidden, the sea gave back the subdued cloud-light in a sort of grey sheen, so common on calm nights at sea, when anything that breaks the surface of the water may be easily seen a considerable distance away.

This second disappearance had a frightening effect on the men. They spent the rest of that night, both watches, sitting in the fo'cas'le and talking about what had happened; their talk wandering off into a dozen ghastly sea superstitions, until at last they jumped every time there came the creak of a bulkhead, as the little brig rolled to some scarcely known swell.

The next day they got a fair wind, which blew away some of their mental cobwebs of ghostliness; but the feeling returned with the darkness, so much so that when, in the middle watch, Tompkins, the man whose wheel it was, stepped in over the starboard washboard, one of the men fairly yelled out with fright, until he saw who it was.

"What you doin' away from the wheel?" they asked Tompkins, as soon as they had their bearings again.

"The Mate said 'e'd give me a spell-oh," said Tompkins, joining the card-party and drawing out his pipe. " 'E've took the wheel hisself an' said I might come forrard till four bells 'E's a all right old cove, if 'e 'as got a tongue on 'im like a bollard!"

And, indeed, big Maulk proved himself in many ways to justify the man's opinion; for he took many a wheel during the next few nights, and let the man go forward for a smoke. At the same time, he was so grim and self-sufficient that he never weakened his authority over them in the slightest way; so that he was as well-liked by the rough sea-dogs forward as is possible under shipboard conditions.

III

"The boy ain't in his bunk, sir," reported one of the men to Maulk, three mornings later.

It was one bell (4:30 a.m.) in the morning watch, and very dark, with a raw, cold feeling coming off the sea that set a shiver through the A.B. as he spoke. He had been sent down to call the cabin-boy to get the galley-fire lit for the morning coffee; and the boy was not in his bunk or anywhere around the pantry.

The Mate stared a moment through the darkness at the man; then, with a grim mutter of oaths, he went below to have a look for himself. Yet, when he returned to the half-poop, he had nothing fresh to report. The boy was certainly gone; and Maulk ordered the man to go forward and light the fire in the caboose and tell the men to have a look around the decks for him. Meanwhile, he would go down to the pantry and get out enough coffee for the morning.

The man went forward along the dark main-deck at a run. He had certainly no stomach for coffee just then, or anything else, except the companionship of the men forward. In his undeveloped brain, he was vaguely impressed by the Mate's callous indifference. If the Mate were hardy enough to be alone about the decks, he wasn't. He gasped as he thought something moved in the greyness around the pumps; then he was past the caboose, and a moment later burst into the fo'cas'le with this fresh news.

Both watches turned out to listen, and they went aft with him in a bunch to the galley, whilst he made the fire; and all the time they talked and kept together, glancing about them, over the rails at the grey sea and about the decks. It was not until the Mate had twice sung out for the man to go aft for the coffee that he went, and then he got the crowd to go with him. Maulk cursed the man and the whole lot of them, paying particular attention to their livers and ancestry in his remarks. He was interrupted by the man at the wheel darting down off the half-poop into the crowd; for the helmsman had suddenly discovered what had happened, and had simply bolted from the wheel.

Maulk jumped down in among the men, hauled the shaking helmsman out bodily, and dragged him bodily to the wheel, where he lashed him by the ankles to the grating, and clouted him into a dazed and silent admission of a more practical and painful kind of fear than his imaginary ones.

Meanwhile, the crowd had gone forward again to the galley and kept the temporary cook company whilst he made the coffee.

"I ain't going to the wheel tonight!" said one man; "not so wot the Mate says." And on this point they all agreed; though none of them had dared to interfere in the case of the unfortunate who was even then steering, lashed by his ankles to the wheel-grating, and unable to see the compass-card, because his gaze was fixed in terror over his shoulder. He feared unutterably what might come up over the taffrail at his back, out of the greyness that lay yet upon all the sea.

But Maulk, the big Mate, walked the half-poop morosely, and presently was singing out along the main-deck to know when his coffee was coming.

IV

That night the men in both watches refused absolutely to go back to the wheel and lookout. Dan'l Templet, the Bo'sun, met the difficulty with his watch by allowing two men to go to the wheel together; but Maulk was different. At first, he seemed to be half-minded to use force, but after a minute of grim silence in which his watch stood tense, he turned on them jeeringly and told them to go forward to their nursemaids, whilst he took the wheel himself And take the wheel he did for the next six nights.

The sixth night was very dark, and the wind fell away into a blank calm a little before midnight, the brig rolling slightly on the slow swells, with her sails slatting and gear and timbers creaking a little mournfully in the quietness that lay black and immense all about her.

At midnight Maulk came up and relieved the Bo'sun. At the same time he cursed morosely a couple of his own watch who came aft to take the wheel, and sent them forward with a jeer, as he had done every night since their first refusal to go alone to the wheel. In any case, there was no actual need for anyone at the wheel; so that he merely tautened up the kicking-tackles, and began to pace the half-poop alone, as usual.

When the Bo'sun came up, four hours later to relieve him, he was not there, nor was he anywhere in the ship. He had vanished as completely as had the three others.

"The Cap'n's punt's gone," said one of the men suddenly to the Bo'sun, who was leading the search. "Look, Bo'sun!"

The man was right. The boat, which hung always inboard from the starboard quarter davits, had disappeared.

"Now, that's almighty rum!" said the Bo'sun, and jumped to the rail. He stared down into the darkness, then turned and whipped out the lamp from the binnacle, and shone the light over the side. It showed the falls dangling loose, with the blocks just dipping into the calm sea as the brig rolled slightly from time to time; but of the punt there was no sign.

"Almighty rum!" muttered the Bo'sun again, to himself. Then he handed the lamp to one of the men and hollowed his hands around his mouth. "Boat ahoy!" But there came no answer; nor any sound of oars out of the distance.

"Now," said Dan'l Templet in a slow voice, speaking to the men who crowded round, peering over the rail into nothingness—"now what should any man make of that? What hell an' devilment have this packet got aboard! The Mate's gone, an' I can't navigate; though I give best to no man on God's earth when it comes to plain seamanship. The Mate's gone, but he never went natcheral, you may stake on that! An' we're lost out here maybe a thousand miles from any land as ever I've heard on. Come down with me, lads, an' I'll take a look at the chart; maybe it'll show where we are. I don't fancy to go below alone."

The Bo'sun led the way down the scuttle, carrying the binnacle-lamp, though the lamp was still burning in the large cabin, as they could tell by the light through the glass of the skylight. In the big cabin they picked up the hanging lamp, and took a look round for the chart, but could find nothing. Then one of the men suggested looking in the cabins that opened off fore and aft. They pushed open the door of the Mate's room, and the Bo'sun shone the binnacle-lamp in.

"Theer's summat on th' boonk-board!" shouted one of the men, who was peering over his shoulder. "Sitha?"

The Bo'sun stepped inside the smaller cabin and held the lamp close, and so, with infinite difficulty he spelled out what was written on a leaf torn out of the log-book, and fixed on to the front of the Mate's bunk, by means of a couple of sail-needles used as nails. The writing on it was beautiful copperplate, and exceedingly brief. It ran:

"Look in the lazarette. See key."

The key in question dangled by its loop of ropeyarn from one of the sail-needles, and fitted the lock in the trap door under the cabin table, which led to the lazarette below, where the ship's stores were kept.

"Now," said Dan'l Templet simply, as he took the key, "I don't fancy to go down there; it may be some new sort of devil's work. We'll get a-plenty of lamps from the lamp-locker, and we'll all go below together. Get some belayin'-pins, some of you!"

They did as the Bo'sun said and came back with him to the big cabin. There Dan'l Templet got under the table and unlocked the trap-door; then, with all his courage, he pulled it wide open and threw the hatch on to the deck of the cabin. The men were kneeling all around, holding their lamps in one hand and a belaying-pin or marlin-spike in the other; some of them had their sheath-knives drawn. Yet not one of them made any motion to descend; instead, there was rather a tendency to draw back from the black gape of the hatchway. It was the Bo'sun who finally led the way. He hauled a length of punt-yarn out of his pocket and bent it to the handle of his lamp; then lowered the lamp to the foot of the ladder which went down into the lazarette.

For maybe a full minute he and the men stared down, but could see nothing unusual. At last Dan'l Templet decided to venture it, and putting his feet down into the hole, began to go crabwise down the ladder, with a muttered word to the men to follow him closely.

Near the bottom of the ladder he thought he heard a vague sound to his left, which made him pause; but the man above apparently had heard nothing, for he continued to go down, and trod heavily on the Bo'sun's head. Dan'l Templet grabbed wildly at the man's foot, swearing automatically, and the two of them slipped and went down in a heap at the foot of the ladder, falling on the lamp and crushing it to pieces.

They got up, the man still yelling at the top of his voice; for he was sure that some infernal thing had caught at him out of the darkness of the lazarette. The Bo'sun caught the man a hard clip on the side of the head, then made one jump up the ladder and caught a lamp from the next man on the rungs. With this he dropped back into the lazarette and held the light over his head.

There was a clamour of shouts and questionings from the men who were even then coming down. But when they saw the Bo'sun standing there unhurt, they hurried to join him with their lamps, and so in a minute the place was full of light. Thus it was that they were able to see immediately an extraordinary sight; for, lying in a row, but about a fathom apart from each other, were three figures that had begun to wriggle about and emit vague, inarticulate sounds.

"Lord save us!" shouted the man who had first seen the writing on the Mate's bunk-board. "See theer! See theer!" He pointed excitedly, holding the lamp forward with the other hand. "Yon's tha Cap'n, an' Bruikson, an' th' lad! Sitha!"

At the Lancashireman's words there was a general surge forward on the part of the men, led by Dan'l Templet. The three figures on the deck of the lazarette had twisted round to them, and their eyes shone queerly bright out of grimed faces and shocks of matted hair. But none of them could move a yard; for they were not only gagged and lashed hand and foot, but tethered by short lengths of rope to staples driven into the skin of the ship.

The three of them were quickly cut loose and helped up into the cabin above.

"Where's yon—Maulk!" old Captain Gaskelt had gasped out with an unmentionable oath, as they cut from his mouth the fiercely bitten piece of wood, which had done for a gag during all the weary days in which he had lain below there.

"Gone!" said Dan'l Templet, "and the punt with him!" He stared at the piece of hard teak which the Captain had chewed into the shape of an hourglass. "G'lord! Cap'n!" he added, "this must a' giv' you hell! Was it the Mate as done it?"

Captain Gaskelt swallowed a stiff tot of rum and passed the jug round. Then he explained how one night, he didn't know now how long ago it was, Maulk had come up behind him during his watch, and nearly choked him to death. The next thing he knew, he came to lying in the lazarette, all lashed up, as he said, like a bale.

Bruikson, the man, had much the same thing to tell; he was, however, careful to hide the truth, which was that he had seen Maulk attack the Captain, but had held his tongue, being a thoroughly callous sort, and had later tried to frighten the big Mate into sharing with him whatever he had gained by killing the Captain; for he had never thought but that Maulk had murdered old Captain Gaskelt and dumped his body quietly overside.

The case of the boy was entirely different. He had heard a sound in the lazarette, the key of which Maulk carried always on him. He had heard the sound, like a sort of knocking, whilst he was in his bunk, and had run into the Mate's cabin to wake him. To his amazement and fear, Maulk had caught him by the throat and threatened to kill him if he uttered a sound. The Mate had then carried him to the trapdoor, unlocked and opened it, and carried him below, where he lashed him up in the same way that he had made the man and the Master fast.

Maulk had not treated his prisoners badly, in many ways. He had fed them twice a day, ungagging each one in turn and attending to their various wants in a grim but not brutal fashion.

But the reason for it all was what bothered the Captain; for, so far as the Bo'sun and the crew could tell him, Maulk had taken no sort of advantage of his temporary command of the ship. The whole of the Mate's action was inexplicable; and thus it remained until daylight, which began to come, clear and cold and calm, a little before eight bells.

V

Captain Gaskelt had taken charge once more. His old knees trembled a little as he stood near the lee-rail, peering away to port; but though he felt utterly tired, his spirit was indomitable, and he was waiting for the fast-coming daylight to show the punt somewhere within the circle of the horizon. He had a man aloft at each masthead, and had promised a pound of tobacco to the one who should first report the boat. Meanwhile, he studied the sea around through his telescope.

As the daylight strengthened, Captain Gaskelt had something of a shock; for what he had taken to be a heavy bank of clouds to the southward began to resolve itself into something more solid. Even as he realised this, there came the hail almost simultaneously from both mastheads:

"Land on the port beam, Sir!"

The morning light came more strongly, and old Captain Gaskelt gave a little mutter of amazement as he perceived what he was staring at. With a slight shake of his old wrists, he adjusted the glass to his eye and stared. Then in a curious voice he turned and hailed the Bo'sun.

"Dan'l," he said, "there's land to loo'ard. Take a look at it an' tell me what you see.... Lord! To think of it... after all these years!" he added to himself, whilst he waited for the Bo'sun to speak.

"It's a hiland," said Dan'l Templet, staring through the telescope. "There's a great peak, as you c'n see, Sir, to the eastern end of it, and there's a most unnatcheral lookin' cross, or the likes of the same, on the side of the peak." He lowered the glass, and the Captain grabbed it from him, whilst the Bo'sun stared down curiously at the Old Man. "Do you mean to say, Sir," added Dan'l Templet, "as yon's the hiland we always thought was a joke of yourn?"

But old Captain Gaskelt never heard him.

"That's it! That's it!" he kept saying under his breath. "Oh, Mister Maulk, you great hog, I forgive you.... That's why you put me away, so as you could take charge an' steer the ship down here.... An' me tellin' you about the island!... An' you knowin' all the time.... Lord! Look at the crossbones! Cut as natural as life!... An' that quiet devil knowed the latitood an' the longytood all the time! An' never a word to me, the sly hog—the sly hog! But I guess he overrun the mark, or else the ship's in a drift, and the current's brought her down on the island during the night. I shouldn't wonder...."

He broke off his mutter and spoke to the Bo'sun; still without ceasing to look through the telescope.

"Turn the men to, Bo'sun, clearing out the starboard boat," he said. "Yon Mister Mate has sure made ashore yon, and we'll catch him yet for his sins. And maybe we'll make our fortunes while we're there, Bo'sun. There's as much gold hid ashore in the Crossbones, they do say, as would buy Jerusalem.... And to think of all the brasted fools I've met while I've been fishin', as was ready to bet there was no such place as the Crossbones!"

He lapsed into brief but subtle profanity, in no wise lacking in vigour, despite its subtlety. The memory of all the men who had laughed at him in many a public-house and saloon in many a seaport came hot upon him. Here was truly a case of he laughs the best who laughs the last.

"And yon devil knew all the time!" he broke out again presently. "Not since I was a boy, Dan'l, have I seen yon blessed sight!" he continued, oblivious of the fact that the Bo'sun had long since gone to assist the men at clearing the big ship's boat. "Not since I was a boy... They do say there's a mint of the gold buried under the crossbones itself," he went rambling on. "To think, all my life I've thought of yon, and there it is!... Bo'sun, are they gettin' that boat cleared?"

VI

Captain Gaskelt beached the boat on a sandy spit of sand that ran out in a long curve, and made a splendid, sheltered landing. The little punt lay there, high and dry where Maulk had hauled it up when he landed some hours before. From the punt there ran a single track of footsteps towards where, some hundred fathoms away, there began the skirt of a dense, gloomy-looking wood, coming surprisingly far down to the beach, and continuing upward over a great rise, which led inward toward the centre part of the island.

"That's the way yon devil went," said Captain Gaskelt, pointing at the footprints. "One of you stay by the boat; the others come along with me." He glanced up at the sky and the sun, then round the horizon. "I hope the weather'll hold calm," he muttered to himself in half-conscious uneasiness.

"Now, lads!" He began to lead the way.

As they neared the place where the sand-spit merged into the upward slope of the island, old Captain Gaskelt's excitement broke out. He looked back over his shoulder at his five men.

"Get a move on you, lads!" he shouted. "There's a million fortunes hid on this island. This is the place they've been looking for these two hundred years. This is where Galt and Ladd and a dozen of them old pirate devils hid their stuff; and we're going to get it. Come on!"

And he began to run along the tracks toward where they entered the trees, a little to the side of a low cliff that stood up to their left, all crowned with a chaos of wild bushes.

The men had been incredibly fired by the Old Man's words, and they pelted after him in a string; and so entered the wood, panting and stumbling over the lacings of undergrowth. Their run dwindled presently into a walk, and soon into a climb; for the side of the island went up very abruptly in that place. Yet the old Captain's excitement was so great that he managed still to keep the lead; and even found breath to shout back odd phrases of:

"Come along, lads! Hey for the old pirates' gold! No more going to sea, men! No more turning out on a dirty night! Come along, lads!"

The men answered back with breathless shouts and climbed furiously, the sounds of their gasps and stumblings going curiously clear through the chilly morning air.

"Keep off there!" roared Maulk's voice suddenly from some unknown place among the trees. "Keep off, Cap'n. I don't wish you no harm, as you should know; but I'll blow you to hell an' out again if you come a step farther!"

"There he is, men!" shouted Captain Gaskelt. "On to him, lads! On to him!"

But as there was no one for them to "on to," they simply stood in their tracks, staring helplessly about them.

Abruptly, there came the heavy bang of a musket, from somewhere below them, and a bullet went splintering the smaller branches over the men's heads; and at that, they turned to their left and bolted forthwith through a clearer space among the trees

"I'll learn you! I'll learn you!" they heard Maulk shouting in a great voice through the trees; and immediately afterward there came the thud, thud, of two other shots and the zipping of the bullets to right and left.

Old Captain Gaskelt was running with the rest. They had not a weapon among them except their sheath-knives; and so were at the mercy of Maulk, unless they could reach some sort of safe shelter.

"Sitha!" shouted the Northman who had formed one of the boat's crew. "Yon cave! Yon cave! Coom on!" And he dashed out of the line of flight toward where a great hole showed in the side of a rock face to their left. The others followed, and within a few seconds they were all under cover in a cave that went winding in into an utter darkness, like a sort of gigantic passage.

" 'E'll never let us go alive!" said one of the men, after they had stood silent a few minutes, listening desperately for any signs of Maulk. "Us know too bloomin' much of this 'ere island! There's the old brig! My oath! I'd give my 'ole bloomin' payday to be safe aboard 'er this bloomin' minnit! The Mate's a bloomin' madman, that's wot 'e is!"

From where they stood they could see out over the sea to the north and west, a roughly circular view-field bounded by the mouth of the cave; and across this field of blue water there was drifting slowly the brig, with her sails slatting ever so gently as she rolled a little from time to time.

"G'Lord!" said Captain Gaskelt abruptly, as a tremendous crash of sound went echoing over the island. "Look!" he added, almost in a shriek, as a great jet of water rose between the shore and the brig. "It's a cannon!"

He broke off into an inarticulate cry as a bright, white shower of splinters shot up into the clear morning air from the starboard rail of the brig.

" 'E's goin' to sink 'er, and then 'e'll murder us just like shootin' a lot of dawgs!" said the man who had spoken before. "Let's out and charge the swine. Maybe we'll be able to knife 'im before 'e outs us all! 'E don't mean one of us to leave 'ere alive!"

With the word, he rushed out through the mouth of the cave into the daylight, waving his sheath-knife. A couple of steps he ran, and then pitched headlong, whilst the thud of a musket sounded through the trees. He lay on the ground, piteously still; and no one followed him.

A second and a third shot from the cannon followed at leisurely intervals; but the shooting was not so good, and they both missed the brig. Then the men in the cave began to cheer; for the Bo'sun was hoisting out the remaining boat; and presently he had it ahead of the vessel, and was towing her out of danger as hard as the men could lay to the oars.

There was presently a fourth cannon shot which, however, fell short of the brig by about half a mile; and after that, through the long, silent, breathless-seeming afternoon, no sound in all the island, save the vague, far noise of the surf to the southward and the lonely crying of sea-birds, wheeling high against a sky that was slowly growing leaden.

"I don't understand 'im 'avin' that cannon," said one of the men; "nor powder nor shot nor nothin' else! What like place is this 'ere hiland, Cap'n?"

"I guess it's one left here by them damned pirates," said Captain Gaskelt, eyeing the sky and the general look of the atmosphere anxiously.... Lord! I don't like the look of the weather! There's a proper southerly buster brewin', or I know nothin'!... What powder and shot.... I don't know; only it looks as if there's been devilment ashore here not such a mighty long time gone. I'd not be s'prised at anything I found down here. It's just Satan's own pet hiding-place for his own spawn! As for the Mate, I'm thinkin' he must have been mixed up in some rum doings, sometime or other in his wicked life. But I've been thinkin' it must have been years gone, now; and him, maybe, lived decent a bit; but broke loose with the chance to get back to the gold he must 'a' known to be here. I don't reckon, somehow, we've any but him to bother with; he'd not go shootin' so free an' easy if there was others; they'd not want him, and he'd not want them; not if it's the gold he's after. We'll do him yet, if the wind'll hold off till dark. We'll make a run for the boats and get away, unless he thinks to stove them…. Good Lord! What's that?"

In through the cave-mouth there came crawling painfully a limp, white-faced man, dragging his left leg, limp and useless from the hip. As he came there sounded outside the bang of a musket, very near, and the heavy ball knocked a shower of rock chippings from the top of the cave-mouth on to the back of the creeping man.

"It's Tauless!" said several voices, shouting the name of the man who had been shot outside, and whom all had supposed to be dead. Then half a dozen hands were dragging him in to safety. As they did so, they heard Maulk outside, shouting in a great voice, shaken with a sort of brutal-seeming laughter:

"I'll learn you! I'll learn you!" he was shouting. "I'll make long pig of you before this time tomorrow. I've blown the brig to hell, and you'll go too, as soon as I get at you!"

They heard his laughter going loud and intentionally threatening through the thin, chill air, echoing with a strange, empty sound from some of the naked rocks and boulders that lay huge around the cleared space out of which their cliff sprang. But after the echoes had died away, they heard nothing for hours, and no one spoke except old Captain Gaskelt, muttering nervous comments to himself on the look of the darker-growing sky. Once he broke out with:

"It's one of the devil's lies about the brig. She got clean away!" He looked round at the men in the half-darkness of the cave, as if he doubted that he had himself seen the vessel towed out of danger.

"She's all right, Cap'n," they assured him. "I wish we was half as right!" One of them crept quietly and cautiously near to the mouth of the cave and peered out. He nodded back to Captain Gaskelt. "She's all right, Cap'n," he whispered over his shoulder. "The Bo'sun's getting the sail off her. They—"

But he never finished; for simultaneously with the startling bang of Maulk's firearm from near by, a heavy bullet struck the rock within a foot of the man's head; and he rolled backward into the cave, swearing with fright, but unhurt. Evidently Maulk was keeping a close watch.

Presently a certain recklessness took the old Captain, and he wandered back into the darkness of the cave, feeling around him, and striking odd matches. The men sat and whispered together in a depressed fashion, but suddenly they heard the Master calling softly to them from some place in the darkness. Then a match was struck, apparently some fifty yards away, shining like an infinitely small star in an utter gloom. They walked toward it, and as the Captain struck a second light they came up with him.

"Follow along, lads," said old Captain Gaskelt; and he led them through a long passage which was presently lighted here and there through shafts or blowholes through the rock. They came out in about a minute onto a shelf of rock that stood out from an immense wall of rock which faced to the south, and went down sheer a hundred feet below.

They were looking out over an extraordinary harbour which seemed to be situated somewhere near the centre of the island, being entirely land-locked, to such an extent that not only could they get no view of the sea to the southward, but they were unable to trace the exact position of the hidden mouth of the harbour, which was entered probably by a winding passage through the irregular rocky sides, which towered up all around.

Lying in this harbour, still floating, despite that they appeared to belong to a period a hundred or more years earlier, were three ancient craft, still carrying to the trained eye a tale of rakishness that suggested their history. In each case they had a heavy gun mounted amidships; though in the biggest of the three vessels the gun carriage had rotted away, and the gun lay upon the deck, amid the wreck of its rotted carriage.

"Them's been pirate ships, I'll bet my davy!" said one of the men. "Old timers as was killin' an' murderin' before you or me was fishin'! But that's a tidy little hooker, and good enough to go to sea in, if she was overhauled."

He pointed to the westward where there lay moored head and stern a beautiful little cutter-rigged vessel, not more than some ten or twelve tons register. Her boom and gaff were unshipped, and it was obvious that she had lain there for many years—maybe a dozen or more. But she was evidently capable of being made seaworthy; and her presence showed the men that the island must have been visited during the past generation.

"There's big guns mounted among them rocks to the southwest," remarked Captain Gaskelt, pointing. "That way must be the entrance. The blessed island's like a fortress. Lord, but I wish I had a good musket in my fist! I'd—"

He broke off, as a great flicker of lightning ran across the dead greyness that now covered all the sky overhead.

"God help us!" he said, "if the weather don't hold till we make the brig." he crossed himself unconsciously, having been brought up a good enough Catholic, though it was long since he had thought of religious things.

For maybe a couple of hours the Captain and the men stood out there on the ledge, looking about for some way of escape, but without finding any, for the cliff, both below and above, went away too steep. They had forgotten the possibility of Maulk finding them there; and suddenly they heard his voice above them:

"Get back there! Get back there!" And immediately the thud of his musket far above. The bullet struck the rock near to the old Captain, and sent a splash of hot lead on to the back of his hand; whilst the echoes of the shot rang back and forth, strangely hollow-sounding across the curious, silent harbour, with its long forgotten craft. "Get back there. I've got you!" came Maulk's roar again; but already they were all in the passage, and Captain Gaskelt was striking a match to show the way.

When they reached the other entrance, the Captain had a look at Tauless, whose wound he had previously bandaged tightly with strips torn off his own shirt. He found the man exhausted, but not suffering much pain; and after a few words with him, turned to the others. "Now, lads," he said, "it'll be dark in less than half an hour. A couple of you off with your jackets and pass me over all your belts. We'll rig up a sling to carry this sick lad. Get your boots off, so you'll make no noise when we go.

VII

The night had come, heavy and black, with an intense stillness upon the island, through which came only the vague, far roar of the southward surf. Every few minutes an immense quiver of violet flame would flit across the dark arch of the night, showing every rock and tree about the entrance of the cave. But there was no thunder.

Old Captain Gaskelt was lying on his stomach at the mouth of the cave, trying to take advantage of the lightning flashes to learn whether Maulk was about.

"Now, lads!" he said at last, over his shoulder, speaking in a whisper. "Lift him easy and don't make a sound. The Lord help us, and we'll do that devil yet. Wait! Now, out you come!"

They came out in their bare feet, carrying their boots. Two of the biggest men had the helpless Tauless on the sling of coats and belts; whilst old Captain Gaskelt led the way, cursing silently as someone stumbled and rattled a loose boulder.

They had just reached the edge of the trees when one of those huge flashes swept over the sky, and they showed, like a lot of stumbling, black puppets, plain for anyone to see.

"I've got you!" roared Maulk's voice; and almost on the instant, as if it were thunder to the lightning, came the immense thud of a cannon high up the slope, and a screaming, whistling shower passed far over their heads.

"Run!" shouted the old Captain. The men obeyed and crashed down through the trees, bumping themselves and the unfortunate man they carried. Yet, so frantic a speed they made that in less than a minute they were down on to the sandspit, and running for the place where the two boats showed plain in two rapidly succeeding flashes of lightning. Behind them, as they ran, the silence of the island was broken by a musket shot; but no one heard the bullet. Then they were come to the boat; and set the wounded Tauless on the sand, whilst they strained to the launching. They heard a far shouting from Maulk, coming strangely clear across the immense silence, and then, just after the lightning had flashed once more, there showed a great red burst of fire, far up on the side of the island; and immediately afterward there came again that screaming, whistling shower of metal through the night. Some of the shot struck the boat; and one man shouted loudly, for he had been hit in the hand. Yet, before the madman on the hill could again fire the cannon, which he must have trained on the boats during the daylight, they had the bigger boat afloat. They lifted Tauless in, and someone hit the man who had been shot in the hand a mighty clout on the head, and bade him stop his yelling.

"Out oars, lads! Smartly now!" shouted old Captain Gaskelt. "Get her off! Get her off! Move handy now! Dear Lord! we'll do it yet before the wind hits us! There's the brig's lights away to the nor'-west. Put your backs into it, men! Put some beef into it, or you'll never smell salt horse again. *Pull!*"

They reached the brig half an hour later; and ten minutes afterward the "southerly buster" broke down on them, in a roar of wind out of the south that was like the roll of an invisible world against them, a stunning pressure of wind, full of froth like blown snow, and a sea behind it that followed black and living and furious.

And somewhere, far in the wake of this grim storm, they lost that mysterious island; for when the dawn broke there was nowhere anything from horizon to horizon save the mad flurrying of the seas, heaving crests of foam forty feet high; and everywhere the bowl of the universe seeming filled with a drunken, raging wind that made all mere human power but a vain thing.

Yet, strange as it may seem to a landsman, old Captain Gaskelt was an extraordinarily contented man. He had perfect faith both in his little brig and in his own seamanship; and both were justified. For, when the storm left them some hundreds of miles to the northward, the brig had not lost a sail or a spar, nor any deck furniture of consequence.

Perhaps old Captain Gaskelt's satisfaction with things in general may be more perfectly appreciated when I explain that down in his cabin, securely locked in his own desk, was a small, heavily tarred canvas bag, that was yet so heavy, despite its smallness, that the sturdy Captain needed both hands to heft it. He had found this bag deposited in the stern of the boat; and had said nothing to the men, being of the safe opinion that division lessens profits as well as labour.

He had no certain knowledge how it had come there; but had reasoned out that his one-time Mate had never shown him any ill-will, and had possibly put the bag there as a little present. In the light of this opinion, the Captain was forced to believe that Maulk had not been particularly anxious to kill any of them; but that his chief intention had been to frighten them away, knowing that the coming storm would blow them some hundreds of miles from the island before there could be any chance of taking a latitude to discover its position.

Possibly Captain Gaskelt's opinion of the matter is correct. In any case, there is no doubting the fact of the bag of gold coin; nor that Captain Gaskelt, like the rest of us, is still anxious to find out where Crossbones Island lies.

One curious thing I must tell in conclusion. The man Maulk must certainly have been unbalanced in many ways; for, when they came to examine the ship's boat, they found no less than twenty-two bent and broken gold coins imbedded in her, which can be explained only by supposing that he had literally loaded the cannon for that last shot with a fortune in gold. What became of the man himself we can only surmise. It is not impossible that he got away, after the storm, in the little craft which the men noticed lying in the western part of the harbour.

Yet, from that day to this, the latitude and longitude of Crossbones Island has remained a mystery. The island itself is a familiar name in many an olden fo'c's'le; and many are the sailors who swear they will yet find it and its enormous wealth of gold, leave the sea, and buy a farm.

But they never do.

The Stone Ship

RUM THINGS!— OF COURSE there are rum things happen at sea— As rum as ever there were. I remember when I was in the *Alfred Jessop,* a small barque, whose owner was her skipper, we came across a most extraordinary thing.

We were twenty days out from London, and well down into the tropics. It was before I took my ticket, and I was in the fo'cas'le. The day had passed without a breath of wind, and the night found us with all the lower sails up in the buntlines.

Now, I want you to take good note of what I am going to say:—

When it was dark in the second dog-watch, there was not a sail in sight; not even the far off smoke of a steamer, and no land nearer than Africa, about a thousand miles to the Eastward of us.

It was our watch on deck from eight to twelve midnight, and my lookout from eight to ten. For the first hour, I walked to and fore across the break of the fo'cas'le head, smoking my pipe and just listening to the quiet.... Ever heard the kind of silence you can get away out at sea? You need to be in one of the old-time wind-jammers, with all the lights dowsed, and the sea as calm and quiet as some queer plain of death. And then you want a pipe and the lonesomeness of the fo'cas'le head, with the caps'n to lean against while you listen and think. And all about you, stretching out into the miles, only and always the enormous silence of the sea, spreading out a thousand miles every way into the everlasting, brooding night. And not a light anywhere, out on all the waste of waters; nor ever a sound, as I have told, except the faint moaning of the masts and gear, as they chafe and whine a little to the occasional invisible roll of the ship.

And suddenly, across all this silence, I heard Jensen's voice from the head of the starboard steps, say:—

"Did you hear *that,* Duprey?"

"What?" I asked, cocking my head up. But as I questioned, I heard what he heard—the constant sound of running water, for all the world like the noise of a brook running down a hill-side. And the queer sound was surely not a hundred fathoms off our port bow!

"By gum!" said Jensen's voice, out of the darkness. "That's damned sort of funny!"

"Shut up!" I whispered, and went across, in my bare feet, to the port rail, where I leaned out into the darkness, and stared towards the curious sound.

The noise of a brook running down a hill-side continued, where there was no brook for a thousand sea-miles in any direction.

"What is it?" said Jensen's voice again, scarcely above a whisper now. From below him, on the main-deck, there came several voices questioning:— "Hark!" "Stow the talk!" "…there!" "Listen!" "Lord love us, what is it?" …And then Jensen muttering to them to be quiet.

There followed a full minute, during which we all heard the brook, where no brook could ever run; and then, out of the night there came a sudden hoarse incredible sound:—ooaaze, oooaze, arrrr, arrrr, oooaze—a stupendous sort of croak, deep and somehow abominable, out of the blackness. In the same instant, I found myself sniffing the air. There was a queer rank smell, stealing through the night.

"Forrard there on the lookout!" I heard the Mate singing out, away aft. "Forrard there! What the blazes are you doing!"

I heard him come clattering down the port ladder from the poop, and then the sound of his feet at a run along the main-deck. Simultaneously, there was a thudding of bare feet, as the watch below came racing out of the fo'cas'le beneath me.

"Now then! Now then! Now then!" shouted the Mate, as he charged up on to the fo'cas'le head. "What's up?"

"It's something off the port bow, Sir," I said. "Running water! And then that sort of howl…. Your night-glasses," I suggested.

"Can't see a thing," he growled, as he stared away through the dark. "There's a sort of mist. Phoo! what a devil of a stink!"

"Look!" said someone down on the main-deck. "What's that?"

I saw it in the same instant, and caught the Mate's elbow.

"Look, Sir," I said. "There's a light there, about three points off the bow. It's moving."

The Mate was staring through his night-glasses, and suddenly he thrust them into my hands:—

"See if you can make it out," he said, and forthwith put his hands round his mouth, and bellowed into the night:— "Ahoy there! Ahoy there! Ahoy there!" his voice going out lost into the silence and darkness all around. But there came never a comprehensible answer, only all the time the infernal noise of a brook running out there on the sea, a thousand miles from any brook of earth; and away on the port bow, a vague shapeless shining.

I put the glasses to my eyes, and stared. The light was bigger and brighter, seen through the binoculars; but I could make nothing of it, only a dull, elongated shining, that moved vaguely in the darkness, apparently a hundred fathoms or so, away on the sea.

"Ahoy there! Ahoy there!" sung out the Mate again. Then, to the men below:— "Quiet there on the main-deck!"

There followed about a minute of intense stillness, during which we all listened; but there was no sound, except the constant noise of water running steadily.

I was watching the curious shining, and I saw it flick out suddenly at the Mate's shout. Then in a moment I saw three dull lights, one under the other, that flicked in and out intermittently.

"Here, give me the glasses!" said the Mate, and grabbed them from me.

He stared intensely for a moment; then swore, and turned to me:—

"What do you make of them?" he asked, abruptly.

"I don't know, Sir," I said. "I'm just puzzled. Perhaps it's electricity, or something of that sort."

"Oh hell!" he replied, and leant far out over the rail, staring. "Lord!" he said, for the second time, "what a stink!"

As he spoke, there came a most extraordinary thing; for there sounded a series of heavy reports out of the darkness, seeming in the silence, almost as loud as the sound of small cannon.

"They're shooting!" shouted a man on the main-deck, suddenly.

The Mate said nothing; only he sniffed violently at the night air. "By Gum!" he muttered, "what is it?"

I put my hand over my nose; for there was a terrible, charnel-like stench filling all the night about us.

"Take my glasses, Duprey," said the Mate, after a few minutes further watching. "Keep an eye over yonder. I'm going to call the Captain."

He pushed his way down the ladder, and hurried aft. About five minutes later, he returned forrard with the Captain and the Second and Third Mates, all in their shirts and trousers.

"Anything fresh, Duprey?" asked the Mate.

"No, Sir," I said, and handed him back his glasses. "The lights have gone again, and I think the mist is thicker. There's still the sound of running water out there."

The Captain and the three Mates stood some time along the port rail of the fo'cas'le head, watching through their night-glasses, and listening. Twice the Mate hailed; but there came no reply.

There was some talk, among the officers; and I gathered that the Captain was thinking of investigating.

"Clear one of the life-boats, Mr. Celt," he said, at last. "The glass is steady; there'll be no wind for hours yet. Pick out half a dozen men. Take, 'em out of either watch, if they want to come. I'll be back when I've got my coat."

"Away aft with you, Duprey, and some of you others," said the Mate. "Get the cover off the port life-boat, and bail her out."

" 'i, 'i, Sir," I answered, and went away aft with the others.

We had the boat into the water within twenty minutes, which is good time for a wind-jammer, where boats are generally used as storage receptacles for odd gear.

I was one of the men told off to the boat, with two others from our watch, and one from the starboard.

The Captain came down the end of the main tops'l halyards into the boat, and the Third after him. The Third took the tiller, and gave orders to cast off.

We pulled out clear of our vessel, and the Skipper told us to lie on our oars for a moment while he took his bearings. He leant forward to listen, and we all did the same. The sound of the running water was quite distinct across the quietness; but it struck me as seeming not so loud as earlier.

I remember now, that I noticed how plain the mist had become—a sort of warm, wet mist; not a bit thick; but just enough to make the night very dark, and to be visible, eddying slowly in a thin vapour round the port side-light, looking like a red cloudiness swirling lazily through the red glow of the big lamp.

There was no other sound at this time, beyond the sound of the running water; and the Captain, after handing something to the Third Mate, gave the order to give-way.

I was rowing stroke, and close to the officers, and so was able to see dimly that the Captain had passed a heavy revolver over to the Third Mate.

"Ho!" I thought to myself, "so the Old Man's a notion there's really something dangerous over there."

I slipped a hand quickly behind me, and felt that my sheath knife was clear.

We pulled easily for about three or four minutes, with the sound of the water growing plainer somewhere ahead in the darkness; and astern of us, a vague red glowing through the night and vapour, showed where our vessel was lying.

We were rowing easily, when suddenly the bow-oar muttered "G'lord!" Immediately afterwards, there was a loud splashing in the water on his side of the boat.

"What's wrong in the bows, there?" asked the Skipper, sharply.

"There's somethin' in the water, Sir, messing round my oar," said the man.

I stopped rowing, and looked round. All the men did the same. There was a further sound of splashing, and the water was driven right over the boat in showers. Then the bow-oar called out:— "There's somethin' got a holt of my oar, Sir!"

I could tell the man was frightened; and I knew suddenly that a curious nervousness had come to me—a vague, uncomfortable dread, such as the memory of an ugly tale will bring, in a lonesome place. I believe every man in the boat had a similar feeling. It seemed to me in that moment, that a definite, muggy sort of silence was all round us, and this in spite of the sound of the splashing, and the strange noise of the running water somewhere ahead of us on the dark sea.

"It's let go the oar, Sir!" said the man.

Abruptly, as he spoke, there came the Captain's voice in a roar:— "Back water all!" he shouted. "Put some beef into it now! Back all! Back all!… Why the devil was no lantern put in the boat! Back now! Back! Back!"

We backed fiercely, with a will; for it was plain that the Old Man had some good reason to get the boat away pretty quickly. He was right, too; though, whether it was guess-work, or some kind of instinct that made him shout out at that moment, I don't know; only I am sure he could not have seen anything in that absolute darkness.

As I was saying, he was right in shouting to us to back; for we had not backed more than half a dozen fathoms, when there was a tremendous splash right ahead of us, as if a house had fallen into the sea; and a regular wave of sea-water came at us out of the darkness, throwing our bows up, and soaking us fore and aft.

"Good Lord!" I heard the Third Mate gasp out. "What the devil's that?"

"Back all! Back! Back!" the Captain sung out again.

After some moments, he had the tiller put over, and told us to pull. We gave way with a will, as you may think, and in a few minutes were alongside our own ship again.

"Now then, men," the Captain said, when we were safe, aboard, "I'll not order any of you to come; but after the Steward's served out a tot of grog each, those who are willing, can come with me, and we'll have another go at finding out what devil's work is going on over yonder."

He turned to the Mate, who had been asking questions:—

"Say, Mister," he said, "it's no sort of thing to let the boat go without a lamp aboard. Send a couple of the lads into the lamp locker, and pass out a couple of the anchor-lights, and that deck bull's-eye, you use at nights for clearing up the ropes."

He whipped round on the Third:— "Tell the Steward to buck up with that grog, Mr. Andrews," he said, "and while you're there, pass out the axes from the rack in my cabin."

The grog came along a minute later; and then the Third Mate with three big axes from out the cabin rack.

"Now then, men," said the Skipper, as we took our tots off, "those who are coming with me, had better take an axe each from the Third Mate. They're mighty good weapons in any sort of trouble."

We all stepped forward, and he burst out laughing, slapping his thigh.

"That's the kind of thing I like!" he said. "Mr. Andrews, the axes won't go round. Pass out that old cutlass from the Steward's pantry. It's a pretty hefty piece of iron!"

The old cutlass was brought, and the man who was short of an axe, collared it. By this time, two of the 'prentices had filled (at least we supposed they had filled them!) two of the ship's anchor-lights; also they had brought out the bull's-eye lamp we used when clearing up the ropes on a dark night. With the lights and the axes and the cutlass, we felt ready to face anything, and down we went again into the boat, with the Captain and the Third Mate after us.

"Lash one of the lamps to one of the boat-hooks, and rig it out over the bows," ordered the Captain.

This was done, and in this way the light lit up the water for a couple of fathoms ahead of the boat; and made us feel less that something could come at us without our knowing. Then the painter was cast off, and we gave way again toward the sound of the running water, out there in the darkness.

I remember now that it struck me that our vessel had drifted a bit; for the sounds seemed farther away.

The second anchor-light had been put in the stern of the boat, and the Third Mate kept it between his feet, while he steered. The Captain had the bull's-eye in his hand, and was pricking up the wick with his pocket-knife.

As we pulled, I took a glance or two over my shoulder; but could see nothing, except the lamp making a yellow halo in the mist round the boat's bows, as we forged ahead. Astern of us, on our quarter, I could see the dull red glow of our vessel's port light. That was all, and not a sound in all the sea, as you might say, except the roll of our oars in the rowlocks, and somewhere in the darkness ahead, that curious noise of water running steadily; now sounding, as I have said, fainter and seeming farther away.

"It's got my oar again, Sir!" exclaimed the man at the bow oar, suddenly, and jumped to his feet. He hove his oar up with a great splashing of water, into the air, and immediately something whirled and beat about in the yellow halo of light over the bows of the boat. There was a crash of breaking wood, and the boat-hook was broken. The lamp soused down into the sea, and was lost. Then, in the darkness, there was a heavy splash, and a shout from the bow-oar:— "It's gone, Sir. It's loosed off the oar!"

"Vast pulling, all!" sung out the Skipper. Not that the order was necessary; for not a man was pulling. He had jumped up, and whipped a big revolver out of his coat pocket.

He had this in his right hand, and the bull's-eye in his left. He stepped forrard smartly over the oars from thwart to thwart, till he reached the bows, where he shone his light down into the water.

"My word!" he said. "Lord in Heaven! Saw anyone ever the like!"

And I doubt whether any man ever did see what we saw then; for the water was thick and living for yards round the boat with the hugest eels I ever saw before or after.

"Give way, men," said the Skipper, after a minute. "Yon's no explanation of the almighty queer sounds out yonder we're hearing this night. Give way, lads!"

He stood right up in the bows of the boat, shining his bull's-eye from side to side, and flashing it down on the water.

"Give way, lads!" he said again. "They don't like the light, that'll keep them from the oars. Give way steady now. Mr. Andrews, keep her dead on for the noise out yonder."

We pulled for some minutes, during which I felt my oar plucked at twice; but a flash of the Captain's lamp seemed sufficient to make the brutes loose hold.

The noise of the water running, appeared now quite near sounding.

About this time, I had a sense again of an added sort of silence to all the natural quietness of the sea. And I had a return of the curious nervousness that had touched me before. I kept listening intensely, as if I expected to hear some other sound than the noise of the water. It came to me suddenly that I had the kind of feeling one has in the aisle of a large cathedral. There was a sort of echo in the night—an incredibly faint reduplicating of the noise of our oars.

"Hark!" I said, audibly; not realising at first that I was speaking aloud. "There's an echo—"

"That's it!" the Captain cut in, sharply. "I thought I heard something rummy!"

"...I thought I heard something rummy," said a thin ghostly echo, out of the night "...thought I heard something rummy" "...heard something rummy." The words went muttering and whispering to and fro in the night about us, in rather a horrible fashion.

"Good Lord!" said the Old Man, in a whisper.

We had all stopped rowing, and were staring about us into the thin mist that filled the night. The Skipper was standing with the bull's-eye lamp held over his head, circling the beam of light round from port to starboard, and back again.

Abruptly, as he did so, it came to me that the mist was thinner. The sound of the running water was very near; but it gave back no echo.

"The water doesn't echo, Sir," I said. "That's dam funny!"

"That's dam funny," came back at me, from the darkness to port and starboard, in a multitudinous muttering "...Dam funny!...funny...eeey!"

"Give way!" said the Old Man, loudly. "I'll bottom this!"

"I'll bottom this...Bottom this... this!" The echo came back in a veritable rolling of unexpected sound. And then we had dipped our oars again, and the night was full of the reiterated rolling echoes of our rowlocks.

Suddenly the echoes ceased, and there was, strangely, the sense of a great space about us, and in the same moment the sound of the water running, appeared to be directly before us, but somehow up in the air.

"Vast rowing!" said the Captain, and we lay on our oars, staring round into the darkness ahead. The Old Man swung the beam of his lamp upwards, making circles with it in the night, and abruptly I saw something looming vaguely through the thinner-seeming mist.

"Look, Sir," I called to the Captain. "Quick, Sir, your light right above you! There's something up there!"

The Old Man flashed his lamp upwards, and found the thing I

had seen. But it was too indistinct to make anything of, and even as he saw it, the darkness and mist seemed to wrap it about.

"Pull a couple of strokes, all!" said the Captain. "Stow your talk, there in the boat!... Again!... That'll do! Vast pulling!"

He was sending the beam of his lamp constantly across that part of the night where we had seen the thing, and suddenly I saw it again.

"There, Sir!" I said, quickly, "A little to starboard with the light."

He flicked the light swiftly to the right, and immediately we all saw the thing plainly—a strangely made mast, standing up there out of the mist, and looking like no spar I had ever seen.

It seemed now that the mist must lie pretty low on the sea in places; for the mast stood up out of it plainly for several fathoms; but, lower, it was hidden in the mist, which, I thought, seemed heavier now all round us; but thinner, as I have said, above.

"Ship ahoy!" sung out the Skipper, suddenly. "Ship ahoy, there!" But for some moments there came never a sound back to us except the constant noise of the water running, not a score yards away; and then, it seemed to me that a vague echo beat back at us out of the mist, oddly:—"Ahoy! Ahoy! Ahoy!"

"There's something hailing us, Sir," said the Third Mate.

Now, that "something" was significant. It showed the sort of feeling that was on us all.

"That's na ship's mast as ever I've seen!" I heard the man next to me mutter. "It's got a unnatcheral look."

"Ahoy there!" shouted the Skipper again, at the top of his voice. "Ahoy there!"

With the suddenness of a clap of thunder there burst out at us a vast, grunting:—oooaze; arrrr; arrrr; oooaze—a volume of sound so great that it seemed to make the loom of the oar in my hand vibrate.

"Good Lord!" said the Captain, and levelled his revolver into the mist; but he did not fire.

I had loosed one hand from my oar, and gripped my axe. I remember thinking that the Skipper's pistol wouldn't be much use against whatever thing made a noise like that.

"It wasn't ahead, Sir," said the Third Mate, abruptly, from where he sat and steered. "I think it came from somewhere over to starboard."

"Damn this mist!" said the Skipper. "Damn it! What a devil of a stink! Pass that other anchor-light forrard."

I reached for the lamp, and handed it to the next man, who passed it on.

"The other boat-hook," said the Skipper; and when he'd got it, he lashed the lamp to the hook end, and then lashed the whole arrangement upright in the bows, so that the lamp was well above his head.

"Now," he said. "Give way gently! And stand by to back-water, if I tell you.... Watch my hand, Mister," he added to the Third Mate. "Steer as I tell you."

We rowed a dozen slow strokes, and with every stroke, I took a look over my shoulder. The Captain was leaning forward under the big lamp, with the bull's-eye in one hand and his revolver in the other. He kept flashing the beam of the lantern up into the night.

"Good Lord!" he said, suddenly. "Vast pulling."

We stopped, and I slewed round on the thwart, and stared.

He was standing up under the glow of the anchor-light, and shining the bull's-eye up at a great mass that loomed dully through the mist. As he flicked the light to and fro over the great bulk, I realised that the boat was within some three or four fathoms of the hull of a vessel.

"Pull another stroke," the Skipper said, in a quiet voice, after a few moments of silence. "Gently now! Gently!... Vast pulling!"

I slewed round again on my thwart and stared. I could see part of the thing quite distinctly now, and more of it, as I followed the beam of the Captain's lantern. She was a vessel right enough; but such a vessel as I had never seen. She was extraordinarily high out of the water, and seemed very short, and rose up into a queer mass at one end. But what puzzled me more, I think, than anything else, was the queer look of her sides, down which water was streaming all the time.

"That explains the sound of the water running," I thought to myself; "but what on earth is she built of?"

You will understand a little of my bewildered feelings, when I tell you that as the beam of the Captain's lamp shone on the side of this queer vessel, it showed stone everywhere—as if she were built out of stone. I never felt so dumb-founded in my life.

"She's stone, Cap'n!" I said. "Look at her, Sir!" I realised, as I spoke, a certain horribleness, of the unnatural.... A stone ship, floating out there in the night in the midst of the lonely Atlantic!

"She's stone," I said again, in that absurd way in which one reiterates, when one is bewildered.

"Look at the slime on her!" muttered the man next but one forrard of ma. "She's a proper Davy Jones ship. By Gum! she stinks like a corpse!"

"Ship ahoy!" roared the Skipper, at the top of his voice. "Ship ahoy! Ship ahoy!"

His shout beat back at us, in a curious, dank, yet metallic, echo, something the way one's voice sounds in an old disused quarry.

"There's no one aboard there, Sir," said the Third Mate. "Shall I put the boat alongside?"

"Yes, shove her up, Mister," said the Old Man. "I'll bottom this business. Pull a couple of strokes, aft there! In bow, and stand by to fend off."

The Third Mate laid the boat alongside, and we unshipped our oars. Then, I leant forward over the side of the boat, and pressed the flat of my hand upon the stark side of the ship. The water that ran down her side, sprayed out over my hand and wrist in a cataract; but I did not think about being wet, for my hand was pressed solid upon stone.... I pulled my hand back with a queer feeling.

"She's stone, right enough, Sir," I said to the Captain.

"We'll soon see what she is," he said. "Shove your oar up against her side, and shin up. We'll pass the lamp up to you as soon as you're aboard. Shove your axe in the back of your belt. I'll cover you with my gun, till you're aboard."

" 'i, 'i, Sir," I said; though I felt a bit funny at the thought of having to be the first aboard that dam rummy craft.

I put my oar upright against her side, and took a spring up it from the thwart, and in a moment I was grabbing over my head for her rail, with every rag on me soaked through with the water that was streaming down her, and spraying out over the oar and me.

I got a firm grip of the rail, and hoisted my head high enough to look over; but I could see nothing... what with the darkness, and the water in my eyes.

I knew it was no time for going slow, if there were danger aboard; so I went in over that rail in one spring, my boots coming down with a horrible, ringing, hollow stony sound on her decks. I whipped the water out of my eyes and the axe out of my belt, all in the same moment; then I took a good stare fore and aft; but it was too dark to see anything.

"Come along, Duprey!" shouted the Skipper. "Collar the lamp."

I leant out sideways over the rail, and grabbed for the lamp with my left hand, keeping the axe ready in my right, and staring inboard; for I tell you, I was just mortally afraid in that moment of what might be aboard of her.

I felt the lamp-ring with my left hand, and gripped it. Then I switched it aboard, and turned fair and square to see where I'd gotten.

Now, you never saw such a packet as that, not in a hundred years, nor yet two hundred, I should think. She'd got a rum little main-deck, about forty feet long, and then came a step about two feet high, and another bit of a deck, with a little house on it.

That was the after end of her; and more I couldn't see, because the light of my lamp went no farther, except to show me vaguely the big, cocked-up stern of her, going up into the darkness. I never saw a vessel made like her; not even in an old picture of old-time ships.

Forrard of me, was her mast—a big lump of a stick it was too, for her size. And here was another amazing thing, the mast of her looked just solid stone.

"Funny, isn't she, Duprey?" said the Skipper's voice at my back, and I came round on him with a jump.

"Yes," I said. "I'm puzzled. Aren't you, Sir?"

"Well," he said, "I am. If we were like the shellbacks they talk of in books, we'd be crossing ourselves. But, personally, give me a good heavy Colt, or the hefty chunk of steel you're cuddling."

He turned from me, and put his head over the rail.

"Pass up the painter, Jales," he said, to the bow-oar. Then to the Third Mate:—

"Bring 'em all up, Mister. If there's going to be anything rummy, we may as well make a picnic party of the lot.... Hitch that painter round the cleet yonder, Duprey," he added to me. "It looks good solid stone!... That's right. Come along."

He swung the thin beam of his lantern fore and aft, and then forrard again.

"Lord!" he said. "Look at that mast. It's stone. Give it a whack with the back of your axe, man; only remember she's apparently a bit of an old-timer! So go gently."

I took my axe short, and tapped the mast, and it rang dull, and solid, like a stone pillar. I struck it again, harder, and a sharp flake of stone flew past my cheek. The Skipper thrust his lantern close up to where I'd struck the mast.

"By George," he said, "she's absolutely a stone ship—solid stone, afloat here out of Eternity, in the middle of the wide Atlantic.... Why! She must weigh a thousand tons more than she's buoyancy to carry. It's just impossible.... It's—"

He turned his head quickly, at a sound in the darkness along the decks. He flashed his light that way, across and across the after decks; but we could see nothing.

"Get a move on you in the boat!" he said sharply, stepping to the rail and looking down. "For once I'd really prefer a little more of your company...." He came round like a flash. "Duprey, what was that?"

he asked in a low voice.

"I certainly heard something, Sir," I said. "I wish the others would hurry. By Jove! Look! What's that—"

"Where?" he said, and sent the beam of his lamp to where I pointed with my axe.

"There's nothing," he said, after circling the light all over the deck. "Don't go imagining things. There's enough solid unnatural fact here, without trying to add to it."

There came the splash and thud of feet behind, as the first of the men came up over the side, and jumped clumsily into the lee scuppers, which had water in them. You see she had a cant to that side, and I supposed the water had collected there.

The rest of the men followed, and then the Third Mate. That made six men of us, all well armed; and I felt a bit more comfortable, as you can think.

"Hold up that lamp of yours, Duprey, and lead the way," said the Skipper. "You're getting the post of honour this trip!"

" 'i, 'i, Sir," I said, and stepped forward, holding up the lamp in my left hand, and carrying my axe half way down the haft, in my right.

"We'll try aft, first," said the Captain, and led the way himself, flashing the bull's-eye to and fro. At the raised portion of the deck, he stopped.

"Now," he said, in his queer way, "let's have a look at this.... Tap it with your axe, Duprey.... Ah!" he added, as I hit it with the back of my axe. "That's what we call stone at home, right enough. She's just as rum as anything I've seen while I've been fishing. We'll go on aft and have a peep into I the deck-house. Keep your axes handy, men."

We walked slowly up to the curious little house, the deck rising to it with quite a slope. At the foreside of the little deck-house, the Captain pulled up, and shone his bull's-eye down at the deck. I saw that he was looking at what was plainly the stump of the after mast. He stepped closer to it, and kicked, it with his foot; and it gave out the same dull, solid note that the foremast had done. It was obviously a chunk of stone.

I held up my lamp so that I could see the upper part of the house more clearly. The fore-part had two square window-spaces in it; but there was no glass in either of them; and the blank darkness within the queer little place, just seemed to stare out at us.

And then I saw something suddenly... a great shaggy head of red hair was rising slowly into sight, through the port window, the one nearest to us.

"My God! What's that, Cap'n?" I called out. But it was gone, even as I spoke.

"What?" he asked, jumping at the way I had sung out.

"At the port window, Sir," I said. "A great red-haired head. It came right up to the window-place; and then it went in a moment."

The Skipper stepped right up to the little dark window, and pushed his lantern through into the blackness. He flashed the light round; then withdrew the lantern.

"Bosh, man!" he said. "That's twice you've got fancying things. Ease up your nerves a bit!"

"I did see it!" I said, almost angrily. "It was like a great red-haired head...."

"Stow it, Duprey!" he said, though not sneeringly. "The house is absolutely empty. Come round to the door, if the Infernal Masons that built her, went in for doors! Then you'll see for yourself. All the same, keep your axes ready, lads. I've a notion there's something pretty queer aboard here."

We went up round the after-end of the little house, and here we saw what appeared to be a door.

The Skipper felt at the queer, odd-shapen handle, and pushed at the door; but it had stuck fast.

"Here, one of you!" he said, stepping back. "Have a whack at this with your axe. Better use the back."

One of the men stepped forward, and we stood away to give him room. As his axe struck, the door went to pieces with exactly the same sound that a thin slab of stone would make, when broken.

"Stone!" I heard the Captain mutter, under his breath. " By Gum! What *is* she?"

I did not wait for the Skipper. He had put me a bit on edge, and I stepped bang in through the open doorway, with the lamp high, and holding my axe short and ready; but there was nothing in the place, save a stone seat running all round, except where the doorway opened on to the deck.

"Find your red-haired monster?" asked the Skipper, at my elbow.

I said nothing. I was suddenly aware that he was all on the jump with some inexplicable fear. I saw his glance going everywhere about him. And then his eye caught mine, and he saw that I realised. He was a man almost callous to fear, that is the fear of danger in what I might call any normal sea-faring shape. And this palpable nerviness affected me tremendously. He was obviously doing his best to throttle it; and trying all he knew to hide it. I had a sudden warmth of understanding for him, and dreaded lest the men should realise his state. Funny that I should be able at that moment to be aware of anything but my own bewildered fear and expectancy of intruding upon something monstrous at any instant. Yet I describe exactly my feelings, as I stood there in the house.

"Shall we try below, Sir?" I said, and turned to where a flight of stone steps led down into an utter blackness, out of which rose a strange, dank scent of the sea... an imponderable mixture of brine and darkness.

"The worthy Duprey leads the van!" said the Skipper; but I felt no irritation now. I knew that he must cover his fright, until he had got control again; and I think he felt, somehow, that I was backing him up. I remember now that I went down those stairs into that unknowable and ancient cabin, as much aware in that moment of the Captain's state, as of that extraordinary thing I had just seen at the little window, or of my own half-funk of what we might see any moment.

The Captain was at my shoulder, as I went, and behind him came the Third Mate, and then the men, all in single file; for the stairs were narrow.

I counted seven steps down, and then my foot splashed into water on the eighth. I held the lamp low, and stared. I had caught no glimpse of a reflection, and I saw now that this was owing to a curious, dull, greyish scum that lay thinly on the water, seeming to match the colour of the stone which composed the steps and bulksheads.

"Stop!" I said. "I'm in water!"

I let my foot down slowly, and got the next step. Then sounded with my axe, and found the floor at the bottom. I stepped down and stood up to my thighs in water.

"It's all right, Sir," I said, suddenly whispering. I held my lamp up, and glanced quickly about me. "It's not deep. There's two doors here...."

I whirled my axe up as I spoke; for, suddenly, I had realised that one of the doors was open a little. It seemed to move, as I stared, and I could have imagined that a vague undulation ran towards me, across the dull scum-covered water.

"The door's opening!" I said, aloud, with a sudden sick feeling. "Look out!"

I backed from the door, staring; but nothing came. And abruptly, I had control of myself; for I realised that the door was not moving. It had not moved at all. It was simply ajar.

"It's all right, Sir," I said. "It's not opening."

I stepped forward again a pace towards the doors, as the Skipper and the Third Mate came down with a jump, splashing the water all over me.

The Captain still had the "nerves" on him, as I think I could feel, even then; but he hid it well.

"Try the door, Mister. I've jumped my dam lamp out!" he growled to the Third Mate; who pushed at the door on my right; but it would not open beyond the nine or ten inches it was fixed ajar.

"There's this one here, Sir," I whispered, and held my lantern up to the closed door that lay to my left.

"Try it," said the Skipper, in an undertone. We did so, but it also was fixed. I whirled my axe suddenly, and struck the door heavily in the centre of the main panel, and the whole thing crashed into flinders of stone, that went with hollow sounding splashes into the darkness beyond.

"Goodness!" said the Skipper, in a startled voice; for my action had been so instant and unexpected. He covered his lapse, in a moment, by the warning:—

"Look out for bad air!" But I was already inside with the lamp, and holding my axe handily. There was no bad air; for right across from me, was a split clean through the ship's side, that I could have put my two arms through, just above the level of the scummy water.

The place I had broken into, was a cabin, of a kind; but seemed strange and dank, and too narrow to breathe in; and wherever I turned, I saw stone. The Third Mate and the Skipper gave simultaneous expressions of disgust at the wet dismalness of the place.

"It's all stone," I said, and brought my axe hard against the front of a sort of squat cabinet, which was built into the after bulkshead. It caved in, with a crash of splintered stone.

"Empty!" I said, and turned instantly away.

The Skipper and the Third Mate, with the men who were now peering in at the door, crowded out; and in that moment, I pushed my axe under my arm, and thrust my hand into the burst stone-chest. Twice I did this, with almost the speed of lightning, and shoved what I had seen, into the side-pocket of my coal. Then, I was following the others; and not one of them had noticed a thing. As for me, I was quivering with excitement, so that my knees shook; for I had caught the unmistakable gleam of gems; and had grabbed for them in that one swift instant.

I wonder whether anyone can realise what I felt in that moment. I knew that, if my guess were right, I had snatched the power in that one miraculous moment, that would lift me from the weary life of a common shellback, to the life of ease that had been mine during my early years. I tell you, in that instant, as I staggered almost blindly out of that dark little apartment, I had no thought of any horror that might be held in that incredible vessel, out there afloat on the wide Atlantic.

I was full of the one blinding thought, that possibly I was *rich!* And I wanted to get somewhere by myself as soon as possible, to see whether I was right. Also, if I could, I meant to get back to that strange cabinet of stone, if the chance came; for I knew that the two handfuls I had grabbed, had left a lot behind.

Only, whatever I did, I must let no one guess; for then I should probably lose everything, or have but an infinitesimal share doled out to me, of the wealth that I believed to be in those glittering things there in the side-pocket of my coat.

I began immediately to wonder what other treasures there might be aboard; and then, abruptly, I realised that the Captain was speaking to me:—

"The light, Duprey, damn you!" he was saying, angrily, in a low tone. "What's the matter with you! Hold it up."

I pulled myself together, and shoved the lamp above my head. One of the men was swinging his axe, to beat in the door that seemed to have stood so eternally ajar; and the rest were standing back, to give him room. Crash! went the axe, and half the door fell inward, in a shower of broken stone, making dismal splashes in the darkness. The man struck again, and the rest of the door fell away, with a sullen slump into the water.

"The lamp," muttered the Captain. But I had hold of myself once more, and I was stepping forward slowly through the thigh-deep water, even before he spoke.

I went a couple of paces in through the black gape of the doorway, and then stopped and held the lamp so as to get a view of the place. As I did so, I remember how the intense silence struck home on me. Every man of us must surely have been holding his breath; and there must have been some heavy quality, either in the water, or in the scum that floated on it, that kept it from rippling against the sides of the bulksheads, with the movements we had made.

At first, as I held the lamp (which was burning badly), I could not get its position right to show me anything, except that I was in a very large cabin for so small a vessel. Then I saw that a table ran along the centre, and the top of it was no more than a few inches above the water. On each side of it, there rose the backs of what were evidently two rows of massive, olden looking chairs. At the far end of the table, there was a huge, immobile, humped something.

I stared at this for several moments; then I took three slow steps forward, and stopped again; for the thing resolved itself, under the light from the lamp, into the figure of an enormous man, seated at the end of the table, his face bowed forward upon his arms. I was amazed, and thrilling abruptly with new fears and vague impossible thoughts. Without moving a step, I held the light nearer at arm's length....

The man was of stone, like everything in that extraordinary ship.

"That foot!" said the Captain's voice, suddenly cracking. "Look at that foot!" His voice sounded amazingly startling and hollow in that silence, and the words seemed to come back sharply at me from the vaguely seen bulksheads.

I whipped my light to starboard, and saw what he meant—a huge human foot was sticking up out of the water, on the right hand side of the table. It was enormous. I have never seen so vast a foot. And it also was of stone.

And then, as I stared, I saw that there was a great head above the water, over by the bulkshead.

"I've gone mad!" I said, out loud, as I saw something else, more incredible.

"My God! Look at the hair on the head!" said the Captain.... "It's growing! It's growing!" His voice cracked again.

"Look at it! It's growing!" he called out once more.

I was looking. On the great head, there was becoming visible a huge mass of red hair, that was surely and unmistakably rising up, as we watched it.

"It's what I saw at the window!" I said. "It's what I saw at the window! I told you I saw it!"

"Come out of that, Duprey," said the Third Mate, quietly.

"Let's get out of here!" muttered one of the men. Two or three of them called out the same thing; and then, in a moment, they began a mad rush up the stairway.

I stood dumb, where I was. The hair rose up in a horrible living fashion on the great head, waving and moving. It rippled down over the forehead, and spread abruptly over the whole gargantuan stone face, hiding the features completely. Suddenly, I swore at the thing madly, and I hove my axe at it. Then I was backing crazily for the door, slumping the scum as high as the deck-beams, in my fierce haste. I readied the stairs, and caught at the stone rail, that was modelled like a rope; and so hove myself up out of the water. I reached the little deck-house, where I had seen the great head of hair. I jumped through the doorway, out onto the decks, and I felt the night air sweet on my face…. Goodness! I ran forward along the decks. There was a Babel of shouting in the waist of the ship, and a thudding of feet running. Some of the men were singing out, to get into the boat; but the Third Mate was shouting that they must wait for me.

"He's coming," called someone. And then I was among them.

"Turn that lamp up, you idiot," said the Captain's voice. "This is just where we want light!"

I glanced down, and realised that my lamp was almost out. I turned it up, and it flared, and began again to dwindle.

"Those damned boys never filled it," I said. "They deserve their necks breaking."

The men were literally tumbling over the side, and the Skipper was hurrying them.

"Down with you into the boat," he said to me. "Give me the lamp. I'll pass it down. Get a move on you!"

The Captain had evidently got his nerve back again.

This was more like the man I knew. I handed him the lamp, and went over the side. All the rest had now gone, and the Third Mate was already in the stern, waiting.

As I landed on the thwart, there was a sudden, strange noise from aboard the ship—a sound, as if some stone object were trundling down the sloping decks, from aft. In that one moment, I got what you might truly call the "horrors." I seemed suddenly able to believe incredible possibilities.

"The stone men!" I shouted. "Jump, Captain! Jump! Jump!" The vessel seemed to roll oddly.

Abruptly, the Captain yelled out something, that not one of us in the boat understood. There followed a succession of tremendous sounds, aboard the ship, and I saw his shadow swing out huge against the thin mist, as he turned suddenly with the lamp. He fired twice with his revolver.

"The hair!" I shouted. "Look at the hair!"

We all saw it——the great head of red hair that we had seen grow visibly on the monstrous stone head, below in the cabin. It rose above the rail, and there was a moment of intense stillness, in which I heard the Captain gasping. The Third Mate fired six times at the tiling, and I found myself fixing an oar up against the side of that abominable vessel, to get aboard.

As I did so, there came one appalling crash, that shook the stone ship fore and aft, and she began to cant up, and my oar slipped and fell into the boat. Then the Captain's voice screamed something in a choking fashion above us. The ship lurched forward, and paused. Then another crash came, and she rocked over towards us; then away from us again. The movement away from us, continued, and the round of the vessel's bottom showed, vaguely. There was a smashing of glass above us, and the dim glow of light aboard, vanished. Then the vessel fell clean over from us, with a giant splash. A huge wave came at us, out of the night, and half filled the boat.

The boat nearly capsized, then righted and presently steadied.

"Captain!" shouted the Third Mate. "Captain!" But there came never a sound; only presently, out of all the night, a strange murmuring of waters.

"Captain!" he shouted once more; but his voice just went lost and remote into the darkness.

"She's foundered!" I said.

"Out oars," sung out the Third. "Put your backs into it. Don't stop to bail!"

For half an hour we circled the spot slowly. But the strange vessel had indeed foundered and gone down into the mystery of the deep sea, with her mysteries.

Finally we put about, and returned to the *Alfred Jessop*.

Now, I want you to realise that what I am telling you is a plain and simple tale of fact. This is no fairy tale, and I've not done yet; and I think this yarn should prove to you that some mighty strange things do happen at sea, and always will while the world lasts. It's the home of all the mysteries; for it's the one place that is really difficult for humans to investigate. Now just listen:—

The Mate had kept the bell going, from time to time, and so we came back pretty quickly, having as we came, a strange repetition of the echoey reduplication of our oar-sounds; but we never spoke a word; for not one of us wanted to hear those beastly echoes again, after what we had just gone through. I think we all had a feeling that there was something a bit hellish abroad that night.

We got aboard, and the Third explained to the Mate what had happened; but he would hardly believe the yarn. However, there was nothing to do, but wait for daylight; so we were told to keep about the deck, and keep our eyes and ears open.

One thing the Mate did, showed he was more impressed by our yarn, than he would admit. He had all the ship's lanterns lashed up round the decks, to the sheerpoles; and he never told us to give up either the axes or the cutlass.

It was while we were keeping about the decks, that I took the chance to have a look at what I had grabbed. I tell you, what I found, made me nearly forget the Skipper, and all the rummy things that had happened. I had twenty-six stones in my pocket and four of them were diamonds, respectively 9, 11, 13½ and 17 carats in weight, uncut, that is. I know quite something about diamonds. I'm not going to tell you how I learnt what I know; but I would not have taken a thousand pounds for the four, as they lay there, in my hand. There was also a big, dull stone, that looked red inside. I'd have dumped it over the side, I thought so little of it; only, I argued that it must be something, or it would never have been among that lot. Lord! but I little knew what I'd got; not then. Why, the thing was as big as a fair-sized walnut. You may think it funny that I thought of the four diamonds first; but you see, I *know* diamonds when I see them. They're things I understand; but I never saw a ruby, in the rough, before or since. Good Lord! And to think I'd have thought nothing of heaving it over the side!

You see, a lot of the stories were not anything much; that is, not in the modern market. There were two big topaz, and several onyx and cornelians—nothing much. There were five hammered slugs of gold about two ounces each they would be. And then a prize—one winking green devil of an emerald. You've got to know an emerald to look for the "eye" of it, in the rough; but it is there—the eye of some hidden devil staring up at you. Yes, I'd seen an emerald before, and I knew I held a lot of money in that one stone alone.

And then I remembered what I'd missed, and cursed myself for not grabbing a third time. But that feeling lasted only a moment. I thought of the beastly part that had been the Skipper's share; while there I stood safe under one of the lamps, with a fortune in my hands. And then, abruptly, as you can understand, my mind was filled with the crazy wonder and bewilderment of what had happened. I felt how absurdly ineffectual my imagination was to comprehend anything understandable out of it all, except that the Captain had certainly gone, and I had just as certainly had a piece of impossible luck.

Often, during that time of waiting, I stopped to take a look at the things I had in my pocket; always careful that no one about the decks should come near me, to see what I was looking at.

Suddenly the Mate's voice came sharp along the decks:—

"Call the Doctor, one of you," he said. "Tell him to get the fire in and the coffee made."

" 'i, 'i, Sir," said one of the men; and I realised that the dawn was growing vaguely over the sea.

Half an hour later, the "Doctor" shoved his head out of the galley doorway, and sung out that coffee was ready.

The watch below turned out, and had theirs with the watch on deck, all sitting along the spar that lay under the port rail.

As the daylight grew, we kept a constant watch over the side; but even now we could see nothing; for the thin mist still hung low on the sea.

"Hear that?" said one of the men, suddenly. And, indeed, the sound must have been plain for half a mile round.

"Ooaaze, ooaaze, arrr, arrrr, oooaze—"

"By George!" said Tallett, one of the other watch; "that's a beastly sort of thing to hear."

"Look!" I said. "What's that out yonder?"

The mist was thinning under the effect of the rising sun, and tremendous shapes seemed to stand towering half-seen, away to port. A few minutes passed, while we stared. Then, suddenly, we heard the Mate's voice:——

"All hands on deck!" he was shouting, along the decks.

I ran aft a few steps.

"Both watches are out, Sir," I called.

"Very good!" said the Mate. "Keep handy all of you. Some of you have got the axes. The rest had better take a caps'n-bar each, and stand-by till I find what this devilment is, out yonder."

" 'i, 'i, Sir," I said, and turned forrard. But there was no need to pass on the Mate's orders; for the men had heard, and there was a rush for the capstan-bars, which are a pretty hefty kind of cudgel, as any sailorman knows. We lined the rail again, and stared away to port.

"Look out, you sea-divvils," shouted Timothy Galt, a huge Irishman, waving his bar excitedly, and peering over the rail into the mist, which was steadily thinning, as the day grew.

Abruptly there was a simultaneous cry:—— "*Rocks!*" shouted everyone.

I never saw such a sight. As at last the mist thinned, we could see them. All the sea to port was literally cut about with far-reaching reefs of rock. In places the reefs lay just submerged; but in others they rose into extraordinary and fantastic rock-spires, and arches, and islands of jagged rock.

"Jehoshaphat!" I heard the Third Mate shout. "Look at that, Mister! Look at that! Lord! how did we take the boat through that, without stoving her!"

Everything was so still for the moment, with all the men just staring and amazed, that I could hear every word come along the decks.

"There's sure been a submarine earthquake somewhere," I heard
the First Mate say. "The bottom of the sea's just riz up here, quiet and
gentle, during the night; and. God's mercy we aren't now a-top of one
of those ornaments out there."

And then, you know, I saw it all. Everything that had looked mad
and impossible, began to be natural; though it was, none the less, all
amazing and wonderful.

There had been during the night, a slow lifting of the sea-bottom,
owing to some action of the Internal Pressures. The rocks had risen so
gently that they had made never a sound; and the stone ship had risen
with them out of the deep sea. She had evidently lain on one of the
submerged reefs, and so had seemed to us to be just afloat in the sea.
And she accounted for the water we heard running. She was naturally
bung-full, as you might say, and took longer to shed the water than
she did to rise. She had probably some biggish holes in her bottom.
I began to get my "soundings" a bit, as I might call it in sailor talk.
The natural wonders of the sea, beat all made-up yarns that ever were!

The Mate sung out to us to man the boat again, and told the Third
Mate to take her out to where we lost the Skipper, and have a final
look round, in case there might be any chance to find the Old Man's
body anywhere about.

"Keep a man in the bows to look out for sunk rocks, Mister," the
Mate told the Third, as we pulled off. "Go slow. There'll be no wind
yet a while. See if you can fix up what made those noises, while you're
looking round."

We pulled right across about thirty fathoms of clear water, and
in a minute we were between two great arches of rock. It was then I
realised that the re-duplicating of our oar-roll was the echo from these
on each side of us. Even in the sunlight, it was queer to hear again that
same strange cathedral echoey sound that we had heard in the dark.

We passed under the huge arches, all hung with deep sea slime.
And presently we were heading straight for a gap, where two low reefs
swept in to the apex of a huge horseshoe. We pulled for about three
minutes, and then the Third gave the word to vast pulling.

"Take the boat-hook, Duprey," he said, "and go forrard, and see
we don't hit anything."

" 'i, 'i, Sir," I said, and drew in my oar.

"Give way again gently!" said the Third; and the boat moved forward for another thirty or forty yards.

"We're right onto a reef, Sir," I said, presently, as I stared down over the bows. I sounded with the boat-hook. "There's about three feet of water, Sir," I told him.

"Vast pulling," ordered the Third. "I reckon we are right over the rock, where we found that rum packet last night." He leant over the side, and stared down.

"There's a stone cannon on the rock, right under the bows of the boat," I said. Immediately afterwards I shouted:—

"There's the hair, Sir! There's the hair! It's on the reef. There's two! There's three! There's one on the cannon!"

"All right! All right, Duprey! Keep cool," said the Third Mate. "I can see them. You've enough intelligence not to be superstitious now the whole thing's explained. They're some kind of big-hairy sea-caterpillar. Prod one with your boat-hook."

I did so; a little ashamed of my sudden bewilderment. The thing whipped round like a tiger, at the boat-hook. It lapped itself round and round the boat-hook, while the hind portions of it kept gripped to the rock, and I could no more pull the boat-hook from its grip, than fly; though I pulled till I sweated.

"Take the point of your cutlass to it, Varley," said the Third Mate. "Jab it through."

The bow-oar did so, and the brute loosed the boat-hook, and curled up round a chunk of rock, looking like a great ball of red hair.

I drew the boat-hook up, and examined it.

"Goodness!" I said. "That's what killed the Old Man—one of those things! Look at all those marks in the wood, where it's gripped it with about a hundred legs."

I passed the boat-hook aft to the Third Mate to look at.

"They're about as dangerous as they can be, Sir, I reckon," I told him. "Makes you think of African centipedes, only these are big and strong enough to kill an elephant, I should think."

"Don't lean all on one side of the boat!" shouted the Third Mate, as the men stared over. "Get back to your places. Give way, there!... Keep a good lookout for any signs of the ship or the Captain, Duprey."

For nearly an hour, we pulled to and fro over the reef; but we never saw either the stone ship or the Old Man again. The queer craft must have rolled off into the profound depths that lay on each side of the reef.

As I leant over the bows, staring down all that long while at the submerged rocks, I was able to understand almost everything, except the various extraordinary noises.

The cannon made it unmistakably clear that the ship which had been hove up from the sea-bottom, with the rising of the reef, had been originally a normal enough wooden vessel of a time far removed from our own. At the sea-bottom, she had evidently undergone some natural mineralising process, and this explained her stony appearance. The stone men had been evidently humans who had been drowned in her cabin, and their swollen tissues had been subjected to the same natural process, which, however, had also deposited heavy encrustations upon them, so that their size, when compared with the normal, was prodigious.

The mystery of the hair, I had already discovered; but there remained, among other things, the tremendous bangs we had heard. These were, possibly, explained later, while we were making a final examination of the rocks to the Westward, prior to returning to our ship. Here we discovered the burst and swollen bodies of several extraordinary deep-sea creatures, of the eel variety. They must have had a girth, in life, of many feet, and the one that we measured roughly with an oar, must have been quite forty feet long. They had, apparently, burst on being lifted from the tremendous pressure of the deep sea, into the light air pressure above water, and hence might account for the loud reports we had eoard; though, personally, I incline to think these loud bangs were more probably caused by the splitting of the rocks under new stresses.

As for the roaring sounds, I can only conclude that they were caused by a peculiar species of grampus-like fish, of enormous size, which we found dead and hugely distended on one of the rocky masses. This fish must have weighed at least four or five tons, and when prodded with a heavy oar, there came from its peculiar snout-shaped mouth, a low, hoarse sound, like a weak imitation of the tremendous sounds we had heard during the past night.

Regarding the apparently carved handrail, like a rope up the side of the cabin stairs, I realise that this had undoubtedly been actual rope at one time.

Recalling the heavy, trundling sounds aboard, just after I climbed down into the boat, I can only suppose that these were made by some stone object, possibly a fossilised gun-carriage, rolling down the decks, as the ship began to slip off the rocks, and her bows sank lower in the water.

The varying lights must have been the strongly phosphorescent bodies of some of the deep-sea creatures, moving about on the upheaved reefs. As for the giant splash that occurred in the darkness ahead of the boat, this must have been due to some large portion of heaved-up rock, overbalancing and rolling back into the sea.

No one aboard ever learnt about the jewels. I took care of that! I sold the ruby badly, so I've heard since; but I do not grumble even now. Twenty-three thousand pounds I had for it alone, from a merchant in London. I learned afterwards he made double that on it; but I don't spoil my pleasure by grumbling. I wonder often how the stones and things came where I found them; but she carried guns, as I've told, I think; and there's rum doings happen at sea; yes, by George!

The smell—oh that I guess was due to heaving all that deep-sea slime up for human noses to smell at.

This yarn is, of course, known in nautical circles, and was briefly mentioned in the old Nautical Mercury of 1879. The series of volcanic reefs (which disappeared in 1883) were charted under the name of the "*Alfred Jessop* Shoals and Reefs"; being named after our Captain who discovered them and lost his life on them.

The Regeneration of Captain Bully Keller

I

CAPTAIN BULLY KELLER MADE the first serious mistake of a triumphal career, as hard-case skipper, when he hammered little Nibby Tompkins, the ship's boy.

He used the end of the mizzen top-sail halyards for this purpose, and the top-sail halyards of a three-thousand-ton, steel, four-masted bark is not suitable rope to lay across the back of a boy of fourteen or fifteen. It is certainly too heavy.

At an early stage of the thrashing, young Nibby had so far forgotten himself as to assure Big Bully Keller that his father would kill him. As Nibby gasped this threat out, between the violent shocks of the heavy rope, it had run literally thus:

"Wait while me feyther sees you! He'll sure kill you, you great beast!"

He had no breath left for further threats. Captain Bully Keller had seen to that, most efficiently. He had finally thrown the half-senseless boy, in a quivering heap on to the mizzen hatch, whence he had been removed later by one of the men, in a soft-hearted moment, to his bunk.

As a result of his lamming, young Nibby Tompkins was a very sick lad when the big steel barque, *Alceste*, ran in through the Golden Gate, and came to anchor off Telegraph Hill, San Francisco.

Captain Bully Keller squared the doctor with a hundred-dollar bill; and little Nibby Tompkins's illness was recorded officially as rheumatism, with the result that there were no awkward inquiries from the authorities ashore. Nor had Captain Keller anything to fear from his crew; for the plain and simple reason that each man feared him like the wrath of God, or, indeed, considerably more. All his various crews learned to fear him entirely in the period of a single passage; for he weighed sixteen stone of brawn and malignant evil, and stood six feet one inch in his gum boots.

His favorite method of becoming "acquainted" with his crews was at once effectual and memorable. On the second or third day out, he would go forward into the fo'cas'le, after the watch below had turned in and was asleep. Here he would pace up and down, taunting the sleeping men in their bunks, that no two of them had the pluck to come out and fight him; which was invariably true, and the rough, hairy sailors would lie sweating; insisting, in a rolling chorus of snores, that each man of them was the one and only remaining relative of the seven sleepers.

Captain Bully Keller would continue his disturbing promenade of the "sleeping" fo'cas'le, expressing his opinion of the sleepers' mixed parentage, in terms and voice that could be heard and appreciated by Mr. Jackson, the pleasant bucko Mate, who walked the short poop, away aft, grinning like a wolf.

Eventually, Captain Bully Keller, having lashed his sides sufficiently to require violent action as a sedative, would spring at the nearest bunks and haul a couple of men out by their hair. He would pile them on the deck of the fo'cas'le in a struggling heap, which he kicked and punched, until, in desperation, they would "go" for him, fighting mad, only to be knocked out of time and place by the Captain's great fists.

If they put up a good fight, he would send the Steward forward, afterward, with a bucket of rum and water. But if he failed to bring them up to the fighting point, he would chase them round and round the decks, in their flannel drawers, kicking and punching them to his entire satisfaction.

Only once had he ever met his match. This was when a big Irish A.B. had jumped out of his bunk, at the first taunt the Skipper had let loose, and had knocked Captain Bully Keller across the fo'cas'le with a mighty and scientific right-and-left punch. And Captain Bully Keller had immediately shown the brute's blood that was in him; for he had drawn his gun and shot the big Irishman through his shoulder; after which, although the man was disabled, he had hammered him into quietness.

There you have the man. He loved fighting. He liked a good fight; but he would fight as foul and ugly as an apache, if he thought there was any danger of someone beating him.

Very few men could say truthfully that they had ever drawn a pay-day out of any ship commanded by Captain Bully Keller. Nor could the men of his latest crew boast otherwise; for they lowered one of the boats, with enormous secrecy and fear, the same night the ship dropped anchor in the bay; and pulled for the shore, sans pay-day and sea-chests.

But had they understood Captain Bully Keller's point of view, they might have experienced less fear, and troubled less about secrecy. He had been awake while they maneuvered with much grease (out of the Cook's slush-tub) to grease the boat's falls and the sheaves of the blocks, so as to insure their running silently when they lowered the boat. And he had merely grinned to himself and let them go; for the boat could be recovered in the morning; and it was a cheap way of getting labour—to have the men all run off without a cent of pay!

The only defect of this system was the difficulty it entailed in getting men. But this was solved by the longshore crimps and shang-hai-houses on the waterfront.

II

The *Alceste* discharged her cargo and went across to the mudflats, to lie up and wait for freights to rise.

By this time, Nibby Tompkins was suffciently recovered to be about the decks again, and as there was no one aboard but Captain Bully Keller, his Mate, Mr. Jackson, and the Steward, Nibby had a vigorous time of it, between dawn and dusk.

Each night, Nibby was further employed in the boat. It was his work to go ashore with the Captain and the Mate, and stand by the boat till they returned, which was often not until well after midnight. Nibby, however, occupied the time usefully enough in sleeping on the bottom boards, rolled up in a piece of old sailcloth, which he kept stored away in the boat for that purpose.

One night, however, just as Nibby was standing up, rolling himself into a sort of human sausage, preliminary to lying down for his accustomed "snooze," a voice hailed him through the dusk from the little wooden jetty to which the boat was made fast. And at the sound of the voice, Nibby both thrilled and shivered; for his father was a stern disciplinarian, almost as stern (though not in any way as brutal) as Captain Bully Keller; and it was his father's voice that had hailed the boat.

"You in the boat, there! Ha! You in the boat, there! Can you tell me where yon ship named *Alceste* is?" came the hail again.

"Father!" said Nibby, in a half-suffocated voice, and shed the wrapping of old sailcloth like a skin.

"It's Nibby boy!" he heard his mother's voice cry out, suddenly. "Nibby! Nibby! Nibby!"

"Hush, Mother!" said his father, quietly.

"Mother," shouted Nibby, and hauled the boat in alongside, by the painter, all his hesitation gone. "Mother!" he shouted, as he leaped up onto the jetty.

A little woman was standing there, in the dusk, beside a short, enormously thick-set, bow-legged man, with a goatee. The little woman gave out a small screech, and ran at the lad. Then her arms were round him, and she was crooning and crying, together, in sudden satisfied contentment.

The short, thick-set man came forward slowly and patted the woman gently on the shoulder. "There, there, Mother! Don't 'ee take on!" he said, in a curiously deep, gentle voice.

"You'll not be hard with him, Joseph?" said the woman, in a stifled, anxious tone.

"Nay, Mother, the lad's made his bed, and he must lie on it; but there's things I've to say to him. Nibby, son, do ye think it was right to your mother, to go running off like this to sea with never a word? Son, I tell you, I would have thrashed you within an inch of your life, had I caught ye three months back. I can't think ye'd any true idee how you would put your mother so in trouble, or you'd never have done the like of such a thing. And the first word we had from you was after ye reached here, tellin' how the Cap'n had laced you good and proper; and well you needed it, son, I'm thinkin'. You've made your bed, and you'll have to lie on it. I come here to bring your mother; for she was breaking her heart with trouble over you. But don't think, son, as I'll stand for you backin' down from your contrac'! You've made your bed, and you'll lie in it! You'll finish this voyage, out and back to Boston, and sign off proper and get your discharge and money, and come home, and maybe you'll have learned a bit sense by then, and found the sea's not like the dime books tell about. What are you doing down in that boat?"

"I'm standin' by her, feyther, till Cap'n an' Mate come back from the drink saloon," said Nibby, loosing himself gently out of his mother's arms and facing his father.

"What time'll they be back, son?" asked Mr. Tompkins, in his quiet, deep voice.

"Gen'rally about midnight," said Nibby. "I sleeps in the bottom of the boat till they comes."

"Where's the ship, son?" asked his father. "Your mother's set that she must see where you sleep and eat, and what-like your clothes is, an' the like. Can we go aboard?"

"Sure, feyther," said Nibby. "Come, Mother an' Dad. I'll pull ye both out in a crack. There's hours 'fore the boat'll be needed."

Ten minutes later Nibby and his father and mother were in the somewhat gloomy, bare, iron-sided fo'cas'le of the *Alceste*.

"An' where do ye sleep, Nibby?" asked his mother.

"Here, Mother, mum," he said, and drew back the rough curtains that he had made out of an old potato-sack.

"Why, Nibby, where's your bed?" asked his mother, in a shocked voice.

"Haven't got one, Mummie," he said. "Hadn't a cent when I come aboard."

"You been sleepin' on them bare boards, all this past three months?" said his mother, and began to cry.

Joseph Tompkins flashed a quick look, that betrayed a sudden grim pride, at this son. But, "I guess you sure got a hard bed to shake up, son," was all he said, in his quiet way. Then, suddenly, as if remembering something, he ordered abruptly: "Strip, son. I'll take a look to see if the Cap'n lambasted you as hard as you said in your letter."

Nibby pulled off his dungaree jumper, and then his shirt, and turned his small but muscular back for his parents to inspect. Even his father, the winner of over sixty fierce ring-fights, let out his breath a little quickly; for though it was a month since the thrashing, the boy's back was still all covered with great dull livid patches, where the flesh had not yet recovered from the crushing and bruising of the heavy top-sail halyards; while in many places the skin was furrowed in huge discoloured wheals.

Nibby's mother neither cried nor said anything for a full minute. Then she spoke, in a queer, fierce breathless voice: "Joseph!" she said, "are you going to stand for that, Joseph?"

Nibby's father said nothing for a little. He was too shaken with an extraordinary new sort of anger—the kind of anger that shakes the she bear when her cubs are molested; but what he said, at last, in his deep voice, was just this, and he meant every word of it:

"Nibby's shore been through it, Mother; but I mean as he shall finish what he begun. I mean as he shall learn his lesson once an' always. But I'm kind-a angry too; for I don't reckon as that's a proper way to lick no lad. We'll go back ashore, wife, to the hotel; an' we'll have a word of prayer about this."

For Nibby's father was that most pungent of combinations—a reformed and deeply religious prize-fighter.

"Nibby," he said, as they left their son at the little wooden jetty, a few minutes later, "here's five doll'rs. Get yourself a bed, son, an' a shirt or two. Me an' your mother'll come down and see you here tomorrow night."

III

Next evening, shortly after Nibby had been left in charge of the boat, his father and mother came along the little wooden jetty, and his father hailed him.

"I've brought you some buckwheats an' bacon-pastries, Nibby," his mother told him, as he hauled the boat alongside the jetty. "They'm not what I'd call proper pastry-cake, but you wait while I gets you to home. I'll shore cook you some an' you'll do fine."

"Do they ever carry passengers in your ship, Nibby?" his father asked him.

"Dunno, Feyther," said Nibby, with his mouth full of bacon pie. "Are ye thinkin' of comin' passenger for the trip home, Dad? Is Mother comin'?"

"Me and your mother has an idee of it, son," replied his father.

"I heard th' Cap'n say today as we was goin' to ship a few runners and go up the river to Crockett on Wednesday, to load grain," said Nibby. "Maybe if you an' Mum was to come alongside in Crockett, casual, an' say as you wanted to go round to Boston, you might fix it up with the old beast. I hope you lams the soul out of him afore we gets back, Dad."

Mr. Tompkins frowned a little. "Ye'll use better language, son, before your mother!" he said, quietly. "An', further, you'll understand, son, not one word as I'm yer feyther. Not one word, mind ye! You've made your bed, an' you must lie on it, an' maybe by the time ye hit Boston again, ye'll have a bit of horse-sense hammered into you. Though I'm not sayin' I'll stan' for the Cap'n using you bad again, the way he done on the v'yage out here. At first, I'll own, I weakened, son, an' I wanted bad to give way to me nat'ral feelin', an' lay the Cap'n out. But me an' your mother's had a deal of prayer about this. An' she reck'ns, same as me, that we can trust the Lord in all things, if we does our best to help ourselves, same time. Me an' your mother will come passengers, if I can fix it up with the Cap'n; an' maybe, son, as I've said to your mother, he may prove a brand as we can pluck from the burnin'."

"I doubt he'd ship you, Dad, if he knew you was my feyther," said Nibby.

IV

"You'm wanted, Cap'n," said Nibby, the following Thursday, as the *Alceste* lay alongside the grain wharf, up in the little wheat-packing township of Crockett.

"Eh?" said Captain Bully Keller. "Who the 'ell wants me?"

"It's an old geezer an' his missus, up on the quay side, Cap'n," said Nibby; "Says he wants to take a passage to Boston."

The Captain's eyes brightened a moment with interest and greed. If he could "nobble" a passenger or two for the run home, he would so work it that no mention of the fact ever reached his owner; and the passage-money would prove very useful to a man of his somewhat exceptional thirst.

He went up on deck, his face less unpleasant than usual. "Mornin', Sir! Mornin', Ma'am!" he said, as he came to the side of the vessel, close to where the old "geezer" and his wife were standing. "I hear you'd like to take the trip home with me. Come aboard. I should think we might fix you up, if you got the dollars."

"Safe right here, an' plenty of 'em, Cap'n," said Nibby's father, slapping the breast of his coat.

The big Captain's hard eyes glinted again, with a quick flash of money-lust. Here was plainly an old "stick" who had the dollars and didn't mind the world hearing of the fact. He promptly named a sum far in excess of what he had meant to ask.

"I'll take you both round, Sir, an' land you in Boston, safe an' sound, an' well fed, for the sum of four hundred dollars for the two of you, paid down on the nail," he said. "Will you come aboord an' look round the ship?"

They climbed down aboard and went the round of the ship, with Mrs. Tompkins striving all the time to get a sight of Nibby, without the Captain noticing.

They concluded the tour of the vessel and came to a pause on the poop, where Mrs. Tompkins stood behind the huge figure of the Captain, and ventured a slight signal of affection to her son, whom she could see swabbing down paintwork, near at hand.

Meanwhile, Mr. Tompkins was talking to the Skipper. "You'll not be a religious man, Cap'n Keller?" he remarked.

"No, Sir," said Captain Keller, firmly, "I'm not what you'd call religious."

Then he realized in a sudden flash of quick cunning that the countrified-looking couple, who proposed to take passage with him, must be given "that way." "But I've a sound respect for religion, Sir—a sound respect," he added, hastily.

Here was a clear four hundred dollars going a-begging, and Captain Keller had considerably more use for gold than for his own soul. He regretted, savagely, that he hadn't seen at once the kind of people these prospective passengers were. They were just the sort of folk to be shy of taking passage with a man that hadn't a "denomination" of his own. He wished he had been less emphatic about his non-religious temperament. Perhaps he could remove the impression—

He was aware suddenly, that Mr. Tompkins was speaking again: "Me an' my missus is sure sorry, Cap'n, you ain't religious," he was saying. "I don't reckon as an unsaved man had oughter go to sea—no, Sir, I sure don't."

"I've a sound respect for it, Sir—a sound respect," repeated the Captain, his great frame shaken with the anxiety of his possible loss. He could see that they felt disinclined now to sail with him. Could he think of nothing to help the scales of decision down on the side he wanted? A desperate thought flashed across him. Could he not turn "religious"? He opened his mouth to get out something or other that would revivify the fast-fading intention of these people to sail with him; but in that moment, Mr. Tompkins continued again:

"But there's hope, Cap'n; there's hope," said the ex-prize-fighter, with a glow of religious fervour in his somewhat sombre eyes. "There's hope, Cap'n. I'm right glad to hear ye say you've a sound respec' for religion. Yes, Sir! Maybe the day of salvation approacheth. Would you come to a bit of dinner with me an' my missus, up at the Pike Restrong? Maybe we can fix this up over a snack, Cap'n. I'd sure like a talk. I've been a great sinner, Cap'n, meself. A great sinner—and the fare, you say, is four hundred dollars. Very good. Maybe we can show you the path, Cap'n. It would be a pleasure to sail with you, if you was regenerate, Cap'n—a great pleasure an' a great privilege. You'll come up to the Pike at seven thirty-sharp, Cap'n?"

"Sure, Sir an' Ma'am," said Captain Bully Keller, feeling immensely hopeful.

"Joseph," said his wife, as they walked away up to the township, "I shore can't feel Christianlike to that man, nohow. I shore don't feel I want to speak to him. The great brute!"

"Aye, Mother," said her husband, quietly. "I guess I understan'; but it would be a great deed to pluck such a brand from the burning. A great deed. We must put our heart bitterness behind us." His eyes still shone with the dull, steady glow of intense fervour that bespeaks the enthusiast.

V

Exactly what happened at that "snack," up at the Pike Restaurant, that night, I do not know; but a remarkably drunk sailor, one of the runners belonging to the *Alceste,* had an extraordinary tale to tell the next morning, which no one in the fo'cas'le believed.

He asserted that, the previous night, having spent no more than a dime on beer, and feeling, as he put it, just nicely hearty, he had drifted in at the doorway of the little Salvation Army hall up in Pine Street.

"Strike me!" he continued; "but them's smart chaps at their job; they are that! I'd not sung mor'n two verses of 'Whiskey is the Life of a Man' when I found myself up on the pen-tent form, with one of 'em on each side of me, prayin' like the divil. Well, mates, I got thinkin', as I *was* there, I might as well let 'em save me, an' be done wiv it, when the next thing I knows, there was the Capting, right on me starboard beam, with that old codger as come aboard today, and his missus, one on each side of him; an' they was prayin' like billy-oh! I never stopped to see the end of it. I was that scared, I thought sure it was the rats as was comin' on me; an' I just come clear out of the place, before them as was convertin' me had done the job proper. I told 'em I wasn't well, and I'd call again. I tell you, mates, it's gospel I'm givin' you—"

And so forth, and much more in the same style; which only excited further violent disbelief, and earnest inquiries regarding the drink saloon where he had been able to achieve so much for the strictly modest sum of one dime.

Whatever we are to think about the matter, the fact remains that Mr. and Mrs. Tompkins *did* take passage with Captain Bully Keller. But, knowing the character of the man, I can scarcely think that even the lure of the four hundred dollars passage-money makes the runner's yarn seem plausible. Yet there is the fact—Nibby's father and mother took passage with Captain Bully Keller, cash paid down!

VI

The way of the transgressor is hard, we are informed; though the hardness is sometimes less evident than poetic justice might desire.

But in the case of Captain Bully Keller, the statement fitted. His conversation became so pruned on the passage home to Boston that his own Mate hardly recognised it. Further, he had to take part in lengthy religious discussions with Mr. Tompkins, until, in self-defense, he took to staying in his cabin and swearing to himself, until some sensation of self-respect returned.

This lasted a little over a week, during which, more and more, old Mrs. Tompkins found herself less and less able to bear herself in Christianlike spirit toward this latest "brand plucked from the burning." She kept remembering the view she had been given of Nibby's terribly bruised and lacerated back; and the power of forgiveness was not in her.

Meanwhile, things were happening. Mr. Tompkins, the ex-prize-fighter, grew more and more fervid in his "religious talks" with the Captain, his gray goatee wagging earnestly by the hour, in admonition and advice concerning the ways and wiles of Satan, of whom few men had more expert knowledge than big Captain Bully Keller. Also, what I might describe as the Captain's boiler-pressure was rising daily.

The lid blew off finally, and with great violence, on the tenth day out. One of the men, a stranger to Captain Bully Keller's record, and not recognising in this much-restrained Captain anything resembling human dynamite, was so ill-advised as to "answer back" the Captain on some trivial point concerning the position of the ship's head, during his trick at the wheel. The result was painful to the man and necessitated his retiring to his bunk for a week to convalesce.

This proved the end of Captain Keller's enforced regeneration. Having, as it might be said, "tasted blood," he cut loose liberally, and went forward to the fo'cas'le to indulge in one of his orgies.

He was concluding a most enjoyable hammering of two of the men's heads together, when he heard the quiet voice of Mr. Tompkins, in the starboard fo'cas'le doorway.

"Cáp'n! Sir! Cap'n!" he was saying in a grieved voice. "You'm backsliding, Cap'n. Take a holt on yourself, Cap'n, an' come away aft with me, an' me an' missus'll help ye wrastle in prayer, to drive the eevil sperrit outen you—come, now, Cap'n. It's never too late—"

"You get to hell out of here, 'fore I smash you, you psalm-singing, chin-wagging goat, you!" bellowed Captain Bully Keller, in his old-time voice.

Mr. Jackson, his bucko Mate, away aft on the poop, heard it, and smiled the only way he could smile, which I've explained earlier. This was something he could understand. The Skipper was himself again.

In the starboard fo'cas'le doorway, Mr. Tompkins, ex-prize-fighter, winner of over sixty first-class heavy-weight fights, hesitated, in conflict with the "natural eevil" which had "riz" up in him at the "brand's" remark. Then Mr. Tompkins won—quite as great a battle, in its way, as any he had ever won in the ring.

"Are you going, you—you, hymn-swiping gazoot, or am I going

to lay you out stiff, to teach you to keep to you own part of the ship!" bellowed Captain Bully Keller, again.

And Mr. Tompkins, ex-prize-fighter, winner of over sixty fights, turned and walked aft slowly, without a word.

VII

"I reck'n I'm standin' right in the shoes of law an' Providence," said Captain Bully Keller, later, in answer to Mr. Tompkin's gentle remonstrances. "I'm Cap'n of this ship, Sir, an' I reckon Cap'n of a ship is the nearest thing to the A'mighty you'll get in this world; an' if I choose to do anything, why, I guess I'm the man as does it; an' I'm right weary o' psalm-singing! An' likewise, Mister, this end of the ship is where you belong, an' don't you need to be told twice again, or maybe I'll forget ye're a passenger and an old wheat-sheaf, an' I'll be giving you a tonic ye'll not forget in a hurry."

"Joseph!" said Mrs. Tompkins's voice, at that moment, from the companion-way, "can I speak with ye a moment, Joseph?"

"Your pardon, Cap'n," said Mr. Tompkins; "the missus wants me a moment."

He crossed the poop to where his wife stood in the companion-way. "Well, M'ria?" he said.

"Joseph," said his wife, very small, and very white-faced with inward anger. "Ye know, Joseph, I've always stood for you bein' converted; an' I just thanked God on me two knees, when ye turned *reeligious*, an' quit fightin', did I not, Joseph?"

"That's so, wife," said Mr. Tompkins.

"Well," said his wife, "me that's for peacefulness an' godliness, an' that's helped pluck many a brand from the burnin', me that thanked God when I won ye to peaceful decent ways, I say, Joseph, go an' fight that man, an' bring him low. I've stood here an' harked to things he's said to ye, an' I'm fair woun' up!" Her voice rose and cracked, shrilly, in a final brief command: "Fight the brute, Joseph! Beat him up good!"

There was a sudden roar of laughter from where the Mate stood on the poop, and the Helmsman grinned broadly; for they caught the last few words of Mrs. Tompkins's injunctions.

The Mate walked forward to where Captain Bully Keller stood near the break of the poop. "She's tellin' the old codger to beat you up, Cap'n!" Mr. and Mrs. Tompkins heard the Mate say, in no modulated voice. "I guess, Cap'n, you've sure riled the old lady!"

Mrs. Tompkins clenched her small, rather thin hands. "Joseph!" she said "Go right now an' beat him up, or you're no husband o' mine!"

"Nay, M'ria," said Mr. Tompkins, in his quiet composed way. "I've had more'n one fight wi' meself, an' I've won. An' you'll be the first to say I was right, when you'm less upset, wife. Maybe I can yet soften him."

Mrs. Tompkins turned and went down the stairs into her cabin, where she sat for an hour, staring at the bulkhead and fighting to drive out the storm that possessed her small body. And meanwhile, up on deck, Mr. Tompkins, ex-prize-fighter, continued with invincible self-command to ply the "soft word"; but with about as much effect as if he had tried "genteel conversation" with a polar bear suffering from a sense of suppressed spiritual injuries.

VIII

"Feyther!" came a shrill cry, early in the morning hours, just after daybreak the following morning. And then the sounds of heavy blows, and of someone sobbing, breathlessly, as each blow was struck. Then again the shrill cry of "Feyther! Feyther!"

At the first cry, Mr. Tompkins, dressed in flannel drawers and shirt, had leaped from his bunk with an agility astonishing in so heavily built a man. And now he was on the companion steps, taking them four at a time, in great muscular bounds.

"Feyther!" came the cry again, shriller.

"Comin', son," said Mr. Tompkins, in his deep voice.

Then he arrived, a quick-moving, human fighting machine, as dangerous as any angry tiger and as precise as a modern quick-firing gun.

Mr. Jackson, the big bucko Mate, was thrown bodily a dozen feet along the poop-deck, and Nibby was picked up, from where the Mate had let him drop—for the man had been ropes-ending the lad with the end of the main brace, and Nibby was being violently sick, owing to the weight of the blows he had received.

As Mr. Tompkins held his son in a position to ease his vomiting, Mr. Jackson got up off the poop-deck, and for the first time realised who it was that had attacked him.

"My beloved oath!" he shouted, and charged down on the ex-prize-fighter. "I'll gi'e you what I was givin' the kid, you bloomin' billy-goat, you!" he roared, and swung a powerful, clumsy right-hand punch at Mr. Tompkin's head.

Mr. Tompkins evaded the punch, and then, with Nibby in his arms, started to run for the companion-way, with the Mate thudding along the poop-deck in his wake.

Abruptly, something new happened—a small thin figure, wrapped in a sheet, darted up through the companion-way on to the poop. It had thin, grey hair, done in three or four spiky plaits, that stuck out from its head at various angles; and it called out a shrill, tense direction: "Put Nibby down, Joseph. I'll tend him. Beat that beast up good, an' look out for the other, he's comin'.'"

Nibby's father lowered his son quickly on to the seat that ran all along the skylight, and jumped to one side. Nibby's mother, small though she was, gathered the boy up against her bosom and glanced over her shoulder, to see how her man dealt with the bucko Mate.

The ex-prize-fighter made a quick job of it, and the bucko Mate (accounted formidable enough against the usual port-sweepings and degenerates supplied by the shangai-houses) made but a pitiable show against the grim fighter he had pursued with such fatuous confidence.

Had Mr. Tompkins been minus his long goatee and eminently respectable side-whiskers, the Mate might have recognized "old Bowleg Jo, the one-ton-punch merchant"; but he was oblivious just then to the fact and, a moment later, to all the facts of life; for the bulk of Mr. Tompkins slid, with an almost incongruous grace, under the bucko's great round-arm-punch, and immediately afterward the Mate's chin made a brief but unforgettable acquaintance with the historic "one-ton-punch" right fist of Mr. Tompkins, and the thud his body made, as it struck the deck, seemed to shake the vessel.

"Look out, Jo-o-seph!" shrilled Mrs. Tompkins; and her husband hove himself round in his track, like a great agile cat, and met the silent ugly rush of Captain Bully Keller, who had just raced up out of his cabin, in time to see the Mate go down senseless on the deck.

Now, this sixteen stone of fight and violent evil was a very different proposition from that of the bucko Mate; and the ex-prize-fighter was well aware of the fact. He side-stepped the charging Captain, and tried a rib punch as he passed under his swing; but the Captain chopped it down in a way that showed he knew more about scientific fighting than Mr. Tompkins had supposed.

The Captain came round on his toes, and jumped in at Mr. Tompkins, hitting right and left at his face. The ex-prize-fighter slipped the right-hand-punch, and pushed up the left, like lightning. As he did this, his left foot went forward, and his left fist traveled upward about eight inches, and struck the underside of Captain Bully Keller's jaw. The Captain's head went back, and Mr. Tompkins brought in his right, with a short radius swing against the side of the Captain's neck.

The blow sounded exactly like a butcher's mallet hitting a piece of lean beef, and the Captain rocked just for one brief instant on his feet. Then he had recovered, for he was as strong as a bullock.

He jumped back a couple of paces and kicked off his slippers. "Now you goat-wagger, I'm going to maul you, by God, yes!" And he dashed in at the easily poised figure of the ex-prize-fighter.

Mr. Tompkins sidestepped him, sliding his head in under the ponderous right-hand swing that the captain left fly, with a deep malignant grunt. As the Captain overshot him, Mr. Tompkins was, just for one brief moment, a little on his rear, and in that instant of time he smote the great stern of Captain Bully Keller with his open left palm, even as an empathic matron "corrects" a child, in a hasty moment.

The sound of the ugly slap rang fore and aft along the decks, and suddenly there was a roar of laughter from forward; for both watchers had streamed out of the fo'cas'le to watch the stupendous spectacle of the invincible Keller getting a hammering—at last!

Now the slap had done no harm, for all that it was so hearty. It was nothing more than a natural ebullition of spirit on the part of Mr. Tompkins at finding himself, with a clear conscience, enjoying all the charm and intense zest of a first-class scrap. But the effect of that same slap on Captain Bully Keller, coupled with the laughter it had evoked, was to turn him temporarily into a madman. Just try to get it—sixteen stone, odd, of muscle and evil berserk rage! That was the particular kind of human tornado that came round, roaring, at Mr. Tompkins.

The Captain made one spring, and caught him by the hair of his head with his left hand, and his goatee beard with the other, and swung him clean off his feet.

The method of attack was somewhat unorthodox, according to Mr. Tompkins's lights, and it lacked nothing of vigour. The Captain swung him around bodily, in a half-circle, with his feet off the deck. Then the hair and beard simultaneously refused duty. They came out in two handfuls, and Mr. Tompkins shot sprawling with a crash on to his hands and knees on the poop-deck.

Captain Bully Keller roared like a great bull and charged down at the smaller man, his hands full of beard and hair. He kicked Mr. Tompkins in the face with his bare foot, cutting a great gouge under his left eye with his nails.

But Mr. Tompkins caught the foot, and Captain Bully Keller promptly fell on him; and as he opened his hands to save himself, the light breeze blew a couple of tufts of hair and beard hither and thither along the poop.

And then Captain Bully Keller got a nasty surprise and a very bad jar to his system, all in one and the same moment. As he sprawled an instant, grabbing for hold a-top of Mr. Tompkins's extremely broad and muscular back, the ex-prize-fighter descended for the first time to rough-and-tumble methods, and slewed half over on his side, and drove his right elbow backward and outward in a terrible jolting elbow-punch under the Captain's jaw.

The blow was a tremendous one, as any fighting man will understand, and would have put ninety-nine men in a hundred to sleep instanter; but, with Captain Bully Keller it merely drove his head back for a couple of seconds and produced a vaguely stunned sensation, followed immediately by a gorgeous riot of toothache; for every tooth in his jaws had been jarred as if by a blow from a hammer.

Then Bully Keller was himself again; but things had changed considerably; for in that brief time of temporary "numbness" on the part of his enemy, Mr. Tompkins had hove himself out from under Bully Keller and was on his feet, waiting for his man.

Nor had he more than a bare half-second; for the Skipper hurled himself up from the deck, with an inarticulate bellowing, and rushed the squat figure of the ex-prize-fighter. Right and left, right and left, he punched, grunting like an animal, with every blow, and had any one of them got home on a vital mark, they would have been enough, literally, to kill an average man! But here Mr. Tompkins was very truly at his own game, and he slipped and side-stepped round a small portion of the poop-deck, with the Captain pursuing him, hitting and grunting, grunting and hitting; but never once reaching him in any fashion calculated to do serious damage.

Then, suddenly, Mr. Tompkins stopped dead in his wonderful circle of retreat, and one leg stiffened behind him rigidly, like a steel bar, at the identical moment that his right fist shot out in one of the famous "one-ton-punches" which had won him so many of his fights.

The tremendous blow took the Captain a little (not more than a full inch) below the point of the jaw, and all of Mr. Tompkins's strength and skill had gone to that blow; moreover, the punch had taken the captain in the midst of his storming rush, and the suddenly rigid leg of the prize-fighter stiffened to take the enormous shock of the sixteen stone man's charge, at the moment of impact.

Captain Bully Keller's jaw cocked up abruptly, in the absurdly helpless fashion that a man's head does go up, when he gets a punch of that kind from a certain angle; his great arms were suddenly adrift, and his ponderous shoulders were all at once untensed from fierce effort to an inexpressible inanition. He went backward one step, two steps, then a third, still with his head cocked up in that absurd way.

Mr. Tompkins dropped his own hands to his sides with a satisfied expression. He knew, from his extensive experience, that he had just administered a knock-out blow, of a foot-energy (if I may so express it, without appearing Irish) of several hundred pounds.

The Captain's body paused a moment, inertly, in its backward stagger. Then, lurched rearward, with one final, dragging step, and seemed on the point of collapsing. And then, in that moment, the Captain's chin came down slowly from its cocked-up angle, and he stared at Mr. Tompkins with half-glazed eyes, his face totally expressionless. It was most extraordinary. The man was knocked out of time and place. It would take him anything from ten minutes to two hours to come round from such a blow as he had received, and here he was still standing on his feet and staring at his opponent.

The ex-prize-fighter stared, silent and fascinated. From away forward there was a low hum of talk that came clear through the chill morning air—just that sound and no other—except the odd creak of the masts, and the whine, whine, of the gear in the leads and blocks, and the odd slat, slat, of the reef-points away up aloft.

And then, in all that silence, Captain Bully Keller spoke, in a queer toneless, creaking voice: "Say," he said, "where am I?" The glazed look left his eyes as he spoke, and his shoulders lost their flaccid appearance; and abruptly, intelligence came into his eyes and face—and then memory.

Mr. Tompkins continued to stare. In all his years of fighting he had never seen a man make such a recovery—the man's vitality must be as stupendous as his physique. Suddenly, Mr. Tompkins got on the defensive. He received the knowledge of the Captain's complete recovery just in time; for in that same moment Captain Bully Keller leaped at him and smashed in a flurry of right and left hand punches.

With a feeling of amazement in his brain, Mr. Tompkins slipped and guarded and sidestepped busily, until the sudden charge had eased a little. The Captain was not hitting quite so hard, which proved that the "knock-out" punch he had received had taken steam from the boiler.

Then Mr. Tompkins saw an opportunity and stepped in smartly. He drove three upper-cuts hard to the old place, and as the Captain gave back he put in a tremendous right-and-left punch, aimed at the mark; but, as he expressed it to himself afterward, the man seemed to have ribs down to his knees. It was like punching into the side of a horse.

Yet the blows had effect; and a minute later he drove in a very heavy punch again, to the jaw, this time a little more on the side, and fairly knocked Captain Bully Keller off his feet.

During the whole of the fight Mr. Tompkins had not yet received one dangerous punch; but now he paid for a moment of carelessness; for the Captain came up off the deck, as quick as a cat, and made one jump at him, and struck, before the prize-fighter's hands were up. The blow took Mr. Tompkins on the forehead, and knocked him literally head over heels, over the low sail-locker hatch.

Captain Bully Keller let out a roar, sprang to the rail, hauled out an iron belaying pin and jumped over the hatch to make an end of Mr. Tompkins.

"Look out, Jo-o-seph!" shrieked Mrs. Tompkins, and loosed Nibby. She ran round to the starboard side, just as the Captain caught her husband by the throat. She dropped the sheet and flew at him—a skinny wraith of wifely devotion. She grasped the pin itself with her two hands, just as the Captain struck, and was hurled bodily a dozen feet, still clinging to the pin; but she had saved her husband; for Mr. Tompkins seized the chance, and hove himself sideways; then jumped, and got safely to his feet, his head singing like a kettle, and his whole system badly jarred.

He whirled round just in time to receive the Captain's rush. He hurled himself at Mr. Tompkins and grabbed him round the body. He made a snap at Mr. Tompkins's nose with his teeth, and, missing this most useful organ, bit his ear.

Then Mr. Tompkins shed all his remaining Christianity and got busy. He uppercut the Captain twice under the jaw, with both fists together, and then, as the Captain's head went back and his great throat lay exposed, he hit him a chopping blow with his right fist, straight upon his Adam's apple.

Captain Bully Keller loosed away, making noises in his throat, and ran around in a circle, still making those noises. And in the midst of his running round and round, the ex-prize-fighter stepped in and hit him handsomely, with every ounce of his strength, one liberal right-hand swing on the side of the point of his jaw.

It may seem a little brutal on Mr. Tompkins's part to have done this at so distressing a moment; but, actually, it had an element of rough mercy in it; for the unconsciousness that followed promptly brought a swift and effectual ease to the bully.

The Captain slid down into a heap on the deck, beaten physically, mentally, and morally.

"Now," said Mr. Tompkins, converted prize-fighter, "maybe I'll win ye yet to the Lord's side." His eyes shone anew with the fervour of grim religious enthusiasm. He stooped and lifted the big man in his arms, with amazing ease, and carried him down to his cabin.

IX

Today there is no such person as Captain *Bully* Keller. After the hammering he received from Mr. Tompkins he lost prestige, and other heavily built sailormen discovered that it was possible to stand up successfully to him. His enormous confidence in himself seemed destroyed, and he became plain Captain Keller, a man who now pays his crews in cash, instead of in the blows that were once so economical and all-sufficient.

He still remembers Mr. and Mrs. Tompkins, passengers from San Francisco to Boston; but without, I may say, marked enthusiasm. Indeed, if you are a smallish man, it is well not to venture the subject.

The Mystery of Missing Ships

I

YES, I PROMISED I'D tell you what happened when I was Master of the *Richard Harvey*—a steam tramp and a fine strong lump of an iron vessel; bought by the French, she was, afterward, an' they asked me to go on running her; but not me!

Mind you, this is a mighty strange business I'm going to tell you about; but it started just ordinary, with one of the blessed Stokers getting blind, paralysed drunk. We'd a cargo of all sorts, and I found afterward he'd got into a case of whisky that one of the stevedores must have stowed forrard on purpose, so as they could get it through the fore hatch.

Well, this joker gets drunk, and when he got below into the heat of the stokehold, he starts to play hell fire and Sally Lunn all at the same time. The Chief, who *wasn't* Scotch, for a wonder, told two of 'em to run him on deck. There were several sorts of a rumpus then, including blood and murder, before they done it, and then they didn't, for they was deader than him.

You see, the silly fool got in some ugly work with his shovel; and while they stood off from him, he started in and smashed all the steam gauges, and the place was full of steam in no time.

That was nothing, if he'd stopped there; but a properly drunk man's got a bit of the madman about him—an' some of a madman's silly sort of murdering cunning. He creeps through the steam to where the main steam pipe was coupled onto the valve, and he lets out with the heavy shovel a dozen mighty, great blows, and then, crack, "chrrrr," the main steam pipe split open—on the engine side of the valve, as we found after—and there was steam at near two hundred pounds and hot as the hereafter roaring round the engine room and the stokehold.

I was on the bridge at the time having a quiet smoke, and I heard shouts down the stokehold, and the the b-z-z-z of steam from the

307

broken gauges; and a minute after came that awful mad "chrrrr" yell of the steam when the main pipe went. The engine-room skylight leaves was flung open in a moment, and the steam cane out in a white smother, roaring till I could think the sky was one solid echo with it. In a minute you couldn't scarce see the decks fore or aft, and the screw had stopped right on the turn.

I knew it was mighty serious by the signs, and I came down off the bridge and across to the skylight like a runaway mare. I could scarce see the skylight already through the volumes of steam rolling along the decks. But my hands got the edge of it, and then in a moment I gave back from the skylight, with my face one scorch of pain, where the smother of steam came boiling out in mighty clouds. I stuffed my fingers into my ears, for I couldn't hear not one sound in all the world but that dead, stunning roar.

Then I got a quick notion, and ran forrard a few yards and fumbled round. I ripped open the fiddley and the stokehold skylight, and got the burning stuff again on my half-raw face. Then I right about and raced for the Second Engineer's berth, but he was out already in his shirt and drawers.

"The skylights!" he shouted, but I caught him by the arm.

"Open! All of 'em!" I roared in his ear. "Look at my face and hands!"

"It's the main steam!" he shouts again at me, looking into the steam, and I was far enough away from the sound just to hear a faint ghost call of what he shouted.

"That's what I'm thinking!" I yelled back.

He ran off to his room again, and I after him. He'd started smearing stuff over his face and hands.

"I'm going down," he said.

"So am I," I told him, and grabbed the tin of dubbin from him and smeared the stuff over my own face and hands. Then we tried for it, with the men all round like ghosts, and shouting to us not to go.

Well, we went down, and I thought my throat and mouth and chest was burned clean out with the first breath I took.

I let the Second lead, for he knew his own place better than me, and we tumbles over a man at the foot of the iron ladders.

I felt him over, and guessed it was the Chief by his beard. We couldn't speak, but the Second helped me get him on to my back, and I went up the ladder while the Second tried for the valve.

I got the man up and out on deck, and sure it was the Chief. Lord! I guess he must have tried for the valve and got into the direct steam, then run blind for the steps and dropped.

I turned to go down, and four of my own deck hands came after me.

"Back, lads!" I shouted. "You can't do nothing!"

But they just shook their heads, meaning they would take their share. And then three of the Stokers ran up, too, with their faces all wrapped up in their blankets to kill the steam.

"Keep back!" I shouted. "You—" And then the roar below stopped, and I knew the Second had got to the valve.

"Thank God for that!" I says out plain and honest. And I turned and looked down and listened to the horrible kind of steamy silence below me in the engine room.

"Johnson!" I shouted down into the dead steam below, that being the Second Engineer's name, but there weren't no answer.

"You can come and help me fetch the Second up," I said to the men that were all pressing round me now,

"Cap'n," said one of my deck hands, "ketch a holt of my arm."

"Go to hell with your arm!" I said, my voice sounding loud and queer in the sudden darned silence.

I knew then I felt a bit rummy, but sailormen got to be shown how to do things, and I went down into the engine room and carried the Second up myself, for I couldn't do less for a man of his breed.

When I got down again the men had found the two Stokers and the madman, all of 'em cooked to a turn, as you might say. There was signs enough about 'em to show they couldn't live again and wouldn't be no use if they could, so I had 'em each shoved into a blanket, with a chunk of coal, and dumped over the side. I did the same with the Chief. I felt we were starting to clear things up a bit then. I never do have no use for dead men aboard a ship. If they're dead, dump 'em, I say, an' always have said.

Lucky there was only the three Stokers below; two of the others was up at the ash shoot and winch, and the other one was in the bunkers, having a row with a trimmer that wouldn't feed coal properly, and I guess they all had cause to thank the Almighty, too.

II

Well, there I was, with a well-found steamship and a bust main steam pipe and one engineer a mile deep under my keel and the other a mighty sick man in his bunk, nearer dead than alive. We carried a Greaser and twelve Stokers, but not even the Greaser was game to tackle the job of splicing up the steam pipe, and I cursed the man, while the Steward dressed my hands and face. Cursing wouldn't mend the pipe, only it eased me to say things. Then I just went down to have a look at it myself.

I couldn't use my hands, but I guess I had the brains I carry under my hat. I had no patience with the Greaser, and I got two of my own deck hands down to unship the pipe and strip away the packing that was parcelled all round the pipe to stop it losing heat, and then I had a good look at the bust. You see, I've a brother as is an engineer, and I've always had a taste that way myself, and I felt I could fix that pipe up to work if I'd only had the use of my hands. But I might do something yet if my lads showed they'd only a bit of gumption in their fingers and thumbs. I'd do the thinking. There was just one good thing about the Greaser; he knew what spares there was, pretty near down to the number and size of every spare bolt and nut; and I told the man plain that he'd good points, for I always give a man his due; you aren't fit or able to run men if you don't.

He'd told me right away there was no spare length of steam piping, but he fished out a fathom of sheet copper a quarter of an inch thick, and I thought I might be able to bend it round the split part of the pipe, first drilling and tapping the pipe.

I told him his notion had good sense, but unless he or my lads had finger skill to get the copper curved round even they'd never make a joint that'd hold steam. You see, the split was on the outside of a curve of the pipe, and a mighty cute bit of work it would take to fit anything round it close enough to hold in the power.

Well, after thinking awhile, I had the Greaser and my couple of lads taking turns with a hand drill, and I put four holes through the pipe on the inner side of the curve. Then I told the Greaser to put a punch in the holes and drive out the burst-in edges of the pipe, where the shovel had driven them inside the pipe. This way. I got the pipe into tolerable shape and the edges of the two-foot split closer; but I wasn't much nearer making the pipe hold steam.

"Is there no elbow piping among the spares as would make a sleeve over this?" I asked the Greaser. "It needn't fit all that close if I can use it the way I want."

But there was no such thing, and I knew it would have to be the sheet of copper.

Well, I started the Greaser and my two lads to bend that sheet of copper, both to the curve of the elbow and the round of the pipe and midnight found them still bending and me still swearing and the split pipe still staring ugly at the lot of us.

"Drop it, men," I said, "and turn in. I'll tell the Second Mate to let you have all night in, and you can call at the cabin door and tell the Steward I said you was to have a tot of grog, and you, too, Greaser."

That pleased them, as is but natural, and poor sort of man I'd be to run men if I didn't know when a man had done his best, even if it were a damned clumsy sort of best.

III

Before I turned in I got a notion to have look at the ship's manifest, and there, sure enough, I hit on something that set me hoping I'd found the thing in the cargo that might help. For there was a consignment of strong iron piping to a Mr. Daylesly, of Gostell, a grain station about sixty miles above 'Frisco. Then, farther on, there was two tons of sheet lead for Ellison, a plumber on the water front.

I went up on deck, meaning to tell Aymes, the Second Mate, to turn his watch to on the fore hatch, where the pipes and the lead was stored. But just as I stepped up into the scuttle, I was taken all aback to hear the Second Mate hailing from the break:

"Ahoy, there! Ahoy, there!" he was singing out. "Where are you coming to? Look where you're coming to!"

Do you know, I got a sudden sick turn for the moment. I guessed in a flash one of them as is in the Bad Business had spotted us, rolling there, broken down. And if you don't know what that is let me tell you it's the modern form of piracy, and it's piracy just as deadly and naked as ever in the old days. Let a vessel break down in mid-ocean and one of these human sharks will smell her out before long, and—well, she becomes one of the missing ships. You don't believe me perhaps? Well, you hark to what I got to tell you first. There's all sorts in the Bad Business, but whalers is worst. They got a sort of free pass to loaf around the ocean doing nought, with more men an' boats to them than's good for 'em. It's like *asking* them to help themselves, sending hard cases to sea fitted up like that—all ready to make trouble. Oh, I know!

"Do you want help, Cap'n?" came a voice out of the darkness.

"No!" I roared, taking the answer out of Aymes' mouth. "Sheer off there! When I want help I'll ask for it. Sheer off there!"

As I sung out I reached for my night glasses out of the box in the companion scuttle, and now I set them to my eyes and stared.

"A whaler," I said to myself, "by his boats. The Lord help us if he's a wrong un!"

You see, the whaler carries a deal of men for her size, and I'd always suspect a whaler quicker than any other craft afloat. They've things too much their own way, and that means crookedness made easy—see? They can run in and out of ports as suits 'em, or loaf about the ocean without anyone thinking they're up to anything funny. No, I never had no use for whaling ships, not when I'm at sea. They've too many men, and they're a rough lot at best, and a deal rougher ordinarily. And what they are at worst—well, I guess I know better than some.

I slipped down in three jumps into my cabin and shoved two big Colts into my side pockets; then back on deck, and went across to Mr. Aymes.

"Is he sheering off?" I asked.

"Yes, Sir," he said. "I didn't care for him running up so close. I don't see what his notion was, but it ain't seamanlike, to say the least of it."

"Mister," I said, "keep your eyes skinned tonight. I've no use for that kind of business. Send a lad down into the lamp locker to trim and pass out all the lamps he can find. If yon vessel sees we're on the go about the decks maybe it'll be as well. I want you to lift the fore hatch and turn your watch and some of the Stokers to work shifting cargo. There's some stuff I want. I'll keep about the decks with you. Whose lookout is it?"

"James Knowles, Sir," he told me.

"I'll have a word with him," I said, and got my second glasses from my cabin. Then I went straight away forrard and up on to the fo'cas'le head.

"Knowles," I said, "keep your eyes open tonight. Here's a pair of glasses. I don't like yon hooker hanging round and offering help so friendly-like where help ain't needed."

"Nor me, Sir, if I may make so bold. I ain't no use for whalers," said the man, who was an old shellback. "Is it the Bad Business you're thinking on, Sir?"

"It's just that, my lad," I told him. "Have you ever come up against it?"

"No, Sir;" he said, "but my brother sailed in the *Alec Thompson*, a big four-master as was reported missing two years ago. That ain't nothin', I know, Sir; but before I signed on last trip I was lookin' in a pawnshop in 'Frisco, and there were his own watch, a good silver one, starin' at me. I knew it by the dial that was made like a draught board of silver an' black enamel. I went in an' asked to have a look at it; all of a shake I was, so that the chap in the shop thought maybe I was on to some funny work, for he wouldn't let me have the watch into my hands at first. When he did I opened the back, for my brother had his name there, with the date of his birth that I'd cut for him myself with a graver; for I've a taste that way.

"Well, Sir, there *had* been something there, for I could see where the case was scraped; but not a thing as I could swear to, only I knew as it were my brother's watch I held in my fist; an' him with the watch in his hand in Liverpool, as I know, when I saw him off, for we set our watches alike, same as we always does before a voyage, and never alters 'em by the ship, but sees which has kep' best time. An' his ship hadn't never been seen since, except reported at sea, once on the line an' once down in these parts, an' then never no more.

" 'This is my brother's watch,' I said to the shopman; 'him that was lost in the *Alec Thompson*. I can swear to it.'

" 'What of it?' he asks me, and I could swear he looked different. 'Here, give it to me,' he says, and snatched it from my hand. 'If you want it pay for it. Hundred dollars is the figure.'

" 'Hundred dollars!' I said. "Why, it didn't cost a quarter that new.'

" 'Hundred's the price to you,' he says, and shoves the watch back into the tray. 'If you want it bring your money with you or keep out. I've no time to waste with the likes of you.' You know, Cap'n, the ugly way them 'Frisco storekeepers have with a sailorman; as if he wasn't nothin' but dirt?"

"Yes," I says, mighty interested. "Did you go for him?"

"No, Sir," he said. "I went out into the street to think how I might get that watch, for I could see the storekeeper were a wrong un, an' never meant me to have it. No sailorman ever has twenty quid to spend on a watch. I'd never believed the odd yarns that's floating round about the Bad Business, but I guess then, Sir, I knew they was Gospel truth; else how did my brother's watch come there, when him an' the ship an' all is at the bottom? Now, I reckon that was just dead proof that there's something in them funny yarns as is always floatin' round, with no one ever to prove 'em or know how they come on the go. An' I guess a store man was a crook, and knew more or guessed more than you or me, Sir, 'll ever know.

"Well, Sir, I went past that window again that evening, but the watch weren't put on sale again; never then or any other time.

"An' then I thought, after I signed on my new ship, an' drew my advance, I'd go in an' see if the store man'd rise to an offer. I bought a new fit-out of togs, so as to look like I had plenty cash; then in I goes.

" 'I've come in for that there watch I looked at a bit back,' I says, as easy as I could.

"He looks me up an' down with a puzzled look, then he remembers me.

" 'You!' he said; an' I could 'a' sworn he'd got a fright. 'Oh, I remember, he goes on. 'We sold the watch awhile back. No, Mister, I don' know the bloke as got it. Sorry,' he says. 'Mornin'.' And out I had to come.

"Now, Sir, if that ain't proof, what is?"

"You needn't try to prove things to me, my lad," I said. "I *know*; but them yarns takes a hell of a lot of proving before any one ashore'll ever take 'em for anythin' more than a sailor's yarn. You keep your eyes skinned tonight, and watch the sea for boats, particular. An' keep your ears open. You ain't going to hear much tonight; for there's a small breeze, but you might chance to hear oars. They carry a long way over water."

"Aye, aye, Sir," he said; and I ran down onto the main-deck, where they were beginning to lift the fore hatch.

IV

There was a deal of stuff to shift before we got down to the piping. There was wire netting of all sizes, by the five hundred and thousand yards, in mighty great rolls, that made the men sweat at the winch to hoist out. Not heavy stuff for its bulk, but heavy enough, and clumsy. And then, at last, we come down to the pipes, and in a minute I saw what I wanted—a pipe elbow-joint couplin'.

I was just pointing which piece I wanted hoisted out, when Knowles sings out, quick an' quiet from the fo'cas'le head:

"They'm comin', Sir! I c'n see four boats in the water, betwixt us an' the whaler."

That looked like my suspicions was right, and I jumped to the rail and took my night glasses from my jacket pocket.

"About a point forrard of the beam, Sir," said Knowles. And then I got them, full in the fuzzy gray night field of the glasses. Four boats there were, right enough—dim, vague sort of things they looked out there in the dark, at that distance; but they were boats, I had no doubt, and I didn't doubt, either, what they was coming for.

"They'm a mile away yet, an' more," I said to Knowles. "Keep your eye on 'em, an' never lose 'em."

I whipped across to the hatch.

"Knock off, there," I said quietly. "Come up out of the hold, you that's down there. There's a matter of three or four boats comin' across to pay us a visit, unexpected, as you might say. I guess they think we ain't up to their little ways.

"What they're coming for won't be no good to you nor me, men; an' they ain't coming aboard here, not while we can stop 'em. If once they does, I guess there's none of us'll draw another pay day.

"One of you bounce out the other watch—smart! Now, then, grab one of these rolls of netting. Rip off the cover. Get the stops off it, and run it along the rail, fore and aft, outside the rigging."

I heard Aymes running forrard. "Four boats, Sir," he said, trying to whisper it, so as the men shouldn't hear. "They'm between us an' the whaler, about a mile away."

"That's right," I said. "Knowles has just reported. Away aft with you, Mister, an' call the Mate and the Third. Tell 'em I want you-all, at once. Roust the Steward out and the cook and carpenter while you're on the job. If you've any shooting gear in your sea-chests, you'd better dig it out as smart as you can. Shift, now!"

"Very good, Sir," he said, and was away at a run; and before he was into the cabin I had the other watch and the rest of the Stokers chasing out of the fo'cas'le.

"Another coil, this side, lads," I sung out. "I'll have the nettin' doubled. We'll give 'em something to dig through. Open two on the starboard side, now. Get moving, there. Pass up them coils of wire rope! Andrew and McCebe, take an end each on this side, outside of everything, and stretch it fore and aft. Jones and Taylor do the same to starboard. Stop it up to the fo'cas'le head, an' the rigging, bridge stanchions, awning stanchions, and the crutch for the after derrick. Move them!—Bo'sun, that you? Good! Get then out some wire for seizings, and pass it round smart."

Believe me, inside of ten minutes that netting was stretched fore and aft, and the upper edge stopped to the wire rope I'd had set up, while the bottom edge they was wiring down, for all they was worth, to the bulwark stanchions, so that there was a wire netting now fore and aft, right round the slip.

The First Mate, Second, and Third was with me long before this; and good men all three, not to mention the Bo'sun, who was a man I've carried these thirteen years. A right clever sailorman, an' mighty good to run men.

I kept the Second Mate and Knowles watching the boats, but they was still near half a mile off, so far as we could judge, which showed they was coming slow, thinkin' we'd not spotted 'em.

The three Mates had revolvers, good, healthy-sized small cannon they was, too; and I'd my two Colt revolvers in my pockets, and that was all the weapons there was in the ship.

"Damn the authorities!" said the Mate. "Why the hell ain't it law as every ship should have to be properly armed before she goes to sea!"

"Damn 'em, by all means!" I said. "But we ain't beat. Pass up some of them bundles of sharp iron garden railin's— Look at that now, Mister! A bit fancy, but as good to kill a man as if that's what they was made for. An' they'll go through the mesh of the wire netting easy. I wouldn't fancy a prod in the face with one of them!

"Have the men shove all them other rolls of wire on their ends, along under the rails. The bulwarks is steel, but I doubt if they'll stop a high-power nickel rifle bullet. Not as they'll try shooting, at first; that ain't their little way. And see as all the water doors is fast shut, top an' bottom flaps."

I went up onto the bridge, and had a look for the boats. They was still a goodish way off in the night, and I guessed they were lyin' on their oars. watchin' us quietly.

I came down and had a word with the Mate.

"They'm out there, Mister," I told him; "maybe six or seven hundred yards off, lying on their oars. I've a notion they're waitin' for us to quiet down. I guess they think we got all hands working double watches on this breakdown. Let 'em go on thinking that, and keep the lamps burning bright about the decks, until they get tired of waitin. The longer they wait, the better I'm pleased, for then it's the nearer to daylight, an' then, maybe, they'll think better of it, an' draw off before they think we've seen 'em. You see, them as messes with the Bad Business aims always to surprise a ship, and never to be seen or known; for, if a dozen shipmasters came in, all with yarns of seeing vessels attacked, the authorities'd have to move; an' there'd be a slump to their dirty trade of knifing, robbing, an sinking'unarmed sailormen.

"But mind, the moment them boats starts to move in on us, douse the lights; for we don't want to be fancy-illuminated targets for them to pot at comfortably out of the darkness. Station the men right round the decks, a couple or three fathoms apart, according to how they pan out, an' explain to them to keep down, out of sight. All they got to do is to jab them fancy garden spikes through the meshes at anyone as tries to come aboard. All clear, that?"

"Yes, Sir," he said.

"I'll take two of the handiest men down with me," I went on. "I'm going into the engine room to see if I can't get yon bu'st steam pipe fixed up. Tell Marti and Telboy to pick up yon piping elbow, and bring it down. The sooner the pipe's fixed, the better, and then we can get the fires lit again an' get of this. The minute them boats begin to come in, mind you, out with them lights, an' report to me."

V

"We'll have to saw the blessed elbow in halves, lengthwise," I told the two men, after they'd tried to fit the burst part of the steam pipe into it. "Get one of them big twenty-inch hacksaws and start up. Come on, lads, it's got to be done!"

For just half an hour by my watch we worked there; me itching to grab the saw from 'em an' show how it should be done; but my hands was too sore, an' all parcelled up by the Steward, except the two trigger fingers, that I'd worked loose for my Colts. All the same, the iron of the pipe cut pretty easy, for it was soft stuff, an' though the men had broke two of the saw blades, I guessed there was enough spares to see us through.

And then I heard the Mate's voice, up at the fiddley, whispering down to me.

"Cap'n!" he was saying."Cap'n, they'm coming!"

"Right," I said. "See the lamps is all out, and go round, and steady the men. Make sure they understand they ain't to show themselves, but just jab through the netting at anyone as tries to come up over the rail. I'm coming right now."

I brought my two putty engineers up with me, and sent them forrard, to take their places along the bulwarks with the others. I went up then onto the bridge, and found the Third Mate there, watching.

"Over there, Sir, just a point foreside the beam," he whispered to me; pointing out into the dark; and I took a good look through my night glasses. The boats were about three hundred yards away, as I guessed, and coming in very quiet and slow and cautious on us. It made me just tingle to see them human sharks coming in on us so sly and silent. I slipped my right fist down into my jacket pocket, an' felt the heavy revolver that was there, with the second in the left pocket, ready for when it was needed. It gave me a good feelin' to touch the gun; and then I got a fresh notion; and turned to the Third Mate.

"Down, smart, now, Mister, into the lamp room, and pass out a couple of flares," I said. "See there's paraffin in the tins. Take them onto the main-deck, and, when I give you the word, light them, and see if you can't just heave 'em slam into the boats. They'll give us a chance to see to pot the devils. Tell the First and Second to be ready with their guns from poop an' fo'cas'le head. Tell 'em not to shoot till you've hove out the flares."

After the Third had gone, I watched the boats creeping slowly up to us, till at last they was not more than a hundred yards away. Then I slipped my glasses into my left hand, and reached for one of the big Colts, with my right.

The boats moved in noiselessly on us, and I could tell they'd got stuff parcelled round the oars and rollocks, so as they'd make no noise.

I scarce breathed, and I guess hardly one of us in the ship was breathing just then. I never heard a sound nor a whisper fore and aft. We might have been a ship full of sleepin' men.

And then, like a lot of damned evil kind of shadders, the four boats came drifting silent alongside. There was never a word spoke in all the boats—I reckon they knew their own ugly business too well—not a word; an' then, very gentle, I heard a little scraping noise along the bulwarks. I guessed they was trying to hook some kind of ladder fixings in over our rail.

By what I was able to see in the dark, the four boats was all along the one side—the port side. I never moved from where I was hid by the weather-cloth dodger, that was lashed up in the forrard angle of the bridge end.

The breeze had dropped now, and there was only a little bit of a damp wind blowing, with no sea at all, so that the night was just grown mighty quiet, and I was able to hear anything.

I knew the Mate and Second would be ready, but I meant to give them devils in the boats the best surprise I could; so I held back from telling the Third to light up and throw the flares over the netting into the boats.

I just harked, for all as I could hark, and I could see dimly, as well. There was men coming, slow an' foxy as big cats, up the side of the ship; and by that I knew they'd got their ladders hooked proper in over our rail. I looks forrard and aft, and I guess each boat must have hooked on two or three ladders; for them dark, crawling lumps was thick on the ship's side, fore and aft.

An' then came a yell from away forrard; an' the same moment a screech from near by, forrard of the bridge, an' then a man screaming somewhere away aft. An' then the thuds of bodies falling into the boats. An' I guess I knew the garden railings was provin' pretty good prodders, like I'd reckoned they would.

"Heave the flares, Mister!" I roared out, in a voice you could have heard a mile away that calm night. "Heave the flares, an' we'll send these devils back home! Heave!"

My word, but the Third was a smart lad! He'd been standin' down under the bridge, with a great clump of lucifers in one fist and a flare in the other, and, before I'd done singing out, he'd lit the first, an' then the second from the first, an' then one of the flares went sailin' up over the netting, and down, bang, into a boat forrard of me; and the second flare he chucked away aft, and it dropped in a boat, too; and such a sight I never saw; for the whole of the starboard side was lit up fore and aft with two great paraffin flares; and, sure enough, there was the four boats, ranged head and stern all along the side, an' a dozen ladders hooked up to our port rail, and men thick on the ladders.

Aft in a flash I saw it, as I leaned outboard over the netting; for the bridge end came over the top of it, and I could see clear. Three of the ladders was empty; an' men a-wriggle, all bloody, as I could see, in the boats under the empty ladders; and then I'd fetched out my second Colt, an' was shooting quick an' steady, right an' left, left an' right; for I reckon I can shoot with a pocket gun. An' every time I fired a man flopped off one of the ladders, thump into the boat under him. An' forrard an' aft, the First and the Second was shootin' from the fo'cas'le head and our bit of a poop-deck, aft. An' all this in a matter of ten to fifteen seconds, not a second more; an' a good twenty men of 'em, what the papers call hors de combat, down there in the boats, an not one of us touched. Never did I see nothing better managed.

But it couldn't last more'n a few seconds, as you can think; for the boats was big, an' full of men. I guess there was a cool hundred in the four boats, an' armed to kill; and before I'd done more than empty my Colts clean out, some one had dumped the flares out into the sea, an' they was shooting back, and the air full of bullets in a moment.

I chucked myself flat on the bridge, an' loaded my two Colts as quick as I could, with my damaged hands. The shootin' was growin' stronger than ever, and I knew I should have been full up with bullets if I'd so much as stuck my head over the rail to take a pot into the boats.

As it was, the canvas dodger I'd been behind was all shot to bits, as I could see, even in the dark, and I could feel odd bits drop on me where I was. The bullets kept hitting the iron stanchion of the bridge, and buzzing off like loopy wasps out over the sea to starboard.

I saw as I could do nothin', stuck up there alone, not daring to show my head; I slid away to leeward, as you might all it, and made one jump down onto the top of my chart-house, and then to the deck.

The shooting made a devil of a row, an' I could hear scarce a thing else; but I went right along the main-deck, fore and aft, an' found the men all as ready as might be, with their garden railings, but never a head coming above the rail to poke at.

The Mate was forrard, lying on his chest on the fo'casle head, seeing as no heads come up over the bow part. You see, as soon as a head came above the rail, it was plain to pot, against the night sky, in spite of the dark.

Away aft, I found the Second Mate, flat on the poop. He'd been touched twice with bullets, but only grazers, nothin' to bother about. And he was takin' care of himself now, and just giving them no more chances.

All the while they was shootin' fifteen to the dozen, and yet never no attempt to attack again; and sudden I tumbled to what it might mean.

I made one run to the starboard side—just in the shadow of the bridge, I was—and then I saw what they was up to. They'd sent two of the boats round from the port side, as quiet as two blessed sharks, and they was haulin' theirselves along the starboard quarter to get amidships, and then to hook on their ladders, and get up quiet an' cut holes in the netting, an' get aboard in the din the others was makin' to port. And then I guess our throats would all have been cut while you could wink twice.

You see, with all that shootin' going on along the port side, we'd not been able to look over without the chance of getting our heads shot to bits, an' so we'd never spotted their plan. It was a good dodge, too.

I slipped across to port like a live shadder, and this man an' that man I picks out, as quiet as you like, an' sends 'em over to starboard, so that I'd got 'em pretty equal divided on both sides the ship in less than the waggle of a duck's stern. Then I looks for the Third, but he'd vanished.

"Where the blazes is yon Third Mate?" I sings out.

"Here, Sir," he said, close to me, coming out of the Bo'sun's locker. "I got a notion, Sir, we wants more lights in them boats," he goes on. "I've a armful of oakum balls here, an' I've soaked 'em with paraffin. I'm going to light 'em, an' sling 'em into the boats, so we can see to shoot again."

"Good for you, Mister!" I said; an' felt the soppin' things in his arms. "The devils have sent two of the boats round to starboard, an' they'm goin' to try to get us in the small of the back, as you might say, while we're admirin' their gun music to port. Now, as soon as I sings out to you, light up an' heave 'em over to starboard. Run first an' warn the two Mates to be ready on the starboard side. We'll get the hogs again, like we surprised 'em to port, an' maybe we'll drop a round dozen before they wake up enough to start shootin'."

"Great, Sir!" he says, an' bolts off; and I then away up quiet onto the bridge, and crept to the starboard end, keeping behind the starboard dodger.

I took out my knife, an' ripped a hole in the canvas, an' peeped down along the ship's side. The two boats was lying close to our side, amidships, an' already they was getting the ladders up into place.

Presently I saw as they'd five ladders up and the men was beginning to get onto them. I knew now was the time, an' I shouted just the three words "Heave, Mister! Heave!"

The Third was smart on the word, too! He struck a bunch of matches before ever the third word was clear out of my mouth. An' he'd hove the second flaming chunk of oakum before I'd got my guns proper to bear. Then I let 'em have it alongside, leaning well over the bridge rail as I fired. And forrard an' aft there came the thump! thump! of the Mates' heavy shooters; while under me the Third got clean up onto the t'gal'en' rail, an' shot down through the wire nettin' into the swarm of 'em.

A wonderful sight it was, too, for the Third had slung five of them flaming balls into the boats before he began to shoot, an' there was the five ladders, with two an' three men apiece on 'em, all froze stiff that one instant with the blaze of light so unexpected, just as they was sure they'd worked the surprise packet on us proper.

Bang! bang! I let out with my Colts, an', away aft, there was the Second Mate's thump! thump! thump! An' under me the Third, belting lead down into the thick of the boatloads of men, an them fallin' slump off the ladders atop of the others, an' yells an' screams an' cursings like I reckon them as goes to hell must be given to. An' forrard, the Mate firin' boomp! boomp! boomp! as steady as a clock running; an' me with my two empty Colts, hot an' smokin' in my hands, before I knew I'd emptied 'em; an' every one of them five ladders stark empty, an' the boats that full of men with the pip, some cursin' and fightin', an' the others screechin', that they hadn't no chance to shoot back for thirty seconds an' more, an' that give me, an' all of us, the chance to load up a gun each an' loose it off into 'em again. An' then they got the last of the lights rolled on an' trampled on, an' a dozen or more of them was shootin' back, an' I'd a bullet through the side of my neck, an' my shoulder gouged with another before I could get out of the way.

I down then on the deck of the bridge; an' a fine fight the men was having to port, as I could hear them; for the other two boats had attacked the same time as we opened on the starboard lot; so as to get us on both sides at once.

I made two jumps to the deck; but I needn't have troubled, for the boats began to draw off from us on both sides, an' we heard 'em pulling away as fast as if the devil was chasin' 'em; which I don't doubt, for crooked work means a deal of trouble dodgin'!

Ten minutes later, with my night-glasses, I saw all four boats join company about five hundred yards off on our port beam, an' pull away for their own vessel. Then I guess the three Mates an' me just shook hands mighty hard.

The we went round the decks; and a sad business it was, for there was two of the Stokers and one A.B. shot as dead as ever men need be; and four of the others was shot in the arms an' shoulders; but not to kill.

I had grog served out all round. Then we put the dead men over the side at once; for I can't abide dead men in a ship. No more can any sailorman as I knows.

An' after that I turned to an' doctored the four men an' the three Mates, for the three Mates 'ud all got nicked, but not one of them, by the wonder of Providence, more than a bad graze. And, after that, the Mate and the Second fixed me up, and we went up again on deck, where we had a bit of a talk, and I showed them that we'd got to get the steam pipe repaired and steam up an away without waste of time; for them devils had been given a kind of broth that would make 'em want our blood pretty bad; and the chances were they'd wait till day-light, an' then come in on us, and finish us, maybe with explosives, or maybe they'd some kind of a gun aboard big enough to blow a hole in our side that would let half the Pacific Ocean in on us in a hurry.

This talk made the three Mates stop their little crowing over what they'd reckoned was just a right, tight little victory. They began to understand that, maybe, there was a lot more of a worse kind of trouble coming to us.

I didn't stop long to talk; but I left the Mates to fix the same kind of watch all round the decks as before and to fetch me the moment they saw anything rummy. Then I went down again into the engine room with the two men I'd last been working with and the two I'd had earlier, trying to fit the copper plate round the elbow of the steam pipe.

I set two of them to their old job of sawing the cover pipe length-wise, and the two others I sent down into the fore hold, to pass up about two hundredweight of sheet lead from among the plumbing stuff that we was carryin' cargo.

I told 'em, to tell the cook, on their way, to get the galley fire in as smart as he could, and to make a devil of a good fire, too. As soon as they'd got the lead cut off one of the big rolls, they was to take it along to the galley an' shove it in two or three of the Doctor's iron saucepans, an' tell him to get it melted as quick as he liked.

"When you done that," I said, "an' while the stuff's meltin', pass me up one of them middle-gauge coils of wire out of the cargo, an' bring it down here, an' your marline spikes; an' look smart, lads, so we can get this darn pipe gadget fixed, an' get off before them devils has another go at us."

VI

My two lads at the hacksaw got through the elbow pipe just after the other two had come down with the wire and their spikes, after shoving the lead on the galley stove to melt.

An' this is the way I shaped to fix up that blessed steam pipe, an' I don't reckon there was ever a main steam pipe in this world as was fixed like that one.

Before I fitted the two halves of the cover pipe onto the steam pipe itself, I cut a good, deep notch with a file in the edges, so as to make a hole through for the lead to be poured in, to fill the space that there was between the steam pipe and the cover pipe; for they wasn't by no manner of means anything of a steam-tight fit.

When I'd done this, I fitted the two halves of the cover pipe together round the steam pipe—at least, that's what I made my men do, and the same with all the other handwork, as you'll understand; for I was putting in the headwork.

When I'd fitted the two halves round the pipe, I set the two men to lash them together with the wire, and to heave the wire taut an' solid with their spikes. When this was done, I'd got what you ought call a metal sleeve fitting loosely round the steam pipe.

The next thing I did was to make the men pack the two ends of the sleeve with oakum, an', while two of 'em was doing this, I sent the others to see how the lead was getting along in the galley. By this time it was coming down, and I stepped up on deck to have a word with my officers and to take a look round.

"We think that's her, Sir," said the First Mate; "only you can't make sure of nothing with the thin mist there is on the sea."

I had a good look through my night-glasses; for, though the dawn was coming, it was still middlin' dark. I could see somethin' off the beam that looked like the dull loom of a ship's hull an' spars.

While I was watchin' it, the men came up to report as the lead wasn't melted yet, an' I sent 'em into the galley an' told 'em to fetch it along the moment it was.

It came broad daylight while the Mates an' me stood watchin'. An' I took a walk forrard, and had a look down the fore hatch, which was still open. There was a mint of pipes of all sizes, from two inches wide to a foot; an' some of them had a pretty hefty lot of metal in them, so that I guessed they was meant to stand a bit of pressure. An' it was while I stood there, lookin' at 'em, that I got the first notion of an idea that I took no particular heed of then; though I thought more about it in a bit.

But just then I heard one of the men at my back sing out, and, when I turned, there was the mist gone away, an' yon ugly devil of a whale ship, with her boats out ahead of her, plain to see, being towed toward us, an' I know then as there was ugly work coming, that we couldn't have no hope to escape from.

The three Mates came running forrard to me.

"They'm busy at something on the poop, Sir," said the Second Mate. "I've just had a-squint from the main rigging; but I can't make nothin' of it all."

"They's stopped towin'," said the First Mate. "Look at that there, Sir! They'm haulin' her round broadside onto us. What do you make of that, now?"

The whaler was something less, maybe, than half a mile away, an' I got a sick feelin' as I saw what they was doin'.

"They'm goin' to sink us," I said, speaking low an' quiet. "They'm goin' to stay off there, where we can't touch 'em, an they'm just goin' to knock holes through us. They've some sort of a gun aft there, on the poop, an' I guess they're loadin' her."

"My God!" said the Mate, and hauls out his revolver.

"Put it away, Mister," I said. "You can't do nothin' that way."

"I'd sooner man the boats, an' go for 'em," said the Third Mate. "If we've got to be wiped out. I guess there'll be a bit of satisfaction in cutting some of them brutes up first."

"You'd never get within a hundred fathoms of her, my laddie," I said. "They'me well fit out with rifles an' there'd not be a live one of us in the boats once we got out on the sea to give 'em a fair chance at us."

"The lead's melted, Sir," said one of my men, coming up to me.

I was watchin' the whaler as he spoke, and spotting as there was no name on her as could be seen, and then, just as I realised what the man was tellin' me, there was a bit of a red flash on the poop of the whaler. I saw it pretty plain, with the morning being grey.

"They're shooting at us," the Third Mate was startin' to say; but he never finished for there was a mighty big jet of water kicked up, about twenty fathom away on the beam, an' then a crash against the ship's side, and one of the big rolls of netting we'd stowed along the bulwarks was flung right out onto the main hatch, an' one of the Stokers with it; an' the two of them things lay there on the hatch, an' the Stoker was just as quiet as the big roll of netting, for he'd been hit with a ball of iron as big as my fist. As for the roll of netting; it had a great dint in the side of it, where the iron chunk had caught it a clip, before it plunked into the Stoker.

An' then, while I still stood there, stiff a bit at what had happened' there came the loud thud of a big gun rolling over the sea, heavy and solidlike.

It was surprisin' the time that bang took to come to us; just a red flash over yonder in the grey mornin', an' a dull, big thump of sound, and a round hole in our bulwarks, as big as the top of a jam pot an' the big roll of wire on the hatch an' the Stoker lyin' as quiet as a baby beside it. Just dead before he knew anything had happened at all.

By Gum! but I felt something begin to boil in me. I went over an' looked at the Stoker an' the dinge in the roll of wire then I walked back to the side again, never sayin' nothing; nor did a man aboard say one word in that blessed moment, only they was all lookin' at me to do something; an', by Gum, but I meant doing something, too, when I got the thing that was come again into my mind properly sorted.

"Look out!" shouted one of the men suddenly.

We had all seen the flash, and we waited in a middlin' sick, helpless sort of way.

The shot hit the water again, this time about ten yards from the ship's side, and kicked up a mighty great chunk of spray, that wet me where I stood. I heard the shot strike our hull before the spray reached me, and afterward I jumped up onto the rail and looked down. There was a hole punched in through our side, not two feet above the water line. All round where the shot had struck the plates was bent in, an' I guessed from that as the shot hadn't as much steam to it as the first one, or it'd have gone clean through, without no dentin' of the plates to speak of.

I took another look at the first hole that was through the bulwarks. This had been punched clean through, an' it'd scarce dinged in the plate at all. By this difference I reckoned they wasn't usin' a *reg'lar* charge of powder, an' that told me as they wasn't usin' ready-loaded cartridges; but just measurin' out loose powder each time. An' by the same reasonin', an' that they was usin' just round iron balls, I reckoned they'd not got no modern cannon, but an old-fashioned piece, as would take time to load an' fire; an' they might take a dozen or maybe five dozen shots before they put a hole through us as would sink us.

I stood a bit, thinkin' all this out, an' then I took a few steps fore an' aft along the deck, to see my way clear; an' no one speakin' a word.

Then one of the men sung out again as they'd fired, an' this time there was no splash, but, the first thing we knew, there was a queer sort of zipp against our metal rail, an' the Greaser was hit with a splinter of sharp iron a yard long that had been stripped off the iron rail by the shot.

An' I guess in that moment I saw how I could do the thing I'd been turnin' over in my mind.

"Handy-billy tackle to the fore hatch!" I roared out. "Aymes, lift the after hatch. Take a couple of men and pass out one of them cases of black powder."

I went down myself into the fore hold an' got a hold of what I needed. I took two of them lengths of pipe that was plainly made of rolled metal an' meant for pressure. It took me five minutes to find just what I wanted; for I was lookin' for two lengths of pipe, with a screw plug in one end of 'em, meant for section ends, I guess I wanted one pipe to fit tight inside the other, so as to double their strength; an' I found just the two of 'em as I was needing. The smaller of 'em had a bore of maybe two or two an' a half inches, an' had a hefty steel screw plug in one end. The bigger pipe just took the smaller one into it, fine an' tight; but, after I'd got 'em on deck, an' before I fitted the smaller one down into the big un, I poured about a quart of melted lead down into the plugged end of the bigger pipe, which was likewise a lot shorter than the thin one.

Then I shoved the thinner pipe down, plug end first, slow an' strong into the bigger pipe, until the butt of it was sweated down solid into the melted lead, an' when they cooled I guess they was like one piece of mighty thick pipe with a narrow bore, an' the length over all would be about two fathoms.

With the lead being ready melted, an' the pipes fittin' into each other so wonderful well, we had the job done in less than five-an'-twenty minutes after I gave the word for the handy-billy.

But them devils in the whaler had been at us all the time, an' four shots more they'd fired with their big gun; but not a one of 'em that had done us any great harm, except that they'd punched two holes through the funnel an' bu'sted the top off one of our port forrard bitts as clean as if it'd been cut.

Every man aboard was on the jump, by this, to get the thing done;

for they saw, by the shape of it, that I'd a notion to make some sort of a shootin' thing, to get back a thump or two at them murderin' swine to the whale-ship.

I'd got half of the men at one of the hand winches, heavin' up a lathe bed out of the fore hold, an' while they was doin' this, three of the other men was takin' one-minute spells an' workin' hell-like-fury with a hand drill to make a touchhole near the butt end of the big pipe-gun gadget.

"Take a man or two, Gilchrist," I said to the Third Mate, "an' rout out a bunch of them window-sash weights an' shove two or three in the galley fire."

"Aye, aye, Sir!" he sung out under his breath; an' was streakin' for the fore hatch before the words was proper out of his, mouth, an' two of the men after him.

As he went, they loosed off again from the whaler, an' the shot hit a iron chunk of the rail clean away, an' the chunk hit the end of the sheep pen, an' killed one of the sheep in a manner that would surprise you, but the shot itself stuck hard an' fast, bedded in the place where it had knocked the iron chunk out of the rail.

I swore a bit, an' then I laughed, for there's nothing like a cheerful grin or two when men is feelin' they'm sure lost an' dead an' done for, if you can't show 'em a way out.

"There'll be fresh meat for dinner today, lads." I said. An' they laughed, too; but it was the way you'll see men laugh when they'm needing to hide how mortal bad they feel.

There was a bit of rifle shootin' from the whaler, off an' on, when we shoved our heads into sight above the rail; but not one of us got touched. They was servin' the big gun slower, an' I guessed they was findin' they'd want to tow in a little nearer, an' maybe that might suit me very well, too.

We got the touchhole bored just after they'd brought the lathe bed aft. An' then they shoved the iron lathe bed on the hatch, an' we lifted the gun, all together, an' laid it along the bed of the lathe, and there we lashed it firm an' solid.

I'd got two irons from the stokehold for rammers, an' a bag of oakum from the Bo'sun's locker, for wads; an' set them to load her.

We put two pint pannakins of black powder into the gun for a test charge, as you might say, an' rammed down a dry oakum wad on the top of it. Then I told the Third to damp another wad, an' work it up good an' hard; an' jamb it down solid on top of the dry oakum.

The Mate had been busy makin' a oakum-n'-paraffin torch on

the end of a long piece of wire, an', after I'd primed the touch hole, he give it to me, with his own box of matches. An' that was the last thing he ever did, for one of the odd rifle bullets took him, just as I was tryin' to get a sight along the pipes at the whaler.

Lord, how I burnt up that moment, inside of me; for I'd always liked the First Mate; but I never said anything, only just nodded to the men as was standing all sick an' white round about, to heave the lathe bed up an inch, an' then to cant her forrard a bit, an' afterward to make fast the handy billy, for a kickin' tackle, to one of the bulwark stanchions.

"Fetch out one of yon hot sash weights," I said; and the Third Mate went off at a jump an' brought one on the galley shovel. All glowin' red, it was. He shoved it in the gun muzzle and rammed it down hard on the wet oakum.

"Stan' clear, all of you!" I said, an' started to light the torch the Mate, as was dead at my feet, had just made.

As I spoke, I saw the flash of the gun aboard the whaler, an' then there was a big splash where the shot had struck the calm sea; about ten fathoms away, an' the same instant, it seemed, the shot came right in over the rail and killed James, an A.B., an' cut the wire in my hand as clean as a pair of shears, then ripped a hole in the starboard bulwark behind me and bashed its way out into the sea.

I wiped my face an' picked up the cut torch again, an' lit it with the Mate's matches; then I took one last look along the pipes, an' saw they pointed clear over the whaler.

"God A'mighty," I said, out loud, "send this where it should go!" An' with just these words I put the burnin' oakum to the touchhole.

There came a flare up in my face, nearly, an' a mighty great flash, an' a bang that made me deaf for an hour after; an' all the decks was full of a mighty great cloud of smoke.

I jumped over the dead Mate, an' ran aft, to be clear of the smoke, for I needed to see where that shot went to.

But I never knew where that shot struck, nor no other man aboard us; only there was a terrible blaze that went up hundreds of feet from the whaler, an' a bang that I could hear, though I was near deaf at the time, as you know; an' there was nothing then to see for a bit but a great bank of smoke right down low on the sea.

No, I've never reckoned to be religious, but that made me feel rummy; for, as I watched, there was great splashes here and great splashes there about the sea, an' I knew, after a moment, as it was bits of yon devil ship, comin' down from a sky that was too sick to let 'em bide up there. An' when the smoke rolled away a bit, there was nothin' under it, nothin' but a blank, naked sea.

An' that's not all; for when I come round to look at the gun I'd made, the whole of the forrard end of it was split, an' I knew it would never throw a shot again; nor any gun on this earth ever shoot the equal of the one shot it did shoot. I guess there must have been a mint of explosive aboard yon whaler.

Yes, I repaired that steam pipe, for I'd only to fill in the space with melted lead between the steam pipe and the outer pipe I'd fitted round the elbow, to make a downright solid steam-tight joint. What's more, I had steam up before evening, an' I run there engines myself, as well as navigated the ship, for the Second Engineer ain't fit at this minute to do more than lie an' count how many beans makes seven.

Yes, I've laid the whole business before the authorities. Oh, aye! We've made our sworn statement before the authorities, but it don't prove nothing, 'cept that; as they put it, "there's been a case of modern piracy." I did my damndest to tell 'em it wasn't just "a case of modern piracy." I told 'em piracy 'd never properly stopped. Things 'd changed, an' piracy with 'em, same as burglars had changed, but they hadn't gone off the earth; an' if the land robbers hadn't died out, with all law an' order against 'em, did they suppose, to goodness, as sea robbery had stopped, right *out there*, away from law and order? I told 'em it never would stop till they put a gun or two into every seagoing ship, so as sailors can protect theirselves.

But, bless you, they said they was much interested in my views on the subject, but they must persist in regarding the regrettable affair as nothing more than an isolated incident. They said the seas was too crowded and well patrolled nowadays for that sort of thing to occur even once without the perpetrators being discovered in the act. Lord! Heard any man ever the like of such blather!

I told 'em about other things I'd come across myself, and they was much interested, unofficially, as you might say; but they couldn't move the matter without I brought sufficient evidence to support each statement I made, They said I should have reported each affair at the time, an' brought my crew forward as witnesses. I told 'em I'd never have taken the trouble to make this statement, let alone the others, if I'd not felt there was evidence all round to make 'em get a move on 'em. I said I was darned if I ever came near 'em again; not if I was witness to the sinkin' of a liner by one of them Bad Business lot. When I said that, the chairman said he must call me to order. My language was improper. Improper! Fancy botherin' about a trifle of language, an' lettin' slide all that same language meant! It just sickened me, an' I said: "Be damned to you for a pack of silly old wimmen. I pray God the whole b'ilin' of you'll be copped by one of them in the Bad Business, an' sunk out in mid-ocean. I reckon you'd wish' then as you'd fixed it up for all ships as go to sea to carry some kind of weapon of defense. An' I guess you'll learn then as the sea ain't quite the highly peaceful, well-patrolled, an' crowded artificial bloomin' lake as you seem to think it. Good day, gentlemen!"

An' out I comes, with them paralysed at my plain speakin'.

We Two and Bully Dunkan

"**D**ON'T GO, MILES," I said. "Better lose your pay-day. It seems
he's got it in for you, and a common sailorman can do nothing
against the after-guard."

"I'm going back, John," he told me. "I swore he'd not haze *me*
out of the ship, and he shan't. He's belted the rest of the crew half
silly, and they've bunked, without drawing a penny. Some of the poor
devils even left their sea-chests. I expect he thinks I'm going to do the
same; but he's mightily mistaken."

This was in 'Frisco. I had just run up against Miles, who had a
badly swollen face, and an ugly scar over his right eyebrow.

"What is it?" I'd asked him. "Been a trip with a Yankee Skipper?"

"Just that, John," he answered me. "Bully Dunkan!"

"Goo' Lor'!" I said. "Were you drunk when you signed on?"

For no free, sober white-man ever sails with Bully Dunkan, not
unless it's that or the hard and stony beach. That is just what it had
been with poor old Miles; and he'd had a Number One rough time
of it; for once, when he explained that he misliked the application of
the Mate's heavy sea-boot to his rear anatomy, the Mate had promptly
knocked him down, having first slipped a big brass knuckle-duster
on his fist, to emphasise his accompanying and entirely unprintable
remarks. This accounted for the scar over my old shipmate's eye.

The swollen face had been acquired at a later date; to be exact,
about a week before the ship reached 'Frisco. It was what I might
describe as the lingering physical memory of an efficiently dislocated
jaw. The dislocation had been the personal and vigourous handiwork
of Bully Dunkan himself. It appears that Miles, one afternoon, so far
forgot his early training as to withhold the other cheek, during one of
the Mate's attentive moods. In fact, I understand that Miles actually
hit the man (Hogge by name and nature) so hearty a wallop with his

fist, that he floored him on the main-deck. The next thing that poor Miles knew was, as he put it, stars. Old Bully Dunkan had come up behind him, wearing felt slippers, and hit him solidly with his fist, on the side of the jaw.

Bully Dunkan weighed two hundred pounds, in his stockings, and his title isn't a fancy one. So when Miles came round, in about ten minutes, and found the Bo'sun and Chips, the carpenter, trying to heave his jaw back into place, he wasn't surprised; but, as he told me, it hurt a lot; which I could believe, by the look of the swelling!

"Well," I told him, "you're a fool, if you try to make the trip back to Boston in her. He'll have it in pretty savage for you."

Miles, however, is a pig-headed brute, when he's fixed on anything; so when he just shook his head, I told him I would sacrifice my bones on the altar of friendship, and sign on for the return trip with him, just to look after him a bit!

"John," he said, in his solemn, earnest kind of way, "you're a friend to tie to. And I'll not try to persuade you not to come—not until you've heard the rest of what I've got to tell you:—

"When we were coming up from Sydney, through the Islands, the Old Man and the Mate went ashore one night in the boat. I was one of the boat's crew, and a chap, called Sandy Meg, was the other.

"We were told to stay by the boat, and lie just off the shore a bit. I thought it was a rummy business; and ugly too; for both the Skipper and the Mate had guns. They were loading them in the boat, while we were pulling ashore.

"Well, they'd been ashore about an hour, I should think, when Sandy Meg nudged me to listen. I heard what he meant, then; for there was a faint, far-off screaming, seeming about a mile or more away; and then there were several shots. I could swear to that.

" 'What do you make of it, Sandy?' I asked him; but he shook his head, and wouldn't answer. Poor devil; they had fairly beaten the bit of spirit out of him. Not that he was ever very wise.

"About half an hour later, I heard someone running, up among the trees; and then I saw the Mate and the Captain coming down to the bench at a run, and singing out to us to bring the boat ashore, smart.

"They fairly raced down the sands, and I could see they were carrying a packet between them; pretty heavy it seemed, and done up in some of that native matting. They hove this down into the bottom of the boat; and I swear it sounded like coin, packed tight. Then they shoved her out and scrambled in, yelling to us to give way, which we did, with the two of them double-banking the oars, and driving her out stern-first.

"We'd got out about three hundred yards, when a man came out of the woods, and ran down the shore, a white man, by the look of him in the moonlight; but, of course, that's half guessing. He knelt down near the edge of the water, and then there was a flash, and something knocked splinters off the port gunnel of the boat, and there was the bang of one of these old Martinis. I recognised the sound!

"By the time he'd loaded and fired twice more, we were too far away to get hurt. He never touched the boat, after that first shot. I saw several other men on the shore; but I suppose they can't have had anything to shoot with.

"Then we were heading away for the ship—she looked like a ghost out on the sea; too far away for the people ashore to recognise anything about her.

"Next day, when I was sent up to lace on the boat-cover, I saw something in the bottom, that made me stare. When I'd reached for it, I found it was a twenty-dollar gold piece. You'll remember the package they dumped into the bottom of the boat! Now what do you make of all that?"

"Ugly!" I said.

"Well," he told me, "*that's* one more reason why I'm going home to Boston in her. I've to get square for these" (he touched the scar and his jaw) "and I reckon the best way to get square with hogs of that kind, is to touch them right on their dollar-marks. Now, are you strong to come, as ever?"

"Stronger," I told him. "Only I guess we'll go heeled. There's sure to be some excitement coming to us this trip. Tell me, where is the lazarette trap—in the pantry, or in the big cabin?"

"Neither," said Miles. "Bully Dunkan sits on the grub hatch, as they say! The hatch of the lazarette is in his own cabin, and opens up under his table. It's no good thinking of that, John. And there's no getting in through the lazarette bulkshead, from the hold. She's stowed up with cargo, solid to the deck-beams. I've thought of all that. I've thought of things for hours at a time; but I can't see how to do it!"

"He drinks pretty heavily, doesn't he?" I asked.

"No," said Miles, "not for him, you know. I've never seen him stupid with it yet. And he sleeps so light, that we always have to go to the wheel on the port side of the poop. His cabin is on the starboard side, and he comes up raging, if anyone walks over his head."

"Do you happen to know what kind of irons they carry?" I asked.

"Yes," he told me. "They ironed Billy Duckworth. He went for the two of them, with an iron belaying-pin, after they had both been kicking him. They laid him out stiff; and ironed him down in the lazarette. Kept him there three days on water. He told me they've got big iron rings, let into the deck of the lazarette, and a chain and padlock. The way they fixed him up, was by handcuffing his two hands together, and then passing the chain over the handcuffs and through one of the rings in the deck, and padlocking him there, like a wild beast."

"Um!" I said; "and of course the lazarette's kept locked?"

"I don't know," he answered. "I don't see it matters anyway. It's not the lazarette that's going to be any use to us."

"Perhaps not," I said. "It certainly sounds a tough proposition. Let's go and have a drink."

II

Bully Dunkan signed me on, in a joyous mood, for him! But I had to ape to be half drunk, or he'd have smelled several kinds of a rat; for free, American white-men don't offer to go promiscuously to sea with him; unless they're either not sober, or they're on the rocks; and I wasn't ragged enough for that yarn to tally-up with appearances.

The ship was a wooden barque of about 500 tons, and Bully Dunkan carried no Second Mate; for the Bo'sun used to stand his watch for him, Marine Law Regulations or not!

The only two of the old crew who had not been run out of the ship, were Miles, and Sandy Meg, the rather soft-witted man who had been in the boat that night with Miles. I found that he had been made acting Steward, as the last man had been run out with the others. I daresay the arrangement suited Bully Dunkan very well; for he never raised Meg's wages, and as acting Steward he remained.

By good fortune, Miles and I were both picked in the same watch—the Mate's. Two days out at sea, there started the usual kind of Bully Dunkanism. One of the men, a big "Dutchman," in a foolish moment, imagined that his two hundred and fifty pounds of brawn and simplicity were the equivalent of Bully Dunkan's two hundred pounds of brawn and hell-fire. As a result, when Dunkan kicked the big Dutchman, the man turned on the Skipper, and held an enormous bony fist under his nose, just through that brief length of time that it took Bully Dunkan to realise the amazing fact.

"Shmell that!" said the huge Dutchman, in his sublime innocence.

Apparently there was something displeasing to the Skipper in the odour of the big Dutchman's homely fist; for he never said a word; but the crack he hit the Dutchman was heard by the watch below in the fo'cas'le.

There was no need for the Bully to accentuate his protest further; but being Bully Dunkan, he—well, he just Dunkanised, and jumped on the big man with his sea-boots, until I was almost angry enough to have interfered.

After all was over, however, the Dutchman was not really badly hurt. His ribs were like the ribs of a horse, and his spirit was like the spirit of a milch cow; and he was a first class sailorman. I have frequently seen them built on these lines, which are much approved by Skippers of the "Yankee Skipper" type.

I had a word with Miles, after this bit of bother.

"See here, Miles," I said, "if that unpleasant person aft, or his pet Hogge try that sort of game again on you, or attempt liberties with this particular American citizen who's talking to you, why then, my friend, we've both got to stick to each other, several degrees closer than the proverbial brother. And if one of us gets a taste of the irons, the other has got to go through it with him. Sumga? So keep those tools and oddments we got in 'Frisco, handy in your pockets, savvy?"

"Yes, John," said Miles, in his sober way. "I think I follow what's in your mind."

And at that I left it.

The next day, in the morning watch, I had an adventure with the Mate. Perhaps I ought to admit that the adventure was less of his seeking than mine; but, I thought perhaps certain plans I had in my head, might as well pass into action, early as late. And, in short, I sought trouble with both hands; so waste no pity on me; but give me what a Frenchman I once knew, called the liniment of your understanding.

I had been set to work on a paunch-mat, for chafing gear; and I decided that a smoke might be a soothing adjunct, to me; though I could hardly say truthfully that I expected the Mate would view it personally as a sedative. That I was right in this conclusion, I soon proved; for the Hogge, happening soon to come along the main-deck, let out a gasp as he came opposite to where I was working, foreside of the main-mast.

I pretended an entire innocence of anything unorthodox; but all the same, I slackened the bite I had on my pipe; for I was too far from a dentist, just at the moment.

The next thing I knew, the Mate (a hefty brute he was too), had made one jump for me. He gripped the pipe and tore it out of my mouth, with a violence that might have left a serious gap, had I not been prepared.

I turned slowly, and looked at him, as mildly as I could. He held the pipe in his fist, by the bowl; and seemed to be a little too full for words.

"Ah!" I said, "was it you who just removed my pipe?"

"Of all——" he began; and became incoherent....

"You shore got some nerve, you have!" was what he finally managed to reduce it to. This is, of course, a strictly expurgated quote.

"You ought *really* to be a little more careful," I explained. "I don't mind you borrowing my pipe; indeed I'll make you a gift of it; for I never care to smoke after other people; but you should really be a little more careful. You might have loosened one or more of my incisors, and dentists do make such awful charges."

"Say!" he shouted, and caught hold of his own throat, in a very ecstasy of deep feeling. "Say!" he shouted again. "Say!..."

He yelled it this time; and if I had never heard despair before, I should recognise it in future.

"I'm listening," I assured him, anxious to help him in every way. "Is it matches you want, or...."

But he relieved himself abruptly, with a remarkable exhibition of energy. In brief, he came for me, nearer mad than sane. I doubt whether anyone had ever spoken him fair and gentle before in all his rough, sinful life; and he was anxious to record his impressions—on me!

Now, I am not a big man; not when compared with the two-hundred-and-fifty pound Dutchman, or even the two-hundred pound Skipper, or the Hogge, who must weigh almost as much. I weigh a hundred and seventy-five pounds, stripped; but then I have fought in the ropes many a score of times, and I am rather unusually strong for a man of my weight; therefore, perhaps, you will understand why I was pleased to accept the Hogge's attentions in as warm a fashion as he could have wished.

He swung two mighty right and left hand punches at my head, which was certainly "not there" when the punches arrived; and he followed this by a second and a third right-and-left, right-and-left, grunting like a hogge, as he hit.

There was a clatter of feet, and good old Miles came racing up, to bear a hand; but I checked him.

"All right," I called out. "The Hogge and I are having a little argument." I slipped under the Mate's right, as I spoke. "Hark to him grunt!" I added, and shot my own right up under the man's unpleasant chin, with the lift of my shoulder under it. He went away from me, all loose, just as a man does who gets a punch of that kind. I went after him, with two steps, and hit him again, this time with a straight left-hand punch right below the point of the sternum.

As I hit, I was vaguely aware that someone had come at me, with a run, and Miles had jumped in between. The Mate concluded his falling movement and hit the deck. He lay as quiet as a tired babe, and I was able to glance round.

I saw that Miles and Bully Dunkan were mixing it, in the prettiest kind of a fight; only that Miles was no match for the Skipper, especially with his face and jaw still so tender, that a touch hurt like a blow.

The next thing I knew, poor old Miles was down and out, on the deck; and that two hundred pounds of Evil and Fight was charging me, in a silent ugly way that meant business.

Now, Captain Bully Dunkan could fight, and he knew how to use his hands; also he weighed almost two stones more than I do. But my years of ring-work stood for all that, and more. I slipped my head under his left drive, countering hard with my left on his nose; for I wished to daze and weaken him a bit, without knocking him out.

He had no *real* foot-work, and he was a little slow; but there was quite enough of the human hurricane to him, as he bored in at me, punching with right and left, to make me careful. I can quite believe that he must have proved a tough proposition for the average rough-and-ready fighter.

Bully Dunkan was no pretty sight, as any boxing man will understand, when you remember that I had landed a hard, straight, left punch on his nose, as he rushed me; but he was not really damaged; and I set out now to knock some of the steam out of him. I had already sidestepped and slipped him all around a twelve foot circle; and it tickled me a little to see the way the men stood about the decks, almost stiffened with amazement, as they realised that I was not "eaten clean up."

I came in suddenly at the Bully; pushed his right up smartly with my left hand, and landed him a hard, solid punch on the side of the jaw; but not heavy enough to knock him out. He rocked back an instant, with his chin snicked up in the air; and I could see that he was all adrift for the moment. Then he steadied, and rushed me, hitting with right and left.

He was panting badly now, and I slid under his left arm, and hit him a good body thump as I passed him. Then I sprang at him from behind, caught him by his two shoulders, put my knee hard into his back, and brought him down with a deuce of a thud onto his broad back. This shook him badly, and took the evil out of him a lot. When he got up, I hit him a right and left punch over the heart, and as he tried to grab me, I uppercut him under the chin, with a straight-armed, right upward swing.

I guessed now that he'd had a lot of the ugliness dazed out of him, and he would not be able to hurt too much, if I let him hit me. However, I had to take some chances; for it's my experience of life, that gold has to be worked and suffered for! Yet, to make sure he was as weak as possible, I stalled off his next rush, with a heavyish left-hand thump in his great bull neck, and a right-hand punch, pretty hard, in the short ribs. Then I let him hit me; but he was gasping heavily, and rocking a little on his feet as he struck, and the blow I took from him, hardly made my eyes water; yet, I threw out my hands, and sagged, and collapsed backwards on to the hatch, with a thud that shook me up a lot more than his punch. And there I lay, never moving.

"Got yer!" roared Bully Dunkan, with a gasp, and aimed a clumsy kick at me, where I lay; but I had so weakened him, that he staggered over sideways, and sat down heavily beside me on the hatch, and was immediately very sick indeed.

I never moved or opened my eyes, and presently, I heard him bellowing weakly for one of the men to go aft and tell the Steward, who, as you know, was Sandy Meg, to bring the irons.

They handcuffed me first, where I lay, apparently unconscious. I could hear Bully Dunkan, sitting near me on the hatch, groaning a little. After they had handcuffed me, I heard them gather round poor Miles, and then came the chink of the cuffs, and I knew that he too was ironed.

"Take 'em aft, Stooard, an' dump 'em down the lazarette," shouted Dunkan. "You, Lang an' Tarbrey an' Mike, give a hand with the hogs, an' one of you others shove a bucket o' water over that fool Mate o' mine, an' fetch him round...."

He broke off, and groaned a bit; then turned suddenly on my "unconscious" body.

"You——!" he said, vilely, and bashed his sea-booted heel a couple of times into my ribs, where I lay; but he broke nothing; for he was still too shaken to be his true self. Then I was picked up, shoulders and feet, and carried aft. I could hear men's feet stumbling ahead of me, and knew they were carrying Miles first; and behind me, there was the voice of Bully Dunkan, cursing; and then a sound of thrown water, by which I knew they were heaving cold water over the Mate.

"They's washing down th' Hogge!" I heard the man mutter who was carrying my feet.... "Carry 'im easy, mate; I'm 'is friend for life an' hevermore, the way he's outed the First Mate an' pasted the Skipper. Ee's a holy terror!"

I gathered that the latter part of the man's remark applied to me; but I kept my eyes shut.

"Wasn't it just swate the way he played round the Ole Man," said the man at my head. (I could tell it was Mike.) "I'm lackin' to know, bejabers, how he come to get knocked out at all, at all!"

It is unnecessary to say that I did not explain that I was entirely un-knocked-out, if I may so put it. I had a secret plan to carry out, and a ship's fo'cas'le is no place to hold secrets long; so I remained knocked-out and limp, to them and all the world of that moment.

Five minutes later, Miles and I were chained down to the floor of the lazarette; and to make sure that it was done right, Bully Dunkan came groaning and cursing down the steep ladder, and locked and tested the padlocks himself. Then he took the keys of the irons from Sandy Meg, and pocketed them; after which he kicked Miles once, and me twice; and I certainly wished I had hit him about a little more than I had. However, I managed to keep silent, and in a minute he had gone, with the Steward and the men. I heard the heavy trap dropped, and afterwards the sound of a key, locking it.

The first part of my plot was achieved. Miles and I were in the lazarette.

III

Poor Miles lay very quiet, where the men had put him. For my part, I ached considerably, and had something of a fight to check the anger that was boiling up in me for the way Bully Dunkan had kicked the two of us, after we were ironed.

But I reasoned myself out of it. I had arranged the whole thing, with a perfect knowledge of the kind of man the Skipper was; and it was hardly logical, I told myself, to be all of a bubble inside me, because I had received the due portion of Dunkanism which I had earned. It was part of the price we had to pay for the saving of Bully Dunkan's soul; for only by affliction could such a one be saved from his thoroughly earned fate. Incidentally, as I have mentioned before, gold is a painful metal to achieve—either slow or painful; and frequently both.

Thus I shook myself, mentally, and became slowly able to delay the shedding of Bully Dunkan's blood.

I leaned towards poor Miles, in the absolute darkness; but I could not touch him; for the ring-bolts, to which we were chained, were evidently calculated to be just sufficiently far apart to prevent unevenly tempered seamen from mingling their tears.

I saw that it was time I brought into use some of the various little preparations which I had made for our adventure. I reached into my pockets and found, first of all, a box of matches and half a candle.

I lit the candle, and stood it on the deck of the lazarette. Then I took, from a small pocket I had stitched in the waistband of my trousers, a sawn handcuff key, such as is used by those apparently clever jugglers, who make their living by persuading unfortunate and credulous people to lock numberless pairs of handcuffs upon them, immediately afterwards retiring into hiding, while they quickly unlock them with a key like the one I held; after which they return to the audience and exhibit the irons (but not the key) and obtain thereby much applause.

The beauty of this key is at once evident. It is like an ordinary handcuff key, only longer in the barrel and made of steel. It is then sawn lengthways down the barrel, so that it is possible to press it on to the screwed end of the bolt that holds a handcuff shut, and then a mere pull opens the cuff, and the prisoner is free. As a key of this kind will fit almost any standard make of cuff, it is an entirely useful pocket adjunct to adventurers, criminals, conjurers and the like!

With this key, I unlocked the cuff on my right wrist, and let the chain that passed over it, from the ring-bolt in the floor, fall on to my knees. I was free.

I took the candle; put the matches in my pocket, and crept over to Miles. He was lying huddled, where they had dropped him, and I set to and straightened him out. Then I unlocked his cuffs, and began to rub his hands. After a bit, I opened his shirt and rubbed his chest, hard; and presently he moved a little.

"Ssh!" I said; for he had suddenly kicked out. "Keep quiet. You're all right. We're down in the lazarette." But he was not conscious enough yet to comprehend me.

Ten minutes later, he was talking to me, a little stupidly at first; but he improved every half minute.

"Have you got your gun on you?" I asked him, as soon as he was all right.

"Yes," he told me. "In my right sea-boot. And I've those candles in my pockets, you told me to carry around, and two boxes of matches. The auger fixing and the screwdriver are in my left boot; and the long narrow canvas sack you made, is wrapped round my waist, under my shirt."

"That's all right," I said. "I've got my automatic in one sea-boot and the narrow saw and the files in the other; and I've got the keys and a dozen half candles and three boxes of matches and the bottle of dope in my pockets; and a belt-full of cartridges under my shirt. We'll do fine. I've even got a little black beeswax, to hide any bright gaps we may have to make with the files."

"John!" he said, suddenly, heaving himself up into a sitting position. "It's just struck me, they've not taken our sheath-knives or our matches or pipes or tobacco or anything. I've got all mine on me. If they had, they'd have discovered the matches and candles and your bunches of keys. They've forgotten! And that means they'll be coming down, as soon as ever they remember, to search us and take them away. They'll never leave us with our matches and sheath-knives, and I'll bet they'll take our tobacco, so as to stop us having even the comfort of a chew."

"By Jove! I'll bet you're right," I said. "It's a mercy you thought of it. Here, out with everything, automatic, auger, screwdriver, candles, matches, the bag—everything! No, leave one box of matches and your pipe and leave a bit of your plug. That'll make them sure you've not hidden anything; and they'll not maul you as much, searching you— see? I'll do the same. Hurry up, man! They may be down any minute."

I had been emptying my pockets and my boots, while I was speaking, and I even slipped off my hidden belt of cartridge-clips. I took the whole lot of things, and wrapped them in my red cotton handkerchief. Then, taking the lighted candle, I went quietly across the lazarette, and hid the stuff behind the bread barrels.

I came back, and locked Miles up again, and afterwards myself, and blew out and hid the candle.

"When they come, you'd better be sitting up," I told him; "so as to be able to guard your face, if he kicks you."

"Right!" he answered. "Where have you put the key for the cuffs? They mustn't find that on you."

"I've put it behind one of these chocks that keep these sugar-casks from rolling," I told him. "I can just reach it, lying down and stretching."

"Good!" he said; and as he spoke, we heard the key put into the lock of the trap door, somewhere above us in the darkness, over to starboard.

The trap was lifted, and an oblong of shadowy daylight showed in the deck above us.

Then I heard the Skipper's voice; he was cursing Sandy Meg, the Steward. Directly afterwards, his feet came into sight, and his bulk blotted out most of the daylight. He reached the bottom of the ladder, and Sandy Meg came down also, carrying a lantern.

Bully Dunkan walked across to us, with the Steward following and holding the lantern up.

"Well now, I do admire that!" he said, stopping in front of Miles. "So you're sitting up on your little hind legs, Sonny, a-ready. That was a tidy clip I landed you, now; don't ye think so!"

He spoke a bit snuffily, because of the punch I had hit him on the nose, which looked emphatically enlarged, in the lantern-light.

"Now, Steward," he went on, "I'm a-going to take away his little pipe an' matches, *and* his knife.... Lie down, you goat, while I go through you!"

This last was to Miles, and Bully Dunkan gave my friend a push with his foot, that rolled him over onto his side. Then the Skipper went through his pockets, and took away everything he had, including his knife.

When he had done with Miles, he came over to me.

"So *you're* come round too, are you!" he said. "Maybe you thought you could hand it out to me; but you was mistook, dear friend.... You was mistook, I tells you!"

He repeated this in a shout, and then, without another word, as if the memory of the way I'd hammered him, drove him mad, he took a swinging kick at me, and got me in the ribs, with a thud that made me feel sick.

Twice more, he kicked me; then bashed me over onto the deck, with his foot, and went through my pockets. He took all he found, also my sheath-knife.

"Mister Hogge will be coming down in a bit, maybe, to have a little word with you," he said, catching hold of my ears, and twisting them brutally until they bled.

I began to regret that I had locked myself up again. Perhaps it was as well; for if I could have got free that moment, I should certainly have tried to kill him.

However, I managed to keep from making a sound; and then he let go, and stood back a step, staring down at me. I bit my teeth hard together for a moment, so as to steady myself. Then I spoke:—

"How is the Hogge, Cap'n?" I said, and stared up at him, smiling as well as I could. "Tell him, with my compliments, I'll be pleased to hear him grunt a bit, any time he likes."

He never answered a word, for a moment; then burst out into a great laugh.

"I'll hand the Mate that," he said. He roared out again into his brute of a laugh. "Oh, my bonny boy, but ye'll hear him grunt, I'm thinkin'. I'll hand him that, sure I will. It'll rat him rank mad."

He turned away, hove the things he had taken from us, down into an empty box on the floor of the lazarette, out of our reach, and went straight away up the ladder, with the Steward following with the lamp. The trap was slammed, and I heard it locked. Then Miles spoke to me:—

"Did he hurt you much, old man?"

"Not to mention it," I said. "It seemed to tickle him about the Mate. If I understand his kind, right, though; he'll never let the Hogge down here. He'd sooner use us to rag the Hogge with. That's just his way. He's got to be unpleasant to someone, or he couldn't keep well. Did he damage you at all?"

"No," said Miles; "but I wanted badly to plug him."

"Never mind!" I answered. "When this business is through, safely, I'm promising myself the pleasure of cutting loose, properly, just for five heavenly minutes on the Dunk."

IV

Miles and I had talked everything over, a score of times before ever I started the row with the Hogge, which had landed us in our much-desired lazarette.

We knew that the money must be in Bully Dunkan's own cabin; for where else in a windjammer would he be likely to keep it! Also we knew that the trap of the lazarette opened directly under his cabin table; and, finally, I had a bunch of "master" keys, and if these wouldn't do, I could possibly unscrew the lock with the screwdriver.

"We'll tackle the job tonight, Miles," I said, after we had sat in the dark for a couple of minutes, listening. "He'll not keep us down here more than a day or two. It would break his heart to have two or three hundred pounds of sailor-flesh sitting idle. He'll probably give us nothing but water, like Billy Duckworth; more power to Billy for going for him! Then he'll boot us out, as soon as he thinks he's put the fear of God into us sufficiently."

"You mean, if we don't do the job at once, we may be out of here again, before we get the chance," he said.

"Just that," I answered. "Things are ideal for us now in every way. One of the minor reasons why I wanted to be ironed safely down here, was so that he could have no suspicion of either of us; for, I tell you, he'll have the whole ship pretty well capsized, and every man and sea-chest aboard, searched, when he finds the loot is gone, like the little song says, away and away-oh!"

"Um!" said Miles. "I never thought of that. I don't see how you're going to hide the stuff, in that case."

"Think again," I answered. "It all works out perfectly. He has the key of this place in his pocket, and therefore he'll never suppose that the money may be down here."

"Um!" said Miles, again. "And how are we going to get it out of here, without his seeing we're loaded up? Why man! The package they hove into the boat that night, must have weighed getting on for a hundredweight, by the sound it made, and the way they carried it."

"The ventilator," I explained. "It comes down through the poop-deck and the cabin-deck, and opens over that top shelf, just behind you. What do you suppose I made the canvas bag that shape for! We'll put the coin into it, and stand it behind the boxes, right under the ventilator. The ventilator is not in use just now, and the cowl is unshipped, and the sleeve it fits on is covered with a brass cap.

"Well, last night, in the middle watch, it was pretty black as you know; so I took a chance, and crept along to the ventilator, and lifted the cap. It's got a ring inside, for lashing it down by. All I did, was to bend on a chest-lashing to this ring, and let the end come down here. Then I put the lid back in place. It's hanging there now, you'll find; and we've only to make it fast to the neck of the canvas bag, and the job will be done, so far as down here is concerned. The rest we can manage when we get shoved on deck again. It'll be just as simple as the job I had, to fix on the chest-lashing. That all clear, man?"

"Yes," he said. "Very neat plan…. Can't we have a light now, and get out of these irons?"

"Wait a bit," I said. "There's someone at the trap, now."

The trap was opened, and Bully Dunkan and the Steward came down again. The Captain had the lantern, and the Steward carried a bucket of water and a cup. This, he set on the deck of the lazarette, midway between Miles and me, where we could both reach it.

Dunkan kicked us each, and examined our irons; after which he grunted in a satisfied way.

"There's something to get your backs up on, my bonny boys," he said, giving the bucket a push with his foot. "It's all you'll get for forty-eight hours. Don't make hogs of yourselves!"

Then he went, laughing viciously, and ushering Sandy Meg before him up the ladder. The trap shut, and we heard the key turn.

"The——!" said Miles, out of the darkness.

"Couldn't have been better!" I whispered back. There's grub all round us, there's water in the bucket; what more could a man want! Wait while I find the key."

V

It was some hours later, and we were both out of the irons again, and standing, listening on the ladder that led up to the trap.

Bully Dunkan was in his cabin, and the Hogge was with him, and there was a constant chink of coin, and a low mutter of talk.

"What's that?" I heard the Hogge say; and I sweated a little; for I was trying my bunch of "master" keys on the lock of the trap, and I had made a bit of a rattle, fumbling there in the shadows and swaying candlelight; and the ship rolling more than a trifle.

"It's yon damn Steward," said Bully Dunkan.... "What is it?" he roared out. "What the devil d'yer want?"

"I got the hot water, Sir, for the grog," I heard Sandy Meg's voice say, faintly, because he was evidently the other side of the cabin door.

"Bless his dear heart an' liver!" said Bully Dunkan. Then, in a lower voice:— "Here, shove this chart over the stuff, while I opens the door."

It was plain to both of us, now, beyond all doubt, that the Hogge and the Captain had the dollars nakedly on the table before them, as one might say; and were counting them, with the door locked. I tell you, it made me feel so close to the stuff, that I could have found it in my heart to open the trap there and then, and wade into the two of them, with the aid of our automatics. Only, of course, this would have been clumsy, and might have ended in my having to send the Dunikan (as Miles would insist on calling him) and the Hogge prematurely to an investigation of those high temperatures which they were daily fitting themselves to appreciate.

I heard the cabin door unlocked and opened; and slammed and locked again. Then Bully Dunkan's voice, in a roar:—

"Drop that, you scow-bottomed down-Easter! Haul them dollar gold-pieces out of yer pocket, right this moment!"

"Say!" said the Hogge, "you quit that talk to me, Cap'n, or there'll be trouble. Say!..."

"You make me tired," said Bully Dunkan. "D'yer suppose I didn't see you! Do you suppose, you damn fool, I'm going blind. Ante up them dollars, Sonny dear, or—!"

"There was a sudden rustle, as if someone had moved quickly; then the Hogge's voice:—

"All right! *All* right! I was only jokin'. I'll tip the stuff up."

"No, Sonny! Sonny!" came Dunkan's voice. "Quit putting your lily-white hands into yer jacket pockets. Just keep 'em right on the table, plain in sight. They're bonny hands. Deary me, Mr. Mate, I'd no idee you took such keer of yer nails!"

I smiled, where I stood on the ladder; for I could picture the great horny black-rimmed nails of the Hogge. Miles, who was holding the candle, below me, laughed out loud; but checked himself in a moment.

It was plain to us, that the Captain had turned from the door, just in time to catch the Hogge weighting himself down with a spare preliminary handful, or two, of gold, before the division of the dollars had been carried out; and it was plain also, that the Captain had drawn his gun on the Hogge. Altogether, an interesting little situation.

I had just discovered a key on my bunch which turned the lock of the trap; and I thought this might be a suitable moment to make a brief investigation of facts.

"Blow out the light, Miles," I said. Then, very gently, I shot back the lock, and pressed the trap up, half an inch at a time, until I could see along the deck of the cabin.

Close to the edge of the trap, was a liberal pair of feet, in unstinted bluchers. I recognised them as the Hogge's, and wondered what he would think, if he suddenly stuck them out further, and encountered the gaping hole of the little hatchway in which I stood! I hoped sincerely that he would keep still.

A little to my right, and standing about a yard away from the table, were the Bully's boots. My ribs recognised them almost before I did. They were painfully familiar acquaintances. I regarded them a moment, with a sudden pleasurable anticipation of what I should eventually do to their owner.

"People who wear leather sea-boots, ought——"

I had got this far in my voiceless soliloquy, when I saw something else, on the deck, to the left of the Hogge's bluchers, and not a foot away from the edge of the hatch. It was the kettle of hot water for their grog, which the Steward, Sandy Meg, had just handed in.

I had a sudden, and, some might say, an apparently insane longing to possess that kettle. I raised the trap a little higher, and reached out my left hand, slowly, until I could grab the kettle handle; and as I did so, the Bully's voice came, suddenly, and seeming abnormally loud and distinct, owing to the previous moments of silence, and to the fact that now there was no longer the thickness of the trap to deaden the sounds in the cabin.

"Don't move, Sonny!" he said; "not one single little blessed inch, or I'll plug you clean as any whistle you ever blowed."

I stiffened, where I was, and I took very good care not to move, as may be imagined. But I was not idle. I'm not that kind! The hatch cover (or trap) was propped open, resting on my head; my left hand was holding the handle of the kettle, and my right hand was free, and with my right hand, I was deaf-and-dumbing (single-hand-code) to Miles, to pass me up my automatic. Then, I realised that he would not be able to read what I was saying, with the candle out; and I was going to risk what I might call a flying retreat, and chance Dunkan's gun.

But, in the very moment, when I was going to jump and let the hatch fall with a crash, Bully Dunkan spoke again:—

"I'm going to go through your pockets, Sonny son," he said, in his quiet, ugly way. And his feet moved, and went towards the Hogge.

Goodness! But I felt the relief. He had not seen me at all! He was still speaking to the Hogge. With the revulsion of feeling, I described myself briefly and exactly in unspoken phrases as a fool of the completest kind. Then, I lifted the kettle down into the hatchway, and lowered the trap (or hatch-cover) noiselessly shut again.

"Matches, quick, Miles!" I whispered.

"What's the kettle for, John?" he asked me, as the candle-flame rose and brightened. "What were you deaf-and-dumbing?"

"I thought the Dunkan had got me," I whispered! "Quick, the dope! This is the hot water for their grog. I'll make them sleep longer than the seven sleepers. I never knew such luck."

He raced for the bottle of "dope" (sleeping-draught, 'Frisco quality!) and handed it up to me. I poured about half of it into the kettle. I dared not risk more; for I felt that neither of them was ready; that is, not from a Christianlike way of looking at the matter. I told Miles to blow out the candle. Then, very carefully, I lifted the hatch-cover again, and put the kettle back, where I had found it under the table.

Bully Dunkan was standing at the back of the Hogge's chair, evidently going through his pockets, in an unemotional but thorough fashion.

"That's all, dear friend," I heard him say. "I guess I got yer gun; so you'll maybe check yer evil propensities. What say now, to the grog?"

"Don't mind if I do," growled the Hogge.

I shut the hatch just in time, as Bully Dunkan reached under the table for the kettle.

Five minutes later, the Hogge grunted, with more than porcine satisfaction.

"That's good stuff, Cap'n," he said. "You're hell-fire an' you got ugly ways I ain't no use for; but I'll allow as you shore can make a grog-stew."

"I believe you, Sonny," said Bully Dunkan; and he also smacked his lips, in a way that was a good second to the Hogge's.

Down in the lazarette, Miles and I held on to each other, and tried to keep it as silent as we could; but that kind of laugh takes a deal of managing!

VI

During the next half-hour, I stood most of the time on the ladder, close up to the trap, listening.

At first, I could hear the Hogge and Bully Dunkan talking, with the constant accompanying chink, chink of money. Once, the Hogge began to grumble, but in a drowsy undertone, that was pleasantly suggestive to me of good, plain, efficient "dope," or knock-out-mixture—to give it only one or two of its varied names.

Abruptly, there came a dull thud on the deck, close to my head, and the sound of a shower of coins.

"Beas'ly... drunk... 'Ogg!" said Bully Dunkan, in a tone of indescribable senility; and with a long pause between each word.

"The Hogge's gone to sleep on the door, and taken half the gold with him, I should judge by the sounds," I whispered down to Miles.

"How's the Dunikan?" he whispered back.

"Seems to be on his last legs," I said; "that is, by the way he's been trying to reprove the Hogge. He's just told him he's a beas'ly drunk 'Ogg; and it took him nearly half a minute to say it.... Ah! there he goes, too!"

For there had come a second thud on the deck, accompanied by a further cascading of coins.

I waited through a long couple of minutes, during which an absolute silence filled the cabin over my head. Then I lifted the trap slowly, and peeped through. The Hogge lay on his side, within a yard and a half of me. He looked crumpled and inert; but peacefully disposed. Bully Dunkan lay sprawled, at the end of the table, his legs under it, and his head lying on one of the Hogge's sea-boots. He had the same expression of peace.

All around the two of them, lay five-, ten-, and twenty-dollar gold pieces. The two men were literally lying in wealth, if not in the lap of luxury. I never saw quite so much gold on the floor at one time, before or since.

"Come along, Miles," I said. "Bring the bag. They sleep as sleep the Innocent that knows no wrong; nor e'er hath taken aught that did belong, to any...."

I ceased declaiming, and went up through the little hatchway; and in a moment, Miles followed, with the long, strong, bolster-like, canvas bag, which I had made for this moment.

"Behold them, dear man," I said. "It's picturesque to see them lie among the gold."

"Good Lord!" answered Miles; "look at the pile on the table."

"I have," I told him. "And I'm not tired yet. Here you are, hold the bag, while I slide it off into it."

This was a short but pleasant piece of work. Then we set-to and picked up all the gold coins that lay about the deck of the cabin. When we had finished, the bag was simply awesomely full.

"Now, Miles," I said, "there are just one or two things to do, before we go below to our humble abode of darkness. We shall have to sacrifice a handful of gold; but we can spare it."

I took a handful out of the mouth of the long, narrow sack, and stepped across to Bully Dunkan's bunk. I unscrewed and opened the port-light that was in the ship's side, just over his bunk. I took several of the coins and laid them on the rebate of the port-hole, just *outside*. Then I placed a coin or two on the brass rim of the port-hole itself, trusting to luck that they would not slip off, with the rolling of the ship.

After that, I spread three or four coins about, in the sunk recess in the ship's side, which contained the port-light. The rest of the handful of gold, I scattered in a trail across the blankets of Bully Dunkan's bunk, in such a way as to lead the glance at once to the port-hole.

"What's it for, John?" asked Miles.

"Just a little way of easing some of the steam out of the search these two will make, when they wake up and find they're deficient in bullion," I told him. "You see, they'll be stumped. Each will suspect the other, and they'll search the ship, pretty well from truck to keelson. For they'll each argue that the gold *must* be in the ship, as no one would steal it, merely to dump it.

"But, if my little plan works, when they come to look round, and see the gold trail to the port, they'll get a horrid idea that one of them may have put the stuff through into the sea, in the mad, silly sort of way a man will do things when he's drunk.

"Of course, this won't stop them from suspecting each other, and it may not stop them from searching the ship; but, whatever happens, the possibility that one of them may have done this, will be always in the backs of their minds, and it will grow, as they fail to find the gold, until they come to the conclusion that they *must* have dumped the stuff overboard themselves.

"You know what a chap can do, in throwing his cash about, and being generally a fool, when he's boozed.... In rum out rhino! I guess it'll seem the only possible explanation, especially as they know they were safely locked in, when they started drinking.

"There's just one other little thing I've got to do."

I hunted round, until I found the drawer where Bully Dunkan stored his rum. Then I took out a couple of bottles, and knocked off the necks. I reached down a couple of clean glasses from the rack by the door, and poured us each a good tot.

"Here's health, Miles," I said. "We've earned it, working like this for the soul-welfare of the Hogge and his master."

"To you, John," said Miles; and we drank.

"Then I dumped the two glasses out of the port, and took the two bottles of rum, and poured it liberally over the Bully and the Ilogge, until they were soaked through, and they smelt to Heaven of the stuff. I took a third bottle, and slopped rum all over the table, and into their empty glasses. Finally, I emptied out what was left of the water and dope, in the kettle, and poured rum into it.

I threw the three empty bottles onto the floor, where I let them roll. I went back to the drawer, and picked up a full bottle. I held this above the others, and let it fall back with a crash. "Drunk men drop bottles, Miles," I observed.

He nodded.

"I guess you don't want them to suspect they were doped," he said. "You're out to make them think they must have gone in for an almightly drunk. That was a cute dodge, putting the rum into the kettle. They'll guess they must have done it, after they got muzzy, and got drinking the stuff neat."

"You've savvied, old friend," I said. "Let's get away below. Phoo! the place smells!"

Miles went down the ladder, half a dozen steps, and I lashed up the neck of the bag of gold with a leather lace out of one of the Captain's drawers. Then I lowered the bag onto Miles' shoulders, and he went slowly down to the bottom of the ladder. There must have been well over a hundred-weight of gold.

I followed Miles, and shut and locked the trap. Miles had already lighted a candle, and we set-to at once, and put the gold behind the row of boxes on the shelf near the deck, right under the place where the cap of the closed ventilator-shaft opened. I had previously fixed two rope grommets in the shoulders of the bag, and to these I attached the hanging end of the chest-lashing, that I had made fast to the ring in the cap of the ventilator-shaft.

"Now, let's store all our tackle away, over behind the bread-casks," I said; "but we'll keep our automatics in our boots, in case the Bully comes down here and cuts loose on us, to ease his feelings. There's no saying what the sweet Dunkan may not be capable of, given a bad head and a sour mouth, an empty gold chest and a full revolver! So we'll keep the little guns handy. Now let us acquire a meal."

Half an hour later, we entered the irons again, and prepared to get some sleep.

"I guess the Bo'sun'll have to keep double watch tonight, John," said Miles, just as I was dozing off.

"Poor beggar!" I answered, and was asleep before he could think of anything else.

VII

I was waked some hours later by a tremendous noise overhead. There were heavy blows on the deck, and Bully Dunkan was shouting, thickly.

"What is it, Miles?" I asked, and sat up in the darkness.

"They're waking up, John," he said.

"They appear to be doing it very thoroughly," I replied. "It sounds as if Dunkan were massaging the Hogge."

"He's bumping his head on the deck," said Miles. "He'll kill him, instead of bringing him round."

"Probably, dear man," I answered; "but I don't think we're out to save the Hogge's bacon! If they finished each other, the world, and the sea especially, would be well shut of them…. Hark to him!"

There was a steady, monotonous bumping now on the deck of the cabin, above. I had no doubt that it was the Mate's head; also, I began to think Miles' prophecy would come right. The bumps were so vigourous, that they made the lazarette resound.

Abruptly, one of the bumps ended, in a curious, breaking sound.

"G'lor'!" said Miles. "Did you hear that? He's broke the Mate's head!"

The heavy blows had ceased, and there was a brief silence.

Suddenly, we both heard the Hogge's voice say, in a dazed tone:—

"Leggo my ears, dam yer! Leggo my ears!"

Miles sighed relief. I could hear him plainly, through the darkness.

"Thought that'd wake yer, my bonnie boy!" said Dunkan's voice. "Where's the gold?"

"Say! What's this blame thing I'm lyin' my 'ead on?" asked the Hogge, still a little dazed-seeming; but palpably returning again to this life.

"Where's the gold?" reiterated Bully Dunkan.

"What's this blame thing I got my 'ead on?" asked the Hogge, again. "It's blame sharp!… Leggo my ears, I tells yer. Leggo!"

There was a short scuffle; then the Hogge's voice again:—

"A broke ceegar-box, you old swine, you! I s'pose you thought it dam funny to bash me down onto that. I'm all cut with the broke wood. Dam your ugly ways!"

"Where's the gold?" asked Bully Dunkan. There was a sharp movement; and then the Hogge's voice, now less dazed than ever:—

"Say! Don't point that blame thing at me. You're too drunk to play with shootin' gear."

"Where's the gold?" asked Bully Dunkan. "I'm goin' to shoot in a minute."

There was a scurrying, lumpish sound, as if the Hogge had sat up suddenly.

"The gold!" he said, in a voice that denoted he was at last awake to the Complete Present. "The gold! Why we was countin' it... on the table. It's there, ain't it? Say! I feel dam bad. How ever much did we put down? I'm all..."

"Where's the gold?" said Bully Dunkan's voice, monotonously.

There were sounds, suggestive of the Hogge's essaying a standing position.

"Say!" he said, after a moment, in a stunned kind of voice, "the dollars is gone! Say...!" He broke off, and I heard his feet go at a clumsy run towards the cabin door. "Say!" he called out, "it's locked! Say, Cap'n! Say! I tell yer the blame door's locked!"

"Where's the gold?" came Bully Dunkan's everlasting reiteration. "You smart Hogge, you! Out with it, or I'll plug yer! Where's the gold?"

There followed a moment's silence.

"No, you blame well don't, Cap'n!" said the Hogge's voice, suddenly full of suspicion. "You don't put that over on *me*, dam yer! You don't foxy *me* that way! No, Siree!"

There was a sudden crash, and a chinkling down on the deck, of broken glass. One of them, probably the Hogge, had evidently thrown one of the empty bottles. There followed the rush of the Hogge's big bluchers, from the direction of the door; and simultaneously, there were two revolver shots, almost together.

Then came the thud of the two men meeting, and through the next five minutes, there was quite high-class trouble up above. Apparently, everything smashable in the cabin got smashed. The thuds, blows, stampings, breathless cussings, and the chorus-crashes of breakages, were impressive and stimulating to listen to.

Finally, it ended.

"That was some row, Miles," I said, through the darkness.

"It was, John," said Miles. "Listen to them now. They're feeling cooler."

The Hogge and Bully Dunkan were apparently collecting themselves. The still uncoordinated fragments refused to attempt clear speech for a time. They wheezed, and achieved odd words and grunts, and displayed a very apparent breathlessness.

Finally, the Hogge amalgamated first.

"Say! You might ha' blame well plugged me, dam your ugly ways!"

"What d'yer want to go slingin' bottles around for, then!" Bully Dunkan managed to articulate, with generous pauses.

They appeared, both of them, to be on the floor; for presently I heard them scrambling and slurring their heavy boots, as they got slowly to their feet.

One of them walked across the cabin, towards the bunk. It was Bully Dunkan; for his voice came the next moment:—

"Look a-here, quick!" he said. "Good Lord! Look a-here!"

The Hogge's bluchers stumbled hastily across the cabin. There was a full quarter minute silence, completely eloquent with horror.

"Say!..." began the Hogge; and was silent again. Then, with simple despair, he said all that he was capable of:— "Say! *All them dollars!*"

Neither man spoke, for maybe a minute after that. They were both acquainted with liquor and its vagaries when imbibed in largish quantity. They both knew that "in liquor," or "full" as they more briefly described it, in the troubled talk that followed, a man will do anything.

"It's worse," said the Hogge, sadly, "than when I got drunk in Val'parazo an' give the bar-man five hundred dollars, all I had. My pay-day for fifteen months. An' next day, he'd not even stand me a drink. Swore I'd not give him a cent. Said he made a point never to take presents."

We heard them moving about.

"I guess this is the kettle, right enough. It's flat; but there's a drop of stuff in it," said Dunkan's voice; and I could hear him tasting something, with a clumsy smacking of his lips.

"It's neat rum," he announced, mournfully. "No wonder we was screwed. I guess we filled the kettle, an' then forgot, an' thought it was water."

"Three empty bottles on the deck," said the Hogge, gloomily, "an' the dee-canter."

There followed a long period of flat silence.

"Guess I'd best go up an' relieve the Bo'sun," said the Hogge, in a sombre voice.

There was no thought of searching the ship. My little plot had worked, just the way I like a plot to work. Bully Dunkan and the Hogge accepted what I might call the Suggestion of the Port Hole, as at once a practicable and a probable solution of the mystery. It tallied both with the teachings of their Experience and the suggestions of their Reason, felt that I had done much to help the cause of temperance.

VIII

We were released some hours later, at midday.

That night, during the Hogge's watch, while he was sleeping soundly and illegally on the weather-seat of the cabin-skylight, I crept up onto the poop, lifted the cap of the ventilator, and hauled on the chest-lashing. Half a minute later, I had the long, narrow-bag up through the ventilator shaft, and beside me on the deck. I cast off the chest-lashing from the cap of the ventilator, and pressed the cap down into place again.

All this, I had managed, without ever rising to my feet; and the bag had been hard to pull up, in that position. Now, I took a look aft over the skylight. It was a pretty quiet night; but very dark. I could hear the Hogge snoring in a most satisfactory fashion; and the man at the wheel just showed vaguely in the light from the binnacle; so I guessed he could not see me. Then, I gripped the bag in my arms, stood up and walked, barefooted, to the lee stairway, where Miles was waiting for me.

"The bo'sun's locker!" I said; and we carried the bag there. Inside the locker, we fastened the door, and I lighted a candle I had ready in my pocket. Then, among all the mucker of chain, chain-hooks, marlin-spikes, serving-mallets, sampson-line, spun-yarn, good Stockholm-tar, and the like, the two of us started to pack the gold into a lot of little canvas bags that Miles and I had made ready for the job. We hurried like mad; for we stood to lose everything, if anyone found us locked in there, at that time of night.

At last, we had all the cash divided up into little bags, about ten or twelve pounds weight each, I should think; and we hid all but four of them at the back of the tar-barrel.

We blew out the candle, unlocked the door, and got out on deck, each of us with a bag in each of the side-pockets of our jackets. We walked forrard into the fo'cas'le, where most of the watch on deck were playing poker, sitting on deck-buckets.

Miles and I opened our sea-chests, and pretended to rummage a bit; and while we were rummaging, we managed to stow away our little bags of gold, without one of the shell-backs seeing us.

We made three more journeys, during the next half hour; and this way, we managed to store the gold away in our sea-chests, without one of all those sinners in that crowded fo'cas'le ever guessing a thing we didn't want guessed! And a good job done, too; when you remember that a fo'cas'le is never empty at sea.

IX

We made a pretty fair passage round; and Miles and I did our best to put up with the Hogge's little ways and Bully Dunkan's, without causing a riot. We each had to stand a kicking or two; and we were each knocked down several times; and we held ourselves back in a way that made me realise what a good Christian must have to go through in this life.

"There's a better time coming," I told Miles. "Keep the lid on until then, old man. We've too much at stake, to risk trouble, till the loot's safe ashore."

The day we reached Boston, Miles and I had a final knocking about from Bully Dunkan and the Hogge, and it took every ounce of our hundred-weight, or so, of hard-earned gold, to enable us to put up with it quietly.

That night, however, we got the stuff safely ashore, and stored it at the house of one of Miles' friends. Then we felt free at last to interview Dunkan and the Hogge, without stint. And my friend Miles was quite as eager as I.

"The Hogge's your mutton," I told him. "The Bully for me! I can still feel where his sea-boot took me in the seat of my pants this morning."

Miles was very well content with the arrangement; and as we both felt we couldn't wait another hour, we decided to go right back to the ship there and then, and see whether Bully Dunkan and the Hogge had got back aboard again.

We met Sandy Meg, returning from the galley to the cabin; and he told us that both of them were in the cabin, and he was just taking their supper aft.

"Sandy Meg," I said, "we're going in to see the Old Man and the Hogge. We're going to tell him we want to be paid off."

"They'll murder you," said Sandy Meg. "The Skipper's rotten to-night. He knocked me flat as soon as the two of 'em come back aboard, just 'cause I'd not got the supper ready. How was I to know they'd be comin' back aboard as soon as this; an' first night ashore, too!"

"Sandy Meg," I said, "you keep out of the cabin for ten minutes. Go up on the poop, and have a free seat in the gallery. You can see what happens, through the skylight. Miles and I are going to paste up those two brutes; and pay them back some of what's coming to them. Don't fret about us. We let them lick us out at sea, for reasons of our own. This is going to be different."

Sandy Meg said never a word; but put his tray down on the main-hatch, silent and grimly joyful, and went up to have his free "gallery seat" through the flap of the open skylight.

Miles and I went in through the door, under the break of the poop, and walked straight into the cabin, where the Dunkan and the Hogge sat, waiting at the table, and looking fretful enough, each of them, to make me think they must have had a poor evening ashore.

"We've come to ask you to pay us off, Cap'n," I said.

They jumped, and then sat silent; neither of them saying a word; being momentarily incapacitated from doing anything else.

"We've come to ask you to pay us off, or else discharge the Hogge, Cap'n," I said. "We don't like being kicked; but it's not dignified being kicked by a grunter. You'll remember, Cap'n, that I remarked once before that he grunted. I think you agreed with me. It isn't dignified—"

But that was all they allowed me to explain. The Hogge snatched up a plate, and it spoiled the maple-wood bulkshead behind me. Then both he and the Captain came for us, with their fists.

There wasn't much room; but quite sufficient; for I'd not come there to play light. As the Bully rushed me, I propped him off with one clean left hand hit in the neck; and the way his stern met the deck of the cabin, was a thing to remember; at least I can't see him forgetting it.

Miles and the Hogge were having a great time of it, over by the end of the table; and before the Bully had got up and rushed me again, Miles had got that brute of a Hogge up against one of the cabin bulks-heads, and was hitting him, quick and monotonous, right and left, right and left, just wherever he pleased. And as he hit, he seemed to be intoning a number of things that the Hogge must have been the better and wiser for hearing.

The Bully was up again by now, and he rushed me, hitting with both hands, like a madman. I slipped clean under his right, and punched him up against the bulkshead, as he tumbled past me.

He came round, like a shot, and took a flying kick at me; but I declined to be at home, and his foot took the edge of the cabin table, instead, and kicked a strip clean off it, fore and aft, about six inches wide.

"Captain, dear," I said, "you'll not have a bit of furniture left; the way you and the Hogge carry on."

He rushed me a third time, putting his head down to butt me in the stomach; but I brought up my knee quickly, and made him straighten wonderfully.

"Now, Bully Dunkan," I said, as he tried twice to hit me with his elbows, "here's what's coming to a brute and a bully and a murderer like you!" And with that, I slipped a left-handed swing of his, and punched him hard on the short ribs with my left hand; then, I crossed in over with my right hand, as his head came forward; and I hit him clean on the side of his chin, close up to the point. I hit with my body and leg to help the blow; and Bully Dunkan went down with a crash, as he had laid many a poor devil of a sailorman out.

Miles had finished now with the Hogge, who lay on the deck, showing no interest in anything; and I decided we had done enough, both for pleasure and for common justice.

"Come along, Miles," I said. "They'll keep in a restful state of mind for a bit, I reckon. Pity we can't lynch them."

Outside on the deck, Sandy Meg nearly hugged us. "My oath!" he said. "My oath; but that did me good to see!"

Miles and I went forrard and rummaged our sea-chests; the chests themselves we decided not to bother with, and presented them to two of the men who were without. Then we said good-bye to the old ship; and went ashore. We had enough to buy new sea-chests, we decided, if ever we were fools enough to need such things again.

The next day, I sent the following letter to Bully Dunkan and the Mate:—

"Dear Captain and Hogge,

"Let me commend to your earnest notice the following observations:—

1.—Handcuffs have keys.

2.—Lazarette-hatches have the same weakness.

3.—Dope (especially 'Frisco quality) is most effective, particularly when put into, say, a kettle of hot grog-water, left on the deck near a lazarette hatch.

4.—Gold, in almost any form; but especially in gold-dollar shape, is a peculiarly useful and likeable metal.

5.—A punch on the point of the jaw is an instant cure for most evils. N.B. How is your jaw? Hope I didn't hit too hard.

6.—Hogges grunt. Get rid of the habit or the Hogge.

7.—There is a little, unknown island, somewhere in the Pacific, known to you and the Hogge. If you will supply us with the latitude and the longitude of same, we shall be pleased to hand the information over to the police, with *all* particulars. Failing which, we must appropriate certain useful metal to our own use.

"From an old shipmate."

The Haunted *Pampero*

I

"**H**URRAH!" CRIED YOUNG TOM Pemberton as he threw open the door and came forward into the room where his newlywed wife was busily employed about some sewing, "they've given me a ship. What ho!" and he threw his peaked uniform cap down on the table with a bang.

"A ship, Tom?" said his wife, letting her sewing rest idly in her lap.

"The *Pampero*," said Tom proudly.

"What! The 'Haunted *Pampero*'?" cried his wife in a voice expressive of more dismay than elation.

"That's what a lot of fools call her," admitted Tom, unwilling to hear a word against his new kingdom. "It's all a lot of rot! She's no more haunted than I am!"

"And you've accepted?" asked Mrs. Tom, anxiously, rising to her feet with a sudden movement which sent the contents of her lap to the floor.

"You bet I have!" replied Tom. "It's not a chance to be thrown away, to be Master of a vessel before I've jolly well reached twenty-five."

He went toward her, holding out his arms happily; but he stopped suddenly as he caught sight of the dismayed look upon her face.

"What's up, little girl?" he asked. "You don't look a bit pleased." His voice denoted that her lack of pleasure in his news hurt him.

"I'm not, Tom. Not a bit. She's a dreadful ship! All sorts of horrible things happen to her—"

"Rot!" interrupted Tom decisively. "What do you know about her anyway? She's one of the finest vessels in the company."

"Everybody knows," she said, with a note of tears in her voice. "Oh, Tom, can't you get out of it?"

"Don't want to!" crossly.

"Why didn't you come and ask me before deciding?"

"Wasn't any time!" gruffly. "It was 'Yes' or 'No.' "

"Oh, why didn't you say 'No?' "

"Because I'm not a fool!" growing savage.

"I shall never be happy again," she said, sitting down abruptly and beginning to cry.

Tears had their due effect, and the next instant Tom was kneeling beside her, libelling himself heartily. Presently, after sundry passages, her nose—a little pink—came out from the depth of *his* handkerchief.

"I shall come with you!" The words were uttered with sufficient determination to warn him that there was real danger of her threat being put into execution, and Tom, who was not entirely free from the popular superstition regarding the *Pampero*, began to feel uneasy as she combated every objection which he put forward. It was all very well going to sea in her himself; but to take his little girl, well—that was another thing. And so, like a sensible loving fellow, he fought every inch of the ground with her; the natural result being that at the end of an hour he retired—shall we say "retreated"—to smoke a pipe in his den and meditate on the perversity of womankind in general and his own wife in particular.

And she—well, she went to her bedroom, and turned out all her pretty summer dresses, and for a time was quite happy. No doubt she was thinking of the tropics. Later, under Tom's somewhat disparaging guidance, she made selection among her more substantial frocks. And, in short, three weeks later saw her at sea in the haunted *Pampero*, along with her husband.

II

The first ten days, aided by a fresh fair wind, took them well clear of the Channel, and Mrs. Tom Pemberton was beginning to find her sea legs. Then, on the thirteenth day out they ran into dirty weather. Hitherto, the *Pampero* had been lucky (for her), nothing special having occurred save that one of the men was laid up through the starboard fore crane line having given way under him, letting him down on deck with a run. Yet because the man was alive and no limbs broken, there was a general feeling that the old packet was on her good behavior.

Then, as I have said, they ran into bad weather and were hove to for three weary days under bare poles. On the morning of the fourth, the wind moderated sufficiently to allow of their setting the main topsail, storm foresail, and staysail, and running her off before the wind. During that day the weather grew steadily finer, the wind dropping and the sea going down; so that by evening they were bowling along before a comfortable six-knot breeze. Then, just before sunset, they had evidence once again that the *Pampero* was on her good behavior, and that there were other ships less lucky than she; for out of the red glare of sunset to starboard there floated to them the water-logged shell of a ship's lifeboat.

In passing, one of the men caught a glimpse of something crumpled up on a thwart, and sung out to the Mate who was in charge. He, having obtained permission from the Skipper, put the ship in irons and lowered a boat. Reaching the wrecked craft, it was discovered that the something on the thwart was the still living form of a seaman, exhausted and scarcely in his right mind. Evidently they had been only just in time; for hardly had they removed him to their own boat before the other, with a slow, oily roll, disappeared from sight.

They returned with him to the ship where he was made comfortable in a spare bunk and on the next day, being sufficiently recovered, told how that he had been one of the A.B.'s in the *Cyclops*, and how that she had broached to while running before the gale two nights previously, and gone down with all hands. He had found himself floating beside her battered lifeboat, which had evidently been torn from its place on the skids as the ship capsized; he had managed to get hold of the lifelines and climb into her, and since then, how he had managed to exist, he could not say.

Two days later, the man who had fallen through the breaking of the crane line expired; at which some of the crew were uneasy, declaring that the old packet was going back on them.

"It's as I said," remarked one of the Ordinaries, "she's 'er bloomin', 'aunted tin kettle, an' if it weren't better bein' 'aunted 'n 'ungry, I'd bloomin' well stay ashore!" Therein he may be said to have voiced the general sentiments of the rest.

With this man dying, Captain Tom Pemberton offered to sign on Tarpin—the man they had picked up—in his place. Tarpin thankfully accepted, and took the dead man's place in the forecastle; for though undeniably an old man, he was, as he had already shown on a couple of occasions, a smart sailor.

He was specially adept at rope splicing, and had a peculiarly shaped marlinspike, from which he was never separated. It served him as a weapon too, and occasionally some of the crew thought he drew it too freely.

And now it appeared that the ship's bad genius was determined to prove it was by no means so black as it had been painted; for matters went on quietly and evenly for two complete weeks, during which the ship wandered across the line into the Southern Tropics, and there slid into one of those hateful calms which lurk there remorselessly awaiting their prey.

For two days Captain Tom Pemberton whistled vainly for wind; on the third he swore (under his breath when his wife was about, otherwise when she was below). On the evening of the fourth day he ceased to say naughty words about the lack of wind, for something happened, something altogether inexplicable and frightening; so much so that he was careful to tell his wife nothing concerning the matter, she having been below at the time.

The sun had set some minutes and the evening was dwindling rapidly into night when from forward there came a tremendous uproar of pigs squealing and shrieking.

Captain Tom and the Second Mate, who were pacing the poop together, stopped in their promenade and listened.

"Damnation!" exclaimed the Captain. "Who's messing with the pigs?"

The Second Mate was proceeding to roar out to one of the 'prentices to jump forward and see what was up when a man came running aft to say that there was something in the pigsty getting at the pigs, and would he come forward. On hearing this, the Captain and the Second Mate went forward at a run. As they passed along the deck and came nearer to the sound of action, they distinctly heard the sound of savage snarling mingled with the squealing of the pigs.

"What the devil's that!" yelled the Second, as he tried to keep pace with the Skipper. Then they were by the pigsty and, in the gathering gloom, found the crew grouped in a semicircle about the sty.

"What's up?" roared Captain Tom Pemberton. "What's up here?" He made a way through the men, and stooped and peered through the iron bars of the sty, but it was too dark to make out anything with certainty. Then, before he could take away his face, there came a deeper, fiercer growl, and something snapped between the bars. The Captain gave out a cry and jumped back among the men, holding his nose.

"Hurt, Sir?" asked the Second Mate anxiously.

"N-no," said the Captain in a scared, doubtful voice. He fingered his nose for a further moment or two. "I don't think so."

The Second Mate turned and caught the nearest man by the shoulder.

"Bring out one of your lamps, smart now!" Yet even as he spoke, one of the Ordinaries came running out with one ready lighted. The Second snatched it from him and held it toward the pigsty. In the same instant something wet and shiny struck it from his hand. The Second Mate gave a shout, and then there was an instant's quietness in which all caught a sound of something slithering curiously along the decks to leeward. Several of the men made a run to the forecastle; but the Second was on his knees groping for the lantern. He found it and struck a light. The pigs had stopped squealing, but were still grunting in an agitated manner. He held the lantern near the bars and looked.

Two of the pigs were huddled up in the starboard corner of the sty, and they were bleeding in several places. The third, a big fellow, was stretched upon his back; he had apparently been bitten terribly about the throat and was quite dead.

The Captain put his hand on the Second's shoulder and stooped forward to get a better view.

"My God, Mister Kasson, what's been here," he muttered with an air of consternation.

The men had drawn up close behind and around and were now looking on, almost too astonished to venture opinions. Then a man's voice broke the momentary silence:

"Looks as if they 'ad been 'avin a 'op with a cussed treat shark!"

The Second Mate moved the light along the bars. "The door's shut and the toggel's on, Sir," he said in a low voice.

The Skipper grasped his meaning but said nothing.

"S'posin' it 'ad been one o' us," muttered a man behind him.

From the surrounding "crowd" there came a murmur of comprehension and some uneasy glancing from side to side and behind.

The Skipper faced round upon them.

He opened his mouth to speak; then shut it as though a sudden idea had come to him.

"That light, quickly, Mister Kasson!" he exclaimed, holding out his hand.

The Second passed him the lamp, and he held it above his head. He was counting the men. They were all there, watch below and watch on deck; even the man on the lookout had come running down. There was absent only the man at the wheel.

He turned to the Second Mate.

"Take a couple of the men aft with you, Mr. Kasson, and pass out some lamps. We must make a search!"

In a couple of minutes they returned with a dozen lighted lamps which were quickly distributed among the men; then a thorough search of the decks was commenced. Every corner was peered into; but nothing found, and so, at last, they had to give it up, unsuccessful.

"That'll do, men," said Captain Tom. "Hang one of those lamps up foreside the pigsty and shove the others back in the locker." Then he and the Second Mate went aft.

At the bottom of the poop steps the Skipper stopped abruptly and said "Hush!" For a half a minute they listened, but without being able to say that they had heard anything definite. Then Captain Tom Pemberton turned and continued his way up onto the poop.

"What was it, Sir?" asked the Second, as he joined him at the top of the ladder.

"I'm hanged if I know!" replied Captain Tom. "I feel all adrift. I never heard there was anything—anything like this!"

"And we've no dogs aboard!"

"Dogs! More like tigers! Did you hear what one of the shellbacks said?"

"A shark, you mean, Sir?" said the Second Mate, with some remonstrance in his tone.

"Have you ever seen a shark-bite Mister Kasson?"

"No, sir," replied the Second Mate.

"Those are shark-bites, Mister Kasson! God help us! Those are shark-bites!"

III

After this inexplicable affair a week of stagnant calm passed without anything unusual happening, and Captain Tom Pemberton was gradually losing the sense of haunting fear which had been so acute during the nights following the death of the porker.

It was early night, and Mrs. Tom Pemberton was sitting in a deck chair on the weather side of the saloon skylight near the forward end. The Captain and the First Mate were walking up and down, passing and repassing her. Presently the Captain stopped abruptly in his walk, leaving the Mate to continue along the deck. Then, crossing quickly to where his wife was sitting, he bent over her.

"What is it, dear?" he asked. "I've seen you once or twice looking to leeward as though you heard something. What is it?"

His wife sat forward and caught his arm.

"Listen!" she said in a sharp undertone. "There it is again! I've been thinking it must be my fancy; but it isn't. Can't you hear it?"

Captain Tom was listening and, just as his wife spoke, his strained sense caught a low, snarling growl from among the shadows to the leeward. Though he gave a start, he said nothing; but his wife saw his hand steal to his side pocket.

"You heard it?" she asked eagerly. Then, without waiting for an answer: "Do you know, Tom, I've heard the sound three times already. It's just like an animal growling somewhere over there," and she pointed among the shadows. She was so positive about having heard it that her husband gave up all idea of trying to make her believe that her imagination had been playing tricks with her. Instead, he caught her hand and raised her to her feet.

"Come below, Annie," he said and led her to the companion-way. There he left her for a moment and ran across to where the First Mate was on the look out; then back to her and led her down the stairs. In the saloon she turned and faced him.

"What was it, Tom? You're afraid of something, and you're keeping it from me. It's something to do with this horrible vessel!"

The Captain stared at her with a puzzled look. He did not know how much or how little to tell her. Then, before he could speak, she had stepped to his side and thrust her hand into the side pocket of his coat on the right.

"You've got a pistol!" she cried, pulling the weapon out with a jerk. "That shows it's something you're frightened of! It's something dangerous, and you won't tell me. I shall come up on deck with you again!" She was almost tearful and very much in earnest; so much so that the Captain turned-to and told her everything; which was, after all, the wisest thing he could have done under the circumstances.

"Now," he said, when he had made an end, "you must promise me never to come up on deck at night without me—now promise!"

"I will, dear, if you will promise to be careful and—and not run any risks. Oh, I wish you hadn't taken this horrid ship!" And she commenced to cry.

Later, she consented to be quieted, and the Captain left her after having exacted a promise from her that she would "turn in" right away and get some sleep.

The first part she fulfilled without delay; but the latter was more difficult, and at least an hour went by tediously before at last, growing drowsy, she fell into an uneasy sleep. From this she was awakened some little time later with a start. She had seemed to hear some noise. Her bunk was up against the side of the ship, and a glass port opened right above it, and it was from this port that the noise proceeded. It was a queer slurring sort of noise, as though something were rubbing up against it, and she grew frightened as she listened; for though she had pushed the port to on getting into her bunk, she was by no means certain that she had slipped the screw-catch on properly. She was, however, a plucky little woman, and wasted no time; but made one jump to the floor, and ran to the lamp. Turning it up with a sudden, nervous movement, she glanced toward the port. Behind the thick circle of glass she made out something that seemed to be pressed up against it. A queer, curved indentation ran right across it. Abruptly, as she stared, it gaped, and teeth flashed into sight. The whole thing started to move up and down across the glass, and she heard again that queer slurring noise which had frightened her into wakefulness. The thought leaped across her mind, as though it was a revelation, that it was something living, and it was grubbing at the glass, trying to get in. She put a hand down on to the table to steady herself, and tried to think.

Behind her the cabin door opened softly, and someone came into the room. She heard her husband's voice say "Why, Annie—" in a tone of astonishment, and then stop dead. The next instant a sharp report filled the little cabin with sound and the glass of the port was starred all across, and there was no more anything of which to be afraid, for Captain Tom's arms were round her.

From the door there came a noise of loud knocking and the voice of the First Mate:

"Anything wrong, Sir?"

"It's all right, Mister Stennings. I'll be with you in half a minute." He heard the Mate's footsteps retreat, and go up the companion ladder. Then he listened quietly as his wife told him her story. When she had made an end, they sat and talked awhile gravely, with an infinite sense of being upon the borders of the Unknown. Suddenly a noise out upon the deck interrupted their talk, a man crying aloud with terror, and then a pistol shot and the Mate's voice shouting. Captain Pemberton leaped to his feet simultaneously with his wife.

"Stay here, Annie!" he commanded and pushed her down onto the seat. He turned to the door; then an idea coming to him, he ran back and thrust his revolver into her hands. "I'll be with you in a minute," he said assuringly; then, seizing a heavy cutlass from a rack on the bulkhead, he opened the door and made a run for the deck.

His wife, on her part, at once hurried to make sure that the port catch was properly on. She saw that it was and made haste to screw it up tightly. As she did so, she noticed that the bullet had passed clean through the glass on the left-hand side, low down. Then she returned to her seat with the revolver and sat listening and waiting.

On the main-deck the Captain found the Mate and a couple of men just below the break of the poop. The rest of the watch were

THE HAUNTED *PAMPERO*   367

gathered in a clump a little foreside of them and between them and
the Mate stood one of the 'prentices, holding a binnacle lamp. The
two men with the Mate were Coalson and Tarpin. Coalson appeared
to be saying something; Tarpin was nursing his jaw and seemed to be
in considerable pain.

"What is it, Mister Stennings?" sung out the Skipper quickly.

The First Mate glanced up.

"Will you come down, Sir," he said. "There's been some infernal
devilment on!"

Even as he spoke the Captain was in the act of running down
the poop ladder. Reaching the Mate and the two men, he put a few
questions rapidly and learned that Coalson had been on his way after
to relieve the "wheel," when all at once something had leaped out at
him from under the lee pin-rail. Fortunately, he had turned just in
time to avoid it, and then, shouting at the top of his voice, had run
for his life. The Mate had heard him and, thinking he saw something
behind, had fired. Almost directly afterward they had heard Tarpin
calling out further forward, and then he too had come running aft; but
just under the skids he had caught his foot in a ring-bolt, and come
crashing to the deck, smashing his face badly against the sharp corner
of the after hatch. He, too, it would appear, had been chased; but by
what, he could not say. Both the men were greatly agitated and could
only tell their stories jerkily and with some incoherence.

With a certain feeling of the hopelessness of it all, Captain Pemberton gave orders to get lanterns and search the decks; but, as he
anticipated, nothing unusual was found. Yet the bringing out of the
lanterns suggested a wise precaution; for he told them to keep out a
couple, and carry them about with them when they went to and fro
along the decks.

IV

Two nights later, Captain Tom Pemberton was suddenly aroused from
a sound slumber by his wife.

"Shish!" she whispered, putting her fingers on his lips. "Listen."

He rose on his elbow, but otherwise kept quiet. The berth was
full of shadows for the lamp was turned rather low. A minute of
tense silence passed; then abruptly from the direction of the door, he
heard a slow, gritty rubbing noise. At that he sat upright and sliding
his hand beneath his pillow, brought out his revolver; then remained
silent—waiting.

Suddenly he heard the latch of the door snick softly out of its catch, and an instant later a breath of air swept through the berth, stirring the draperies. By that he knew that the door had been opened, and he leaned forward, raised his weapon. A moment of intense silence followed; then, all at once, something dark slid between him and the little glimmer of flame in the lamp. Instantly he aimed and fired, once—twice. There came a hideous howling which seemed to be retreating toward the door, and he fired in the direction of the noise. He heard it pass into the saloon. Then came a quick slither of steps upon the companion stairway, and the noise died away into silence.

Immediately afterward, the Skipper heard the Mate bellowing for the watch to lay aft; then his heavy tread came tumbling down into the saloon, and the Captain, who had left his bunk to turn up his lamp, met him in the doorway. A minute was sufficient to put the Mate in possession of such facts as the Skipper himself had gleaned, and after that, they lit the saloon lamp and examined the floor and companion stairs. In several places they found traces of blood which showed that one, at least, of Captain Tom's shots had got home. They were also found to lead a little way along the lee side of the poop; but ceased altogether nearly opposite the end of the skylight.

As may be imagined, this affair had given the Captain a big shaking up, and he felt so little like attempting further sleep that he proceeded to dress; an action which his wife imitated, and the two of them passed the rest of the night on the poop; for, as Mrs. Pemberton said: You felt safer up in the fresh air. You could at least feel that you were near help. A sentiment which, probably, Captain Tom *felt* more distinctly than he could have put into words. Yet he had another thought of which he was much more acutely aware, and which he did manage to formulate in some shape to the Mates during the course of the following day. As he put it:

"It's my wife that I'm afraid for! That thing (whatever it is) seems to be making a dead set for her!" His face was anxious and somewhat haggard under the tan. The two Mates nodded.

"I should keep a man in the saloon at night, Sir," suggested the Second Mate, after a moment's thought. "And let her keep with you as much as possible."

Captain Tom Pemberton nodded with a slight air of relief. The reasonableness of the precaution appealed to him. He would have a man in the saloon after dark, and he would see that the lamp was kept going; then, at least, his wife would be safe, for the only entrance to his cabin was through the saloon. As for the shattered port, it had been replaced the day after he had broken it, and now every dog watch he saw to it himself that it was securely screwed up, and not only that, but the iron storm-cover as well; so that he had no fears in that direction.

That night at eight o'clock, as the roll was being called, the Second Mate turned and beckoned respectfully to the Captain, who immediately left his wife and stepped up to him.

"About that man, Sir," said the Second. "I'm up here till twelve o'clock. Who would you care to have out of my watch?"

"Just as you like, Mister Kasson. Who can you best spare?"

"Well, Sir, if it comes to that, there's old Tarpin. He's not been much use on a rope since that tumble he got the other night. He says he hurt his arm as well, and he's not able to use it."

"Very well, Mr. Kasson. Tell him to step up."

This the Second Mate did, and in a few moments old Tarpin stood before them. His face was bandaged up, and his right arm was slipped out of the sleeve of his coat.

"You seem to have been in the wars, Tarpin," said the Skipper, eyeing him up and down.

"Yes, Sir," replied the man with a touch of grimness.

"I want you down in the saloon till twelve o'clock," the Captain went on. "If you—er—hear anything, call me, do you hear?"

The man gave out a gruff "aye, aye, Sir," and went slowly aft.

"I don't expect he's best pleased, Sir," said the Second with a slight smile.

"How do you mean, Mister Kasson?"

"Well, Sir, ever since he and Coalson were chased, and he got the tumble, he's taken to waiting around the decks at night. He seems a plucky old devil, and it's my belief he's waiting to get square with whatever it was that made him run."

"Then he's just the man I want in the saloon," said the Skipper. "It may just happen that he gets his chance of coming close to quarters with this infernal hell-thing that's knocking about. And by Jove, if he does, he and I'll be friends for evermore."

At nightfall Captain Tom Pemberton and his wife went below. They found old Tarpin sitting on one of the benches. At their entrance he rose to his feet and touched his cap awkwardly to them. The Captain stopped a moment and spoke to him:

"Mind, Tarpin, the least sound of anything about, and call me! And see you keep the lamp bright."

"Aye, aye, Sir," said the man quietly; and the Skipper left him and followed his wife into their cabin.

V

The Captain had been asleep more than an hour when abruptly something roused him. He reached for his revolver and then sat upright; yet though he listened intently, no sound came to him save the gentle breathing of his wife. The lamp was low, but not so low that he could not make out the various details of the cabin. His glance roved swiftly round and showed him nothing unusual, until it came to the door; then, in a flash, he noted that no light from the saloon lamp came under the bottom. He jumped swiftly from his bunk with a sudden gust of anger. If Tarpin had gone to sleep and allowed the lamp to go out, well—! His hand was upon the key. He had taken the precaution to turn it before going to sleep. How providential this action had been he was soon to learn. In the very act of unlocking the door, he paused; for all at once a low grumbling purr came to him from beyond the door. Ah! That was the sound that had come to him in his sleep and wakened him. For a moment he stood, a multitude of frightened fancies coming to him. Then, realising that now was such a chance as he might not again have, he turned the key with a swift movement and flung the door wide open.

The first thing he noticed was that the saloon lamp had burned down and was flickering, sending uncomfortable splashes of light and darkness across the place. The next, that something lay at his feet across the threshold—something that started up with a snarl and turned upon him. He pushed the muzzle of his revolver against it and pulled the trigger twice. The Thing gave out a queer roar and flung itself from him halfway across the saloon floor; then rose to a semi-upright position and darted howling through the doorway leading to the companion stairs. Behind him he heard his wife crying out in alarm; but he did not stay to answer her; instead, he followed the Thing voicing its pains so hideously. At the bottom of the stairs he glanced up and saw something outlined against the stars. It was only a glimpse, and he saw that it had two legs, like a man; yet he thought of a shark. It disappeared, and he leaped up the stairs. He stared to the leeward and saw something by the rail. As he fired, the Thing leaped and a cry and a splash came almost simultaneously. The Second Mate joined him breathlessly, as he raced to the side.

"What was it, Sir?" gasped the officer.

"Look!" shouted Captain Tom, pointing down into the dark sea.

He stared down into the glassy darkness. Something like a great fish showed below the surface. It was dimly outlined by the phosphorescence. It was swimming in an erratic circle leaving an indistinct trail of glowing bubbles behind it. Something caught the Second Mate's eyes as he stared, and he leaned farther out so as to get a better view. He saw the Thing again. The fish had two tails—or they might have been legs. The Thing was swimming downward. How rapidly, he could judge by the speed at which its apparent size diminished. He turned and caught the Captain by the wrist.

"Do you see its—its tails, Sir?" he muttered excitedly. Captain Tom Pemberton gave an unintelligible grunt, but kept his eyes fixed on the deep. The Second glanced back. Far below him he made out a little moving spot of phosphorescence. It grew fainter and vanished in the immensity beneath them.

Someone touched the Captain on the arm. It was his wife.

"Oh, Tom, have you—have you—?" she began; but he said "Hush!" and turned to the Second Mate.

"Call all hands, Mister Kasson!" he ordered; then, taking his wife by the arm, he led her down with him into the saloon. Here they found the Steward in his shirt and trousers, trimming the lamp. His face was pale, and he started to question as soon as they entered; but the Captain quieted him with a gesture.

"Look in all the empty cabins!" the Skipper commanded, and while the Steward was doing this, the Skipper himself made a search of the saloon floor. In a few minutes the Steward came up to say that the cabins were as usual, whereupon the Captain led his wife on deck. Here the Second Mate met them.

"The hands are mustered, Sir," he said.

"Very good, Mister Kasson. Call the roll!"

The roll was gone over, each man answering to his name in turn. The Second Mate reached the last three on the list:

"Jones!"

"Sir!"

"Smith!"

"Yessir!"

"Tarpin!"

But from the waiting crowd below, in the light of the Second Mate's lantern, no answer came. He called the name again, and then Captain Tom Pemberton touched him on the arm. He turned and looked at the Captain, whose eyes were full of incredible realization.

"It's no good, Mister Kasson!" the Captain said. "I had to make quite sure—"

He paused, and the Second Mate took a step toward him.

"But—where is he?" he asked, almost stupidly.

The Captain leaned forward, looking him in the eyes.

"You saw him go, Mister Kasson!" he said in a low voice.

The Second Mate stared back, but he did not see the Captain. Instead, he saw again in his mind's eye two things that looked like legs—human legs!

There was no more trouble that voyage; no more strange happenings; nothing unusual; but Captain Tom Pemberton had no peace of mind until he reached port and his wife was safely ashore again.

The story of the *Pampero*, her bad reputation, and this latest extraordinary happening got into the papers. Among the many articles which the tale evoked was one which held certain interesting suggestions.

The writer quoted from an old manuscript entitled "Ghosts," the well-known legend of the sea ghoul—which, as will be remembered, asserts that those who "die by ye sea, live of ye sea, and do come upward upon lonely shores, and do eate, biting likeye shark or ye deyvel-fishe, and are drywdful in hunger for ye fleyshe of man, and moreover do strive in mid sea to board ye ships of ye deep water, that they shal saytisfy theire dryedful hunger."

The author of the article suggested seriously that the man Tarpin was some abnormal thing out of the profound deeps; that had destroyed those who had once been in the whaleboat, and afterward, with dreadful cunning, been taken aboard the *Pampero* as a cast-away, afterward indulging its monstrous appetite. What form of life the creature possessed, the writer frankly could not indicate, but set out the uncomfortable suggestion that the case of the *Pampero* was not the first; nor would it be the last. He reminded the public of the many ships that vanish. He pointed out how a ship, thus dreadfully bereft of her crew, might founder and sink when the first heavy storm struck her.

He concluded his article by asserting his opinion that he did not believe the *Pampero* to be "haunted." It was, he held, simple chance that had associated a long tale of ill-luck with the vessel in question; and that the thing which had happened could have happened as easily to any other vessel which might have met and picked up the grim occupant of the derelict whaleboat.

Whatever may be the correctness of the writer's suggestions, they are at least interesting in endeavoring to sum up this extraordinary and incomprehensible happening. But Captain Pemberton felt surer of his own sanity when he remembered (when he thought of the matter at all) that men often go mad from exposure in open boats, and that the marlinspike which Tarpin always carried was sharpened much to the shape of a shark's tooth.

The Real Thing: 'S.O.S'

"BIG LINER ON FIRE in 55.43 N. and 32.19 W.," shouts the Captain, diving into his chart-room. "Here we are! Give me the parallels!"

The First Officer and the Captain figure busily for a minute.

"North, 15 West," says the Master; and "North, 15 West," assents the First Officer, flinging down his pencil. "A hundred and seventeen miles, dead in the wind!"

"Come, on!" says the Captain; and the two of them dash out of the chart-room into the roaring black night, and up onto the bridge.

"North, 15 West!" the Master shouts in the face of the burly Helmsman. "Over with her, smart!"

"North, 15 West, Sir," shouts back the big Quartermaster, and whirls the spokes to starboard, with the steering-gear engine roaring.

The great vessel swings round against the night, with enormous scends, smiting the faces of the great seas with her seventy-feet-high bows.

Crash! A roar of water aboard, as a hundred phosphorescent tons of sea-water hurls inboard out of the darkness, and rushes aft along the lower decks, boiling and surging over the hatchways, capstans, deck-fittings, and round the corners of the deck-houses.

The ship has hit the fifty-mile-an-hour gale full in the face, and the engine telegraph stands at full speed. The Master has word with that King of the Underworld, the Chief Engineer; and the Chief goes below himself to take charge, just as the Master has taken charge on deck.

There is fresh news from the Operator's Room. The vessel somewhere out in the night and the grim storm is the S.S. *Vanderfield*, with sixty first-class passengers and seven hundred steerage and she is alight forrard. The fire has got a strong hold, and they have already lost three boats, smashed to pieces as they tried to launch them, and every man, woman, and child in the boats crushed to death or drowned.

"Damn these old-fashioned davits!" says the Master, as he reads the wireless operator's notes. "They won't lift a boat out clear of the ship's side, if she's rolling a bit. The boats in a ship are just ornaments, if you've not got proper machinery for launching them. We've got the new derricks, and we can lower a boat, so she strikes the water, forty feet clear of the side, instead of bashing to pieces, like a sixty-foot pendulum, against our side!"

He shouts a question over his shoulder, standing there by the binnacle:

"What's she doing, Mister Andrews?"

"Twenty and three-quarter knots, Sir," says the Second Officer, who has been in charge. "But the Chief's raising her revolutions every minute... She's nearly on to the twenty-one now."

"And even if we lick that we'll be over five hours reaching her," mutters the Master to himself.

Meanwhile the wireless is beating a message of hope across a hundred miles of night and storm and wild waters.

"Coming! The R.M.S. *Cornucopia* is proceeding at full speed in your direction. Keep us informed how you are...."

Then follows a brief unofficial statement, a heart-to-heart word between the young men operators of the two ships, across the hundred-mile gulf of black seas:

"Buck up, old man. We'll do it yet! We're simply piling into the storm, like a giddy cliff. She's doing close on twenty-one, they've just told me, against this breeze; and the Chief's down in the stokeholds himself with a fourteen-inch wrench and a double watch of Stokers! Keep all your peckers up. I'll let you know if we speed-up any more!"

The Operator has been brief and literal, and has rather understated the facts. The Leviathan is now hurling all her fifty-thousand-ton length through the great seas at something approaching a twenty-two knot stride; and the speed is rising.

Down in the engine-room and stokeholds, the Chief, minus his overalls, is a coatless demi-god, with life in one hand and a four-teen-inch wrench in the other; not that this wrench is in any way necessary, for the half-naked men stream willing sweat in a silence broken only by the rasp of the big shovels and the clang of the furnace-doors, and the Chief's voice.

The Chief is young again; young and a King tonight, and the rough days of his youth have surged back over him. He has picked up the wrench unconsciously, and he walks about, twirling it in his fist; and the Stokers work the better for the homely sight of it, and the sharp tang of his words, that miss no man of them all.

And the great ship feels the effect. Her giant tread has broken into an everlasting thunder, as her shoulders hurl the seas to port and starboard, in shattered hills of water, that surge to right and left in half-mile drifts of phosphorescent foam, under the roll of her Gargantuan flanks.

The first hour has passed, and there have been two fresh messages from that vessel, flaming far off, lost and alone, out in the wild roar of the waters. There has been an explosion forrard in the burning ship, and the fire has come aft as far as the main bunkers. There has been a panic attempt to lower two more of the boats, and each has been smashed to flinders of wood against the side of the burning ship, as she rolled. Every soul in them has been killed or drowned, and the Operator in the burning ship asks a personal question that has the first touch of real despair in it; and there ensues another little heart-to-heart talk between the two young men

"Honest now, do you think you can do it?"

"Sure," says the Operator in the *Cornucopia*. "We're doing what we've never done at sea before in heavy weather. We're touching within a knot of our 'trials' speed—we're doing twenty-four-and-a-half knots; and we're doing it against *this*! Honour bright, old man! I'll not deceive you at a time like this. I never saw anything like what we're doing. All the engineers are in the engine-room, and all the officers are on the boat-deck, overhauling the boats and gear.   We've got those new forty-foot boat derricks, and we can shove a boat into the water with 'em, with the ship rolling half under. The Old Man's on the bridge; and I guess you're just going to be saved all right... You ought to hear us! I tell you, man, she's just welting the seas to a pulp, and skating along to you on the top of them."

The Operator is right. The great ship seems alive tonight, along all her shapely eight hundred feet of marvellous, honest, beautiful steel. Her enormous bows take the seas as on a horn, and hurl them roaring into screaming drifts of foam. She is singing a song, fore and aft, and the thunder of her grey steel flanks is stupendous, as she spurns the mutilated seas and the gale and the bleak intolerable miles into her wake.

The second and third hours pass, and part of the fourth, in an intermittent thunder of speed. And the speed has been further increased;

for now the Leviathan is laying the miles astern, twenty-nine in each hour; her sides drunken with black water and spume—a dripping, league-conquering, fifty-thousand-ton shape of steel and steam and brains, going like some stupendous Angel of Help across the black Desolation of the night.

Incredibly far away, down on the black horizons of the night, there shows a faint red glow. There is shouting along the bridge.

"There she is!" goes the word fore and aft. "There she is!"

Meanwhile the wireless messages pulse across the darkness: The fire is burning with terrible fury. The fore-part of the *Vanderfield's* iron skin is actually glowing red-hot in places. Despair is seizing everyone. Will the coming *Cornucopia* never, never come?

The young Operators talk, using informal words.

"Look out to the South of you, for our searchlight," replies the man in the wireless-room of the *Cornucopia*. "The Old Man's going to play it against the clouds, to let you see we're coming. Tell 'em all to look out for it. It'll cheer them up. We're walking along through the smother like an express. Man! Man! we're doing our 'trials' speed, twenty-five and a half knots, *against this*. Do you realise it—*against this!* Look along to the South. Now!"

There is a hissing on the fore-bridge, quite unheard in the roar of the storm; and then there shoots out across the miles of night and broken seas the white fan-blaze of the searchlight. It beats like an enormous baton against the black canopy of the monstrous storm-clouds, beating to the huge, thundering melody of the roar and onward hurl of the fifty-thousand-ton rescuer, tossing the billows to right and left, as she strides through the miles.

And what a sight it is, in the glare of the great light, as it descends and shows the huge seas! A great cliff of black water rears up, and leaps forward at the ship's bows. There is a thunderous impact, and the ship has smitten the great sea in twain, and tossed it boiling and roaring onto her iron flanks; and is treading it into the welter of foam that surrounds her on every side—a raging testimony, of foam and shattered seas, to the might of her mile-devouring stride.

Another, and another, and another black, moving cliff rises up out of the water-valleys, which she strides across; and each is broken and tossed, mutilated from her shapely, mighty, unafraid shoulders.

A message is coming, very weak and faint, through the receiver:

"We've picked up your searchlight, old man. It's comforted us mightily; but we can't last much longer. The dynamo's stopped. I'm running on my batteries...." It dwindles off into silence, broken by fragments of a message, too weakly projected to be decipherable.

"Look at her!" the officers shout to one another on the bridge; for the yell of the wind and the ship-thunder is too great for ordinary speech to be heard. They are staring through their glasses. Under a black canopy of bellied storm-clouds, shot with a dull red glowing, there is tossed up on the backs of far-away seas, a far-off ship, seeming incredibly minute, because of the distance; and from her fore-part spouts a swaying tower of flame.

"We'll never do it in time!" says the young Sixth Officer into the ear of the Fifth.

The burning ship is now less than three miles away, and the black backs of the great seas are splashed with huge, ever shifting reflections.

Through the glasses it is possible now to see the details of the tremendous hold the fire has got on the ship; and, away aft, the huddled masses of the six-hundred-odd remaining passengers.

As they watch, one of the funnels disappears with an unheard crash, and a great spout of flame and sparks shoot up.

"It'll go through her bottom!" shouts the Second Officer; but they know this does not happen, for she still floats.

Suddenly comes the thrilling cry of "Out derricks!" and there is a racing of feet and shouted orders. Then the great derricks swing out from the ship's side, a boat's length above the boat deck. They are hinged, and supported down almost to the draught line of the ship. They reach out forty feet clear of the ship's side.

The Leviathan is bursting through the final miles of wild seas; and then the telegraph bell rings, and she slows down, not more than ten or twelve hundred yards to windward of the burning hull, which rises and falls, a stupendous spectacle on the waste of black seas.

The fifty-thousand-ton racer has performed her noble work, and now the work lies with the boats and the men.

The searchlight flashes down onto the near water, and the boats shoot out in the "travellers," then are dropped clear of the mighty flanks of the Mother Ship.

The Leviathan lies to windward of them, to break the force of the seas, and oil bags are put out.

The people in the burning ship greet the ship with mad cheers. The women are hove bodily into the seas, on the ends of lines. They float in their cork jackets.

Men take children in their arms, and jump, similarly equipped. And all are easily picked up by the boats, in the blaze of the rescuer's searchlights that brood on leagues of ocean, strangely subdued by the floods of oil which the big ship is pumping onto the seas. Everywhere lies the strange sheen of oil, here in a sudden valley of brine, unseen, or there on the shoulder of some monstrous wave, suddenly eased of its deadliness; or again, the same fluorescence swirls over some half-league of eddy-flattened ocean, resting between efforts-tossing minor oil-soothed ridges into the tremendous lights.

Then the Leviathan steams to leeward of the burning ship, and picks up her boats. She takes the rescued passengers aboard, and returns to windward; then drops the boats again, and repeats the previous operations, until every man, woman, and child is saved.

As the last boat swings up at the end of the great derricks aboard the *Cornucopia* there is a final volcano of flame from the burning ship, lighting up the black belly of the sky into billowing clouds of redness. There falls the eternal blackness of the night... The *Vanderfield* has gone.

The Leviathan swings round through the night, with her six hundred saved; and begins to sing again in her deep heart, laying the miles and the storm astern once more, in a deep low thunder.

Jack Grey, Second Mate

I

SHE STEPPED ABOARD FROM one of the wooden jetties projecting from the old Longside wharf, where the sailing ships used to lie above Telegraph Hill, San Francisco. She rejected almost disdainfully the great hand extended by the Second Mate to assist her over the gangway.

The big man flushed somewhat under his tan, but otherwise gave no sign that he was aware of the semi-unconscious slight. She, on her part, moved aft daintily to meet the Captain's wife, under whose wing she was to make the passage from 'Frisco to Baltimore.

At first it seemed as if she were to be the only passenger in the big steel barque; but, about half an hour before sailing, a second appeared on the little jetty, accompanied by several bearers carrying his luggage. These, having dumped their burdens at the outer end of the gangway, were paid and dismissed; after which the passenger, a gross, burly-looking man, apparently between forty and forty-five years of age, made his way aboard.

It was evident that he was no stranger to sea-craft; for without hesitation, he walked aft and down the companion-way. In a few minutes he returned to the deck. He glanced ashore to where his luggage remained piled up as he had left it, then went over to where the Second Mate was standing by the rail across the break of the poop.

"Here, you!" he said brusquely, speaking fair English, but with an unfamiliar accent. "Why don't you get my luggage aboard!"

The Second Mate turned and glanced down at him from his great height.

"Were you speaking to me?" he asked quietly.

"Certainly I was addressing you, you—"

He stopped and retreated a pace, for there was something in the eyes of the big officer which quieted him.

"If you will go below I'll have your gear brought aboard," the Second Mate told him.

The tone was polished and courteous, but there was still something in the grey eyes. The passenger glanced uneasily from the eyes to the great, nervous hand lying, gently clenched, upon the rail. Then, without a word, he turned and walked aft.

The *Carlyle* had been two days at sea, and was running before a fine breeze of wind. On the poop the Second Mate was walking up and down, smoking meditatively. Occasionally he would go to the break and pass some order to the Boatswain, then resume his steady tramp.

Presently, he heard a step on the companion stairs, and, the moment afterward, saw the lady passenger step out on deck. She was very white, and walked somewhat unsteadily, as if she were giddy.

She was followed by the Captain's wife, carrying a rug and a couple of cushions. These the good woman proceeded to arrange on the Captain's own deck-chair, after which she steadied the girl to a sitting position and wrapped the rug around her knees and feet.

Abruptly, in one of his periodic journeys, as the Second Mate passed to windward of the place where they were sitting, the voice of the lady passenger reached him. She was addressing the Captain's wife, but was obviously indifferent whether he heard or not.

"I wish that man would take his horrible pipe somewhere else. The smell of it makes me quite sick!"

He was aware that the Captain's wife was trying to signal to him behind the girl's back; but he made no sign that he saw. Instead, he continued his return journey to the break of the poop, with a certain grimness about the corners of his mouth.

Here he proceeded to walk athwartships, instead of fore and aft, so that now he came nowhere near to the girl whose insolent fastidiousness had twice irked him. He continued to smoke; for he was of too big a mind to give way to the smallness of being huffed over the lady's want of manners. He had removed from her presence the cause of her annoyance, and, being of a logical disposition, saw no reason for ceasing to obtain the reasonable enjoyment of his pipe.

As he made his way to and fro across the planks, he proceeded to turn the matter over in his own calm way. Evidently she regarded him—if she thought at all about him—as a kind of upper servant; this being so, it was absurd to suppose that there was an intentional rudeness, beyond such as servants are accustomed to receive in their position of living automata. And here, having occasion to go down on to the main-deck to trim sail, he forgot the matter.

When he returned to the poop, the girl was sitting alone; the Captain's wife having been called below to attend to her husband who had been ill enough to be confined to his bunk for upward of a week.

As he passed across the planks, he cast occasional glances aft. The girl was certainly winsome, and peculiarly attractive, to such a man as he, in her calm unknowing of his near presence. She was sitting back in the chair, leaning tiredly and staring full of thought out across the sea.

A while passed thus, perhaps the half of an hour, and then came the sound of heavy steps coming up from the saloon. The Second Mate recognised them for those of the male passenger; yet the girl did not seem to notice them. She did not withdraw her gaze from the sea, but continued to stare, seeming lost in quiet thought.

The man's head appeared out of the companion-way, then the clumsy grossness of his trunk and fat under-limbs. He moved toward her, stopping within a couple of yards of her chair.

"And how is Miss Eversley?" the Second Mate heard him ask.

At his voice, the girl started and turned her head swiftly in his direction.

"You!" That was all she said; but the disgust and the undertone of something akin to fear were not lost upon the Second Officer.

"You thought—" began the man in tones of attempted banter.

"I thought I had seen the last of you—forever!" she cut in.

"But you see you were mistaken. If the sickness of the sea hadn't claimed you for the last two days, you would have discovered earlier that regret for my absence was wasted."

"Regret!"

"My pretty child—"

"Will you go away! Go away! Go away!" She put out her hands weakly with a gesture of repulsion.

"Come, come! We shall have to see much of one another during the next few weeks. Why—"

She was on her feet, swaying giddily. He took a step forward, as if with an unconscious instinct to bar her passage.

"Let me pass! She said, with a little gasp.

But he, staring at her with hot eyes, seemed not to have heard her. She put up a hand to her throat, as if wanting air.

"Allow me to assist you below."

It was the deep voice of the Second Mate. His naturally somewhat grave face gave no indication that he was aware of any tensions.

"I will attend to that," said the male passenger insolently.

But the officer seemed to have no knowledge of his existence.

Instead, he guided the lady to the companion-way, and then down the stairs to the saloon.

He left her in the charge of the Captain's wife telling the latter that the sea air had proved too much for the lady.

Returning on deck, he found the passenger standing by the opening of the companion. He had it in his heart to deal with the person in a fashion of his own; but the fellow had taken the measure of the big officer and, though full of repressed rage, took good care to invite no trouble.

On his part, the Second Mate resumed his steady tramp of the deck; but it may be noted that his pipe went out twice, for his thoughts were upon the girl he had helped below. He was pondering the matter of her repulsion for the male passenger. It was evident that they had met elsewhere, probably at the port where the *Carlyle* had picked them up. It was even more evident that the girl had no desire to continue the acquaintance, if it could be named as such.

Upon this, and much more to the same effect, did he meditate. And so, in due time, the First Mate came up to his relief.

II

Three days later, the Captain died suddenly, leaving his wife helpless with grief at her loss. By this time, Miss Eversley had gathered strength after her bout with seasickness, and now did her best to comfort the poor woman. Yet the desolate wife would not be comforted; but took to her bunk as soon as her husband had passed into the deep, and there stayed, refusing to be companied by anyone. This being so, Miss Eversly was, perforce, left greatly to her own devices, and her own company; for that of Mr. Pathan, the other passenger, she avoided in a most determined manner.

This was by no means an easy matter to accomplish, save by staying in her berth; for did she go upon the poop, the man would, in defiance of all her entreaties or commands, pursue her with his hateful attentions. Yet help was to come; for it happened one day that, the poop being empty save for the man at the wheel, with whom, however, Pathan seemed curiously familiar, the fellow took advantage of the opportunity to try to take her hands. He succeeded in grasping her left, making the remark:

"Don't be so skittish, my pretty. What are your hands, when I am to have the whole of you?" And he laughed mockingly.

For answer, she tried to pull away from him, but without success. "You see, it's no good fighting against me!"

She glanced round, breathlessly, for help and her gaze fell upon the Helmsman, a little, hideous dago who, with an evil grin upon his face, was watching them. At that, she went all hot with shame and anger.

"Let go of my hand!"

"I shall not!"

He reached his left out for her right, but she drew it back; and then, as if with the reflex of the movement, clenched it and struck him full in the mouth.

"Beast!" she said with a little savage note in her voice.

The man staggered a moment; for the blow had been shrewdly delivered, and his surprise almost equalled the pain. Then he came back at her with a rush. The man was no better than some bestial creature at the moment. He seized her about the neck and the waist.

"—you!" he snarled. "I'll teach—"

But he never finished. A great knuckled hand came between their faces, splaying itself across his forehead. His sweating visage was torn from her. A rough, blue-sleeved arm comforted his neck mightily, tilting his chin heavenward. His grip weakened upon her, then gave abruptly, and she staggered back dizzily against the mizzen rigging.

There came a sound of something falling. It was a very long distance away. She was conscious of the Second Mate in the immediate foreground, his back turned to her; and beyond him, her gross-featured antagonist huddled limply upon the deck. For a moment neither moved; then the man upon the deck rose shakily, keeping his eye mateward.

The big officer never stirred, and the passenger began backing to get the skylight between him and the Second Mate. He reached the weather side and paused nervously. Then, and not till then, the officer turned his back upon him, and, without vouchsafing a glance in the direction of the girl, walked forward toward the break of the poop.

As she made to go below, she heard the little steersman mutter something to the defeated man; and he, now that he was in no instant danger of annihilation, raised his voice to a blusterous growl. But the big man?

III

The fore-hands of the big steel barque *Carlyle* were a new lot who had been signed on in 'Frisco, in place of the outward-bound crew of Scotch and Welsh sailormen, who had deserted on account of the high pay ruling in 'Frisco. The present crowd was composed chiefly of "Dutchmen," and in each watch, consisting eight men and a boy, there were only two Americans, one Englishman, and a German. The remainder were dagos and mixed breeds.

The two Americans were in the First Mate's watch, the Englishman and the German being with the Second's crowd, and the whole lot of them, white, olive and mixed, were about as hard a "rough-house" crew, scraped up from the water-front, as one could find, and acceptable only because of the aforementioned high wages and shortage of men.

And, to complete the number of undesirable aboard, there was Mr. Pathan, the half-breed passenger.

Finally, Mr. Dunn, the First Mate, was a nervous little man, totally unfitted to handle anything more than an orderly crew of respectable Scandinavians. The result was that already his own watch had been once so out of hand he had been forced to call upon the Second Officer to help him maintain authority; since when, automatically, as it were, the Second Mate had taken, though unofficially, the reins of authority into his own hands.

Thus the situation five days after leaving port, on the homeward passage.

A week had passed.

"If you please, Sir, I'd like a word with you."

It was the big Boatswain who spoke. He had come halfway up the poop ladder, and his request was put in a low voice, yet with an apparently casual air.

"Certainly, Barton! Come up here if you have anything about which you wish to speak."

"It's about the men, Sir. There's something up, an' I can't just put me finger on it."

"How do you mean, something up?"

"Well, Sir, they're gettin' a bit at a loose end, an' they're gettin' a bit too free-like with their lip if I tells 'em to do anythin'."

"Well, you know, Barton, I can not help you in that. If you can not keep them in hand without aid, you'll never do it with."

" 'Tisn't exactly that, Sir. I can handle a crowd right enough along with any man; savin' it be yourself, Sir—" with an acknowledging glance at his officer's gigantic proportions "—but there's somethin' in the wind, as is makin' 'em too ikey. It's only since the Cap'n went, an' it's my belief as yon passenger's at the bottom of it!"

"Ah!"

"*You* noticed somethin' then, Sir?" asked the Boatswain quickly.

"Tell me what makes you think the passenger may be in anything that is brewing?" said the Second Mate, ignoring the man's question.

"Well, for one thing, Sir, he's too familiar with the men. An' I've seen him go forrard to the fo'cas'le of a night when 'twas dark. Once I went up to the door on the quiet, thinkin' as I'd get to see what it was as he was up to; but the chap on the lookout spotted me an' started talkin'. I reckoned he meant headin' me off; so I asked him to pass me down the end of me clothes-line, for a bluff, an' then I made tracks."

"But didn't you get any idea of what the fellow was doing in the fo'cas'le?"

"Well, Sir, it seemed to me as he was palaverin' to 'em like a father; but as I was sayin' I hadn't time to get the bearin's of what was goin' forrard. Then there's another matter, Sir, as—"

"And you might tell the man, while he's up, to take a look at the chafing gear on the fore swifter," interjected the Second Mate calmly.

The irrelevancy of this remark seemed to bring the Boatswain up all standing, as the saying goes. He glanced up at the officer's face, and in so doing the field of his vision included something else—the very one of whom they were talking. He understood now the reason of the Second's apparently causeless remark; for that keen-sensed officer had detected the almost cat-like tread approaching them along the poop-deck, and changed the conversation on the instant.

For a couple of minutes the Boatswain and the Second Mate kept up a talk upon certain technical details of ship work, until Mr. Pathan was out of hearing.

"I reckon as he thought he'd like to know what it was we're talkin' about, Sir," remarked the Boatswain, eyeing the broad back of the stout passenger.

"What is this other matter that you want to speak to me about?"

"Well, Sir, some of the hand 'as got hold of booze somehow. I keeps smellin' of 'em whenever one of 'em comes near me, and I reckon as he—" jerking his head in the direction of Mr. Pathan "—is the one as is givin' it to 'em."

The Second Mate swore quietly.

"What's his game, Sir? That's what's foozlin' me. I thinks it's time as you looked inter the matter!"

"If I thought—"

"Yes, Sir?" encouraged the Boatswain.

But whatever the Second Mate thought, he did not put it into words. Instead, he asked the Boatswain if he were of the opinion that nay of the forecastle crowd were to be depended upon.

"Not one of 'em, Sir! There isn't one as wouldn't put a knife inter you if he got half a chanst!"

The second nodded, as if the man's summing-up of the crew were in accordance with his own ideas. Then he spoke.

"Well, Barton, I cannot do anything till we know more definitely what is in the wind. You must keep your eyes open and report to me anything that seems likely to help."

Behind them they heard again the pad of Mr. Pathan's deck shoes.

"You had better overhaul the sheaves in those main lower top-sail brace blocks," he remarked for the benefit of the listening passenger. "That will do for the present."

"Very good, Sir," said the Boatswain, and went down the ladder onto the main-deck.

IV

It was in the afternoon watch, and Miss Eversley was sitting with a book in her lap, staring thoughtfully out across the sea.

Forward of her, the Second Mate tramped across the break of the poop. When she had appeared on deck, he had been pacing fore and aft along the poop, but had kept since then to the fore part of the deck.

Of the male passenger there was no sign. Indeed, since the big officer's "handling" of him, he had kept quite away from her, so that at last she was beginning to find her stay aboard not at all unpleasant. Occasionally the girl's glance would stray inboard to the great silent man, smoking and meditating as he paced across the planks.

It was curious (she recognised the fact) how often of late she had found her thoughts dwelling upon him. He was no longer a nonentity—something below the line of her horizon—but a man, and a man in whom she was beginning to be interested. She remembered now—what at the time she had scarcely noticed—her casual ignoring of his proffered aid as she stepped aboard. It had seemed nothing then to her, no more than if she had casually rejected the aid of a footman; but now she could not comprehend how she had done it.

From this her memory led her to that distinctly-to-be-regretted remark about his smoking. She watched him, and realised the more completely as she did so that she would be vitally afraid to do such a thing again; for, all unaware to herself, the manhood of the man was mastering her. Yet, at this time, she had no realisation of the fact; nothing beyond that she was interested in him, perhaps somewhat afraid and certainly a little desirous of knowing him.

On the Second Mate's part, he was thinking of other things than her. The preceding day he had been obliged to step down on the main-deck to exert authority, and had succeeded only by laying out a couple of the crew. That the disaffection was due, in part at least, to Mr. Pathan he had very little doubt; but no proof that would justify him in putting the man in irons, as he had determined to do the very moment such was forthcoming. Also, he knew that the Captain's death had unsettled them, and that there were vague ideas among them that now they were under no obligation to obey order. It was doubtless, along these lines that Pathan was working with them, and the thought made the big officer grit his teeth.

"Look out, Mr. Grey!"

The words came shrill and sudden in the voice of Miss Eversley, and the Second Officer turned sharply from where he had stopped a moment to lean upon the rail. He saw that she was on her feet, her arm extended toward him, while her gaze flickered between him and aloft. In the same instant, there was a sort of sogging thud behind him.

His stare had followed the girl's, and for an instant he had seen the dark face of one of the crew over the belly of the mizzen top-sail; then he had twisted quickly to see the reason for that noise, though already half comprehending the cause. In that portion of the rail over which he had just been leaning was struck a heavy steel marlinspike, the sharp point thereof appearing below, for it had penetrated right through the thick teak.

For a moment he looked at it, while his face grew quietly grim. Then he turned and walked toward the mizzen rigging. From here he could look up abaft the mast. Thus he saw the man who had dropped the spike making his way rapidly from aloft.

Getting into the lower rigging, the man—who proved to be one of those the Second Mate had floored the previous day—called out in broken English his regret for the accident; but the officer, knowing how little of an accident there had been about the affair, said nothing. Then, as soon as the creature put foot on the deck, he caught him by the nape of the neck and walked him forward to where the spike stood up in the rail.

Below on the main-deck stood several of the crew, watching what would happen, and fully prepared to make trouble if they got the half of a chance. They saw the Second Officer grasp the embedded spike with one great hand, then with apparent ease bend it from side to side till it broke, leaving in the rail that portion which had penetrated.

Immediately afterward, quite coolly, and calculating the force of the blow, he struck the man with it upon the side of the head, so that he went limp in his grasp; then he laid him down gently on the hencoop and bade a couple of them come up and carry him to his bunk. And this, being thoroughly cowed, as was the Second Mate's intention, they did without so much as a murmur.

As soon as the men were gone with their burden, he walked aft to where the girl stood.

"Thank you, Miss Eversley," he said simply. "I should have been spitted like a frog if you had not called."

She made no pretense of replying, and he looked at her more particularly. She was extraordinarily pale, and staring at him out of frightened eyes. He noticed also that she held to the edge of the sky-light as if for support.

"You are not well?" he said, and made as if to support her.

But she warded him off with a gesture.

"What a brute you are!" she said in a voice that would have been cold had it been less intense.

He looked at her a moment before he replied, as if weighing the use of speech.

"You don't understand," he remarked at last, calmly. "We have a rough crowd to handle, and half measure would be worse than useless. Won't you sit down?" And he indicated the chair behind her.

"It—it was butchery!" she remarked with a sort of cold anger, and ignoring his suggestion.

"Very nearly—if you hadn't called." There had come a suggestion of humour about the corners of his mouth.

"I—"

She groped backward vaguely for the chair, and seemed unconscious that it was his hands which guided her there.

"Now, see here, Miss Eversley. You must really allow me to be the better judge in a matter of this sort. I can not afford to sign for the long trip, in only for your sake."

"For my sake!" Her voice sounded scornful. "In what way does it concern me?"

The grimness crept back into his face and chased away the scarcely perceptible humour.

"In this way," he replied in a voice as nearly cold as her own but for a certain almost savage intensity. "I, and I alone, am keeping matters quiet aboard here; for I may as well tell you at once that the First Mate does not count for this much—" and he snapped his finger and thumb "—among the crowd we've got in this packet. They're quiet at present only because they're afraid of me."

"What do you mean?" She asked the question with a brave assumption of indifference, to which her frightened eyes gave no support.

"How does it matter to me whether your men are quiet or not?"

He looked at her a moment quietly and with something in the expression of his face that would have been contempt had it not been tempered by a deeper emotion.

"Listen!" he said, and she quailed before his masterfulness. "If that spike had done its work just now, you had been better dead than here. Do you think—"

He did not finish but turned from her and walked along the deck, leaving her gazing at the nakedness of a hideous possibility.

V

A week passed in quietness, and, though the Second Mate and the Boatswain between them had kept a strict watch upon the male passenger's movements, there had been nothing that could be looked upon with suspicion; for they had no knowledge of the tightly folded notes flipped to the Helmsman, and by him conveyed forward, and read for the delectation of the mutinous crowd in the forecastle.

It was extraordinary that Pathan should discontinue so abruptly his nocturnal visits to the men. Possibly he had caught a stray word or two of the Boatswain's confabulation with the Second Mate, and so taken fright. Whatever it was; the fact remained that it was impossible to come upon anything which would justify their putting him out of the way of doing mischief. Even the Boatswain's complaints about the men's behavoiur seemed to be lacking foundation during this time, and altogether the ship appeared to be quieting down nicely.

Though there had seemed of late little need for anticipating trouble, yet the Second Mate had his doubts but that there was something under his apparent calm, and, having his doubts, took the precaution to carry a companionable weapon in his side pocket.

In the end, events proved that he was right; for, one afternoon on watch, the Boatswain, chancing to have physical trouble with one of the men, the rest of the watch closed in upon him in a mob. At that the Second Mate went down to take a turn, which turn he took to such a tune that he had three of them stretched out before they were well aware that he was among them. They were beginning to give before his onslaught when suddenly he heard Pathan's voice, away aft, singing out:

"Get onto him, lads! Now's your time! Give the bully a taste of his own sort!"

At that the rest of them turned upon him with a rush, leaving the sadly mauled Boatswain to himself. And now the Second Mate showed of what he was made. They were clinging onto him like a lot of weasels—gripping his legs to trip him, grasping at his hands and arms, and climbing on his back. One of these latter having clasped hands under his chin, was doing his utmost to throttle him.

This the Second Mate foiled by unclasping the fellow's dirty paws and pulling him bodily over his head, bringing him, with a continuation of the movement, crashing down upon those of his attackers immediately in front. At the same instant, the Boatswain, being by now somewhat recovered, lain hold upon one of those in the rear and hauled him off. Even as he did so, there came the sound of a pistol shot.

The Second Mate hove himself round carrying the mass of clinging men with him. He saw Pathan coming along the decks toward them at a run. In his hand was a pistol, with the smoke still rising from it. Upon the deck lay the Boatswain. He was kicking and twitching; for it was he whom the passenger had shot.

"You—skunk!" roared the Second Mate. He caught two of his attackers by the hair of their heads and beat their skulls together so they became immediately senseless.

He saw Pathan halt within a dozen feet of him and aim straight at his head. He had been dead the following instant, but that there happened a diversion.

A white face flashed into the field of his vision, and the next moment Miss Eversley had thrown a handful of some whitish powder into the man's face. The pistol dropped with a thud, and from Pathan there was nothing save a mixture of gasps and shouts, violent sneezing, and coughs that broke off oddly into breathless blasphemy.

The Second Mate shouted incoherently. Then the girl was upon his assailants, throwing handfuls of the powder into their faces; whereupon they loosed him, as if their strength had gone from them, and fell to much the same antics as had Pathan. Some of the powder rose and assailed the Second Officer's nostrils, so that he sneezed violently. It was pepper!

He turned to the girl. At her feet lay the tin with which she had wrought his relief. She herself was standing, crying and sneezing along with the rest, and trying to wipe her eyes with a peppery handkerchief.

The Second Mate's glance noted the pistol dropped by Pathan, and he stepped over, and, picking it up, put it in his pocket. Between him and the group of sneezing, choking men lay the body of the Boatswain. A lot of the pepper had been spilt upon his upturned face, yet he moved no whit. He was quite dead.

"What's happened, Mr. Grey?" asked a thin voice at his elbow.

"Rank mutiny!" he replied.

"Whatever shall we do?" returned the voice, the owner of which was the First Mate. "Whatever shall we do?"

"Nothing," said the Second Mate shortly.

He turned from the Mate and bellowed to the other watch who were coming aft in a body, having been aroused by the noise.

"Now then, my lads! Up forrard with you! Smartly!" And he pulled out his revolver.

They went backward with a surge as he covered them.

"Back into the fo'cas'le! Don't stir till I tell you!"

The threatening weapon, backed by the determination of the man, overawed them and they went quickly.

"Close that door!" he roared.

It was closed immediately. Then he turned his attention to those around. Miss Eversley was standing near, her cheeks white, but her eyes and nose very red. It was plain to him that she was all of a tremble and like to fall, so that, without more ado, he took her by the shoulders and led her to a seat upon a spar lashed along by the bulwarks.

"Now, don't faint," he commanded.

"I'm not going to," she said soberly.

He left her hurriedly; for the men, having recovered from the effects of the pepper, were gathered in a clump and eyeing him doubtfully. To the right, Pathan had got upon his feet. It is just possible that in another moment they would have been upon him, which would have meant the loosing of the other watch, had he not acted with decision.

"Cyrone and Andy," he shouted, facing them squarely, "aft with you, and tell the Steward to pass out the irons!"

At the word, Andy started aft to obey. But Cyrone, one of those who had been foremost in the trouble, made no move.

"Cyrone!" said the Second Mate.

The man had done well to understand the dangerous quiet in his tone; but he did not. Instead, with unbounded insolence, he turned to the fellows surrounding him.

"Who for the irons, hey? They for we! I know! I know!" he shouted excitedly, and broke off into an unintelligible jargon of words.

"Cyrone!"

"For to—you go!" shouted the wretch in reply. It was evident that he was depending on the others to back him up.

The Second Mate said no word, but raised his pistol. The men about Cyrone scattered to each side. They had seen the Second Mate's eyes. In that last moment the fellow himself must have come suddenly into knowledge; for he started back, crying out something in an altered tone.

There was a scream from Miss Eversley, which blent with the sudden crack of the weapon; then Cyrone staggered and fell sideways on to the hatch. There was an instant of strange silence, broken by a dullish thud on the deck behind.

"Jardkenoff, go along with Andy for those irons," said the Second Mate in a level tone.

At his order the whole of them had started forward like frightened animals.

Jardkenoff ran past him, crying "Yi, yi, Sir!" in a shaking voice.

While they were gone for the irons, the Second Mate bade the others lift the bodies of the Boatswain and Cryone on to the hatch. Then he looked round to discover the cause of that thud upon the deck. He saw that Miss Eversley had fallen forward off the spar onto her face, and at that he hastened to lift her. Fortunately, she had escaped injury, at which unconsciously he sighed relief. Then, taking her into his arms, he carried her to the hatch, singing out to one of the men by name to run aft to bring the Steward with some brandy.

All this while, Pathan, the passenger, had stood in a dazed fashion beside the main-mast. Now, thinking he perceived a chance to steal aft to the temporary safety of his room, he began to sidle quietly away. It was no use, for the Mate's voice pulled him up short before he had gone a dozen feet.

"You will stay where you are, Mr. Pathan!" was all that he said.

When the irons came, the Steward accompanied them, carrying a glass full of brandy. This, under the eye of the Second Mate, he proceeded to administer. At the same time, the officer was superintending the ironing of Pathan. By the time that this was accomplished, Miss Eversley had begun to come to a knowledge of her surroundings, and presently sat up. Before this, however, the Second Mate had seen to it that Pathan was removed to the lazarette, for he would not have her upset further by sight of the murderer.

As soon as she was strong enough, he gave her his arm and led her aft to her cabin. In the saloon they came upon the Captain's wife sitting limply in one of the chairs. At their entrance, she started up, and cried out something in a frightened voice. The poor woman seemed demented and quite incapable of rational speech. It was evident that the scene on deck—which apparently she had witnessed—had, in conjunction with her recent loss, temporarily unsettled her mental balance.

With difficulty they persuaded her to go to her room, after which the Second Mate returned to the deck, with the intention of trying to put a little heart into the nonentity whom Fate had placed above him in the scale of authority.

That evening, in the second dog watch, the body of Cyrone was, by his orders, ignominiously dumped over the side without ceremony, and with a piece of rope and holystone attached to his feet.

VI

The following day it was a somewhat cowed lot of men who came aft, at the Second Mate's bidding, to the funeral of the Boatswain. Nor did his opinion of them, expressed tersely after the body had gone down into the darkness, help to reassure them. He told them that, at the first sign of further insubordination, he would shoot them down like the dogs they were; that, in future, there should be no afternoon watch below, and that work should be continued right through the two dog watches. On learning this, there came a slight murmur, expressive of discontent checked by fear, from the men grouped below the break.

"Silence!" roared the Second Officer, and whipped out a pistol from his side pistol.

Instantly the murmur ceased; for the men, as was the Second's intention, realised that he would stop nowhere to enforce his commands. And there was still vividly in their minds the execution of Cyrone.

As the men went forward, the First Mate ventured a weak protest against the Second's measure.

"You'll have 'em murdering us, Mr. Grey, if you go on like that! Why don't you speak to 'em nicely?"

The Second Mate looked down upon his superior. At first his glance denoted impatient contempt; but after the first moment an expression of tolerance spread over his features as he took in the other's almost pathetic weakness of face and figure.

"I believe you read the Bible, Mr. Dunn?"

"I—I—" began the Mate, flushing slightly. "Yes—perhaps I do sometimes. Why?"

"Well, you should know how little use swine have for pearls."

"You think, then, Mr. Grey—"

"I'm certain. That scum would take kindness for a sign of weakening on our part, and then—"

He made an expressive gesture.

"I wish to God we were home!" said the Mate fervently.

"You cheer up, Mister!" replied the big officer. "If you have any trouble with your lot, don't stop to talk—shoot!"

"It's an awful thing to take a life."

"It's a necessary thing sometimes. And, besides, you have only to bang on the deck for me, and I'll be up in a brace of shakes."

And so, after a few more words of encouragement to the frightened man, the Second left him in charge, and went below for a sleep.

True to his word, the Second Mate kept the mutinous crowd of sailormen hard at it from dawn to dusk. Even the First Mate, inspired by his example and encouragement, made a brave attempt to follow in his wake. As the Second Mate put it, "Sweat the flesh off their bones, and they'll be too tired to use their dirty brains." Also, he was the more confident of keeping them in subjection, now that Pathan was safely ironed in the lazarette.

Thus, at last, matters seemed in a fair way to tend to a happy ending of the troubles that had beset them so far. Yet of one person this could not be said; for the mental condition of the Captain's wife showed no signs of improvement. Fortunately, she was in no way violent and gave little trouble, her state being that of one suffering from melancholia in one of its quieter forms.

Then one morning if was discovered she was missing. A search was made through the ship, but without success. She was never found. Evidently the poor creature had crept on deck sometime during the night and gone overboard.

From this, onward, nothing disturbed the monotony of the voyage for many days. The Second Mate kept the crew well in hand, in no way abating rigourous treatment of them, so that did he but raise a hand they jumped to do his bidding.

And now of Miss Eversley. Day by day the girl had found her thought centering on the Second Mate. The horizon of her mind seemed bounded by him. She caught herself watching his least gesture as he paced the poop in his meditative fashion, or gave some order to the crew. Did the First Mate relieve him, so that he could go below for a sleep, the deck seemed strangely empty, the wind chilly, the sea dull and uninteresting. Yet when he relieved the First Mate, how different! Then the wind was warm, the sea full of an everlasting beauty; the deck, nay, the very planks of the deck, companionable.

And so she grew into the knowledge that she loved him, even to the extent of looking forward to her future life as a hideous blank, if he were not to share it; while he—silly man! He would break off his walks to sit and chat with her; but of that which she most desired to hear, not a word. Yet, by his eyes, she guessed that he cared; but for some reason—possibly because she was so much alone—he said nothing.

And so, at last, she might have come to aid him in spanning the gulf that remained between them; but that fate, in its own terrible way, took a hand.

VII

"Mr. Grey! Mr. Grey! Jack! Jack!"

The Second Mate woke with a start and leapt up in his bunk.

Miss Eversley was standing in the doorway of his berth.

"Quick! They've killed the First Mate! And they're coming down—now! Pathan has been let out, and he's with them!"

Even before she had made an end of speaking, the Second Mate had reached the floor with a bound. He snatched the revolver from under his pillow, and ran into the saloon.

From the doorway, giving into the companion stairs came the sounds of whispering, and the padding of many bare feet descending. He made a quick step to meet them; but the girl caught his arm.

"Don't, Jack! Don't!" Then, as he still hesitated: "For my sake—remember! Oh! Is there no place?"

She stopped, for the Second Mate had caught her by the arm and was running her toward the fore part of the saloon. His wits, slightly bewildered by sleep, had flashed instantly to their normal clearness under the stress of her terror. He realised that, for her sake alone, he had no right to throw away his chances of life.

Just as the foremost of the mutineers stepped silently into the dimly lighted saloon, the big officer pushed open the door of the foremost berth on the port side and thrust Miss Eversley in. At the same moment, the man at the other end discovered and gave a yell to announce the fact.

The following instant he lay dead, and the man behind him shared the same end. This caused a temporary hesitation on the part of the attackers, and in that slight interval the Second Officer slipped into the berth after the girl, slammed the door, and locked it.

"Stand to one side," he whispered to her.

As she did so, he hurled himself at the forward bulkhead of the berth. One of the boards started, and he attacked it again, the noise he was making drowning that of the mutineers in the saloon.

CRASH! The momentum of his effort had made a great breach in the woodwork and taken him clean through into the absolute darkness of the sail-locker beyond.

In a moment he was back. He caught the girl by the wrist and helped her through. Even as he did so there came a loud report in the saloon, and a bullet stripped off a long splinter on the inner side of the door as it came through.

Immediately, the Second Officer raised his weapon, and fired—once—twice. At the second shot there came a sharp outcry from one of those beyond the door, and then three shots in quick reply. They hurt no one, for the big officer had bounded into the sail-locker. He had dropped his emptied weapon into his side pocket, and was helping Miss Eversley over the great masses of stowed sails.

In the half of a minute he whispered to her to stand. An instant he fumbled, and she heard the rattle of a key. Then a square of pale light came in the darkness ahead of her, and she saw that he had opened a trap in the steel bulkhead that ran across the poop.

The following instant she was in darkness; for the huge bulk of her companion completely filled the aperture as he forced himself through. The light came again, and then she saw his head silhouetted against it in the opening.

"Give me your hand," he whispered, and the moment afterward she was standing beside him on the deck, under the break of the poop.

For an instant they stood there, scanning the decks, but every soul, saving the Helmsman, had joined in the attack. Through the opening behind them came the sound of blows struck upon the door of the berth which they had just quitted. No time was to be lost; for the moment that the brutes discovered that rent in the woodwork of the berth, they would be after them.

A sudden idea came to the Second Officer. He shut down the door of the vertical trap and locked it. The men would search the sail-locker for them, now that it was shift and fastened; while, if he had left it open, they would have been on their track immediately.

"Forrard to the half-deck," he muttered, and they ran out into the moonlight.

Now the half-deck was a little, strongly built steel deck-house, situated about amidships. It had one steel door on the after end; and once they were in, and this shut, they would be comparatively safe, at least for the time being.

Abruptly, as they ran, there came a muffled outcry, and they knew that the door to the berth had been broken down They reached the half-deck, and, while Miss Eversley sprang over the washboard, the officer ran to slip the hood which held the door back. Even as he reached up his hand there came a shout from the poop. They were discovered.

There came a thudding of rapid feet, and he saw the whole remaining crew of the boat tumbling hurriedly down the ladder on to the main-deck. At that critical instant he found that the hook was jammed. He riddled at it a moment; but still it refused to come out of its eye.

The running men were halfway to him, howling like wild beasts, and brandishing knives and belaying-pins. In desperation he caught the edge of the door, put one foot against the side of the house, and tugged. An instant of abominable suspense; then the hook gave, parting with a sharp crack. Through the very supremeness of his effort, he staggered back a couple of paces; before he could regain the door to shut it, a couple of the men who had outstripped the others, leaped past him and into the half-deck, with a cry of triumph.

He heard Miss Eversley scream; then the third man was upon him. The Second Mate tried to slam the door in his face, but the fellow jammed himself in between the door and side of the doorway. At that the big officer caught him by the chin and the back of the head, and plucked him into the half-deck by sheer strength. Then he brought the door to, and slipped the bolt, just as the rest of the men outside hurled themselves against it.

From the girl there came a cry of warning; and, in the same instant, the loud clang of some heavy missile striking the door by his right ear. He whirled round just in time to receive the united charge of the three he had imprisoned with himself in the deck-house.

Fortunately there was a sufficiency of light in the berth; for the lamp had been left burning by the former occupants when they left to join the attack on the after-guard.

Two of the men had their knives. The third stooped and made a grab for the iron belaying-pin which he had just thrown at the officer. Him the Second Mate made harmless by a kick in the face; then the other two were upon him.

He snatched at the knife-hand of the man to the right, and got him by the wrist; tried to do the same to the other and missed. The fellow dodged, rushed in and slashed the Second Mate's shirt open from the armpit to the waist, inflicting a long gash, but the next instant was hurled across the berth by a terrific left-hand blow.

The Second Mate turned upon the man whose wrist he had captured. His fingers were hurting intolerably, for the fellow was tearing at them with the nails of his loose hand so that they were bleeding in several places. He caught the wretch by the head, jammed the left arm under his chin, and leaned forward with a vast effort. There was a horrid crack, and the man shuddered and collapsed.

There came a little gasp of horror from the girl, who was crouched up against the corner by the starboard side. The Second Mate turned upon her.

"Turn your face to the bulkhead, and stop your ears," he commanded.

She shivered and obeyed, trembling and striving to stifle back a tumult of sobbing which had taken her.

The officer stooped and removed the knife from the hand of the dead man. Upon the door behind him sounded a perfect thunder of blows. Abruptly, as he stood up the glass of the port on the starboard side was shattered, and a hand and arm came into the light.

The Second Mate dodged below the line of the bunkboard. There was a loud report and a bullet struck somewhere against the ironwork. He ran close up to the bunk, still keeping out of sight, then rose upright with a sudden movement and grasped the pistol and the hand that held it, leaned forward over the bunk, and struck with his knife a little below the arm. There came a howl of pain from outside and the body fell away from the port, leaving the loaded pistol in the Second Mate's grasp.

Not a moment did he waste, but slammed-to the iron cover over the port and commenced to screw up the fastening. It was stiff, so that he had to take both hands to it, and because of this he placed the revolver down upon the bedding of the bunk.

This came near to causing his death, for, suddenly, as he wrestled with the screw, a hand flashed over his shoulder and grabbed the weapon. Instinctively the Second Mate dodged and swung up a defending arm. He struck something. There was a sharp explosion close to his head, and then the clatter of the falling weapon.

By this he had got himself about and saw that the two whom he had temporarily disabled were upon him. Before he could defend himself, one of them struck him with the iron belaying-pin across his head. It sent him staggering to the floor.

As he fell, a scream from Miss Eversley pierced to his dull senses, and he got upon his knees, gasping and rocking, yet still full of the implacable determination to fight. For all his grit he would have been dead but for the girl. He had grasped the legs of one of his assailants; but was too dazed and weakened to put forth his usual strength.

The second man raised the heavy pin for another smite, but it never fell. To the Second Mate, wrestling pointlessly, there sounded a dull thud and a cry. Something fell upon him all of a heap, as it were, and he was brought to the deck upon his side; yet he had not relaxed his somewhat nervous grip upon the man's legs, so that the fellow came down with him.

For perhaps the half of a minute he held on stupidly while the man struggled violently to get away. Then, almost abruptly, nerve and reasoning-power came back to him, and in the same instant a violent pain smote him between the left shoulder and the neck. He got upon his knees, hurling the dead body of the other man from off his shoulders with the movement.

He was now above his opponent, and at once attempted to capture the fellow's knife. In this he was not at first successful, with the result that he sustained a second stab, this time slitting open the front of his shirt, and cutting his breast. At that, growing inconceivably furious, he regarded not the knife, but smote the man with his bare fist between the eyes and again below the ear, and so shrewd and mighty were the blows that the fellow died immediately.

Perceiving that the man was indeed dead, the Second Mate got himself upon his feet. He was breathing deeply, and his head seemed full of a dull ache.

He took his gaze from the bodies at his feet, and glanced around. Not two yards distant stood Miss Eversley. She had a revolver in her right hand. At that, the Second Mate understood how he had escaped with his life. Yet he had no thought of thanking her; for the horror in her face warned him not to do anything that might increase her realisation of what she had done. Instead, he made two steps to her, and took her in his arms.

With the feel of his arms about her, she dropped the pistol and broke into violent weeping. And he, having some smattering of wisdom, held his peace for a space.

Presently the extreme agitation of the girl passed off, and she sobbed only at intervals. Later still she spoke.

"I shall never be happy again."

And still the Second Mate preserved the sweet wisdom of silence.

"Never, never, never!" he heard her whispering to herself.

And so, in a while, she calmed down to quiet breathing. For a space they stood thus, and on the decks all about the little house was silent, save for the occasional pad, pad, of a bare foot, as those without moved hither and thither.

VIII

The day had come and passed, and it was again night.

Within the house things could be seen but dimly, for the lamp was turned no more than a quarter up; and of oil they had no supply beyond the quantity within the lamp itself. Fortunately, there was no immediate need to worry about water; for the water breaker, lashed to the port end of the table, was a quarter full, owing to the Boatswain's and the Carpenter's dislike for soap and water.

As for food, an examination of the bread barge in one of the empty lower bunks showed him that there was enough biscuit to keep the two of them crudely fed for some days, provided they were careful. In the food cupboard there was also a half a bottle of ship's vinegar, about half a pound of ship's salt port, some sugar in a soup-and-bully tin, and about three pounds of black molasses in a big seven-pound pickle jar; all of these being the usual savings of rations that might be found in the food locker of any other lime-juicer, windjammer in all the seven seas.

He had, aided by the girl, bound up his wounds, which were not sufficiently serious to trouble him with anything more than a constant smarting; and though he had bled a good deal, he was so full of life and vitality that he was scarcely aware of the loss, except that he was abnormally thirsty; which fortunately the water in the breaker enabled him to quench freely. Yet, all the same he held this need somewhat in check, for they must never run short of the precious fluid.

During the day a certain amount of light had driven in between the crevices about the door. Beyond this there had been none, for the ports were all protected by their iron covers. Fortunately, as the Second Mate had discovered, all of them had been fastened on the preceding night, previous to their making a refuge of the house; all, that is, save the one through which they had been attacked. To this fortunate happening it is probable they owed their lives.

In the corner of the house to the right of the door there was a grim mound. The Second Mate had spread a couple of blankets over it to hide its full horror from the eyes of the girl; yet, by this very act, he had made it almost more unbearable than if he had left them in all the stark awesomeness of uncovered death.

Out upon the decks was quietness. Indeed, all through the day there had been but one attempt to molest them, and this the Second Mate had foiled by quickly opening one of the after ports and firing into the thick of the attacking party. In this way he was persuaded that he could have held the house for as long as it pleased him to do so but for the insurmountable obstacle that confronted him in the shape of lack of ammunition. Yet, even as it was, it was plain to him that the repulse he had given them was likely to keep them at a respectable distance—at least for some while. For, out of a crew of sixteen deck hands, six had already been killed and several wounded

In the brief time he had been at the port he had gathered something of the methods they had been about to apply to the felling of the door. They had rigged up a spar on a tackle, so as to form a rough sort of battering ram; yet, in the brief attempt that he had permitted them, the machine had proved unsuccessful, for the suspending had been too long and the rolling of the ship had caused the spar to swing across the after end of the house, in the fashion of a clock pendulum, so that at one moment the business end of the ram was opposed to the door, and another to some portion of the end of the house.

In spite of the failure of the attackers, the big officer was well aware that with a more perfect appliance, and no ammunition with which to beat them off, they would not be long in forcing the door. And then....

The second night of the imprisonment had come. The Second Mate had gone to the door and was listening; but beyond the pad of a bare foot, or hum of hoarse voices, there was nothing to tell of the watchers about the decks.

For her part, the girl was busying herself clearing away the few eatables from which they had been making a meal. This done, she hesitated a moment, then went over to the Second Mate.

"Let me stay up tonight and watch, Jack. You have not had any sleep, and I have slept most of the day. I could wake you up the moment anything happened."

The big man put a hand on each side of her shoulders and looked down upon her with a grave half-smile.

"Do, Jack! You can trust me," she urged.

"Trust you, little girl," he replied. "Yes, child, with a thousand lives if I had them."

"Then you will let me stay up and watch?"

He shook his head slowly.

'There will be no need tonight, at any rate. They cannot get at us without noise. We may both sleep."

This he said to quiet her entreaties; for he had no intention to allow her to sit alone in the darkness with her thoughts, and that blanket-covered mound, while he slept. More, he wished her to sleep; for he had a project which he hoped to carry out during the hours of darkness.

For a moment she stood looking up at him in the half-light. Then she slipped her hands onto his shoulders.

"Then I will say good night, Jack, for we must save the oil in the lamp."

The Second Mate stooped and kissed her.

"Good night, Mary," he said gravely.

"Good night," she whispered, kissing him in return.

Then she left him and went behind the blanket which he had rigged up before the bunks on the starboard side.

A space of about two hours passed, during which the Second Mate lay awake listening. Presently, realising that the girl was asleep, he got up and quietly opened the door of the house. He listened a minute and found no one about; then swiftly he carried out each of the dead bodies onto the deck and left them there. He returned to the house and locked the door.

All at once, from outside the door, there rose an outcry. At that, he knew that the dead had been discovered. The outcries sank to a subdued murmur; for there had come fear among the men. Yet from thence onward, the door was never left unguarded day or night.

IX

The morning of the fourth day of their imprisonment dawned, and the Second Mate was awakened by a noise of hammering close against the port on the left side of the door. He jumped from his bunk quietly, and crept softly to the one on his right. He had the revolver in his hand.

Very cautiously he unscrewed the fastening of the iron cover, and glanced out, but could see no one. For a little he listened, and between the blows he caught a murmur of talk some little distance away. Abruptly he recognised Pathan's voice. At that, quickly but silently, he unscrewed the fastening of the glass and opened it. He thrust his head out and looked to the left.

Close to him, and right in front of the door, stood one of the men. He held the muzzle of a clumsy ship's musket, the butt resting on the deck. The Second Mate remembered having observed this same antique weapon hanging in the Steward's pantry. It was evident that they were but poorly supplied with firearms.

Beyond the guard, he made out a couple more of the men fixing a heavy piece of timber across the other port. Evidently they had hit upon this plan of preventing his interfering with their operations. With the two after ports blocked they could do much as they pleased.

Suddenly a sharp exclamation on his right startled the Second Officer. He glanced round. There was Pathan fumbling with his revolver.

Instantly the Second Mate snatched his head in to the shelter of the house. Almost at the same moment there sounded a thunderous bang close to the left. He heard Pathan give a scream of pain breaking off into a blatter of cursing.

At the risk of his life he shoved his head out. Pathan was nursing his right hand, while big tears of pain were running down his cheeks to that strange accompaniment of blasphemy. On the deck, close to his feet, lay the shattered butt of his revolver. The Second Mate twisted to the left for a brief glance. He saw that the guard was sitting upon the deck, rubbing his right shoulder. He looked woefully scared, while near by lay the cumbrous weapon with which he had been armed.

What had happened was now clear to the big officer. The man had fired at the protruding head—but a fraction too late—with the result that the bolt, with which the gun had been loaded, had stricken the passenger's revolver, destroying it and wounding his hand.

Even as the solution came to the officer, the guard had reached for his gun and scrambled to his feet. In another moment he would have clubbed the Second Mate, but that a bullet sent him twitching to the deck.

The Second Mate turned his pistol upon Pathan. Could he but rid the ship of that fiend, all might yet be well.

Yet, as he pressed the trigger for the second time, his elbow was jogged from within the house. He swore between his teeth and tried another shot, only to be warned by the unsatisfying click of the hammer that his ammunition had come to an end.

He drew away from the port with an angry gesture, and well it was for him that he did so, for one of the two at work upon the port, seeing that the weapon was empty of cartridges, had run at him with a hammer. The blow missed, and the following instant the Second Mate had slammed the covers and fastened up the port.

He turned and found the girl standing by him.

"Do you know," he said a trifle sternly, "you made me miss Pathan when you touched me. If I had shot that wretch the men would have been glad enough to come to terms."

He was hot with his failure, or he had not spoken so to her. And she, having but touched him because of the fear which had seized her at his rashness in so exposing himself, burst into crying; for she had been sorely overstrained with the rough happenings of late.

At this his anger left him and he made to comfort her, so, for that morning they sat together, she taking little heed of the various sounds about the house which told him that the fiends outside were preparing to batter down the door. They had covered up the second port immediately after his closing of the cover, so that he had no means of knowing how matters were progressing beyond such as his ears, trained in ship-craft, could tell him.

Very slowly the day passed to its close. He knew that the final struggle was at hand; but he did not by any means consider their chances of life beyond hope; for he knew that the crew had been greatly reduced, so that, could he but avoid the fire of the big musket, he might slay Pathan and put the rest to flight. Yet he had no knowledge but that the house might be their prison for a day or two longer; though, beyond that time they could not hope to stay, for of food they had but little, and less water.

The day had been a fine one, as they could tell by the light which came through the crevices around the somewhat loosely fitting door, and when at last the evening came, the girl went to the door to try to get a look at the sunset.

"Come and look, Jack," she said suddenly, after a period of silence.

He turned from the water breaker at which he was busy emptying the last few drops.

"What is it, Mary?"

His voice was perhaps a trifle uneasy, for he had made the discovery that there was left only half a pannakin of water. During the last two days of their imprisonment he had been limiting his allowance; for he would not see her stinted, and now, through some mischance, the spigot, which someone had fixed near the bottom of the little cask, had been loosened, and the small quantity of the imperative liquid which had been theirs was all squandered save for the drainings which he had emptied into the enameled mug.

He came across to where she stood. For the moment he was minded not to tell her, then, remembering because of the fiends outside, that a clear knowledge of their position was her due, he told her not only of this matter but of the likelihood of the crisis being near at hand.

When he had made an end, she reached up one hand to his shoulder, then held out the other for the mug. She drew him down to the crevice through which she had been peering.

"See," she said, "did you ever see such a sunset?" Her voice dropped. "And it may be our last, Jack." She patted his shoulder as she spoke. "You know, boy, I may only be a silly girl, but I know nothing but a miracle can save us."

It was the first time she had spoken out so plainly, and he, having nothing to answer, stared out blindly into the dying glory outside.

In a little, perhaps the half of a minute, she drew him back somewhat and held the little mug up before them

"We will drink it together, darling," she whispered, and bent her hand over and kissed the brim, then handed it to him; but he was not deceived.

"Fair play, little woman. You have drunk nothing."

He passed it back to her, and she, knowing him, sipped a little, then held it up to him and made him drink from her own hands. He was hideously thirsty, but controlled himself to one gulp only; then took the mug from her and set it down upon the table. For the end was not yet, and she might have need of it 'ere then.

It was almost dark in the berth, for the oil of the lamp was done this long while, the only light they had coming through the crannies about the door.

For a while the two of them stood together. He was deep in pondering as to when the attack would come. Probably as soon as it was dark; for, of course, they could not be absolutely sure that he had no further supply of cartridges.

She for her part was leaning forward, peering through the narrow opening at the red splendour of the sun's shroud. Once or twice she ran her fingers up and down this crack, as if she would fain enlarge it. Possibly the tips showed outside, for her hands were very slender; yet, however it may have been, it is certain that one of the devils upon the deck was attracted and crept up on tip-toe. Inside, the girl, staring out, saw something come abruptly between her and the sun. The Second Mate saw it at the same moment, else she had been dead on the instant.

He pushed her from him, out of a line with the crack, and in so doing brought himself almost directly opposite. There came a sudden spurt of flame into the semi-darkness of the house, and a tremendous report up against the door. The girl gave a little scream which almost drowned her lover's moan of pain, but not quite.

"You are not hurt, dearest?" she cried out loud.

For a moment he did not answer, and in that quick silence she heard a man outside laugh brutally.

The Second Mate had his hand up to his eyes and was very silent. In the dimness of the place she saw that he was swaying upon his feet.

"Jack," she said in an intense whisper of fear. "Are you hurt?"

She caught his wrist with a gentle hold. Still he did not reply. Beyond the door she heard the murmur of voices, and odd words and fragments of sentences drifted to her uncomprehending brain.

"—for?"

"Fiddlin' at the door!"

"—bust! The gun's busted!"

"Thank God!" It was the Second Mate who had spoken, and the girl loosed her hands from his wrists in her astonishment. Then, with a sudden applying of his words to satisfy the desire of her soul—

"You are not hurt, then, dear?"

"A—a little. My eyes—"

"What? Let me see!" But he swung round from her.

"Can you get me some—something for a bandage?" There was a desperate levelness in his tone.

He took two or three uncertain steps across the floor, as if bewildered. She followed him. He took his hands from his face and moved his head from side to side, as if peering about the house. Abruptly, he turned and blundered into her clumsily. She would have fallen, but that he caught and steadied her.

"Jack! Oh, Jack!" she cried, for even in the dimness of the place she had caught a glimpse of where his eyes ought to have been.

"It's all right, little woman," he replied in a voice that was nearly steady. "I—can't see very well while the pain's bad." He had covered his face again with his hands.

She answered nothing. She was tearing one of her undergarments into strips, and trying to quiet her sobs.

X

The night had come. The Second Mate, the upper portion of his face swathed in wrappings, was seated on the sea-chest below his bunk. The girl was sitting by him, and their right hands were clasped.

The crack along the edge of the door had been stuffed up with a strip of blanket. Upon the edge of the table was stuck a tiny fragment of candle, and by the light of this she was reading slowly the betrothing passage from the Solemnisation of Matrimony—that in which the man plights his troth. The Second Mate was repeating the words after her.

Presently they had made an end and the girl slipped her hand gently from his; then, taking hold of his in turn, she read in a firm voice that passage in which the woman gives her troth. At the end, she released the Second Mate's hand and drew a ring from off one of her finger. This she put gently into his hand. Then, having given him her left, he slid the ring on her third finger, repeating the meanwhile, after her, the passage which she whispered to him.

And after that they sat awhile, too full of thought for speech.

Presently the candle went out abruptly, and the two were alone in the darkness.

From the deck beyond the door came an occasional mutter of

speech, an occasional padding of feet and an occasional creaking of gear, and the two within sat and waited.

Toward midnight the moon rose and limned the outline of the door in pale light. Presently the girl spoke.

"The moon has risen, Jack."

She rose from his side and moved to the door. Perhaps she might be able to see what the crew were busied at. Abruptly, as she stooped forward to peer, something struck the door a tremendous blow, filling the interior of the house with a deafening, hollow boom. She cried out in fear, and even as she cried came the second blow and the crack of a breaking rivet.

She realized that the attack had begun, and groped a moment for the matches. She struck one and examined the door. To the casual glance it was unharmed; but by the light of the third match she made out that a rivet in the bottom hinge was snapped. By this, a dozen blows had been dealt, and yet, from the Second Mate, seated upon the sea-chest, no sound.

All at once, he spoke.

"Come here, Mary."

She came to him quickly, wondering, half consciously, at the strange harshness of his tone. By the light of the match which she carried, she saw that he had in his hand the revolver.

"It's no good, Jack," she said despairingly, thinking he had a mind that she should use it in their defense. "There are no cartridges!"

"I kept—one," he said with a jerk, and still in that unnatural voice.

He reached out his left hand to her. And at that she comprehended, and comprehending shrank back with a little wail.

"O-o-h! O-o-h! Jack!" she sobbed, with a sudden plumbing of the abyss of mortal terror.

There came a louder crash on the door, and then the Second Mate's voice.

"Mary!"

She went up to him, quivering.

"Not yet, Jack! Not yet!"

He put his left arm round her.

"Mary!" he said, and the fierce agony which possessed him spoke out in his voice. "Tell me when the door begins to go!"

And she knew that the time of the door's standing was the span of her life.

At each ringing thud of the ram she could feel the place quiver. By now it had become a steady, almost rhythmic *boom, boom, boom,* which, as a rivet gave, blent into a crash. The inside of the steel house was like the inside of a great drum.

And so a minute passed, and another, and still the door stood, while that dread booming beat out the knell of the two within—he grim for very fear of himself, and she shaking because of the thing that was to happen, and still with some room in her soul for his sufferings, yet unable to say anything; for in those last moments he had become her executioner as well as her lover, and there were things she could not say to the two.

Boom! Boom! Boom! Crash!

"Mary?" His voice sounded like the cry of a lost soul, and the love in the woman answered to it. Yet the physical terror of death was upon her.

"The—the door—is—is—stop! It's only the bottom hinge had broken. It isn't down yet!"

Crash! Crash! Crash!

The girl, all of a shiver, turned suddenly and put her arms round his neck.

"Kiss me, Jack!"

Crash! Crash!

He repelled her for a moment then, drawing her to him, kissed her goodbye.

Crash! C-r-a-s-h!

"Don't! Don't! Not yet! It isn't down yet! Give me—give me as long as you—you can!"

For the arm about her shoulders had tightened with a sudden grip. Then abruptly—

"Have you—have you a—a—a knife, Jack?"

He took his arm from about her and brought something from behind, which he held out for her to take.

She saw it faintly by the glimmer of moonlight that came through the shaken door.

"No, no, no!" she cried, and shuddered. "You—you take it! Give me the pistol. I—I can see."

He gave up the revolver to her and shifted the knife to his right hand. Even as he did so, the door crashed in. He felt the girl thrill in the grip of his arm; then her right hand went up, and, an instant later came the click of the hammer, but no report—the cartridge had missed fire. She had aimed at a dark figure beyond the doorway, which she had recognised as Pathan. Yet the cruelty of fate denied her even the consolation of knowing that she died leaving her lover not at the mercy of that creature.

She cried out her dismay, and then again in terror, for the grip of the Second Mate's arm warned her that the end had indeed come. There came the rush of feet along the deck, and the blaze of a flare. Then Pathan's voice:

"Don't hurt the girl!"

She caught so much of it. Then the touch of her lover's fingers upon her breast made her quiver. She felt his right arm go back for the blow.

"Oh, my God, help me! Help me! Help me!" he heard her whispering desperately, and it shook him badly in that supreme moment. But, for the love he bore her, he meant that there should be no faltering in his stroke. Abruptly, the girl felt him start violently, and he began to quiver from head to feet. He cried out something in a strange voice.

"Oh, my God!" he said in a sort of whispering, husky shout. "I can see! I can see! Oh, my God, I can see! We're going to win! Mary, Mary! We're going to win! I can see! I can see! I can see! I tell you, I can see!"

He loosed her and put both his hands up to his bandages, which had slid down onto his nose, and tore them away in a mad kind of fashion, while the girl stood limp and sick against him, still half-fainting.

"I can see! I can see!" he began to reiterate again.

He seemed to have gone momentarily insane with the enormous revulsion from utter despair to hope. Suddenly he caught the girl madly into his arms, staring down at her through the darkness. He hugged her savagely to him, whispering hoarsely his refrain of:

"I can see! I can see! I tell you I can see!"

He held her a single instant or two like this; then he literally tossed her into one of the upper bunks.

"Don't move!" he whispered, his voice full of the most intense purpose. "I'm going to get square with that brute now. There's a chance for both of us. Here, take the knife in case I don't manage. Just lie still, whatever happens. You must be out of the way. I could tackle a hundred of them now."

He was silent, listening. By the sound of the men's voices, the Second Mate knew that they had halted some little distance from the doorway. There they hung for a few moments, no man anxious to be the first to face the big officer. For they had no knowledge of his blindness.

Then he caught Pathan's voice urging them on.

"Go on, lads! Go on! There won't be much fight left in him!"

At that, a feeling of dismay filled him. It was evident that Pathan was not going to head the attack, and he might die without ever getting his hands on him.

From the irresolute men came a shuffle of feet. Then a man's voice rose—

"Trow de flare into ze hoose."

To the Second Mate the remark suggested a course of action. He threw himself upon a sea-chest, so that his face could be seen from the doorway. He kept perfectly still. If the man threw the flare into the house they would see his bandaged face and think him dead. It might be that the coward Pathan would venture to come into the place—then!

Thud! Something struck the floor near him.

He kept his eyes shut. He could see no light; but the smell of burning paraffin was plain in his nostrils. He listened intently and seemed to catch the sound of stealthy footsteps. Abruptly, a voice just without the doorway shouted:

"They're both dead! Both of 'em!"

"What?"

It was Pathan's voice. He heard the noise of booted feet approaching at a run. They hesitated one instant on the threshold, then came within, and a surge of barefoot pads followed. The booted feet came to a stand not two yards away.

For an instant there was silence, a bewildered, awestruck silence. Pathan's voice broke it.

"My God!" he said. "My God!"

Immediately afterward he screamed, as the huge, blood-stained form of the big officer hurled itself upon him. There were cries from the men, and a pell-mell rush to escape. Someone fell upon the flare and extinguished it.

There was a shivering silence. It was filled abruptly by the beginning of a sobbing entreaty from Pathan. This shrilled suddenly into a horrid screaming. The men were no longer trying for the doorway, for the Second Mate had got between it and them. They could see him indistinctly against the moonlight beyond. He was flogging the steel side of the house with something. Beyond the hideous thudding of the blows, the house was silent.

One of the crouched men, tortured to madness, threw a belaying-pin. The next instant the Second Mate hurled himself among them. He had the battered steel door for a weapon, and the edge of it was as a ploughshare amidst soil.

Amid the cries of the men, the side of the house rang out a dull thunder beneath the weight of some blind, misdirected blow.

Most of the men escaped upon their hands and knees, creeping out behind the man who smote and smote. They got to the forecastle upon all fours, too terrified and bewildered even to get to their feet. There, in the darkness, behind closed and barred doors, they sat and sweated, in company of those who had hesitated to enter the house.

Presently the ship was quiet.

The berserker rage eased out of the Second Mate and he perceived that the house was empty, and the mutiny truly ended. He cast the heavy steel door clanging through the open doorway out on to the main-deck, a dripping testimony of a man's prowess against enormous odds.

He stood a moment, breathing heavily. Then, remembering, he wheeled round in the darkness to where, in the gloom of the upper bunk, the girl lay shivering, with her hands pressed tightly over her ears.

He caught her up in his great arms, with the one word, "Come!" and stepped through the open doorway into the moonlight, the fallen door ringing under his tread. Then, Master of his ship, he carried her aft to the cabin.

A Fight with a Submarine

YOU DON'T BELIEVE IN miracles, don't you? Well, I do, and I'll tell you why, if you care to listen. A miracle happened to me this last October, out in the North Sea. Oh, I'm not telling you whereabout, nor where we were bound for; but I don't mind telling you we got the shock of our lives when a darned brute of a German submarine came alongside of us, shoved up a quick-firer out of a sort of hatch foreside of the conning-tower, and batted a shell bang across our bows.

Not being either a hero or a man-of-war, but just an average aggregate of flesh and blood and bones born and bred in the ways of common sense in the port of St. John's, Newfoundland, I rang the telegraph to stop, pretty smart; and when our way was off us, she slid alongside near enough to talk, and the officer in command, a snorty sort of person, sung out to me to lower our dinghy, with a couple of men, and pull across to her.

"Do you want me?" I asked.

"No!" he said in English good enough to go down anywhere. "Stay where you are, Cap'n, and keep order. If anyone starts any funny business, just understand I'll sink you before you can say your prayers. Be smart with that boat. I want it."

Well, of course, I sent the boat, and she came back in about ten minutes with three thumping, greasy, great Germans, and a cute little dumpling of an officer, partly gold lace, and the rest bad manners and thirst.

First thing he did was to go for the manifest, and the second was a bottle of "Black and White." The third thing was to start in on my own special brand of cigars, and the fourth was *to tell me to keep out of my own cabin!* Suffering Jehoshaphat! But the little brute was nearer Kingdom Come that same moment than he'll ever guess, till he gets there! They say there's something in the blood of Newfoundlanders that makes it boil at the thought of the most tepid insult. And this wasn't an affront of the brand marked "extra mild."

However, I kept the stopper on, and shoved my gear into the First Mate's room, and he went into the Second's and pushed poor old Welby into the bottom bunk. I felt sorry for Welby, but I guess we all had our troubles!

They were busy all day—the German thieves, I mean—carting stuff across in the boat. They took charge entirely, and I was told if I showed on deck they'd shove daylight through me. The same with the two Mates. And I understood from the Steward, who was allowed to go along the decks to the galley, that the men had been told to keep in the fo'cas'le.

I couldn't quite twig what the whole game was. It was something more than stocking their larder and filling up with oil from the Engineers' store-room. They kept us going at about quarter speed, I judge, and from the tell-tale in the saloon I could see they'd altered the course a couple of points more to the norrard. There was something ugly in view, and I'd have given a whole lot to shove a spoke in their wheel and mess up their little plans.

Well, after thinking it over I began to get the beginnings of a plan in the back of my mind that would start something on the enemy, and I went to call the Mate to talk things over with me.

"Come into my room, Mister Belston," I said. "I've been thinking this confounded business over, and I've got an idea."

The Mate climbed out of the top bunk, and the Second Mate, Mister Welby, shoved his head out of the bottom one.

"Not you, Mister Welby," I told him. "If we have a crowd in my room that fat German hog'll get smelling seven kinds of rats, and that won't do. The Mate will tell you what I've got to say when he comes back."

I went back to my room, and the Mate followed me in his shirt and trousers.

And then, you know, I'd no more got the business opened up to Mister Belston when the Steward knocked gently on the door and shoved his head in.

"Sir," they're talking German. The submarine's right alongside, an' him—" he jerked his thumb over his shoulder to mean the officer who had been put in charge of my ship, "—he's gassing back. I been listening through the pantry port-hole, only I don't know no German. You do, don't you, Sir? It's dark in there, an' maybe you'd hear something as would be useful—"

"Good man, Steward," I said, interrupting him. "Get along and keep cave for me. Mister Belston, you stay here, quiet. I'll be back in a minute."

I went across to the pantry, which was dark, and told the Steward to get out and keep watch in the hood companion-way, and let me know the moment he saw anyone coming along to come below. Then I shut myself into the pantry so that the light from the saloon would not show my through the port. After that I got close up to the port-hole, and started to listen for all I was worth.

The submarine was lying within two fathoms of our side, and the conning-tower was almost level with my face. The night was absolutely still and calm, and I could hear every word. What was more to the point, I'd picked up enough German in my schooling days in St. John's to be able to understand all that was said; and what they were saying was just plain life and death to every man aboard, and to others as well.

Of all the cold-blooded brutes that ever sailed God's seas, they were the—well, judge for yourself, then you'll realise just how much chance any of us had got of being alive the following night, unless I could start in and work a small miracle.

The officer in the mouth of the conning-tower did the bulk of the talking. He was the boss. What he said I can put briefly. Here's the point. They were planning to use the old Narcissus as a stalking-horse. They'd got inside information from some darned traitor who traded into Hartlepool, so it seemed, and was the Mate of a small coaling steamer in the Dutch trade. He gets hold of information from a German bum "agency" ashore, and peddles it round to those beggars on the trip to Holland. My oath! I swore if I ever came out alive there'd be a new Mate to that steamer, and he'd make a hole in the sea just big enough to hold him through Eternity!

They'd got the news from this chap that a Battle Squadron was going North, and they were aiming to take my ship right across their track and lie hid under our lee until the squadron was quite close up to us. Then they were going to slip out and bust off all the torpedoes they'd got into the middle of the fleet; and they'd reckoned they were absolutely certain to get at least a couple of our Dreadnoughts. They simply gloated about it, until I was ready to let loose with my automatic and make one less, at any rate, of that little lot. And then came the final thing—the limit— The *it* of German milk of human kindness and decency!

Listen! As soon as the English Battle Fleet was sighted, *we* were to be shot, so as to ensure that there would be no danger of our giving any sort of warning signal at the crucial moment. Wasn't that just German! Efficiency gone mad! And, as all extremes are bound to do, defeating its own ends; for that last detail, when I told it to the Mates, made them ready to go right slam down into the hell and pluck the Kaiser himself by the moustache out of the biggest pot of brimstone there. I guess when men know they've got to die they ain't exactly particular what risks they run to get a chance of living and getting even. That may be Irish; but, by the Lord, it's like a lot of Irishisms I've heard from Paddys toiling in the mists on the Great Newfoundland Banks; it's plain sense!

Of course, all this fresh news altered my half-cooked plans, and I just loaded the Mate up with all I'd learnt, and sent him back into his room to prime the Second Mate, and make him as ready for murder and sudden death as the two of us were already!

Well, we held a War Council later and settled something that meant quick death or sudden delivery for the whole lot of us.

First of all I told the Steward to keep on the watch, and to start coughing the moment he heard anyone coming. Then I went over the whole plan again, and told the Mates exactly what to do.

They were to lash me up in my bunk and gag me. As soon as I heard the other officer come below with the man who seemed always to attend him wherever he went, I would groan in such a way as to call their attention. They'd come to see what was the matter, and the two Mates who would be waiting were to bash them on the head with a couple of bootjacks (excellent "bashers" are bootjacks too!) and tie them up. The bashing was not meant to break anything, but just to daze them a bit and make them easy to handle.

Then they would haul the dinghy alongside, shove some grub and water into her, and take the German officer and one or two of his men and "get."

"You see," I finished up, "the submarine will be bound to go searching for you as soon as she finds you're gone; otherwise, if you get ashore with your men, or reach a patrol, it'll be all U.P. with her little plan to use us to stalk our ships. And while she's gone, why I guess we'll coax our old engines to take us away out of his before she gets back. And she'll never sink us *before* going, because she'll look to catch you and be back in three or four hours, and if we're sunk, well, we'd be no use as a stalking-horse—eh?"

The whole thing worked excellently next day. I heard the officer and his companion (a sort of senior seaman, I fancy, who was apparently dry-nursing him!) come down into the saloon. Then I groaned, and I heard them stand a moment to listen. I groaned again, and they came to my cabin door which was opened and looked in over each other's shoulder, as you might say.

"Mein Gott!" said the officer.

"Mein Gott!" said the man. Then I saw my two Mates behind them, and the two bootjacks got in a useful thump apiece on their thick German heads.

Exactly ten minutes later the two of them were lashed up solidly and gagged, and laid on the floor of my cabin to groan in unison with me. We all groaned.

My two Mates and the Steward went on deck in search for the two other men. One was at the wheel, and the other was sleeping in my chart-house. Both got bashed, and lashed up and gagged. Then the Second Mate took the wheel, while the Mate went forrard and routed out a man to steer, whilst he and the Second Mate got busy on other things.

The dinghy was towing astern. They hauled her up quietly and shoved Armours' tinned beef, water, whisky, hard biscuit, Dutch cheese and other etceteras into her. Then they came below and carried the German officer on deck and lowered him quietly into the dinghy. They collared also the two German sailormen and lowered them on top of their officer.

Then they came down and told me that they were going, and just how many sorts of fool I had been to refuse to come with them and to threaten to prevent them from leaving the ship. They said they would steer West-Sou'west, which should take them into the Firth, and there hand their prisoners over and start a warship off to us. After that they elevated thumbs of insolence to their separate noses and therewith departed, leaving the German leading seaman on the floor of the cabin to keep me company.

Seven hours and a half later the people in the submarine came aboard. They must have smelled a rat. Perhaps they hailed us and go no answer; and then, when they sang out for the dinghy, well, there was no dinghy. Result, I guess they came right in along side of us, and shoved half-a-dozen men aboard with rifles.

When they found the German leading seaman and me they cut us both loose, and then started to rough-house me; but the German who had been lying on my cabin floor explained all *he* knew, and they had no excuse to keep on taking it out of me. All the same, they were pretty beastly! I guess it's just in the blood, and they can't help it.

Well, as soon as they'd got all the details they put a hustle on. They shoved a handy-billy tackle down through the engine-room skylight, and what do you think the cunning devils did! They lifted off the lead of the high-pressure cylinder and lowered it aboard their own craft.

"Good Lord!" I thought to myself, "that snuffs out the cut-and-run plan!" But naturally I said nothing.

They weren't more than half an hour on this job, and after that they rummaged the flag locker and took every bit of our bunting. It was pretty plain that they meant that we should have no chance to fly signals during the few hours they expected to be away in chase of the boat. I got hoping that these signs meant they would leave no one aboard on guard; but I soon saw I was mistaken; for after holding a bit of a pow-wow on my poop, the commanding officer cleared off and left two armed Germans aboard under the control of the man who had been lying on the floor of my cabin.

"Cap'n," sang out the Commander of the submarine, after he'd got aboard his own craft again, "I'm trusting you to keep order while I'm gone. If you don't, well, my men know what to do, and there'll not be one of you left alive by the time I get back. So, I'd be wise, if I were you, Cap'n."

"I'll be wise, right enough," I told him. "I guess wisdom's best policy just now!"

"At a premium, Cap'n," he said, and called down the speaking-tube to go ahead. I could hear him laughing for a minute afterwards as the submarine glided like a fish into the darkness.

I leant over the pop rail and watched her for a bit. She was evidently not going more than half speed, and I guessed the German officer was anxious not to get too far before daylight lest he should overshoot the boat in the dark.

You see, he'd got the course the boat would steer from the German sailorman who had been on the floor of my cabin when my two Mates made so many unnecessary explanations!

I grinned to myself; but all the same, I was deuced anxious; for unless I could bottle up those three armed Germans, and unless Mac could see some way to do the impossible, and unless I could carry out another notion or two of mine, why, I couldn't see anything but a mess, and a bad mess, inside the next twelve hours or so, with good-bye to all hopes of ever seeing the good port of St. John's again at the end of it. For whether the submarine found the boat or not we could expect her back before the day was half through. You see, she'd never miss a chance go get her torpedoes off at the ships she was laying for.

Anyway, the first problem was how to get rid of those three big Germans.

Six hours later I went on deck, but the leading seaman person wanted to show he was Lord of Creation and ordered me below without bothering to be polite about it. And because I didn't exactly jump to do his bidding he gave me a poke in the ribs with the butt of his rifle just to make his meaning clear. It was! And I went!

In a way I was rather pleased. I felt more like killing a man or two than I did. I never was much good at the cold-blooded act. But now! Well, you try a German rifle-butt in your ribs if you want the edge taken off some of your finer scruples. It's effective!

I sat a bit in the saloon and smoked, then I thought I would risk going through the alley-way to Mac's room and have a word with him. When I got there, however, Mac was not in his bunk, and I knew he must be down in the engine-room. So I thought I'd risk a bit more and follow him there. I did.

But on the fiddley I stopped; for things were happening, right there before me.

Mac was up at the open head of the high-pressure cylinder, with his rule and a pair of dividers in one hand and a piece of chalk in the other. At the moment, however, he was not taking measurements, but looking up at the engine-room skylight. As I looked up also I heard someone say from the engine-room below:

"Vat yoous do mit dat cylingder. Gome away dis von momengt, or tead I shood yoous!"

"Two of 'em, begowb!" I heard Mac mutter as he stared down now into the engine-room below.

There were certainly two of them! One, the leading seaman, with his head shoved under the leaf of the open skylight, and the other, a big brute, who must have gone down the engine-room stairway and entered through the stokehold doorway.

"Get away from that cylinder," said the German in the skylight, speaking such perfect enough English, or rather American, that it seemed to carry me straight back home. "Get away right now, or I'll sure lead you up solid so you'd sink a thousand miles. I will, by Josh!"

He began to pass his rifle in through the opening of the skylight; and right then Mac acted.

"Ye'll do phwat!" he said; for he's an Irish Mac, not a Scottie. "Ye'll do phwat!"

He said never another word, but let fly with one of the big holding-down nuts from the cylinder-head. The nut took the German in the chest with a thump like a drum, and the man went white and gasped a moment. Then, deliberately, and before I could conceive he would really do such a thing, he shot poor old Mac through the middle of his forehead, and Mac flopped a moment soft and quiet over the edge of the cylinder. Then rolled with a dull, sickening thump to the floor of the engine-room.

Then I was awake, as you might say. There's one thing in favour of an automatic; it's quicker in the change-speed gear, and I drilled the German's forehead with two .38 holes, one above each eye—one for payment and the other for good measure.

He hung there, dead; half of him one side of the skylight-coaming, and the other half the other. But I'd no time to think about him; for something split away a great piece out of the peak of my cap, and the same moment the engine-room loomed again to a rifle-shot. The German down below had loosed off at me.

However, I'd no need to bother about him. The Second Engineer and two of the Stokers got him on the run, and what they did to him was sufficient and a bit over. Only, of course, Mac was a good boss and well liked, and I can't say I blame them.

I heard someone running along the after well-deck then, and I stepped out with my automatic in my fist. It was the third German, and the moment he saw me with the automatic in my hand he let drive. So did I. It was a draw, I should fancy, for we both missed!

Before he could work the bolt I let drive again, and got him through the right forearm. But he was plucky, right enough. He snapped the bolt back and forward and fired from his hip. The bullet took away the whole of my right coat-pocket without touching me. It's queer what tricks a bullet will play at times.

I fired again, and got him in the left hand, and at that he ran all the way after to the poop, crying aloud with the pain of it. I was sorry for the beggar; but he was still dangerous, for he had taken his rifle with him; and the next thing I knew, he snapped off a shot at me from behind one of the after ventilators.

He missed me by a mile. I guessed he was shaking too much, and I felt he couldn't hit me now, except by a fluke; so I just rushed him, for I was sick of the killing, though I knew the brutes would not have hesitated to shoot the whole crowd if we hadn't got them going right from the first.

He managed another shot as I ran at him, which was the best he made, for it nicked the left side of my neck, and I bled like a pig; but it was nothing more than a shallow gouge; and the following instant I'd taken the rifle from him and he was sitting on his head.

Afterwards I whistled for the Steward, and the two of us bandaged him up and carried him down and locked him in the spare cabin on the starboard side. Then I got busy.

I had poor old Mac put in his berth, and the two Germans were shoved on the forehatch under some canvas. Then I went for the Second and Third Engineers and told them what I wanted doing.

It seems there is an old high-pressure cover in the store-room that has been there for many a voyage, and Mac had been planning to make a try at fitting it on in place of the other, so that we could get up steam and be away before the submarine returned.

We got the cover out of the store-room, and while the Engineers tried it for the fit, I had all my deck hands running around on a special job of my own. The old packet fairly hummed with energy let loose.

"Well?" I asked a bit later when I went back to the engine-room. "How is it, you two? Can it be made to fit?"

"Yes, Sir," said the Second. "All the bolt holes don't come in to the same places, and we'll have to drill four new ones, and we'll have to pack her up, but I reckon we can do it, only it'll take time." I nodded, and left them to get at it; for they are good men, both of them, and I knew they'd do their darndest. But, as you can guess, I was anxious as a maggot on a hot brick. However, I'd business of my own to do, and I did it, and between whiles I paid visits to the engine-room, and I'll own to a prayer or two; for there would be no sort of mercy shown us once the submarine came back, as jolly well I knew.

Two hours passed, and I'd paid three visits to the engine-room. The Donkey-man and two Stokers were taking one-minute spells at a geared hand-drill which the last two engineers were tending in a pretty earnest sort of way.

The fourth time I went they'd got the four holes drilled out by hand, and a weary job it had been with the poor tools they'd got, and the cylinder cover, of course, proving to be extra hard stuff, just for sheer cussedness.

The sixth time I went along all hands were busy, working like madmen, with sheet copper and cold chisels cutting gout packing to raise the cylinder head, which was not enough domed to give sufficient clearance to the newer-pattern piston.

"Mister Melbray," I said to the Second Engineer, "it's four hours and twenty minutes since that darned submarine went away looking for the dinghy. I guess we can look for her back any time inside the next hour or so; an' if she finds us here like this it'll be bye-bye for all of us. How long do you reckon you'll be now before you can put steam through your gadgets?"

"Another half-hour, maybe, Cap'n" he told me; "an' even then, it's God help us, I'm thinking, if we can't make a good steam-tight job of this. She'll have to do all she knows to get anywhere before that darned submarine be on top of us, if we don't get shifting before she gets near us. What do you reckon those U-submarines can do on the surface, Sir?"

"The Lord knows," I told him. "No one knows, really; but I understand they're supposed to run up to fifteen knots in fine weather, that is."

He shrugged his shoulders in a sort of hopeless fashion, but he never stopped working for a moment.

"Give us another twenty or thirty minutes, Cap'n," he said at last. "I'll try her then; and I guess we'll blow something adrift before we let them come up on us."

I went away again. I had sent a man aloft to keep a lookout all around, but there were no signs of the submarine; though, as a bit of a breeze had sprung up, she wouldn't be so easy to see in the broken water if she were running with only her periscope out.

I walked the poop, pretty anxiously, for the next ten minutes; then I got more philosophical, and decided the whole job wasn't worth indigestion. So I came below and had a smoke. At the end of the half-hour I walked forward to the engine-room and shoved my head in the skylight.

"Well?" I asked.

"Just going to put the steam through her, Cap'n," said the Second Engineer.

He was sweating, and the and the Third Engineer and the Donkey-man were heaving away pretty fierce on a four-foot spanner, compressing the sheets of copper packing to a steam-tight "consistency."

And then, from my man aloft, came the yelp of:

"Submarine on the port beam, Sir! Submarine on the port beam! She's dead on the beam, Sir; about four miles off, I reck'n. ....*She ain't got the boat!*" He yelled that out with triumph. Then, in a different voice: " 'Less they've sunk her!"

"That's all right, my lad!" I said to myself. "Don't worry."

You see, when the two Mates explained their proposed course with such exact detail in my cabin, well—they were remembering that they were going to leave one German behind just for the one purpose of passing on that bit of information. I need hardly say that the boat steered a very different course indeed! That would have been one comfort, whatever else happened.

I shoved my head in the engine-room again to see how they were managing. As I did so, the engine began to turn over slowly. The Third was at the main steam-valve giving her steam gently, and the Second and the Donkey-man were standing anxiously by the high-pressure to see how the packing held the steam. It held fine, and the Second grinned up at me as pleased as Punch.

"Good man," I said, and pulled out my head and bellowed for a man to go to the wheel; for the old *Narcissus* had started to forge slowly ahead.

I went to the side and grinned down like a delighted maniac at the water moving past our side as our speed increased. Then there was a yell from the man aloft.

"They'm shootin', Sir! They'm shootin'!"

As he yelled I heard the scream of a high-velocity shell from the submarine's six-pounder, and cr-rash, a regular hole was bust in our steel bulwarks on the port side about thirty feet foreside of me, for the shell struck there and burst, the bits cracking and thudding viciously all over the place. I should never have imagined that six pounds of iron would have gone so far in the spreading line. It sounded like half a hundred-weight.

No one was hurt, and I made one jump for the bridge and rang the telephone for full speed ahead.

"Shove your helm over hard-a-port!" I shouted at the man at the wheel.

As the old *Narcissus* started to pay off I saw a flash aboard the submarine, now about two and a half miles away, or perhaps a bit less. And then, almost in the same instant, the queer, beastly "meeee" whine of the high-velocity shell crowding the wide miles into a couple of seconds. "Mee-owww," it went, changing its note in a queer fashion as it came for us. Then "cr-rash" again, and the whole top of the engine-room skylight seemed to fly up in a shower of glass splinters.

I grabbed the speaking-tube to the engine-room.

"Anyone hurt?" I called.

After a few moments the Third Engineer's voice answered:

"It got the Second, Sir. He's dead. The engine's all right, though," he said. He sounded calm enough, and I sent a man for the Steward to go down to the engine-room and see if the Second was quite knocked out. Then I turned and looked for the submarine again. She was right astern now and seemed to be gaining only slowly. As I stared I saw the flash of the gun again, and then once more came the beastly whine of the shell.

"Bang!" it struck the middle steel bridge-stanchion which supports the center of the bridge. This is a stout three-inch stanchion of solid steel. The shell gouged away a piece as easily as if it had been putty and burst with a stunning crash direction under the bridge. Two of the middle planks were blown up on end, and in three places fragments of shell struck clean up through the deck of the bridge penetrating right through the heavy planks. One of these fragments killed the man at the wheel, and I jumped to steady the helm, while I sung out for another man to come aft.

I looked round with a feeling of despair. The whole sea was empty of shipping from horizon to horizon, and I didn't pretend to hide the fact that nothing short of a miracle could save us; for the German wasn't out to coddle us, I could bet on that!

The Steward came up on the bridge and reported that the Second Engineer was headless and therefore unmistakably dead. I told him to give a hand to carry the dead Helmsman down on to the main-deck hatch, and then bring a flag and cover him. I guessed we'd be gone inside twenty minutes; but we might as well be decent.

I was just beginning to get sentimental over the old folks at home and saying a last farewell, as it were, to all my pals in Newfoundland I should never see again, when I caught suddenly the "meeee" scream of another shell coming. "Meeee-oww, cr-rash!" ...It ripped a monstrous great chunk out of the funnel, about half of it; and it seemed to me I felt our speed drop right then in that same moment.

Then one, two, three, four...one after the other they loosed off at us as fast as they could work the quick-firer. The air seemed one whining scream as the four shells came "Cr-rash! Cr-rash! Cr-rash! Cr-rash!" The rest of the funnel vanished. The wheel, and the man at it, went in a flying cloud of spokes and torn flesh and clothing, and the aftermast was punched clean through, and the chart-house was wrecked. My Steward was wounded, and I saw one of the deck boys limping along the main-deck.

"Jehoshaphat!" I said; "we're done!" ...I didn't even know I was bleeding all down my face where a shell-splinter had cut me.

Two more shells came Thud! Thud!—dull ugly thumps away aft in the stern of her that told me the Germans had started now to sink us in real earnest. You never saw such deliberate murder!

"Cr-rash!" came another shell, higher this time, and killed the boy who was limping along the deck.

I stared round and round the horizon in despair. I sung out to the man aloft to know whether he could see anything. He simply shook his head in a hopeless, silent sort of way.

I found myself praying aloud in a fierce sort of fashion for a miracle to happen; for nothing but a miracle could save us now.

And suddenly, like the voice of God:

B-A-N-G!

It was coming from somewhere ahead of us on the starboard bow, but precious close.

I raced across to the starboard end of the bridge:

B-A-N-G!

The miracle had happened. A long gray shepe was tearing through the sea, firing as she went.

I was one of our latest submarines that had just bobbed up:

B-A-N-G!

I whipped round with my binoculars and stared at that murdering brute astern.

"Flash!"

I was just in time to see her go straight down into Hades with all her devils aboard of her. The shell from the submarine ahead had hit her slap at the base of the conning-tower, and she just simply vanished—went!

No, there was no miracle about it; not if you want to argue. But I don't!

The dinghy was overhauled and my two Mates and the Greaser taken aboard by the submarine, one of our latest type on patrol duty. The poor old *Narcissus* foundered inside of half an hour.

But, by the Lord, I'm a believer in miracles from now onwards.

Revenants
(or Posthumously Published
Stories of the Sea)

Revenants
(or Posthumously Published
Stories of the Sea)

In the Danger Zone

S.S. Futerpe. January 31ˢᵗ, 1918.
Out from Liverpool.

"SUB—MAR—EEN—ON—th' starr—boarrd—boww, Sir!" came
the far-drawn-out hail of the man aloft.

"There she is!" I said, reaching into the box under the rail for my
glasses. What I had expected had happened. "Muster all hands aft, Mr.
Perry," I called to the Second Mate. "I'll take charge."

I walked over to the starboard end of the bridge and took a look
for the submarine. I couldn't spot her at first; but in about half a minute
I could see her three periscopes. She looked to be submerged right
to about the top of her conning-tower. At least I thought I could see
the top of the conning-tower every now and again between the seas.
But it wasn't easy to see.

I guessed that she'd be quite six or seven miles away, and judging
by the fact that her three periscopes were all in a line, she was not
making towards us.

That puzzled me quite a bit, for if she were out sinking helpless
British merchant vessels, why didn't she come for us and get it over? I
couldn't see her making any bones about it. And why was she running
submerged, as if she wanted to keep out of sight? I guessed it was
not likely to be mercy, but plain, hard reason—which is the god the
Germans imagine they worship, poor devils!

Anyway, as you can suppose, I took a look around for something
that might account of their actions, from a Germanic point of view.
Then I understood. There was a big Ballett Line vessel coming down
from the norrard, and the submarine was keeping out of sight lest the
big Ballett Liner should alter her course. It was clear to me that the
submarine was plainly aiming to get the two of us, without having to
do any superfluous chasing.

However, I wasted less than five seconds, once I'd realised the
situation. I made one dive for my chart-house, and banged out a

427

warning to her on my wireless (my own personal plant). My word, but she didn't require two tellings.... By the time I got out onto the bridge again she had ported her helm, and was heading to the East'ard; and, by Jove, the submarine didn't take long to show her little plan; for she started after her. She knew all right that we were a slow packet, and she could pick us up any time she wanted; but the other was a big 19-knot vessel and carried passengers as well as cargo, and in addition she was a whole heap more valuable a vessel—three sound Germanic reasons for sinking her as soon as possible.

However, with the start she had, I was fairly confident that the submarine could never come near enough to her to do any damage, and I knew that as soon as the German officer realised this for himself, back would come the brute and take it out of us. And, to be frank, I've always thought the cold-water method of going to heaven distinctly unattractive!

"The men are mustered aft, Sir," said the Second Mate at this moment.

"Very good," I answered, and I stepped to the front of the bridge. "Men," I said, "there's a German submarine away out on the beam. I've no doubt she means to try to sink us. There's one of the Ballett Line vessels away to the Norrard; but we can't look for help from her, and I've just warned her off. I guess we've got to help ourselves. And we're going to put up a fight before that German water-rat gets us!"

There was quite a healthy little fighting yelp from them at that. They're a crowd of Britishers, thank goodness! A man knows where he is with a lot of grousing Cockneys and Scotsmen. They grumble like blazes every time they get a chance; but when the tight time comes they're right there. I guess the right time had come right then!

"Any of you men been in the Naval Reserve?" I asked.

"Me, Sir," said a big fellow, named Gatley.

"Good!" I told him. "Anyone else?"

But not another one of them had ever been anything but plain shellbacks all their lives.

"Well," I said, "I guess I'll have to manage with Gatley.

I turned to the First Mate:

"Mister Alfred," I said, "turn all hands to number three hatch, and break out those cases marked machinery. You'll remember I told you to have them stored right in the mouth of number three."

"Very good, Sir" said the First Mate, and carried the crowd off.

The chief thing to do was to take advantage of the extra time we should have to make every possible preparation to fight off that murdering under-water devil, away there on the beam. It wasn't a bit of use trying to run for it, except to gain time. Our top speed, with a Stoker cussing on the safety valve, was 12.9; and I guessed the big submarine would be able to manage an easy eighteen, on the surface.

No, what we'd got to do, was to put the helm over, as I'd already done, get up all the steam possible and run to the best of our ability, so as to gain an extra hour or so. For the rest, it was trust in God, and do our number one best. I certainly had no notion of doing anything else.

"Well, George," I heard the Chief Engineer saying from the foot of the starboard bridge-ladder. "What's all this about a German submarine?"

"Come up, Mac," I told him. "Things are looking ugly, and we've got to put our heads together."

Mac came up, rubbing the sleep out of his eyes; for he's a worker, and stands his own watch every night, instead of trusting to his Third. He came up now, buttoning his waistcoat; and I gave him the details.

"I'll start my bucks right on the job this blessed moment, George," he said, as soon as he'd got my plan. He looked as nearly joyful as I've ever seen him. "I get your notion; and I think it's got sense to it. I'll take charge of my lads on deck, and I'll keep Mister Alec below. He'll make those Stokers sweat!"

The last idea seemed to give him particular pleasure, and he started off at a run; but stopped on the port steps to fire back a question:

"Ye don't think they'll try torpedoes, George?"

"No," I said. "Torpedoes cost quite some money, as you should know, Mac. And I don't suppose even these new super-subs will carry more than about twenty. They're luxuries kept for special occasions and war craft. We'll get the humble but quite effective German fourteen-pound shell in our ribs. She may, of course, carry a twenty-two-pounder; but I have my doubts, Mac."

"I'm thinking the size needn't worry us," I heard Mr. MacCall saying to himself, as he went down the steps. "A fourteen-pound shell in the right place will send us all to hell, I'm thinking, as quick as a four-inch!"

"Mr. Perry," I sung out, over the bridge rail, "come up here and take the bridge for a few minutes. Keep your glasses on the submarine."

"Very good, Sir," said the Second; and I went down then to see how the First Mate and his gang were getting on at number three hatch.

I found things humming, and told the Mate to send for Chips and get the three cases marked C_2, C_3 and C_4 opened in the hatch. That would save rigging gear to hoist them out.

"While Chips is busting these cases," I told him, "take some of the hands, Mister, and roust out some of that dunnage from the forepeak. There's some six-by-six timber there, and we shall want them in a bit."

"Now then, Chips," I said, when he came along with his tools, "get going smartly now!"

I jumped down into the hatch myself, and grabbed a hammer and a chisel. Inside of five minutes we had the lid of the long case, marked C_2, lifted clean off. And there she was, resting sweetly in her chocks.

Gatley, the A.B. who had been in the Naval Reserve, let out a yelp.

"Jeerusalem! She's a pom-pom! That's to say she's got the build of one, to my eye; but she's mighty short in the barrel."

"Come and have a look at her," I told him, and he jumped into the hatch and "felt" the gun over.

"She's a bit new to me, Cap'n," he said. "I reckon she's a two-pounder, or maybe three. But she's that short in the barrel she'll never throw far. She'll never punch through the top of yon submarine, Sir, not in a month of Sundays; not 'nless she were right close up. And I don't reckon she'll come up near to be plugged. She'll put us down and out a couple miles away."

"Jove!" I said. "I believe you're right, Gatley. But, anyway, she's the best we can manage at short notice!"

And then, like a flash, a plan struck me. I vaulted out over the coaming of the hatch and ran aft to the chart-house.

"She's rigged her wireless, Sir," said the Second Mate, as I came up to him.

I nodded.

"Get me the code book," I said, interrupting him. "Toggle these hoists together and get the first one hoisted as soon as she gives up trying to overhaul the liner—see?"

This was the message:

"Carrying bullion. One hundred thousand pounds. Anxious. Are you British?"

The Second Mate looked a bit puzzled for a moment. Then he grabbed round for my plan.

"That's a smart notion," he said, reaching for the flag halyards. "You're betting that he'll not care to sink us till he's got that fancy bullion.... Is that it, Sir?"

"Largely," I told him. "You see, Mister, the Mate and I have just discovered a gun in a case in number three hatch. But Gatley, that old Naval Reserve man, says it's too short in the barrel to carry far, and I guess he's right. Unless we can coax that darned submarine close up to us, before she starts cutting loose on us, well, I guess we shall be in a hole—that'll reach the bottom of the Atlantic. That gave me the notion to try this dodge. She can't know that I wirelessed the other packet about her; for, as you've just said, she's only now rigged her own. I'm going to pretend I *think* she's British, but am keeping out of her way till I'm sure. I expect they'll think that I've got softening of the brain; but I don't mind, as long as they don't think I've got anything more dangerous! They're bound to feel interested in all that case! A hundred thousand, I think I said. Better make it five hundred thou, while we're on the job. She'll feel bound to have a try for that little lot. It'd break my heart, let alone a German's, to sink five hundred thousand golden quidlets. Well, when he comes to get it, I guess we'll hand him something so hard as cash any day—eh? That's if we can only drop across some ammunition to fit the gun."

The Second Mate smiled a little when I said that last bit. He's sailed with me before, I'd better mention, and he's a smart lad. But he made no comment, like a wise man.

"Now then, Mister," I said, "stand by ready with that lot and get 'em strung out when I give you the word. But don't mention them to Mister Andrews. I haven't time to keep making explanations. The Second grinned again, and I bolted off down to get hold of Mac.

"I've had to change my plans, Mac," I told him. "We've got the gun uncovered, but she's a short brute, and she'll never punch a hole through anything unless it's right close up to her."

I explained to him my latest dodge, and told him just how I was rearranging various details.

"Instead of keeping that brute astern all the time now, Mac, by running for it, while we tried long pots," I told him, "I'll have to port the helm a bit, as soon as we're ready, so as to let her drop in easily from the starboard beam after she's given up chasing the other packet. She'll probably put a shot across our bows then, and if that doesn't stop us, smack will go your engines, Mac!"

Mac swore suddenly as the reality of the whole beastly business hit him.

"What you'd best do," I went on, "is to take those six-by-six timbers the Mate's routing out and shove them up on the starboard side of your engines. Then shove in some hatches across them, on edge and put your trimmers and Stokers on the job of filling in the space between them and the ship's side with coal—as much as you can pack in. That way you may save the engines, and, please God the powers that be, we shall have a good use for 'em yet!"

Mac approved of my plan and went off at a good lick, and I ran down on to the main-deck to tackle number three hatch again. The other two cases marked C$_3$ and C$_4$ had been broken open. C$_3$ contained the mountings and shield for the gun, and C$_4$ held a thousand rounds of ammunition, which Gatley was examining curiously.

"Well?" I said, "what is it?"

"New to me, Sir," he replied. "But it looks good stuff. They're mighty long shells—considering the bore. They must weigh a matter of nigh five pound each. I reckon, if we can get 'er to come near enough, I could plug 'er; though you'll remember no man can swear how he's a-goin' to shoot with a gun he's never tried out."

"Quite so," I agreed. "We're just going to do our best, Gatley.... Now then, all of you, bear a hand here and lift this gun—altogether now. Steady!"

Half an hour later we had her mounted in my chart-house. The Chief came up himself to give us a hand in assembling her, and taking it all round, we made a smart job if it, I reckon. She was mounted just inside the starboard doorway, and by opening the door she commanded all the sea to starboard.

I had Chips spike the stand down to the deck of the chart-house, and while he was doing this, I turned all hands on to the job of shifting several tons of corrugated galvanised iron roofing from number four hatch. We were carrying five hundred tons of this, and I remembered it suddenly.

I was packed in quarter-ton slabs, with tarpaper between, and I felt as pleased as a pig with a new hind leg when I remembered it. I sent for Mac and suggested that he shove some loads of it down the ash-hoists, and stow it between the starboard boiler and the side of the ship. It should keep anything out, if only he got enough of it packed around.

Mac was positively ecstatic with delight at the notion, for he'd been worrying about his boilers all the time.

Meanwhile, I had all my deck-hands lumping it up amidships and storing it around the chart-house—all except the doorways, and these I protected as much as possible by laying the stuff down on its side, so as to protect the base of the gun—not to mention my legs!

When I'd enough of the stuff packed around the house to keep out a modest fifteen-inch shell, I put one of our mooring-chains round and round the lot waist high, and set it up taut with a handy-billy tackle to hold the lot in place. It was quite a job getting in and out of the chart-house! Finally, to hide my patent armour-plate, I made the hands spread the poop awning over the top of the chart-house, as if to dry, so that it hung down and covered everything except the upper half of the starboard door, which I meant to keep closed until the last moment, so as to have the gun hid.

Then I made everyone turn-to and give Mac a hand to finish getting his engines and boilers protected, and just as Mac sung out that we could do no more, unless it was pray harder than he was doing, which he didn't think possible, Mr. Perry, whom I'd told to stay on the deck bridge, sent down word that the Ballett liner was almost out of sight, and the submarine seemed to have given up the chance and be steering for us at full speed.

I ran up on deck to the bridge.

"Get those flag-hoists up," I said. "I'm not going to use the wireless. He'll ask too many questions, and I may get tripped and make him suspicious. If he notices the aerials he may think it's broken down, and that we're forced to use the flag-hoists instead. And, of course, he'll never answer you.

"All you men on deck!" I said; "get down into number four hold out of the way. Stow that galvanised iron round you. You'll be safe down there. If I whistle, come up on the run. The Steward will serve out grog to you. You've worked well, men. Now get a move on you, my lads. Take a chain-hook each, or anything hefty you can find, and nurse it till you hear from me. Don't smoke.... Gatley, I shall want you in the chart-house."

"Aye, aye, Sir," he said, and went. Then I turned to Mac and gave him some final instructions that made his eyes shine like razors.

"George! I'd do it, if I was to die next minute!" he said. "The murdering brutes! You leave it to me. But I'll look to you to give the word."

"I'll blow my whistle twice," I said. "Then you'll know what to do!"

I left him bellowing orders to his "black squad," and raced up to the chart-house.

The next hour held life or death for every man of us. And I meant it to be LIFE!

"I'll take the bridge," I told Andrews. "You'd better stay. I may want you. There's that Zilchrist at the wheel. I fancy he's got nerve enough to stick here till I tell him to shunt. So I guess we're all right at present....Mr. Perry, you get into my chart-house with Gatley and stand by to lend him a hand. Mac's sending me up the Second Engineer to stand by handy, in case anything goes wrong with the gun. Keep the port door open for the Mate and me, in case we have to do a hefty bunk for shelter.... Got your revolvers?"

"Yes, Sir," replied both men, and hauled them out to show me.

"That's all right," I said, "but mind, *no* shooting until I give the word. If we bungle this job it's going to be Kingdom-Come for all of us inside the next forty or fifty minutes, so go wisely!"

When I got back to the bridge I reached for my glasses, meaning to take a look around to locate the submarine again, for I'd long ago ordered the lookout down from aloft.

But there was no need now for glasses to spot the brute. She was less than two miles away, fully unsubmerged.

I saw now that she had two conning-towers, with a narrow platform or deck reaching between them, well up above the sea. There were about a dozen men on this platform, and away foreside of the forrard conning-tower there was another bunch of men.

When I got the glasses focused on them I saw that they were busy round a long gun, that looked like a twenty-four or twenty-five pound quick-firer. They were getting ready for their beautiful murder game. I heard my First Mate swear under his breath as he spotted what they were up to. Then, suddenly, he called out:

"Look out, Sir!"

I had seen the same thing. They had swung the gun around until it looked to be pointing right at us. Curiously enough, I had a feeling it would hit the Mate, and it was plain that he felt I was the one in most danger. The psychology of this is curious.

There came a quick, reddish flash, and then we saw that the gun had been trained nowhere at us, but a little ahead of the ship, for a shot struck the sea, about twenty fathoms in front of our bows, and kicked the spray fifty feet in the air. Directly afterwards came the intensely harsh, sharp *bang* of the gun, and I knew the fight was on.

"Ring down to 'stop,' Mr. Alfred," I said. "We'll not give the beggar any unnecessary excuse to start messing up the engine-room."

The Mate made one dash at the engine-room telegraph, pumped the lever back and forth quickly, and brought it over to "Stop."

The answer came "by return," and almost in the same instant the screw stopped turning. I guess Mac must have been waiting with his hand on the throttle, for he was mighty anxious not to invite shell practice among his boilers and machinery. And I don't blame him either! A shell in the boilers means just plain hell, with frills.

However, their lordships in the submarine were obviously of the "*must*-be-obeyed" kind, as they proceeded to prove instanter.

You see, naturally, a Bessel carries some headway on her for a couple of minutes after stopping her engines. But the brutes chose to ignore this fact. They had not hoisted the "heave-to" signal before firing the gun, and only now did they do so. The following instant there was a second flash from the gun, and then *crash*, and a blaze of red fire on our starboard side. The whole vessel quivered fore and aft. The devils had fired a live shell slam into our broadside just where they guessed our engines to be.

I rushed to the side and stared over. There was a whopping great tear in our plates, about three feet by two feet, right opposite the engine-room, but fortunately well above the water-line. I guessed however, this had been no attempt to *sink* us; nor should we be sunk until they had been aboard for the "cash" I'd advertised so widely. They were merely being a little masterful.

I ran to the telephone and 'phoned down to Mac, but felt better when I heard that my proposal had saved the engines, for the shell had been held back by the shield of coal which Mac had built at my suggestion.

"The rotten cowards!" said Mr. Alfred. "The darned rotten cowards!"

He was leaning over the end of the bridge beside me, looking almost absurdly wrathful.

"I agree, Mister," I said "and if I'm not mistaken they'll give us one or two more, just for the sheer pleasure of the thing.... Ah! I thought so!"

For as I spoke I caught the flash of the gun again; and then, abruptly, there was a flash all round the capstan on our fo'cas'le head, and a stupendous bang. Then a tremendous splash over on the port side of the ship.

There was a cloud of black smoke for a couple of seconds where the shell had struck, but this cleared, and then I saw we were minus the capstan; also there were some flames starting in the deck of the fo'cas'le head.

"Mister Alfred," I said, "call up a couple of the men and go forrard and shove some water over that fire. Fill all the deck buckets and leave them handy on the main-deck."

"Very good, Sir," said Mr. Alfred, and went away on the job. As he ran down the starboard steps the gun on the big submarine flashed out again, and the next instant they'd punched as pretty a round whole in our foremast as you'd want to see; only, for some reason, the shell never exploded. When the shells were coming I noticed they made a queer noise, like "Meeeee," which always seemed to alter into "Meeeee-oooooo-oooww" as the shell "arrived." Then, of course, the smash of the explosion. Only, in the case of this last shell, it made only a queer, curious sort of "zip" when it struck the mast, and afterwards I saw it strike the water and chuck up a great spout of sea and spray about a mile away to port. But the most curious effect was the way the steel mast acted after the blow. It vibrated just like a gigantic tuning-fork, and the whole ship seemed to thrill and thrum to it for nearly half a minute; but, of course, there was no sound that we could hear.

After the first, second, and third shots (which I fancy were fired partly for sheer pride of marksmanship and partly to cower us to a suitable degree of shaky-kneedness), there were no more gun-shots. Instead, the thumping great submarine came straight for us at top speed, about eighteen knots, I should guess, with the sea one white boil over her fore whaleback. In less than ten minutes she was within half a mile of us, and I can tell you I thrilled—a sort of mad excitement—all down my spine when I realised that in another minute she would be near enough for us to make a bit of a show for our lives; that is, if our gun had any sort of punch at all, and if Gatley really knew his business and could get the hang of her in time to get a shot home where it would do the most good—or harm!

Mr. Alfred was back now from putting out the fire and filling the deck buckets. He had sent the men down number three hatch again, and he came to report about the fore-capstan. I didn't want to hear about the fore-capstan, though, and I didn't wait for the details, but sent him off to my chart-house at a run to tell Gatley not to open fire, whatever he did, until I gave the word.

At first my notion had been to open fire as soon as ever the submarine was well within our range; but now I'd a different plan. I knew they'd be after that "fairy-gold" of ours, and that would mean they'd have to put a boat in the water and come aboard. If they did this, they'd certainly run up quite near, which would be all to our advantage; and also there would be some diversion among them when they were getting the boat out (I know what launching a boat from a submarine means). And in the midst of that same diversion we might get a useful shot or two home before they knew what was troubling their innocent little lives.

On she came, right up to within two hundred fathoms of us; then cut off her spark and came in, with the way she had on her, until she rounded-to, flat on our starboard beam, less than fifty fathoms away.

Then came the next move, as smart as you like. A long hatch opened, right under the bridge-deck between the two conning-towers. Two men reached down into the hatch and brought out a couple of tackles, which they hooked to ring-bolts in the under part of the bridge-deck.

Three men tailed on then to each tackle, and up came as bonny a Berthon collapsible boat as ever I've seen. They ran the tackles out on runners that were fixed in under the bridge-deck until the collapsible was clear of the open hatch. It was a grand moment, but I was so darned interested I forgot to sing out to Gatley to let drive! They spread the boat, and a man jumped in, and then they slid her down the rounded side of the submarine into the water. They chucked off the tackles and held her by the painter, while a very unshaven officer and eight men tumbled into her, all armed with revolvers and swords. The painter was cast off, and they out oars to start for my ship.

And then, suddenly, I realised that I was letting the ideal moment go. "Gatley!" I roared out; "Gatley, FIRE!"

I heard the starboard door of my chart-house fly open, and, almost simultaneously, there came a devil of a BANG, and then a complete silence, except for someone swearing in the chart-house.

The shell from our gun missed the submarine by yards. Went right over her, in fact, and kicked up a fine healthy spout of sea-water, which suggested that the gun had got plenty of punch, if we could only apply it where it was badly needed—from our point of view!

The people aboard the submarine looked absolutely stupefied for a moment or two. I was watching them through my glasses. If an infant cow had made a likely try at tossing the boss bull of the herd, he couldn't have looked more bewildered than did that lot of German scuttlers. And the best of it was, as I twigged at once, they couldn't decide at all which part of the ship the shot had been fired from, for the awning, hanging loosely over the chart-house, more than half hid the open doorway, and the corrugated iron across the lower part hid a good deal of the rest.

"For the Lord's sake, shoot, Gatley!" I sung out, in more of a sweat than I should have thought possible. "You're going to lose the chance!"

That seemed to put some movement into the Germans, for they were near enough to hear my voice easily, and the next thing I knew was: Crack! Crack! Crack! The men in the collapsible were loosing off their rifles at me, and the air was full of the "whang" of their confounded bullets.

The Mate gave a sudden yell of pain, and in the same breath almost shouted:

"Look out for the gun, Sir! They're going to shoot again!"

"Looks a bit that way, Mister," I said. "Suppose we vacate this highly exalted eminence."

And with that we both made one jump to the deck and behind my chart-house.

As we did so the whole starboard side off the bridge flew up in a red volcano of fire and smoke, with a crash and a smash that nearly stunned the two of us where we stood. For a couple of seconds it rained burning splinter and chunks of wood in twenty different directions. Then I looked at the Mate. "I've a notion that's what the newspapers at home describe as a providential escape," I said.... You much hurt, Mister?"

"N—no Sir," he said. "I got a bullet graze, I suppose it was, up on the bridge; but it's stopped hurting."

I'd hardly waited for his reply, for I was into the chart-house, through the port door in a moment. I found the atmosphere in there pretty near as concussive as the shell-fire outside. The gun had jammed, in some one of those silly ways that hopper-fed guns will jam, and what the Second Engineer and Gatley between them were saying to it, with the aid of a spanner, was sheer inspiration—though the gun didn't seem to stop being jammed!

"Good Lord," I said, after I'd had a glance at the gun, "shove the trip-lever right over, for the Lord's sake, and get her going. I thought you understood guns, Gatley! And you, Mister Engineer, I'm surprised you couldn't tumble to a simple thing like that!"

I pushed them, one on each side of the gun, out of my way, grabbed the trip-lever (for lifting the net cartridge from the hopper), and shoved it hard over (Gatley had only pushed it two-thirds over), and then with a good swing forward I jumped the next cartridge into place, shoved the lever back again, and the gun stood ready to fire. And in that moment—CRASH! the whole chart-house rocked, and the forrard starboard top corner went up in a fountain of splintered steel, woodwork, glass, and part of my glass-rack.

Then I got busy. I shouldered the shoulder-pad of the gun, forced her muzzle well down, and pulled the firing lever.

BANG! went the gun—a stunning, deafening bang, and great Scott, how I yelled with delight!—the long gun on the submarine upended right on its stern, looking a very drunken sort of cannon indeed, squatting on the middle of a twisted-looking, automatic, disappearing pedestal, that I guessed couldn't disappear in a hurry any more, for my shell had gone slap bang crash into the middle of the works.

I wrenched the trip-lever right over again, and went through the loading movements, which took about two seconds a cartridge. As I did so I wigged the tremendous silence in the place, and glanced over my shoulder to see what was wrong. The Second Engineer and the First Mate were trying to stop poor old Gatley bleeding, but I saw in a moment it was no use. But, Lord! how mad it made me.

I jammed the lever well over, depressed the gun a little more, and brought the muzzle round on to the forrard conning-tower. Then I pulled, and BANG!...CRASH! The shell hit the conning-tower, smack, and burst; but when the smoke blew away the conning-tower was still there, though with a deuce of a great skew-whift dint in it. I guess that conning-tower must have been built of three or four-inch steel. I'd heard something about these super-submarines being armoured, but I'd not thought of it particularly. And now I got suddenly anxious, as you can think.

I wrenched the trip-lever backwards and forwards smartly, and sung out to the second Mate to leave poor old Gatley to the Second Engineer, and feed more cartridges into the hopper, and likewise to stand by to keep on feeding 'em in. You see she carried three cartridges at a time in the hopper, and I meant to keep emptying it, if I could.

Bang! I tried a shell slam down onto the fore whale-back of the submarine; but she must have been armoured all her length above water, for the shell only gouged a bright scoop in the metal and glanced off into the sea, just as it burst.

"Darn it all!" I said, and tried two more farther aft. I knocked the bridge-deck between the conning-towers all to pieces, and about six men that were on it went to sea in penny numbers. She was a good little gun, right enough, and if she'd only had the punch I'd have felt happy.

But I wasn't. I was darned anxious. The men were dodging all over the whalebacks of the submarine—racing towards the after conning-tower as I thought. They'd slammed down the heavy hatch-covers of the boat-hatch, and I tried a shell at the place, to see if I could get through there, but they were too solid.

Suddenly I heard my First Mate let out a yell behind me.

"They've another gun aft there, Sir! Look!"

I saw what he meant now, and realised why the submarine's crew had been racing towards the after end, for the leaves of a big gun-hatch in the whale-back had risen up on end (hydraulic, I suppose), and up from beneath them was rising silently a long gun, and a big one, too! By the look of it, I guessed it was one of the four-point-one, German high-velocity guns, with which they arm their light cruisers. And a very big and powerful gun for a submarine. She could blow us into minced iron in just the time it would take to load and fire her. It was like German notions of shipbuilding to put their biggest stuff aft, so they could use it in fighting a running stern action. Cute beggars!

But you can guess I didn't stop just then to admire German methods and cute ways. I turned my little fire-spitter and loosed off three of my small shells as fast as ever I could work the trip and the firing levers. The first missed clean, and went skipping across half a mile of sea, chucking up hefty little gouts of water. The second went through one of the crowd of Germans around the gun, and "dived" without exploding. The third struck the gun-pedestal bang, and splashed red fire and death every way in the middle of the gun's crew. When the smoke cleared, the after whale-back was literally a shambles.

As I looked I saw that the long muzzle of the four-point-one was swinging round, and I realised that some of the gun crew were training her from the hatch, which made a fine protection for them. In another moment they would have the gun trained, and I worked the trip-lever furiously, only to discover that the Second Mate had let me run out of "fodder." Lord! how I swore; and then in the middle of my swearing the long four-point-one roared out, almost in my face it *seemed*. But, by Jove! I shall always have a high respect for galvanised iron roofing in future. It'll keep anything out, rain *or* shells—provided you've got enough! We had enough—about six feet of it, stacked on edge round the chart-house, and the four-point-one ate about a solid yard of 'em, then burst, and I thought the chart-house had gone—what with the jar of the concussion and the crashing of falling sheets of disorganised and badly mutilated iron-roofing.

I discovered I was still quite alive, and much the same as before; but I realised I shouldn't be long if I let another of those brutes arrive! I turned on to the Second Mate, to swear some more, and then found that he'd managed to fill the gun-hopper with ammunition in the middle of the excitement, and held a further supply in the crook of his left arm—ready.

"Good man!" I roared, and drove the trip-lever back and forwards. Then snatched at the firing-lever, took a smart aim, and let drive. Yes, I'll admit I had strong religious promptings as I fired, for if the shell did nothing I couldn't see anything nearer at hand for all of us than a mighty sudden death inside the next five-seconds; for though the shell from the four-point-one had failed to reach us, it had stripped away almost all of my patent armour-plating at the after end of the house.

The shell from my squat little quick-shooting cannon hit the long German gun on the left-hand side, just above the top of the pedestal, right among the training gear. BANG! she went, and the air was full of disassociated gun machinery. I jammed the trip-lever back and forth, and shoved four shells, one after the other, slam down into the hatch out of which the gun pedestal rose. I sent them so quickly that the concussion of the bursting shells followed each other in a regular Crash! Crash! Crash! Fire and smoke and vague wreckage of men and iron vomiting up out of that death-pit. And then, at the fourth shell, I must have got onto the magazine, for—B-O-O-M—a monster great column of fire roared up out of the gun-hatch, and the after whale-back of the submarine was driven clean under water by the shock. The after part continued to go down, and the queer-looking bow of the submarine came up into the air for quite a hundred feet, rising steadily and slowly—a strange, "aluminum-bright" shape of metal, like a monstrous fish built of steel. The long, sharp bows rose up, and seemed to veer in towards us, hanging a moment almost over our heads, as it seemed high as our mast-heads. Then, CRASH! There came a second roar of sound, muffled, because it was under water. And immediately, in one swift, terrible movement, the great thing went sliding down and was gone.

I stared, half stunned. I could hardly realise it had happened. I kept staring at the sea, with the shoulder–pad of the quick-firer still to my shoulder. It seemed incredible. One moment the bows of that underwater monster standing like a vast steel cigar, far up out of the sea, and now—absolutely nothing except, here and there, far over the water, odd splashes, as blown-up wreckage came down from enormous heights.

I heard a huge crash on the main-deck, and the Mate ran out to see what had happened.

"It's part of their gun, Sir," I heard him shout. "It's fallen aboard and smashed right through the main-deck into number two hold. Part of it's sticking out. I—"

He quit talking suddenly and dived back into the chart-house, yelling something fresh. In the same instant I heard the loud reports of several rifles.

"It's the men that were in the Berthon, Sir!" he shouted, holding his left arm near the shoulder. "They got me, damn them! They've got aboard! What are we going to do now, Sir—?"

I pushed him to one side and jumped to the door, pulling out my revolver. As I shoved my head out there came a regular volley of bullets all around me, bursting like the crack of a whip on the steel of the port side of the chart-house. I got a sight of the officer who had been in charge of the Berthon. He was dodging behind a ventilator, about ten yards away. I took a snap at him, right through the thin arm of the ventilator, and got him too! Five or six rifles crashed out from different parts of the bridge-deck, and I sampled a bullet through the "thick" of my neck. I saw it was time to act pretty quickly, unless I was going to have all hands massacred by the brutes. I grabbed my whistle and blew twice—two good shrill blasts. And the second blast was lost in a fierce roar of steam, and a pressure, I should judge, of a couple of hundred pounds to the square inch. I had arranged this with Mac, in case we were boarded, and he had turned the main-steam through some flexible metal feed-piping he'd got; and with this invention of hell he was searching out every crevice of the bridge-deck with something a little more terrible than the fingers of Death himself.

I will say nothing of that last scene. It was necessary, but it is horrible; and afterwards all the ship lay very quiet under a deadly steamy silence. Mac had done his part of the beastly work that had been shoved on us.

Old Golly

"THE SKIPPER'S A TOUGH, you bet!" said Johnstone, one of the few men who had stayed in the *El Dorado* for the trip home. "He stiffened out Old Golly on the passage out, and he'd have got his bloomin' neck jolly well stretched, I'm thinkin', if it had been a British port. I s'pose they thought one nigger more or less didn't matter all that much. Anyway, he got off."

"Say, you might just tell what did happen," remarked Grant, an ordinary seaman who had signed on for the trip home. "Was it with a gun?"

"No," replied Johnstone. "Got him in the back of the neck with an iron pin. Hove it at him, you know. I didn't see it, but the chap at the wheel said Old Golly just went at the knees all in a heap, and never said a word 'cept 'Golly!' That's what the old fool was always sayin'; so we used to call him Old Golly."

"What had he done, Mate?" asked one of the other watch who was standing by, listening.

"None of us knew," said Johnstone. "Except the Old Man 'd been drinkin' some, or he'd never have let fly just goin' into harbour."

"No, it was a darned shame, anyway," said one of the men. "I liked Old Golly. So did everyone for that matter."

This was in the fo'cas'le the second day out from 'Frisco, in the second dog-watch. That same night something peculiar happened.

It had breezed up a bit during the first half of the eight-to-twelve watch (midnight), and at four bells the Second Mate had the three royals clewed up. Johnstone went up to the main, one of the AB's to the fore, and a 'prentice to the mizzen. The rest of the men forrard went into the fo'cas'le to stand by in case they should be wanted.

Presently, Johnstone walked in through the starboard doorway and dropped onto one of the chests where he sat panting.

"What's up lad?" asked Scottie, one of the older men. "Ye're bleedin' like a pig."

"Where?" said Johnstone in a curious voice. "Where—I mean who's bleedin'?"

"Look, your face!" cried several of the men together, having glanced up at Scottie's remark. "You're cut bad and as white as a sheet. What's happened?"

Johnstone put his hand up to his face and drew it away quickly to look at it. "My oath!" he muttered, and he reached for his towel.

"What's happened, anyway?" asked Tupmint, the oldest sailorman on their side. "Has the Old Man been gettin' onto you?"

"It was up in the main," said Johnstone. "I'm blimed if I don't half think there's somethin' up there. I could have sworn I heard someone say somethin' up in the main-mast, and then I got a hit in the eye, but I didn't know I was cut. I came down pretty smart, I can tell you. I may have done it then. Lord! I don't mind sayin' I had a fright!"

"That all?" said Tupmint contemptuously. "We thought the Old Man had been gettin' outer your track. Guess you've just been fancyin' things!"

"Come 'ere, lad, an' I'll fix your face for ye," said old Scottie.

Johnstone crossed over to Scottie's sea-chest, and the older man, turning up an old pillowcase which he tore into strips, used it for bandages.

"What was it ye heard, son?" he inquired, as he adjusted the strips of cotton. "I'm askin' 'cause I ken last night I heard somethin' when I was up there." He looked keenly at Johnstone.

"What was it you heard?" asked Johnstone, staring back at him.

"I'm askin' _you_, lad," replied the old sailor.

"Well," said Johnstone, "I thought it was with the talk we've had lately about the old nigger. I——" he hesitated.

Scottie nodded.

"Ye needn't fear, son, that I'm goin' to laugh at ye," he said. "Seems we both heard the same thing." He stopped bandaging to fill and light his pipe.

"What would Old Golly want to do it for?" queried Johnstone, simply. "We treated him fair and square in the fo'cas'le. I guess he'd want to get even with the Old Man, not us sailormen forrard."

There was questioning in the man's tone; but old Scottie shook his head.

"We tret him pretty fair, lad, 'cause we _had_ to, and part 'cause he wasn't a bad sort. But he could lick any man in here, an' I guess that was what made us pretty civil. All the same, I don't see why we should get it. No, I don't. Glad I'm not the Old Man, son!"

Three nights later the port watch had a taste of something curious. It was in the middle watch from midnight to four a.m., and an ordinary seaman had been sent up to loose the main-royal. He went up over the main-top, and climbed into the top-mast rigging; then suddenly he let out a yell, and jumping into the backstays, came down to the decks like lightning, burning all the skin from his hands in his rapid descent.

"What the blazes is wrong with you?" cried the Second Mate. "I'll teach you to kick up a shindy and play the fool. Get up! And smart, or it'll be the worse for you!"

"There's a nigger in the top, Sir! I daren't. I daren't," gasped the youth.

"A nigger in your pants!" yelled the Second Mate. "Up! And smart with that royal, or I'll half kill you!" And the lad—truly between the devil and the deep blue sea—went. He reached the top again, caught at the grab-line, raised his head to a level and peered over. Down on deck the men watched him curiously; for there had already gone a whisper round the forecastle that there was something queer up the main, though Scottie and Johnstone were the only men who had actually experienced anything; the others having merely got the atmosphere of the thing from the vague talk that Johnstone's condition and remarks had created forward.

"Get a move on!" roared the Second, as the youth paused; and the A.B., apparently seeing nothing to frighten him, went up over the top and climbed into the top-mast rigging. They could see him only vaguely here because of the shadow of the top-sail; but he appeared to have paused again about level with the lower masthead.

"Get a move on!" again shouted the Second. That same instant the lad screamed out:

"Don't touch me, Golly! I never did nothin' to you!" And directly after he began to yell something at the top of his voice, evidently frightened out of his wits. And then in the midst of his shouting, he fell headlong out of the darkness, struck the shrouds once and bounded off into the sea.

Simultaneous, frightened cries came from all the men about the decks; then the Second began to sing out orders and to take steps to save the youth. But the lad must have sunk at once, for no one ever caught sight of him again, though a couple of life buoys were flung and the boat got out and kept rowing round and round for several hours.

Both watches had been roused out, and the Skipper and the First

Mate were on deck. When at last the boat was once more hoisted aboard, a tremendous and excited discussion took place on the poop.

"Golly be darned!" roared the Skipper. "He's dead meat these three months, and I'll have no ghosts in my ship!"

He turned to the Second Mate. "Take a couple of men up the main right away and just find out what's up there. If any of the hands is playin' the goat, I guess they'll wish they was dead twice over when I've done with 'em!"

The Second Mate, for all his bullying ways, had plenty of pluck; but he plainly disliked the job before him and suggested that a couple of lanterns would assist the search. With these, and two of the men who found courage to go when they knew that he would lead the way, he went up the main-rigging. He climbed over the main-top, first passing his lantern up to see what was there; but he saw nothing. Then he went right on up to the cross-trees, and finally searched all the yards. But no sign was there of any living man up among the lofty spars and gear.

Coming down, he made his report, and the Skipper ordered a thorough search of the ship; but this also produced nothing, so that the sturdy unbelief of the Old Man was faced with the necessity of inventing some more normal explanation of the mystery than obtained credence in the forecastle. But what he achieved in this direction no one ever learned, for he not only kept his mouth shut on the subject in the future but showed a strong dislike to having it discussed by the Mates in his presence. From all of which it may be imagined that he believed more than he knew, as is the way with most of us.

During the rest of the night which followed this incident, there was no more sleep in the forecastle; for both watches sat up to talk about what had happened, and to listen to and comment upon Johnstone's earlier experiences, and his views and opinions thereon, which were now regarded as gospel.

"I'll never go up that stick again alone as long as I'm in this blimy packet!" concluded Johnstone. "Not if they was to put me in irons, I won't! I tell you, Old Golly's up there, an' he'll not rest till he's coaxed the Old Man up, an' finished him, same as he finished Grant (meaning the A.B.). You see if I ain't right! The Old Man don't know what fear is, an' he'll go, sure as nuts."

A fortnight passed after this, and the Mates arranged matters as far as possible so that none of the men need go aloft after dark. One night, however, the Skipper came up rather later than usual, and after taking a turn or two of the poop, he turned to the First Mate.

"How is it, Mister," he asked, "that you've got that main r'yal fast?"

"Well, Sir," replied the Mate, and then he hesitated, not knowing just how to put the thing.

"I'm listening, Mister!"

"Well, Sir," began the Mate again, "after what's happened, I thought it best to go easy with sending the men aloft at night."

"Just what I thought, Mister! Send a lad up to loose that sail right away. You're nigh as soft as the men!"

"There's something very queer, Sir—" began the Mate in answer.

"You don't *say*, Mister!" interrupted the Skipper, snorting. "Meanwhile, as I'm not interested, s'pose you just toot that whistle of yours and send the boy up."

The Mate made no reply but blew his whistle and gave the order, which was received by the watch in an incredulous silence; for it had by now become an accepted supposition among the men that no one should leave the deck after nightfall, except the safety of the ship depended on it. And now this order!

The Mate repeated it, but was still greeted by a silence. Then before the Mate could take any further steps, the Skipper was down off the poop and among the watch. He caught two of the men by their throats and banged their heads savagely together; then, going for the biggest man there, he took him by the shoulders and booted him with a half a dozen heavy kicks to the main rigging.

"Up with you, my lad!" he shouted, giving him a final kick to help him on to the rail. Dazed with the handling he had received, the man halted, still so afraid of what might be up there that he was uncertain whether the Captain's kicks were not the lesser of two evils.

"Up, you fathom of pump water!" yelled the Captain, jumping after him. The man, a Dutchman, ran all the way up the main lower-rigging squealing, the Captain after him, giving him the weight of his fist at every third ratline. The man raced over the top and scuttled clumsily up the top-mast rigging. Then the Skipper came down again, feeling "good," as he described it.

Having loosed the royal in doublequick time and lighted up the gear, the Dutchman came down, hand-over-fist, in a frightened hurry. At the main-top, just as he was reaching his foot down for the fut-tock-rigging, he shouted something in a loud voice and made a jump into the main rigging. He landed about halfway down, carried away three ratlines, and came through bodily on to the main-deck with a crash.

The rest of the watch picked him up and carried him forward to his bunk where, however, he was found to have done no great damage to himself, being merely badly bruised and stunned. When he recovered sufficiently to speak, he insisted that he had seen a great black giant standing at the top. And not a man in the forecastle but felt that Svensen was telling the truth.

Away aft, however, the Captain was jeering the Mate. "Nigger! Nigger be damned!" he bellowed, as he walked up and down. "Funk! Just blue cussed funk! Funk and fancy, that's all the ghosts there is aloft in this packet, an' I don't allow *them* to bother me in my ship. No, Sir! Pity he didn't break his bloomin' neck!"

From that time onward whenever there was anything to be done aloft at night, the two Mates got into the way of going up with their men to give them a bit of heart.

"There's sure somethin' queer up there at nights," the First Mate told the Second. "I was up with my lot in the middle watch, an' comin' down over the top, I heard Old Golly speak out close to my ear, as plain as you like."

"If it comes to that," said the Second. "I thought I heard somethin' two nights ago when I was up. I couldn't be sure, though."

"It sounds darned silly," said the First. "But there it is, you know. Svensen swears he saw him, but I wouldn't take too much heed of that if it hadn't been for the A.B. *He* must have seen something."

That same night it breezed up a bit hard, and the First Mate, whose watch on deck it was, clewed up the main topgallant—the fore and the mizzen having been taken off her the previous watch.

"Up an' make it fast lads," he sang out, and was the first to jump on the sheerpole.

"Where are you goin', Mister?" shouted the Captain's voice at that moment from the poop.

The Mate called back an explanation.

"You'll please to come right up here, Mister," replied the Captain. "This is your part of the ship. I keep A.B.'s for goin' aloft and," he concluded in a fierce shout, "they're goin', Mister, without coddlin'!"

With that, he was down on to the main-deck among the men, who gave way before him in all directions. "Up, you old women!" he roared. "Up!" And seizing the nearest man he hove him bodily onto the rail.

The man caught the sheerpole and climbed into the rigging, while three others scrambled hurriedly after him. There, as they realised through their haze of fright that there might be something even worse than the Skipper to face, up above in the darkness, they came to a pause and crouched on the ratlines.

"What!" roared the Skipper, and after them he went with a bound.

At that, they began to run aloft, followed by the Captain, who hammered the last man over the top. The man, in his fright, went clumsily and, in getting out of the futtock-rigging, his foot slipped and came down on the Skipper's face, causing him to swear horribly as he hurled himself up over the top, that he might "sock it to him good!" The A.B., realising what he had done, raced his hardest, tried to climb over the back of the man above, and it was in this position that the Captain caught him.

"My oath! I'll skin you!" he shouted, hitting at him blindly in the dark.

The man yelled, and the A.B. above him began to curse. The Skipper jumped a ratline higher; but before he could hit again, the men heard something say, "Golly! Golly!" quite softly out of the shadows of the maintop.

The Captain hove himself round and then—how it happened no one ever knew—he had missed his grip and was falling.

He fell over the forward end of the top, and the bight of the clew-garnet caught him and broke his back. They found him hanging there, limp and silent, when they raced down from the threatening heights of the lofty main-mast.

Two days later, the First Mate, now acting Captain, found something that seemed to be a partial explanation of the mystery. He had gone aloft with the Boatswain to take a look at the heel of the main top-mast; which the latter said was rotten. Afterward, he went a bit farther up, trying the top-mast with his knife as he went. He was standing on the lid which loosely covered the head of the hollow steel main-mast, when suddenly he heard, apparently under his feet, someone saying, "Golly! Golly!"

For a moment he experienced a horrible thrill of superstitious fear; but the Boatswain was quick to recognise the sound now that there was no darkness to breed fancies.

"It's the scoop-pump, Sir," he explained. "The last Old Man had it fitted. It were like a fancy of his; but it never acted proper. It comes up inside the mast, and there's a screw nozzle just foreside of the mast above the pin-rail. His idea was that, when the ship's goin' through the water, she'd scoop the water up with a sort of shovel-flange of iron that's fixed to 'er bottom, just where the pipe opens out into the water. There's a lever to pull the scoop up, but I s'pect the pin's slipped!"

This, indeed, proved to be the case; and when the long disused lever inside the hollow main-mast was once pulled up into its place, so as to close the lower end of the pipe to the sea, there was never any more talk of hearing Old Golly whispering in the main-top. The hollow steel mast had carried the noise of the gurgling water upward, giving a curious, semi-human quality to the sound, so that in the dark, windy nights it could certainly be thought that a low voice kept muttering the word, "Golly! Golly!"

Yet, though this may have been the cause of the sounds which had been heard odd times by the men aloft, not a man in the forecastle believed it. Their explanation of the ceasing of the haunting was different. As Johnstone put it: "I told you he'd go up. Old Golly'd never have rest till he got level. If he hadn't got him that time, he'd have got him in the end!"

He stopped and nodded significantly at the other men. And all the men nodded back in solemn assent.

Demons of the Sea

"COME OUT ON DECK and have a look, 'Darky!' " Jepson cried, rushing into the half-deck. "The Old Man says there's been a submarine earthquake, and the sea's all bubbling and muddy!"

Obeying the summons of Jepson's excited tone, I followed him out. It was as he had said; the everlasting blue of the ocean was mottled with splotches of a muddy hue, and at times a large bubble would appear, to bust with a loud "pop." Aft, the Skipper and the three Mate could be seen on the poop, peering at the sea through their glasses. As I gazed out over the gently heaving water, far off to windward something was hove up into the evening air. It appeared to be a mass of seaweed, but fell back into the water with a sullen plunge as though it were something more substantial. Immediately after this strange occurence, the sun set with tropical swiftness, and in the brief afterglow things assumed a strange unreality.

The crew were all below, no one but the Mate and the Helmsman remaining on the poop. Away forward, on the topgallant forecastle head the dim figure of the man on lookout could be seen, leaning against the forestay. No sound was heard save the occasional jingle of a chain-sheet, or the flog of the steering gear as a small swell passed under our counter. Presently the Mate's voice broke the silence, and, looking up, I saw that the Old Man had come on deck, and was talking with him. From the few stray words which could be overheard, I knew they were talking of the strange happenings of the day.

Shortly after sunset, the wind which had been fresh during the day, died down, and with its passing the air grew excessively hot. Not long after two bells, the Mate sung out for me, and ordered me to fill a bucket from overside, and bring it to him. When I had carried out his instructions, he placed a thermometer in the bucket.

"Just as I thought," he muttered, removing the instrument and

451

showing it to the Skipper; "ninety-nine degrees. Why, the sea's hot enough to make tea with!"

"Hope it doesn't get any hotter," growled the latter; "if it does, we shall all be boiled alive."

At a sign from the Mate, I emptied the bucket, and replaced it in the rack, after which I resumed my former position by the rail. The Old Man and the Mate walked the poop side by side. The air grew hotter as the hours passed, and after a long period of silence broken only by the occasional "pop" of a bursting gas bubble, the moon arose. It shed but a feeble light, however, as a heavy mist had arisen from the sea, and through this, the moonbeams struggled weakly. The mist, we decided, was due to the excessive heat of the sea water; it was a very wet mist, and we were soon soaked to the skin. Slowly the interminable night wore on, and the sun arose, looking dim and ghostly through the mist which rolled and billowed about the ship. From time to time we took the temperature of the sea, although we found but a slight increase therein. No work was done, and a feeling as of something impending pervaded the ship.

The fog horn was kept going constantly, as the lookout peered through the wreathing mists. The Captain walked the poop in company with the Mates, and once the Third Mate spoke and pointed out into the clouds of fog. All eyes followed his gesture; we saw what was apparently a black line, which seemed to cut the whiteness of the billows. It reminded us of nothing so much as an enormous cobra standing on its tail. As we looked it vanished. The grouped Mates were evidently puzzled; there "erred to be a difference of opinion among them. Presently as they argued, I heard the Second Mate's voice:

"That's all rot," he said. "I've seen things in fogs before, but they've always turned out to be imaginary."

The Third shook his head and made some reply which I could not overhear, but no further comment was made. Going below that afternoon, I got a short sleep, and on coming on deck at eight bells, I found that the steam still held us; if anything, it seemed to be thicker than ever. Hansard, who had been taking the temperatures during my watch below, informed me that the sea was three degrees hotter, and that the Old Man was getting into a rare old state. At three bells I went forward to have a look over the bows, and a chin with Stevenson, whose lookout it was. On gaining the forecastle head, I went to the side and looked down into the water. Stevenson came over and stood beside me.

"Rum go, this," he grumbled.

He stood by my side for a time in silence; we seemed to be hypnotized by the gleaming surface of the sea. Suddenly out of the depths, right before us, there arose a monstrous black face. It was like a frightful caricature of a human countenance. For a moment we gazed petrified; my blood seemed to suddenly turn to ice water; I was unable to move. With a mighty effort of will, I regained my self-control and, grasping Stevenson's arm, I found I could do no more than croak, my powers of speech seemed gone. "Look!" I gasped. "Look!"

Stevenson continued to stare into the sea, like a man turned to stone. He seemed to stoop further over, as if to examine the thing more closely. "Lord," he exclaimed, "it must be the devil himself!"

As though the sound of his voice had broken a spell, the thing disappeared. My companion looked at me, while I rubbed my eyes, thinking that I had been asleep, and that awful visitation had been a frightful nightmare. One look at my friend, however, disabused me of any such thought. His face wore a puzzled expression.

"Better go aft and tell the Old Man," he faltered. I nodded and left the forecastle head, making my way aft like one in a trance. The Skipper and the Mate were standing at the break of the poop, and running up the ladder I told them what we had seen.

"Bosh!" sneered the Old Man. "You've been looking at your own ugly reflection in the water."

Nevertheless, in spite of his ridicule, he questioned me closely. Finally he ordered the Mate forward to see if he could see anything. The latter, however, returned in a few moments, to report that nothing unusual could be seen. Four bells were struck, and we were relieved for tea. Coming on deck afterward, I found the men clustered together forward. The sole topic of conversation with them was the thing which Stevenson and I had seen.

"I suppose, Darky, it couldn't have been a reflection by any chance, could it?" one of the older men asked.

"Ask Stevenson," I replied as I made my way aft.

At eight bells, my watch came on deck again, to find that nothing further had developed. But, about an hour before midnight, the Mate, thinking to have a smoke, sent me to his room for a box of matches with which to light his pipe. It took me no time to clatter down the brass-treaded ladder, and back to the poop, where I handed him the desired article. Taking the box, he removed a match and struck it on the heel of his boot. As he did so, far out in the night a muffled screaming arose. Then came a clamour as of hoarse braying, like an ass, but considerably deeper, and with a horribly suggestive human note running through it.

"Good God! Did you hear that, Darky?" asked the Mate in awed tones.

"Yes, Sir," I replied, listening—and scarcely noticing his question—for a repetition of the strange sounds. Suddenly the frightful bellowing broke out afresh. The Mate's pipe fell to the deck with a clatter.

"Run for'ard!" he cried. "Quick, now, and see if you can see anything."

With my heart in my mouth and pulses pounding madly, I raced forward. The watch were all up on the forecastle head, clustered around the lookout. Each man was talking and gesticulating wildly. They became silent, and turned questioning glances toward me as I shouldered my way among them.

"Have you seen anything?" I cried.

Before I could receive an answer, a repetition of the horrid sounds broke out again, profaning the night with their horror. They seemed to have definite direction now, in spite of the fog which enveloped us. Undoubtedly, too, they were nearer. Pausing a moment to make sure of their bearing, I hastened aft and reported to the Mate. I told him that nothing could be seen, but that the sounds apparently came from right ahead of us. On hearing this, he ordered the man at the wheel to let the ship's head come off a couple of points. A moment later a shrill screaming tore its way through the night, followed by the hoarse braying sounds once more.

"It's close on the starboard bow!" exclaimed the Mate, as he beckoned the Helmsman to let her head come off a little more. Then, singing out for the watch, he ran forward, slacking the lee braces on his way. When he had the yards trimmed to his satisfaction on the new course, he returned to the poop and hung far out over the rail listening intently. Moments passed that seemed like hours, yet the silence remained unbroken. Suddenly the sounds began again, and so close that it seemed as though they must be right aboard us. At this time I noticed a strange booming note that mingled with the brays. And once or twice, there came a sound which can only be described as a sort of "gug, gug." Then would come a wheezy whistling, for all the world like an asthmatic person breathing.

All this while the moon shone wanly through the steam which seemed to me to be somewhat thinner. Once the Mate gripped me by the shoulder as the noises rose and fell again. They now seemed to be coming from a point broad on our beam. Every eye on the ship was straining into the mist, but with no result. Suddenly one of the men cried out, as something long and black slid past us into the fog astern.

From it there rose four indistinct and ghostly towers, which resolved themselves into spars and ropes, and sails.

"A ship! It's a ship!" we cried excitedly. I turned to Mr. Gray; he, too, had seen something, and was staring aft into the wake. So ghostlike, unreal, and fleeting had been our glimpse of the stranger, that we were not sure that we had seen an honest, material ship, but thought that we had been vouchsafed a vision of some phantom vessel like the *Flying Dutchman*. Our sails gave a sudden flap, the clew irons flogging the bulwarks with hollow thumps. The Mate glanced aloft.

"Wind's dropping," he growled savagely. "We shall never get out of this infernal place at this gait!"

Gradually the wind fell until it was a flat calm, no sound broke the deathlike silence save the rapid patter of the reef points, as she gently rose and fell on the light swell. Hours passed, and the watch was relieved and I then went below. At seven bells we were called again, and as I went along the deck to the galley, I noticed that the fog seemed thinner and the air cooler. When eight bells were struck, I relieved Hansard at coiling down the ropes. From him I learned that the steam had begun to clear about four bells, and that the temperature of the sea had fallen ten degrees.

In spite of the thinning mist, it was not until about half an hour later that we were able to get a glimpse of the surrounding sea. It was still mottled with dark passages, but the bubbling and popping had ceased. As much of the surface of the ocean as could be seen had a peculiarly desolate aspect. Occasionally a wisp of steam would float up from the nearer sea, and roll undulatingly across its silent surface, until lost in the vagueness which still held the hidden horizon. Here and there columns of steam rose up in pillars, which gave me the Impression that the sea was hot in patches. Crossing to the starboard side and looking over, I found that conditions there were similar to those to port. The desolate aspect of the sea filled me with an idea of chilliness, although the air was quite warm and muggy. From the break of the poop the Mate called to me to get his glasses.

When I had done this, he took them from me and walked to the taffrail. Here he stood for some moments, polishing them with his handkerchief. After a moment he raised them to his eyes and peered long and intently into the mist astern. I stood for some time staring at the point on which the Mate had focused his glasses. Presently, something shadowy grew upon my vision. Steadily watching it, I distinctly saw the outlines of a ship take form in the fog.

"See!" I cried, but even as I spoke, a lifting wraith of mist disclosed to view a great four-masted barque lying becalmed with all sails set, within a few hundred yards of our stern. As though a curtain had been raised, and then allowed to fall, the fog once more settled down, hiding the strange bark from our sight. The Mate was all excitement, striding with quick, jerky steps, up and down the poop, stopping every few moments to peer through his glasses at the point where the four-master had disappeared in the fog. Gradually, as the mists dispersed again, the vessel could be seen more plainly, and it was then that we got an inkling of the cause of the dreadful noises during the night.

For some time the Mate watched her silently, and as he watched the conviction grew upon me that, in spite of the mist, I could detect some sort of movement on board of her. After some time had passed, the doubt became a certainty, and I could also see a sort of splashing in the water alongside of her. Suddenly the Mate put his glasses on top of the wheel box and told me to bring him the speaking trumpet. Running to the companion-way, I secured the trumpet and was back at his side.

The Mate raised it to his lips, and taking a deep breath, sent a hail across the water that should have awakened the dead. We waited tensely for a reply. A moment later a deep, hollow mutter came from the barque; higher and louder it swelled, until we realized that we were listening to the same sounds which we had heard the night before. The Mate stood aghast at this answer to his hail; in a voice barely more than a hushed whisper, he bade me call the Old Man. Attracted by the Mate's hail and its unearthly reply, the watch had all come aft, and were clustered in the mizzen rigging, in order to see better.

After calling the Captain, I returned to the poop, where I found the Second and Third Mates talking with the Chief. All were engaged in trying to pierce the clouds of mist which half hid our strange consort, and arrive at some explanation of the strange phenomena of the past few hours. A moment later the Captain appeared carrying his telescope. The Mate gave him a brief account of the state of affairs, and handed him the trumpet. Giving me the telescope to hold, the Captain hailed the shadowy barque. Breathlessly we all listened, when again, in answer to the Old Man's hail, the frightful sounds rose on the still morning air. The Skipper lowered the trumpet and stood with an expression of astonished horror on his face.

"Lord!" he exclaimed. "What an ungodly row!"

At this, the Third, who had been gazing through his binoculars, broke the silence.

"Look," he ejaculated. "There's a breeze coming up astern." At his words the Captain looked up quickly, and we all watched the ruffling water.

"That packet yonder is bringing the breeze with her," said the Skipper. "She'll be alongside in half an hour!"

Some moments passed, and the bank of fog had come to within a hundred yards of our taffrail. The strange vessel could be distinctly seen just inside the fringe of the driving mist wreaths. After a short puff, the wind died completely, but we stared with hypnotic fascination, the water astern of the stranger ruffled again with a fresh catspaw. Seemingly with the flapping of her sails, she drew slowly up to us. As the leaden seconds passed, the big four-master approached us steadily. The light air had now reached us and, with a lazy lift of our sails, we too began to forge slowly through that weird sea. The barque was now within fifty yards of our stern, and she was steadily drawing nearer, seeming to be able to outfoot us with ease. As she came on she luffed sharply and came into the wind with her weather leeches shaking.

I looked toward her poop, thinking to discern the figure of the man at the wheel, but the mist coiled around her quarter, and objects on the after end of her became indistinguishable. With a rattle of chain-sheets on her iron yards, she filled away again. We meanwhile had gone ahead, but it was soon evident that she was the better sailor, for she came up to us hand-over-fist. The wind rapidly freshened, and the mist began to drift away before it, so that each moment her spars and cordage became more plainly visible. The Skipper and the Mates were watching her intently, when an almost simultaneous exclamation of fear broke from them.

"My God!"

And well they might show signs of fear, for crawling about the barque's deck were the most horrible creatures I had ever seen. In spite of their unearthly strangeness there was something vaguely familiar about them. Then it came to me that the face which Stevenson and I had seen during the night belonged to one of them. Their bodies had something of the shape of a seal's, but of a dead, unhealthy white. The lower part of the body ended in a sort of double-curved tail on which they appeared to be able to shuffle about. In place of arms they had two long, snaky feelers, at the ends of which were two very humanlike hands equipped with talons instead of nails. Fearsome indeed were these parodies of human beings!

Their faces which, like their tentacles, were black, were the most grotesquely human things about them, and the upper jaw closed into the lower, after the manner of the jaws of an octopus. I have seen men among certain tribes of natives who had faces uncommonly like theirs, but yet no native I had ever seen could have given me the extraordinary feeling of horror and revulsion which I experienced toward these brutal-looking creatures.

"What devilish beasts!" burst out the Captain in disgust.

With this remark he turned to the Mate and, as he did so, the expressions on their faces told me that they had all realised what the presence of these bestial-looking brutes meant. If, as was doubtless the case, these creatures had boarded the barque and destroyed her crew, what would prevent them from doing the same with us? We were a smaller ship and had a smaller crew, and the more I thought of it the less I liked it.

We could now see the name on the barque's bow with the naked eye. It read: *Scottish Heath*, while on her boats we could see the name bracketted with Glasgow, showing that she hailed from that port. It was a remarkable coincidence that she should have a slant from just the quarter in which yards were trimmed, as before we saw her she must have been drifting around with everything "aback." But now, in this light air, she was able to run along beside us with no one at her helm. But steering herself she was, and although at times she yawed wildly, she never got herself aback. As we gazed at her we noticed a sudden movement on board of her, and several of the creatures slid into the water.

"See! See! They've spotted us. They're coming for us!" cried the Mate wildly.

It was only too true; scores of them were sliding into the sea, letting themselves down by means of their long tentacles. On they came, slipping by scores and hundreds into the water, and swimming toward us in droves. The ship was making about three knots, otherwise they would have caught us in a very few minutes. But they persevered, gaining slowly but surely, and drawing nearer and nearer. The long tentacle-like arms rose out of the sea in hundreds, and the foremost ones were already within a score of yards of the ship, before the Old Man bethought himself to shout to the Mates to fetch up the half-dozen cutlasses which comprised the ship's armoury. Then, turning to me, he ordered me to go down to his cabin and bring up the two revolvers out of the top drawer of the chart table, also a box of cartridges which was there.

When I returned with the weapons, he loaded there and handed one to the Mate. Meanwhile the pursuing creatures were coming steadily nearer, and soon half a dozen of the leaders were directly under our counter. Immediately the Captain leaned over the rail and emptied his pistol into them, but without any apparent effect. He must have realised how puny and ineffectual his efforts were, for he did not reload his weapon.

Some dozens of the brutes had reached us, and as they did so, their tentacles rose into the air and caught our rail. I heard the Third Mate scream suddenly, and turning, I saw him dragged quickly to the rail, with a tentacle wrapped completely around him. Snatching a cutlass, the Second Mate hacked off the tentacle where it joined the body. A gout of blood splashed into the Third Mate's face, and he fell to the deck. A dozen more of those arms rose and wavered in the air, but they now seemed some yards astern of us. A rapidly widening patch of clear water appeared between us and the foremost of our pursuers, and we raised a wild shout of joy. The cause was soon apparent; for a fine, fair wind had sprung up, and with the increase in its force, the Scottish Heath had got herself aback, while we were rapidly leaving the monsters behind us. The Third Mate rose to his feet with a dazed look, and as he did so something fell to the deck. I picked it up and found that it was the severed portion of the tentacle of the Third's late adversary. With a grimace of disgust I tossed it into the sea, as I needed no reminder of that awful experience.

Three weeks later we anchored in San Francisco. There the Captain made a full report of the affair to the authorities, with the result that a gunboat was dispatched to investigate. Six weeks later she returned to report that she had been unable to find any signs, either of the ship herself or of the fearful creatures which had attacked her. And since then nothing, as far as I know, has ever been heard of the four-masted barque *Scottish Heath*, last seen by us in the possession of creatures which may rightly be called demons of the sea.

Whether she still floats, occupied by her hellish crew, or whether some storm has sent her to her last resting place beneath the waves, is purely a matter of conjecture. Perchance on some dark, fog-bound night, a ship in that wilderness of waters may hear cries and sounds beyond those of the wailing of the winds. Then let them look to it; for it may be that the demons of the sea are near them.

The Wild Man of the Sea

CHE "WILD MAN OF the Sea," the First Mate called him as soon as he came aboard.

"Who's yon wild-looking chap you've signed on, Sir?" he asked the Captain.

"Best sailorman that ever stepped, Mister," replied the Master. "I had him with me four trips running out to 'Frisco. Then I lost him. He went spreeing and got shipped away. I dropped on him today up at the shipping office and was glad to get him. You'd best pick him for your watch if you want a smart man."

The Mate nodded. The man must be something more than average smart at sailoring to win such praise from old Captain Gallington. And indeed he soon had proof that his choice of the lean, wild-looking straggle-bearded A.B. was fully justified for the man became almost at once by general consent the leading seaman of the port watch.

He was soaked in all the lore of the sea life and all its practical arts. Nineteen different ways of splicing wire he demonstrated during one dog-watch argument; and from such practical matters went on to nautical "fancy-work," showing Jeb, the much-abused and half-witted deck boy belonging to his watch, a queerly simple method of starting a four-stranded Turk's-head; and after that he demonstrated a manner of alternating square and half moon sinnet without the usual unsightliness that is so generally inevitable at the alternations.

By the end of the watch, he had the whole crowd round him, staring with silent respect at the deft handiwork of this master-sailorman, as he illustrated a score of lost and forgotten knots, fancy-whippings, grace-finishings and pointings, and many another phase of rope work that hardly a man aboard the *Pareek,* sailing ship, had even so much as heard the name of. For they were mostly of the inefficient "spade and shovel," suji-muji, half-trained class of seamen, with most of the faults

460

of the old shellback, and too few of his virtues, the kind of sailorman
who lays rash and unblushing claim to the title of A.B. with an effron-
tery so amazing that he will stand unabashed at the wheel which he
cannot handle, and stare stupidly at the compass-card the very points
of which he was unable to name. No wonder that Captain Gallington was emphatic in his satisfaction at getting one genuine, finished
sailorman signed on among the usual crowd of nautical ploughboys.

And yet Jesson was not popular in the fo'cas'le. He was respected,
it is true, not only for his sailorman's skill, but because his six-feet-
odd-inches of wire-and-leather body very early made it clear to the
others that its owner was the strongest man aboard, with a knowledge
of the art of taking care of himself that silenced all possible doubts
in a manner at once sufficiently painful to be obvious.

As a result the whole fo'cas'le was silent and deferent when he
spoke, which was seldom; and had not his seamanship and his fighting
powers been so remarkable he would have been stamped by his insensate fellow A.B.'s as hopelessly "barmy." His good nature was often
manifest; for instance, he kept most of the other men's look-outs in
his watch, when of course he was not at the wheel. He would go up
and relieve the lookout man, much to that individual's delight and half
contempt; and there with his fiddle he would sit on the crown of the
anchor playing almost inaudible airs of tremendous import to himself.

Sometimes he would pace round and round the "head," chaunting
breathlessly to himself in a kind of wind-drunken delight, walking
with swift, noiseless strides in his endless circling.

Behind all his taciturnity, Jesson was fiercely kind-hearted in a
queer impulsive way. Once, when Jeb, the deck-boy in his watch, was
receiving a licking from one of the men, Jesson, who was eating his
dinner, put down his plate, rose from his sea-chest and, walking across
to the man, lugged him out on deck by his two elbows.

His treatment of the man was sufficiently emphatic to ensure
that Jeb was not in future kicked into submission; and as a result the
much-hazed lad grew to a curious sort of dumb worship of the big,
wild-looking sailorman. And so grew a queer and rather beautiful
friendship—a wordless intimacy between these two—the wild, silent,
strange-mooded seaman and the callow youth.

Often at night, in their watch on deck, Jeb would steal up silently
on to the fo'cas'le head with a pannakin of hot and much-stewed tea;
for the Doctor—i.e., the Cook—had an arrangement with the deck-
boy in each watch by which the lads would have his fire ready lighted
for him in the morning, and in return were allowed to slip into the

galley at night for a hook-pot of tea out of the unemptied boilers.

Jesson would take the tea without a word of thanks, and put it on the top of the capstan, and Jeb would then vanish to the main-deck where he would sit on the fore-hatch listening in a part-understanding dumbness to the scarcely audible wail of the violin on the fo'cas'le head. At the end of the watch, when Jesson returned Jeb his pannakin, there would often be inside of it some half-worked-out fancy-knot for the boy to study, but never a word of thanks or comment on either side.

And then one night Jesson spoke to the lad as he took from him the accustomed pannakin of hot tea.

"Hark to the wind, Jeb," he said, as he put down the pannakin on the head of the capstan. "Go down, lad, an' sit on the hatch an' let the wind talk to ye."

He handed something across to the boy.

"Here's the starting of some double-moon sinnet for ye to have a go at," he said.

Jeb took the sinnet and went down to his usual place on the fore-hatch. Here, in the clear moonlight, he puzzled awhile over the fancy-sinnet, and speedily had it hopelessly muddled. After that, he just sat still with the sinnet in a muddle on his knees, and began half-consciously to listen to the wind as Jesson had bid him—And presently, for the first time in his life, he heard *consciously* the living note of the wind, booming in its eternal melody of the Sailing-ship-Wind, out of the foot of the foresail.

With the sound of five bells, deep and sonorous in the moonlight, the spell of the uncertain enchantment was broken; but from that night it might be said that Jeb's development had its tangible beginning.

Now the days went slowly, with the peculiar monotonous unheeding of ailing-ship days of wandering on and on and on across the everlasting waters. Yet, even for a sailing-ship voyage, the outward passage became so abnormally prolonged that no one of the lesser shellbacks had ever been so long in crossing the line; for it was not until their eighty-fourth day out that the equator was floated across, in something that approximated an unending calm, broken from hour to hour by a catspaw of wind that would shunt the *Pareek* along a few miles, and then drop her with a rustle of sails once more into calm.

"Us'll never reach 'Frisco this trip!" remarked Stensen, an English-bred "Dutchman" one night as he came into the fo'cas'le, after having been relieved at the wheel by Jesson.

At this there broke out a subdued murmur of talk against Jesson which showed plainly that the big sailorman had grown steadily more and more unpopular, being less and less understood by those smaller natures and intellects.

"It's his b—y fiddlin'!" said a small Cockney named George. No one remembered his other name, or indeed troubled to inquire it.

It was the inevitable, half-believed imputation of a "Jonah," and as will be understood, they omitted none of their simple and strictly limited adjectives in accentuating the epithet.

The talk passed to a discussion of the quality of beer sold at two of the saloons down on the waterfront, and so on, through the very brief catalogue of their remembered and deferred pleasures, till it finally fizzled out into sleepy silence, broken at last by Jeb putting his head through the port doorway and calling them out to man the braces. Whereat they rose and slouched out, grumbling dully.

And so the *Pareek* proceeded on her seemingly interminable voyage; the calm being succeeded and interleaved by a succession of heavy head gales that delayed them considerably. In the daytime, Jesson was merely a smart, vigourous wild-haired seaman; but at night, mounting his eternal lookout on the fo'cas'le head, he became once more the elemental man and poet, pacing and watching and dreaming; and anon giving out his spiritual emotion in scarcely audible wild melodies on his fiddle, or in a sort of sonorous chaunting spoken in undertones, and more and more boldly listened to by Jeb who, day by day, was being admitted to a closer, though unobtrusive, intimacy with the big seaman.

One night when Jeb brought him the usual pannakin of tea, Jesson spoke to him.

"Did you listen, Jeb, to the wind as I told you?"

"Yes, Sir," replied the boy. He always gave him "Sir;" and indeed, the title had more than once slipped out from the lips of some of the A.B.s; as if, despite themselves, something about him won the significant term from them.

"It's a wonderful night tonight, Jeb," said the big seaman, holding the hot pannakin between his two hands on the capstain-top, and staring away into the greyness to leeward.

"Yes, Sir," replied Jeb, staring out in the same direction with a kind of faithful sympathy.

For maybe a full two minutes, the two stood there in silence; the man clasping and unclasping his hands around the hot pannakin, and the boy just quiet under the spell of sympathy and a vague, dumb understanding. Presently the big man spoke again:

"Have ye ever thought, Jeb, what a mysterious place the sea is?" he asked.

"No, Sir," replied Jeb, and left it at that.

"Well," said the big man, "I want ye to think about it, lad. I want you to grow up to realise that your life is to be lived in the most wonderful and mysterious place in the world. It will be full of compensations in such lots of ways for the sordidness of the sea-life, as it is to the sailorman."

"Yes, Sir," said Jeb again, only partly understanding. As a matter of fact, as compared with his previous gutter-life, it had never struck him as being sordid; and as for the mystery and wonderfulness of the sea, why, he had possibly been ever so vaguely conscious of them right down somewhere in the deep of his undeveloped mind and personality; but consciously, his thoughts had run chiefly to keeping dry; to pleasing the men, his masters; to becoming an A.B.—a dream of splendour to him—and for the rest, to having a good time ashore in 'Frisco up at the saloons, drinking with the men, like a man! Poor sailor laddie! And now he had met a real man who was quietly and deliberately shifting his point of view.

"Never make a pattern of the men you sail with, Jeb," said the big man. "Live your own life, and let the sea be your companion. I'll make a man of ye, lad. It's a place where you could meet God Himself walking at night, boy. Never pattern yourself on sailorman, Jeb. Poor devils!"

"No, Sir," repeated Jeb earnestly. "*They* ain't sailormen, them lot!" He jerked his thumb downward to indicate the rest of the A.B.s in the fo'cas'le beneath them. "But I'll try to be like you, Sir; only I couldn't be, so how I tried," he ended wistfully.

"Don't try to be like me, Jeb," said Jesson in a low voice. He paused a moment, then lifting the pannakin, he sipped a little of the hot tea and spoke again.

"Take the sea, lad, to be your companion. You'll never lack. A sailor lives very near to God if he would only open his eyes. Aye! Aye! If only they would realise it. And all the time they're lookin' for the shore and the devil of degeneration. My God! My God!"

He put the pannakin down and took a stride or two away as if in strange agitation; then he came back, drank a gulp of tea and turned to the lad.

"Get along down, Jeb, and stand by. I want to be alone. And remember, lad, what I have told ye. You're living in the most wonderful place in the world. Lad, lad, look out on the waters and ye may see God Himself walking in the greyness. Get close to the glory that is round ye, lad; get close to the glory.... Run along now, run along."

"Ay, ay, Sir," replied Jeb obediently, and he went down noiselessly off the fo'cas'le head, confused, yet elated because his hero had condescended to talk with him, and also vaguely sanctified in some strange fashion as if, somehow—as he would have put it—he "was jest coined out o' church."

And because of this feeling, he spent quite a while staring away into the greyness to leeward, not knowing what he wanted or expected to see. Presently the wail of the violin stole to him through the darkness, and quietly mounting the lee steps to the head till his ear was on a level with the deck of the head he stayed listening until the big man ceased his playing, and began to walk round and round the head in his curious fashion, muttering to himself in a low voice.

Jeb listened, attracted as he always was by these moods of the big sailorman. And on this night, in particular, Jesson walked round and round for a long time just muttering to himself; once or twice stopping at the lee rail for some silent moments during which he appeared to be staring eagerly into the grey gloom of the night. At such times Jeb stared also to leeward with a feeling that he might see something.

Then Jesson would resume his walk round and round the head with long, swift, springy noiseless strides, muttering, muttering as he went. And suddenly he broke out into a kind of hushed ecstatic chaunt, yet so subdued that Jeb missed portions here and there, strive as he might to hear all.

Then the man's voice trailed off into silence. The sudden hush was broken by a muttered remark from the starboard side of the main-deck.

" 'e's proper barmy!"

Jeb glanced quickly to windward and saw dimly against the greyness of the weather night the forms of two of the men crouching upon the starboard steps leading up to the rail.

"A b—y Jonah!" said another voice.

Some of the men had been listening to Jesson, and certainly without appreciation. Down stole Jeb from the port ladder, and took up his accustomed seat on the fore hatch. He had a kind of savage anger because the men were secretly jeering his sailor-demigod; but he was far too much afraid of them to risk making himself evident, and so he crouched there, listening and wondering. And even as he waited to hear what more they had to say there came the Mate's voice, sharp and sudden along the decks:

"Stand by the t'gallant ha'lyards! Smart now!"

A heavy squall was coming down upon them, and Jeb, having called out the men in the fo'cas'le, raced away aft with the rest to stand by the gear in case they had to lower away. He stood staring to windward as he waited, seeing dimly the heavy black arch of the squall against the lighter grey murk of the night sky; and then, even as he stared, he heard in the utter quietness the curious whine-whine of the distant rain upon the sea, breaking out into a queer hiss as it drove nearer at tremendous speed. Behind the swiftly coming hiss of the rain-front there sounded immediately a low, dull sound that grew into an uncomfortable nearing roar; and then, just as the first sheet of that tremendous rain smote down upon them, there was the Mate's voice again:

"Sheets and ha'lyards! Lower away! Clewlines and buntlines! Lower away! Lower away! Lower awa——"

His voice was lost in a volume of sound as the weight of the wind behind the rain took them; and the vessel lay over to the squall, over, over, over, whilst the whole world seemed lost in the down-thundering rain and the mad roar of the storm.

Jeb caught the Mate's voice, faintly, and knew that he was singing out to lower away the top-sails. He fumbled his way aft, groped and found the pin; then cast off the turns and tried to lower; but the heavy yard would not come down for the pressure of the wind was so huge that the parral had jammed against the top-mast, and the friction of this, combined with the horrible list of the ship, prevented the yard coming down.

A man came dashing through the reek; hurled the boy to one side, and threw off the final turns of the hal'yards, roaring out in a voice of frightened anger:

"It's that b——y Jonah we've got on board!"

There came the vague shouting in the Mate's powerful voice, of "Downhauls! Downhauls!" coming thin and lost through the infernal darkness, and the dazing yell of the squall and the boil of the rain. The vessel went over to a more dreadful angle so that it seemed she must capsize. There was an indistinct crashing sound up in the night, and then another seemingly further aft, and fainter. Immediately after, the cant of the decks eased, and slowly the vessel righted.

"Carried away!... Yes, Sir... The main-top-mast... Carried away! Look out there!... Mizzen!... Look out there!"

A maze of shouting fore and aft, for the squall was easing now and it was possible to hear the shouts that before had been scarcely audible, even at hand. The other watch was out on deck and Captain Gallington was singing out something from the break of the poop....

"Stand from under!" There was a fierce loud crash almost in the same moment, and a man screaming, with the horrible screaming of a man mortally hurt. Everywhere in the darkness there was lumber, smashed timber, swinging blocks, wet canvas, and from somewhere amid the wreckage on the dark decks the infernal screaming of the man, growing fainter and fainter, but never less horrible.

The squall passed away to leeward, and a few stars broke through the greyness. On the deck all hands were turned-to with ships' lamps investigating the damage. They found that the main-top-mast had carried away just below the cross-trees, also the mizzen t'gallant. On the main-deck, under the broken arm of the main t'gallant yard one of the men, named Pemell, was found crushed and dead. One other man was badly hurt, and three had somewhat painful injuries, though superficial in character. Most of the rest had not escaped bad bruises and cuts from the falling gear.

The vessel herself had suffered considerably, for much of the heavy timber had fallen inboard, and the decks were stove in two places and badly shaken in others. Also the steel bulwarks were cut down almost to the scuppers where the falling mast had struck.

Through all that night and the next day into the dog-watches, both watches were kept at it with only brief spell-ons for food and a smoke. By the end of the second dog-watch Chips had managed to repair and re-caulk the decks, whilst the wreckage had all been cleared away, and the masts secured with preventer stays pending Chips getting ready the spare main top-mast and mizzen t'gallant-mast.

All that day while they worked, there had lain in the Bo'sun's locker, covered with some old sail-cloth, the man who had been killed by the falling spars; and when finally the men had cleared up for the night, Captain Gallington held a brief but grimly piteous service to the dead which ended in a splash overside, and a lot of superstitious sailormen going foward in a very depressed and rather dangerous mood.

Here, over their biscuits and tea, one of them ventured openly to accuse Jesson of being a Jonah and the cause of all that had happened that night before, also of the calms and the head gales that had made the voyage already so interminable.

Jesson heard the man out without saying a word. He merely went on eating his tea as though the man had not spoken; but when the stupid sea yokel, mistaking Jesson's silence for something different, ventured on further indiscretions, Jesson walked across to him, pulled him off his sea-chest, and promptly knocked him down on to the deck of the fo'cas'le.

Immediately there was a growl from several of the others, and three of them started up to a simultaneous attack. But Jesson did not wait for them. He jumped towards the first man and landed heavily and, as the man staggered, he caught him by the shoulders and ran him backwards into the other two, bringing the three of them down with a crash. Then as they rose, he used his fists liberally, causing two of them to run out on deck in their efforts to escape him. After which, Jesson went back to his unfinished tea.

Presently, the night being fine, he took his fiddle and went on the fo'cas'le head, where as usual he relieved the lookout man who hurried below for a smoke.

Meanwhile, there was a low mutter of talk going on in the fo'cas'le—ignorant and insanely dangerous—dangerous because of the very ignorance that bred it and made it brutal. And listening silent and fierce to it all sat Jeb, registering unconscious and heroic determination as the vague wail of the violin on the dark fo'cas'le head drifted down to him, making a strange kin-like music with the slight night airs that puffed moodily across the grey seas.

" 'Ark to 'im!" said one of the men. " 'Ark to 'im! Ain't it enough to bloomin' well bring a 'urricane! My Gord!"

"I was once with a Jonah," said the Cockney. " 'e near sunk us. We 'eld a meetin', both watches, an' 'e got washed overboard one night with a 'eavy sea, 'e did! That's 'ow they logged it, though the Mate knowed 'ow it was reely; but 'e never blamed us, or let on 'e knowed. We couldn't do nothin' else. And we'd a fair wind with us all the way out, after."

With heads close together, amid the clouds of thick tobacco smoke, the low talk continued till one of the men remembered Jeb was near, and the lad was ordered out on deck; after which the doors were closed, and ignorance with its consequent and appalling brutality made heavy and morbid the atmosphere as the poor undeveloped creatures talked among themselves without any knowledge of their own insanity.

Up on the fo'cas'le head the violin had hushed finally into silence, and Jesson was walking round and round in that curious noiseless fashion, muttering to himself and at times breaking out into one of his low-voiced chaunts. On the lee ladder crouched Jeb listening, full of his need to explain to the big man something of the vague fear that had taken him after hearing the men talk.

Then suddenly, his attention was distracted from the man's strange ecstacy by a murmur from the direction of the weather ladder.

" 'ark to 'im. My Gord, if it ain't enough to sink us. Just 'ark to that blimy Jonah... 'ark to 'im!"

Whether Jesson heard or felt the nearness of the men who had come sullenly out on deck, it is impossible to say; but his low-voiced, half-chaunting utterance ceased, and he seemed to Jeb, out there in the darkness, to be suddenly alert.

One by one the men of both watches came silently out on deck, and Jeb had nearly screwed up his courage to the point of calling out a vague warning to the unconscious Jesson when there came the sound of footsteps along the main-deck, and the flash of the Mate's lantern shone on the lanyards of the preventer gear. He was making a final uneasy round of the temporary jury-stays with which the masts had been made secure; and as the men realised this, they slipped quietly away, one by one, back into the fo'cas'le.

The Mate came forrard and went up on to the fo'cas'le head, felt the tension of the fore-stay and went out on to the jibboom, testing each stay in turn to make sure that nothing had "given" or "surged" when the main upper-spars went. He returned and, with a friendly word to Jesson, came down the lee ladder and told Jeb he might turn in "all standing," and get a sleep.

But Jeb did not mean to turn in until he had spoken to Jesson. He looked about him, and then stole quietly up the lee ladder, and so across to where the big sailor was standing, leaning against the fore side of the capstan.

"Mister Jesson, Sir!" he said, hesitating somewhat awkwardly abaft the capstan.

But the big man had not heard him, and the lad stole round to his elbow and spoke again.

"That you, Jeb?" said the A.B., looking down at him through the darkness.

"Yes, Sir," replied Jeb. And then after hesitating a few moments, all his fear came out in a torrent of uncouth words....

"An' they're goin' to dump you as soon as she's takin' any heavy water, Sir," he ended. "An' they'll tell the Mate as you was washed overboard."

"The grey rats destroy the white rat!" muttered the big sailorman as if to himself... "Kind to kind, and death to the un-kin—the stranger that is not understanded!" Then almost in a whisper: "There would be peace of course.... Out here forever among the mysteries.... I've wanted it to come *out here*.... But the white rat must do justice to itself! By— Yes!"

And he stood up suddenly, swinging his arms as if in a strange exhilaration of expectancy. Abruptly, he turned to the deck-boy.

"Thank ye, Jeb," he said. "I'll be on my guard. Go and get some sleep now."

He turned about to the capstan head and picked up his fiddle. And as Jeb slipped away silently, barefooted, down the lee ladder there came to him the low wailing of the violin, infinitely mournful, yet with the faint sob of a strange triumph coming with a growing frequence, changing slowly into a curious grim undertone of subtle notes that spoke as plainly as Jesson's voice.

A fortnight went by and nothing happened, so that the lad was beginning to settle down again to a feeling of comfort that nothing horrible would happen while he was asleep. By the end of the fortnight, they had hove both the new main top-mast and new mizzen t'gallant mast into place, and had got up the main royal and t'gallant mast, and the rigging on both main and mizzen set up. Then, in slinging the yards there were two bad accidents. The first occurred just as they got the upper top-sail yard into place. One of the men named Bellard, fell in the act of shackling on the tie, and died at once. That night in the fo'cas'le there was an absolute silence during tea. Not a man spoke to Jesson. He was literally, in their dull minds, a condemned person; and his death merely a matter of the speediest arrangement possible.

Jesson was surely aware of their state of mind; but he showed no outward signs of his awareness; and as soon as tea was over, he took his violin and went away up on to the fo'cas'le head, while down in the fo'cas'le the men sent Jeb out on deck, and talked hideous things together.

Three days later when all the yards and gear were finally in place again, Dicky—the deck-boy in the other watch—was lighting up the gear of the main-royal when he slipped in some stupid fashion, and came down; but, luckily for him, brought up on the cross-trees with nothing worse than a broken forearm which Captain Gallington and the Mate tortured into position again, in the usual barbarous way that occurs at sea in those ships that do not carry a doctor.

On deck, every man was glancing covertly at Jesson, accusing him secretly and remorselessly with the one deadly thought—"Jonah!"

And, as if the very elements were determined to give some foolish colour to the men's gloomy ignorance, the royal had not been set an hour before an innocent-looking squall developed unexpected viciousness, blowing the royal and the three t'gallants out of the bolt-ropes. The yards were lowered, and all made secure.

This was followed, in the afternoon watch, by a general shortening of sail, for the glass was falling in an uncomfortably hasty fashion. And surely enough, just at nightfall, they got the wind out of the north in a squall of actual hurricane pressure which lasted an hour before it finally veered a little and settled down into a gale of grim intention.

When Jeb was called that night for the middle watch, he found the ship thundering along under foresail and main lower top-sail, driving heavily before the gale, Captain Gallington having decided to run her, and take full advantage of the fair wind. He struggled aft to a perfunctory roll-call.... the Mate shouting the names into the windy darkness, and only occasionally able to hear any of the men's answering calls. Then the wheel and the lookout were relieved, and the watch below struggled forrard through the night and the heavy water upon the decks on their way to the fo'cas'le.

The Mate gave orders that the watch on deck were to stand-by handy, under the break of the poop, and this was done; all the men being there except Jesson who was on the lookout, and Svensen who was at the wheel.

Until two bells the men stayed there under the break, talking and growling together in orthodox shellback fashion, an occasional flare of a match making an instantaneous picture of them all grouped about in their shining wet oilskins and sou'westers; and outside beyond the shelter of the break, the night, full of the ugly roar of the wind and the dull, heavy note of the sea... a dark chaos of spray and the damp boom of the wind. And ever and again there would come a loud crash as a heavy sea broke aboard, and the water would burst into a kind of livid phosphorescent light, roaring fore and after along the decks as it swirled in under the dark break among the waiting men in great glimmering floods of foam and water.

At two bells, which no one heard because of the infernal roaring of the wind and the harsh, constant fierce noises of the seas, Jeb discovered suddenly that several of the men had slipped away quietly forrard through the darkness of the storm. Sick with fright, he realised why they had gone and, fumbling his way out from under the break of the poop, he made a staggering run for the teak support of the skids. Here he held on as a heavy sea broke aboard, burying him entirely beneath a mountain of fierce brine. Gasping for breath, mouth and nostrils full of water, he caught the temporary life-line that had been rigged, and scurried forrard through the dazing roar and the unseen spray that stung and half-blinded him from moment to moment.

Reaching the after end of the deck-house where was the galley and the sleeping place of "Chips," the Bo'sun, "Sails" and the "Doc," he fumbled for the iron ladder and went up, for he knew that the lookout was being kept from the top of the deck-house owing to the fact that the fo'cas'le head was under water most of the time.

Once having warned Jesson, he felt quite confident that the big sailorman would be able to take care of himself. And Jeb meant to stay near in the lee of the galley skylight so as to be on hand if anything were attempted.

Creeping right on to the forrard end of the house he failed to find Jesson. He stared around him into the intolerable gloom of the storm that held them in on every side.

He shouted Jesson's name, but his voice disappeared in the wind, and he became conscious of a dreadful terror, so that the whole of that shouting blackness of the night seemed one vast elemental voice of the thing that had been done. And then, suddenly, he knew that it was being done then, in those moments, even while he crept and searched of the dark house top.

Shouting inaudibly as he hove himself to his feet, he made a staggering run across the sopping house-deck. His foot caught something, and he went crashing down on his face. In a frenzy he turned and felt the inert, sagging thing over which he had stumbled. Groping swiftly and blunderingly for the face, he found it was more or less clean shaved, and knew it was not Jesson, but evidently one of the men who had attacked him.

The boy raced forrard again, across the top of the house. He knew just where to go. One blind leap to the deck, from the port forrard corner of the house, and he went crashing into a huddle of fighting men whose shouts and curses he could only now hear for the first time in the tremendous sound of the elements. They were close to the port rail, and something was being heaved up in the gloom... something that struck and struck, and knocked a man backwards, half dead, as Jeb came down among them.

He caught a man by the leg and was promptly kicked back against the teak side of the house. He lurched to the rail, all natural fear lost in fierce determination. He cast off the turns of the idle top-sail ha'lyards and wrenched madly at the heavy iron belaying-pin. Then he sprang at the black, struggling mass of men and struck. A man screamed, like a half-mad woman, so loud that his voice made a thin, agonised skirl away up through the storm. The blow had broken his shoulder. Before Jeb could strike again, a kicking boot took him in the chest and drove him to the deck, and even as he fell a strange inner consciousness told him with sickening assurance that knives were being used. Sick, yet dogged, he scrambled to his feet: and as he did so the black, gloom-merged struggling mass became suddenly quiet, for the thing that they had fought to do was achieved. An unheard splash over-side among the everlasting seas, and Jesson the sailorman, the white rat among the grey, had taken his place "out there among the mysteries."

Immediately Jeb was upon the suddenly stilled crowd of men, striking right and left with the heavy pin. Once, twice, three times! And with each blow the iron smashed the bone. Then, swiftly, he was gripped by fierce, strong hands, and a few minutes later the *Pareek*, sailing ship, was storming along in her own thunder, a mile away from the place where the developed man and the crude boy had ended their first friendship, and begun a second and ever-enduring one among the "sea palaces and the winds of God."

Jesson had killed two men outright with his fists in his fight for life. The rest of the crew—both watches had assisted—dumped these men and afterward reported them as having been washed overboard by the same sea that took the man and the boy! To the same cause they were able to attribute with safety the injuries they themselves had received during the fight.

And while the night went muttering things with the deep waters, in the fo'cas'le under the slush-lamps the men played cards unemotionally.... We'll have a fair wind tomorrow," they said. And they did! By some unknown and brutal law of Chance, *they did!*

But, in some strange psychic fashion peculiar to men who have lived for months lean and wholesome among the winds and the seas, both the Mate and the Master suspected something of the truth that they could neither voice nor prove. And because of their suspicions they "hazed" the crew to such an extent, that when 'Frisco was reached all hands cleared out—sans pay-day, sea-chests and discharges!

And in the brine-haunted fo'cas'les of other old sailing-ships, they told the story to believing and sympathetic ears; and foolish and ignorant heads nodded a sober and uncondemnatory assent.

The Habitants of Middle Islet

"THAT'S 'ER," EXCLAIMED THE old whaler to my friend Trenhern, as the yacht coasted slowly around Nightingale Island. The old fellow was pointing with the stump of a blackened clay pipe to a small islet on our starboard bow.

"That's 'er, Sir," he repeated. "Middle Islet, an' we'll open out ther cove in er bit. Mind you, Sir, I don't say as ther ship is still there, an' if she is, you'll bear in mind as I told you all erlong as there weren't one in 'er when we went aboard." He replaced his pipe, and took a couple of slow draws, while Trenhern and I scrutinised the little island through our glasses.

We were in the South Atlantic. Far away to the north showed dimly the grim, weather-beaten peak of the Island of Tristan, the largest of the Da Cunha group; while on the horizon to the Westward we could make out indistinctly Inaccessible Island. Both of these, however, held little interest for us. It was on Middle Islet off the coast of Nightingale Island that our attention was fixed.

There was little wind, and the yacht forged but slowly through the deep-tinted water. My friend, I could see, was tortured by impatience to know whether the cove still held the wreck of the vessel that had carried his sweetheart. On my part, though greatly curious, my mind was not sufficiently occupied to exclude a half conscious wonder at the strange coincidence that had led to our present search. For six long months my friend had waited in vain for news of the *Happy Return* in which his sweetheart had sailed for Australia on a voyage in search of health. Yet nothing had been heard, and she was given up for lost; but Trenhern, desperate, had made a last effort. He had sent advertisements to all the largest papers of the world, and this measure had brought a certain degree of success in the shape of the old whaler alongside of him. This man, attracted by the reward offered, had volunteered information regarding a dismasted hulk, bearing the name of the *Happy Return* on her bows and stern, which he had come across during his last voyage, in a queer cove on the South side of Middle Islet. Yet he had been able to give no hope of my friend finding his lost love, or indeed anything living in her; for he had gone aboard with a boat's crew, only to find her utterly deserted, and—as he told us—had stayed no time at all. I am inclined now to think that he must unconsciously have been impressed by the unutterable desolation, and atmosphere of the unknown, by which she was pervaded, and of which we ourselves were so soon to be aware. Indeed, his very next remark went to prove that I was right in the above supposition.

"We none of us wanted to 'ave much truck with 'er. She 'adn't a comfortable feelin' 'bout 'er. An' she were too dam clean an' tidy for my likin'.'"

"How do you mean, too clean and tidy?" I inquired, puzzled at his way to putting it.

"Well," he replied, "so she were. She sort of gave you ther feelin' as 'er crowd 'ad only just left 'er, an' might be back any bloomin' minnit. You'll savvy wot I mean, Sir, when you gets aboard of 'er." He wagged his head wisely, and recommenced drawing at his pipe.

I looked at him a moment doubtfully; then I turned and glanced at Trenhern, but it was evident that he had not noticed these last remarks of the old seaman. He was far too busily engaged in staring through his telescope at the little island, to notice what was going on about him. Suddenly he gave a low cry, and turned to the old whaler.

"Quick, Williams!" he said, "is that the place?" He pointed with the telescope. Williams shaded his eyes, and stared.

"That's it, Sir," he replied after a moment's pause.

"But—but where's the ship?" inquired my friend in a trembling voice. "I see no sign of her." He caught Williams by the arm, and shook it in sudden fright.

"It's all right, Sir," exclaimed Williams. "We ain't far enuff to the Sutherd yet ter open out ther cove. It's narrer at ther mouth, an' she were right away up inside. You'll see in er minnit."

At that, Trenhern dropped his hand from the old fellow's arm, his face clearing somewhat; yet greatly anxious. For a minute he held on to the rail as though for support; then he turned to me.

"Henshaw," he said, "I feel all of a shake—I—I—"

"There, there, old chap," I replied, and slipped my arm through his. Then, thinking to occupy his attention somewhat, I suggested to him that he should order one of the boats to be got ready for lowering.

This he did, and then for a little while further we scanned that narrow opening among the rocks. Gradually, as we drew more abreast of it, I realised that it ran a considerable depth into the islet, and then at last something came into sight away up among the shadows within the cove. It was like the stern of a vessel projecting from behind the high walls of the rocky recess, and as I grasped the fact, I gave a little shout, pointing out to Trenhern with some considerable excitement.

The boat had been lowered, and Trenhern and I with the boat's crew, and the old whaler steering, were heading direct for that opening in the coast of Middle Islet.

Presently we were amongst the broad belt of kelp with which the islet was surrounded, and a few minutes later we slid into the clear, dark waters of the cove, with the rocks rising up in stark, inaccessible walls on each side of us until they seemed almost to meet in the heights far overhead.

A few seconds swept us through the passage and into a small circular sea enclosed by gaunt cliffs that shot up on all sides to a height of some hundred odd feet. It was as though we looked up from the bottom of a gigantic pit. Yet at the moment we noted little of this, for we were passing under the stern of a vessel, and looking upwards, I read in white letters *Happy Return*.

I turned to Trenhern. His face was white, and his fingers fumbled with the buttons of his jacket, while his breath came irregularly. The next instant, Williams had laid us alongside, and Trenhern and I were scrambling aboard. Williams followed, carrying up the painter; he made it fast to a cleet, and then turned to lead the way.

Upon the deck, as we walked, our feet beat with an empty sound that spelt out desolation; while our voices, when we spoke, seemed to echo back from the surrounding cliffs with a strange hollow ring that caused us at once to speak in whispers. And so I began to understand what Williams had meant when he said "She 'adn't a comfortable feelin' 'bout 'er."

"See," he said, stopping after a few paces, " 'ow bloomin' clean an' tidy she is. It aren't nat'ral." He waved his hand towards the surrounding deck furniture. "Everythin' as if she was just goin' inter port, an' 'er a bloomin' wreck."

He resumed his walk aft, still keeping the lead. It was as he had said. Though the vessel's masts and boats had gone, she was extraordinarily tidy and clean, the ropes—such as were left—being coiled up neatly upon the pins, and in no part of her decks could I discern any signs of disorder. Trenhern had grasped all this simultaneously with myself, and now he caught my shoulder with a quick nervous grasp.

"See her, Henshaw," he said in an excited whisper, "this shows some of them were alive when she drove in here—" He paused as though seeking for breath. "They may be—they may be—" He stopped once more, and pointed mutely to the deck. He had gone past words.

"Down below?" I said, trying to speak brightly.

He nodded, his eyes searching my face as though he would seek in it fuel for the sudden hope that had sprung up within him. Then came Williams' voice; he was standing in the companion-way.

"Come along, Sir. I aren't goin below 'ere by myself."

"Yes, come along, Trenhern," I cried. "We can't tell."

We reached the companion-way together, and he motioned me to go before him. He was all a-quiver. At the foot of the stairs, Williams paused a moment; then turned to the left and entered the saloon. As we came in through the doorway, I was again struck by the exceeding tidiness of the place. No signs of hurry or confusion; but everything in its place as though the Steward had but the moment before tidied out the apartment and dusted the table and fittings. Yet to our knowledge she had lain here a dismasted hulk for at least five months.

"They must be here! They must be here!" I heard my friend mutter under his breath, and I—though bearing in mind that Williams had found her thus all those months gone—could scarcely but join in his belief.

Williams had gone across to the starboard side of the saloon, and I saw that he was fumbling at one of the doors. It opened under his hand, and he turned and beckoned to Trenhern.

"See 'ere, Sir," he said. "This might be your young leddy's cabin; there's feemayles' things 'ung up, an' their sort of fixins on ther table—"

He did not finish; for Trenhern had made one spring across the saloon, and caught him by the neck and arm.

"How dare you—desecrate—" he almost shrieked, and forthwith hauled him out from the little room. "How—how—" he gasped, and stooped to pick up a silver-backed brush which Williams had dropped at his unexpected onslaught.

"No offence, Mister," replied the old whaler in a surprised voice, in which there was also some righteous anger. "No offence. I wern't goin' ter steal ther bloomin' thing." He gave the sleeve of his jacket a brush with the palm of his hand, and glanced across at me, as though he would have me witness to the truth of his statement. Yet I scarcely noticed what it was that he said; for I heard my friend cry out from the interior of his sweetheart's cabin, and in his voice there was blent a marvellous depth of hope and fear and bewilderment. An instant later he burst out into the saloon; in his hand he held something white. It was a calendar. He twisted it right way up to show the date at which it was set. "See," he cried, "read the date!"

As my eyes gathered the import of the few visible figures, I drew my breath swiftly and bent forward, staring. The calendar had been set for the date of that very day.

"Good God!" I muttered; and then:—"It's a mistake! It's just a chance!" And still I stared.

"It's not," answered Trenhern vehemently. "It's been set this very day—" He broke off short for a moment. Then after a queer little pause he cried out "O, my God! grant I find her!"

He turned sharply to Williams.

"What was the date at which this was set?—Quick!" he almost shouted.

Williams stared at him blankly.

"Damnation!" shouted my friend, almost in a frenzy. "When you came aboard here before?"

"I never even seen ther blessed thing before, Sir," he answered. "We didn't stay no time aboard of 'er."

"My goodness, man!" cried Trenhern, "what a pity! O what a pity!" Then he turned and ran towards the saloon door.

In the doorway he looked back over his shoulder.

"Come on! Come on!" he called. "They're somewhere about. They're hiding— Search!"

And so we did; but though we went through the whole ship from stern to bow, there was nowhere any sign of life. Yet everywhere that extraordinary clean orderliness prevailed, instead of the wild disorder of an abandoned wreck; and always, as we went from place to place and cabin to cabin, there was upon me the feeling that they had but just been inhabited.

Presently, we had made an end to our search, and having found nothing of that for which we looked, were facing one another bewilderedly, though saying but little. It was Williams who first said anything intelligible.

"It's as I said, Sir; there weren't anythin' livin' aboard of 'er."

To this Trenhern replied nothing, and in a minute Williams spoke again.

"It aren't far off dark, Sir, an' we'll 'ave ter be gettin' out of this place while there's a bit of daylight."

Instead of replying to this, Trenhern asked if any of the boats were there when he was aboard before, and on his answering in the negative, fell once more into his silent abstraction.

After a little, I ventured to draw his attention to what Williams had said about getting aboard the yacht before the light had all gone. At that, he gave an absent nod of assent, and walked towards the side, followed by Williams and myself. A minute later we were in the boat and heading out for the open sea.

During the night, there being no safe anchorage, the yacht was kept off, it being Trenhern's intention to land upon Middle Islet and search for any trace of the lost crew of the *Happy Return*. If that produced nothing, he was going to make a thorough exploration of Nightingale Island and the Islet of Stoltenkoff before abandoning all hopes.

The first portion of this plan he commenced to put into execution as soon as it was dawn; for his impatience was too great to allow of his waiting longer.

Yet before we landed on the Islet, he bade Williams take the boat into the cove. He had a belief, which affected me somewhat, that he might find the crew and his sweetheart returned to the vessel. He suggested to me—searching my face all the while for mutual hope—that they had been absent on the preceding day, perhaps on an expedition to the Island in search of vegetable food. And I (remembering the date of the calendar) was able to look at him encouragingly; though had it not been for that, I should have been helpless to aid his belief.

We entered through the passage into that great pit among the cliffs. The ship, as we ranged alongside of her, showed wan and unreal in the grey light of the mist-shrouded dawn; yet this we noticed little then, for Trenhern's visible excitement and hope was becoming infectious. It was he who now led the way down into the twilight of the saloon. Once there, Williams and I hesitated with a certain natural awe, whilst Trenhern walked across to the door of his sweetheart's room. He raised his hand and knocked, and in the succeeding stillness, I heard my heart beat loud and fast. There was no reply, and he again rapped with his knuckles on the panels, the sounds echoing hollowly through the empty saloon and cabins. I felt almost sick with the suspense of waiting; then abruptly, he seized the handle, turned it, and threw the door wide. I heard him give a sort of groan. The little cabin was empty. The next instant, he gave out a shout, and reappeared in the saloon holding the same little calendar. He ran to me and pushed it into my hands with an inarticulate cry. I looked at it. When Trenhern had shown it to me the preceding day it had been showing the date 27th.; *now it had been altered to the 28th.*

"What's it mean, Henshaw? what's it mean?" he asked helplessly.

I shook my head. "Sure you didn't alter it yesterday—by accident?"

"I'm quite sure!" he said.

"What are they playing at?" he went on. "There's no sense in it—"
He paused a moment; then again:— "What's it mean?"

"God knows." I muttered. "I'm stumped."

"You mean sumone's been in 'ere since yesterday?" inquired Williams at this point.

I nodded.

"Be Gum then, Sir," he said, "it's ghostses!"

"Hold your tongue, Williams!" cried my friend, turning savagely upon him.

Williams said nothing, but walked toward the door. "Where are you going?" I asked.

"On deck, Sir," he replied. "I didn't sign on for this 'ere trip to 'ave no truck with sperrets!" and he stumbled up the companion stairway.

Trenhern seemed to have taken to notice of these last remarks; for when next he spoke he appeared to be following out a train of thought.

"See here," he said. "They're not living aboard here at all. That's plain. They've some reason for keeping away. They're hiding somewhere—perhaps in a cave."

"What about the calendar then. You think—?"

"Yes, I've an idea that they may come aboard here at night. There may be something that keeps them away during the daylight. Perhaps some wild beast, or something; and they would be seen in the daytime."

I shook my head. It was all so improbable. If there was something that could get at them aboard the ship, lying as it did surrounded by the sea, at the bottom of the great pit among the cliffs, then it seemed to me that they would nowhere be safe; besides, they could stay below decks during the day, and I could conceive of nothing that could reach them there. A multitude of other objections rose in my mind. And then I knew perfectly well that there were no wild beasts of any description on the Islands. No! obviously it could not be explained in that manner. And yet—there was the unaccountable altering of the calendar. I ended my line of reasoning in a fog. It seemed useless to apply any ordinary sense to the problem, and I turned once more to Trenhern.

"Well," I said, "there's nothing here, and there may be something, after all, in what you say; though I'm hanged if I can make head or tail of anything."

We left the saloon and went on deck. Here we walked forward and glanced into the fo'cas'le; but, as I had expected, found nothing.

After that we bundled down into the boat, and proceeded to search Middle Islet. To do this, we had to pull out of the cove and round the coast a bit to find a suitable landing place.

As soon as we had landed, we pulled the boat up into a safe place, and arranged the order of the search. Williams and I were to take a couple of the men apiece, and go right round the coast in opposite directions until we met, examining on the way all the caves that we came across. Trenhern was to make a journey to the summit, and survey the Islet from there.

Williams and I accomplished our part, and met close to where we had hauled up the boat. He reported nothing, and so did I. Of Trenhern we could see no trace, and presently, as he did not appear, I told Williams to stay by the boat while I went up the height to look for him. Soon I reached the top and found that I was standing upon the brink of the great pit in which lay the wreck. I glanced round and there away to the left, I saw my friend lying on his stomach with his head over the edge of the chasm, evidently staring down at the hulk.

"Trenhern," I called softly, not wanting to startle him.

He raised his head and looked in my direction; seeing me, he beckoned, and I hurried to his side.

"Bend down," he said in a low voice. "I want you to look at something."

As I got down beside him, I gave a quick glance at his face; it was very pale; then I had my face over the brink and was staring into the gloomy depth below.

"See what I mean?" he asked, still speaking scarcely above a whisper.

"No," I said. "Where?"

"There," he answered, pointing. "In the water on the starboard side of the *Happy Return.*"

Looking in the direction indicated, I now made out in the water close alongside the wreck several pale, oval-shaped objects. "Fish," I said. "What queer ones!"

"No!" he replied. "Faces!"

"What!"

"Faces!"

I got up on to my knees and looked at him.

"My dear Trenhern, you're letting this matter affect you too deeply— You know you have my deepest sympathy. But—"

"See," he interrupted, "they're moving, they're watching us!" He spoke quietly, utterly ignoring my protest.

I bent forward again and looked. As he had said, they were moving, and as I peered, a sudden idea came to me. I stood up abruptly.

"I have it!" I cried excitedly. "If I'm right it may account for their leaving the ship. I wonder we never thought of it before!"

"What?" he asked in a weary voice, and without raising his face.

"Well, in the first place, old man, those are not faces, as you very well know; but I'll tell you what they very likely are, they're the tentacles of some sort of sea monster, Kraken, of devil-fish—something of that sort. I can quite imagine a creature of the kind haunting that place down there, and I can equally well understand that if your sweetheart and the crew of the *Happy Return* are alive, they'll be inclined to give their old packet a pretty wide berth if I am right—eh?"

By the time I had finished explaining my solution of the mystery, Trenhern was upon his feet. The sanity had returned to his eyes, and there was a flush of half-suppressed excitement on his hitherto pale cheeks.

"But—but—but—the calendar?" he breathed.

"Well, they may venture aboard at night, or in certain states of the tides, when, perhaps they have found there is little danger. Of course, I can't say; but it seems probable, and what more natural than that they should keep count of the days, or it may have just been put forward thoughtlessly in passing. It may even be your sweetheart counting the days since she was parted from you."

I turned and peered once more over the edge of the cliff; the floating shapes had vanished. Then Trenhern was pulling at my arm.

"Come along, Henshaw, come along. We'll go right back to the yacht and get some weapons. I'm going to slaughter that brute if he shows up."

An hour later we were back with a couple of the yacht's boats and their crews, the men being armed with cutlasses, harpoons, pistols and axes. Trenhern and I had each chosen a heavy shellgun.

The boats were left alongside, and the men ordered aboard the wreck; and there, having brought sufficient food, they picnicked for the rest of the day, keeping a keen watch for signs of anything.

Yet when the night drew near, they manifested considerable uneasiness; finally sending the old whaler aft to tell Trenhern that they would not stay aboard the *Happy Return* after dark; they would obey any order he chose to give in the yacht; but they had not signed on to stay aboard of a ghost-ridden craft at night.

Having heard Williams out, my friend told him to take the men off to the yacht; but to come back in one of the boats with some bedding, as he and I were going to stay the night aboard the hulk. This was the first I had heard on the matter; but when I remonstrated with him, he told me I was at perfect liberty to return to the yacht. For his part he had determined to stay and see if anyone came.

Of course after that, I had to stay. Presently they returned with the bedding, and having received orders from my friend to come for us at day-break, they left us there alone for the night.

We carried down our bedding and made it up on the saloon table; then we went on deck and paced the poop, smoking and talking earnestly—anon listening; but nothing came to our ears save the low voice of the sea beyond the kelp-belts. We carried our guns; for we had no knowledge but that they might be needed. Yet the time passed quietly, except once when Trenhern dropped the butt of his weapon upon the deck somewhat heavily. Then indeed, from all the cliffs around us, there came back a low hollow boom that was frightening. It was like the growl of a great beast. At the bottom of that tremendous pit it presently became exceedingly dark. So far as I could judge, a mist had come down upon the Islet and formed a sort of huge lid to the pit. It was about twelve o'clock that we went below. I think by that time even Trenhern had begun to realise that there was a certain rashness in our having stayed; and below, at least, if we were attacked, we would be better able to hold our own. Somehow such vague fear as I had was not induced by the thought of the great monster I believed I had seen close to the vessel during the day; but rather by an unnameable something in the very air, as though the atmosphere of the place were a medium of terror. Yet—calming myself with an effort—I put down this feeling to my nerves being at tension; so that presently, Trenhern offering to take the first watch, I fell asleep on the saloon table, leaving him sitting beside me with his gun across his knees.

Then as I slept, a dream came to me—so extraordinarily vivid was it that it seemed almost I was awake. I dreamt that all of a sudden Trenhern gave a little gasp and leapt to his feet. In the same moment, I heard a soft voice call "Tren! Tren!" It came from the direction of the saloon doorway, and—in my dream—I turned and saw a most beautiful face, containing great wondrous eyes. "An angel!" I whispered to myself; then I knew that I was mistaken and that it was the face of Trenhern's sweetheart. I had seen her once just before she sailed. From her, my gaze wandered to Trenhern. He had laid his gun upon the table, and now his arms were extended towards her. I heard her whisper "Come!" and then he was beside her. Her arms went about him, and then, together, they passed out through the doorway. I heard his feet upon the stairs, and after that my sleep became a blank, dreamless rest.

I was aroused by a terrible scream, so dreadful that I seemed to wake rather to death than life. For perhaps the half of a minute I sat up upon my bedding, motionless in a very frost of fear; but no further sound came to me, and so my blood ran warm once more, and I reached out my hand for my gun. I grasped it, shook the clothes from me and sprang to the floor. The saloon was filled with a faint grey light which filtered in through the skylight overhead. It was just sufficient to show me that Trenhern was not present, and that his gun was upon the table, just where I had seen him place it in my dream. At that, I called his name quickly; but the only answer I received was a hollow, ghostly echo from the surrounding empty cabins. Then I ran for the door, and so up the stairs onto the deck. Here, in the gloomy twilight, I glanced along the bare decks; but he was nowhere visible. I raised my voice and shouted. The grim, circling cliffs caught up the name and echoed it a thousand times, until it seemed that a multitude of demons shouted "Trenhern! Trenhern! Trenhern!" from the surrounding gloom. I ran to the port side and glanced over—Nothing! I flew to starboard; my eyes caught something—many things that floated apparently just below the surface of the water. I stared, and my heart seemed suddenly quiet in my bosom. I was looking at a score of pale, unearthly faces that stared back at me with sad eyes. They appeared to sway and quiver in the water; but otherwise there was no movement. I must have stood thus for many minutes; for, abruptly, I heard the sound of oars, and then round the quarter of the vessel swept the boat from the yacht.

"In bow, there," I heard Williams shout. " 'ere we are, Sir!" The boat grated against the side.

" 'ow 'ave" Williams began; but it seemed to me that I had seen something coming to me along the deck, and I gave out one scream and leapt for the boat. I landed on a thwart.

"Push off! Push off!" I yelled, and seized an oar to help.

"Mr. Tren'ern, Sir?" interjected Williams.

"He's dead!" I shouted. "Push her off! Push her off!" and the men, infected by my fear, pushed and rowed until, in a few moments we were a score of yards distant from her. Here there was an instant's pause.

"Take her out, Williams!" I called, crazy with the thing upon which I had stumbled. "Take her out!" And at that, he steered for the passage into the open sea. This took us close past the stern of the wreck, and as we passed beneath, I looked up at the overhanging mass. As I did so, a dim, beauteous face came over the taffrail, and looked at me with great sorrowful eyes. She stretched out her arms to me, and I screamed aloud; for her hands were like unto the talons of a wild beast.

As I fell fainting, Williams's voice came to me in a hoarse bellow of sheer terror. He was shouting to the men:—

"Pull! Pull! *Pull!*"

The Riven Night

CAPTAIN RONALDSON HAD LOST his wife. This much we knew, and when the stern-visaged man came aboard to take command, it was I, the eldest apprentice, who stood at the gangway and passed his "things" aboard. One quick glance I have in his face as he passed me, and the world of sorrow that lurked in those sombre eyes touched me with a feeling of intense pity; though I knew little, save that he had lost his wife after a brief space of married life. Afterwards I learnt something of their story. How he had fought and saved to make sufficient to marry the woman he loved. How for her sake he had lived straightly and honourably, working at his profession until at last he had obtained a Master's certificate. Then they had married, and for six brief weeks' joy had been theirs; and now—this!

During our outward voyage the Captain was grimly silent. He acted like one who had lost all interest in life. As a result, the two Mates after a few attempts to draw him into conversation left him pretty much to himself, which indeed was what he apparently desired.

We reached Melbourne after an uneventful voyage and, having discharged and reloaded, commenced the homeward passage: the strangest and weirdest, surely, that ever man took. Even now, I scarce know what was real and what not. Sometimes I'm almost persuaded that the whole dread incident was a fearsome dream, were it not that the things which happened (things I cannot explain away) have left all too real and lasting traces.

We had a tedious passage with continual headwinds, heavy gales, and long calms, and it was during one of these that the strange thing I have to tell of befell.

We had been out a hundred and forty-three days. The heat had been stifling, and thankful I was when night came, bringing its shade from the oppression.

It was my "timekeeping," and I walked the lee side of the poop sleepily.

Suddenly the Second Mate called me up to wind'ard. "Just have a squint over there, Hodgson; I seemed to see something just now," and he pointed out into the gloom about four points on the port bow.

I looked steadily for some minutes but could see nothing. Then there grew out of the darkness a faint, nebulous light of a distinctly violet hue. "There's something over there, Sir," I said. "It looks like one of those corpse-candles."

The Second had another long look, and then went for his night-glasses. For some time after, he watched the thing at intervals, taking short hurried strides up and down the poop between whiles. Evidently he was puzzled; so was I for that matter. The light was not that of another vessel; it appeared to be, as I have just said, more of the nature of a corposant, or "corpse-candle."

Presently the hail of the "lookout" came hollowly aft. "Light on the port bow, Sir."

"Thanks for nothing," I heard the Second Mate mutter: then louder, "Aye, Aye."

There was not a breath of wind. The "courses" had been hauled up to prevent chafing, and we were lying silently in the night.

A little later, after a prolonged gaze, the Second again called me to him and asked if I thought the light any plainer. "Yes, Sir," I replied. "It's much plainer and larger too, Sir."

For a while he was silent.

"Queer thing, Sir." I ventured after a bit.

"Damned queer!" he replied. "I shall call the Old Man soon if it comes any closer."

"Perhaps it's not moving," I suggested. The Second Mate looked at me a moment moodily, then stood upright with a sudden movement.

"I never thought of that," he cried. "You think we may be in a current taking us towards it?" I nodded silently.

He went to the side and looked over, then returned irritably. "I wish to heaven it was daylight!" he snapped. In a while he looked again; then an exclamation of surprise came from him quickly, and turning, he handed the glasses to me.

"See if you can see anything queer about it," he said.

I had a long look, then passed them back to him.

"Well?" he questioned impatiently.

"I don't know, Sir," I answered. "It beats all I've seen while I've been fishing: it seems tons larger too."

"Yes, Yes!" he growled, "but don't you notice anything about the shape?"

"Jove, yes, Sir, I do now you mention it. You mean it looks like a great wedge? And the colour, Sir, it's wonderful. You might almost fancy..." I hesitated somewhat shyly.

"Go on," he grunted.

"Well, sir, you could almost fancy it was a tremendous valley of light in the night."

He nodded appreciatively, but said nothing.

An hour passed, and the thing grew visibly. From the main-deck came a subdued hum, the voices of the watch discussing the strange phenomenon in awestruck tones.

It could be seen plainly now with the naked eye, a great chasm of violet light like the opening of a huge valley into dreamland.

The Second Mate beckoned to me, and I went quickly.

"Take the poop," he said, "and keep your eyes lifting while I go and call the Old Man."

"Very good, Sir," and he went below. Presently he came up again.

"Can't make him hear at all," he said uneasily. "Better run down and call the Mate."

I did, and in a few minutes he joined the Second on the poop.

At first the Mate did little but stare astonished at that uncanny sight, while the Second Mate told him what little we knew. Then we went to the chart room and presently returned. I saw him shake his head in answer to question from the Second, and after that they watched that growing mystery in silence. Once the Mate said something, and I thought I caught the words "luminous clouds," but was not certain.

On we moved. The sight grew vaster.

A little later the Second Mate had another try to wake the Captain, but returned unsuccessful.

Down on the main-deck had gathered the whole crew. Once a man's voice rose blasphemously. There was a growing mutter of anger, and the blasphemer was silent. Time passed slowly.

The gulf of light rose right up into the midnight sky spreading fan-wise, and vanishing into further space. We were apparently some two miles from it when I heard the First Mate whisper something and go back to our binnacle. When he came back I heard him mutter hoarsely that we were drifting directly into the thing. The words were caught by some of the crew and passed round quickly in accents of fear.

Strange to say, no light came to us from the rift and this, I think, made it the more spectral and unearthly. The two miles had dwindled down to half, and I saw the Second Mate raise his glasses and look towards where the gulf had joined the sea. In fearful curiosity my gaze followed his, and there came to me a fresh feeling of dread as I saw that the point of the shimmering wedge seemed to drive far below the surface of the silent deep.

Still nearer, now but a hundred yards from that luminous gulf. I stared but could see nothing.

Nearer, and I looked up one slope of the riven night showing like the side of an eternal mountain.

The ship's bows drifted into the light. A moment, and I saw the foremast with its maze of ropes loom ghostly against that weird effulgence.

The Mate spoke jerkily.

"Damn!" he said, and was silent.

I looked forrard again and stared, terrified.

The fore-part of the ship had vanished. In place rolled a sea of violet clouds out of which rose grotesquely the frightened face of the lookout man. Further aft came the impalpable billows of mist. Forward of the foremast, nothing showed save that frightened face.

The ship drove forward and the main-mast faded into nothingness. I saw the crew in the waist stare fearfully out of those trembling waves of mystery. A moment later it was upon me, and I found myself submerged in an ocean of violet shades that gleamed wondrously.

The two Mates still stood together, and I saw them look bewilderedly at one another, though neither spoke. I looked astern and saw a mighty shape of blackness, with a glimmer of dark waters. It was the night we had left.

Slowly, as my faculties began to work, I saw things more plainly. Afar on my left rose a vast range of shadowy peaks, showing ghostly. Between them and where I stood rolled an immensity of luminous misty waves that fluctuated eternally.

To the right, the eye swept away into unutterable distances, and over all reigned an intolerable silence. A coldness like that of a tomb crept over me. I shivered. Once the brooding silence was broken by a moaning, as of a distant wind.

Presently I put out my hand through the winding mist and felt something hard; it was the rail running across the break of the poop. I looked down, but could see nothing. I took a step forward and stumbled against a hard object; it was a hencoop, and gropingly I sat down on it. I felt strangely tired and bewildered. How long I sat there it would be difficult to say. Time seemed to have no part in that dread place. The cold grew more intense, and I have an indistinct memory of shivering through an indeterminable space of time.

Suddenly there came again that windy moan, and then a cry of indescribable fear from many voices, followed by a sound as of whispering in the sky. I leapt to my feet and looked to where I had last seen the crew. There they were, all huddled together like frightened children, their eyes staring fearfully upwards into the void. Instinctively my gaze followed theirs. At first I could not make out what it was they watched so steadfastly; but slowly there grew out of the mists shapes, shapes clothed mistily, that watched us with great sombre eyes. Nearer they came, and looking towards the distant mountains, I saw dusky masses of clouds sweeping steadily from their towering heights in our direction. On they came, and as they drew nearer I saw that they were not clouds, but legions upon legions of those spirit forms. Still they came, floating like great clouds of intelligence above us. The weird sight impressed me terribly. I felt that the end of all things was approaching. Then as I watched, a strange thing happened. From those unnameable beings above, there drove a single dim enshrouded figure. It came headlong like a storm-driven cloud, and stopped before the crowd of cowering sailors. Then, as the wrappings of a shroud, rotten with extreme age might fall away shewing the corpse within; so did the dusky mist slip away and reveal to my astonished gaze—not a corpse, but the face and figure of a lovely young girl. I gave a gasp of astonishment, and leaned forward to get a better look; even as I did a tall form sprang from amongst the crowding sailors and shouted hoarsely.

"Mary! Mary!" it said, and ended in a harsh scream. It was Langstone, one of the A.B.'s. The girl put one ghostly hand to her heart, and I saw the handle of a sailor's sheath-knife showing starkly. What she meant, I could not at first make out. Then Langstone's voice rose shrilly, "Mary! Mary! Forgive...." He stopped abruptly. The girl-spirit after that one accusing gesture had turned away coldly and unforgivingly. I saw Langstone give a despairing glance at the shrinking men, then with a cry of "God help me," he leapt away out into the purple billows, and faintly to my ears as though from miles beneath my feet came the sound of a far distant splash, and then a long dread silence.

In a while I looked again towards those gloomy heights, but now I could no longer see the spectral hosts; instead it had grown wonderfully clear, and far into the void I saw a speck of snow-white fleece which grew rapidly larger as I watched, until presently it floated just overhead, and I made out a tender, womanly face smiling down upon me. It was the face of my mother who a short year previously had passed into the arms of the Great One. I took a step forward and held my arms out supplicatingly—I felt as though the tumultuous beating of my heart would suffocate me. I called "Mother," first softly, then loudly, and saw the dear lips move tremulously. Then even as I watched, it faded and like a dream was gone. For some moments I stood looking tearfully and unbelievingly upwards, until sorrowfully it was borne upon me that she had indeed gone.

A moment it seemed, and a voice spoke. The words came to me muffled, as though through mists of eternity—unmeaning they seemed and unreal. A dreamy feeling stole over me. I felt disinclined to listen. Again the voice came and I roused myself to catch the words. Two words only, but they woke me thoroughly. The sound echoed from the far heights with a tender insistence: "My Love! My Love! My Love!" And presently a step sounded, muffled and soft. I turned, and lo! the Captain's face showed palely. He was looking up into the wide with a rapt expression. I looked also, but though I searched earnestly, could see nothing. Suddenly I heard again the vague murmur of a deep splash, and glancing down quickly, could nowhere see the Captain. I stood confounded. The cry above had ceased. Then it seemed I saw a shadowy form with a face like that of the Captain's, float upwards into the violet twilight.

And thus, stupified, I stood waiting; waiting for I knew not what.

Presently I roused myself and made my way gropingly towards where I judged the side of the vessel to be. In a while my hand rested on something that I knew to be the rail running along the port side of the poop, and thus I leant upon it and peered over and down into the strangeness of that unearthly sight. Sometimes I looked and saw nothing, save the illimitable deeps of that billowy, misty ocean. It seemed to me as though ages passed over my head and still I watched dreamily. At times I dimly saw weird things that peered up at me and vanished. Thus I stood, and the monotony of time passed over my head in silent aeons. Then, it might have been halfway through eternity, something drove up out of the boundlessness, a dull green glow that shone lividly through the purple gloom of that infinite mystery. Steadily it grew, a cold malicious gleam that frightened me, and in a while, looking far to my left I saw another ghostly glimmer strike through that dark-hued sea.

Brighter grew the brilliance of those lights until their vivid greenness smote intolerably up into the violet impalpableness like two transparent pillars through which played a shiver of lambent flame, and suddenly the murky vastnesses beneath were heaved upwards into a mighty wave that drove towards us threateningly. Yet ere it reached us, my eyes had seen something, something terrible—eyes that blazed out of mystery, and beneath, lips—white, vast and slobbering had opened, disclosing the blackness of an everlasting night. Then, like an awesome wall that reached up into the nothingness above and blotted out everything, the wave was upon us, and instantly we were wrapped in a surging blackness that seemed to weigh down upon us and suffocate. My head began to sing queerly and I felt my knees give weakly. Then the blankness of unconsciousness swept over me, and I passed into dreams.

I opened my eyes and looked around bewilderedly. For a moment I saw things through a violet haze. It passed, and I saw that the sun was shining brightly. I glanced aloft, noting that a fresh breeze of wind filled the sails; then down on deck to where the two Mates still stood, just as I had seen them last. Even as I gazed, the Second Mate stood upright and yawned, then looked round him in a puzzled manner. As he did so, his eyes fell upon the Mate still sleeping. The Second stared stupidly a moment, then put out his hand and shook his superior roughly.

"What the devil's up, Mr. Gray?"

The Mate jumped and swore quickly.

"What the hell's the matter with you?" Then seeming to realise that he was not in his bunk, he rubbed the sleep out of his eyes and looked around—dazed.

The Second Mate spoke again, "Blarst!" and stared over the break of the poop. The Mate turned slowly and looked also. I heard him give a little gasp. Wondering what it was they eyed so earnestly, I ran to the break and glanced down on to the main-deck. Great God! What a sight. There, lying on the deck and huddled on the top of one another, lay the crew. The watch on deck, and the watch below, mixed up in an inextricable senseless heap. As we watched them, one of the men stood up shakily. His lips moved, but no words came. I saw the two Mates look at one another, and their eyes were full of doubt. Then the First Mate turned and tottered to his room. The Second Mate said nothing but continued to watch the men, as at intervals they rose and with suspicious, bewildered looks stumbled forrard. Some cursing there was, yet most preserved a glum and vacant silence. True, a little Frenchman—excitable like all his nation—started to question volubly, but ceased in surprise at the blank looks that were cast upon him. During the day, and indeed the rest of the voyage, the subject was strictly tabooed. It was as though each one of us felt afraid to admit that which according to our knowledge could not be.

Strangely enough, seen in this light, no surprise was expressed when the Captain's and Langstone's disappearance was formally announced. Instead, each one received the news tacitly. All, that is, except the little Frenchman, who swore softly in several languages at the—to him—incomprehensible behaviour of his comrades.

Once, a few days later, I had some work to do for the First Mate in the cabin. On the table was the Log book, and with a mingled dread I turned up the date of that fearsome night. There I found the following entry:

Lat.—S. Long.—W Heavy gales. About 2 A.M. shipped a tremendous sea which washed Captain Ronaldson and Langstone, one of the A.B.'s, overboard.

At the bottom were the signatures of the two Mates.

The Heaving of the Log

MR. JOHNSON, THE SECOND Mate of the *Skylark*, was a character in his way, and a very disagreeable one. His systematic bullying of the boys aboard shewed the nature of the man; while his language was coarse and lurid.

His bullying would often take the form of making some wretched youngster sit up on the main royal-yard (about 150 to 160 feet above the deck) during the whole four hours of the midnight watch: or perhaps it would be a cuff across the head, or a kick with a heavy sea-boot; and, being a big man, none of them had the heart to retaliate, knowing he would make it an excuse to take it out of them the more. Then he had petty provoking ways of annoying. He would never give them seaman's work if he could help it; instead he would put them to painting and tarring, scrubbing and cleaning, and any dirty work he could find or make for them. In addition he would, at the least excuse, keep them up in their watch below, thus depriving them of much of their time for sleep and recreation. Added to these grievances was the fact that the man himself was a poor sailor, slovenly in his work, and pandering to the men by allowing them to shirk their duty. Lastly he was guilty of the unpardonable crime of sleeping in his watch on deck, thus imperilling the safety of the ship, and the lives of all aboard.

Knowing the sort of man the boys were under, the reader will more readily understand the incidents of the following story.

The night is dark, and the four-masted barque *Skylark* is ploughing along, some twelve knots an hour, before a fine southerly breeze; it is ten p.m. and four bells have just rung out sharply on the fresh night air, followed by the Second Mate's hoarse cry: "Heave the log!" in answer to which, three youths, ranging in age from fifteen to eighteen, run quickly up the poop ladder, and away aft; where, while one holds the reel (a large wooden spool affair, on which is wound the log-line), another gets the glass (a sand glass used for timing), and the third stands by, waiting to give a hand in hauling in the line, after the log has been hove. The Second Mate then takes the end of the line, with its little canvas bag attached, and hauling some of the slack line off the reel, makes a loose coil, and throws it over the stern. As the water catches and fills the bag, the line starts to fly out; then as the "white rag" affixed to the line passes over the taffrail, the Second Mate shouts: "Turn!" to the holder of the glass, which he does instantly, and when the last grain has run out, he in turn shouts: "Stop!" Whereupon the waiting apprentice grips the flying line, and takes a quick hitch around a belaying-pin, until his companion, having put the glass away, comes to his assistance; without which he could never haul the line in, such is the power of the water upon the little bag at the end of it.

After reeling up the log-line two of the boys, Erntuck and Jute, go down to the berth; leaving Bell, whose "time" it is, to walk up and down the lee side of the poop. As he paces the narrow length of deck, he occasionally glances to the windward, at the man who had made himself so disliked.

Mr. Johnson has seated himself on a hencoop, and Bell knows well, that if he stays there, he will probably fall asleep, when he (Bell) will be able to slip down to the warm berth, instead of shivering on "Mount Misery," as they term the poop.

Down in the berth the 'prentices are discussing various topics, chief of which is the "Second's" many delinquencies. "The Second Mate's asleep again," says Bell, entering the half-deck at this instant.

"What, again!" growls Erntuck, "that makes five times in a fortnight. The old beast!"

"Yes," chimes in Jute, "and it would serve him jolly well right if the old man caught him, he would log him and no mistake, and serve the bully right too."

"By Jove! I'll tell you what boys," says one of the other watch, "the old beggar was ragging Bell, wasn't he? about being asleep when he sung out to heave the log. Well I'll tell you what to do; as soon as one bell is struck: go quietly up, and get the log ready for heaving; then when all is right, just take a bit of a turn round his neck with the slack of the line, and then heave the log over and shout: 'Turn.' That'll wake him, and if it doesn't, I'll bet the jerk the line gives will, and you can swear it was an accident, that the line got foul of him; and he won't dare to say much, because you'll have seen he was asleep."

There was a roar of laughter at this plan, and after discussing it awhile, they agreed to carry it out, especially as the Second Mate was sitting sleeping on a hencoop close by the log-reel, and it would there-fore be quite possible for him to be entangled with the line, without his being able to prove that it had been done purposely.

Seven bells are struck, and word is passed round to the watch on deck as to what is going forward, with the result that when one bell goes (at a quarter to twelve), and the trio go onto the poop to carry their scheme into operation, there is quite an audience to view the fun.

Very quietly and gingerly the three conspirators steal aft to their stations. Bell slips the log-reel noiselessly from its becketts; Erntuck gets the glass and stands silently by; while Jute gathers up a coil of slack line in his hand. Then he glances round; by the light of the bin-nacle lamp he sees that the Helmsman wears a broad grin, shewing he had a good inkling of what is going on. While from farther for'rard he can distinctly hear murmurs of amusement from the rest of the watch gathered there. Up till now he has been rather afraid of play-ing a trick on the Second: but at the sound of the men's smothered laughter, his fear quickly vanishes, and with a half-smile, he takes a couple of loose turns round the Second Mate's neck, and throws the bag overboard, then when the "white rag" flashes past him, shouts: "Turn!" The shout rouses the officer instantly, and he jumps as if he had been shot. Turning to Jute he roars: "What the devil do you mean by making that noi—"

At that instant the slack line tightens round his neck with a tre-mendous jerk, bringing his head in violent contact with the taffrail. From the group of men for'rard a subdued guffaw of irrepressible laughter breaks forth, in which the three apprentices are unable to resist joining. All has happened in the space of a few seconds: and Jute, stooping down, with a quick turn of the wrist, disengages the line from around Mr. Johnson's neck; when to his astonishment, instead of turning round, and giving vent to bad language, the man drops all in a heap on the deck. Jute seizes one of the binnacle lamps and throws the light on the man at his feet then gives a shout of horror to see his head partly twisted round in an unnatural manner. A hurried examination shews that the sudden jerk must have broken his neck, and the Second Mate is dead.

The Sharks of the *St. Elmo*

"I T'S AS STRANGE A place today as it was a thousand years ago," said Captain Dang, nodding his head out to sea where many vessels rode at anchor and busy tugs churned up the waves into flying foam. "And in a million years it'll be just the same," he added. "Just the same. It can be found out."

He was an extraordinary man, was Captain Dang. I had run into him quite by chance on the harbour pier. Years ago I had been a very youthful Second Mate of his and as such had known him for a perfect gentleman, a good master and the possessor of an unlimited vocabulary of Scotch, Irish and Americanism. Ashore he was the most reserved of men—stern, faultlessly dressed and speaking perfect English. At sea he rolled fore and aft, dressed in rough pilot-cloth, bellowed with laughter, chewed plug tobacco with an almost indelicate zest, and—culminating atrocity—wore lavender kid gloves!

To find him in a talkative mood ashore was something fresh, and knowing something of his adventurous past and with time to waste till joining my ship, I waited for the yarn I knew would be coming.

"It's as much a mystery today as ever," he said, "and no one knows better than me. Mystery on the waters and below. I remember when I was in the old *St. Elmo*—steam and sail she was—trading between 'Frisco and the Teapot—that's China—I came across a mighty curious thing. We left 'Frisco early Tuesday morning, and by eight bells Wednesday afternoon we were losing our steam for some monkey reason or other, and scarcely doing more than three knots. What little wind we had was right ahead, and so we'd a harbour furl on everything so as to offer no more resistance than possible.

Captain Dang spat into the blue waters of the bay. "If I can tell you, lad, it's the devil's own job to sail in one of these auxiliaries.

"Three knots was about our wind mark all the first dog-watch, and

497

then it dropped to two, and the sea did likewise. It was like a great, smooth lake. Smooth-heave, smooth-heave, and our speed at two knots.

"And then we saw the sharks. One of the lads spotted them first and let out a yell fit to wake the dead.

" 'Sharks! Millions of 'em!' he yelled, and jumped onto the pin-rail to get a better look, followed by the rest of us.

"I tell you, lad, it wasn't only a strange sight, it was a downright dreadful sight. There seemed to be thousands and tens of thousands of sharks following the vessel, strung out on each side of the wake as far as you could see. And they weren't only astern, mind you, but away out on the beam as far as I could see; and some of the brutes right in alongside, swimming easy with a gentle wriggle of their tails to keep 'em going just our speed.

"I saw this much from the starboard rail, and then I went across to port to have a look that side. It was the same there. You could see them just under the water, and now and then their backfins and sometimes the whole of their ugly backs coming right out of the water into sight, and then under again. What got me the most was the way some of them kept hugging close up against the side of the ship so that you could spit on the water over 'em, and watch the brutes look up at you as knowing as devils.

"I reckon our speed had dropped to almost a knot and a half an hour by this, and the blaspheming engineers sweating and tinkering below. The poor Greasers had been at it all that blessed night for the engines developed new complaints mostly every hour.

"I was Bo'sun at the time and soon knew I was in for a picnic as both old Cap'n Moss and the First Mate, Mr. Nathaniel, were drinking. They'd been as drunk as lords ever since we cleared the Golden Gates, and a jolly good thing for us that Mr. Jackson, the Second, was a sober little man—a little envious, discontented rat of a man, but sober for all that.

"Well, by the end of the second dog-watch," continued Captain Dang, having paused a moment to bite an immense chew out of a plug of tobacco, "there wasn't any more wind than you could put in your hat, and that isn't a lot, I'm thinking. Consequent, the sea was just like glass except for a bit of a slow heave that went under it, and there, away on each side of us, I could see the sharks breaking the water gently with their backs in ten thousand different places at once. It was strange to stand and watch the night come down on all that, and to think what it would mean if there was any going aloft! You just try to imagine what it would be like to go out on one of the yards above all that lot of hungry fish—keep your mind on it a moment, lad, it'll do you good!

"And away after the Old Man and the Mate were sitting straddle of the saloon skylight, drunker than ever, and singing "Ben Bowline" worse than any gramophone.

"I wasn't taking any watches being Bo'sun, but I kept on deck all the first watch, being unable to sleep anyway. I had an uneasy feeling which the men had too, for I heard them talking superstition and death, and chattering by the fathom on the decks.

"Many a time that watch I went to the side and took a look over. Once I lit a bull's-eye lantern we used for clearing up the ropes at night and shone it down over the side. Some of the men saw what I was doing and ran to have a look. There, right under the light, was the head and eyes of the biggest shark I'd ever seen. Snugged right up against the side of the ship he was, just squirming his tail as gently as a lady's fan so as to give him way through the water the same speed as we were moving. And he looked up at the lantern as knowing and devilish as you please. I tell you, lad, there was the intelligence of a man or a monster in that great brute. I could see knowledge in his eye. It's a queer thing to say, but it's true. One of the men called out: 'He's looking at us, lads, he knows as much as we do,' and I guess he was right, only the beggar knew a good deal more in some strange fashion, and you'll agree with me when I'm done telling you.

"When I shunted the beam of light out a bit from the ship's side, we could see a string of sharks hefty enough to make sausage-meat of any man living. Everywhere we shone the light we could see the black-looking fins and backs of thousands and thousands moving here and moving there, all coming after the ship. You never saw such a sight.

"Then Mr. Jackson got singing out to know what the devil we were doing with that light, so I dowsed it, but I didn't feel like turning in. It was all so rummy. I shall always say there was something queer about that night.

"When the boy called me in the morning, I asked him if the sharks had gone.

" 'No,' he said, 'it's worse than ever—more of 'em. And,' he added, 'the engines have broken down proper an' we're stuck in a dead calm!'

"Well, I cut out on deck then in my drawers to have a look for myself. There wasn't a breath of wind, and both the sea and the sky had a bit of a leaden look. The sea was just as smooth as glass except round about the ship. You never saw anything like it. It was just alive with sharks.

"I got up onto the spar top-sail and looked over the port rail. The sharks were packed so close about the ship you couldn't see blue water between them. I could hear the ship rub against 'em when she rolled a little. There they lay wonderfully quiet, close in to us. Just a bit of a wriggle this way or that, and from time to time one of the brutes would shove his great head clean up out of the water across the back of another and lie like that for five minutes or so, as if he was staring up at us.

"Further out the beggars weren't so thick, but they were swimming around. You could see their fins and backs showing right up out of the water at times, and once we saw a fight amongst them. The sea frothed and boiled for a few seconds. I guess if any were killed they just got eaten up as quick as you could wink.

"The silly Mate tried to harpoon some of the brutes and got a fright for his pains. He comes up, as drunk as you please, at seven bells, sees the sharks and starts rubbing the sleep out of his eyes. Then he sends a boy for the harpoon out of the lamp-locker, and when he'd got it bent onto a bit of ratling-line he lets fly. Well, you never saw such a fuss. It was like hell waked up suddenly. The shark that was struck with the iron did the flip-flap, of course, and every shark near him made a mighty rush at him so that they all piled up into one great wriggling heap, clean above the sea level for a moment. Lashing, biting, you couldn't see a yard in front of you for the clouds of water and foam and blood that was thrown everywhere, all in a moment. When it quieted down, there wasn't any harpoon or ratling-line or shark either. I guess after that the Mate was just as well pleased to let 'em alone. The fight among themselves made us all feel they'd be aboard by their thousands if we didn't leave them alone. And you know, lad, she wasn't a big packet, the *St. Elmo*, and she hadn't all that much freeboard. Oh, it was pretty easy to get imagining things with all that lot of devils lying round us.

"It was a queer, uncomfortable day that followed. The men had all got it into their heads that there was a Jonah aboard—funny creatures sailors are! And the Engineers crowd was nearly as bad. They'd taken the engine room skylight and lifted it clean off, and all the starboard side of the deck littered with their steam gadgets. I asked them if they were making a new engine but only got cursed for my cheek. Poor devils, the Chief had kept them hard at it till they were dead beat.

"The Old Man came up about five bells in the forenoon watch with a bottle of whisky in his fist and a big pint mug. He goes to the side and looks down, very solemn.

" 'Have you seen 'em, Mister Nathaniel?' I heard him asking the Mate after he's looked awhile.

" 'Yes, Sir,' replied the Mate.

" 'Well, I'm glad you've got 'em too, Mister,' said the Captain gravely. And with that he filled his mug with whisky and drank it off neat. He was a rum old stick.

"Things went on like that for three days. No wind, no steam, no nothing. Only the sharks and the bad talk from the Engineers little crowd. Forrard in the fo'cas'le the men would scarcely speak to one another. Each one suspected the other of being a Jonah. I tell you, I'm not joking. When men of that level of intelligence get a superstitious idea into their heads it may mean downright murder. I know for a fact that if any one of you had got named outright for a Jonah causing all our trouble he'd have been put overboard as sure as nuts after dark. Oh, yes he would, and that was why I was knocking about at night and keeping an eye on the men in case they got up to some mad wickedness with the funk they'd got.

"In the afternoon watch on the third day we got a light bit of a breeze astern, and the Mate sings out for the watch to loose sail. At first some of them hung back, not liking to go out on the yearyards above all those brutes in the sea; but I saw it had to be done, so I gave them a lead and we got the job done. Nasty work it was too, looking down on those thousands and thousands of waiting brutes right under our feet when we were out on the yards. How you like it, lad?

"We got the sail on her, and the old packet began to move through the water, perhaps a couple of knots an hour. And mighty strange it was to see those close-packed sharks begin to get a move on too, wriggling their tails and bodies so as to just keep speed with the ship, all of them as if they were tied to her by invisible strings. It was a queer sight and gave me a queer feeling.

"All that week it was the same, sometimes the wind shunted us along a couple of knots an hour, or less, and sometimes it dropped to a dead calm. The men were getting that nervous we could hardly get 'em off the decks at night to go aloft.

"Twice during that week the Engineers got the engines running, but they came to a stop again each time in less than an hour, and there was the whole bag of Greasers up to their necks again, doing their fancy repairs. That old packet wasn't in a fit state to leave port, and that's the truth of it.

"And so things went along. The second week might have been seven years instead of seven days, and all the time the Skipper and the Mate on the drink, and the little Second Mate looking more and more discontent, as if he wanted to take a bite out of someone, and small blame to him.

"At night I used to go out and listen at the rail, and I tell you lad, it was mighty queer to hear the sharks rubbing their hides against the skin of the ship. I got to fancying things at last, same as the men, only worse because, you see, I knew more. I grew to thinking there was something in the air at night—all manner of queer thoughts—that something was trying to entice me to go over the side—into the sea. You'd understand fast enough if you'd been there. It seemed to me the very air about the ship was tainted—as if it smelt of shark. It's hard to explain—and then to shine the lantern down at night and see some of those great brutes looking up at you, waiting, sort of cunning, and their eyes as intelligent as the eyes of a bad man. No wonder I got fancies!

"One of the men, Jellott, must have had them too, for one night I woke about three bells in the middle watch. There was a devil of a hullabaloo, men shouting and the noise of churning water close to the ship. I came running out and saw a lot of men on the port side away in the darkness. They were all shouting and some of them were running about the deck as if they'd gone mad. But what took me most was that awful noise of water outside the ship, as if the sea was boiling. And in a moment I guessed what it was.

"Catching hold of the first man I could, I shook him.

" 'It's Jellott, Bo'sun,' he stuttered. 'At least we think it is.'

"That was all, but it was enough. The noise outside the ship quietened pretty quickly, but all the men could tell me was that Jellott had sung out something, and then they'd heard the noise of the sharks fighting. Anyway, the Second who'd come along called the roll and there was no Jellott, sure enough. We got the bull's-eye then and shone the light out over the seas. It was as calm as glass, with the sharks packed close up round the ship the same as ever, looking up quiet and knowing at the light. But no one saw anything of Jellott. And we didn't put out a boat, neither, my lad!

"Now, away aft, things were getting into a pretty pickle. The little Second Mate was the only one that kept any sort of a watch, for the Skipper and the Mate were rarely sober, and when they were sober they were not fit to live with, what with bully-ragging all hands and scrapping up on the poop between themselves. Oh yes, there's queer doings at sea, though they do say nothing ever happens on the liners.

"The third week passed without a breath of wind, the sails just hanging in the ropes, and none of them furled as they might have been to save chafing, for the simple reason that not a man alive would leave the decks. I tell you, there was a mighty funk on our chests.

"On the Friday of the third week, the Mate and the Skipper drank themselves speechless, and the Steward had to take them in hand. The Second sent for me, and together we lashed the two of them in their bunks, and they'd both have been better if we'd done it earlier.

" 'You'll have to take the Mate's watch, Bo'sun,' said the Second when we'd finished tying those two loonies up.

" 'Very good, Sir,' I replied. 'I've got my Mate's ticket.'

"And so I had, but he didn't know it till then, and you should have seen him stare. You see, I'd signed on as Bo'sun being unable to get a Mate's billet and my cash was running low.

"Well, we fixed it up that way and took watch and watch. I remember now on those dark nights I'd stand by the poop rail and listen to that beastly noise of the sharks rub-rubbing themselves against the side of the ship, and now every now and again there were splashes out in the dark where some of the brutes were swimming about and worrying the smaller ones.

"It was while I was pacing Mount Misery in this fashion, and with plenty of time to think, that I got a notion, and an ugly notion it was. I fired it off at the Second Mate when he came up to relieve me at the end of the watch.

" 'Mr. Jackson,' I said, watching his face by the light of the lantern from the standard binnacle, 'I've been thinking that there's a reason for these brutes round this ship.'

"He looked at me in a queer sort of way but said nothing.

" 'Mr. Jackson,' I went on, 'there's dead men in this packet, and you know it, Sir.'

" 'I know nothing, Bo'sun,' he'd said, still looking at me in that queer way.

" 'But you suspect something, Sir,' I went on, looking at him hard.

"He shook his head. 'I've neither share nor part in it, Bo'sun,' he replied.

" 'Maybe not, but the Old Man and the Mate have,' I told him looking him straight in the face.

" 'I know nothing about it, Bo'sun,' was all he would say, but I knew there'd been some dirty work going on, and that he had some idea of it all, too. What was troubling his little soul was the fact that he's been given no share of any money there was knocking around.

"Now, I said nothing more for five minutes or so while I took a turn to and fore across the break of the poop. Then it got plainer to me that there was something pretty wrong aboard, and that there was big money in it, somehow. The way the two men were drinking showed that. It was just the way two men like the Skipper and the Mate would act if they'd cut loose a bit, standing either to make a heap of money or get into trouble. If the Mate hadn't been in it with the Skipper, it wasn't likely the Old Man would have let him be on the drink. And that's how I sized it all up, looking down over the ship's side into the darkness, and thinking what an unpleasant sort of death was lying so precious a few feet below my nose.

" 'I'm going down to have a look at the ship's papers, Mr. Jackson,' I told the Second Mate.

"He just shrugged his shoulders in a way he had, and from that I gathered that he had spoken the truth when he said he was out of it.

" 'Please yourself,' he muttered. 'You do it on your own responsibility, mind. Remember, I'll have nothing to do with it, one way or the other.... Anyway, you'll find nothing.' He turned his back on me and then called out, 'I had a look myself... I had a notion there might be something wrong.'

"I laughed. 'I guess you'd more than a notion,' I told him. 'I expect you know more than you're ever likely to own up to!'

"And with that I went straight down into the Captain's cabin where the Old Man, lashed up securely, was chattering to himself and staring up at the desk over his head. He was saying something over and over to himself all the while I was rummaging through the papers. At last I got the hang of it:

" 'Fifty dead Chinamen all in a row!
Fifty dead Chinamen all in a row!
Fifty dead Chinamen all in a row!'

"When I realised what it was he was saying, I was struck in a heap and stopped rummaging, for I tumbled to it all in a moment. Once I'd cut loose from superstition I knew that it was a pretty uncomfortable explanation that was going to explain away all those sharks waiting so patiently round the ship. I knew they were waiting for something.

"But what?

"I stood a moment or two watching that old devil lashed up to his bunk, but he never stopped his queer singing:

" 'Fifty dead Chinamen all in a row!
Fifty dead Chinamen all in a row!

Fifty dead Chinamen all in a row!'

"I left him staring up at the deck planks above him and went to find the Second Mate.

" 'Mr. Jackson,' I said, 'I'm going forrard to have a talk with the men, and if I were you, Sir, I'd have a look over the taffrail and not bother about what you may hear.'

"He looked at me doubtfully a moment.

" 'It's all right, Mister,' I assured him. 'I'll keep them in hand, never you fear.'

"Anyway, he took the hint and wandered aft as natural as you please to watch the beauties of the night.

"And then, lad, I went forrard to the fo'cas'le and routed out all hands.

" 'Now, my men,' I said to them, 'if you want to see an end to all this Jonah business you're so mad about, come along with me and lift the main hatch. And go as quiet as you can or I'll break some of your necks for you. One of you boys go and call the Carpenter and tell him I want him.'

"Well, we got the hatches lifted and I sent for the bull's-eye lamp, lit it, and shone the light round the cargo that was showing. I was soon quite sure that what I had guessed was right. I jumped down onto the cargo, took a grip of a mighty great hogshead and gave the thing a heave. Sure enough, I could stir it, and that was enough for me, for by rights it should have been so heavy that nothing short of a tackle and the winch could have moved it.

" 'Now, lads, out with it onto the deck!' I ordered.

"We lifted it pretty easily, and I told Chips to knock up the hoops and let us have a look inside. I don't mind telling you, lad, I had a queer feeling in the pit of my stomach.

"Chips got at his job as quietly as he could, and while I held up the light he shoved in his chisel and lifted out the head of the great tub while the men crowded round to look in.

"The next moment they all gave back, for sure enough inside that tub was a dead man. And a Chinaman at that.

" 'My God!' cried Chips, and dropped his hammer with a thump on the deck, making us all jump.

" 'And there's forty-nine more of 'em, boys,' I told them. 'Come on, there's nothing to be afraid of in a dead Chinaman. We'll get the lot out and dump them. You'll not get rid of those sharks otherwise.'

"But it took a bit to get the men going. They weren't for touchin' those barrels, but I put a bit of courage into a few, and the rest followed, shoving the opened hogshead away aft a bit by the house till we could get all the others up. And a mercy it was we did, and a greater mercy that I didn't give word to dump it overboard straight away.

"It took us nearly three hours lifting out those forty-nine tubs, and opening them to make sure we'd got the right ones. I was right all along, for fifty was the number all told and a body in each. A pretty ghastly business it was too, with the deck full to those great tubs and their contents and then to think what was waiting just outside the iron skin of our packet.

"And then we got the surprise of our lives, for out of one of the tubs a white arm started to wave.

"The men went off like a parcel of women, slap into the fo'cas'le and screaming like a lot of idiots. Chips nearly knocked the lantern out of my hand, and I confess I didn't feel too steady myself.

"The next thing I knew were two arms coming out and a voice which helped to assure me that whatever was in that hogshead was certainly not dead, Chinaman or no Chinaman. Anyway, to cut the story short, we got the beggar out and laid him out on the deck. He was too feeble to stand. You wouldn't believe it but for every question we asked him, he asked us two in his queer pidgin English. It took us some time to get the whole story clear, and a pretty dirty story it was. There wasn't a dead man among the lot. They were all as wick as wick in no time. You can't kill a Chinaman anyway. In some cunning fashion, the hogshead had been made to let air in and, although they were all drugged, they all seemed none the worse after their experience.

"As far as we could understand them, it seems they all belonged to a political society whose great idea was to get rid of their present figurehead and put up another. However, as it happened, there was plenty of power at the back of the government; for all these men were tracked down, caught and drugged with one of their devilish drugs and popped into the barrels. Then they must have been shipped aboard our vessel to be carried off secretly to China where each one was to be made an example of if he landed there alive. From what Chin-chin told me, the Chinese government had no power to touch them so long as they remained in 'Frisco, as theirs was a political offense. That was why they were all being shipped back where the government could deal with them openly and make an example of them. And a precious near thing it was for them. If it hadn't been for those engines breaking down, they'd have been in the Kingdom by this time.

"And speaking of the engines, I've thought sometimes that there was more in that than met the eye, as you might say. There were several Chinamen among the Stokers and Trimmers, and two Chinese Greasers. Now, did they have a bit of a game with the works so to speak? Why did our engines keep breaking down, eh? I've sometimes thought those Greasers had been put up to the job by someone in the know. But there, I may be mistaken. Anyway, it was a lucky thing for Chin-chin that he waved his arms when he did, or they'd all have gone overboard. And I guess it was a lucky thing for me too. I didn't do so badly out of it. Some of those Chinamen were worth more than you'd think—unless, of course, you know Chinatown Down 'Frisco way.

"Hushed up, did you say? Oh yes, it was all hushed up, right enough. The Skipper and the Mate when they got sober didn't want any talk, no fear, and the Chinamen didn't want any either, poor beggars. They were all too feeble after their drugging to want any arguments, I can tell you. And what the shellbacks said didn't matter a tinker's cuss, for they're always drunk ashore, and no one cares a darn what they say, or believes a word of it either. So when the engines started running again—and they got going all right—we just turned right back and landed our 'cargo' on the quiet.

"Now, would you believe it, lad, when daylight came there wasn't a shark in sight! Nothing but the sea. Now, what did *they* know? That's what I'm always asking myself. *Who* told them? Eh? It's a queer place is the sea, a queer place. A mighty big, queer, blue mysterious place, and the mysteries that it holds will never be known this side of Eternity, my lad. Aye, it's a queer place, and well I know it.... And to think I nearly dumped the whole fifty of 'em! Just think of it! My word! just think of it!"

"Sailormen"

"ALL HANDS ON DECK! Shorten sail!" A few minutes later we are out on the wet, slippery deck, fully dressed in oilskins and heavy sea-boots. All around and overhead is deep blackness, while away to windward the weird phosphorescent loom of light, caused by the oncoming squall tearing the wave tops into foam, only serves to intensify the stormy darkness of the night. Ever and anon, some white-topped mountain heaves its briny head above the weather bulwarks, descending with a roar and swirl upon our heads, burying us beneath tons of water and foam.

"Stand by t'gallant halyards... Lower away!... Man the clewlines and buntlines." Next instant, above the roar of the squall, comes the deep, hollow thuttering of the sail, as the wind, catching it aback, tears it to ribbons. "Up aloft, and furl!" comes the order, and away I go, followed by five of the hands. Being first on the yard, I lay out to windward with Joe Norton (New Zealand Joe, we call him) next to me—a fine, strapping young fellow. The wind is lashing the torn sail in one continuous thunder, causing the yard, with the six men on it, to quiver like a steel spring. It is too dark to attempt to dodge flying ends; we must take our chance. Slowly and surely, despite the darkness and storm, we manage to get the sail in hand. Joe holds it. I feel under the yard for the gasket. While doing so a fiercer gust, filled with sleet, strikes the ship. I hear a cry; "My God, hold on all!" I stop breathing. Far down, some hundred feet below, distinct, in spite of the roar of the storm, I hear a sickening thud that seems to vibrate through the ship. I stretch out my hand to touch Joe. Shout his name. He is not there. Then I know and go dizzy. The man farther in on the yard is violently sick. For some minutes I can only hold on and pray. Soon as may be, we get the gaskets round the sail; and then down from aloft as best we can, feeling for each ratline, and holding on like death.

508

We reach the deck. No need to ask of those below.

In one of the deck-houses a dim oil-lamp lights up one of the tables, on which lies a long, still form, covered with an old ensign. 'Tis New Zealand Joe.

By the Lee

"WHERE THE HELL ARE you running her off to? Look where you're going, man! You'll have us by the lee!" and the burly Mate grasps the spokes of the big wheel and puts forth his strength to assist the weary Helmsman in heaving it down.

They are off Cape Horn. Midnight has passed, and the murderous blackness of the night is slit at times with livid gleams that rise astern and hover, then sink with a sullen harsh roar beneath the uplifting stern, only to be followed by others.

The straining steersman snatches an occasional nervous glance over his shoulder at these dread spectres. He does not fear the foam-topped phosphorescent caps; but shudders at the hollow blackness that comes beneath. Occasionally, as the ship plunges, the binnacle light flares up, striking a reflected gleam from that moving gloom, and shewing living walls of water poised above his head. At moments such as these, he looks ahead resolutely. The threatening death behind is not to be borne.

The storm grows fiercer, and hungry winds howl a dreadful chorus aloft. At times comes the deep hollow booming of the main lower top-sail.

The man at the wheel strains desperately. The wind is icy cold and the night full of spray and sleet, yet he perspires damply in his strenuous fight with death.

Presently, the hoarse bellow of the Mate's voice is heard through the gloom:

"Another man to the wheel." It is time. Unaided, the solitary, struggling figure guiding the huge, plunging craft through the watery thunders, is unable to cope longer alone with his task, and now another form takes its place on the lee side of the groaning wheel, and gives its strength to assist the master hand through the stress. An hour passes: the Mate stands silently swaying near the binnacle. Once his voice comes tumultuously through the pall: "God damn you! Keep her straight; do you want to send us all to Hell?"

There is no reply; none is needed. The Mate knows the man is doing his utmost, and so struggles forrard, and is swallowed up in the blackness.

With a tremendous clap, the main top-sail leaves the ropes and drives forward upon the fore mast—a dark and flickering shadow seen mistily against the sombre dome of night. The ship steers madly in swooping semi-circles, and with each one she looks death between the eyes. The hurricane seems to flatten the men against the wheel, and grows stronger.

The sooty night becomes palpably darker, and nothing can be seen save those foamy giant forms leaping up like grasping hands astern; then sweeping forward overwhelmingly.

Time passes—

A human note comes out of the night. It comes from the Mate standing unseen, hidden midst the briny reek:

"Steady!" it rises to a hoarse scream, "For God's sake, steady!"

The ship sweeps up against the ocean. Things vast and watery hang above her for one brief moment. Then....

The morning is dawning leaden and weary, like the face of a worn woman.

The light strikes through the bellying scum o'er head and shews broken hills and valleys carven momentarily in liquid shapes.

The eye sweeps round the eternal desolation.

Tossed on a briny mountain, something shews briefly, a piece of wreckage perchance, or a body....

A Note on the Texts

WHENEVER POSSIBLE, TEXTS FOR this series have been based on versions that were published in book form, preferably during Hodgson's lifetime. The major exceptions to this rule are the stories that appear in volumes edited by Sam Moskowitz. Moskowitz was known to have access to original manuscripts and other source materials. Some stories were published only in serial form, and have been taken from those primary sources.

Over the years, many of Hodgson's stories have appeared under variant titles, which are noted below. As a rule, the titles used in this series are based on the first book publication of a story, even if the story previously appeared under a different title, in serial form.

Specific textual sources are noted below. The only changes that have been made to the texts have been to correct obvious typographical errors, and to standardize punctuation and capitalization. British and archaic spelling has been retained.

The Ghost Pirates is based on the 1909 Stanley Paul & Company edition.
"The Silent Ship" (AKA "The Phantom Ship," AKA "The Silent Ship Tells How Jessop Was Picked Up") is based on its publication in *The Haunted Pampero* (Grant, 1991). It was originally published as "The Phantom Ship" in *Shadow No. 20* (October 1973).
"A Tropical Horror" is based on its publication in *Out of the Storm* (Grant, 1975). It was originally published in *Grand Magazine* (April 1905).
"The Voice in the Night" is based on its publication in *Men Of Deep Waters* (Eveleigh Nash, 1914). It was originally published in *Blue Book Magazine 6, No. 1* (November 1907).
"The *Shamraken* Homeward-Bounder" (AKA "Homeward Bound") is based on its publication in *Men Of Deep Waters* (Eveleigh Nash,

1914). It was originally published in *Putnam's Monthly 4, No. 1* (April 1908).

"Out of the Storm" is based on its publication in *Out of the Storm* (Grant, 1975). It was originally published in *Putnam's Monthly 5, No. 5* (February 1909).

"The Albatross" is based on its publication in *Out of the Storm* (Grant, 1975). It was originally published in *Adventure 2 No. 3* (July 1911).

" 'Prentices' Mutiny" (AKA "Mutiny") is based on its publication in *At Sea* (Necronomicon Press, 1993). It was originally published in *Wide World Magazine 28, No. 5*; *28 No. 6*; and *29, No. 1* (February, March, and April 1912).

"On the Bridge" (AKA "The Real Thing: On the Bridge") is based on its publication in *Men Of Deep Waters* (Eveleigh Nash, 1914). It was originally published in *Saturday Westminster Gazette No. 5899* (April 20, 1912).

"The Derelict" is based on its publication in *Terrors of the Sea* (Grant, 1996). It was initially published in *Red Magazine No. 88* (December 1, 1912).

"The Island of the Crossbones" is based on its publication in *Terrors of the Sea* (Grant, 1996). It was initially published in *Short Stories 80, No. 4* (October 1913).

"The Stone Ship" (AKA "The Mystery of the Ship in the Night") is based on its publication in *The Luck of the Strong* (Eveleigh Nash, 1916). It was originally published as "The Mystery of the Ship in the Night" in *Red Magazine No. 126* (July 1, 1914).

"The Regeneration of Captain Bully Keller (AKA "The Waterloo of a Hard-Case Skipper") is based on its publication in *At Sea* (Necronomicon Press, 1993) as "The Waterloo of a Hard-Case Skipper." It was originally published in *Red Magazine No. 134* (November 1, 1914).

"The Mystery of Missing Ships" (AKA "Ships that Go Missing") is based on its publication in *All Around Magazine 11, No. 2* (December 1915).

"We Two and Bully Dunkan" (AKA "The Trimming of Captain Dunkan") is based on its publication in *The Luck of the Strong* (Eveleigh Nash, 1916). It was originally published as "The Trimming of Captain Dunkan" in *Red Magazine No. 128* (August 1, 1914).

"The Haunted 'Pampero' " is based on its publication in *The Haunted Pampero* (Grant, 1991). It was originally published in *Short Stories 89*, No. 2 (February 1918).

"The Real Thing: 'S.O.S' " is based on its publication in *Cornhill Magazine 3rd Series,* No. 247 (January 1917).

"Jack Grey, Second Mate" (AKA "Second Mate of the Buster") is based on its publication in *Adventure 14, No. 3* (July 1917). It was initially published in *Red Magazine No. 98* (May 1, 1913), as "Second Mate of the Buster."

"A Fight with a Submarine" is based on its publication in *Canada in Khaki* (January 25, 1918).

"In the Danger Zone" is based on its publication in *Canada in Khaki* (June 1919).

"Old Golly" is based on its publication in *The Haunted Pampero* (Grant, 1991). It was originally published in *Short Stories 92, No. 6* (December 1919).

"Demons of the Sea" (AKA The Crew of the Lancing) is based on its publication in *Terrors of the Sea* (Grant, 1996). It was initially published in *Sea Stories Magazine 6, No. 5* (October 5, 1923).

"The Wild Man of the Sea" is based on its publication in *The Haunted Pampero* (Grant, 1991). It was originally published in *Sea Stories Magazine* (May, 1926).

"The Habitants of Middle Islet" is based on its publication in *Deep Waters* (Arkham House, 1967). It was originally published in *Dark Mind, Dark Heart* (Arkham House, 1962).

"The Riven Night" is based on its publication in *Terrors of the Sea* (Grant, 1996). It was initially published in *Shadow No. 19* (April 1973)

"The Heaving of the Log" is based on its 1988 Strange Company chapbook publication.

"The Sharks of the *St. Elmo*" (AKA "Fifty Dead Chinamen All in a Row") is based on its publication in *Terrors of the Sea* (Grant, 1996). It was initially published in chapbook form by Strange Company in 1988.

"Sailormen" is based on its publication in *Terrors of the Sea* (Grant, 1996).

"By the Lee" (AKA "The Storm") is based on its publication in *Terrors of the Sea* (Grant, 1996). It was oringally published in a slightly different form as "The Storm" in *Short Stories* (December 1919).

The Complete Fiction of William Hope Hodgson is published by
Night Shade Books in the following volumes:

The Boats of the "Glen Carrig" and Other Nautical Adventures
The House on the Borderland and Other Mysterious Places
The Ghost Pirates and Other Revenants of the Sea
The Night Land and Other Perilous Romances
The Dream of X and Other Fantastic Visions